PEN
T



Born in 1934 in Faridpur, now in Bangladesh, Sunil Gangopadhyay came as a refugee to Calcutta in 1947, following the partition of India. The family suffered extreme poverty initially and Sunil, though only in his teens, was forced to find employment. He still managed to continue his education, taking his Master's degree from Calcutta University.

Sunil began his literary career as a poet, starting the epoch-making magazine, *Krittibas*, in 1953. His better-known poetry collections are *Eka ebang Kayekjon* (1958), *Amar Swapna* (1972), *Bandi Jege Achhi* (1974) and *Ami ki Rakam Bhabe Benche Achhi* (1975). Storming into the field of the novel with the trendsetting *Atma Prakash* (1966)—a powerful portrayal of the frustration and ennui of the youth of Calcutta—he soon rose to become the leading and most popular novelist of Bengali. *Sei Samai* (1982), which won him the Sahitya Akademi Award, and *Purba Paschim* (1989) are among his best novels.

*

Aruna Chakravarti took her Masters and Ph.D. degrees in English Literature from the University of Delhi. She has held the post of reader in one of the affiliated colleges of the university for many years and is, at present, its principal. She is also an author and translator of repute.

Her first translation, *Tagore: Songs Rendered into English* (1984) won the Vaitalik Award for excellence in literary translation. Her translation of Sarat Chandra Chattopadhyaya's immortal classic *Srikanta*, is deemed her best work, having won the prestigious Sahitya Akademi Award for 1996. *Srikanta* was published by Penguin India in 1993. She has also written a biography of Sarat Chandra, entitled *Sarat Chandra: Rebel and Humanist*.

PENGUIN BOOKS
THOSE DAYS

Born in 1934 in [illegible], now in Bangladesh, Sunil Gangopadhyay came as a refugee to Calcutta in 1947, following the Partition of India. The family [illegible] initially, and [illegible] to look for full-time employment. He still managed to continue his education, gaining his Master's degree from Calcutta University.

[illegible] his literary career as a poet, starting the epoch-making magazine *Krittibas* in 1953. [illegible] poetry collections are [illegible] (1972), [illegible] (1975) and [illegible] (1975). Storming into the field of the novel with [illegible] *Atmaprakash* (1966)—a powerful portrayal of the frustration and ennui of the youth of Calcutta—he soon went on to become the leading and most popular novelist of Bengal. *Sei Samay* (1982), which won him the Sahitya Akademi Award, and *Pratham Alo* (1996) are among his best novels.

Aruna Chakravarti took her Master's and Ph.D. degrees in English Literature from the University of Delhi. She has held the post of reader in one of the affiliated colleges of the university for many years and is at present its principal. She is also an author and translator of [illegible].

Her first translation, *Tagore Songs*, rendered into English (1993), won the [illegible] Award for excellence in literary translation. Her translation of Sarat Chandra Chattopadhyay's [illegible] is deemed her best work, having won the prestigious Sahitya Akademi Award for [illegible]. [illegible] she has also written a biography of Sarat Chandra entitled [illegible] *Women*.

SUNIL GANGOPADHYAY

# *Those Days*

Translated by Aruna Chakravarti

PENGUIN BOOKS

Penguin Books India (P) Ltd, 11 Community Centre, Panchsheel Park, New Delhi-110017, India
Penguin Books Ltd., 27 Wrights Lane, London W8 5TZ, UK
Penguin Putnam Inc., 375 Hudson Street, New York, NY 10014, USA
Penguin Books Australia Ltd., Ringwood, Victoria, Australia
Penguin Books Canada Ltd., 10 Alcorn Avenue, Suite 300, Toronto, Ontario M4V 3B2, Canada
Penguin Books (NZ) Ltd., 182-190 Wairau Road, Auckland 10, New Zealand

Published in the Bengali as *Sei Samai* by Ananda Publishers Pvt. Ltd. 1981, 1982

Published in English translation as *Those Days* by Penguin Books India (P) Ltd. 1997


10 9 8 7 6 5 4 3

Typeset in Palatino by Digital Technologies and Printing Solutions, New Delhi

*To Milu and Akhil . . .*

# *Introduction*

When Penguin India approached me with a request to translate Sunil Gangopadhyay's *Sei Samai,* I found myself, I must confess, somewhat at a loss. I had read the book twice and loved every moment of it but the thought of rendering it into English was daunting. For one thing it was a marathon project—two volumes of closely printed text running into nine hundred and seven pages! And that was not all. I was instructed to compress the matter and bring it down to five hundred pages. I wrote to the author, whom I had met several times, and asked him to suggest areas that might be deleted without disturbing the intrinsic pattern of the book. But he, very graciously, wrote back to say that he would leave that to me, having full faith in my abilities.

Thus, with the responsibility fully and squarely on my shoulders, I sat down to take stock of the situation. And to my surprise, I found that the task was not so formidable after all. The English language lends itself, quite naturally, to greater precision than the Bengali. So, a certain amount of tightening could be achieved without undue strain. Discreet deletions here and there took care of the rest.

There was another hurdle that had to be overcome. The characters of *Sei Samai* speak the lively dialect of nineteenth-century Calcutta. I researched a bit, trying to find a corresponding dialect in English. Then, rejecting every one I found as unsuitable, I decided to make my characters speak plain twentieth-century English with a few Bengali phrases and exclamations thrown in for the ambience. The effect, I find, is not too much at variance with the original. I hope my Bengali readers will share this view.

And now—a few words about *Sei Samai*. The novel, appearing in serial form in *Desh* over a period of two and a half years and published in two volumes in 1981 and 1982, respectively, presents a bold and startling deviation from the Marxian search for man's salvation that was Sunil's forte in his work of the sixties and seventies. *Sei Samai* is a period novel set in nineteenth-century Bengal. It explores the cross-currents of social, political and intellectual life in the city of Calcutta during the period generally referred to as the Bengal Renaissance. This period, in the opinion of Shibnath Shastri, stretches through the two decades between 1825 and 1845. 'Those twenty years,' he writes in his *Ramtanu Lahiri and Bengali Society of the Time*, 'ushered in a new era in the history of Bengal. There was an awakening in the realms of politics, religion and education such as had never been witnessed before.' Sunil Gangopadhyay tries to reconstruct this awakening in *Sei Samai* but the time-frame of his novel is different. 'My personal view,' he writes in his epilogue to *Sei Samai*, 'is that the Bengal Renaissance, as we understand it, manifested itself not in the span between 1825 and 1845 as Shibnath Shastri suggests but in the three decades between 1840 and 1870.'

The novel has a vast canvas against which the lives and destinies of a number of historical figures of the time are traced. Many fictional people and events find their place, too. In fact, one of the unique features of the novel is the deftness with which the author weaves the actual and the purely fictional into the tapestry of his story. Another is the quality of his voice—rational, analytical and totally without bias.

Sunil Gangopadhyay's attempt is to synthesize two approaches to history. Like his illustrious predecessor, Bankim Chandra Chattopadhyaya in *Durgésnandini*, *Mrinalini*, *Chandrasékhar* and *Anandamath*, he tries, on the one hand, to explore the reality of historical events and reconstruct them as faithfully as possible. On the other, he moulds history to the point where it embodies a vision. History is both symbolical and prophetic in *Sei Samai*.

The characters of *Sei Samai*, historical and fictional, are flesh and blood human beings, caught between two worlds—one old, decrepit and dying by degrees and the other struggling to be born. They are all protagonists; all engaged in a struggle—some to keep alive and perpetuate the old, others to hasten its death and bring about the birth of the new. The characters are historically authentic for the most part and so is the world they people. Yet, *Sei Samai* is not history. Sunil Gangopadhyay makes that amply clear. '*Sei Samai* is a novel—not a historical document,' he writes in his epilogue. 'History is a record of palpable facts. Fiction is not. The fiction writer, even when depicting historical truth, has to invest it with the light of the imagination.' Thus, Sunil's historical characters think, act and feel as he sees them do in his mind's eye. Vidyasagar speaks a rough and ready tongue and weeps at the slightest provocation. Debendranath Thakur exchanges the highest philosophical ideas with Rajnarayan Basu over a glass of wine. Harish Mukherjee goes drinking and whoring with the lowest of the low and Madhusudan Datta has homosexual yearnings for Gourdas Basak.

Readers have questioned these aspects of the book and indicted the author for taking unwarranted liberties. Sunil answers their charges with the words: 'We Indians believe in idol worship and cannot rest in peace till we have deified those we respect . . . But blasphemy is an excellent component of great literature—a most useful one, too. When an attack, true or fabricated, is directed against an illustrious personage of a previous age and time, the consequent situation is fraught with controversy. And in the analyzing that invariably follows new light is sure to be shed and a better perspective acquired. T.S. Eliot's near murder of Shelley did not destroy Shelley. It sparked off a curiosity leading to greater awareness in the mind of the reader. I have been accused of belittling the great sons of our land. I submit that I have done nothing of the kind. If, in the interest of realism, I've depicted some of them as having feet of clay, I consider that I've done no wrong.'

One agrees with Sunil. The creative writer is beholden to no one. Something or someone fires his imagination. He gives expression to it through a chosen medium. He is answerable only to himself for it is his bounden duty to be faithful to his own thoughts and perceptions. The reader is at liberty to accept or reject his work—in part or as a whole.

The creative writer, when recreating historical figures, is at a serious disadvantage. Barring certain events which are recorded history and an anecdote or two, perhaps made popular by repeated usage, he has little matter on which he can fall back. There is, therefore, no option for him except to enter into an imaginary dialogue with his characters. He has to penetrate their minds and keep pace with their steps—physical and mental. There are many who will challenge this kind of identification and dismiss it as false and frivolous. But the creative writer, in my opinion, should be given that liberty. He should feel free to interact with his characters and make them think and speak. Only, he shouldn't strike a false note. And he won't do so if he remembers to keep them within their time and context.

A point that has consistently plagued readers of *Sei Samai* is the true identity of Nabin Kumar Singha. Is his character based on that of Kali Prasanna Singha's or isn't it? If it is, why has the author changed his first name? And why is his paternity cast under a cloud? And if it isn't, why is the translation of the Mahabharat and the authorship of the lively *Hutom Pyanchar Naksha* attributed to him? And the book, interestingly enough, is dedicated to Kali Prasanna Singha.

Anticipating these questions, Sunil tells us that though Nabin Kumar's life and character bear a slight resemblance to those of 'a certain historic personage who died while still a youth', the reader should not make the mistake of seeking complete identification. Nabin Kumar and Kali Prasanna Singha were both scions of wealthy landed families, possessed extraordinary intellectual powers and died young. But here the resemblance ends. Practically nothing beyond these facts is known of Kali Prasanna Singha. Nabin is a product of Sunil's imagination—a dynamic character of a tremendous range and amalgam of qualities; a compound of strengths and weaknesses. Spoiled, arrogant and vain, he was forceful, brilliant and humane. Moreover, he is portrayed as striving, consciously and constantly, to better himself.

Though Nabin is the one character whose life and destiny are linked, albeit tenuously at times, with all the characters of *Sei Samai*, Sunil Gangopadhyay does not project him as its hero. If there is a hero at all it is Time. Time is the central character and the focal point of the novel. In order to invest this abstraction with flesh and blood and make it a living entity, Sunil Gangopadhyay had to have a symbol. Nabin Kumar is that symbol. His name, Nabin, meaning 'new', is a pointer to the part he is to play in the novel. 'Oh! Time that is yet unborn!' he scribbles on a scrap of paper just before his death. 'I salute you.'

Nabin dies before fulfilling his dearest wish—that of hearing 'the cannon booming at midnight a hundred times, ringing out the old and ringing in the new—the twentieth century', but his spiritual successor, the young scholar and thinker, Pran Gopal, will do so. In fact, at the end of the book, he already does so—in the imagination. 'Looking out into the night he heard its footsteps in the distance and his eyes glowed with the light of another—a more glorious world.'

**Aruna Chakravarti**

# *List of Characters*

## The Singhas of Jorasanko

Ram Kamal Singha - a wealthy zamindar
Ganganarayan - his elder son
Nabin Kumar - his younger son
Bimbabati - his wife
Kamala Sundari - his mistress
Leelavati - Ganganarayan's first wife
Kusum Kumari - Ganganarayan's second wife
Krishna Bhamini - Nabin Kumar's first wife
Sarojini - Nabin Kumar's second wife
Dibakar - Steward of the household
Sohagbala - his wife

Chintamoni, Matu - maids

Duryodhan, Nakur - servants

## The Mukhopadhyays

Bidhubhushan Mukherjee - A lawyer
Soudami - his wife

Narayani, Bindu, Suhasini - his daughters

Pramgopal - Suhasini's son

The Malliks of Hatkhola

Jagai Mallik - A wealthy old man

Kaliprasad } - his sons
Chandikaprasad

Aghornath - his grandson
Durgamoni - Chandika's wife

The Dattas of Khidirpur

Rajnarayan Datta - a wealthy lawyer
Madhusudan - his son
Jahnavi Devi - his wife
Henrietta - Madhusudan's second wife

Others

Dwarkanath Thakur - A wealthy banker and stevedore
Debendranath - his son
Keshab Sen - Debendranath's disciple
Jagamohan Sarkar - A rich babu of Calcutta
Ishwar Chandra Vidyasagar - An educationist and social reformer
Madanmohan Tarkalankar - his friend
Shreesh - his pupil
Harish Mukherjee - a journalist
David Hare - an educationist
John Bethune - an educationist
Ramgopal Ghosh } - followers of Derozio
Dakshinaranjan Mukhopadhyay
Ramtanu Lahiri
Pyarichand Mitra - a writer
Kishorichand Mitra - a writer
Kishorichand Mitra - his brother
Rani Rasmoni - A wealthy woman of Calcutta

Mathur - her son-in-law
Heeramoni - a courtesan of Calcutta
Raimohan Ghosal - her paramour
Chandranath - her son
Harachandra Samanta - her lodger
Goopi - a jeweller
Trilochan - a tenant farmer
Thakomoni - his wife
Dulal - his son
Mr Mac Gregor - an English planter
Golok Das - his steward
Devi Lal - Bindu's abductor
Mansaram Chhadiwala - a resident of Varanasi
Munshi Amir Ali - a Muslim lawyer
Janab Abdul Latif Khan - a landowner
Jadupati Ganguly - Nabin Kumar's friend
Deenabandhu Mitra - a playwright
Surya Kumar Goodeve Chakravarti - a doctor
Bhujanga Bhattacharya - Rent collector of the Singha estates
Gourdas Basak - Madhusudan's best friend

# *Book I*

# Chapter I

The child was born seven months and ten days after conception. Stifling in the secret recess of his mother's womb, the little mass forged ahead, before his time, from darkness to light.

Babu Ramkamal Singha sat watching the sun setting over the Mahanadi river, when a boat came across the water, swift as an arrow, to where the bajra, a large two-storeyed boat, was anchored. His faithful gomosta, Dibakar, the steward of his household, leaped out, his face tense with anxiety, and Ramkamal's heart beat painfully fast. Bimbabati was no more! He was sure of it. Dibakar shared his fears. He had left his mistress lying unconscious, dangerously ill. Words of comfort failed him. 'We must leave tonight, Karta,'[1] was all that he could say. 'Ukil[2] Babu sent me to fetch you.' Tears welled out of Ramkamal's eyes. Bimbabati was the goddess of his home and hearth—the source of all his fortunes. He rose, and climbing down the steps to the chamber he shared with Kamala Sundari, he said, 'Everything is going with her, Kamal. Nothing in the world can give me pleasure—from this day onwards.'

Kamala Sundari soothed his brow with gentle fingers. Her eyes grew moist at the thought of Bimbabati. She had seen Bimbabati bathing in the Ganga. She had gazed at her from a distance and marvelled at her beauty—as celestial and dazzling as the Goddess Durga's. Kamala Sundari was not fit to be her handmaid. It was amazing that a man with a wife like Bimbabati should go to other women; should change mistresses every three years. Kamala Sundari's complexion was a polished ebony; Bimbabati's, rich cream, suffused with vermilion. Perhaps, that was why Ramkamal always picked dark-skinned women for his mistresses. Men were strange creatures.

Pouring some brandy into a silver glass, she held it to his

---

1 Master.
2 Lawyer.

lips. 'Drink,' she coaxed, 'or you'll feel weak and ill.' Ramkamal pushed the glass away. 'I don't want anything—anymore,' he said fretfully. 'Don't bother me, Kamal. Get out of my sight.'

Kamala Sundari went and stood by the window. She shook down her hair till it streamed out in the wind. Her eyes gazed out on the river, where the last flames of the setting sun licked the water with greedy tongues. 'This is the beginning of the end,' she murmured to herself. 'Who knows where my fate will take me now?' Ramkamal lay on his luxurious bed and moaned in agony. The bajra had begun its return journey to Calcutta.

Three days later, Ramkamal stood before his palatial mansion in Jorasanko. As he stepped through the large iron gates or deuri, the wail of a newborn infant came to his ears. Knitting his brows he looked questioningly at Dibakar. But Dibakar shook his head. He hadn't known, either, that his mistress's agony was the travail of childbirth. Besides, who had ever heard of a seven-month foetus seeing the light of the world?

Ramkamal Singha was forty-seven years old. Fifteen years ago he had taken Bimbabati as his third wife. The other two had died before they attained puberty. He remembered his first wife, Lakshmimoni, very faintly, but his second, Hembala, was only a blur. Bimbabati had brought good fortune with her from the day she stepped through the deuri—a little bride of nine. The Singhas had prospered. Everything Ramkamal touched had turned to gold. But Bimbabati had one sorrow. She was barren and could not give her husband a son. Everyone, including Bimbabati, had urged Ramkamal to remarry but he wouldn't hear of it.

Ramkamal hurried up the stairs to the landing where Bidhusekhar was waiting. An astute lawyer and a man of the world, Bidhusekhar was Ramkamal's lifelong friend, guide and counsellor. Bidhusekhar's heart was as large as his brain was agile, and Ramkamal trusted him implicitly.

'Is it all over?' Ramkamal asked his friend. Bidhusekhar caught him in an embrace. 'You are here,' he said. 'Now I have nothing to fear. Have a wash and something to eat. You can hear the details later.' Ramkamal fixed his eyes on Bidhusekhar's face. 'Tell me first,' he cried passionately, 'if Bimbabati is alive. Tell me if I shall see her again!'

Their arms around each other, the two friends stood at the door of Bimbabati's chamber. She lay on her large bedstead, very still, her hands crossed over her breast. Her face was unnaturally pale. Three English doctors sat with grim faces on the velvet couch to her right. On her left, the famous Kaviraj Deen Dayal Bheshak Shastri stood, eyes closed, chin sunk into his breast. A south Indian ayah stood in one corner, holding a tiny bundle wrapped in a kantha sheet. It was from this bundle that the wailing came, a sound loud enough to set any father's heart at rest. The child was healthy and would live. But Ramkamal's new-found paternity left him cold. His only concern was Bimbabati.

'Is it all over?' he asked again, his voice hoarse and unsteady.

'No,' Bidhusekhar answered, 'there is life in her yet. Sati Lakshmi Bimbabati has waited for you to come to her. She won't go without seeing you and taking leave of you.'

Ramkamal ran towards Bimbabati's bed but Surgeon Gordon rose swiftly from the couch and stood before him. 'Don't disturb her, please,' he said. 'There are enough chances that she will survive.' Ramkamal stared at him with a dazed expression. 'Let me sit by her,' he begged. 'Let me touch her once. I won't speak a word.' Surgeon Gordon glanced briefly at Bidhusekhar and stepped aside. Then, taking a gold watch from his pocket, he watched the seconds tick away. Ramkamal removed his *nagras* and moved softly, on naked feet, to his wife's bedside. His heart beat painfully. A strange smell was in the air. Was it the smell of death? He placed a hand on Bimbabati's brow. How cold and clammy it was! Forgetting his promise, he cried out in a cracked voice,' Bimba! Bimba! Open your eyes and look at me. See, I'm here by your side.' But the cry did not reach Bimbabati's ears. She lay cold and lifeless as stone.

Surgeon Gordon looked up in alarm. 'Please, please,' he begged. The kaviraj opened his eyes and said, 'Call upon God, Singhi Moshai![3] If He wishes it, all will be well.' Ramkamal controlled himself with an effort and moved away from the bed, ashamed of his childish outburst before such eminent

---

3 Sir.

physicians. As he stepped forward to leave the room, Bidhusekhar called after him, 'Don't you wish to see your son?' He signalled to the ayah and she came up to Ramkamal, holding out the bundle for him to see. A tiny mass of flesh lay in the kantha, so tiny, it looked more like a kitten than a human child. But it was alive. The crying was lusty and the little arms flailed the air angrily. Ramkamal sighed and wondered why the child had been born, only to kill its mother. He had never missed not having a son and he didn't want one at the cost of Bimbabati. He pressed two gold coins into the ayah's hand and hurried out of the room.

Over the next seven days a fierce battle raged, with death on one side and the mortals on the other. And then, on the eighth day, Bimbabati opened her eyes. 'Where am I?' she asked. Ramkamal had just sat down to his midday meal when the news came. He pushed away his *thala*, rose and made his way to Bimbabati's room. 'You are in your own home, Bimba!' he said. 'This is your room and this your bed. And I, your husband, am here by your side. You've given birth to a male child. Do you know that?'

But Bimbabati's eyes were vague and unfocussed. 'What happened to me?' she asked. 'Did I die?'

'Oh no! Why should you die? You—'

'I must have been dreaming. I thought I was passing through strange lands—crossing rivers and forests and climbing high mountains. There were huge tunnels as dark as pitch. But there was light beyond them, so bright it dazzled my eyes!' She sat up with a jerk. 'My son!' she cried. 'Where is my son?' The ayah laid the newborn infant on Bimbabati's lap but Bimba stared at it blankly. 'Who is this?' she cried. 'This is not my son. My son is much bigger.'

Ramkamal stroked his wife's hair and said gently, 'You were pregnant. Don't you remember? This is the child of your womb.' The child was not crying any more. It lay, sleeping quietly, in the kantha. Bimbabati stared at it for a long while. Then her eyes cleared and tears dropped from them on to the infant's cheek. She gathered it close and kissed the damp brow. Looking up at her husband, she said, 'Ganga? Where is Ganga?'

Ramkamal turned to the servants who crowded at the door. 'Fetch Ganga,' he commanded. 'Where is the boy?'

'He's gone to study at the *firinghee pathshala*, Karta,' one of them answered.

'*O go*, send for him,' Bimbabati begged. 'I want to see him. I haven't seen him for so long.'

Ramkamal ordered one of the servants to run and fetch Ganga from school. Then, turning to Bimbabati, he said, 'You must rest now. Ganga is coming.'

'You thought I was dead, didn't you?' Bimbabati smiled at her husband. 'But I wasn't dead! I fell into a deep, deep sleep. And in my sleep I travelled . . . '

Bimbabati's widowed sister-in-law, Hemangini, said, 'Have something to eat, Chhoto Bou![4] You've had nothing but medicine all these days.'

'I'm not hungry, Didi.' Bimba clasped the baby to her breast, as if afraid someone would snatch it away. 'My body and mind are suffused with joy. I feel I've drunk a whole pot of *amrita*.'

After a while Ganga was brought into the room. He was a handsome lad of fourteen, with a sweet, shy face. Bimba took him in her arms and stroked his face and hair. 'Did you think your mother was dead, Ganga?' she cried. 'Why didn't you come to me?'

'*O lo*, don't talk so much,' Hemangini admonished. 'You'll be fainting again. Your face is as pale as a ghost's.'

Ramkamal was alarmed. They said that a flame flickers into life just before it goes out altogether. Was that what was happening to Bimbabati? 'Lie down, Bimba,' he said. 'I've asked Kaviraj Moshai to come and take a look at you.'

'Don't fear for me any more. I won't die. I haven't seen you for so long. I haven't seen Ganga for so long. My poor Ganga looks so pale! Have you had your meal, Ganga?' Ganga nodded. 'Call me Ma, Ganga! I haven't heard you call me Ma for so many days.'

'Ma,' Ganganarayan said in a trembling voice.

'Come, sit on the bed. See, you have a baby brother. You'll love him, won't you?'

Ramkamal's ancestral home was in the village of Baksa in Hooghly district. Many years ago, his grandfather left the

---

4 Younger daughter-in-law.

village to seek his fortune in the city of Calcutta. Fortune favoured him and he gained considerable wealth and repute in the salt trade. Over the years he even managed to find a place in the exalted circles of Calcutta's elite. But just as this branch of the family prospered in every way, the rest of the tree shrivelled up and fell into decline. Ramkamal kept no links with his native village till, one day, he heard a story so strange that it appeared in the leading English papers. A woman had left her one-year-old son on the portico of the nine-jewelled temple of Sri Sri Raghunath Jiu in Ramkamal's ancestral village of Baksa. When caught, she had admitted her guilt but said she had abandoned her infant because she couldn't bear to see it starve to death before her eyes. She had left the babe at the feet of Sri Sri Raghunath Jiu in the hope that it would be saved, following which she would take her own life.

The woman was a widow. On making enquiries Ramkamal learned that her dead husband was his cousin, twice removed. Protective of his family name, he had the woman and her child brought to his mansion in Jorasanko, where many such had found shelter. Ramkamal's mother was a generous, kind-hearted woman and no one who came to her door was ever turned away. The house was full of poor relations. At least fifty *thalas* were laid out at each meal. But whereas the others lived in cramped quarters on the ground floor, the newcomers were given a large, airy room upstairs and all the comforts the house could provide. Yet the woman wept often and suffered from bouts of depression. She lived only six months from the day she had come under Ramkamal's roof but, before she died, she placed the baby on Bimbabati's lap and begged with tears in her eyes, 'Take care of him, Didi.'

The child was Ganganarayan. On his mother's death, Bimbabati took him to her bosom and made him her own.

Believing Bimbabati to be barren and knowing that the blood of his forefathers ran in the child's veins, Ramkamal decided to adopt Ganganarayan with full ceremony. That was five years ago. Then a strange thing happened. As Ganga approached manhood, his face and form developed a striking resemblance to Ramkamal's. Everyone who saw Ganga commented on the fact. Some even went so far as to say that the adoption ceremony was a facade and that Ganganarayan was

Ramkamal's natural son. After all, everyone knew of Ramkamal's weakness for women. It was quite possible that he had kept a mistress in his native village and that Ganga was her son. The adoption ceremony, they said, had been arranged to legalize Ganga's inheritance. Such rumours were rife and many believed them. But not Bidhusekhar. When he heard them he laughed aloud. He was not one to be swayed by scandalous gossip.

Bimbabati believed that Sri Sri Raghunath Jiu had heard her prayers and sent Ganga to her. Ganga was such a lovely boy—gentle and sensitive, extremely intelligent and of a scholarly bent of mind. Already, at fourteen, he knew Sanskrit and Persian and was learning English at the *firinghee* school. There was no doubt in anyone's mind that Ramkamal's vast estates would be safe in Ganga's hands.

Now, of course, the situation had changed. But Ramkamal still had his doubts. Would the child survive? It was so tiny—no human child, surely, was that small. Also, it didn't sleep as much as other infants did. It stayed awake most of the day and cried and laughed incessantly. It was said that a new-born, used to the darkness of the womb, shuts his eyes against the light of the world for a month or two. But not this one. It looked with unblinking eyes at everything and everyone and laughed with a tinkling sound whenever a finger was wagged at it.

Ramkamal avoided the child for the first few days. Even when he went to see Bimbabati he wouldn't look at it. He didn't wish to form any emotional ties with one who was destined to leave the earth. He had Ganganarayan, his son and heir, and he was satisfied. Then, gradually, a change came over him. His own flesh and blood drew him like a magnet. Now he was seen in Bimbabati's chamber several times a day. He would gaze at the tiny face and form, hear the tinkling laugh and marvel at the infant's strength. Who would have thought that a foetus of seven months and ten days would have so much life force?

Something else left him wondering. All these years he had thought himself incapable of impregnating a woman. Bimbabati, of course, believed that the flaw was in her. But Ramkamal knew the truth. He had planted his seed in many women but not one had taken root. If he had had a son, even from a whore, he would have given him his name and paternity and proclaimed him successor to the family estates. But that was not to be! Ramkamal's manhood had been proved before the world, not by a lowly strumpet but by his high-born, beauteous wife. Whenever he thought of this miracle, happiness and gratitude surged through his blood in waves.

Bimbabati sat with the child on her lap, waiting for her husband to come to her. The moment he entered, both pairs of eyes automatically fell on the sleeping child.

'Have you seen his eyes?' Bimbabati whispered. 'They are like yours. The mouth too. Only his brow is like mine.'

Ramkamal smiled. Women were absurd creatures. Where, in that tiny mass of flesh, could one find any resemblance to anyone?

'How do you feel, Bimba?'

'I am well.' Peace and contentment shone in Bimba's eyes. 'You must look after yourself. I'm no good to you now.'

'You musn't worry. Ma and Bara Bouthan[5] are looking after me.'

'Is Ganga asleep? Has he had his meal?'

'Doesn't he come to you?'

'He hasn't come today. I was told he was studying when I sent for him. He has never seen me lying around in bed; it makes him shy, I think.'

'Children often get like that when brothers and sisters are born. I was nine when Kusum Kumari came. I felt Ma didn't love me any more. All she cared for was Kusum—'

'Ganga is much older. He'll understand.'

'Bimba! Can you love the two equally and in the same way?'

'Why not? I haven't carried Ganga in my womb. But he is no less to me because of that.'

'Bidhu says there is bound to be trouble between the two. It is always so between real and adopted children. So many cases come up in court—'

'Ganga will never fight his brother.'

'Even if Ganga doesn't, this one might. What if he grows up to hate Ganga?'

A hurt expression came into Bimbabati's eyes. 'Why do you

---

5 Elder sister-in-law.

say such things?' she cried. 'Nothing like that will happen. They will live the way brothers should.'

'I hope so. I'll divide my properties equally between them and draw up a legal document. They'll both be rich—' Even as he said the words, Ramkamal thought, 'Equally! Why equally? Why should Ganga get an equal share with my own flesh and blood? What will my son think of me when he grows up and discovers the truth? Will he not consider it injustice?' Ramkamal laughed aloud.

'What is it?' Bimbabati asked.

'Blood is a strange thing, Bimba! It pulls at a man and weakens him. I found myself wondering why the two should inherit equally. After all, Ganga isn't . . .'

'I'll never think like that. I'll love them both equally, as long as I live.'

'If you can do that, I can too. You are their mother, but I'm their father, am I not?'

Bimbabati recovered her full strength in the next few days, to the amazement of the doctors who were still in attendance. No one had expected both mother and child to survive. Ramkamal's mother, Soudamini, busied herself in arranging pujas and charities. The poor were fed. Brahmins were given alms and their blessings sought for the newborn. While all this was going on, the family priest was studying the position of the stars and planets at the moment of birth and recording his observations. Then, one day, he read out the horoscope. The child would be a man of destiny! His fame would spread far and wide and he would bring honour to his family name. Bimbabati had held a jewel in her womb!

The child was named Nabin Kumar. On the twenty-first day after his birth Ramkamal entered Bimbabati's room to find her sitting on the floor, suckling her babe. Ganga sat behind her, his cheek resting on her shoulder.

'Beautiful!' Ramkamal murmured. Tears stood in his eyes and, for some strange reason, for the first time after his return, he remembered Kamala Sundari. Hurrying downstairs, he ordered Dibakar to get the carriage ready. He would go to Janbazar, to Kamala Sundari's house.

## Chapter II

The shop was shut for the day but Goopi, the goldsmith, was inside, working by the light of a lamp, when the wicker door was pushed open and Raimohan entered. So tall that his head touched the roof, Raimohan was quite a dandy. He wore a dhoti of fine Shimle weave and a yellow banian. A striped Shantipuri chador hung from his neck and a string of jasmine from his wrist. On his feet were shoes of fine English leather. His sudden appearance did not surprise Goopi for Raimohan came quite often and always at that hour. Pushing a stool towards him Goopi said, 'Sit, Ghoshal Moshai.'

Raimohan sat on the stool, his knees sticking up in the air. Then, taking a brass *dibé* from his pocket, he helped himself to paan and offered some to Goopi. The fire was hot and the sweat rolled down Goopi's face in fat, oily drops. Stretching out a hand, he said, 'I'll have one. Now, Ghoshal Moshai, tell me the news.'

'The hottest news of today is that Churo Datta's whore was stabbed last night in her room. She was found this morning, her face stuck in a pool of blood.'

'Which whore? He has many, so I hear.'

'The Bowbazar one. She was my Heeremoni's neighbour.'

'Tchk, tchk. She was very beautiful, wasn't she?'

'That she was. One of the brightest stars has fallen from the Calcutta sky. You should have heard Churo Datta's wails. Men don't weep so loud at the death of a wife!'

'But who could have stabbed her? It takes courage to come near a keep of Churo Datta's.'

'Have you tried?'

'*Ram kaho*! *Ram kaho*! Who am I? The smallest of small fry. I only hear of such women; I've never seen any.'

'I have a feeling it is Churo's own handiwork. The bird was fluttering her wings and would have flown. Rasik Datta had his eye on her. Churo couldn't allow that. He kicks out his women—not the other way around.'

'*Ram kaho*! *Ram kaho*! What is the world coming to? Tell me more.'

'I was in Chetlaganj this morning. The rice boats have arrived. Rice will be cheaper this season . . .'

'So the boats have arrived, have they? The rice we've been getting these last three months—*Ram kaho*! I heard the cannon being fired from the fort, boom boom, this evening. Is some big saheb coming from across the water?'

'Some director of John Company. His name is—*doos*! I forget his name.'

'Are you on your way back home, Ghoshal Moshai?'

'Home? At this hour? Are my limbs pickled that I should dawdle home at dusk and chew the cud all night? Do you hear music, Goopi?'

'Hunh. Where is it coming from?'

'From Jorasanko. The Thakurs are celebrating a birth. Dwarkanath has been blessed with a grandson. An English band is playing.'

'Haven't you been invited?'

'Today's entertainment is for the sahebs. There'll be wine and dancing girls. The natives are being fed tomorrow. I don't need an invitation. I just walk in wherever there's a feast.'

'Which of Dwarkanath's sons is the father?'

'His eldest, Debendranath. Deben Thakur's first child, a girl, died at birth. So there is much rejoicing over this one.'

'These Thakurs are experts in squandering money. Debendranath will be worse than his father.'

'Won't he? Don't you remember the time he spent a lakh on Saraswati Puja? Even Dwarkanath was shocked.'

'I hear he wears pearls and diamonds on his feet.'

'Feet? On his shoes, Goopi. On his shoes.'

'What is the world coming to!'

'These Thakurs have so much money, they don't know where to keep it. I hear the money in that house is not counted. It is weighed on a pair of scales. Debendranath went to study in Hindu College—*chhi*! a filthy den of *mlechhas*. Druzo Saheb is dead and gone but his disciples are even worse. You think they care about caste and morals? Dwarkanath took his son away and set him to manage the estates. And what does he do? He throws away money with both hands! He's some wastrel, that boy, for all he's only twenty-three years old.'

'To your advantage,' Goopi cut in with a grin.

'And now, Ramkamal Singhi has a son. All these years he has reaped the harvests of others. And now it *seems* his own seed—'

'Seems! Why do you say seems?'

'I don't believe everything I'm told, Goopi. Singhi's wife was brought to bed of a son. But who knows who fathered it?'

'*Aha, chhi chhi! Ram kaho*! Don't say such things. Everyone knows that Ramkamal's wife is a Sati Lakshmi—as pure as she is beautiful.'

'Sati! There isn't a sati left in the country after Bentinck Saheb passed the law.'

'What law? What has the saheb done?'

'*Chha*! The *mlechha* of *mlechhas* passed a law against sati. Women will not burn with their husbands any more. Did you know that, Goopi? The satis just disappeared overnight. Show me one woman who is a sati.'

Goopi was nervous of such talk. He had a wife and children, and a living to make. He shrugged his shoulders and changed the subject. 'Tell me about yourself, Ghoshal Moshai. How is life treating you?'

In answer, Raimohan drew out a gold chain from his pocket. 'Have a look at it,' he said. 'How much will it fetch?' Goopi turned the chain over in his hand and inspected it closely. 'Where did this come from?' he asked. 'How many chains do you have, Ghoshal Moshai?'

'This is my grandson's.'

'Aha! Don't sell it, Ghoshal Moshai. Don't sadden the child's heart.'

'I don't give a crow's foot for the child's heart. Besides, he isn't around to get saddened. He died last year and went to Heaven. There's so much gold there, Goopi, he can roll in it. Now weigh it quickly—'

Goopi knew Raimohan was lying and Raimohan knew that Goopi knew. Yet they played this game every time Raimohan brought something to sell. Raimohan looked on with a hawk's eye while Goopi fiddled with the scales. No one knew how old Raimohan was. He had been around for years and years. But if anyone asked him his age, he answered, 'Twelve or thirteen. Don't you see my armpits are as smooth as a newborn's?' Raimohan had no hair on his body. He had no flesh either. Only a thin yellow skin, stretched tight as a drum over a row of bones, making him look taller than he really was. His nose stuck out cadaverously in the air and his eyes gleamed with the cunning of a hunted fox. Raimohan made his living by sniffing around in rich men's houses.

'The gold here is, hum, one and a half bharis.'

'You swung your hand, you rogue. I saw you.'

'I didn't. See here.'

'All goldsmiths are thieves. Well, how much is it?'

'One and a half bharis, exactly. At nineteen rupees a bhari it will come to—'

'Gold is selling at twenty, you cheat!'

'That's the price of ripe gold.'

'And I've brought you raw gold, have I?'

Goopi wouldn't give a paisa more than twenty-eight rupees and Raimohan would not take a cowrie less than thirty. At last, after a heated debate, a compromise was reached. Tucking twenty-nine rupees into his pocket, Raimohan rose from the stool and, bang, his head hit the beam. Rubbing the sore spot ruefully, Raimohan walked out into the night.

A moon shone in the sky and light streamed from the lanterns people carried in their hands. It was Saturday evening and Chitpore Street was chock-a-block with men, horses and bullocks. A few yards from Goopi's shop Raimohan came upon a phaeton, stuck between two bullock carts. The coachman yelled curses from the box and, at the window, a babu's face appeared, calling fretfully, 'Death be on your heads. Let go, I say, let go.' One of the bullocks swung its tail in agitation, smacking the babu squarely on the jaw. Crrack! The coachman's whip descended on the hapless creature's back, making him start nervously. The cart came unstuck, slipped and slithered and landed in a ditch. *'Arré! Arré*! Stop it. Hold it!' The crowd ran after the cart while, oblivious of the cries and the swinging of lanterns, a procession passed. Two drummers in the lead beat out a frenzied rhythm and men with flaring torches brought up the rear. The people swayed and sang:

He dances, nude, with tangled locks.
Bhola—*bom*—Bhola!
Swinging skulls on naked chest
Bhola—*bom*—Bhola!

Raimohan walked with them, his lips curved in a smile. Suddenly, a figure got dislodged from the swaying mass and fell, with a thud, at Raimohan's feet. 'I'm Peyara from Chhikeshto Bagan,' a face blubbered in the dark. 'Sorry, I'm Chhikeshto from Peyara Bagan. What are you, sir? A palm tree?' Three women, standing together under a tree, giggled loudly. All three had red silk kerchiefs in their hands.

'Careful, careful! Are you hurt?' Raimohan helped the drunk to his feet.

'Oh, no. I just swung a little like a boat in a high wind.'

'Have a paan, Moshai.' Raimohan held out his *dibé*.

'Give me, give me!' The three wenches snatched the *dibé* from Raimohan's hand and crammed paan into their mouths. Then one of them swayed lasciviously towards Raimohan and touching the string of jasmine on his wrist, said huskily, 'Who is this for, beloved? Put it around my neck.'

'No, mine, mine!' the other two clamoured while the first pulled at his hand, saying, 'Come to my room, dear heart.'

'*Ja* Baba!' Gaping at the scene, the drunk muttered, 'Am I a soiled banana leaf that no one wants me?'

Raimohan pulled himself loose and, chucking the three girls under their chins, walked on. Passing Hedo Lake, where a fat black priest guarded a pile of fat black Bibles, while a thin white priest preached a sermon, he came to Bowbazar and stood before a two-storeyed house. 'Heeremoni! O Heeremoni!' he called from the bottom of the steps. 'Can I come in?'

A pretty girl in a blue spangled sari leaned over the banister. 'You!' she cried, amazed. 'Aren't you afraid of coming here after what happened last night?'

'Where do I hide when I'm afraid, my Heeremon bird, but in your nest? Who do I have but you?

'Death be on your head, you corpse! There's no one in the street except you.'

'Wonderful! Then no one will come to you. I can stay all night.'

Raimohan climbed the steps and walked into Heeremoni's room. A thick carpet lay on the floor, covered with fresh white sheets. On the wall nearest the door hung a picture of a cat with a fish in its mouth. Next to it was one of Goddess Kali of Kalighat. A little boy, barely a year old, lay sleeping on the sheet, his head resting on a red velvet cushion.

'I skulked around the neighbourhood a bit this morning,' Raimohan said. 'There were a lot of policemen about.'

'Two white sahebs were here. They were also police, I think.'

'This is an important death, Heere. Churo Datta's whore! Not you or me. I wouldn't be surprised if the governor-general came to see Moti Bibi's carcass.'

'*Aha go*! What a terrible death! Her body was cut to ribbons.'

'That is why I keep telling you not to play the nesting game. Flit from branch to branch, my dear, and peck at whatever fruit you fancy.'

'I said to Moti, "Be careful. Churo Babu is an evil man with a vile temper". But would the strumpet listen? "I don't give a crow's leg for your Churo Babu", she said, her nose in the air. And see what she gets for her arrogance.'

'Let her rot in hell. Tell me why are you all dolled up if no one is coming to you? Is it for me?'

'Hunh! For him who hasn't two blind cowries to rub together in his purse. I dressed up because I like looking pretty.'

Raimohan slapped his banian pocket and the twenty-nine rupees jingled merrily. 'Two blind cowries! Ha, ha ha! I've brought you a hundred rupees tonight, my Heere Rani. Send the servant out for a bottle. We must celebrate our night together.'

'Let me take the child to the other room. You'll start screaming your head off as soon as the first drop hits your stomach.'

'I'll sing to you, Heere. I've written a song—'

'I know the kind of songs you write. About the rich babus of Calcutta—'

'O Hari! That I do for a living. For you I've written a romantic song. A delicious little song for you to sing in your delicious little voice.'

Raimohan looked on with a lively interest as Heeremoni

prepared to carry her son out of the room. 'He has a sweet face,' he said. 'Whose child is he?'

'Mine.'

'I know that. Who is the father?'

'Is that any of your business? God has given him to me and—'

'Which god? There are so many gods in rich families. Is he from the house of the Dattas? Or the Thakurs? Or the Sheels, the Malliks, the Debs, the—'

'Will you shut your mouth?'

'The boy isn't mine, is he? I know I'm not one of the gods that come to you. I'm only the dog that licks their feet. Still—'

'I'll give you seven licks with the broomstick, you scum of the earth!' Heeremoni pulled aside the heavy velvet curtain that separated the two rooms and disappeared from view. Raimohan always came to Bowbazar at the heels of some big babu. The babu did the spending; Raimohan had the fun. It was very rarely that he came alone and, when he did, it was always to Heeremoni. She was new to the profession, only seventeen and very pretty.

Raimohan stretched out his long legs and sipped from his glass in the style of the babus whose toady he was. 'Sing a song for me, Heere,' he commanded.

'You said you would sing tonight.'

Raimohan shut his eyes and, wagging his head from side to side, hummed softly:

On a silver tree with leaves of gold
Sits a bird with a jewelled eye.
Heeremon, Heeremon—she whistles sweet
At every passer-by.

He put out a hand and pinched Heere's cheek. Suddenly, there was a loud knocking at the door and Heeremoni's servant came running in. 'Sarkar Babu!' he stuttered, 'Sarkar Babu is coming.'

'Jagamohan Sarkar!' Raimohan jumped up.

Heeremoni's brows came together. 'Why are you running away?' she cried.

Raimohan bit his tongue and shook his head. 'Sarkar Moshai is here. What am I in comparison? A bedbug—nothing more.'

'No.' Heere caught his hand and held it firmly. 'You will stay. Ramdas, tell Babu I'm not well. I can't see him tonight.'

'No, Heere, no. You musn't do that.'

'Why not? I want you to stay. I want to hear that lovely song again.'

'*Arré*! Babus like Jagamohan Sarkar can make you rich. I'm a pauper and a parasite. I told you I had a hundred rupees. I was lying—'

'Don't you dare talk like that, you ingrate. Have I ever asked you for money? I have enough money of my own.'

'Even if you do, don't send Sarkar Moshai away. He's working so hard for the women of our country—he'll be mortally hurt if a woman shows him the door.'

'Then get out, you bastard. Just get out and never show me your face again.'

'Aha! Don't be so cruel, my Heeremon bird. Love me a little before bidding me goodbye. Everyone kicks me about. But you musn't. *Arré*! *Arré*! Sarkar Moshai is coming up the stairs. I hear his footsteps. Where are my shoes?'

The house shook under the weight of the great babu of Calcutta as he tottered up the steps with the servant's help. His huge body swayed on unsteady feet as he rapped on the door with his gold-headed cane.

'If I were a bird I would fly out of the window,' Raimohan whispered. 'Now what do I do? Where do I hide?'

'You're trembling,' Heeremoni whispered back, 'like a blackbird in a storm.'

'*Koi go*, Heeremoni!' Jagamohan Sarkar called out in a voice loud with liquor. 'Why do you keep me out?.'

A gleam came into Raimohan's eyes. Smiling wickedly, he put a hand on one hip and swayed and pirouetted.

'Have you gone crazy?' Heeremoni stared.

'Open the door, Heeremoni,' the great voice boomed.

'I'm not well tonight. I can't let you in.'

'I have a cure for all your ills, dearie. Just let me in.'

'Open the door,' Raimohan whispered. 'I'll hide in the next room. Don't breathe a word.'

Jagamohan Sarkar lumbered into the room and collapsed on

the velvet cushions. Then, putting his hand on the vast sea of his stomach, he blew out a great bubble of smelly wind. 'You look very well, Heeremoni,' he said coyly. 'Your face grows more beautiful by the hour. If only I were a humming bee I could sit on it!'

'I was wondering,' Heeremoni said by way of an answer, 'what made you come to me when there are so many others in the city.'

'I love you, Heeremoni. I think of you all the time. I can't come as often as I used to because I'm neck deep in good work. I'm so busy, I barely have time to eat and sleep. You must make up to me tonight for all the nights I've lost.'

'You look hot. Let me fan you. Shall I make you some sherbet?'

'Sherbet!' Jagamohan laughed till the tears stood in his eyes. 'After all the wine I've drunk?' Then, sobering down, he asked, 'Why were you trying to get rid of me?'

'It is very late. I was about to go to bed.'

'I can't get to a whorehouse till well past midnight. A lot of young rascals hang about my gates, waiting to catch me. Doing good and noble work has its disadvantages. One lives in perpetual fear of being caught. Why are you sitting so far from me, dearie? Come closer. Take me in your arms and put my head on your breast. I'm so lonely! So lonely!'

From a crack in the door, Raimohan watched the scene.

# *Chapter III*

It is said that Nabin Kumar learned to crawl at five months . . .

One morning, Bimbabati left the house in a palki to take her customary dip in the Ganga, leaving the baby in the care of her trusted maid, Chintamoni. Chinta washed and fed the child and put him to sleep in Bimba's bed. She had barely left the room when she heard a thud and hurried back. The child lay on the ground and a thin stream of blood ran from a cut on his forehead. But instead of wailing and screaming, he giggled at Chinta and, crawling away from her, hid under the bed. Chinta grew pale with horror. She was sure the child was possessed. Not daring to touch him, she stood helplessly at the foot of the bed and called out to him: 'O Chhoto Babu![6] O Chhoto Babu!'

Then, when Nabin Kumar was only eight months old, he stood up one day and walked on unsteady legs from the room to the verandah, startling Bimbabati and her maids. There was more to come. Bimbabati was fond of birds and kept many as pets. Long verandahs ran on all the floors of the house in Jorasanko, from the beams of which hung cages of all shapes and sizes. And in the cages could be seen every kind of bird—myna, bulbul, koel and heeremon. Bimbabati swung them in their perches and fed them gram, soaked in water, with her own hands while little Nabin toddled along after her, the end of her sari bunched up in his little hands. Every morning after her puja, Bimba stood before the myna and tried to teach him to talk. 'O myna, say Radhe Krishna,' she would repeat over and over again in her sweet voice. The foolish myna only pecked and chattered and rolled its red eyes at Bimbabati. But little Nabin said, suddenly one day, in a voice as clear as a bell, 'Radhe Krishna.'

Nabin was exactly eight months and seventeen days old when this incident took place. A wave of ecstasy ran through

6 Young master.

Bimbabati. Not Ma; not Baba; not Dada—the first words her baby had spoken were God's name in a near perfect accent. She had heard Chintamoni say, often enough, that the child was possessed by an evil spirit. Bimbabati half believed her for Nabin's precocity was unnatural. Besides, a child born before his proper time was prone to many ills. But hearing him say Radhe Krishna, her fears vanished. Her child was safe! No evil spirit would dare come near him. She picked him up in her arms and ran to her husband's bedroom.

Ramkamal was a late riser. Rudely shaken out of his sleep, he sat up in bed and stared at his wife as, speechless with excitement, she laughed and cried and kissed the child, wildly, over and over again. Ramkamal was quite confounded. It was Nabin who set his father's fears at rest. He said, once again in a voice like a clockwork doll's, 'Rade Kisso.'

Gradually, word spread that a prodigy had been born in the house of the Singhas of Jorasanko. And, indeed, Nabin could sing, dance and recite verses from the time he was one year old. Wherever he was, he became the centre of attention. The sight of Nabin entertaining a circle of adults was a common one. Most of his spectators enjoyed his performance and egged him on but there were some who looked away in embarrassment. There was something odd about the boy. His arms and legs were so jerky and angular—they seemed carved out of wood. A pair of unnaturally bright eyes glittered from a face that was well formed but totally without charm or sweetness. Many believed that he was a freak of nature and wouldn't survive infancy. A leading weekly of the time, *Samaj Darpan*, carried news of the boy. Mr Marshman of Srirampur wrote the following lines:

'Babu Ramkamal Singha, resident of Jorasanko, has been blessed with a son at the ripe old age of forty-seven. The child's name is Nabin Kumar. His presence has brightened up the ancestral mansion and brought much happiness to the lives of his parents. Nabin Kumar is renowned for his piety. Tears of joy stream from his eyes whenever he sees an image of a god or a goddess. The child is only one year and two months old'.

While Nabin basked in the limelight, Ganganarayan became more of an introvert every day. He was a shy youth who avoided people as a rule. Now, with Nabin holding court, he kept himself almost totally out of view. He had left the *firinghee* school a year ago and joined Hindu College. A new world, an enchanted world of the imagination, opened before him. He was on a voyage of discovery.

Not mad but bound more than a madman is!
Shut up in prison, kept without my food
Whipped and tormented . . .

Ganga walked back and forth, declaiming Shakespeare in the privacy of his room. Romeo's speech! Even as he declaimed he heard Captain Richardson's voice in his ears. Captain Saheb's voice had a tremendous range and a whole gamut of inflections. He could roar like a lion and coo like a dove, all in one breath. While reading the play he modulated his voice to suit all the characters: Capulet, Horatio, Romeo—even Juliet. The boys were so quiet—you could hear a pin drop. Even a wild, indisciplined boy like Madhu listened with rapt attention.

Ganganarayan was now old enough, in his father's opinion, to start learning the management of the estates. It was time he had a wife, too. After careful search and deliberation it was decided that Lilavati, the seven-year-old daughter of Gokul Bosu Moshai of Bagbazar, would make a fitting bride for Ganganarayan. But Ganga's ears turned a fiery red every time his marriage was mentioned. He didn't want to marry a seven-year-old. He had no idea of what to say to her. Besides, there was some mystery in the business of matrimony which he couldn't fathom. Of late, Bindubasini had started teasing him about it.

Bindubasini was Bidhusekhar's third daughter and Ganga's playmate from infancy. They took lessons together, too, from Shib Ram Acharya, a Sanskrit pandit who lived in Bidhusekhar's house and tutored his children. Every morning he journeyed to Srirampur for he was one of the staff of Sanskrit pandits employed by Mr Marshman for his paper, *Samaj Darpan*. Bindu was very intelligent and had a great love of learning. This love turned into a passionate devotion after the death of her husband and her return to her father's house. Bidhusekhar had five daughters but no son. His youngest, the eight-year-old Suhasini, was to be wed in the month of

Agrahayan[7]. A match between Ganga and Suhasini would have been ideal except for the fact that Bidhusekhar was a Brahmin and Ramkamal a Kayastha.

Bidhusekhar was not only a Brahmin; he was a Vaidic *kulin*. His daughters could be given in marriage only to boys from *kulin* families. Marriages, in this community, were arranged almost from the moment of a girl's birth. The actual ceremony took place later, at an appropriate time. Bidhusekhar had formed such alliances for all his daughters. But Bindu was dogged by ill-luck from the moment she was born. The boy from Krishnanagar, with whom her betrothal had taken place, died before she attained her seventh year. Thus Bindu was caught in the strange state of being widowed before she was wed. Another *kulin* match was ruled out for her. After a lot of trouble Bidhusekhar managed to find a *moulik* family, a strain or two lower than the high *kulin* family to which she had been promised, willing to take her.

The sky was a flaming red the night Bindu got married. A terrible fire raging in the Pathuriaghat area of Calcutta had turned night into day for two whole days. And under that flaming sky, the eight-year-old Bindu walked behind her husband, away from her father's house, weeping because she was leaving her dolls and playmates behind. A year and a half later, she returned weeping in the same way—the sindoor wiped away from the parting of her hair.

Bidhusekhar had a flourishing practice in the civil courts of Calcutta, his renown nearly touching that of Rajnarayan Datta's. He was enormously wealthy, too. Yet, unlike his friend, Ramkamal, he never thought of adopting a male child. He had decided to keep his youngest son-in-law (the boy with whom Suhasini was contracted) in his house and to teach him the management of his money and estates. But his hopes were dashed. The boy took two wives even before his marriage to Suhasini was solemnized. Enraged at what he considered a betrayal, Bidhusekhar broke off the betrothal. This caused a flutter in *kulin* circles for no girl's father had dared to do such a thing before. But Bidhusekhar's money took care of everything.

---

7 Mid-November—Mid-December.

The murmurs died down and another boy was found. He was a student of Sanskrit College, very poor but very meritorious and from a *kulin* family of the purest strain.

On her return to her father's house, Bindubasini did not resume her play with the dolls she had abandoned. She was pushed, instead, into a playhouse of vast dimensions and had to spend her days in the service of a larger, more demanding doll. Her father had said to her in a voice shaking with emotion: 'Give over crying, my child. Withdraw from the world and dedicate yourself to God. From this day I entrust our household deity, Janardan, to your care. Think of Him as the husband you have lost and of the rest of us as your children.' This advice, lofty as it was, was not easy to follow for a girl who was barely nine and a half years old. In the beginning, Bindu tried hard to obey her father. Her coarse white *than* wrapped clumsily about her, she sat for hours with closed eyes before the image of Janardan. But before she knew it she fell asleep, curled up on the grass mat. Her mother often found her thus.

Now, of course, Bindu was in and out of the puja room, every morning and evening. The rest of her day she spent with her books. She was getting to be a fine scholar of Sanskrit and Bengali, even better than Ganganarayan. 'Ganga!' she would take him up imperiously, 'Explain, *"Vigyanarthan manushyanang manah purbang prabartate"*.' 'The mind of man desires knowledge,' was Ganga's careless answer, at which Bindu smiled and shook her head. 'Not so easy. Man desires knowledge of reality. Then he wants more. He wants to identify with it and become one with it. And if his desire is not realized anger and frustration set in. *"Tat prapya kamang bhajate roshanang dwija satvam"*.'

Ganganarayan smiled to hear such big words, tumbling from Bindu's childish lips. 'This isn't poetry,' he said scornfully. 'All this dry philosophy does not interest me.'

'Dry philosophy!' Bindu snapped. 'What do you know of Sanskrit? Just because you've read a few pages of English—'

'If you could read English you, too, would think as I do,' said Ganganarayan, who really found Sanskrit dull and drab in comparison. 'What exquisite verses their poets write! And how many books they have! Macaulay Saheb has said that all the books of our country wouldn't fill a shelf of a European library.'

'Has your Macalu Saheb seen the Mahabharat? Ask him how many shelves just that will fill?'

'Why do you study so hard, Bindu? What good will your Sanskrit do you? You won't open a *tol*.'

'I study for my own pleasure.'

Shib Ram Acharya was a thin, shrivelled-up old man. His knees shook whenever he spoke and the hookah in his hand rattled in sympathy. His room, on the ground floor, was dark and damp and cluttered with piles of dusty tomes and manuscripts, which he pored over whenever he found the time. Though weak and emaciated in body, he had a voice of thunder. He loved teaching—Ganga and Bindu in particular for they were intelligent and eager to learn. Bindu's other sisters lacked her enthusiasm though all of them could read and write. Girls in Brahmin households were better educated than in others. Ganga had observed that. His own mother, Bimbabati, didn't know one letter from another.

One Saturday evening, Shib Ram Acharya returned from Srirampur and, washing his hands and feet, sat down to his *jap*. When he opened his eyes, he saw his pupils waiting for him. He enquired after Ganga's family—his little brother in particular—lit his hookah and pulled at it gravely.

'Pandit Moshai!' Bindu said, shuffling her feet restlessly. 'You promised to read Kalidas this evening. *Meghdoot*—'

'*Meghdootam*! Hunh.' Acharya Moshai shook his knees agitatedly. Then he said, 'Bindu, my child! I have been wanting to say something to you but couldn't find the opportunity. You have learned enough. I have nothing more to teach you.'

'Nothing more!' Bindu repeated in a wondering voice. 'You always say knowledge is like an ocean with no end to it. Besides, I've learned so little.'

'It is enough for a woman. You don't need—'

'No, no, Pandit Moshai, 'Bindu interrupted wildly. 'What will I do? How will I spend my time if I'm not allowed to study?'

'No one can prevent you from reading on your own.'

'On my own! But I haven't even completed *Mugdha Bodh*. And I know so little of Sanskrit grammar. Ganga says there are many books of poetry in English. But, surely, *Meghdoot* is superior to them all. Read *Meghdoot* to us, please, Pandit Moshai.'

'No, Bindu. A woman should not read *Meghdootam.*' Pandit Moshai shook his head and looked down at his feet. Bindu's face turned pale. She sensed, with a sickening pull in the pit of her stomach, that there were barriers she had to respect; that she, as a woman, could only go a little way and no further.

Ganganarayan had sat silently all the while. The Acharya's words puzzled him. Why should Bindu give up her lessons?

'Will you stop teaching me as well, Pandit Moshai?'

'Oh no. You can come to me whenever you like.'

'Then why not Bindu? What has she done?'

'A woman has no right to advanced education. It goes against the laws of our religion and society. Bindu has learned enough to read a few religious texts by herself. That should suffice. *Meghdootam* is out of the question.'

'Then leave it. Let us get on with the Mahabharat.'

The Acharya sighed and pulled at his hookah. 'I see I'll have to tell you the truth,' he said at last. 'Bindu's father wants her lessons discontinued. She has turned fifteen and—'

'Does that mean you won't teach me any more?' Bindu asked angrily.

'If your father does not allow it, what can I do?'

Bindu's face crumpled. She bit her lip, trying hard not to cry. This was too big a blow! She couldn't bear it and ran out of the room. The old man sighed and muttered, 'It is time I left the city and took a house in Srirampur. I'm old and all this rushing about wearies me.'

Ganga sat glum and guilt-ridden. He wondered why Bidhusekhar had put an end to Bindu's education. Bindu had said that she studied for her own pleasure. Why did her father have to snatch away the only happiness she knew? Bindu was such a sweet, simple girl. This would break her heart. And Pandit Moshai would have to leave. Ganga would miss the old man.

'Who will teach me if you leave, Pandit Moshai?' he asked. The old man looked at him out of his rheumy eyes: 'The age of Sanskrit is over, Ganganarayan,' he said. 'You are fortunate to be studying English in an English College. Had I stayed on here a little longer, I would have learned a few words from you. English is the language of the day!'

Ganganarayan touched his tutor's feet and took his leave. It was time he went home. It would soon be dark. But he had to find Bindu first. Bindu was so sensitive—she might do something rash. She might tear her books and throw them away because her lessons had been discontinued. Then, what would she do? How would she pass her days? Ganga realized that long years of loneliness and misery lay ahead of her. Women were not allowed to read *Meghdoot*. What was there in *Meghdoot*? He had to find out.

Looking for Bindu he turned a corner of the verandah and came upon Suhasini. She sat on her maid's lap, eating rice and milk. Suhasini would never eat anything by herself and had to be fed. Bidhusekhar had engaged a Brahmin maid for the purpose.

'Where's Bindu, Suhas?' Ganga asked.

'I don't know. I haven't seen her.'

'Look in the puja room,' the maid suggested. 'I thought I saw her go in there.'

As Ganganarayan moved towards the puja room Suhasini called after him, 'Ganga Dada! Who is to get married first? You or I?'

'This little one can't wait to get married,' the maid smiled indulgently.

Ganga rolled his eyes at Suhasini. 'Wait and see what happens. I'll tell your husband you don't eat your rice and milk and he'll box your ears.'

Suhasini balled up her little hands and flailed the air. 'I'll box him, too,' she cried.

Ganga knelt at the door of the puja room and bowed his head to the ground. Then he called softly, 'Bindu.' There was no answer. Ganga craned his neck forward and searched the room. It was empty. She wasn't in her own room either. 'Perhaps she's sitting with her mother,' Ganga thought. Then he remembered that Bindu preferred to be alone whenever she was unhappy or upset. He went up to the roof and found her leaning on the parapet, looking out to the west where the sun was setting. Behind her the sky was a midnight blue, brushed with threads of silver. In front of her all was fire and gold. Her straight, slim form, robed in widow white, stood silhouetted against the flaming sky. Suddenly, Ganga remembered her wedding day. It seemed such a sky appeared over and over again in Bindu's life! He wanted to console her. 'Don't cry Bindu,' he wanted to say. 'I'll teach you whatever I know; whatever I learn in college.' He stole up behind her and put out a hand to touch her back. But something stopped him. Some primary instinct told him all was not as it had been. Pandit Moshai had referred to Bindu as a woman, not once but many times. When did Bindu become a woman? Till yesterday she was a girl—a laughing, boisterous girl, who teased and chatted with Ganga. Today, she had become a woman. How could he touch her?

Ganganarayan's hand fell to his side.

# Chapter IV

Ganganarayan walked to college everyday. His classmates came riding in palkis and hackney coaches but Ganga preferred to walk even though, being the son of a rich zamindar, he could have come riding in a phaeton. He enjoyed the half-hour walk from Jorasanko to Pataldanga every morning. He looked around him as he walked and observed what went on in the streets.

On reaching the crossing one morning he was startled to see a stream of boys run from the college gate towards Gol Dighi, where a crowd had collected. Curious to know what was going on, Ganga followed them. Opposite Gol Dighi was Madhav Datta's bazaar, where various bad characters floated about. Drunks were often caught stealing from the kebab shops. Drug addicts lurked in the shadows of the ganja shops, waiting for their chance. If the shopman left his goods unguarded for even a minute, they pounced on them and carried them off. If a thief was caught, he was shown no mercy. Shopkeepers and pedestrians fell on him with equal fury and beat him black and blue. Sometimes, a college boy was caught stealing and when that happened, fights broke out between the students and the public. Students stole mostly from ganja shops for they were not allowed to buy the stuff. Hare Saheb had forbidden the shopkeepers to sell ganja to the boys.

On one occasion, a shopman had caught a boy stealing ganja and dragged him over to Hare Saheb. Hare Saheb was, ordinarily, a vague, gentle, old man who couldn't hurt a fly. But when he heard that his order had been flouted, he flew into a violent rage. 'Kashi! Bring my whip,' he called out in a terrible voice and when it arrived, he laid it about, quite mercilessly, on the boy's back and buttocks.

On another occasion, Hare Saheb had flogged Ganga's friend, Banku Datta. Banku hadn't stolen ganja. He had been caught taking lessons from Mr Sendis of the Mirzapur Mission. When the matter was reported to Hare Saheb he sent for Banku.

He had a whip in his hand and his face was red and angry. After the flogging was over, Hare Saheb had wept over Banku's bleeding back. He had washed the wounds with warm water and said tenderly, 'Pay attention to your studies, dear boy. Don't addle your brains with religion. There is plenty of time for that.' Hare Saheb had become doubly careful after Derozio Saheb's ignominous dismissal. He knew that if rumours of proselytising the boys spread, guardians would be seriously disturbed. Already, a number of boys had been withdrawn from Hindu College and enrolled in Gour Adhya's Oriental Seminary.

Ganganarayan ran in the direction of Gol Dighi, where many of his friends could be seen in the crowd. Bholanath, Banku, Beni and Bhudev stood together, their faces tense with anxiety. Ganga came up to them and asked, 'What's the matter?'

'Madhu,' Beni answered. 'He's gone mad again.'

Ganga elbowed his way through the crowd and came to Madhu, where he sat on the grass in the centre, a bottle of brandy in his hand. '"I am like the Earth", he declaimed, the words slurring in his mouth, '"revolving round the self-same sun". Boy—' Ganga shivered. Madhu was becoming an alcoholic. He used to drink in the evenings. Now he drank day and night. The reek of liquor was foul on his breath twenty-four hours a day. The other day Mr Carr had reprimanded him quite sharply.

Madhu's palki lay abandoned on the grass a little distance away from where he sat. The two servants who accompanied him wherever he went stood about helplessly, not daring to raise him to his feet and take him away. Madhu treated them like slaves. He would kick and curse one minute and shower them with gold coins the next. Till recently, Madhu had worn pyjamas and achkan to college. Now he wore an English coat through the year—summer and winter. Ever since he started wearing English clothes, his drinking had become heavier and less restrained.

Madhu crinkled his eyes at Ganganarayan and smiled. 'Ah! Ganga. You're still here. Have the others run away? "Seasons both of joy and sorrow, I have, like her, as I run". Boy—' Beni pushed his way through the crowd. 'Madhu,' he cried. 'Our teachers walk down this road to college. If they see you in this state—'

'If they do?' Madhu's lip curled derisively. 'What then? Silly Beni-like talk!' He raised the bottle high above his head and swung it to and fro. 'Come hither . If you have courage—have a sip,' and then poured the neat brandy down his own throat.

'If Carr Saheb hears about this,' Bhudev said nervously, 'he's very strict. He might—'

'I hate that damned fellow, Carr!' Madhu bellowed. 'This will do me no harm. None whatever.'

'Hush,' Beni admonished. 'You're out of your mind. How can you use such language for your own teacher?'

'Get up, Madhu.' Banku pulled him by the arm. 'Aren't you coming to college?'

'No—o—o.' Madhu shrugged his shoulders elegantly, like a Frenchman.

'You haven't attended classes for a week. Aren't you going to study any more?'

'Of course, he is,' Bhudev answered for Madhu. 'Come, Madhu. Come with me to class.'

'You go. You goody, goody boys! You go to class. I'm not going.'

'Shh,' Bholanath whispered. 'There's Reese Saheb.'

The boys turned their heads to see their mathematics teacher, Mr Reese, pass the railings of Gol Dighi. He had an umbrella over his head. His steps were slow and measured and his eyes contemplative. 'That fellow!' Madhu cut in carelessly. 'Are you afraid of him? I'm not.' The boys waited till Mr Reese passed out of sight. Bhudev laughed. 'You are scared of him,' he said. 'You may deny it but you are.' Madhu brought the bottle of brandy to his lips and took a deep draught. Then, patting his narrow chin, he said, 'I'm Madhusudan Datta, Esquire. I'm not afraid of anyone.'

'Shall I call him?' Bhudev challenged. 'He was a soldier in Napoleon's army. He'll pick you up like a bundle of straw and carry you to class.'

'Call him,' Madhu said arrogantly. 'Let us see him carry me to class.'

'Come, Madhu,' Bhudev coaxed. 'We don't like it when you're not with us.'

'Why not? When there are so many bright stars among you?'

'We may be stars,' Banku answered for Bhudev. 'You are Jupiter.'

'There's an essay competition in college today. You may win the prize again, Madhu.' Bhudev tried to use all his powers of persuasion.

'A fig for your scholastic fame!' muttered Madhu.

'You really won't come to college any more?'

'No. I hate college. I hate Carr.'

'But why? You broke the rules. That is why Carr Saheb reprimanded you.'

'I shall go back when D.L. returns. The others have less learning than I. What can they teach me?'

'You mean you'll give up your studies if Richardson Saheb does not return?'

'Yes.'

'Get up, Madhu. Be reasonable.'

'You be damned—'

Ganganarayan had not spoken a word all this while. Now he stepped up to Bhudev and whispered in his ear, 'Shall I call Gour? Madhu will do as he says.'

'Y—yes.' Bhudev considered the proposal. 'You may be right. Run to college and fetch him.'

Gourdas Basak stood at the gate, deep in conversation with two students of Sanskrit College. Ganga drew him aside and told him what had happened. 'What can I do?' Gour shrugged his shoulders indifferently. Gourdas was a handsome boy, slim and fair, with gentle eyes and arched eyebrows that met above a shapely nose. His lips and chin were finely cut—soft and feminine. Gour never failed to attract attention even when he stood in a crowd. Ganga ignored Gour's excuses and, clutching his hand, dragged him over to Gol Dighi. Pushing through the crowd, they stood in front of Madhu. 'You've been drinking again,' Gour said, shaking his head sorrowfully. Madhu jumped up and caught Gour in a passionate embrace. 'Gour! Gour!' he cried, kissing him tenderly on both cheeks. 'I'm seeing you after so long. So long. I come to college only for your sake but I don't find you. I went to the Mechanical Institution but you weren't there either. Seven long letters I wrote you but you—you sent a pigmy-sized letter in reply. Why, Gour, why?'

Blushing with embarrassment, Gour tried to disengage himself but Madhu would not let him go. He was taller and bigger than Gour and he held him against his chest with all the strength of a drunkard. Gour repeated, 'You've been drinking again, Madhu.'

'Why shouldn't I drink?' Madhu demanded belligerently. 'Doesn't Richardson drink? Doesn't he have fun with girls? That is why he loves poetry. That is why the world is so beautiful in his eyes. Don't you remember what he said? "To cold and vulgar minds how large a portion of this beautiful world is a dreary blank". I love poetry, Gour! Poetry widens the sphere of our purest and most permanent enjoyments. I'll be a great poet some day. As great as Byron. You'll see! You'll write my biography—'

'Very well,' Gour cut in. 'Be a great poet! But you gave me your word you wouldn't come drunk to college.'

'Did I? I can't keep my word. It is true, Gour, I can't keep my word. Bhudev can. Banku can. Ganga can. Even Rajnarayan can. But I can't. You mustn't be angry with me, Gour. I love you so much! I can't live without you. But you don't love me half as much. You promised to come to my house but you didn't.'

'How romantic!' A voice jeered from the crowd. 'This is as good as a love scene between Radha and Krishna.'

'People are making fun of you,' Bhudev whispered in Gour's ear. 'Take Madhu away from here.'

Madhu heard nothing. He fixed his large, sombre eyes on Gour's face and continued as if nothing had happened. 'I'll keep one promise only. I promised you I'd go to England and so I will. I sigh for Albion's distant shore.'

'Let me go, Madhu,' Gour sighed. 'I'll never be a poet, so I must go to college.'

'Oh! no,' Madhu made his voice sound exactly like Mr Richardson's. 'I beseech you. "Lo! Raised upon this vast aerial height, this realm of air . . ." No one will go to college today. You'll all come home with me. Bhudev, Beni, Banku and Ganga—' His left arm still around Gour, he stretched the right one towards his other friends.

The crowd had thickened in the meantime and jeers and catcalls could be heard. These came mostly from the students of Sanskrit College. The two colleges stood in close proximity, but there was no love lost between the students. The boys of Hindu College, barring a few free scholars, came from wealthy and distinguished families. Compared to them, the boys of Sanskrit College looked shabby and rustic. They wore no shirts but came to college with udunis around their shoulders. But, for all their unassuming appearances, their tongues were as sharp as blades and they knew how to wound with words. Using Madhu's dark skin and Gour's very fair one as the subject of their taunts, they let loose a flood of metaphors, punctuated with bursts of mocking laughter.

Lurching a little, Madhu made his way out of the crowd. One hand gripped Gour's wrist and the brandy bottle swung gently from the other. Coming to where his palki stood, he stopped short. One palki would not hold all his friends. Turning his face towards the Pataldanga crossing, he put two fingers under his tongue and blew a sharp whistle. Two palkis came rushing towards him at the sound. All the bearers knew him and hastened to serve him for this young babu was amazingly generous with his tips. 'To Khidirpur,' shouted Madhu when his friends were comfortably seated in the three palkis.

Madhu's father, Rajnarayan Datta, was enormously wealthy. His house in Khidirpur was like a palace in size and splendour. Its inmates, however, were few for Rajnarayan Datta was an intensely self-centred, pleasure-loving man and did not encourage poor relations and parasites. Barring two women from his native village of Sagardari, who served his wife, Jahnavi Devi, no other of his kin had found place in his household. Rajnarayan Datta was very proud of his home and had no intention of sharing its luxuries with others. One of the things he enjoyed most was good food. He kept a number of cooks who prepared scores of delectable dishes everyday. He had no scruples about enticing good cooks away from English households with offers of higher wages. If a dish was not to his taste, he sent for the cook and threw it in his face. All the food in the house was of high quality but the mutton pulao was best. It was so delicious that to eat it once was to remember it forever. Madhu's friends often said, 'As the Czar of Russia is the greatest of all kings, so mutton pulao is the king of all foods.'

Madhu was the only child and the apple of his mother's eye. Five of the fourteen servants in the house were there only to serve him. They had strict instructions from their mistress to keep a vigilant eye on Madhu's needs and desires. His slightest wish had to be indulged. Rajnarayan Datta, too, was besotted with his son.

Madhu was only eighteen. Yet his poems were appearing in the *Bengal Spectator*, the *Calcutta Literary Gazette*, the *Comet* and other English papers and journals. Rajnarayan Datta's pride in his son was phenomenal. His colleague in court, Bidhusekhar Mukherjee, once said to him, 'Your son's English is so good—he'll be shitting on the heads of the sahebs in a couple of years.' Bidhusekhar's comment had sent a thrill of pleasure through Rajnarayan. The white-skinned bastards thought themselves the crown of creation! Now they would know that natives were every bit as good as them. Lying back on his velvet couch and inhaling the rich scented smoke from the long stem of his *albola*, Rajnarayan's gaze would often rest on Madhu's dark head and in a gush of affection, he would press the tube of the *albola* into his son's hand. Madhu was to have everything he wanted. Dozens of wine bottles arrived for Madhu from the wine merchants. His father cleared the bills without demur. The house of Hamilton had instructions from Rajnarayan to send samples of all the pomades and perfumes that were shipped out from England. Madhu would make a selection and vast quantities would be ordered.

Madhu liked to tease his father by asking for things that were very difficult, if not impossible, to procure. His father accepted the challenge whenever it came and sent his underlings to scour the city and bring back whatever it was. Then he would take it to his son and, his eyes twinkling, ask triumphantly, 'Isn't this what you wanted? And now—what is next on your list?' It was a game father and son played all the time. Of course, what Madhu asked for most often were books.

Madhu played a different game with his friends. 'Close your eyes, boys,' he would command, 'and ask for any delicacy you fancy. I'll have my servants serve it to you in five minutes.' And, indeed, he could and did. Whatever it was they asked for—fried chicken, curried mutton,. cottage cheese fritters or egg candy—his servants brought it up piping hot in a few minutes. Five or six clay ovens burned day and night in Rajnarayan's kitchen and a variety of dishes were kept ready for no one knew what Madhu would ask for and when.

There were days, however, when not a morsel passed through Madhu's lips; when he spent hour after hour, brandy decanter by his side, reading and drinking. No one was allowed to disturb him then. He would drink himself into a stupor, after which servants would carry him upstairs and put him to bed.

Five servants stepped forward to greet their young master as he stepped out of the palki with his friends. Madhu brought out a handful of silver coins from his coat pocket and, handing it to one of them, barked out the command, 'Pay the bearers.' Then, stretching his arms out wide, he cried, 'Heigh ho! Heigh ho!' Walking through the portico, the boys entered an immense hall, from the centre of which a flight of marble steps curved upwards. At the first step, Madhu warned his friends, 'If you meet my father pay no attention to him.' The boys stared. Rajnarayan Datta was an arrogant man with a towering personality. But he was unfailingly courteous to Madhu's friends and enquired after their welfare each time he saw them. He was particularly fond of Ganga, whose father, Ramkamal Singha, was a personal friend.

'Don't talk to him even if he talks to you,' Madhu said, tightening his jaw. 'You must make it clear that you are on my side.'

'Have you quarrelled with your father, Madhu?' Banku asked.

'Yes.' Madhu gave the door of his bedroom a vicious kick. It flew open and the boys entered. Madhu went straight to a cupboard; on its shelves rows of crystal glasses and decanters glittered and sparkled. Taking out glasses Madhu began pouring brandy into them. 'Come, boys. Your health,' he said, and raising his own glass to his lips, drained the contents down his throat. The boys stood, silent, watching the scene. Only Gour said uncomfortably, 'You're drinking again, Madhu!'

'Why shouldn't I drink? It is a happy day—one of the happiest of my life. My friends are all here. Come, Bhola! Won't you have a drink, Ganga?'

Bhudev had got off the palki midway and gone back to the college. He always managed to get out of these awkward situations. He loved Madhu but avoided coming to his house.

'I'm a poor boy,' he often said. 'Hobnobbing with rich people is not for me.' Ganga had never seen Bhudev in Madhu's house. Ganga shivered as Madhu pressed the glass of brandy into his hand. He remembered something Bindu had said to him a few days before he joined college. 'All the boys of Hindu college drink,' she had said. 'Will you drink, too, Ganga?'

'No, Bindu. I'll never touch wine or spirits.'

'I've seen drunks in the street. *Chhi! Chhi!* I can't imagine how boys from respectable families can get like that. Don't come near me if you start drinking, Ganga.'

'I won't—ever,' Ganga had said. 'I swear it.' And he had touched Bindu's hand and sealed his oath.

The glass trembled in Ganga's hand. Gour touched the brandy to his lips and asked, 'What is the quarrel about? What has your father done, Madhu?'

'He wants me to marry a puling infant, seven or eight years old. I refuse—absolutely. Rajnarayan Datta cannot make me.'

Beni, Banku and Bholanath had been married for some time now. Gour, though not married, was contracted. They took the whole thing lightly. 'That is nothing to get agitated about,' Gour said. 'If your father wants you to marry, you must obey him—that's all.'

'Marry! A crybaby of seven? No. Never. She'll have tantrums all day and snot will run down her nose.'

'You won't find an older girl if you scour all the Kayastha households of Calcutta. She'll grow. Girls grow fast. In three or four years you'll see—'

'I refuse to marry the girl of my father's choice. "Alas! they know not that I die of pains that none can heal".'

Ganganarayan sighed. A similar fate awaited him. His soul rebelled against the thought of marrying a seven-year-old but he lacked Madhu's courage. He could not flout his father.

'Every boy makes a scene just before marrying,' Beni the know-all said ponderously. 'Then he bows to the inevitable. Madhu will, too. It is only through marriage that the patriarchal line is perpetuated. It is our bounden duty—'

'Duty!' Madhu roared. 'You wait and see me doing my duty!'

'If your father insists, you'll have to obey. How long can you hold out?'

Madhu picked up the brandy bottle. 'Rajnarayan Datta dare not insist. If he tries any tricks with me, I'll punish him so badly, he'll remember it all his life.'

# Chapter V

Madhu threw off his coat and opened the door of a wooden closet with a flourish. Inside, in rows, hung English suits of every hue and shade. 'Which one shall I wear, Gour?' he turned to his friend. Before Gour could speak Beni burst out impatiently, 'Why are you changing your clothes? Are you going out?'

'No, I'm not going out. I'm happy here with you all.'

'Then why did you throw off your coat?'

'I can't wear the same clothes for more than two hours. I don't know how you can. It is disgusting! Choose something for me, Gour. Do you like this gold brocade?'

Though Madhu had asked for Gour's opinion, Beni could not help giving his. Beni and Madhu rubbed against one another constantly. Beni was jealous of Madhu. His father, though rich, too, was a miser and gave him a very small allowance. 'Gold brocade!' he jeered. 'On this warm afternoon! I deplore your taste, Madhu.'

'As I deplore yours. I love to see those clouds of golden dye float graceful over yon blue expanse. Look at the sky, Beni. That glorious, golden light—'

'I don't see any golden light. All I see are dark clouds, massing in the east. It is going to rain any minute.'

'You don't have the eyes of a poet,' Banku murmured snidely.

Madhu put on his coat of gold brocade and paced restlessly up and down the room. His face shone with brandy fumes and a strange light came into his eyes. 'Why are you so jumpy?' Beni couldn't help needling Madhu. 'Why don't you sit quietly for a while?' Madhu gave a great roar of laughter. 'I can't sit quietly. I can't. I can't.' Lifting his chin the way Captain Richardson did when reading Hamlet in class, he cried, 'I am like the earth, revolving around the self-same sun. Boy! Why don't you fellows drink? Your glasses are full to the brim. Drink, Banku. Come on, Bhola.'

At this moment a servant entered, bearing two huge platters of smoking kebabs. 'Ah! My favourite.' Madhu's eyes danced. 'Taste them, boys. They are made of the tenderest veal. Only three months old. Delicious!' Ganga shivered. Only the other day a cow had given birth in the shed behind Ganga's house. The newborn had pranced merrily around its mother and then run towards the pond. It had a plump, snowy body and huge eyes, so dark, they seemed lined with kohl. It would be about three months old now.

The other boys helped themselves. Beni bit greedily into a large one but it was too hot and it burned his palate. He danced up and down—his mouth wide open. Finally, with a great effort he swallowed the burning lump and exclaimed, 'Bravo! This meat is as soft as butter. Delicious!'

'Does your father allow beef in the kitchen?' Gour asked, nibbling delicately on his own.

'In this house my word is law.'

'We'll have a grand time when Madhu gets married,' Banku said. 'You'll have nautch girls to entertain us, won't you Madhu?'

'We can have nautch girls whenever you want. I don't have to get married for that.'

'Oh, come on! Your father has made up his mind and—'

'My father's father can make up his mind for all I care.'

'I'll tell him to fix the day some time this winter,' Banku went on relentlessly. 'We'll hire a bajra and go for a pleasure cruise on the river. Kamala can come with us. She's the best dancing girl in Calcutta.' And, saying this, he glanced out of the corner of his eye at Ganga. Ganga knew about his father's interest in Kamala Sundari. She was a reputed nautch girl of the city, only eighteen, with a face and form that seemed carved out of black marble.

'I hope Madhu's father finds him a girl as dumpy as a pot of molasses,' Beni said with unconcealed malice.

'Are you on my father's side?' Madhu roared.

'Hush,' Gour admonished. Madhu calmed down immediately. A note of pain crept into his voice. 'Why are Beni and Banku saying these things to me? Don't they know my feelings?'

'You said you would punish your father,' said Beni, twisting the knife deeper. 'How do you propose to do that?'

'I'll run away from home and—'

'Ha! Ha!' Beni gave a shout of laughter. 'Who will provide you with your English suits and brandy bottles, away from home? You'll have to eat clouds and drink air in place of veal cutlets and wine.'

'I don't give a damn! I'll eat clouds and drink air but I wont come back.'

'No, Madhu,' Gour said gently. 'Don't be unreasonable. Your parents love you. They are doing their best for you. Don't break their hearts.'

'I must. Do you know what that great poet of England, Alexander Pope, once said? He said that to follow poetry one must leave both father and mother.'

'Poets say many things,' Beni cut in with a sneer. 'They don't practise what they preach. No one can—'

'I can and I will.'

Ganganarayan stood up. 'I must go home now,' he said.

'Why?' Madhu turned to him. 'You haven't drunk a drop. Your glass is full.' He jumped up and caught Ganga by the hand. 'No one leaves my house without a meal. You must have something before you go.'

'No, Madhu. I'm not hungry.'

'Then have a drink. One sip—' Madhu brought the glass to Ganga's lips.

'No. I don't drink.' Ganga pushed the glass away. In the scuffle, the glass fell from Madhu's hand, the rich golden liquid soaking the flowered Persian carpet. Madhu didn't give it a glance. He picked up his own glass and tried to force it between Ganga's lips.

'Drink,' he commanded.

'Leave me alone, Madhu.' Ganga folded his hands in supplication. 'I don't drink and never will.'

'Have a kebab then. Begad! They must be cold by now.'

'No. There's a calf in our cowshed. I love it. I can't eat calf meat.'

'Don't call it calf meat, you yokel. Call it beef.' This was from Beni.

'That's the trouble with you all,' Madhu cried angrily. 'I'm sick of you and your Hindu chauvinism. Beef and wine are the best of foods. Meant to build strong people and strong nations! Look at the English, the French, the Russians! They all eat beef and drink wine. That is why they are mighty conquerors. That is why they write the best poetry. And we Hindus! We shave our heads, eat greens and squeal when other nations slap us in the face.'

'The only meat I really enjoy is beef,' said Beni with the smug pomposity of the pseudo rebel.

'Well,' Ganga said, 'there are so many of you eating beef and drinking wine. You are enough in numbers to reform the Hindus. Leave me out of it.'

'Coward!' hissed Beni.

'Everyone can't be a social reformer.'

'Ganga is a stick in the mud. He is completely closed to new ideas.'

Seeing the other boys gang up on Ganga, Madhu came to his rescue. 'I've made fools of you all,' he declared, grinning wickedly. 'These are mutton cutlets—not veal. My mother would never allow beef in the kitchen. Trust me, Ganga. Rajnarayan Datta's son does not lie. Taste one of these.' But Ganga had made up his mind. He was leaving. No one could stop him. The others rose too for they had a long way to go. Madhu was surprised. He hadn't expected their departure quite so soon. He grasped Gour by the hand and begged, 'Don't go, Gour. What will I do if you all go away? I'll start drinking again.'

'It is getting late. I must go,' Gour said uncomfortably.

'No, you mustn't. If you go away, I'll drink a whole bottle.'

'All right. All right.' Gour smiled indulgently. 'I'll stay for a while.'

The moment Gour agreed to stay, Beni, who had risen with the others, sat down. 'I'll stay too,' he declared. 'I'll go back with Gour.' Neither Gour nor Madhu welcomed the suggestion but Beni was too thick-skinned to notice. He walked across to a marble-topped table, piled with books and picked out two. 'Can I borrow these, Madhu?' Madhu hated anyone fiddling with his books but he said magnanimously, 'Take as many as you like. Only leave the *Life of Byron* alone. I'm reading it.' Then, glancing out of the window, he said, 'My palki bearers will take you home if you wish to go now. Once they go off for their meals, they won't come back till evening. You'll have to hire a palki.'

'I'll go then. Aren't you coming, Gour?'

'No.' Madhu spoke for Gour. 'He'll stay with me all day. Maybe all night, too.'

'All night!' echoed Beni.

'No, no,' Gour exclaimed, blushing. 'How can I stay all night? You go home, Beni. I'll stay a while longer or Madhu will start drinking again. As soon as I've calmed him down a bit, I'll go home.'

'Do that.' Beni smiled a crooked smile. 'Who can handle him the way you can? Be sure to love him a little. Oh! Madhu, I must ask you a question. Promise you won't take offence.'

'What is it?'

'Why did you refer to Gour as *she* in the acrostic you wrote last week? Of course, Gour is very beautiful. He can easily be passed off as a woman. But—'

'Who told you that the poem was addressed to Gour?' Madhu asked gravely. 'Most of my poems are dedicated to Gour. Does that mean he is the subject of them all?'

'But acrostics are written on a certain principle, aren't they? The first alphabet of every line, arranged chronologically, make up the name of the person to whom the poem is addressed. D. L. was telling us about acrostics the other day. And it was after hearing him that you wrote the poem. I remember some of it. "Go oh! Simple lay! And tell that fair, oh! Tis for her, her lover dies"!'

'You haven't even learned to read poetry,' Madhu interrupted impatiently. 'Don't forget you are reciting the verses of a poet of the calibre of Lord Byron.'

'I'm no poet. If I had your talent I would have written a poem about Gour.'

'The bearers are getting ready to leave—'

'Stop them. I'm going.' Beni rushed out of the room. Madhu went with him to the stair landing, then came back and shut the door. 'Good riddance!' he said laughing. 'That son of a miser ran like a rabbit the moment he thought he would have to pay for a palki. Now there's no one between us. Gour and Madhu! Madhu and Gour!' He gave a sigh of satisfaction and embracing Gour, kissed him warmly on both cheeks.

'Don't be silly, Madhu.' Gour blushed and pushed him away. 'You embarrass me, sometimes—you behave so oddly.'

'Oddly! Why? I am passionately fond of your company. As I am of you.'

'You heard what Beni said.'

'Beni he damned!'

'No, Madhu. You go too far sometimes. It you persist in behaving like this, I'll have to stop coming to your house.'

'Is that why you've been avoiding me?'

'You have so many friends. Why do you dedicate all your poems to me?'

'Because I love you best. See what I've got for you.' Madhu pulled out a drawer and lifted a case of fine morocco leather. Inside, twinkling and sparkling on blue velvet, lay two exquisitely carved crystal jars. 'This is a French pomatum. And this—lavender water. You said you liked the scent of lavender.'

'You spend too much money on me, Madhu! Only the other day you gave me essence of forget-me-nots.'

'Yet you forget me. Don't talk of money, Gour. I can give up everything I have for your sake. I've decided to commission a portrait of yours—to look at when you are not with me. I'll sell all my clothes to pay for it.' Madhu closed his eyes and murmured, '"All kind, to these fond arms of mine! Come! And let me no longer sigh". Beni is a fool but he was right about that acrostic. It was written for you.'

'You really mean to leave college, Madhu?' Gour changed the subject, his cheeks flaming.

'Not if Richardson returns—'

'But reading poetry isn't everything. You haven't attended the mathematics class for—'

'I hate it. Besides, I'm a poet. What do I have to do with mathematics? Shakespeare could have become a Newton if he wished but Newton could never, never, have become a Shakespeare.'

'And the Bengali classes—'

'Bengali! I refuse to waste my time on a language fit for servants. Fie upon it!'

'Hare Saheb has issued a ruling, making attendance in Bengali compulsory. Those who are short won't be allowed to sit for the exams.'

'A fig for the exams! As for Hare Saheb—I have no opinion of him. He's eaten fish curry and rice for so many years that his English blood has turned native by now.'

'I have a profound respect for Hare Saheb. And I don't agree with what you said about Bengali. Some of the finest poetry has been written in Bengali. Bharatchandra and Ishwar Gupta—'

'Pooh! You call Bharatchandra a poet? He is a pigmy compared to Wordsworth and Byron. As for Ishwar Gupta, I can write verses like his as easily as I sit here.'

'You can write verses in Bengali?'

'Of course, I can. But I don't care to. I hate the native languages. Sanskrit smells of beggarly Brahmins and Bengali of the lower classes.'

'I'm told you are a frequent visitor at Keshto Banerjee's house. Are these his ideas?'

'I do visit him but my ideas are my own.'

'Does he have a pretty daughter? Do you go there for her sake?'

'My dear Gour!' Madhu gave a roar of laughter. 'You are jealous. Your cheeks are as red as roses. Why didn't you tell me you resent my visiting a woman?' He put his arms around his friend and said between kisses, 'Don't be angry with me, Gour. I love you. I love you more than any woman.'

'Don't be ridiculous, Madhu!'

One arm around Gour, Madhu dragged him to the adjoining bedroom and pushed him on the bed. 'Thou hast forgotten thy promise of honouring my poor cot with the sacred dust of thy feet! . . . Fulfil your promise tonight, Gour. Sleep in my bed.'

'I must go home.' Gour sat up, thoroughly alarmed.

'No, Gour. I won't let you go.' Kneeling on the ground, Madhu put his hands on Gour's thighs. 'Take my head in your lap, Gour,' he begged.

'What madness is this?'

'The other day when I knelt before you with my notepad on your lap, you pushed it away. Dear Gour—

I thought I would be able
(Making thy lap my table)
To write that note with ease:
But ha! Your shaking

Gave my pen a quaking.
Rudeness never I saw like this.

Why, Gour, why? I love you more than anything in the world but you don't return my love. You reject me every time I come near you. I express my yearning in poetry but it doesn't touch your heart—'

'You're drunk, Madhu! Let go. Let go, I say.'

'No, no, no.'

Gour was really angry now. He pushed Madhu away with all his might. Madhu lost his balance and fell, his head striking the floor with a thud. Gour stood watching him gather himself together but made no effort to help. Madhu sat up and looked at Gour with the eyes of a dumb animal. 'You pushed me away!' he said in a dazed voice. 'You! Gour! Now I have no one left in the world. I'll go away from you all—so far away that no one will find me. I won't trouble you any more.'

# Chapter VI

Like many of his peers, Babu Bishwanath Motilal had made his money in salt. In the early years of Company rule, fleets of foreign ships had borne away India's wealth across the seven seas and returned empty, tossed about on the waves like egg-shells, till someone discovered the expediency of weighing them down with the cheapest commodity Britain could afford—salt. India had plenty of salt of her own, yet a way was found by the 'nation of shopkeepers' of selling salt in Indian markets. With favourable laws and the active assistance of native agents, indigenous traders were pushed out of business and British salt took over. Over the years many of the same agents bought up large shares and became partners in the business with their British masters. In fact, much of the wealth of the new Calcutta aristocracy had its origins in salt.

Bishwanath Motilal was one such great babu of Calcutta. A man of phenomenal wealth, he had, in his old age, divided up his estates among his sons and spent his days in the company of amateur actors, musicians and athletes. Among his properties was a bazaar, which he gifted to a favourite daughter-in-law, in consequence of which it came to be called Bow Rani's Bazaar. Gradually, the entire locality was referred to as Bow Rani's Bazaar or Bowbazar—the latter gaining currency from repeated usage.

Bowbazar was the chief trading centre of Calcutta and hummed with activity day and night. It had many houses of ill repute for it was the fashion, among the Calcutta elite, to keep mistresses in Bowbazar. Muslim prostitutes from the west—among them fine singers and dancers—found their way here and gave the locality class and character. Wine flowed freely in the inns and there were rooms with beds and women in them for the convenience of the itinerant trader.

But Bowbazar was not all business and pleasure. It boasted of a Kali temple, with a deity so famed for her benevolence that even sahebs and memsahebs brought offerings and asked for boons. Another feature of Bowbazar was the boarding houses set up to accommodate the growing influx from the villages surrounding Calcutta. The sight of a fine mansion transformed into a honeycomb of messes, was not uncommon in the lanes and alleys of Bowbazar. Some kindly babu might rent a set of rooms in such a house and cram it with sons, nephews, even distant kin from his native village. Assured of a roof above their heads and four good meals a day, the boys hung around till work was found for them or seats in some school or college.

Two such boarding houses stood side by side in Panchanantala Lane. One was run by a God-fearing Brahmin named Jairam Lahiri. It had two rooms and a thin strip of a verandah in which thirteen boys were lodged. Jairam Babu left early each morning for his office in Khidirpur and returned late at night. Sometimes he accompanied his British master on a tour of the mofussils, staying away three or four days at a stretch. Consequently, he had little time or opportunity to study the characters of his protégés and being too good himself, saw no evil even when it stared him in the face. Idlers and wastrels for the most part, his wards took full advantage of his blindness and trust. They quickly assimilated the worst traits of city life and became a nuisance in the neighbourhood. Three out of the thirteen were schoolboys—that is, their fees were paid regularly by Jairam Babu. But the older boys wouldn't let them go to school. They made them hang around the house and do all the domestic work and treated them like slaves. The sight of a little one rubbing oil into the hefty flanks of a big one or drawing buckets of water from the well and pouring them over his head was not uncommon.

The worst of the lot was a hulking youth named Haravallabh. He was a monster of depravity, feared and hated for miles around. Even Jairam Lahiri was aware of some of his activities and had asked him to leave more than once. Three times he had found Haravallabh a job and said, 'It is time you moved on, boy, and found a place of your own.' But Haravallabh had got the sack each time and returned to his benefactor. He had clutched Jairam's feet and wept so bitterly that the latter was forced to take him back. Haravallabh was a huge, hefty fellow, as dark and hairy as an ape. His main occupation was terrorizing the working men of the neighbourhood and getting money out of them. Each pay day he skulked in the shadows of the lane, ready to fall on an unsuspecting babu and relieve him of his cash. He was aided in this task by one of the three little boys mentioned above—a mischievous imp of a boy call Ramchandra. It was universally agreed that Ramchandra should have been rightly named Hanumanchandra for he was as cunning as a monkey and up to as many tricks. The 'ape' and the 'monkey' were inseparable. If they weren't out in the lanes they were up on the roof, smoking ganja and drinking cheap liquor. On Jairam's frequent absences from Calcutta, Haravallabh and his followers brought in cheap prostitutes from the streets and got so drunk and rowdy that the neighbours quaked in fear. Babies were startled awake in their cradles and hushed by anxious mothers. Husbands ignored the burning glances of their wives and went back to sleep, not daring to interfere with the goings-on a few doors away.

One night, a young woman ran screaming out of the house, with Haravallabh close behind her—a coil of rope in his hands. He was completely drunk and, as he chased her, he slurred and sang, 'Come, beloved! Take my pleasure garland and hang it upon your breast.' The girl, though a common prostitute and used to rough handling, couldn't allow him to put a rope around her neck. She ran from this door to that, banging and screaming in panic. But all the houses were dark and silent—their inmates not daring to light a lamp, leave alone open their doors.

In one house alone, an oil lamp burned and in front of it, poring over a manuscript, sat a slender, large-headed youth of twenty or twenty-one. He had been completely absorbed in what he was reading, till the frightened screams and drunken bawling crashed into his consciousness. He rose and, tiptoeing past the sleepers who lay everywhere, he came to the door and opened it. There was no light in the street and he could see nothing at first. Then, as his eyes grew accustomed to the dim starlight, he discerned two shapes. A man was dragging a woman by the hair and saying in a voice that the youth recognized instantly, 'You dare play tricks with me, you filthy whore! You've taken money to pleasure me. I can do whatever I like with you.' The youth sighed. He wanted to rush up to

Haravallabh and pull the girl away. But he knew he hadn't the strength. Besides, by the time he made them out, Haravallabh had dragged her in and shut the door.

The house in which the youth lived was also a mess run by a Brahmin called Thakurdas Bandopadhyaya. Thakurdas Babu earned ten rupees a month, on which he fed and educated three sons, five nephews and all of his kith and kin who came up from the village to seek employment in the city. Thakurdas Bandopadhyaya's mess was as different from Jairam Lahiri's as day is from night. All the boys were studious and painstaking. His eldest, Ishwar, was a renowned student of Sanskrit College and received a stipend of eight rupees each month, which he handed over to his father. He had another great talent. He could compose Sanskrit verses of such brilliance that he invariably carried off the prize money of fifty rupees at competitions. But, outstanding scholar and versifier though he was, he was as stubborn as a mule and wouldn't budge from a position once he had taken it. His father would get so exasperated with him at times that he would beat him till he was half-dead. But the beatings left Ishwar untouched, so his father gave them up. Now he looked at him sadly, sighed and said, 'This son of mine is like an ox, with his head screwed on the wrong way.'

Ishwar had passed out from college a few months ago and joined the office at Fort William. The pay was good at fifty rupees a month, and his job was to teach British civilian officers Sanskrit and Bengali. Just as the British knew that to rule India they had to understand her first and to do so they would have to learn her languages, so Ishwar knew that to understand the British and their ideas of governance, he would have to learn their language. Now he studied English and Hindi in the mornings before leaving for Fort William and, on his return, cooked the evening meal, helped his brothers with their homework and then, after everyone was asleep, lit the lamp and read and wrote far into the night.

Returning from Fort William one evening, Ishwar stopped at a grocer's and asked for half a pice worth of Bengal gram. Suddenly, a heavy hand descended on his shoulder and a voice boomed in his ear, 'Have you turned peasant, you son of a Brahmin? What will you do with so much gram? Sow it in your fields?' Ishwar turned around. It was Madanmohan. Madan was some years older than Ishwar but they had studied together in childhood and were close friends. Madan's head was shaved all over except for one tuft that sprang from the back like the wick of a lamp. He had a generous nature and a hearty laugh.

'I'll make a good peasant,' Ishwar answered, smiling. 'As a child I was often out in the fields with a sickle in my hand .'

Madan bought puffed rice and offered some to his friend. 'You have a sickle in your mouth,' he said. 'You don't need one in your hand. Who'll eat all the gram?'

'Well! There are eleven of us at home. Soaked gram makes a cheap and tasty evening snack.'

'But you've bought enough for thirty—'

'My brothers will wolf it down. They eat and shit and shit and eat all day long. If some of the gram is left over I put it in the pumpkin curry we have with our rice at night.'

'Gram in the evening; gram at night! What do you have for breakfast?'

'Ginger.'

'Ha! Ha! No wonder you enjoy such superb health.'

The two friends walked down the street till they reached the mouth of the lane leading to Ishwar's mess. Here, Haravallabh held court with his band of followers. They slapped their thighs and laughed uproariously at a curd-seller who stood weeping and cringing before them. All around were broken pots and spilt curd. Ishwar knew, without being told, that these boys had assaulted him and robbed him of his curds and that some of the pots had got broken in the tussle. He stepped forward, his nostrils flaring, but Madanmohan pulled him back. 'Are you mad?' he cried. 'Do you want to get into a fight with these savages?'

'But they've broken the curd-seller's pots! How can one stand by and allow such a thing?'

'Ignore it and come along.'

'How can I ignore it? Can I shut my eyes as I walk or stuff my ears with cotton?' Then, turning to the curd-seller, he said, 'I'll compensate your loss. Come to me tomorrow. No, come the day after tomorrow. Do you see that white house? I live there.'

'Heh! Heh! Heh!' Haravallabh cackled through his nose. 'The son of a governor has arrived on the scene. Now everyone can go home and rest easy.'

'Look at his stomach!' Ramchandra sang in a shrill falsetto. 'Silk on the outside; rats squealing inside.'

'Don't be foolish, Ishwar.' Madanmohan dragged his friend away. 'You can't take responsibility for all the ills of the world.'

'No. But I can do my best and I will.'

'You're a big man now and—'

'I'm a poor man but I am big.'

The two boys entered the house and sat on the bed. Ishwar turned to his friend. 'Now what would you like to eat?' he asked, smiling.

'Don't offer me soaked gram,' Madan pleaded laughing. 'Or ginger. You're earning good money. Send out for some sweets.'

Ishwar loved treating his friends. 'I'll do that,' he said and called out to his younger brother. 'Sombhu! Go to the sweet shop at the bend of the lane and bring some *sandesh* and *motichoor*. Tell the confectioner I'll pay him later.'

'Talking of *motichoor*, I recall a shlok you composed on Saraswati Puja some years ago. I remember it well—

*Luchi, kochuri, motichoor, shobhitang*
*jilipi, sandesh, gaja birajitang*
*Yashya prasaden phalara magna ma*
*Saraswati Ma Jayatannirantam.*'

'You do remember it!' Ishwar laughed delightedly. 'I had forgotten—'

'How can you hope to remember your own verses when you're so busy learning those of others by rote?'

'Come to the kitchen,' Ishwar invited his friend. 'I'll set a plank for you by the door. We can talk while I do the cooking.'

Thakurdas Bandopadhyaya was away at the village and Ishwar was now the head of the family. He had to be very careful for money was tight. His second brother had been wed some months ago and the family was heavily in debt. The two boys entered the kitchen. It was dark and musty and cockroaches flew about the damp walls.

'*Baap ré*!' Madan stared at the wheeling insects. 'If you're not careful, you'll be cooking a pumpkin and cockroach curry one of these days.'

Ishwar grinned. He had found a cockroach in his curry bowl

one night and, lest others discover it and leave off eating, he had swallowed it without turning a hair. Anyway, cockroaches, they said, were good for asthma and the Chinese ate them with pleasure. Rubbing a couple of flints together, Ishwar lit the kindling already arranged on the clay stove by the servant, Sriram. Shombhu picked and washed the rice and set it on the fire in an earthen pot. The rice boiled over and Ishwar drained it. Then he cooked *dal* and pumpkin curry and fried some delicious-smelling poppy seed fritters. Madanmohan's mouth watered. 'I'd like to stay back and eat what you've cooked,' he said.

'Why don't you? Have your meal with us and spend the night here.'

After the meal, the two friends lay down and talked far into the night.

Suddenly, Ishwar said, his face flushing and twitching with embarrassment, 'Madan! I want you to listen to something I've written. Shall I read it out to you?'

'What is it? A new shlok?'

'No. This isn't Sanskrit. It is a piece of prose writing in Bengali.'

'Bengali! And prose at that! What's wrong with you, Ishwar? Bengali prose is jaw-breaking; unreadable—'

'I agree with you. The texts I teach in Fort William are unreadable. And that is precisely the reason I've taken to it. I want to strip the language of its trappings and mould it anew.'

'You're wasting your time. No one will read Bengali prose.'

'Even if the language is simple and easily comprehended?'

'Even so. The literary among us will not abandon Sanskrit and the pragmatic will turn to English. There's no place for Bengali—'

'My idea was to create a language for the masses.'

'Well! Get on with it. Let's hear what you've written.'

Ishwar pulled out a sheaf of papers from under his pillow. He had given up the quill some months ago and bought a pen with an English nib. '"Narad entered Mathura,"' he read, '"and addressed Kanso O king you smile and look on at Jadov and the gopis and have not a care for the ones who—"'

'Go slow,' Madan interrupted 'What do you think you're doing? Driving a phaeton?'

'No, Madan, I'm reading the way Bengali prose is read. The English use commas, full stops, question and exclamation marks. That's how their prose becomes living and dynamic. Poetry can get along without these for it has a rhythm and cadence of its own. But not prose. I've decided to introduce punctuation marks in Bengali.'

'You've sold yourself, body and soul, to the British and are eternally singing their praises. But how could you imagine that punctuation marks could be grafted on to our language?'

'Why not? They lend the language lucidity and precision. Just listen to this.

"In the meantime, Balaram and the gopis went to Jashoda and said, '*O go*! Krishna has stuffed a ball of clay in his mouth. We keep telling him to take it out but he won't.' The loving mother, Jashoda, ran to her son and tweaking his cheek, said angrily, 'You've been eating clay again, you naughty boy! Come home this instant and see what I do to you'."'

'Stop! Stop!' Madan cried out in alarm. 'Do you call this prose? This is the language of peasants, most common and vulgar. Who will want to read such stuff?'

Ishwar's face fell. 'You really think so?' he asked anxiously. 'No one will want to read it?'

'No one. This isn't prose. It sounds like the bickering of children. Why do you waste your time writing such rubbish?'

'Bickering of children!'

'Exactly. "You've been eating clay again, you naughty boy! Come home this instant and see what I do to you". Ha! Ha! This isn't literature. It is the nagging of illiterate women. Why must an acclaimed Sanskrit scholar like you write such trifling nonsense? People will laugh at you.'

Ishwar's nostrils flared a little and his neck stiffened. But he kept himself in rigid control for Madanmohan was his friend—one he loved and respected. 'You see no future for Bengali, then?' he asked gravely.

'I didn't say that. It is possible to write poetry of a sort in Bengali. I've seen some verses, containing moral instruction for women and children. They are passable. But prose—no. Bengali lacks the weight and substance necessary to contain prose.'

'I thought of publishing this *Basudev Charit* of mine.'

'Don't dream of it. It won't be worthy of a Sanskrit scholar like you.'

Ishwar sighed and put away his papers. 'Perhaps you are right,' he said ruefully. 'Bengali does lack the clarity and dignity of English. It can't contain prose.'

# Chapter VII

In Bidhusekhar's household, the wheels of the morning had come to a grinding halt. It was past noon and the house was dark and still. The midday meal over, the inmates enjoyed a brief siesta. Even the maids and serving men snatched a few winks in their cramped quarters. Only Bindubasini lay, wide awake, on the floor of the puja room. Her body burned as if with a fever and her eyes were hard and jewel bright.

Gusts of hot wind blew in from the window. The garden below shimmered with heat. All was silent. Only two crows, perched on the window sill, looked at Bindu with anxious eyes and cocked their heads and chattered to one another. 'What ails the girl?' they asked, not comprehending how or why the bright, beautiful child, full of fun and mischief, had transformed herself into a woman—a dull, listless woman with weary eyes.

It was the eleventh day of the new moon—a day of rigid fasting for Hindu widows. But Bindu had fasted on Ekadasi ever since the day she had returned to her father's house—a little widow of nine. Fasting, she had romped and played with her sisters. She had sat with her books and, swaying from side to side, had learned her Sanskrit shloks by rote. 'Fasting doesn't bother me one bit,' she had announced proudly, more than once. 'The ancient rishis went without food and water for months while they meditated in the mountains. Even Amba of the Mahabharat—' 'My little girl is getting to be as learned as a guru,' her mother had laughed indulgently and patted her head. 'She can't open her mouth without quoting from the Vedas and Puranas.'

One day, Bindu's fourth sister, Kundamala, complained to her mother, 'Ma! Do you know what Sejdi[8] does on Ekadasi afternoons? She swims from one end of the pond to the other. She drinks water on the sly. I'm sure of it.' 'What rubbish!'

8 Third sister.

Bindu retorted, her face flaming. 'Sri Bhadra's buffaloes wallow in that pond all day. Can I drink that water?' And she nearly puked at the thought. Bindu's mother shuddered and scolded Kunda. 'Durga! Durga! What a vile tongue you have, Kunda! To accuse a virgin widow of drinking water on Ekadasi! Even to hear of such a thing is sin.' Kunda was a child still. She had no idea of the pains and pressures of widowhood. She thought Bindu was lucky to be staying on with her parents instead of in a strange household. 'Even I can fast on Ekadasi,' she declared. 'What a fuss is made over Sejdi the day after. She gets such lovely things to eat—sweets and snacks and almond sherbet.'

'Silly girl!' her mother laughed, tears glittering in her eyes. She looked at Bindu and sighed.

Kundamala was married in due course but, unlike Bindu, she was not called upon to experience the joys or sorrows of widowhood. Lost and lonely in the great household of her zamindar father-in-law, she had wept for her mother and come back to her as often as she could. Then, when she was only twelve years and four months old, she died. Her husband, made fortunate by her death, brought home another eight-year-old with an enormous dowry before the year was out. Kundamala's memory lingered for a while in the world she had lived in and then faded away . . .

And, then, one day, Bindu discovered that she was a girl no more. She had had her first shock when after three years of widowhood, she had seen blood. She hadn't known what it was and had thought some dread disease had struck her. She had hidden herself in her room, terrified at the thought that she was dying, too, like Kundamala. Her mother, Soudamini, had found her two days later. Soudamini's devotion to her husband was phenomenal and she spent all her time in his service. The care of her children and the running of the great household of which she was mistress was left wholly to the servants. There were days when she didn't even see her children. On being informed of Bindu's odd behaviour, she had come into her room and, a quick glance confirming what she had guessed already, had stroked the girl's head and said gently, 'Is this why you are hiding yourself, you silly girl? It is nothing to be ashamed of. It happens to all women. This is the way God made us.'

So Bindu became a woman! So girls become women and

ready to bear children even when they are widowed as infants. For Nature has its own laws and does not recognize the laws of men.

But, though her body was now that of a grown woman, Bindu still enjoyed the freedom of her girlhood. She climbed trees and played rough games with her sisters. She marched up to Acharya Moshai every evening, a pile of books under her arm, and demanded her lessons. She chatted and argued with Ganganarayan for hours. At most her mother would shake her head and say, 'Girls mustn't be so rough, Bindu.' Her father always smiled indulgently. She had never heard a harsh word from his lips. And, then, one day, when she was exactly fourteen years, seven months and eleven days old, she had become a woman in the full sense of the word. Her father had sent for her and said, 'There is no need for you to take lessons any more. You are a woman now. What will people say? It is time you dedicated yourself to the service of Janardan.' Bindu was beside herself with fury. How unfair God was! Why had he changed her from a girl to a woman? But Bidhusekhar's word was law. The next day her books—handwritten manuscripts of parts of the Mahabharat and some Sanskrit and Bengali books, printed at the press in Srirampur—were taken away from her. She had been passionately attached to them and their absence left her dazed and bereft.

Bidhusekhar's moral principles were of the highest order. As a *kulin* male he could have enjoyed the privilege of polygamy. But he took to himself only one wife. He kept no mistresses either. His friend, Ramkamal, had done all he could to introduce him to the pleasures of the flesh, without success. Just as Bidhusekhar hadn't succeeded in weaning Ramkamal away from the low company he kept. The two, though good friends, had different natures. Ramkamal was generous but weak and self-indulgent. And, as such men usually are, he was a fatalist. Bidhusekhar was calculating, exploitative by nature, astute and intelligent. His lips and chin were firm and bore the stamp of confidence and character. Ramkamal's body was soft and slothful; Bidhusekhar's sharp and straight as an arrow. Bidhusekhar had never touched wine or spirits in his life. His one grievance against Rammohan Roy was his addiction to liquor. There were many who had disliked the Raja at first but changed their views when they heard of his death in distant England. But not Bidhusekhar. Even now, whenever the Raja's virtues were extolled at any gathering, Bidhusekhar clicked his tongue and said, 'But do you think he was right in encouraging drinking the way he did? He didn't drink much himself, of course. But can everyone exercise the same restraint? All these drunks lolling about in the gutters! I hold the Raja responsible.' 'You've never tasted wine in your life, Bidhu,' Ramkamal answered, smiling. 'What do you know of the exquisite pleasure it holds? Try draining a bottle and lolling in the gutter for once. You'll see what you've been missing all these years.' Bidhusekhar dismissed this advice with a wave of his hand and went on, 'I don't approve of his setting up English above Sanskrit either. Have you considered the consequences? A few pages of English and our boys are turning insolent and disobedient. I rue the day the Raja and the Rabbit came together.' 'Don't forget, Bidhu Bhaya,' a third voice jeered, 'that the goodly sum you earn each month is owing to English.' A few years ago the language of the courts had been changed from Persian to English and Bidhusekhar had kept an English tutor and learned the language.

Bidhusekhar and Ramkamal had been held together by a strong bond of love ever since they could remember. They had stood by one another in their triumphs and defeats and shared each other's joys and sorrows. Though they were nearly the same age, Bidhusekhar looked on Ramkamal as a younger brother. Many years ago, an astrologer from Varanasi had predicted a short life for Ramkamal, in consequence of which Ramkamal was assailed, from time to time, by fears of death. At such moments he would cling to his friend's hand and beg, 'You'll look after my family and estates when I die, won't you, Bidhu?' As a matter of fact, Bidhusekhar looked after everything even when Ramkamal was alive. His word was law in the Singha household. Even if a servant was caught stealing, Bidhusekhar was sent for. 'You are so busy with your friend's affairs—you have no time for your own,' Soudamini grumbled from time to time. But that was far from the truth. Bidhusekhar watched over his own household with a hawk's eye and acted whenever he thought it necessary. Like the day he put an end to Bindu's lessons. A full-grown widowed daughter was a responsibility he did not take lightly. Brahmin widows must not look on the faces of non-Brahmins on Ekadasi. The house was full of servants. So Bidhusekhar decreed that Bindu must spend the day, alone by herself, in the puja room.

But what was wrong with Bindu? Why was she so changed? She had never felt hunger or thirst on Ekadasi. Why did she now? And what were these new yearnings that went beyond hunger and thirst; that made her limbs burn and her eyes glitter like those of a wild cat's?

She hardly ever saw Ganganarayan these days. He came very rarely and, even when he did, he never came upstairs, never asked for Bindu. The ingrate! There was a time when she was his only friend; when he was too shy and tongue-tied to talk to anyone else. Now he was going to college and had many friends. Ganga had started drinking. Bindu was sure of it. She had read in the *Samvad Prabhakar* that the boys of Hindu College drank liquor and misbehaved in the streets. And Ganga had sworn on her head that he would never touch liquor! Why swear an oath if you are too weak to keep it? If Bindu could catch him just once, she would give him a tongue-lashing he wouldn't forget in a hurry.

On the rare occasions that Ganga came to the house, he could be heard arguing with Bidhusekhar. Ganga stood in awe of his own father but was frank and open with Bidhusekhar. Bidhusekhar had petted and pampered him as a child; had taught him religious verses and loved him as tenderly as he did his own daughters. And now, Ganga had turned atheist and argued with Bidhusekhar about the worth of religion.

Ramkamal Singha being away on a tour of his estates, Ganga had come to seek Bidhusekhar's permission to attend his friend, Banku's sister's wedding. Bidhusekhar asked a number of questions regarding the arrangements and gave his consent on one condition. Ramkamal's steward, Dibakar, would accompany Ganga. Ganga wasn't pleased but there was no question of disobeying Bidhusekhar. 'It is time you were wed too, my boy.' Bidhusekhar smiled at Ganga. 'It isn't enough to go around, enjoying other people's weddings. How old are you?' Ganga stood, silent, his head hanging in embarrassment. 'Let me see,' Bidhusekhar continued. 'You were born in

Bhadra.[9] That makes you sixteen—no, seventeen years old. Seventeen and still unwed! What will people say? The period of mourning is over in the bride's family and we haven't even set a date. Your father expects me to remember everything. But don't worry, son. We'll arrange a grand wedding for you this winter.'

Worry! Marriage was the last thing on Ganga's mind. Rebellious murmurs rose in his heart but they dared not touch his lips. 'After the wedding,' Bidhusekhar continued, quite oblivious of Ganga's feelings, 'you can start learning the management of the estates. You've had enough of college and—'

'Khuro[10] Moshai!' Ganga broke in desperately. 'I have two years left—'

'So what? What use is college to you now? You've learned to read and write English. You can even write essays. That's quite enough. After all, you're not aiming to be an Englishman's clerk. Your father will leave enough money to last you for generations.'

Ganga knew argument was useless. Pleading might have some effect. 'Please, Khuro Moshai,' he begged. 'Allow me to attend college for another two years.'

'Listen, Ganga. I was only fourteen when I joined Sherwood Saheb's office as junior clerk. I've been earning my living since then. Your father managed thousands of rupees worth of business from the age of fifteen. And you are seventeen—'

'Education wasn't considered important then.'

'Are you trying to tell me we are less educated than you?'

'You are self-educated, Khuro Moshai! If you could attend one lecture of Mr Richardson's, you would want to hear him again and again.'

'Richardson! That drunken rogue? Are the boys in his charge? The School Society should have dismissed him years ago.'

'They have. He has been dismissed,' Ganga cried out hastily. 'He's not here any more. He's in Madras.'

---

9 Mid-August—Mid-September.
10 Uncle.

Bidhusekhar burst out laughing. 'Then why are you so keen on attending college? Listen, son. Too much English education is not good for our boys. It is spoiling them for everything else. Moral instruction is the only instruction worth having. The country has been going to the dogs ever since the white rabbit turned brown.'

'White rabbit? Oh! You mean Hare Saheb.'

'He's a madman. He came here to sell watches and look at him now. What call has an Englishman to behave like a native? And why does he take it upon himself to tell us what is good for us? He claims he is educating our youth. As if we weren't educated before he came. The day he sold his business to Grey Saheb, the newspaper headline read, "Old Hare turned Grey". Education! I know what they teach in that college of yours. Godlessness and insolence! That's what they teach. Anyway, that's neither here nor there. You are a man now, Ganga. It is time you took on some responsibility. Your father and I are getting old. We may die, suddenly, some day . . . Forget about English and start learning the business.'

Bindu stood on a first floor verandah and heard every word of what passed between Ganga and her father. So Ganga's education, like hers, was coming to an end. She felt a stab of pain and a rush of joy immediately afterwards. Bewildered by her own conflicting emotions, she gazed stony-eyed as Ganga went out of the house. He dragged his feet as he walked and his face was pale and drawn.

These thoughts and many others passed through Bindu's head as she lay on the floor of the puja room. Her throat was on fire and her tongue was stiff and brittle and crackled with thirst. Her heart thumped painfully against her ribs. She felt desolate; cast out by everyone who knew her. She turned her head and the tears gushed out of her eyes and fell, drop by drop, on the floor.

After a long time she sat up and wiped her eyes. And then she noticed her tears gleaming on the marble. Without stopping to think, she put out her tongue and licked them up. But they were only tears—they didn't even dampen her tongue. Only a taste of salt filled her mouth. The next moment she had caught up the end of her sari and was rubbing her tongue vigorously.

She was a widow and she had tasted water on Ekadasi. She had sinned. Would God punish her for drinking her own tears?

'Bindu! Bindu!' It was a man's voice—half strange; half familiar. But what man would call out to her at this hour? She ran to the window. There was a garden below, with a pond in the middle. A star-apple tree, covered with blossoms, stood on one bank. The hot wind stirred in its branches and the powdery pollen drifted down and fell on the water. Bindu opened the door and came to the stair landing. Her father wasn't home. She could go down if she wished. But Bindu was very sensitive; very proud. She would obey her father's decree even if it killed her. She went back to the puja room and sank down on the floor. And then the voice came again, louder and more insistent. Bindu sat up. Sweat broke out from every pore of her body—a cold sweat that made her shiver even in the heat of the afternoon. She had recognized the voice. It was Aghornath's—her husband, Aghornath, whom she had known so briefly so many years ago in Rajpur village. A dim remembrance floated up from God knew what subterranean depths—of a fourteen-year-old youth, strong as a bull and ruddy as a *gora,* with flashing eyes and long, black hair, calling out to her from the topmost branches of the guava tree. 'Bindu! Bindu!' he called out to his child bride and threw down the largest, ripest guavas for her to eat.

He was calling out to her now. But he was dead. Bindu had seen him die with her own eyes. Had he came back from the land of the dead to claim her and take her away? Bindu was frightened and burst into tears. She wanted to run to her mother and lie down beside her but pride, sharper even than fear, kept her body stiff and inert. The tears kept pouring down till they formed a little pool on the floor.

At last, exhausted with weeping, Bindu sat up. This time she made no attempt to drink her tears. She fixed her gaze on Janardan—a figure of burnished gold, six inches high. The exquisitely chiselled lips were curved in a smile. Bitterness welled up in Bindu's heart. He was cruel, cruel. He smiled while Bindu suffered. Suddenly, a red hot rage swept through her. Why should she go with Aghornath to the land of the dead? She would live here with the living. Her father had said that

Janardan was her husband. She brushed aside the flowers that covered it and took up the dazzling image in her hand.

Under the length of cloth that covered her, Bindu's body waited warm and tender. She felt strange new stirrings within her; a quiver in the pit of her stomach; a melting in her thighs. She pressed the hard gold against her newly swelling breasts and moaned and whispered, 'Give me! God oh! God give me.'

# Chapter VIII

The city was divided in two. On the bank of the river where the old fort stood, southwest of Lal Dighi or the Great Tank, was the Sahebpara—a cluster of neat bungalows which housed the British. The wide, beautiful Court House Street ran through this area. Further south, nestling among leafy trees and shrubs, lay the famous Chowringhee and beyond it, Burial Grant Road. Here were thick jungles, dotted with pleasure mansions, owned by the rich white elite. Much of the jungle had been cleared away for the building of the new fort and for the broad expanse of open land that formed a buffer zone between it and the first houses of the city. This was called the Esplanade . . .

The natives inhabited the northern part of the city. Apart from teachers and priests and, sometimes, a trader or two, no whites could be seen walking the streets here. The British kept away from the natives, by and large, coming together only occasionally at parties hosted by the rajas and zamindars of Calcutta. It was said that even Englishmen vied with each other to get invited to Prince Dwarkanath's parties—so magnificent were they. Likewise, the natives avoided the British residential area, particularly at night. Rumour ran rife about drunken *goras*, skulking about the maidan and beating up innocent natives. So terrifying were the stories circulated that even pilgrims to Kalighat took care to return well before dusk.

Crossing Lalbazar, on his way to Sahebpara, the first sight that met the traveller's eye was the towering pinnacle of the Supreme Court of Calcutta. One of the first actions of the British on establishing their colony was to set up a court of law. Justice and fair play, the rulers claimed, were engrained in the British character and constituted the cornerstone of their administration in India. This claim went undisputed. The natives genuinely believed that the British were here to dispense justice. Raja Nanda Kumar's hanging was a memory that had faded. After all, that was fifty or sixty years ago.

Though ruled by Great Britain, India was not yet numbered

among her dominions. The East India Company still held the lease but did not wield absolute power for it was answerable to parliament, which sat in London. In consequence, the rulers were forced to take heed of the native point of view when formulating their policies. They had to be particularly wary of social customs and traditions for these were inextricably linked with religion.

In the early days of the British presence in India, ruler-ruled interaction was confined to masters and servants. Barbers, cooks, sweepers, ayahs and pimps, though despised by the whites, were indispensable to them for they were the first to pick up a few words of English. Later, the study of English became fashionable and the best families started sending their boys to English schools. And this was when the British made two important discoveries. One, that India was not the land of dark superstitions and primitive cults they had been taught to believe. Two, that upper class Hindus despised the *mlechha* foreigner no less than the ruling class did the native. This knowledge was disconcerting for what master likes to be held in contempt by his slave?

Then, over the years, there was a shifting of attitudes. Worn out by centuries of misrule, natives welcomed the law and order British rule represented. No one regretted the passing away of the nawabs for their regime evoked only memories of decadence, opulence and senseless cruelty. Siraj-ud-doulah, Mir Kasim and Pratap Aditya were to be mythologized into tragic heroes in the plays of twentieth-century dramatists but at that time they were viewed only as rapists and murderers. Not that rapists and murderers had disappeared from the land. Far from it. But they could be brought to trial and justice obtained. There was a case in which a youth named Haragobinda, scion of the wealthy Basak family of Calcutta, was sentenced to life imprisonment for torturing and raping a minor girl called Kshetramoni. That a boy whose father owned lakhs worth of property could be serving a sentence for raping a poor village girl was unheard of! Girls like Kshetramoni had been bought and sold for twenty or thirty *tankas* only a few years ago. Natives respected this aspect of British rule and slowed their steps in reverence when approaching that venerable edifice, the Supreme Court, on their way to Sahebpara. They were to discover, later, that justice was a flexible commodity in the hands of the rulers, to be stretched and twisted at will.

Dusk had settled on the city and the streets were deserted. On the marble steps that rose in an imposing flight to the court's portico, a little group of humans could be seen huddled over their pots and bundles. Trilochan Das, a middle-aged peasant from Bhinkuri village in Kushthia district, his wife, Thakomoni, and children, Dulal and Golapi, stared around them in dismay. They had walked five days and five nights, then crossed the Hoogly by boat, landing at Armenian Ghat only that afternoon. Their first encounter with the city had frightened them. Never had they seen so many houses and people all together.

Trilochan farmed the zamindar's land but two consecutive droughts had impoverished him and he hadn't been able to pay the landlord's dues. Then, only a few days ago, his house had been burned down, and he was now both homeless and penniless. Trilochan Das was only one among many who were suffering the consequences of the Permanent Settlement.

Trilochan did not even know that the zamindari had changed hands. He knew all about sowing and harvesting; which clouds brought rain and which canker fed on the ripe grain. He knew that the tenant had to pay the zamindar's dues and, if he couldn't, he had to fall at his feet and beg for mercy. Trilochan had stared, gaping like an idiot, when a new steward, accompanied by fierce lathi-wielding guards, had approached him and demanded three times the amount he usually paid. He hadn't understood. Neither had the other tenant farmers who shared the same fate. The guards had beaten them mercilessly, looted their homes, then set them on fire.

In the olden days the system was more flexible. The zamindar paid the Company a portion of whatever he could collect from his tenants. The latter knew what their master was like for he lived among them and they shared a common interest. However greedy or rapacious he might be, the zamindar maintained his tenants in times of difficulty for when were dues ever collected from dead men? Now the situation had changed. A permanent arrangement had been made. The zamindar was contracted to pay a fixed sum each year. How he got it out of his tenants was his business. The Company would not interfere.

In the wake of the Permanent Settlement, a new breed of landed gentry came into being. The trading community of Calcutta, grown wealthy on salt, cloth and cork, bought up estate after estate and set up as zamindars. But they did not live among their tenants. They built mansions in Calcutta and lived lives of sloth and luxury, while their agents squeezed the life blood out of the peasants and, in cases of default, seized their land.

A luxury that was gaining in fashion was the promotion of the arts. Education, music and religious ritual flourished on the blood and bones of an impoverished peasantry. Landless and penniless, the latter flocked to Calcutta in the belief that if one fell at the master's feet and begged for mercy, all would be well.

Trilochan didn't even know his master's name. All he knew was that he lived in Calcutta. Trilochan saw the house he sought in his mind's eye—a large, imposing mansion, with a high iron gate and a red turbaned sentry on guard. He wouldn't have much difficulty locating it for surely the zamindar's house was larger than all the other houses! But on stepping into the streets of Calcutta he got a shock. For there were hundreds of imposing mansions, with hundreds of red turbaned sentries on guard. No one knew anybody here. Dazed and frightened, Trilochan clutched his children by their hands and, dodging the traffic, ran this way and that till he reached the safety of the Supreme Court. This building was even more majestic than the others. It might be his master's house. But where were all the people? The doors and windows were barred and all was silent. Being a holiday, the court was closed.

Darkness had set in. The children were hungry and tired and whined unceasingly. Thakomoni sat motionless, the edge of her sari pulled low over her face. Swarms of mosquitoes, the size of baby sparrows, buzzed around them and bit viciously into their arms and necks. Trilochan slapped himself several times in a frenzy. But not even the buzzing and stinging evoked a response from Thakomoni. Only when Trilochan, enraged beyond endurance at the children's whining, slapped them vigorously on their cheeks, did Thako hiss behind her veil,

'Don't lay hands on the children, you lout. If you can't put rice in their mouths, don't knock them about either.'

'Why don't they eat *chiré*?' Trilochan turned on his wife menacingly. 'Can't you give them *chiré*? If I hear another sound I'll thrash them till the bones rattle in their bodies.'

'Why did you bring us here?' Thako began to sniff. 'I want to go back to Bhinkuri.'

These were Trilochan's sentiments, exactly. But he couldn't admit it. 'What is left there, woman?' he snapped. 'Our land's been taken from us and our house burned. Do you want to sleep under the trees?' Thakomoni's reply to this outburst was to the effect that, as far as she could see, no great arrangements for their stay had been made here either. Trilochan's mouth shut with a snap but rage simmered within him. He glared at the scattered bundles that held his worldly possessions. There was some *chiré* left in the pot and some lumps of jaggery. But the children were tired of chewing dry *chiré*. They had been doing so for the last five days and their jaws ached and their mouths hurt. They wanted hot rice, salt and chillies.

At last, weary with weeping, the children sat up and ate some of the *chiré* and jaggery. Then the boy climbed down the steps and urinated, with a great splatter, on one wall of the edifice of justice. Returning, he said, 'I'm thirsty.'

'*Haramzada*!' was his father's loving reply.

'I'm thirsty. I want some water,' the boy set up a wail. The girl hiccuped painfully and even Thako joined the chorus. 'Get us some water. Are we to die of thirst?' Trilochan cursed beneath his breath. Emptying the contents of one pot on to a kantha, he stood up. He knew there was a lake nearby. He had noticed it on his way back from the river ghat. 'Take Dulal with you,' Thako said but Trilochan didn't want her advice. He picked up the pot without a word and walked out into the night.

Trilochan walked a little distance, then afraid of losing his way, looked back to ascertain the direction he had come from. He started counting his steps (that is what country folk did when lured away from their paths by the will o' the wisp) till he reached the edge of the lake. A litter of jackals started up at his approach and skulked away, snarling, scattering the glow-worms that winked and sparkled in great globes of swinging light. Weird sounds of whoor, whoosh, whoor assailed his ears and he could see strange shapes in the distance. They were horses, come to crop the grass that grew thick and juicy by the lake. But Trilochan didn't know that. He trembled with fear and goose bumps broke out all over his body.

Trilochan stepped into the water. Through force of habit he flailed his arms to push away the water hyacinth that covered every village pond with a film of green. But this was the Great Tank; the 'Loll Diggy' of which the Sahebs were so proud, and its water stretched out in a great sheet, clean and clear, in the moonlight. The sahebs fished in the Lal Dighi and took walks by its banks. Natives were banned entry into this area though horses weren't.

Trilochan washed his hands and feet and rinsed his mouth. Then, drinking his fill, he dipped his pot into the water. When he stood on the bank once more, he was astonished to see what looked like two demons, bearing down on him with murderous looking lathis. They were British sentries but their faces and uniforms were exactly like those of the Nawab's soldiers of half a century ago. Enormous sideburns disappeared into whiskers, black and fierce, and eyes flaming with ganja glared menacingly. Grabbing Trilochan by the neck, they rained blows on his back and shoulders. Dazed with pain though he was, Trilochan's heart leaped up with joy. These were the zamindar's guards, he told himself, and soon he would be led to the master and all would be well. The only trouble was that his wife and children were not with him. '*O go!*' he cried. 'My woman is sitting on the steps, waiting for me. I came to get water for the children—' Another shower of blows! The pot fell from Trilochan's hand and broke and the precious water was spilt all over the grass. The guards ran their hands expertly around his waist. Their search yielding nothing; they kicked and pushed him even more roughly and bore him off to the police station.

Meanwhile, Thakomoni sat like a brooding mother bird, her children nestling under her wings. Hours went by and her husband did not return. She grew numb with fear but what else could she do but wait? Suddenly, a snarling of jackals came to her ears and then a rumble of gun shots. Jackals often entered a saheb's compound at night and were shot at from the windows.

Exhausted with weeping and begging for water, the boy fell asleep, his head lolling on the steps. But the girl tossed and turned and hiccuped again and again. Then, when the moon rose behind the church steeple, she retched violently and vomited all over the white marble. Thako was frightened. She clapped her hand over the girl's mouth but it was no use. When had cholera ever been choked off like that? Between her vomits the girl cried for water. Her brother, Dulal, woke up at the sound of her voice and set up a wail of his own. 'Baba! Baba *go*!' he cried piteously. His father didn't hear him but two other men did. They patrolled the street, not the court house, but they came forward to see what was going on. Lifting his lantern, one of them peered into Thakomoni's face. Seeing she was young and healthy, he winked at his companion. They could pretend to take her to the police station and then . . .

*'O go!'* Thako sobbed.' My husband is lost and my daughter is dying! What shall I do? Where shall I go?'

'Get off those steps, you whore,' the men rushed towards her and tugged at her sari. And, at that moment, Golapi retched and vomited again. The men turned tail and ran. They had seen the vomit by the light of the moon and knew it for what it was. The girl's voice had grown feeble by now but she went on repeating like a clockwork doll, 'Water! Water!' The six-year-old Dulal could not bear his sister's agony. He stood up and asked his mother, 'Shall I get some water, Ma?'

Dulal walked down the street, looking around him apprehensively. He wasn't sure where the lake was but he had seen it on his way and knew that it was quite near. His little chest felt tight with pain. Why had his father not returned? He lifted up his voice and called, shrill and penetrating, into the night, 'Baba! Baba *go*!' Not a soul responded. Only a horse, just released from harness, came clip-clopping down the road and nearly knocked him down. Frightened, he ran back to his mother. Golapi continued retching and vomiting till the first shimmer of grey appeared in the east. Then she sank into a profound slumber.

The moon had set and a cool breeze sprang up, scattering the tattered wisps of cloud above Thako's head. A delicious shudder passed through her hot, sweaty limbs. Her lids slipped down over burning eyes, as heavy as stones. Her head sank on her breast and, within seconds, she lay sprawled on the cool marble, her sleeping children around her.

The sun rose high over the horizon but the sleepers didn't awake. Passers-by stopped short and stared in wonder at the scene. A peasant woman and her son lay sleeping on the steps of the highest court of justice in the land. And, a little distance away, a little girl lay in a pool of vomit and faeces—her limbs cold and stiff with death. Flies as big as bumble bees buzzed around her and settled on her blue lips and eyelids.

Boom! Boom! The sound of the cannon being fired from the fort startled Thakomoni out of her sleep. It was seven o'clock. She sat up quickly and, seeing the puzzled faces before her, picked up her dead daughter and clasped her to her breast.

# Chapter IX

Dislodging Thakomoni was not easy. She had all the stubborn arrogance of a woman born and bred in a village. Besides, fear and a sense of defeat had made her desperate. She sat motionless, her children close beside her, the comments from the crowd washing over her like water on a yam leaf.

'Get out of here, you slut! Do you know where you are sitting?'

'Send for the doms. Get the place cleaned up at once or the sahebs will be furious.'

'Now the whole city will catch the contagion! Couldn't these country pests find somewhere else to die?'

'Save me, Ola Bibi! Save me!' This was accompanied by a flinging of cowries on the steps where the dead girl lay.

But in every chorus, a dissenting voice can be heard. 'Oh! The poor little boy!' someone murmured from the crowd. 'He'll get the cholera, too, if he hasn't already. Run away, son, or you'll die, too.'

Jhama jham! Jhama jham! the sweepers entered, lashing the ground viciously with giant broomsticks. And behind them came the chowkidars—the same drug-eating hulks who had run away last night. They had slept in their huts till dawn and now came forward, flourishing their authority with much sound and fury.

'Get out of here, you shameless whore!' they snarled at Thako. 'Get off those steps.'

Thakomoni cowered before them, growling and whimpering like an animal that had strayed away from its lair in the woods. Her eyes rolled in terror and the hackles rose on the back of her neck. She tightened her grip on her dead daughter. The sweepers swept zealously till they discovered a profound truth. They weren't doms. Why should they touch the dead? Besides, who knew what caste the corpse was? They continued sweeping the steps, studiously avoiding the area where Thako sat with her children and bundles, finished their work and went home.

The chowkidars had, in the meantime, fetched the scavengers. These were women in colourful saris, with pretty faces, slim waists and heavy breasts. But their tongues were as sharp as knives and everyone feared them. The ones who worked for the sahebs were the worst. The walked the streets like queens and bore chamber pots on their heads as proudly as if they were crowns. Their hips swung and their silver girdles rippled over plump buttocks as they poured the dirty slops the sahebs made into that holiest of holy rivers, the Ganga. If they touched anyone in their triumphal march (and they took care to do so), no one dared voice a protest.

The two scavengers climbed the steps and clacked their tongues noisily at Thako, the chowkidars and the spectators. No one understood what they were saying but the sight of two pretty women, screaming and gesticulating, was interesting enough. The crowd looked on with pleasure. Thako and her children were forgotten and the two scolding women became the cynosure of all eyes.

Suddenly, a hush fell on the crowd and the two women froze in their places. The chief bailiff of the court, an Englishman called Andrews, had come up quickly and now stood surveying the scene gravely. The natives called him Idrus Saheb and feared him for his cruelty. Andrews was not of those of his race who wouldn't sully their hands by touching a native. On the contrary, he enjoyed cuffing and knocking them down on the slightest pretext. It was rumoured that he had once kicked his gardener so viciously in the stomach that the latter had vomited blood for two whole days. All the sahebs had congratulated him on the power of his kick. Idrus Saheb didn't speak a word. He threw a baleful glance at the scavengers, at which one made a rush at Thako and dragged her up by the hair and the other snatched the child from her breast. Thako fought and screamed but mother love wasn't stronger than the arms of the scavengers. Seeing them bear her daughter away, she ran after them, screaming. She wondered what kind of place the city was, where a man goes to fetch water and does not return; where people stand by and laugh when a child is snatched away from a mother's breast. Poor Thako did not know that her daughter was dead. She ran after the scavengers, begging and pleading till, reaching the river, they threw the dead girl, with a swing of their powerful arms, into the swirling water. Undaunted, Thako jumped into the river and retrieving the body, started running in the opposite direction. As if by running away she could escape this grisly hell, swarming with demons, and return to the safety of her village.

This side of the Ganga was a vast burning ghat but only a few had the means to cremate their dead. The poorest simply threw the corpses into the water. Others left them half-burned for want of sufficient wood. The ground was littered with bones and putrid flesh, over which monstrous argalas slipped and slithered in droves. A horrifying stench hung in a sky darkened with clouds of flapping vultures. At places the ground was cleared and a path cut for bathers to make their way to the river. But even here, human limbs and skulls could be found and vultures could swoop down on the living as well as the dead.

The river brimmed over her banks, heaving and straining with the weight of her water. Barges and boats dotted her surface, some stealing stealthily along her banks; others riding proudly on her crest. Most of them were crude and wooden but a few steel ones could also be seen for the British had recently introduced mechanical ships. Sometimes a ship might knock another down or get overturned in a storm. Then the broken frame, together with its contents, was auctioned off. On such occasions the businessmen and stevedores of Calcutta crowded at the ghat and a frenzied bidding took place.

Exhausted with weeping and running, Thako sank by the path that led to the river and rent the sky with wails to her lost husband. Trilochan did not make an appearance but a few chandals looked on interestedly. Suddenly, a palki came swinging along and stopped a few yards away from where Thako was sitting. The curtains parted and a maidservant, holding an infant in her arms, stepped out.

Sitting inside the palki was Bimbabati. She had come for her ritual bathe in the Ganga and had brought Nabin with her. He was two years old now and so naughty and wilful that she never felt safe when he was out of her sight. Even in the few minutes that it took her to bathe he would get into some mischief. On one occasion he had flung off Chinta's hand and run towards the river. Now Dibakar came with Chinta and kept a close watch on the child.

The bearers picked up the palki and made their way towards the river, shouting, 'Stand aside! Make way!' The bathers recognized the palki from its crest and moved away respectfully. The bearers then stepped into the water and dipped the palki, with Bimbabati in it, seven times. Then they paused in midstream for their mistress would now make her obeisance to the sun. Bimbabati sat inside, serene and radiant like a goddess of beaten gold. Closing her eyes in reverence she brought her palms together . . . Boom! Boom! The cannon from the fort warned the bathers that the tide was coming in. The bearers moved hastily towards the shore. Parting the curtains, Bimbabati said, 'I hear a child crying. Who is it, Chinta?' Thako's tears were spent by now but Dulal cried on and on. Bimba's heart melted with pity. She couldn't bear to see a child suffer.

'There's a woman sitting on the path, holding a little girl in her arms,' Chinta said. 'There's a boy beside her. He's the one who is crying.'

'Why?'

'Who knows?' Chinta said carelessly. 'He might be starving.'

A shadow fell on Bimbabati's face. The world was so beautiful! Yet there was so much suffering in it. So many children starved to death!

'Call Dibakar,' she commanded.

Dibakar came and stood by the palki. Bimba avoided talking to him directly. 'Tell Dibakar to bring the woman and her son to the house, Chinta,' she said. 'We are leaving now. They can come later.'

'As your worship commands,' Dibakar murmured deferentially but inside he seethed with indignation. The mistress was constantly picking up riff-raff from the streets and bringing them home. He walked up to Thako and squatted by her.

'The girl is dead,' he said conversationally. 'Why do you hold her in your arms? What did she die of?'

Dibakar was an astute man and Ramkamal's right hand. Gently, persuasively, he got the whole story out of Thako and Dulal. After a while he was even able to convince Thako that her daughter was dead and ought to be thrown into the Ganga.

Even now her soul might be in torment. Soothed by his kind words and, not knowing what else to do, Thako laid her dead child in the water and taking Dulal by the hand, walked behind Dibakar till they reached the house in Jorasanko. She did not know that this was the house her husband had sought so desperately; that the master of the house was the zamindar of Bhinkuri.

At the deuri of the mansion, a fat white gentleman stood leaning on his stick. Dibakar knew him by sight. He was Hare Saheb. Dibakar stooped respectfully and touched his feet.

'Is this Ganganarayan's father's house?' Hare Saheb enquired in his quaint Bengali. 'I've come to see Ganganarayan.'

Meanwhile, Thako and Dulal were so struck with the size and splendour of the house before them that they stared open-mouthed in wonder and shrank from entering it.

'Go in, child,' Dibakar said to Thako in a patronizing tone. 'Go in and meet the mistress. She has promised you shelter. What is there to fear?'

Thako sank to her knees and sobbed piteously. 'My husband! He's lost in this great city. Where must I look for him? *O go*! Where shall I find him?'

'Come, come.' Dibakar clicked his tongue in embarrassment. 'He'll be found—never fear. We'll do something. Now go in and talk to the mistress.'

'What is the matter? Why is the woman crying?' Hare Saheb asked curiously.

'Husband lost, sir. Crying, crying on Ganga bank. Little girl, sir—meaning daughter, sir. Die this morning. Very poor, sir.' Dibakar volunteered all this information in his inimitable English.

But Hare Saheb did not laugh. He had stood all this while, feet crossed at the ankles in Lord Krishna's pose. Now the tears poured down his cheeks. He was growing old and found human suffering harder to bear than ever before. Wiping his streaming eyes, he asked, 'Your mistress will give them food and shelter? Very kind—most generous.' Then, taking a rupee from his pocket, he put it in Dulal's hand and said, 'Come to me when you are older. I will take you in my school.'

Dibakar ordered the guard to take Thako and her son to the mistress and, turning to Hare Saheb, said obsequiously in

Bengali, 'Come this way, sir. Honour the house with the dust of your feet.' He led the Englishman to a room on the first floor, where Ramkamal and Bidhusekhar sat discussing business over their *albolas*. They looked up in surprise but before Dibakar could say a word, Hare Saheb had brought his palms together and introduced himself. 'Gentlemen! Your servant, David Hare.'

Under the shock of white hair that rarely saw a comb, Hare Saheb's face was strong and ruddy, with three deep furrows marked on the brow. The power of his limbs, encased in loose trousers and a long white coat, belied his years. Seating himself, he said, 'I've come to enquire after Ganganarayan. He has absented himself from college for a fortnight now. Is he ill?'

'Oh no,' Ramkamal answered quickly. 'He's quite well.'

'Why doesn't he attend his classes then?'

'Doesn't he? I didn't know—'

Bidhusekhar knew the reason or thought he knew. It was he who had advised Ganga against attending college and Ganga's obedience pleased him. He had never cared for Hare Saheb and was convinced that the dissolute ways of the young were owing to him. He had heard that Hare Saheb encouraged boys of good families to study medicine, with the consequence that Brahmin boys were messing about with low-caste cadavers. Besides, the education Hare imparted had not a trace of moral instruction in it.

'Ganga is to be wed,' he said shortly. 'That may be the reason—'

Hare Saheb felt the blood rush to his face in angry surprise. But he controlled himself with an effort and said, 'That is good news and I look forward to the feast. But how long do your weddings last? A fortnight?'

'He isn't married yet,' Ramkamal answered with a smile. 'The rites are to be solemnized in a few months time.'

'Why has he left college then? Is the thought of marriage driving all other thoughts out of his head?'

'He hasn't left college,' Ramkamal soothed the angry white man. 'Why should he? He'll go again from tomorrow.'

Bidhusekhar stirred in his chair. He was extremely annoyed at his friend's naïveté. But before he could say a word,

Ramkamal hastened to play the host. 'What is your drink, sir?' he asked Hare Saheb. 'Brandy? Wine? Beer?'

'Nothing. I don't drink.'

Ramkamal was shocked. An Englishman who didn't drink was as big an aberration as a lion which ate grass. What a strange man this David Hare was!

'Then have something to eat. Some sweetmeats, perhaps—'

'Could you call Ganganarayan? I would like to speak to him.'

'Certainly, certainly.' Ramkamal rose hurriedly and went into the house, calling, 'Ganga! Ganga!' Returning, he seated himself and began ostentatiously, 'Sir, your presence in my humble abode does me honour. A great educationist like you; one who has spent his life in selfless service—' Hare Saheb's lips curled in a smile. He raised a hand and checked Ramkamal's effusions with the words, 'You are two eminent men of the land. I need your help.' Bidhusekhar frowned and pulled deeply from his *albola* but Ramkamal folded his hands humbly and said, 'I gave a large donation when the college was founded—'

'I don't deny your generosity,' Hare Saheb answered. 'But I am in need of more than that. You must give me your moral support.'

At this moment, Ganganarayan came into the room. He was blushing a little and looked shamefaced. Hare Saheb rose from his chair with the words, 'I'm taking him back to college, gentlemen. I hope you have no objection.'

'None at all. None at all,' Ramkamal said hastily before Bidhusekhar could say a word.

Turning to Ganga, Hare Saheb said in a stern voice, 'You have absented yourself from college without leave. You will be punished—' Just then, Chinta came into the room, carrying Nabin. And wonder of wonders! Instead of shrinking away from the strange white man, Nabin beamed at him and put out his arms. Hare Saheb drew the infant to him and nuzzled the soft neck. 'He is clean and well cared for,' he said. 'Whose child is he?'

'Mine,' Ramkamal said proudly. 'He's my younger son.'

'He's a beautiful child and very intelligent.' Then, returning the boy to his nurse, Hare Saheb walked out, taking Ganganarayan with him. But Nabin would not let him go. He howled so loudly that Hare Saheb was forced to come back. Taking Nabin in his arms once more, he tossed him high up in the air. Nabin gurgled with pleasure.

'Good! Good!' Hare Saheb said. 'He's not afraid of falling. He's a fine boy and will be a great man some day. Mark my words. A man famed throughout the land—'

# Chapter X

Ganganarayan was unmoved by Hare Saheb's threat of punishment. What he felt most was surprise at seeing him in his own house so early in the morning. He was aware, of course, of the keen interest the white man took in his pupils. If a boy missed college for some days at a stretch, Hare Saheb went personally to enquire after him. If a boy was ill, Hare Saheb sat up nights, nursing him. But he had recently been appointed commissioner of the lower courts and had become very busy in consequence. He had much less time now for his pupils.

David Hare had been a successful man of business till he decided to join the campaign for educating the native. Absorbed in the task, he had neglected his business and, having refused an honorarium from all the educational institutions he had established, was now practically penniless. He had even refused the salary that went with his appointment as secretary of the Medical College of Calcutta. The court appointment was a ruse by the government to enable the great educationist to spend his last years in comfort.

Hare Saheb walked out of the Singha mansion, tapping his stick briskly before him. One hand rested heavily on Ganga's shoulder. 'Who is that man?' he asked suddenly. 'The one who was sitting with your father?'

'My uncle,' Ganga answered. 'My father's childhood playmate and lifelong friend.'

'Hunh! Have you ever seen a likeness of Sir Francis Bacon?'

Ganga shook his head.

'If you had, you would have seen the resemblance. Quite striking—the eyes particularly. I've seen a lot of Indians who look exactly like Europeans. Only the colour is different.'

A little further on, Hare Saheb stopped and asked Ganga, 'Are you hungry? Have you had breakfast?'

'Yes, sir.'

'Tell me the truth. I won't despoil your caste by feeding you from my kitchen. I'll buy you food from a confectioner.'

'No, sir, I've had breakfast,' Ganga said firmly although, as a matter of fact, he hadn't. He had left the house in a hurry and hadn't had time for a meal.

'What have you eaten?' The Englishman probed.

'Milk—' Ganga began.

'Only milk?'

'Mangoes, bananas and sweetmeats.'

'Very good. Why are your feet so languid then? Walk briskly, boy. Match your steps to mine.' Then, a little further on, he asked, 'Do you know where Bholanath lives? Your classmate, Bholanath?'

'Yes sir. In Shimle.'

'Jagamohan Sarkar's house?'

'Jagamohan Sarkar is Bhola's uncle. They live in separate houses, standing side by side.'

'We are going there. Bholanath is ill—seriously ill. I'm surprised you know nothing about it. You will stay there all day and nurse him. That will be your punishment for staying away from college.'

A tremor of ecstasy passed through Ganga's frame. He had this feeling whenever he came near Hare Saheb. He hadn't seen anyone who was less concerned for himself or happier serving his fellowmen.

'I need Jagamohan Sarkar's help for my new project,' Hare Saheb went on. 'He is in favour of educating the women of the country.'

'Are you thinking of opening a school for girls?' Ganga asked eagerly.

'Why do you ask?' Hare Saheb knitted his brows. 'Do you have any objection?'

'Far from it. I welcome the idea. But can it be possible?'

'Why not? Everything is possible if young men like you come forward. The Female Society was set up some years ago and a school started. But the Calcutta aristocrats refused to send their daughters. You like to keep your women in ignorance.'

'I'm not one of them—'

'Jagamohan Sarkar has promised to help. I hope to be able to open a school for girls very soon now. If God gives me another ten years, I'll see the spread of female literacy in the land before I die.'

Ganga was suddenly reminded of Bindu. How bitterly she had wept when her books had been taken away from her! 'Will widows be allowed to study in the school?' The words left his lips before he could stop them. Hare Saheb's gaze rested on Ganga's face for a few moments. Then he said, 'What did you say just now? Repeat it, boy.'

'Will widows be allowed to study in the school?'

'You should be ashamed of asking me that question. Will you send your widows to my school? They who are denied the light of the sun—who can show them the light of knowledge? Listen, Ganga. I'm not a Hindu but my heart is wrung when I think of the deprivations Hindu widows suffer. Women are our mothers. How can we treat them like slaves?' Ganga's eyes glistened. He walked on in silence, his head bowed. Hare Saheb patted him on the back and continued, 'Use the education you are receiving to work for their uplift. Try to change the attitude of your countrymen. I'm an alien here. People don't trust me where their women are concerned.'

They walked on till they came to Jagamohan Sarkar's house, Hare Saheb nodding and exchanging greetings with the men who met him in the street. He had lived in this country for twenty-two years and everyone knew him. But, for some reason, Hare Saheb was not himself. He looked withdrawn and distraught. It was a very hot morning and sweat poured down his red face and neck.

Bhola's father, Birajmohan, and Jagamohan Sarkar were brothers. Of the two, Jagamohan was richer and better known among the Calcutta elite. He was a self-made man, grown wealthy in the export-import business. Sarkar, Auddy and Sons was a famous export house. But Jagamohan knew that wealth was not enough to earn the respect of his countrymen. To do that he needed another image. He took English lessons from Mr Sherwood and hung around reformers and missionaries. At one time he had even thought of embracing Christianity. All that, however, was in his youth, and had long since been forgotten. Now he celebrated Dol[11] and Durga Puja with more pomp and splendour than even the Malliks. And, like his peers, he

---

11 Holi.

nurtured a group of sycophants for that was the fashion. Jagamohan donated generously to public charities, wrote burning articles on the plight of the peasants and worked for the uplift of women.

In the vast reception room of the mansion in Shimle, Jagamohan Sarkar sat in state, surrounded by his courtiers. On his right stood a tall, thin man with a long nose. This was our old friend, Raimohan Ghoshal. He had managed to worm himself into Jagamohan's favour and was now quite indispensable to him.

Jagamohan saw Hare Saheb at the door and, raising his vast bulk with difficulty, came forward hastily. 'Mr Hare!' he exclaimed theatrically, 'Welcome to my humble home. I'm blessed this day that a great soul like David Hare has deemed it fit to step over my threshold.' Then, pausing for breath, he said in an everyday voice, 'I was thinking of you just a while ago. I'm starting my school from next month. Here, in this house. Radhakanta Deb, Raja of Shobhabazar, has expressed his approval of the scheme. Sit down, sir, and I'll tell you everything.'

'That is good news.' Hare Saheb remained where he was, his hand resting on Ganga's shoulder, and continued, 'I'll do all I can to help. One question, though. Where will you find teachers?'

'I've written to the British and foreign school societies and Dwarkanath Babu has promised to speak to the officers. I'll meet all the expenses myself. If I get even one lady teacher, the rest will be easy. I'm calling my school Female Pathshala.'

'Another question. Will females come to the Pathshala?'

'Of course, they will—'

'Your own daughters?'

'Alas! I have no daughters. But I've gone from house to house and spoken to the ladies. "Mothers all!" I've said. "Our country is awakening from a deep sleep! The long dark night is giving way before the first light of dawn. Our sisters and daughters are still enmeshed in ignorance and darkness. Let us open our doors to them and let them fill their eyes with the light of knowledge." But the problem, Mr Hare, is this. Many people, even the highest of the high in the city, believe that book-learned women are liable to lose their husbands. Have you ever seen such crass ignorance and stupidity?'

'What about women who have lost their husbands already? They can't be widowed twice, surely. This young man was asking me if widows will be allowed to study in the school.'

'Widows? What is the use of educating widows? Who is this boy?'

'I'm Bholanath's classmate, Ganganarayan Singha,' Ganga replied. 'My father is Ramkamal Singha.'

Jagamohan's brows came together. Ramkamal Singha stood three or four steps higher in the social ladder than himself and Jagamohan was envious of him. 'Don't listen to him,' he said sharply, looking directly at Hare Saheb. 'Such talk will undo everything. The presence of widows in our households keeps us pure and sanctified. Their self-denial and chastity cleanses us of our sins. Only Hindu women are capable of such immense sacrifice.'

'True! True!' Raimohan cackled, sticking his neck out like a stork. 'Words of wisdom, indeed!'

'Raja Radhakanta Deb has written a book about women's education,' Jagamohan went on enthusiastically. 'He has proved that women of ancient India were as learned as the men. It was with the coming of the Muslims that the confinement of women became necessary. Did you know, sir, that Timurlane was responsible for the darkness and ignorance our women have fallen into? But we'll show them the light—little by little.'

'Raja Bahadur hasn't breathed a word about educating widows.' Raimohan put in his bit for what it was worth. Jagamohan threw a burning glance in Ganga's direction and continued, 'Even to think of such a thing is a sin. As it is people are not ready to send their daughters to my school. So many reports come to my ears. I've even heard it said that I'm a man of loose morals and I'm trying to corrupt—'

*'Chhi! Chhi! Chhi!'* Raimohan interrupted loudly, tweaking his nose and ears in an excess of indignation. 'To accuse you of loose morals! You, who are like a god! My curses on their heads. May they rot in hell!'

'People don't know me as you do, Raimohan,' Jagamohan sighed and looked thoughtful.

'Well!' Hare Saheb's voice broke into this sentimental scene.

'You are a wise man and will take the best course. Let us forget about widows for the present and begin our work with young, unmarried girls.'

'Thank you, Hare Saheb. Now, another question. Shall girls study the same texts as boys? I feel a separate text should be written for them, with more moral instruction in it. Can the School Book Society help?'

'I'll speak to them and let you know. But where is Bholanath? I came to see him. I hear he is sick. What is wrong with him?'

'Bholanath? Oh, yes. I've heard he's been purging and vomiting for the last three days,' Jagamohan answered carelessly. He was a great man and had great tasks before him. He had no time to waste on the maladies of mere nephews.

Ganga sighed as he walked out of the door with Hare Saheb. 'There is nothing for you in this life, Bindu,' he said to himself. 'Wait for the next. But who knows where your fate will take you? You may be a widow again!' He shivered involuntarily. Hare Saheb turned to him as if he had read his thoughts. 'Things will change, dear boy,' he said gently. 'Widows will come to my school one day. If only God gives me another ten years!' Ganga's depression deepened. Ten years was a long time. Could Bindu wait that long?

Bhola's father, Birajmohan, came down the stairs as they entered the adjoining house. Seeing Hare Saheb, he rushed up to him and seized his hands. 'Bhola is dying, Hare Saheb!' he howled like a child, 'but you are here! You are here!' Then, wiping his streaming face, Birajmohan led the two upstairs to a room where Bhola lay in a deathlike stupor. Placing a hand on his son's brow, he said, 'Baba Bhola! Open your eyes and see who is here.' A tremor ran through the boy's frame and he opened his eyes slowly and painfully. But they were dim and unfocussed and seemed to have sunk deep into his face. Then, before anyone knew what was happening, he retched and vomited over the sheets and floor.

'Cholera,' Hare Saheb muttered to himself. 'It strikes the city every summer. The rains must come soon or . . .' Then, addressing Birajmohan, he said, 'Could you fetch me a mop and a bucket of water? Be quick.' The moment Birajmohan left the room, Hare Saheb turned to Ganga and said, 'You Hindus have no sense of hygiene. A sick room should be spotlessly clean or the infection will spread.' The mop and water arrived and Hare Saheb proceeded to change the sheets and wash the floor with his own hands. Bhola's mother and aunt, who had come into the room on learning of the Englishman's arrival, were appalled at the sight and stood by, silent and helpless. Birajmohan tried to snatch the mop away but Hare Saheb wouldn't let him. He cleaned the room meticulously. Then, his task completed, he said, 'I must go now. But I'm leaving this boy behind. Nursing Bhola will be his responsibility. Can I have a clean piece of cloth?' A little girl of about ten, who stood by the door, looked up at his words and, tearing a strip of her sari in a flash, handed it to the Englishman. Ganga recognized her for it was only a few months ago that he had attended Bhola's wedding. She was Bhola's bride, Mankumari, and had been sent for from her father's house on account of his illness. Hare Saheb soaked the strip of cloth in clean water and wiped Bhola's face and mouth. 'Fight the malady, my dear boy,' he murmured. 'The world is beautiful. Don't leave it. No, Bhola. We won't let you go.'

Bhola lay cold and lifeless as stone. His limbs contracted painfully from time to time and tears glistened in the corners of his eyes. Hare Saheb now turned to Bhola's father and asked, 'Do you have faith in the new medicine? Can I send for a doctor from the Medical College?'

'We have faith in you, Saheb,' Bhola's mother answered for her husband. 'We'll do whatever you say.'

'Well, then. I'll write a note for a student of mine. Send someone with it as soon as you can.' Handing over the note, Hare Saheb rose to leave. 'See me in college tomorrow morning,' he commanded Ganga, 'and bring me news of Bhola.' Hare Saheb had barely reached the door when Mankumari let out a piercing wail. Everyone looked up, startled. Hare Saheb turned back. His lip trembled and tears trickled down his cheeks. 'Ma!' he said gently. 'Do not despair. While there is life there is hope.' Then he walked away, out of the room, as quickly as he could.

Ganga was not destined to take news of Bhola to Hare Saheb. He didn't stay long in the house after Hare Saheb's departure for, fearing that he might catch the infection, Bhola's parents insisted that he leave. 'Go home, Baba,' Bhola's mother pleaded over and over again. 'Your mother will be worrying about you.'

And, then, early next morning, Banku came panting and breathless into his room and cried out in a trembling voice, 'Ganga! A terrible thing has happened. Come quickly.'

'Why? What? Is Bhola—? '

'I have no news of Bhola. Hare Saheb is dead!'

The two friends stared at one another for a moment and then burst into tears. In their pale, drawn faces, shock and terror were etched in painful lines for the news was too strange, too frightening. How would they continue to live in a world in which Hare Saheb was no more? Only for a few moments, however. Then they began running—down the stairs, out of the gate and into the street. Not waiting to send for a palki they ran, barefooted, all the way to Lalbazar—where Hare Saheb lived. The house was Grey Saheb's and they could see it from a distance. There was a crowd before it, the size of which had never been seen in the city of Calcutta. Never had so many natives collected together to offer their respects to an Englishman. Derozio's disciples were all there, together with the great babus of Calcutta. The students of Hindu School, past and present, had turned out in large numbers. Ganga's own friends stood in a corner. Even Madhu, who rarely rose before noon, was there. He had a rough tongue but a very soft heart. Every now and then, he averted his face and dashed the tears out of his eyes.

From the murmurs in the crowd, Ganga gathered that Hare Saheb had waken up around midnight, racked with severe stomach cramps and vomiting. The pain had grown more excruciating and the vomits more frequent as the night wore on. But, with his habitual stoicism, he had borne it all in silence. Then, when the night was drawing to an end, he had sent for his head bearer and said, 'Go to Grey Saheb and tell him I'm dying. And send a message to the undertakers. Ask them to prepare a coffin.' On hearing this, the bearer had wept so loudly that many of the neighbours had heard him and rushed over to Grey Saheb's house. Grey Saheb, himself, had come running into his friend's chamber and, seeing his condition, had sent for a doctor from the Medical College. For the rest of the night, Hare Saheb's favourite pupil, Sub Assistant Surgeon Prasanna Mitra, had kept vigil by his bedside. On his applying a blister to lessen the pain, Hare Saheb had begged, 'Remove the blister,

Prasanna, dear boy! Let me go in peace.' And, with the first streaks of dawn, Hare Saheb had passed away.

A sea of landaus, phaetons and pedestrians stretched as far as the eye could see as the coffin emerged from Grey Saheb's house. The sky was overcast and thunder rumbled in the air, growing louder with every passing minute. Then, as Reverend Charles Eyre signalled to the pall-bearers to move forward, the storm broke. Strong winds and torrential rain lashed at the mourners, whipping up their hair and tearing at their clothes. But not one stopped or left the procession. Slowly, with bowed heads, they made their way to Gol Dighi for Hare Saheb's mortal remains were to rest, not in the British cemetery, but near the college he had built and loved. His funeral expenses were to be borne by the general public.

Ganga remembered Hare Saheb saying only yesterday, 'The rains must come soon or . . . ' He had willed the rain to come by offering himself. The cholera had claimed its last victim of the year and was now laid to rest. Walking through the water, Ganga heard Hare Saheb's voice in his ears, 'If God gives me another ten years . . . ' He had wanted to live. He had said the world was beautiful. He had wanted to do more, much more for this land that wasn't his own.

The tears poured from Ganga's eyes and blending with the rain, pattered down silently to his feet.

# Chapter XI

Dusk was setting in when Raimohan entered Goopi's shop. Seating himself on a bamboo stool, he opened his *dibé* and helped himself to paan in a lordly manner.

'Ah, Ghoshal Moshai,' Goopi greeted him enthusiastically. 'You haven't graced my shop with the dust of your feet for months. Have you forgotten your wretched servant, Goopi?'

'Wretched servant!' Raimohan echoed, cackling like a diabolic hen. 'You've grown a fine, fat paunch for one so wretched, Goopi.'

'Don't eye my paunch, Ghoshal Moshai. It is all I've got. Poor men must have something.'

'What about the second storey you've added to your house?'

'That's just it. That's why I have nothing left. Not a cowrie.'

'How about inviting me to a feast of *luchi* and sweetmeats to celebrate your penury?'

'Certainly, certainly. When a Brahmin like you graces my humble abode with the dust of—'

'No dust. I can't promise any dust in this terrible weather. Mud—if you like. Here in Chitpur, water collects in the streets at the sight of a cloud. But why such abject humility all of a sudden, Goopi?'

'Well! You're a big man now. At one time you had nothing but your legs. Then I saw you riding a palki. Now you're driven about in a phaeton.'

'Ah! This is just the beginning, Goopi. You'll see me sitting in landaus and victorias before I'm through. My own, my very own!'

'Wasn't the phaeton your own? The one in which you were sitting when I called out to you the other evening?'

'*Arré*, no. That was Ramkamal Singhi's.'

'I heard you were hobnobbing with Jagamohan Sarkar. When did you abandon him for Ramkamal Singha?'

'I didn't abandon him. I've got them both in my net, wriggling together like twins.'

'You're a great man! Do me a good turn, Ghoshal Moshai. I hear Ramkamal Singha's son is to be wed. He'll spend a lakh of rupees—'

'A lakh? You make me laugh, Goopi. A lakh will be robbed and squandered by his toadies. I've heard he's giving the bride jewellery worth two and a half lakhs.'

'Then let me have the making of some of it. I beg you, Ghoshal Moshai. Even fifty thousand worth will do.'

A wicked smile contorted Raimohan's face. 'What if I do better than that? Don't forget Bidhu Mukherjee is also planning a grand wedding for his daughter.'

'Bidhu Mukherjee the lawyer?'

'Himself. Ramkamal's friend, guide and philosopher.'

'If you are so kind—' Goopi wrung his hands in anticipation of the glorious future ahead of him.

'I'll expect a commission. An anna to a rupee.'

'Whatever you say.'

'Then give me an advance.'

'But, Ghoshal Moshai!' Goopi was aghast. 'I have nothing with me just now. Let me do the job first, then, when I get my payment, I'll give you your commission to the last cowrie.'

'Don't talk nonsense, Goopi. Don't you know how these things are done? I'll have to bribe the watchmen to keep the other goldsmiths out. Can I do that without money?'

'But, believe me, Ghoshal Moshai—'

'Look, Goopi. If you don't want my help, say so straight out and I'll go to Madhav.' Then, in a softened tone, Raimohan added, 'I came to you first because I love you. I'm taking all this trouble for your good. Don't you understand? If you do as you are told I'll sneak you into the household. Then, in a matter of months, Goopi the lizard will turn into Goopi the crocodile. Come! Fifty rupees at the very least.'

'Thirty.'

'That's the trouble with you, Goopi. You'll haggle over a few cowries when lakhs of rupees are at stake. Will you never change?'

'Thirty-five then. Believe me, I don't have—'

'Raise it j-u-u-st a little. Let's clinch the deal at forty-five. That's final. I'm not the man to weep over a few rupees. Buy the children some sugar balls and candy with the rest and tell them their uncle sent it.'

Goopi sat silent, admitting defeat. He was no match for Raimohan and he knew it. Giving away money was an ordeal worse than death for Goopi but Raimohan's vision of the future was too tempting. So many goldsmiths had made their fortunes by securing the patronage of a rich babu. Sighing and contorting his limbs painfully, he unhooked the pouch from his waist and, taking out forty-five rupees, placed them one by one on Raimohan's outstretched palm. Beaming with satisfaction at his own rapacity, Raimohan offered Goopi a paan from his *dibé*. 'Leave everything to me,' he said magnanimously. 'Just get ready to add a third storey to that house of yours. You'll have so much money, Goopi—you'll need more storage space.'

'Give me some news of the city, Ghoshal Moshai.'

'The news! Hmph! All people can talk about is the pestilence. Cholera is raging in the city and people are dying like flies. The Ganga is choking with corpses. Ships are getting stuck—there are so many.'

'*Ram kaho*! Tell me something else.'

'Well! Dwarkanath has returned from *Bilet*.'

'*Bilet*!' Goopi's eyes rolled in his head. 'Are you telling me that he crossed the black water? What's left of his caste, Ghoshal Moshai?'

'Big men don't have to worry about caste. If you try to make a dent in it, whoosh, a silver slipper will come flying at you.' Grinning wickedly, he fondled Goopi's fat chin with fingers as thin and sharp as the claws of a crab. 'Now for business,' he said. 'I want to buy a chain. A small one will do.'

'You? Buy a chain? Are you taking another wife, Ghoshal Moshai?'

'*Chup*! Show me what you have.'

Goopi took out a wooden box, containing six or seven chains of different weights and patterns. Fingering a fine mob chain, Raimohan commanded, 'Weigh this, Goopi.' Though small, the chain was heavy—one and a half bharis exactly.

'Thirty-five rupees,' Goopi announced.

'Oh! yes?' Raimohan sneered. 'When I come to sell I get nineteen rupees a bhari and—'

'My labour, Ghoshal Moshai! You'll pay for my labour, won't you?'

'You'll charge me for your labour, you base ingrate? After all I've done for you?'

After half an hour's haggling, the price agreed upon was thirty-two rupees. Packing the ornament in a little box, Goopi said, 'This is an ordinary chain. Not good enough to hang on a houri's neck. Why don't you take the one with the locket? It would look fine on a fair breast.'

'Hmph! And you'd make a fine profit.'

Blushing furiously for some reason, Raimohan hurried out of the shop and bang—his head hit the lintel. 'The money! The money!' Goopi waddled after him like an agitated duck. 'Of course, of course. I quite forgot.' Raimohan took out his *jeb* with a flourish and counted out thirty-two rupees out of the forty-five he had just received. A faint smile lurked in the corner of Goopi's mouth. He had turned the tables on Raimohan. The chain was the identical one the latter had sold him for twenty-nine rupees.

On his way to Bowbazar, Raimohan paused for a moment outside the mansion of the Thakurs of Jorasanko. Then, sighing a little, he walked on. He had tried his best to worm himself into Dwarkanath's favour but had been cruelly rebuffed. Dwarkanath hobnobbed with white folk these days and held natives in contempt. Raimohan had had no luck with the son either. In the first flush of manhood, Deben Thakur had been a dissolute wastrel and had raised the hopes of the prime toadies of Calcutta. But he had changed of late. He didn't care for music and dancing or wine and women any more. He sat poring over Sanskrit texts, great, heavy tomes, morning, noon and night. Wasn't that unnatural? And selfish? What were poor men to do if the rich turned away from the pleasures of the world? Deben Thakur had his followers but they were not Raimohan's type. They had faces of sheep and bleated incessantly about heaven knew what. Raimohan couldn't fathom them. 'Give him time,' Raimohan mumbled as he went along. 'He's a zamindar's son, after all. A tiger cub will want to taste blood—sooner or later.'

Passing Bowbazar, Raimohan's feet slowed down as they approached Kamala Sundari's house. Kamala was the finest dancer in the city and her protector, Ramkamal Singha, loved showing her off to his friends, unlike his peers who preferred to keep their mistresses in purdah. There would be a great performance tonight for Ramkamal had procured a percussion master from Lucknow, at great expense, to be her accompanist. Kamala's face and form were as dark as night and her ghagra and odhna the colour of fire. She was like a smouldering coal from which tongues of flame leaped and darted as she swirled round and round to ecstatic cries of '*Kyabat*! *Kyabat*!' When the excitement of the audience reached its peak, as Raimohan knew from experience, Ramkamal rose from his seat and, twining an arm around the lascivious waist, drew his mistress into the bedroom and shut the door.

Light streamed from the windows and the tapping of tablas and jingling of *ghungroos* floated down to the street below. But Raimohan did not stop. He quickened his slowing steps with resolution and walked past the house of temptation. Pitter! Patter! The rain fell in a steady drizzle and Raimohan darted this way and that, stepping across puddles and potholes on his long storklike legs.

Raimohan had been born with a flair for music, which he had chiselled and perfected at the feet of masters in his stormy youth. Now, in his prime, he used this gift to make a living. But it still had the power to move him. When he saw Kamala Sundari dancing, it wasn't her he saw. He was carried beyond her; beyond the hall packed with drunken revellers, to realms undreamed of in his day-to-day existence. His head turned back in longing but he steeled himself and walked on. He hadn't seen Heeremoni for over a week and he felt faintly guilty.

Passing the mosque, he stopped by a pond that gleamed pale green in the twilight and washed his feet. Then, shoes in hand, he stood outside Heeremoni's door. The house was dark and its windows barred like a house of death. Not a soul stirred. Heere's servant had left her. Raimohan knew that. There was a Hindustani woman the last time he was here but she, too, seemed to have disappeared. Was Heeremoni—? His legs shook a little as he groped his way up the stairs and stepped gingerly into the room. At first he could see nothing for there was no light. Only a dull glow came from a pile of chaff, smouldering in a clay bowl. Then, his eyes getting accustomed to the dim light, he espied a female figure lying on the carpet at his feet.

'Heere! Heeremoni!' he called in a choking voice.

'You? You're here again?'

Raimohan crossed over to the other end of the room, where a pile of jute stalks, smeared with sulphur, stood stacked in a corner. Taking one, he pushed it into the burning chaff, then, on its bursting into flame, took it in his hand and walked over to where the sick woman lay. 'Where are the candles, Heere?' he enquired conversationally. 'And I want a *gamchha*. My hair is soaking wet. Why, Heere—?' Peering down, his heart missed a beat. Heere's face, turned upwards towards the light, was pale and translucent like a dying moon. The shadows of death lurked under her eyes and over her skeletal form. But her voice, though faint, had not lost its rancour.

'You're here again, you death's head! Get out. Out of my sight.'

'Why, Heere? What have I done? Why do you drive me out so cruelly?'

'I'm dying. Don't you understand, you fool? Do you want to die too?'

'Chandu? Where's Chandu?'

'He's sleeping in the next room.'

'At this hour? Has he eaten anything?'

'That's none of your business.'

'*A Molo*![12] Why do you snap at me every time I open my mouth? I love the boy. Can't I even ask if he's had something to eat? Where's the woman I saw the other day? The one who was doing the cooking and cleaning?'

'I don't know.'

Raimohan sighed. Heeremoni was as arrogant as ever even though she lay at death's door. She wouldn't take any help from Raimohan. If he tried giving her money, she flung it on his face. Mother and son were alone in this mausoleum of a house—penniless and unprotected. What would become of them? Even if thieves broke in and robbed and killed them both, no one would ever know. Rising, he went into the adjacent room and brought the sleeping boy to Heeremoni. Looking on the flower-like face, streaked with drying tears, Raimohan's heart

---

12 'Death be on you!'

was wrung with compassion and bitterness welled up within him.

'Tell me, Heere,' he said in a harsh whisper. 'Tell me who fathered your boy and I'll drag the bastard to your feet by the hair of his head—'

'Again! You dare utter those vile words again? Get out of my sight, you villain. He's my son and mine alone.'

Raimohan stared. What sort of a woman was this? She was hardly twenty and a prostitute. Deceiving and betraying were part of her profession. Yet, even now, when she lay dying, she refused to break faith. Unchaste though she was, she had the fidelity of a Sita; a Savitri. Liar, swindler and cheat that he was, he couldn't understand her.

'If it is Jagamohan Sarkar,' he tried again. 'The scoundrel pokes his head into every door—emancipating women. The only house he's forgotten is this one. I'll fix him. I'll tell the whole world he—'

'I've told you a thousand times it isn't him.'

'Very well, then, I'm Chandu's father from this day onwards.'

'No, you're not. He has no father. When I die, he'll die with me.'

'Oh no, he won't. See here.' He took out the gold chain from his pocket and put it around the child's neck. 'He's mine from this day onwards. I've adopted him. See how the gold glimmers against his skin.'

'Take it off. Take it away,' Heere screamed. 'Heaven knows from where you stole it!'

'I swear to you I didn't steal it. It's mine. I've earned it. I couldn't come empty-handed the day I was adopting a son—could I? Another thing. I'm staying in this house from today. I won't listen to a word you say. But first I must go out and buy some food. Don't think I'll let you slip through my fingers that easily.'

Heeremoni said no more. Tears of exhaustion oozed out of her eyes and fell on the pillow. Raimohan stroked her worn face and neck and whispered, 'I won't let you go, Heere. I need you. I'll have my revenge on the whole bunch of bastards. Just get well and we'll do it together.'

# Chapter XII

Now let us go back a few hundred years—to the time when General Khan Jehan Ali ruled Jessore with a charter from his Imperial Majesty of Delhi. Khan Jehan died in 1458, some years before the birth of Sri Chaitanya Dev. Our story, however, is not about him but about a servant of his—an obscure figure, whose name and dates are not to be found in the annals of history. In fact, we know nothing about him except that he was a Brahmin who lived in Piralya village and was passionately in love with a Muslim girl. In course of time, he married her, embraced Islam, and was given the name of Mahmud Tahir. However, according to the custom of the times, he was better known as Piralyaee, meaning, "of Piralya", which again, in course of time, found an excellent Muslim equivalent in Pir Ali.

Hinduism doesn't believe in conversion. On the contrary, it is ever eager to push its own people out of the fold. Not so the other religions of the world. Islam welcomes new entrants; even offers incentives. Pir Ali, by virtue of his conversion, became the owner of a prosperous pargana named Chengutia and a wealthy and renowned landowner.

It is commonly believed that the convert's zeal for partaking of beef far exceeds that of the Muslim born to the faith. This was never truer than in Pir Ali's case. Not only did he enjoy eating beef above all other meats, he was forever pointing out its merits to his friends and followers.

It is said that Pir Ali once played a cruel joke on his Brahmin dewans, Jaidev and Kamdev. The story goes like this. It was the month of Ramzan and the fasting Pir Ali sat discussing business with his dewans and other officers of state. He held a lemon in his hand, which he sniffed from time to time. Suddenly, one of the brothers, Jaidev or Kamdev, exclaimed, 'Wazir Saheb! You've broken your roza.' On Pir Ali's looking up in surprise, he explained, 'Smelling is half-eating—so our shastras say.' Pir Ali smiled into his beard. Under his cap an idea started forming in his head.

Some days later he held a huge durbar in the audience hall of his mansion in Chengutia. All the eminent Hindus of the estate were invited. While they sat talking, Pir Ali signalled to one of his attendants and, within a few minutes, a procession of cooks streamed into the hall. They bore flaming *chulas* in their hands, topped with *handis* full of beef chunks, sizzling in gravy and emitting clouds of fragrant steam. Some of the guests fled from the hall; others covered up their noses with their udunis. But Pir Ali wouldn't allow Jaidev and Kamdev to do either. 'Why do you run away?' he exclaimed, grasping their wrists with iron hands. 'Smelling is half-eating according to your shastras. Why don't you finish the meal you've only half-eaten?'

On being received among the faithful, Jaidev and Kamdev were given the names of Jamaluddin and Kamaluddin, along with lavish presents of money and jagirs. However, by the same law that decrees 'smelling is half-eating', the conversion of one member of a family to another faith affects the others. Jaidev and Kamdev's brothers, Ratidev and Sukdev, found the guilt of their brothers' conversion placed, fairly and squarely, on their shoulders. They were ostracized by other Hindus; their water became unacceptable and they came to be called Pirali Brahmins.

Unable to bear the pressures of his life in the village, the childless Ratidev disappeared one night and, in all probability, became a sanyasi. But for Sukdev there was no escape. He was a family man, with a daughter and a sister of marriageable age. Where could he find suitable grooms, with the Pirali stigma stamped on his family? He decided to wield the one weapon in his possession—money. With the power of money he was able to secure two Brahmins—Mangalananda Mukhopadhyaya of Phoole for his sister and Jagannath Kushari of Pithabhog for his daughter. The alliance with Sukdev enriched the two men considerably but the Pirali stigma fell on them, too, and they were to carry it for all generations to come.

Now let us leave all the others aside and follow the fortunes of Jagannath Kushari. The Kusharis were the original inhabitants of Kush village as the Gangulys were of Gangul. Over the years, however, many of them left Kush and settled elsewhere—in Sonamukhi village of Bankura; Pithabhog of Khulna; and Kaikirtan village of Dhaka. Of the entire clan, the

Kusharis of Pithabhog claimed the longest and most illustrious lineage. It is said that King Adishoor of Goud invited five Kanauji Brahmins of the purest strain to settle in his kingdom. These were the first Aryans to set foot in non-Aryan Bengal and it is from them that the five great Brahmin clans—Sandilya, Vatsa, Bharadwaj, Kashyap and Sabarna—were derived. Kshitish, the founder of the Sandilyas, had a son called Bhattanarayan who, it is commonly believed, authored the Sanskrit drama, *Benu Samhara*. The Kusharis claimed their descent from Bhattanarayan and, being Sandilya in *gotra*, were referred to as Bandoghati or Bandopadhyaya. But their illustrious ancestry could give them no protection against the Pirali stigma and they continued to suffer untold persecution at the hands of their purer counterparts.

Now let us skip a few hundred years and take up our narrative at the point of time in which Panchanan Kushari and his uncle, Sukdev, left their native village to seek their fortune. In their wanderings they reached the estuary at Gobindapur. There was little habitation here. Only a few fisherfolk lived in a little cluster of huts, straggling along one bank. Panchanan and Sukdev were instantly recognized as Brahmins—their dhotis of fine raw silk, thick *shikhas* springing out of shaven heads and exceedingly fair complexions offering no clue to their lowly status in the Brahminical hierarchy. The inhabitants of Gobindapur greeted them with the utmost deference and begged them to settle in the village. And since Brahmins were only second to God, Panchanan and Sukdev were addressed by the lordly title of Thakur.

Already, at that time, the three villages of Sutanuti, Gobindapur and Kalikata were providing the foundations of the new city of the British. The estuary of Gobindapur (the Adi Ganga of today) was being dredged and widened for easier movement of ships and cargo. Sometimes, interaction became necessary between the Englishmen employed in the task and the villagers. At such times the two Brahmins would be sent for. Assuming that Thakur was their family name and unable to articulate it correctly, the Sahebs called them Tagaure or Tagore. These Thakurs or Tagores and their progeny were the first stevedores and contractors of the new port city. They supplied provisions to the foreign ships that sailed up the river and held contracts for nearly all the building that was going on. On the ruins of the old fort (razed to the ground by Siraj-ud-doulah), the new Fort William was rising and the Maratha ditch was being dug to rid Calcutta of the Borgi menace. The fortunes of the Tagore family swelled with the rising power of the British and with the passing of the years, its Kushari and Pirali origins were quite forgotten.

With wealth came jealousies and quarrels and a family rift. Neelmoni and Darpanarayan were two brothers who lived together in their palatial mansion in the prestigious Pathuriaghat area of the new city—the ancestral dwelling on the banks of the estuary having been abandoned several generations earlier. Neelmoni did business abroad and sent all his earnings home to his younger brother, who managed the estate. But Darpanarayan was greedy and grasping. When Neelmoni wanted to retire from business and settle down, Darpanarayan declared that the Calcutta property was all his—he having managed it and added to it all these years. Making over one lakh of rupees to his brother, he made him sign a document, renouncing all other rights. And so it came about that one wild, rainy night, Neelmoni walked out of his ancestral home with his wife and children, the family deity, Narayanshila, in his hands. However, a Brahmin has no difficulty finding shelter and Neelmoni was no exception. The famous Seth Vaishnavcharan, a man of phenomenal wealth, took him in. This Vaishnavcharan had made his money in Gangajal, that is, Ganga water, an essential commodity in Hindu homes and worth its weight in gold in lands beyond the Ganga.

Among the gifts Vaishnavcharan showered on the homeless Brahmin was a piece of land in Jorasanko. With the money in his possession, Neelmoni bought up the surrounding land and built a fine mansion. And here, the broken branch of the Tagore family took root, growing in time into a magnificent tree that towered over the original.

On Neelmoni's death, the eldest of his three sons, Ramlochan, inherited the estate. He had a good head for management and not only was he successful in keeping the family and estate together, he added largely to the latter. He eventually came to be numbered among the wealthiest men of the city. Ramlochan worked hard all day but made it a point to relax in the evenings. Dressed in a magnificent kurta and dopatta, with a coronet on his head, he was seen every evening, riding out to the maidan in his own tanjam, an elaborate palanquin. He would take the air for a couple of hours and then, on his way home, stop at the houses of friends and relatives and enquire after their welfare. He went often to the house in Pathuriaghat (the two families were reconciled by now) to bow his head before his forefathers and invoke their blessings, stopping at every temple and shrine on the way and offering obeisance.

Ramlochan was a great connoisseur of the arts. Unlike other wealthy men of the city, he was not satisfied with watching the antics of nautch girls. He invited ustads from the west to perform in his audience hall and poets—among them the famous Horu Thakur and Ram Basu—to recite their verses. The entertainment he proffered was famed for its quality throughout the land.

Ramlochan had no son. His wife, Aloka Sundari, had delivered a stillborn daughter and had been barren ever since. Once hope was gone of having a child of their own, the couple decided to adopt Ramlochan's nephew, Dwarkanath. Ramlochan had hoped to supervise the boy's education and raise him to be a great scholar but he was not given the time. Dwarkanath was only thirteen when Ramlochan passed away. However, his education continued under the supervision of his foster mother, Aloka Sundari, and his own elder brother, Radhanath. He took lessons from Sherbourne Saheb (Hindu College was founded several years later), who ran a school in the house of the native Christian, Kamal Basu. Sherbourne was only half-English—his mother being a Bengali and the daughter of a Brahmin. But Sherbourne, far from being ashamed of the fact, proclaimed it proudly. Here Dwarkanath studied *Enfield's Spelling and Reading Book, Universal Letter Writing, Complete Letter Book, English Grammar* and the *Tutinama* or *Tota Kahini*.

When Dwarkanath was eighteen, he took over the responsibilities of the estate. But what he inherited was not enough to satisfy his ambition. His dynamism and capacity for hard work was phenomenal. Within a few years he had distinguished himself as a law agent—settling disputes in land matters with a practised legal eye—and had risen to the position of dewan to the British government. He had added largely to his inherited estate, buying up pargana after pargana, and was now a very wealthy man. But Dwarkanath wanted more. He realized that while land brings respectability, big money comes from trade, the Goddess Lakshmi being notorious for her propensity to flit from buyer to seller. His business interest gradually extended itself over a variety of fields—banking, insurance, silk, indigo, shipping and coal. Dwarkanath's ancestors had been stevedores. Dwarkanath became a shipping magnate—launching a business in equal partnership with an Englishman. That the founding of the Carr, Tagore and Company was a historical event is borne out by a letter written by the governor-general, Lord William Bentinck, congratulating Dwarkanath for being the first Indian to make joint business possible between Europeans and natives.

As a matter of fact, Lord Bentinck was mistaken. There was an Indian before Dwarkanath—one Rustomjee Cowasjee, who had founded the Rustomjee, Turner and Co. several years earlier. When the fact came to light, the newspapers were obliged to change the report. The term, 'first Hindu', replaced 'first Indian'. For Rustomjee was not a Hindu. He belonged to the community of fire-worshippers, the Zoroastrians, who had fled Iran to escape Muslim persecution and had settled on the west coast of India. Rustomjee had sailed from distant Bombay and arrived in Calcutta—the hub of industrial activity of the time. His shipping business had flourished and soon his vessels carried cargo as far east as China and as far west as Africa. Dwarkanath, never content with being second, kept a close watch on Rustomjee's career till the shipping magnate's death, some years later, left him sole master of the field.

Doing business with the British, Dwarkanath discovered that there were two types of Englishmen in India. The first clung fiercely to a self-image of ruler and master and held natives in contempt. But these men, as his friend, Rammohan Roy, pointed out, came from a lower strata of English society. They were shareholders and paid servants of a small company and were held in no great esteem in their own country. Too much power had rendered them corrupt and arrogant and too much money—immoral and debauched. But there were others, liberated, enlightened men, whose voices, sensitive and articulate, rose against exploitation and abuse; who respected the native and worked for his uplift.

Although Dwarkanath believed the coming of the British to be a blessing for strife-torn and misruled India, he sensed the indignity of being governed by foreigners and resolved to earn the respect of the rulers. He understood, even more clearly than Rammohan Roy, that to achieve this Indians must seek the help of this second type of Englishman. A short sojourn in England sparked off another discovery. Dwarkanath realized that the English in England were quite different from their counterparts in India. They treated him as an equal—even a superior. He was fêted and entertained by earls and dukes, visited by famous men, Charles Dickens, the novelist, among them, and presented to her Royal Majesty, the Queen. On the voyage out he had carried expensive presents for the people of England. Returning home he brought one for his own. This was a man by the name of Thompson, a champion of human rights and one who had denounced slavery in a series of fiery speeches only a short while ago in America. In inviting him to India, he had a design—a deep, dark one.

On a cold winter morning, Dwarkanath's ship sailed up the river. Crowds of people stood on the quay to welcome him home. As the ship touched the jetty, Dwarkanath came out and stood on Port Said deck. A smile of triumph lit up his face. He had been told that no native ever returns alive from across the black water. Even Rammohan Roy hadn't. He, Dwarkanath, had returned in full health and strength. And here were his countrymen waiting to receive him. Dwarkanath waved his hand in greeting.

'I'm alive,' he shouted.

# Chapter XIII

At one end of the city stood a firing range, where soldiers practised all hours of the day. Dum! Dum! The surrounding area reverberated to the sound of the shots. And Dumdum it came to be called . . .

Dwarkanath's villa at Belgachhia lay on the road to Dumdum. The finest pleasure mansion in the city, it was surrounded by sprawling gardens of lush green, in which flowers of every scent and hue bloomed in designer beds. The silvery waters of the Moti Jheel meandered through the trees. And in it grew the rich red and violet blue lotus that poets love. At the centre of the lake stood a little island with a summer house, in front of which a naked Cupid smirked beside a marble fountain.

Inside the mansion, the huge reception rooms were hung with the finest paintings and tapestries and decorated with busts and statues of famous sculptors. Long mirrors of Belgian glass reflected the many colours of the Mirzapuri carpets on the marble floors and caught the flames from the hundred candlestick chandeliers. Exotic orchids and ferns hung from the balustrades of the wrought iron stairs.

One evening, a few days after his return from England, Dwarkanath stood in his summer house, entertaining his friends. It was a mixed gathering for Dwarkanath no longer believed in separate entertainments for whites and natives. Among his guests were some of India's leading industrialists and intellectuals, British lawyers, magistrates and members of the council. All eyes were turned to him, where he stood—a regal figure in his embroidered shawl and brocade robe. A heavy gold chain, encrusted with gems, hung from his neck and below his jewelled turban his eyes flashed with spirit and intelligence. In his hands he held a book bound in morocco leather. This was the journal he had kept during his travels abroad. He had recorded all his experiences faithfully in it and now he read parts of it aloud for the benefit of his guests.

'Is it true you sought audience with the Lord of the Christian world, his Holiness the Pope, and that it was granted to you?' an Englishman asked.

'Quite true,' Dwarkanath answered, smiling.

'And is it also true that you refused to bare your head before him?'

'It is. But His Holiness was not offended. I explained to him that in our culture we cover our heads before superiors.'

The English ladies and gentlemen exchanged glances of disapproval but Dakshinaranjan Mukhopadhaya, a follower of Derozio, said firmly, 'Prince Dwarkanath was right in following our own tradition of showing respect.'

'Did you follow the same principle in England?' another voice queried.

'Yes, sir. I must admit that the English in England are quite open in these matters. They show more respect for our culture than you do. On one occasion I kept a duke and duchess waiting for me over an hour while I performed my puja. I made my apologies later, and they were graciously taken. And on another—I must tell you about it. I was in the Palace one afternoon on the invitation of the Queen. I had expressed a wish to see the royal nursery and Lady Littleton was my guide. Your future king, the Prince of Wales, and his little sister were playing in a corner. I gazed at them for a long time, marvelling at their beauty. They looked like little angels in their white muslin and pearls. "How are children supposed to greet adults in your country?" Lady Littleton asked. "Can they shake hands?" "Certainly," I answered. "We pat them on their heads and bless them." At a sign, the royal children came forward and put out their hands. I drew them to me and stroked their cheeks.'

Not one of the present company had even seen the Prince of Wales, let alone shaken hands with him. To think that this native had had the good fortune! And he had even dined with Her Majesty!

'Well, well,' Dwarkanath's cousin, Prasanna Thakur, drawled in his perfect English. 'We've been hearing of the glories of England all evening. But tell me, do they have gardens in England as beautiful as this one in Belgachhia?' Gardens! Dwarkanath suppressed a sigh. He had been so proud of his garden till he had seen those of England. 'Brother,' he answered, 'compared to some of the gardens of England this one is a hole. The garden at Chatsworth—the country seat of the Duke of Devonshire—has every kind of tree and flower that grows on the face of this earth.'

'What else did you see in England that impressed you greatly?'

'Oh! I nearly forgot. The white races have made a tremendous discovery. They have imprisoned a djinn and made it their slave.'

'What do you mean?'

'Have you not heard the story of the djinn in the bottle? It is in the *Arabian Nights*. Well, the modern djinn is steam. You won't believe it but huge iron wagons, joined together in rows, are being pulled by steam. The track on which they run is called a rail road. I have sat in them myself in the city of Manchester in England and Cologne in Germany.' Then, after a pause he added, 'Steam is being used for so many purposes! For printing. For mining coal. I visited the shipyard in Liverpool for I had ordered two ships before I sailed. One of them, the *Dwarkanath*, has a steam engine. With the power of three hundred and fifty horses. Reflect, gentlemen! What a mighty demon it is!'

Flushed with wine and excitement, the company cheered and clapped for here was a native who had visited their motherland—a land many of them hadn't even seen. The evening wore on. Suddenly, one of the guests, a journalist from *Friend of India*, asked bluntly, 'Mr Tagore. Do you think you can ever go back to the glorious England you have just described? It is rumoured that your countrymen are ostracizing you for crossing the Black Water and insist on your performing some penitential rites. Will they include the partaking of cow dung?' Some of the company smiled snidely at this—others averted their faces to hide their amusement. Dwarkanath's face darkened. *Friend of India* made it a point to pitch into him from time to time. He could and did ignore it. But this man had touched a vulnerable spot. It was true that penance was being demanded of him by the very Brahmins he had nurtured for years. He hated them for their mindless orthodoxy and unbridled arrogance. Would Hindus remain in their well of ignorance and folly for all time to come? Would they never see the light? He turned to his interrogator and said in a sombre voice, 'You may also have heard that the late Raja Rammohan Roy was my friend and counsellor. From him I have learned to reject all the blind prejudices that have attached themselves to our religion. If I'm driven out of the Hindu fold I shall not despair. I shall build another religion and society—more liberal and humane. I can do it. I have the power.'

'Will your family support you? Will your son—Debendranath?'

'Of course he will. He is a good boy, with strong filial affections. It was he who made the arrangements for this evening.' Then, raising his voice, he called out to the servants to send Debendranath to him. Minutes passed but no one came. Dwarkanath gathered up the shawl that trailed on the floor and, with a murmured apology, left the room. Crossing over to the verandah he came upon a little knot of servants, huddled together.

'Where is Debendranath?' he asked in a voice of thunder. 'Was he not here just now?'

'No, Karta Moshai.'

'Go, fetch him from wherever he is. Tell him I want him immediately.'

The servants ran to do his bidding but something in their manner puzzled him. He suddenly remembered Debendra's conduct on a similar occasion some years ago. Dwarkanath was hosting a dinner in honour of Miss Eden—Lord Auckland's sister—and had given Debendranath charge of the arrangements. He had a purpose in this. He wanted to impress upon his son the wisdom of making and renewing contacts with eminent men and women of the land. He wanted him to understand that such entertainment, expensive though it was, was necessary in business. Debendranath had done all he had been commanded to do but when the time had come for him to be presented to his father's guests, he had disappeared. Remembering that incident Dwarkanath's face flushed with anger. He strode purposefully out of the summer house, crossed the bridge that connected it with the mainland, and stood on the lawn. The servants ran helter-skelter at the sound of his footsteps and the nayeb, who was the rent collector of the estate, hid himself behind a tree. He would never have the courage to give the master Debendra's message, which was, 'Tell Baba Moshai I'm going home. I don't feel too well this evening.'

Dwarkanath couldn't understand his son. What was wrong with the boy? Some years ago he had taken to spending a great deal of money. One Saraswati Puja he had bought up all the marigolds of the city to offer to the deity. Dwarkanath hadn't approved. Lavish entertainment of the type that was going on tonight was more useful, in his opinion, than lavish rituals. Dwarkanath had wanted to teach his son the value of money and had, in consequence, given him a position in the bank. He had also made him a partner in Carr, Tagore and Co.

Dwarkanath realized that his son disliked associating with the white-skinned foreigners. Was it because his English was weak? Surely, a couple of tutors could remedy that! How could a son have no pride in his father and no respect for his friends? If he hated the English so much, how would he do business with them?

Dwarkanath looked up at the star-studded sky. He felt lost and lonely. He was the greatest man in the land but he had nothing—nobody. His parents were dead these many years. His wife, too, had passed away. He had hoped to mould his son in his own image but had failed. No one loved him. People feared him, hated him, envied him but did not love him. 'Why should I waste myself in this country?' he thought. He would sail away again, across the seas to distant lands, where people loved and admired him.

# Chapter XIV

It was midnight. Debendranath sat in an easy chair on a balcony in the mansion at Jorasanko. It was a winter night, with a piercing wind, but Debendranath felt no chill. Under his silk wrapper his breast heaved in agitation. He had run away from the summer house in Belgachhia, unable to bear the sight of his father's guests wallowing in the pleasures of the flesh. His father would be angry and offended. He was a lion of a man, with a domineering temper, and could brook no contradiction or disobedience. But Debendranath didn't care. A verse from the Kathopanishad ran round and round his head.

For such fools as drown in the wine of wealth and power
The other world ceases to be.
For such fools who lose sight of the other world
Death is the sole reality.

Try as he would he could not escape these words. Like the beat of a drum they pounded in his head and heart. He looked up at the sky and thought it was time he came to a decision. He was twenty-six years old, yet he lived in his father's shadow. His father valued only the power and riches of the world and expected Debendra to do the same. He had no knowledge of the thoughts that tortured his son night and day.

What is the purpose of life? The question had flashed across his mind several years ago. It was the night before his grandmother died. He had loved her dearly and had accompanied her on her last journey—to the Ganga. She lay on the ground, her head resting on the bank and the water lapping her feet. A group of Brahmins chanted, 'Ganganarayan Brahma' over and over again in her ear.

Debendra sat on a mound, a little apart, and watched the scene. The sound of rushing water filled his ears and snatches of kirtan came wafting along with the wind. He looked up at the moon-washed sky and thought, 'What is the purpose of life?' He was the son of the most important man in the land. He could spend all the money he wanted. He had only to express a wish and it would be fulfilled. But, at the end of it all, what? Death! Death was the sole reality. A wave of disenchantment swept over him for the things he had valued all these years—money, power over others, lavish and gracious living. 'This mound of sand is a good enough seat for me,' he thought. 'What need have I of gilded chairs and Persian carpets?' With the first glimmer of dawn he returned home, his soul quivering with ecstasy . . .

Next day, at noon, Dwarkanath's foster mother, the pious Aloka Sundari Devi, passed away. Just before drawing her last breath, she rested her gaze on her beloved grandson as he stood in the water by her side. Laying one hand on her breast, she pointed upwards with the other. Debendra watched her, his eyes bright with unshed tears, and understood. She was pointing to Heaven—to that other world—and bidding him not to lose sight of it.

After all the rituals were concluded, Debendranath turned himself into a wishing tree. Friends, cousins and acquaintances could walk into his rooms at any time of the day or night and take away whatever they wanted. Furniture of carved ebony, fine paintings, marble-topped tables and statues were anybody's for the asking. Even his clothes—the handsome shawls and brocade robes that he had acquired during his brief phase of self-indulgence—now changed hands. For himself he kept only the barest minimum.

The vibrant joy he had experienced on the bank of the Ganga did not last. Instead, a slow pain welled up in his heart at the thought that he had been shown only half the light. He had realized that the pursuit of the material was negative activity. But in what lay the positive? Where was the path that would lead him to the Eternal Joy and Eternal Calm that was God? Who was God and where was He?

In his youth he had believed that the Shalgram, the Vishnu emblem that his father worshipped, was God. He had devoted himself to Durga, Jagatdhatri and Saraswati with fanatical zeal, and every day, on his way to and from college, he had made his obeisance to Sidheswari in the temple of Thanthaniya and begged her for success in the examination. Now, of course, he realized that God did not dwell in these graven images; in these four-armed and ten-armed statues of stone and iron. But, then, where did he dwell? What was his true image? Many of Debendra's college friends had turned atheist and some had embraced Christianity. But Debendra would not do either. He wanted to discover God on his own.

And so his quest began. Sometimes it became too painful to be borne. He found himself withdrawing from the world around him. He would run away from the bank and crossing the Ganga, sit under a tree in the garden at Shibpur. Darkness filled his soul. Even the sun seemed devoid of light. Pain tore at his eyeballs and wove its streaky strands around his heart. He tried to find what he sought in the works of western scholars. Hume and Locke were very popular with the new generation of educated youth but Debendranath could not subscribe to a philosophy that saw nothing beyond the reality of the world; that placed the natural above the divine and preached scepticism in place of faith. He had no use for the philosophy of pantheism either. He shuddered to think of what would happen if man allowed nature to master him. Debendranath turned to his Sanskrit texts for relief. Sometimes, he thought he saw a gleam of light. Then, all was dark again.

One morning as he walked down the stairs, he came upon a leaf torn from a book. Taking it in his hands he saw that it contained some verses in Sanskrit. He read them through but could make no sense of them. His resident tutor, Shyama Charan Pandit, couldn't either. 'Send for Ramchandra Vidyabagish,' he suggested. 'I seem to have heard something like this in the doctrines of the Brahmo Sabha.'

Debendra's heart missed a beat. Was the Brahmo Sabha still in existence? Who was in charge now? Ramchandra Vidyabagish? A strange restlessness seized Debendranath. Where had the leaf come from? Was it a portent? Was he in sight of his goal at last?

The Brahmo Sabha had been established by Rammohan Roy for the worship of the One True God. All monotheists, be they Hindus, Muslims, Jews or Christians, were welcome to participate and they did so in large numbers. Vidyabagish had been with the Raja right from the start. He had wanted to use the Brahmo Sabha as a forum for the dissemination of Vedantic

Hinduism but Rammohan had not agreed. He had felt no need for a new religion. He only wanted to unite all those kindred souls who believed that one formless omniscient being presided over the universe. Debendranath remembered sitting by the Raja's side, as a boy, in the prayer hall of the Brahmo Sabha, listening to hymns sung in English and Persian. There were also two singers of Hindu devotional songs, called Vishnu and Krishna, and a pakhawaj player called Ghulam Abbas.

After the Raja's death in England, the Brahmo Sabha would have closed down altogether, if it had not been for Dwarkanath. Rammohan Roy's own son, Ram Prasad, was an orthodox Hindu and took little interest in it. The whole country was crying out against the Brahmo Sabha and the conservatives among the Hindus, seeing it as a threat to their religion, set up a sabha of their own. Dwarkanath felt he owed it to his friend to keep his beloved institution alive but he was a Hindu, too, and could not accept its doctrines.

Rammohan was very fond of Debendranath. On the eve of his departure for England, he had called at the house in Jorasanko to take leave of the Prince. Just before he rose to depart, he said, 'Where is Debendranath? I wish to see him before I go.' When the young Debendranath stood before him, the Raja took his hands in his and said, 'Brother Debendra'—he called him 'brother' as a joke—'I know your father. He is a worldly man. You—only you can do my work for me when I'm gone.' Recalling these words, shame filled Debendranath's soul. How could he have forgotten them? How could he have wasted his time in vain pursuits? He had visited the Brahmo Sabha only out of curiosity. It had fallen into a severe decline. Ramchandra Vidyabagish read extracts from the Upanishads every evening but hardly anyone came. On one of Debendranath's visits a shower of rain had come on suddenly and a few people had taken shelter in the prayer hall. Vidyabagish, for whom an audience was a rarity, launched on his discourse with great enthusiasm. But the rain stopped in the middle and the people picked up their baskets and bundles and departed. The incident had amused Debendranath and he hadn't been there since.

That evening Debendranath sent for Ramchandra Vidyabagish. After exchanging the usual courtesies, Debendranath handed him the leaf he had found and said, 'Do you recognize the text from which this is torn? And can you explain what is written in it?' Vidyabagish took it in his hands and examined it closely. Then, he said, 'These are verses from the Ishopanishad and the leaf seems to have been torn from the Brahmo Sabha compilation of Sanskrit texts. How did this get here?'

'That I cannot say,' Debendranath replied. 'Kindly explain the verse to me.'

*Ishavasyamidam sarvam jatkincha jagat*
*Tena tyaktena bhunjitha ma gridha kasyasidhvanam.*

Ramchandra recited the verse, then proceeded to explain it thus. 'Literally translated it means, "Enclose the world in the spirit of God. Take what he has given and enjoy it". What has God given Man? Himself—is it not? Enjoy that supreme of all gifts. Give up everything else and retain only God.'

Debendranath sat like a figure of stone. His quest was over. He had found what he sought. God has given himself to Man! What more could anyone want? The torn leaf had carried the voice of God to his tortured, searching soul.

Debendranath wanted to share his new-found philosophy with his friends. Consequently, the Tatva Ranjini Sabha was born. A year later the name was changed to Tatva Bodhini. At first it was housed in a small, dark room on the ground floor of the mansion in Jorasanko—away from the eagle eyes of the master. Here, Debendranath and his followers met once a month and heard discourses and readings from the Vedas and Vedantas. These secret meetings were conducted by Ramchandra Vidyabagish. Then, on one anniversary of the Tatva Bodhini Sabha, Debendranath decided to bring it out into the open. On his invitation, a large number of people collected in the house at Jorasanko. Debendranath made a fiery speech, denouncing idol worship and upholding the doctrine of monotheism. Few in the audience understood what was being said but Debendranath's purpose was served. The Tatva Bodhini Sabha had hit the consciousness of the people who mattered.

Within a few days of this event, Debendranath realized that there was little to be gained by keeping the Tatva Bodhini Sabha and Brahmo Sabha separate. And so, the two were merged and their discourses held in the prayer hall of the Brahmo Sabha.

Having reached this far, Debendranath paused a while. He saw his path before him, straight and clear, but he hesitated before taking the next step. He was not sure of how his countrymen would react. He had offended and hurt his father. His kinsmen were not happy with him. But having realized God, he could not stop. He had to share his experience with others. It was in this frame of mind that he had run away from the garden house at Belgachhia. And on that night, sitting on the balcony and looking up at the starry sky, he had taken a vow . . .

On the seventh day of Poush,[13] Debendranath Tagore initiated himself at the hands of Acharya Ramchandra Vidyabagish and became a Brahmo. Rammohan Roy had instituted the Brahmo Samaj. Debendra founded a new religion—the Brahmo Dharma. 'There can be no dharma without Brahma,' he explained to his band of faithful followers, who had taken the vows with him. 'And Brahma cannot be realized without dharma.'

And thus it came about that the Vedantic Hinduism that had been the life-long preoccupation of Ramchandra Vidyabagish was given a new identity and name.

13 15th December-15th January.

# Chapter XV

Dibakar's wife, Sohagbala, held undisputed sway over the kitchen and servants' quarters and ruled the inmates with a rod of iron. There were eighteen in all—each one's work apportioned according to merit and experience. The master had three personal servants, the mistress three maids to wait on her. Four servants attended the two sons of the house. Even the master's widowed aunt and sister-in-law were allowed a personal maid each. The old mistress had died the year before and the two women who had attended her had no work allotted to them yet. They sat around all day, gossiped and ate paan, to the annoyance of the other servants. A vast number of cooks, gardeners, milkmen, washermen, palki bearers, coachmen and darwans made up the rest of the staff in the mansion of Jorasanko.

The house had two kitchens. One catered exclusively to the tastes of the gentry—the master, the mistress and their two boys. The other doled out coarse, common food to poor relations, hangers-on and servants. Behind the house was a huge garden, with a pond in the middle. At one end of the garden stood a row of palm leaf huts. These were the servants' quarters. Beyond them lay the lavatory pits.

A sound of wailing came from one of the huts. Sohagbala wrinkled her nose in distaste. The beggarly wench the mistress had picked up from the river ghat was at it again. Moaning and groaning and beating her breast! As if hers was the first husband who had deserted his woman. As for losing a daughter—well, it was a blessing as far as she, Sohagbala, could see. Sohagbala hated her and her filthy brat. Ignorant rustics, with the country moss still thick on their skins! The mistress had given her instructions to look after them. Look after them, indeed! The mistress would forget all about them in a few days and then—then they would be at Sohagbala's mercy.

Two hefty men servants dragged the six-year-old Dulal to the verandah, where Sohagbala sat on a marble block—mistress of all she surveyed. She was enormously fat. Her huge breasts protruded like mountains out of the fine cotton sari that encased them and rolls of fat billowed down her waist, melting into gigantic buttocks. Beneath the bushy eyebrows, her face was hot and angry. Sloshing a mouthful of blood-red spittle into her shining brass spittoon, she packed a fresh paan into her mouth and glared balefully at the trembling lad. He was naked except for the filthy strip of cotton that covered his manhood. And he was young—very young and tender. Fixing her eyes on him she spoke in a voice that sent a tremor through the boy's frame.

'What does that slut, your mother, think she is? A guest in this house? It is over a month now and all you two do is eat mountains of rice. Not a spot of work is to be had out of either of you. From today you must work for your rice. No work—no rice.' Raising her voice she called out to a servant: 'Fetch a basin and mop and give them to the boy. You, boy! Wipe down the floor of the verandah and the steps.' There was a servant whose allotted duty was to wipe the floors of the eight verandahs in the house but Sohagbala was determined to make Dulal work for his living. The maids and servants were delighted. A clay basin full of water was brought in. A maid dipped a piece of sacking into it and handing it to the bewildered Dulal, said roughly, 'Get going, boy. Don't stand there, staring like an owl.'

Dulal obeyed. He didn't mind the work. In fact, he preferred it to sitting with his mother in the darkness of the hut. Here, there was so much to see and hear. He watched round-eyed as two enormous carps, still struggling and gasping for breath, were dashed on the floor of the courtyard. Two maids with huge *bontis,* commenced scaling and cutting up the fish. Sohagbala shouted instructions: 'Keep the heads aside. The master is away. They needn't be sent upstairs. Count the pieces and show them to me. You, Duryodhan! What are you doing here? Go into the kitchen and get on with the *kheer*. And Panchi, you little harlot. You haven't fed the birds yet, I'll warrant. What? There's no gram left? Two sacks full were brought in this month. I saw them with my own eyes. Have you been feeding birds or elephants?'

Before Panchi could make a suitable reply, Dulal created a diversion by upsetting the basin. It broke into two and water ran down the verandah into the courtyard. The women who were cutting the fish sprang up, screaming, 'Death take you, you death's head. What are you doing?' Sohagbala fixed her fiery orbs on the trembling lad and said, 'I knew he would do something vile the moment I saw him—the wretch. Grab him by the ears, Nakur, and give him a sound thrashing.' At this point, Thako appeared on the scene and snatching her son away from Nakur's grasp set up a wail. '*O go*! Ma *go*. Don't beat him. He is only a little boy. A poor fatherless—.' '*O ré! O ré!* Stop her. Gag her mouth with a twist of straw,' Sohagbala screamed at the other servants. 'If Ginni[14] Ma hears her we'll all be in trouble.' Two servants grabbed Thakomoni and forced her down to the ground. One pinioned her threshing arms and the other clamped his heavy hand on her mouth. Sohagbala rose from her stool (she never did so, as a rule) and stood over the terror-stricken girl. 'I'm warning you, young woman,' she said menacingly, 'if I hear your voice once again I'll have you tied down with ropes and flung into the pond. You don't know me.' Looking up at the monstrous apparition towering over her, Thako's blood froze. This woman could do anything. She could kill them both and not turn a hair. The conviction shattered the last of her resistance and from that moment onwards, Thako surrendered to the inevitable.

The very next day, Thako was set to work, wiping the floors of the eight great verandahs on the ground floor. From time to time, a maid came to inspect her work and pointing at invisible stains, made her do it all over again. She was scolded and beaten and kept without food for the slightest fault—real or imagined. And thus, in time, she became an efficient and experienced servant. The sea of tears she had held in her bosom dried into a desert. She understood, as never before, that the past was dead for her. The little hut by the canal in Bhinkuri village, where her husband's forefathers had lived; the rose apple tree in front and the strip of paddy field behind were gone forever. She would never feed the cow again nor pick the ripe nuts that fell from the areca palms growing wild around the hut. She would never see the sky as it hung over the canal—huge and dark and heavy with monsoon clouds. A wave of nostalgia swept over her. It

14 Mistress.

was like a dream; like a vision from a past existence. She forgot the poverty and cares of her old life. She remembered only the freedom. However small the hut, however hard the life, she was mistress there. She was queen of her husband's home and heart. Here she was a slave of slaves and she would remain so till the day of her death. And her son after her. He would never know the fierce independence his father knew. He would never feel the touch of the soil. Why? Oh! Why did the zamindar's men set her hut on fire? Why did her husband go out to fetch water and never return?

Thako could not understand the people around her. Life in the palm leaf huts was so different from the life she knew. Marriages between servants and maids were ruled out but adultery and fornication went on unheeded. Social pressure was exerted only when a woman grew great with child. Then she was treated with a cruelty that made Thako's flesh creep.

A maid called Matu (Thako didn't know what her real name was) worked in the house. She was a widow, about eighteen or nineteen years old. She was caught one day, eating bits of burned clay from a broken pot. The moment the news was brought to her, Sohagbala knew what had happened. Matu was pregnant and the child had quickened. Sohagbala sent for the girl and demanded fiercely, 'Who is the man? Tell me at once or I'll pull your tongue out with a pair of tongs.' Matu said nothing at first. She stood where she was, her head hanging in shame. But Sohagbala would not let her off. At a signal from her Duryodhan grabbed Matu by the hair and knocked her down so violently that the poor girl shrieked out the truth. It wasn't one of the servants. It was the gardener's boy, Rakhu. Which Rakhu? The one who had left for his village three months ago and never returned. Sohagbala and the other servants exchanged glances. They knew what had to be done.

That evening, before the lamps were lit, two servants stood on either side of the courtyard, holding a thick rope in their hands. Here Sohagbala dragged in the protesting Matu. 'Jump,' she commanded. 'Jump from this side of the rope to that.' Matu clutched her swelling abdomen and looked fearfully at the rope which was stretched three feet above the ground. The two men who held it looked like demons in the darkness of the courtyard. 'I cant,' she wept piteously. 'Don't make me, Gomosta Ma. I'll fall and die.' 'You dare open your mouth, you shameless whore,' Sohagbala hissed, her eyes burning in the dark like a leopard's eyes. 'Jump or I'll kick you across.' She put out a hand and yanked the sari off Matu's body. Then, stepping over to the naked girl, who stood there still clutching her belly, she slapped her several times across the face. 'Jump,' she said between clenched teeth.

The men who held the rope knew their job. As Matu jumped this way and that, they fiddled with the rope, raising and lowering it with quick movements. Thus Matu found the rope lashing her breasts one moment and twining around her feet the next. She fell with a thud, then rose and fell again. There was a roar of laughter each time she fell. This exercise was carried out every evening for a whole week but the stubborn creature in Matu's womb would not be dislodged. 'Let me go,' Matu begged. 'I'll leave the city and go far away, where no one knows me. I'll not trouble you any more.' But Sohagbala would not allow that. A young widow, roaming the streets with a child in her womb, was a shocking aberration. She would be torn to pieces by the men. Besides, it was grossly immoral. And Sohagbala would never condone immorality. The little bitch should knock her head on Sohagbala's feet in gratitude. For, was not Sohagbala trying to save her from a fate worse than death?

The next ordeal devised for Matu was to carry an enormous clay basin, brimming over with boiling starch—a basin so heavy that it took three men to lift it on to her head—to the pond a hundred yards away. This would work in two ways. The weight on her head would put pressure on her womb and abort the foetus. Or she might slip on the dripping starch and fall, basin and all. The impact of the fall and the burns from the starch would kill her and her unborn child. But the strangest thing happened. Matu walked to the pond and back for ten whole days without falling. And all the time her middle swelled triumphantly till it took on the shape of a Hetampuri pumpkin.

Now Sohagbala was compelled to take a drastic step. The child would be born any day now and the wails of a newborn infant would reach the ears of the master and mistress. And she would be in trouble for in her was vested the responsibility of maintaining law and order in the servants' quarters. She knew of a votaress in the temple of Chitteswari who dabbled in roots and herbs, and to her she dispatched a trusty servant with a letter. The servant returned the next day, a bunch of dried roots and half-a-dozen balls of some sticky black substance knotted in his *gamchha*. These had to be ground to a paste with molasses and fed to the pregnant girl. Two men servants pounced on Matu as she hid behind a tree near the pond and dragged her into Sohagbala's presence. Then, forcing her down to the ground, they poured the stuff down her throat. 'Go to sleep, child,' Sohagbala said. 'You'll deliver in the morning.'

Matu died at cockcrow. She had tossed and turned all night on the floor, groaning and foaming at the mouth. Gasping for breath she had begged piteously, 'Take me out into the open. *O go*, take me out where there is some air. I can't breathe—' But no one had answered or come near her. And after a while she had begged no more. The tiny being that had clung so tenaciously to life might have tried to force its way out of her dead womb but had not succeeded. With the first glimmer of dawn all was over.

Matu's body lay in the hut for a whole day and night. Then, two scavengers arrived and, bundling her body into a grass mat, tied it to a pole. Slinging the pole on their shoulders, they carried it to the Ganga and flung it into the water. No one noted her disappearance. No questions were asked.

Thako was not particularly moved by Matu's fate. A widow carrying on an illicit relationship was bound to come to a bad end. But Matu's ghost haunted her. For nights together after her death, Thako woke up in a cold sweat. She had seen Matu standing over her, grinning from ear to ear. Immediately afterwards, Matu had fallen to the ground and foaming at the mouth and grinding her teeth, she had looked at Thako with pleading eyes and begged, 'Take me out into the open. *O go*! Ma *go*! I can't breathe—'

In her terror, Thako clung to Dulal and would not let him out of her sight but, child that he was, he would slip away whenever he could and wander all over the house and grounds. He would throw stones at the ducks and run after the calf. Most of all, he liked to creep up the huge staircase and, hiding in the shadows, watch the goings-on in Bimbabati's wing. One evening, as he crouched on the landing, watching a servant light the candles in the chandelier, he was caught by Nabin Kumar. 'Who is there?' Nabin called out imperiously to the small black face peering between the banister rails. 'Come here at once.' Dulal obeyed, trembling. But Nabin was in a benign mood. Taking a *sandesh* from a bowl beside him he thrust it at Dulal. 'Eat,' he commanded.

From that day onwards, Dulal became Nabin's playmate. Nabin fed him *sandesh* every day. In return, Dulal did whatever he commanded. Though both were children, they knew instinctively that one was master and one servant. Nabin could make the most obnoxious demands on Dulal but Dulal always obeyed readily and cheerfully. One day it might be Nabin's whim to enact the Goddess Kali. Then he would stand on Dulal's chest, his tongue hanging out and eyes staring. Or he might make Dulal lie on his stomach and pretend he was a peacock while Nabin rode on his back as Kartik.

One day Nabin took it into his head to make Dulal rub his nose on the floor. Dulal didn't know how—he had never done it before—so Nabin had to teach him. In the middle of the demonstration, Ganganarayan walked in and, picking up his little brother, asked in amazement, 'What are you doing, Chhotku?'

'Dulal is so stupid—he doesn't know how to rub his nose on the floor. I'm teaching him.'

Ganganarayan gave a roar of laughter. 'He doesn't know but you do. This is very funny.' He was in a hurry, so he put Nabin down and left. 'You do it now,' Nabin commanded Dulal. Dulal touched his nose gingerly to the white marble. He didn't like this game very much. 'Let's play at something else, Chhoto Babu,' he pleaded. But Nabin had to have his own way. He screamed so loudly that Chintamoni and Dibakar came running in. 'You little wretch,' Chinta stormed. 'You should eat dirt in gratitude that you're allowed to play with the young master,' and Dibakar grabbed Dulal's ears and boxed them soundly. Baring his teeth at the boy, he thundered, 'I'll have your head chopped off if you dare disobey Chhoto Babu.'

Dulal went down on his hands and knees and proceeded to rub his nose all the way down the long verandah. Nabin went after him, a brightly coloured stick in his hand. 'Hat! Hat!' he brought the stick down on Dulal's back. 'Come on, horsy! Come on, donkey! Harder! Rub harder!' And his innocent laughter rang through the house like peals of silver bells.

# Chapter XVI

The wedding dates were set within a few days of one another—Ganganarayan's on a Monday and Suhasini's on the Thursday of the same week. The arrangements for both were made by Bidhusekhar for Ramkamal had of late lost interest in everything other than his evenings with Kamala Sundari. Everything was provided for on a lavish scale. Each invitation card was sent on a silver salver, along with two embroidered shawls, two saris woven by the Muslim weavers of Dhaka, a pair of gold encrusted iron bangles and two vials of attar. Rows of tailors worked from dawn to dusk for all the servants were to have two new outfits each. The sky resounded for miles with the sound of flutes and drums and the air was redolent with the delicious odours that rose from the cooking pits. Tapping his gold cane smartly before him, Bidhusekhar moved rapidly from one house to another, supervising the arrangements with an eagle eye.

On the night ordained for the ceremony, Ganganarayan married Lilavati—the eight-year-old daughter of the Bosus of Bagbazar. And the next day bride and bridegroom stood before the lion gates of Ramkamal's mansion, a train of liveried servants behind them. Ganga's mother, Bimbabati, came forward to welcome her daughter-in-law. Taking up the little bundle of red silk and gold in her arms, she pointed to a clay oven on which an enormous wok of boiling milk brimmed over and asked in her high, sweet voice, 'What do you see, Ma?' Lilavati had been taught the answer by her mother and aunt but, overcome with shyness, she said nothing. She hid her face against her mother-in-law's shoulder and would not look up. One of the women who surrounded Bimba came up and whispered in the little bride's ear, 'Say, "I see my household brimming over."' After a couple of attempts, Lilavati repeated after her in a fluty voice, 'I see my household brimming over,' and put her face again on Bimba's shoulder. Then, the rituals concluded, conches were blown, the women ululated and the couple were taken in.

Released from the nuptial knot, Ganga was free to breathe at last. He felt flooded with relief. Getting married was a nightmare. Last night, after the ceremony, he had been besieged by at least two hundred women. One tugged at his hair, another his ears. There was one—a pretty woman of sixteen or seventeen—who asked him riddles and pinched his cheeks when he couldn't answer. At one moment he found himself sitting alone on the jewelled settee. Lilavati had disappeared. Then the women clamoured, 'Which one is your wife? You must find her out from among us or you'll have to go back alone.' Ganga looked helplessly around him. He had thrown the briefest of glances at Lilavati during the Shubho Drishti, when the bride and bridegroom look at each other for the first time, and could not recognize her now. He scanned one face after another. Every time his glance rested a little longer than usual, the brazen hussy would titter, 'Oh! So you like me best, do you? Why didn't you tell me that before I got married?' And the other women would roar with laughter. At last, in desperation, he took a bold step. Grasping the wrist of the prettiest girl he could see, he announced, 'I've found her. This is my wife.' The girl twisted and turned and tried to pull her hand away. But Ganga would not let her. At last one of the women said, 'Take care, dear bridegroom. You may be a great scholar but our Kanaklata's husband is a wrestler and will knock you down. Let her go.'

'No, I shan't.' Ganga rolled his eyes at the gathering. Defeated, the women produced Lilavati. Putting her on her husband's lap, the women warned, '*O lo*, Lila! Keep him on a leash. He's all set to bring you a co-wife.'

Removing his elaborate wedding garments, Ganga donned a simple dhoti and shawl and came down to the drawing room, where his friends were waiting. Tonight was Kal Ratri—the evil night—and he mustn't see Lilavati's face. No one would miss him. The women were busy with the bride. The men were in the garden, drinking and watching the dancing of nautch girls. Even the drummers and flute players had drunk themselves into a stupor. Only the servants could be heard, quarrelling over their share of *luchi* and sweetmeats. It was the beginning of February and there was a chill in the air.

'Where's Madhu?' Ganga's eyes took in the company at a glance.

'Gone to hell,' Rajnarayan said with a grimace. 'Where's the brandy? Aren't you going to offer us a drink?'

'Why didn't he come? I begged him to—'

'Forget about Madhu,' Beni advised patronizingly. 'Don't take his name on this auspicious day.'

'Why not?' Ganga scanned the faces of his friends. Some were sad, some embarrassed.

'What is wrong with Madhu?' Ganga put a hand on Gour's shoulder. 'Tell me, Gour.' A shadow passed over Gour's face. 'I didn't want to tell you. Not today, at least,' he said haltingly. 'Madhu has run away.'

'Run away?'

'Yes. He wants to become a Christian. The missionaries are hiding him from his father.'

'The Lord Bishop himself—no less,' Rajnarayan drawled. He had already drunk more than was good for him and the words slurred in his mouth. 'He's kept Madhu tucked away in Fort William. No one will ever see him again.'

Fort William! Ganga was aghast. 'How do you know they are not keeping him against his will?' Gour shook his head. 'I went to see him,' he said sadly. 'He was ecstatic. Full of plans. "How could you do this to your mother, Madhu?" I began but he shut me up. "Not a word, Gour. Not a word about my past. I am a new man. My soul yearns to reach the feet of Jesus. I've written a hymn for the occasion. Would you like to hear it?" Then, Madhu recited his hymn. It was the worst poem I've heard or read in my life. Full of oily sentiments. Haranguing our religion and praising Christianity.'

'But Madhu was turning atheist,' Ganga said in a puzzled voice. 'He was quite taken in by Theodore Parker's book. I've never heard him expressing any religious sentiments.'

'You think Madhu believes in Christianity?' Beni sneered. 'The missionaries have promised to send him to England if he becomes a Christian—'

'Who advised him to run away from home? Was it Krishnamohan Bandopadhyaya?'

'Of course it was. That sly fox, Katty Keshto, is at the bottom of it. When Madhu's father confronted him he answered as coolly as you please, "Your son is not a child, Rajnarayan Babu. He is an adult with a mind of his own. However, if you think otherwise, why don't you tell him so"? There's another fellow in the plot. Do you know Nabin Mitra? The boy who was baptized last year. He worked on Madhu too. He told him that the missionaries would send him to England as soon as the rituals were concluded.'

'I have a feeling this was Madhu's way of getting out of a Hindu marriage,' Rajnarayan said. 'He has always maintained that Hindu girls are ignorant and backward and he would never accept one of them as wife. His father was putting pressure. So Madhu put out his wings and flew out of the cage—straight into the arms of Christ.'

Ganganarayan sighed. He shared Madhu's sentiments about Hindu girls but he had succumbed to pressure. He had hated the rituals. He hadn't even glanced at Lilavati. But he had endured it all. He lacked Madhu's courage. For a long time after his friends had left, Ganga thought about Madhu. Would he ever see him again? Would Madhu's father—his stern, domineering, ruthless father—ever forgive him? And, suddenly, he found himself thinking—not of Madhu but of Lilavati. Madhu was Madhu and Ganga—Ganga. Ganga would never do what Madhu had done. He wouldn't hurt anyone—least of all his sweet little child bride. He had made promises to her at the sacrificial fire. He would keep those promises. He would love her and cherish her and keep her from harm.

On Thursday evening, the street outside Bidhusekhar's house was packed with vehicles for all the wealthy and distinguished men of the city had received invitations for Suhasini's wedding. Ganga stood at the gates, receiving the guests. The first to arrive was Mahatab Chand Bahadur, the adopted son of the Raja of Bardhaman. Then came Narasingha Rai Bahadur, the younger son of Sukhomoy Rai—Raja of Posta; then, the Raja of Shobha Bazar, followed by that crown of the Hindu community of Calcutta, Raja Radhakanta Deb. And then on the heels of these august personages, glittering with gold and gems, Debendranath Thakur walked in. The contrast was too stark to be missed. Debendranath wore a plain dhoti and kameez and not a speck of gold adorned his person. The shawl draped on his shoulders was as white as milk but his skin was whiter. Against its folds, his face and hands gleamed like moonlight. After Debendranath came the famous educationist, Ramkamal Sen—his five-year-old grandson Keshab with him. Debendranath knew Ramkamal Sen for he was his father's friend. Exchanging a few words and chucking little Keshab under the chin, he passed on, stopping to greet the next arrival, Satya Saran Ghosh, Raja of Bhukailash, on the way. Then, in rapid succession, Ramgopal Ghosh, Rasik Krishna Mallik, Ramtanu Lahiri, Dakshinaranjan Mukhopadhyaya and Tarachand Chakravarti arrived. They had been Derozio's disciples in their youth and fiery reformers. But now they were old and content with the world.

The boy Bidhusekhar had chosen for Suhasini was called Durga Prasad Bandopadhyaya. He was poor but very meritorious. A brilliant student of Sanskrit College, he was now studying law. With him were his friends—Ishwar Chandra Vidyasagar, Madanmohan Tarkalankar, Mahesh Chandra Shastri, Ramnarayan Tarkaratna and Dwarkanath Nyayaratna. When Ganga's own friends came, he asked eagerly, 'What news? Is it over?'

'Yes,' Gour answered despondently.

'Were you there?'

'Yes. But I caught only a brief glimpse. We weren't allowed to speak.'

'The church at Mission Row was swarming with policemen and soldiers,' Bhudev said. 'Have you ever heard of a baptism being conducted under police protection? The English have become totally shameless. They'll convert the whole of India. They won't allow one Hindu to remain in the country.'

'Did Madhu look happy?'

'We hardly saw him. There was a ring of dukes and lords around him. You've never seen anything like it. Never has a native been so honoured! Only two Indians were allowed inside the church. One was Madhu and the other our black jewel, Katty Keshto. He was the government approver.'

Just then, someone called out to Ganga and he had to go. Later, much later, when the guests had eaten and the ceremony was about to begin, Ganga suddenly thought of Bindubasini. He hadn't seen her for days. Where was she? Ganga felt a pang of guilt. She was his childhood playmate and he had forgotten her. But was it just that? Hadn't he forgotten her because he had willed himself to do so?

He went from room to room but could not find her. Then creeping up the stairs, he came to the door of the prayer room. The house blazed with lights but here all was dark and silent. As his eyes got used to the gloom, he discerned a figure in white, sitting on the floor. It was Bindu. She was alone, truly alone for even Janardan had deserted her. That bright gold god now sat in state in the nuptial hall—the principal witness to the union that was taking place. Bindu's hair streamed down her back. Her eyes were shut and her body swayed like that of a votaress in a trance.

'Bindu!'

The cry did not startle her. She turned gently around. 'Ganga!' she said, a little smile playing around her mouth. 'How is your little bride? I must go and see her—'

'Why didn't you come to the wedding? And today—today is Suhasini's wedding day. Why aren't you downstairs with the other girls? What are you doing here all alone?'

'You're still a child, Ganga,' Bindu smiled at him indulgently. 'I am a virgin widow. I mustn't show my face on any auspicious occasion. Don't you know that?'

Ganga stood as if turned to stone. A wave of self-reproach swept over him. Bindu was his. He loved her. He couldn't live without her. And yet—yet he had allowed himself to be caught in the net his father had spread for him. He had wronged Bindu. Together they could have created a heaven on earth. And all he had done was deny her. He strode into the room and caught the little figure in his arms. 'Bindu! Bindu!' he whispered against her hair. 'You're mine and mine alone. I can't, I won't live without you.'

'No, Ganga,' Bindu disengaged herself gently. 'You mustn't say that. You have a wife now. You must love her and be happy with her and I 'll be happy in your happiness.'

# Chapter XVII

Rajnarayan Datta was suffering from insomnia. Night after night he tossed and turned on his bed, eyes staring into the dark. His heart burned with shame and anger. How dare his son bring him to such a pass?

The zamindar of Rakhutia had come to see him the previous evening. The man had aged twenty years in these few days. His face was white and strained and his eyes had sunk deep into their sockets. Stepping down from his landau, he had stood at the gate, hands resting on a silver cane. 'Dattaja,' he had said in a quavering voice. 'You owe me an explanation.'

'Come into the house, Rakhutia raj,' Rajnarayan Datta had begged him. 'Let us console one another. We are both victims of a common misfortune.'

But the old man had remained standing. 'You arranged the marriage with full knowledge of your son's intentions,' he had said. 'My daughter's reputation is gone. I am ruined!' Rajnarayan Datta had stood transfixed. How dare the old man make such an accusation? Was Rajnarayan Datta a common liar? A pimp and cheat! The blood had rushed to his head. His limbs had trembled with rage. But he had controlled himself and said, 'My heart grieves for you. I would have saved your daughter's reputation if I had another son. Believe me, I had no knowledge of my son's intentions. You say you are ruined but am I not equally so?' Rakhutia had turned and walked away even before the sentence was concluded. Ignoring Rajnarayan's pleas, he had stepped into his landau and driven off.

Rajnarayan Datta had swallowed the insult and gone back into the house. He admitted his guilt. He should never have arranged the marriage. The poor girl would never find a husband now. The contract papers had been signed, the date fixed and the invitations sent out. No boy of good family would take a girl who was pre-contracted. Rajnarayan Datta paced up and down the hall. A low moan escaped him from time to time. What had he done to deserve such a fate? Had he not lavished all the love and care in the world on his son? And the same son, his only son, had turned him into an object of mockery. His wife, Jahnavi Devi, was dangerously ill. She hadn't recovered from the shock. To whom could he turn for consolation?

'Bara Khuro[15]!' His nephew, Pyarimohan, came into the room. 'I've done all I could to bring Madhu back home. But he won't even talk to me. Shall I send for Reverend Krishnamohan? He is ready to come and see you.'

'Reverend!' Rajnarayan's head shot up. 'That scavenger of a Brahmin who sold his religion for a few rupees! If he dares to step over my threshold I'll set my guards on him.'

'Madhu is staying in Father Dealtree's house. We must bring him back.'

'No.'

'You are too harsh on him. Khurima[16] will die if she doesn't see him soon.'

'You don't understand, Pyari. He won't come. Why should we submit ourselves to such humiliation?'

'Madhu is my brother and I don't care for the humiliation. I will bring him home if it takes me twenty years.'

'You'll only be wasting your time.'

'We must act quickly, Bara Khuro, or we'll be too late. The missionaries are sending him to England. That is why Madhu—'

'That is why Madhu—? What is wrong with me? Don't I have the money to send my son to England twenty times over? I didn't because I know of his weakness for English women. He would have married a cat-faced mem the minute he landed. Phoh! Jaundiced bitches, stinking to high heaven! Did you know they bathe only once a week? And my wonderful son says our girls are stupid and ignorant! Just because they cover their heads and keep within the house as decent girls should and do not prance around in heeled shoes and stockings. I had planned to send him next year after he was safely married. Why couldn't he have waited?'

'That's the trouble with Madhu. He has no patience. But I'll

---

15 Elder uncle.
16 Aunt.

bring him back. He's our Madhu still, isn't he? We'll make him go through a course of penitential rites and then—'

But penitential rites were the last thing on Madhu's mind. He enjoyed living in Archbishop Dealtree's house and was thrilled with all the publicity he was getting. So many conversions had taken place in Calcutta but not one had caused such a stir. Madhusudan Datta was a name to be reckoned with. But Madhu missed his friends, Gour in particular. Why hadn't Gour come to see him? Taking up a pen he proceeded to write a letter. A Bengali phrase came to his mind. But no—he wouldn't write in Bengali. He was a Christian now and would use King's English.

'Do come to see me, Gour. Take a day off from college and come to the old church on Mission Row. I'll pay for your palki. I have plenty of money.

Come, brightest Gourdas, on a hired palki.

And see thy anxious friend, M.S.D.'

But, still, Gour didn't come. Madhu wrote another letter.

'My dear friend,

A poet once said to his beloved, "Can I cease to love thee? No." I say the same to my dearest, my closest, my sincerest friend . . . How are you, Gour? Don't think I've forgotten you. I'll never forget you. You mustn't, either . . . My poems are to be published in London. Can you believe it? How is Beni? I dislike him and he dislikes me but I've been thinking of him a lot lately. I think of all my friends. What fun you must all have had at Ganga's wedding! And Bhudev? Did he get his medal? Why don't you come? I said I'd pay for your palki . . .'

Gour came this time but he brought Pyarimohan with him. Madhu came forward eagerly to embrace his friend but stopped short on seeing Pyarimohan. 'You've come again, Pyaridada!' he said indignantly. 'I've told you I can't accept your proposal. I can't and I won't.'

'Come home, Madhu. Your mother is—'

'Don't call me Madhu. My name is Michael,' and he winked and laughed like a naughty child who had outwitted his parents.

'I promised your mother I'd take you back—' Gour began.

Madhu became serious in an instant. 'Ask anything of me, Gour,' he said shaking his head, 'but not that.'

'Why not? What is wrong with going home?' Pyari said. 'Khurima is crazed with grief. She's the kindest, most loving mother in the world. How can you hurt her so, Madhu?'

'You say the same things every day, Pyari Dada. I've told you I can't—'

'Then listen to me, Mr Michael M.S. Dutt,' Gour cut in sharply. 'Don't ever ask me to come to you again. If our request means nothing to you—'

'Don't be angry.' Madhu placed a hand on Gour's knee. 'You don't know what you're asking of me. Don't I long to see my mother's face? Don't I yearn for her caresses? But I can't go home. My father will set his guards on me and keep me prisoner.'

'No. You'll be free to stay or leave as you choose. No one will force you. I give you my word.'

Madhu thought for a minute or two. 'All right,' he said. 'I'll go.'

'Come.' Pyarimohan stood up. 'The palki is waiting.'

'Not today,' Madhu cried out in alarm. 'There's a memorial service in the church—'

'That's in the evening,' Gour said dismissively. 'Why can't you come now? If you don't, you needn't come—ever. I'll never ask you again.'

Madhu shrugged and rose from his chair. 'Let's go, then.'

Pyari hadn't exaggerated. Jahnavi Devi lay on her side on the floor of her chamber. Her hair streamed down her back in a tangled mass. 'Ma!' Without stopping to remove his shoes, Madhu rushed to her side. The call shook her out of her stupor. 'Who is that?' she cried, starting up, and seeing her son, clasped him in her arms. Weeping bitterly, she called out his name again and again. 'Madhu! Madhu! Madhu! Madhu! Why did you do this to me, my son? How could you wound me so cruelly?'

'Why do you weep, Ma?' Madhu said. 'Look at me. Am I not your Madhu? I've changed my faith but nothing else. I'm still your son—'

'The sahebs snatched you away from me.'

'No, Ma. No one has any power over me. I went away of my own free will and I've come back to you, have I not?'

'You won't go away again?' A shadow fell over the floor. Madhu looked up. Rajnarayan Datta stood at the door, his face stern and solemn. Madhu's back stiffened. Only a year ago these two had been friends. Now they were adversaries, measuring one another.

'I've been talking to the priests,' Rajnarayan Datta said without preamble. 'There's a simple solution. All I need to do is feed five hundred Brahmins and give them shawls. And you must stand neck deep in the Ganga, partake of *pancha gavya*[17] and utter a few mantras. That is all. The earlier we carry out the rites the better. We'll fix the date for some time this week.'

'Baba!' Madhu rose and faced his father. 'I'm a Christian because I believe in Christianity. And I'll never reconvert. Never! Not if the sun starts rising from the west. I consider Hinduism to be a religion of barbarians and I've rejected it once and for all. Now I am a member of the civilized nations of the world. I'm as good as an Englishman.'

'Get out of my sight,' Rajnarayan Datta roared, his face convulsed with rage. 'Unnatural son! May I never see your face again.' He stormed out of the room, muttering as he walked down the long verandah. 'Venomous snake! Infidel! He's no son of mine. I'll disown and disinherit him. I'll wipe him out of my head and heart—' Then, stopping short, he thought, 'But I have no other son. Who will perform the last rites over my body? Must I be condemned to hell everlasting?' Standing where he was, he took a vow. He would marry again. He would—he must have another son.

Madhu was initially relieved at his father's attitude for now no one would press him to go home. But, within a few days he started feeling the pinch of poverty. He wanted to resume his studies but Hindu College would not enrol Christians. The only place he could go to was Bishop's College. But that was expensive and Madhu had no money. He had had so much all his life. He had thrown it around. And now he was a pauper. Hearing of his son's desire to continue his education, Rajnarayan Datta made arrangements for a sum of hundred rupees to be paid to him every month. For, angry and bitter though he was, he couldn't allow his son to live on charity.

Bishop's College had been set up for the education of

---

17 Five products of the cow.

European youth. However, in the last few years it had enrolled some Indian Christians, of whom Michael Madhusudan Dutt was one. Madhu was the brightest student of Bishop's College. His flair for the classical languages—Greek, Latin, Hebrew and Sanskrit—never ceased to astonish his teachers. But Madhu was wild and unruly and often disrupted college discipline. The first time was when he came dressed in a black cassock and four cornered hat like the European boys. The teacher stopped his lesson and stared in dismay. The boys tittered and the principal came running in. 'Dear boy,' he said, 'if you must wear a cassock let it be a white one.' 'No, sir,' Madhu answered firmly. 'Either I dress exactly like the European boys or I wear Indian attire of my own choice.'

'All right then,' the principal said. 'Let it be the latter.'

Next morning Madhu created a sensation. The boys left their classes and stood gaping at him as he walked down the corridor in a brocade tunic, embroidered scarf and a high turban of coloured silk. A meeting was convened that very day to discuss Madhu's conduct and decide on the action to be taken against him. The college authorities would have struck Madhu's name off the rolls if it were not for Krishnamohan Bandopadhyaya's intervention. He advocated a milder approach for too harsh a verdict might anger the natives. Boys from good families would hesitate to convert if such discriminations were practised too openly. The authorities decided to act on Krishnamohan Babu's advice. And next day onwards Madhu was permitted to come to college in a black cassock and cap like the white boys.

On another occasion Madhu picked up a quarrel with the steward. He had been studying hard all day—reading Homer and Virgil in the original—and had left his books on hearing the sound of the dinner gong. He was hungry and looked forward to the dinner, particularly the wine, which was light and refreshing. But that night the steward passed him by, neglecting to fill his glass. He didn't understand it at first and waited for his turn. Then he noticed the steward filling up the glasses of the European boys and systematically passing over the natives. Madhu stood up, his eyes blazing. Putting two fingers under his tongue, he emitted a sharp whistle, then crooking a finger at the steward, called out imperiously.

'Why haven't you filled my glass?'

'There wasn't enough to go around,' the steward mumbled.

'Then you should have served us all half a glass each. Isn't that a more civilized way?'

'I've received instructions to serve the white boys first. If there's any left—'

'You be damned,' Madhu roared, knocking back his chair. 'Those instructions be damned.'

Then, picking up his empty glass, he dashed it to the floor. Not content with that he snatched up the glasses of the other Indian boys and hurled them about till the dining hall resounded with the sound of splintering glass.

# Chapter XVIII

Nabin Kumar took up the chalk in his hand at the age of five. His mother was keen on starting his education, for though completely unlettered herself, she valued it in others. Her father and brothers were illiterate; her husband, though exceedingly wealthy, was almost equally so. But her son, Ganganarayan, had advanced far in his studies and was, in consequence, gentle, refined and modest. Bimba wanted her younger son to follow in the elder's footsteps. There was nothing of his father in Ganga. He did not drink; neither did he keep a mistress. He worked hard all day at the family business and spent his evenings in the company of his friends. These friends, too, were not spoiled scions of wealthy houses but intellectual young men who loved nothing better than to exchange views on politics, literature and religion. These days the audience hall resounded not to the tinkle of wine glasses and ankle bells but to the sound of impassioned young voices.

Bidhusekhar was very happy with Ganganarayan. Despite his education in Hindu College, Ganga had not turned Christian like his friend Rajnarayan Datta's son. Nor had he joined the band of heretics that Debendranath Thakur nurtured. He had applied himself seriously to the family business and was learning fast. He had, besides, shown considerable administrative ability on his inspection tours of the parganas. What pleased Bimba and Bidhusekhar most was the fact that there was no jealousy or rivalry between the brothers. Ganga loved his brother dearly, and Nabin, for all his naughtiness with others, honoured and obeyed Ganga.

The arrangements for the ceremony fell on Bidhusekhar for Ramkamal was away on a pleasure tour of northern India. In reality, he had rented a palatial mansion in Varanasi and was living there for the last six months with Kamala Sundari. Bimba did not resent Kamala Sundari for when at home, Ramkamal was Bimba's devoted slave. 'You are my Lakshmi, Bimba!' he never failed to remind her. 'All I have is owing to you. If it makes you unhappy I won't leave your side for a moment.' At these times Bimba hastened to assure Ramkamal that his absences did not make her unhappy. He must do whatever he wished for in his happiness lay hers.

Bidhusekhar chose three eminent Brahmins for the chalk ceremony. The first was the elderly Rammanikya Vidyalankar—assistant secretary of Sanskrit College. The second was Durgacharan Bondopadhyaya. An eminent scholar of Sanskrit and English, Durgacharan had taught for a while in Mr Hare's school, then decided to join Medical College and become a doctor. He had passed with honours and had dedicated himself subsequently to a lifetime of service to the poor and deprived. Bidhusekhar liked and respected Durgacharan, for despite his English education, he hadn't given up native ways. Durgacharan suggested the name of Ishwar Chandra Bandopadhyaya for the third Brahmin. Ishwar Chandra hailed from Midnapore. He was exceedingly ugly in appearance but a scholar of unmatched brilliance. He had been honoured with the title, 'Vidyasagar', some years ago and now held the post of chief pandit in Fort William College.

Ishwar Chandra recognized Bidhusekhar the moment they were introduced. 'Moshai!' he said. 'You don't know me but I know you. I was present at your daughter's wedding. My class fellow, Durgaprasad Bandopadhyaya, is your son-in-law. I will never forget the feast! Is it the custom in your family to kill off the bridegroom's party with too much food?' Bidhusekhar burst out laughing. After some more pleasantries had been exchanged, he said, 'My friend, Ramkamal Singha, has a son of five—a very bright and intelligent boy. It is our desire that he takes up the chalk this Saraswati Puja. I've come to entreat you Brahmins to conduct the ceremony and give him your blessings.'

'Will a feast be arranged for us?' Durgacharan asked, tongue in cheek.

'Glutton!' Ishwar Chandra exclaimed with mock severity. 'You will die of overeating one day.'

'I am a Brahmin, brother! How can I resist good food? Gluttony runs in my blood.'

'You'll honour us Brahmins with shawls, I suppose?' Ishwar Chandra asked Bidhusekhar. 'And gold?'

'Certainly, certainly,' Bidhusekhar hastened to assure him. 'Everything will be done according to custom. My friend is very generous.'

'Then listen to me, Moshai! I have no objection to conducting the chalk ceremony in your friend's house. But I shall do it on my own terms. I shall go empty-handed and come back so. No shawls, no money—not a cowrie shall be thrust on me. Do you agree? If not—I decline your invitation.'

Bidhusekhar stared in amazement. He had never heard anything like this before. 'I earn fifty rupees a month,' Ishwar Chandra continued. 'That is quite enough for me. Durgacharan earns eighty rupees. He does not need charity either. If you wish to spend some money on the occasion, don't waste it on Brahmins. Pay for the education of some poor but meritorious students. That will be true charity.'

'As you wish.' Bidhusekhar rose to depart when Durgacharan said, 'Speak for yourself, Ishwar. And for me, if you will. But don't make any commitment on behalf of Rammanikya Vidyalankar. He is old and has a numerous family. He needs money. My suggestion is that he be given our shares as well as his own.'

'You are right,' Ishwar conceded. Then, turning to Bidhusekhar, he said, 'That is settled, then. But help the poor students if you can.'

'I'll remember that,' Bidhusekhar promised.

'Another thing. I'm a vegetarian and I eat very frugally. Feasting in rich men's houses does not agree with me. I shall only partake of fruit.'

'Here I part ways with Ishwar,' Durgacharan cried jovially. 'I am a glutton and I shall regale myself on *luchi* and sweetmeats.'

The day of the chalk ceremony arrived. The puja concluded, little Nabin, bathed and dressed in new white silk, was brought before the Brahmins, where they sat on velvet asans, floor mats, facing the image of Goddess Saraswati. Rammanikya Vidyalankar and Durgacharan Bandopadhyaya uttered a few mantras and blessed the boy. But Ishwar Chandra did neither. 'Where is the chalk?' he asked. 'And where is the slate?' After the articles had been pulled out from the mound of flowers under which they were buried, he took Nabin on his lap and put the chalk in his hand. Holding it in his own, he wrote the thirteenth letter of the Bengali alphabet, *ka*. 'First a straight line down,' he guided the little fingers. 'Then another—so—and another—so. Like half a kite, then a little hook—so. Now we've written a *ka*.'

'*ka*,' Nabin repeated like a parrot, his unnaturally bright eyes gleaming like jewels.

Ishwar Chandra let go of Nabin's hand. Nabin bent over his slate and scribbled something on it. Looking down, Ishwar Chandra saw another *ka*—a crooked but unmistakable *ka*—next to the one he had written.

'What does this mean?' He looked up in surprise. 'Does the child know how to write?' 'No, he doesn't,' Bidhusekhar said. Everyone crowded around the still scribbling Nabin. Was it possible that someone had taught him to write?

Ishwar Chandra wiped the slate clean and said, 'Let me see. Can you write now?' And, to his utter amazement, a row of *kas* appeared on the slate like magic.

The three Brahmins stared at one another. Durgacharan took up the slate and wrote the English letter A, and then B after it. Handing it to Nabin he said encouragingly, 'See if you can write these two letters, my child.' Nabin grinned and bending over the slate, wrote them effortlessly.

'I have never seen a child like this before,' Durgacharan said. 'He's a prodigy.'

'He learned to walk and talk long before his time,' Bidhusekhar said, smiling proudly. 'And his horoscope says he will be famed for his learning throughout the land.'

'Keep a close watch on his health,' Durgacharan said. 'May the child be granted a long life.'

Bimbabati sat with her women, beyond the bamboo curtain. Her heart felt fit to burst with pride. The awe and admiration with which these eminent Brahmins gazed upon her son removed all the fears that still lurked within her breast. Now she knew that her son was special. He was a genius and, therefore, different from other children.

'Is my chalk ceremony over, Dada?' Nabin asked as Ganga picked him up and prepared to carry him out of the room.

'Yes, Chhotku. You had a very good chalk ceremony. Now you must have something to eat.'

'What about Dulal? He must have a chalk ceremony too. Call him.'

Ganganarayan did not know who Dulal was. Going up to his mother, he asked, 'Who is Dulal?'

'I don't know, child,' she answered. 'It may be the little servant boy he plays with.'

'Dulal! Dulal!' Nabin set up a wail. 'Call him. I want Dulal.'

Thakomoni stood at the edge of the crowd, holding her little boy tightly by the hand. She heard Nabin's cry and her heart quaked with fear. Who knew what would happen now? She slipped away, pulling Dulal after her, and sought the refuge of her own hut.

That evening Nabin accosted Dulal. Showing him his newly acquired slate and chalk, he said, 'You didn't have a chalk ceremony, Dulal. You'll be a dunce all your life.' Dulal had seen it all from afar. The goddess sitting on her white swan, with a mountain of *sandesh* before her! He had hoped for some but he didn't get any.

'Come,' Nabin said encouragingly. 'I'll conduct your chalk ceremony. Take the chalk in your hand. First a straight line down. Then another—so and another—so. Like half a kite. Then a little hook—so. Now we've written a *ka*. Have you learned to write before? Now write A and then B. Now you may touch my feet. May you be granted a long life, my child.'

# Chapter XIX

With the sudden death of Rammanikya Vidyalankar the assistant secretaryship of Sanskrit College fell vacant. There were many contenders for the post but the sahebs were no longer interested in employing elderly pandits from village Sanskrit schools or *tols*. They wanted someone young and dynamic and their choice fell on an ex-student of their own—a brilliant scholar named Ishwar Chandra Bandopadhyaya. Released from his contract in Fort William College on the recommendation of the education secretary, Mr Moet, himself, Ishwar Chandra took up his new appointment. But he had to see his parents first and give them the news. So, one morning, he set off with his brothers for his ancestral village in Midnapore. The journey, though long, was easy and leisurely. From their mess in Bowbazar, the boys walked to the river bank in Hatkhola. Crossing over, they climbed the bank at Shalikha, after which all they had to rely on were their legs. It was the month of Baisakh[18], when squalls came on—sudden and frequent. At such times they sheltered under the trees. Reaching Masat village, they left the highway and started walking cross country over fields and furrows; across hedges and ditches. It was dusk by the time they reached Rajbalhat by the bank of the beautiful and fiercely flowing Damodar. During the rains the river swelled to the size of an ocean—violent and terrible. Even now, though considerably shrunk in the summer heat, it ran lusty and strong. No boat was available that night, so the travellers returned to Rajbalhat. They had rice with them—puffed and beaten—and molasses. Mixing them together, they swallowed the mess with great gulps of water. This done, seeking a wayside inn, they took shelter for the night.

Rising at dawn they crossed the Damodar, then walked ten miles to Patul. After a brief rest in a relative's house they set off

18 Mid-April—Mid-May.

again for their final destination—the village of Birsingha, where their parents lived. It was two o' clock in the afternoon when the boys reached home. The inmates of the household were overjoyed to see them—more so, perhaps, because their visit was unexpected. Old Thakurdas Bandopadhyaya had resigned from service the year Ishwar joined Fort William College. His contemporaries had warned him against taking this drastic step. His son was supporting him now but was there any guarantee that he would do so all his life? What would become of him then? Who would give him a job? But Thakurdas knew his eldest son. The boy was irreligious but loyal and sincere. He had a strong sense of duty. He would never abandon his parents for, in his heart, they took the place of the gods he disdained.

Though the hour for a midday meal was long past, Ishwar's mother got busy cooking for her sons. His wife, Deenamayi, sat with her mother-in-law in the kitchen, as custom decreed that a young wife may not look upon her husband's face in the light of the day. After greeting his parents, Ishwar set out to meet the neighbours. His first visit was to his tutor, Kalikanta Chattopadhyaya. Kalikanta was old and feeble and almost blind. But, dim as his sight was, he recognized Ishwar, playing hide and seek with the village boys on the patch of land in front of the house. '*O go,*' he called out to his wife, excitedly. 'Just see who is here.' Then, putting his head out of the window, he shouted at Ishwar to come into the house.

'In a little while, Pandit Moshai!' Ishwar shouted back. 'Let me finish the game.'

After a few minutes Ishwar came panting into the room. 'I'm out of practice,' he said between breaths. 'I never get time for a game in Calcutta.'

'Are you a child that you play with children?' Pandit Moshai stroked his back affectionately. 'You are a great man now. Assistant secretary of Sanskrit College! Do you know, Ginni,' he turned to his wife, 'our Ishwar hobnobs with sahebs all day long. He's one of the most important men in the land—'

'Our own Ishwar!' Pandit Moshai's wife smiled benignly. 'He was such a little runt of a boy! And so naughty! How old are you now, Ishwar?'

'Twenty-six.'

'You don't look that old. You're still like the little boy you were.'

'Do your students obey you?' Pandit Moshai asked.

'In Fort William I used to teach sahebs. If I could control them, why would I have trouble with rice-eating Bengali boys?'

After a few minutes more of casual conversation, Pandit Moshai asked, 'Would you like to come to Kheerpai with me, Ishwar?'

Kheerpai was Ishwar's father-in-law's village. He hardly ever went there. And now there was even less reason to do so since his wife was here in Birsingha.

'Why are you going to Kheerpai, Pandit Moshai?' he asked. 'You look far from well. You should not undertake these long journeys at your age.'

'What can I do? A marriage proposal has come for me and—'

'A marriage proposal! For you?' Ishwar asked, amazed.

'Yes, my boy. I'm not very keen but they won't take no for an answer.'

Ishwar stared at his guru's face. It was as placid and benign as ever. There was no change of expression on his wife's face either. Kalikanta Chattopadhyaya was a *bhanga kulin*[19] and marrying was his ancestral profession. He kept one wife with him in his house. The others he condescended to visit from time to time, earning good money each time he did so. Ishwar was aware of this. Yet what he had just heard filled him with disgust and hatred.

'I'm helpless Ishwar,' Kalikanta said, noting his expression. 'The *pathshala* does not run as it used to. The collections I make from my existing in-laws are not enough to keep me in comfort. I must earn some money.'

'How old is the girl?' Ishwar asked.

'Nine,' Kalikanta answered. 'Her father is, quite naturally, anxious to wed her. It is not easy to keep such a great hulk of a girl in one's house. He has been begging me to help him out. Besides, he is ready to pay me well.'

'How many years do you expect to live?' Ishwar asked in a

19 A Brahmin belonging to a *kulin* family which had at some time failed to observe *kulin* restrictions.

hard voice. 'What provision are you making for the girl in the event of your death?'

'Provision? I make provision?' Kalikanta gave a short laugh. 'Look at it this way, Ishwar. If I don't marry the girl, her father will lose his place in the order. He'll be ostracized by one and all.'

'You have a son. Why don't you get the girl married to him?'

'I have other plans for Srinath. He's to be wed too, soon. I've told you. I'm badly in need of money.'

Ishwar rose to depart. Waving aside the sweet rice balls his Guru Ma brought for him to eat, he folded his hands and said, 'Forgive me. Not a drop of water passes through my lips in this house from this day onwards.' Touching his guru's feet, he added, 'Guru Moshai! This is the last time I set foot in your house. You will never see me again.' And, with this, he stormed out of the door. Kalikanta and his wife stared at him as if he had gone mad. 'O Ishwar!' they called after him. 'Where are you going? Is anything wrong? O Ishwar!' Ishwar neither stopped nor answered. Anger and shame surged through him. Could nothing be done to stop this accursed custom that victimized *kulin* girls so cruelly? If respected, educated men like Kalikanta Chattopadhyaya could use it to their own advantage so shamelessly, what could be expected of illiterate rustics? He remembered an incident that occurred in his college days. His teacher, Shombunath Bachaspati, had brought home a child bride at the age of eighty. Ishwar had seen her once, on the old man's insistence, and the memory haunted him to this day. Bachaspati died within a few months of the nuptials and the girl became a widow. No one knew what became of her. Ishwar's eyes burned at the thought and hot tears trickled down his cheeks.

Back at home, Ishwar's mother, Bhagavati, set her son's meal before him. She had taken a lot of pains and cooked all his favourite dishes—fish, caught fresh from the pond, and thick, creamy *kheer*. But Ishwar had no appetite. 'Give me a little *dal-bhat*, ma,' he said. 'I can't eat anything more.'

'But why? I cooked all this for you—'

'I'm used to *dal-bhat*. I've eaten it all my life. Why should I eat fine foods now? Thousands of people die of starvation every day. When I think of them—'

'I'll feed the poor one day. I promise you. But you must eat, too.'

Ishwar sat in silence for a while. Then he said, 'Ma! On my way to and from the mess house I pass the milkmen's quarters every day. The calves are tied with strong ropes during milking time, lest they run to their mothers. Is it right to deprive sucklings of their mother's milk so that men may eat delicacies like *kheer*? Is it not for infants that milk flows from their mothers teats? I've stopped drinking milk. I don't eat meat and fish either.'

Now Bhagavati was really alarmed. 'What are you saying, Ishwar?' she cried. 'How can you survive without milk and fish? You work so hard. You need nourishing food.' Taking a piece of fried fish from his *thala*, Bhagavati held it to her son's lips. 'Eat this,' she pleaded. 'For my sake.' Ishwar's brothers sniggered. They were aware of their brother's new fad. They also knew how stubborn he could get. But Ishwar surprised them by taking the piece of fish from his mother's hand. 'I will,' he said. 'But take away the rest, Ma. And the *kheer*. Milk won't pass through my lips in any form, now or ever.' Thakurdas stood by, puffing at his hookah. 'Give over trying, Brahmani,' he said placidly. 'Leave this mule of ours alone to do as he wills.'

Ishwar returned to Calcutta after a few days. He had left the village at the age of nine and had visited it regularly from time to time. He had enjoyed these visits. He had romped and played, bathed in the pond, breathed the pure air and returned happy and refreshed. But this time he came back to the city sad and despondent. He had seen the poverty and misery of the villagers, their ignorance and blind faith. Could nothing be done to improve their lot? Education, he thought, was the only way. Education held up a mirror through which a man learned to view and assess himself.

Back in Calcutta, Ishwar set himself seriously to the task of reorganizing the college. He found chaos and laxity everywhere. Though housed in a concrete building, the college was run like a village *tol*. Teachers and students alike came and went as they pleased. No teaching was done on the first and eighth days of the new moon. No new text was opened on the twelfth, thirteenth, fourteenth and fifteenth. The sight of a pandit, sleeping through a hot afternoon, with a favourite pupil fanning him, was not a rare one. Boys excused themselves from class and hung about in groups outside the toilet, regaling each other with the erotic verses they found scattered freely in their texts. Ishwar changed all that. He decreed that every day would be a working day—barring Sunday. Students would be allowed out of the class only one at a time. Students would carry wooden cards to establish their identity and teachers would apply for leave of absence from the college. Teaching would begin punctually at ten-thirty in the morning and teachers and students must all keep time. The elderly among the pandits found this last order particularly irksome. But Ishwar was firm. Without saying a word(for many among them were his own teachers) he enforced discipline in his own inimitable way. Every morning at ten-thirty, he stood outside the college gate and greeted the latecomers with a smile and a glance at the watch in his hand. And for pandits who couldn't resist a nap, he had the hilarious advice, 'Keep a snuff box with you, Pandit Moshai. Push the snuff deep into your nostrils and sneeze the sleep out.'

Meanwhile, an incident occurred that increased his popularity with his students. Since Sanskrit College and Hindu College stood adjacent to one another, matters of common interest often came up and the heads of the two institutions sorted them out. On Ishwar Chandra's first visit to Mr Carr, the latter threw a brief glance at the simple commoner, clad in homespun, and decided that there was no need for extending any courtesy. Putting his leather-shod feet on the table within inches of Ishwar Chandra's disproportionately large shaven crown, out of which the Brahmin's *shikha* sprang out thick and strong, Mr Carr asked in a voice of easy contempt, 'Well, Pandit! What do you require of me?' Ishwar Chandra's limbs quivered with humiliation but he did not react. Controlling his anger he said what he had come to say and departed. He did not report the outrage nor did he forget it. He simply bided his time till the opportunity came for him to avenge himself.

A few days later, Mr Carr came into his room. Ishwar Chandra put up his dusty slipper-clad feet on the table right under Carr's nose and asked carelessly, 'Yes, Saheb, what can I do for you?' Carr, unlike Ishwar, did not bother to control himself. Trembling with anger he stormed out of the room. In the next few days, the story, considerably embellished with each telling, spread all over the city. The boys of Sanskrit College crowed over their counterparts of Hindu College. Mr Carr reported the matter to the education secretary and added the words, 'This is an affront to the white race. No European should tolerate it.' Mr Moet sent for Ishwar Chandra and demanded an explanation, which the latter gave readily. Looking thoroughly bewildered, he said, 'But I had no intention whatsoever of insulting Mr Carr! Since that was the way he greeted me when I went to see him, I presumed it to be the proper form of salutation in your country. I did not keep my feet on the floor, as I usually do, for fear of upsetting him.' Mr Moet's lips twitched and he burst out laughing. He wrote in his report: 'Pandit Ishwar Chandra Vidyasagar is the bravest and most intelligent Bengali of my acquaintance.'

However, despite this victory, Ishwar resigned from the post of assistant secretary after three months, following a clash of wills with the secretary, Rasamay Datta. The latter had supported Ishwar's plans for reorganizing the college in the hope that the credit for it would come to him. But it didn't work out that way. Ishwar Chandra became increasingly popular with the students. The incident with Carr put him in the limelight and won him the respect of the more liberal among the sahebs. Threatened and frustrated at the turn of events, Rasamay Dutta started putting obstacles in the way of Ishwar's plans for reform. Objections were raised every now and then for no reason at all. Never one to compromise with injustice, Ishwar Chandra handed in his resignation.

'Are you mad, Ishwar?' his friend Durgacharan said to him. 'To relinquish the assistant secretaryship of Sanskrit College upon a whim! Everyone is shocked. Do you know what Rasamay Datta is saying? "The young man is very hot-headed. What does he propose to do now? Starve?" He is quite right—'

'Tell him,' Ishwar answered, smiling, 'that I'll peddle vegetables for a living but I won't work in an institution where I'm humiliated.'

# Chapter XX

Bindu dreamed that she was in heaven. She lay on a bed of flowers, looking up at the radiant form that stood by her side. The gems flashed and sparkled from his crown of gold; his lips smiled kindly at her. Bindu knew him. He was Vishnu, the Lord of the world, and he had come to her in a form she recognized. Janardan! Janardan had come for her. Putting out his hands he said, 'Why are you sad, Bindu? Come, come to me . . .' Bindu started up. Her dream shattered, she looked straight into Ganganarayan's eyes. 'Why, Ganga!' she exclaimed. 'What—?'

Ganga sat on the floor of the puja room, gazing on Bindu's face. It was like a newly opened lotus—creamy white, with dewdrops clinging to the petals. Bindu had grown into a woman of surpassing beauty. Her hair rippled down to her tiny waist, thick and soft as a monsoon cloud. Her breasts swelled out of her thin sari—burgeoning and luxurious. The curve of her thigh had the sharp edge of a Persian broad sword. 'Beautiful! You're beautiful, Bindu,' Ganga groaned. 'I can't bear the waste. I'm going mad.'

'Don't be silly, Ganga,' Bindu cut in with a smile. 'Tell me about yourself. How are you? How is the little bride? Why don't you bring her home?'

'She weeps for her mother. She's still a child. She's of no use to me.'

'That's nonsense. Bring her home. I'll teach her to be a wife.'

'She's happy with her dolls—'

'You'll be her doll from now on. All husbands are—sooner or later. Didn't you know that?'

'I want a companion—not a serving maid. She's unlettered—'

'But you aren't. Why don't you educate her?'

'I don't care about her. I want you, Bindu. I can't live without you.'

'Are you mad? You mustn't say such things.' Bindu shivered

and looked about her apprehensively. 'Go out of the room. Go home, Ganga.'

'The house is empty. No one will see us.'

'Why?' Bindu's eyes were huge and soft in the twilight. 'Why is no one at home?'

'They've gone to Srirampur, to my uncle's house.'

Bindu suppressed a sigh. She was a widow. She wasn't allowed to cross the threshold. No one cared about her. Her own parents and sisters had forgotten her existence. She lived in exile—in the puja room—banished from the rest of the world.

'Your uncle's house?' She asked and a little smile quivered on her lips. 'Then what are you doing here?'

'I didn't go. I've been burning with fever for the last three days. You know nothing and care nothing about me.'

'Fever!' Bindu leaned forward anxiously and laid a hand on his brow. 'Why, you're hot! Why are you here? Go home and rest.' Her soft breasts brushed against his chest and he could hold himself no longer. Clasping her in his arms, he kissed her face and neck, again and again, with hot trembling lips. Thoroughly alarmed, Bindu pushed him away. 'The fever has made you delirious, Ganga,' she cried. 'Go home.'

'I won't go home. I love you. I must have you. How can you live the way you do?'

'I have my Janardan—'

'I'll break your Janardan into a thousand pieces—'

'Don't be silly, Ganga.'

'I'm mad. Mad with love for you. I can't eat. I can't sleep. But you don't care. You don't care one bit.'

'That's not true. I do care.'

'Then why do we starve ourselves? What does Janardan give you in return for all your devotion? He is nothing, Bindu. He is only an image.'

'Have you turned Brahmo?' Bindu asked with a bitter smile. 'I hear you go to Deben Thakur's house every day.'

'How do you know?'

'I know everything about you. Listen, Ganga. Why do you creep in here like a thief because the house is empty? You are a prince. Behave like one. Forget me. I'm fated to suffer.'

'I can change your fate.'

'No one can do that. You remember the day my books were

taken away from me. I was angry then. I didn't understand. But now I know. I'm a woman and a widow and deprivation is my lot.'

'No, no.' Ganga caught her in his arms but this time Bindu slipped away from his grasp and ran out of the room, up the stairs, to the terrace. Ganga ran after her and found her crumpled up in a heap on the floor, weeping bitterly. 'Sin!' she cried between sobs. 'Sin! Don't tempt me, Ganga. I don't want to go to hell.'

'Do you care for someone else? Tell me the truth.'

'How can you ask me that? Don't you know the truth? Can't you feel it in your heart?' Bindu sat up and dashed the tears away from her eyes with an angry gesture. 'I'll kill myself before I surrender my body to you or to anyone else. You know me. I don't make idle threats.'

'That means you don't love me. I understand. I won't come here any more. I swear it.'

Bindu said nothing. She sat, eyes lowered, chin resting on her knees. After a minute or two, Ganga walked away. The next few days were passed in torment. Ganga lay on his bed, restless and feverish. He was twenty-one and a man, and he needed a woman. He could take his pick of the courtesans of Calcutta if he felt so inclined. He had enough money. But he had no use for them. He didn't want his wife either. His body was in a fever for Bindu and his soul yearned for her. He tried to distract himself by visiting Deben Thakur whenever he could. His old friend and contemporary from Hindu College, Rajnarayan Basu, had given up his atheism and turned to the new doctrine. He had found employment as a translator and it was he who had taken Ganga to one of Deben Thakur's meetings. Ganga had found himself irresistibly drawn to Debendranath. The remarkable ease with which he explained and interpreted the obscure Sanskrit of the Upanishads never failed to impress Ganga. But following the quarrel with Bindu, even Debendranath's discourses offered no comfort.

Then, one evening, he went again and stood outside the prayer room of Bidhusekhar Mukherjee's house. 'I've failed, Bindu,' he said in a choking voice. 'I couldn't keep my word. I couldn't stay away from you.'

'Come in, Ganga,' Bindu said softly. Her voice was warm

and sympathetic like a mother's, gently soothing a wayward child. But kindness and sympathy were not enough for Ganga. He wanted more. He vowed he would break her resistance and make her his own. He came every day and remonstrated with her. Why was she throwing away her chance of happiness? What was there for her in her father's house? Why couldn't they run away together to some distant land, where no one knew them? Why couldn't they begin all over again? But Bindu wept and pleaded, cajoled and threatened by turns and would not give in. 'Don't tempt me, Ganga,' she begged. 'Don't push me to the point where I must kill myself. Hell will swallow me up if I—'

'Then let us die together,' Ganga cried vehemently and taking her in his arms, strained her resisting body tight against his chest.

Soudamini stood outside the puja room and watched the scene with eyes that seemed turned to stone. The household had gradually woken up to the fact that something was going on and one of the maids had informed her mistress. Her senses returning, Soudamini called out in a terrible voice, 'Bindu!' The couple sprang apart. 'Die! You accursed one. Die!' Bindu's mother screamed in a choking voice. 'To commit adultery before God! Have you no shame? No fear of hell? Do you live only to bring shame and ruin on us all? And Ganga! A beautiful, pure boy like my Ganga. You try to corrupt him with your evil arts.'

'You are wrong,' Ganga said, his head lowered in shame. 'I am to blame. Not Bindu. I forced her to—'

'Come away from her,' Bindu's mother cried hysterically. Then, pushing the quiet, unresisting girl further into the room, she pulled Ganga away and locked the door. 'Her father will punish her as she deserves,' Soudamini announced. Then turning to the servants who stood huddled together, she said, 'If news of this leaks out of the house, I'll have your tongues plucked out of your mouths.'

'But I'm the guilty one,' Ganga pleaded over and over again. 'I used force on her. Why do you blame Bindu?'

Bidhusekhar was in the house when all this was happening. He heard Soudamini's voice raised in anger and came up to investigate. 'Don't punish her, Khuro Moshai,' Ganga turned to him. 'Punish me if you will. The fault is mine.' Bidhusekhar threw him a burning glance and said quietly, 'Come with me.' Leading him down the stairs and out of the house he climbed into his waiting phaeton and beckoned to Ganga to follow. Ganga thought Bidhusekhar was taking him home to expose him before his parents and demand punishment. But the horses went on and on till, entering Bowbazar, they stopped before the temple of Kali. Bidhusekhar stepped down and taking Ganga's hand in an iron grip, led him to the innermost recess of the shrine. 'Ganga,' he said in a sombre voice. 'No one will hear of the events of tonight. Neither your parents nor anyone else. I swear that before Ma Kali. But you must swear an oath, too. Swear that you renounce Bindu from this day onwards. That you will never attempt to set eyes on her or speak to her again.'

'I'll do whatever you command. Only promise me you won't punish Bindu. She is innocent.'

'I promise.'

Then Ganga prostrated himself before the image of Kali and swore that he would not look on Bindu's face or speak to her as long as he lived.

A few days later Ganga discovered that Bindu had been sent away. He ran to Bidhusekhar and demanded excitedly, 'Khuro Moshai! You swore before Ma Kali you wouldn't punish Bindu—'

'I have kept my oath,' Bidhusekhar answered placidly. 'I haven't hurt her in any way. She is well and happy. If anything—I've made it easier for you to keep your oath. Bindu is in Kashi. You will never see her again.'

# *Chapter XXI*

Dwarkanath set sail once more. He had been unhappy, lately, in his own country. His eldest son's behaviour had hurt and annoyed him. Besides, he had no friends left. He commanded respect and admiration wherever he went but true love—that which springs from the heart—was denied to him. He had worked hard for many years and amassed an enormous fortune, but now he thought, 'For whom?' His heirs, he was convinced, lacked the ability to keep it together, much less add to it. He decided that he would enjoy the years left to him. He would buy every luxury the world could provide. He would go to Europe. He was known there and respected. The food and wine were excellent and so were the women.

On his departure he left strict instructions with Debendranath to send to him, every month, one lakh of rupees for his expenses abroad—a sum with which one could buy five thousand bharis of gold. Though he didn't admit it, Dwarkanath was a little uncertain about his reception during his second sojourn on foreign shores. Last time he had been fêted and lionized by royals and aristocrats, being the first traveller from the 'exotic Ind' they had heard and read about but never seen. He decided to keep the enchantment alive by dazzling their eyes with lavish displays of wealth. He travelled with a large retinue which included his son, Nagendranath, nephew, Nabin Chandra, his English secretary, English physician and half a dozen servants. There were, besides, four students from the Medical College, two of whom had been sent for higher education abroad by the British government in India. The other two were his own protégés. His first task on landing was to find lodgings for the six boys and make arrangements for their education. This obligation over, he was now free to dedicate himself solely to the pursuit of pleasure.

On his last visit Dwarkanath had taken interest in the scientific discoveries of the West and its industrial development. He had wished to emulate the foreigners and import their ideas and machinery. But this time he was indifferent, both to the needs of his country and to the expansion of his own business empire. Food and wine, music and dance, the theatre and opera were his sole concerns. He devised magnificent entertainments to which the cream of English society was invited. Even the queen and her consort (the queen's husband was not the king in England) expressed their delight at the fabulous gifts he had brought for them and invited him to the palace on several occasions. Dwarkanath surrounded himself with lords and ladies, earls and dukes, poets and painters, and basked in the glory his wealth and status had procured for him. He had proved to the ruling race, for the second time, that a native could be their equal in every way.

Attending a session of British parliament, an idea struck him. The members were all democratically elected. Why, then, couldn't an Indian sit in parliament? And who better than himself was fitted for the role? He conveyed his views to the prime minister but was dismayed at the response he got. A shade of embarrassment crept over the latter's manner as he dismissed such a possibility. The idea of a native sitting in parliament was inconceivable, he said. Only Christians had the right. Stung to the quick, Dwarkanath retorted, 'Why? Hinduism and Christianity have flourished, side by side, for centuries. There is no contradiction in their doctrines. Hindus worship God the same as you do. Why can't a Hindu sit by the side of a Christian in parliament?'

'Do you believe Jesus Christ to be the son of God? Those who don't are infidels—according to our tenets.'

The argument was becoming unpleasant. Both gentlemen realized it and changed the subject. But the bitterness remained in Dwarkanath's heart. From this point onwards in his life, he felt an ebbing away of the admiration he had always felt for Christianity. He found that underneath the veneer, Christians were as hidebound and narrow as the Brahmins he loathed in his own country. He coined the phrase 'Brahmins in black robes' for Christian priests. He made cuttings of the scandals that appeared in papers and journals concerning the clergy and pasted them in an album, and whenever a friend or guest (usually a European) eulogized Christianity, he brought it out and showed it to him.

From England Dwarkanath proceeded to France, where he received a grand ovation. He was invited to the palace at Versailles and introduced to the King's wife and sister—an unheard of privilege for a foreigner. The King, Louis Philippe, became a personal friend. The French nobility, the ladies in particular, were charmed by his handsome figure and the exquisitely embroidered Cashmere shawls that hung carelessly from his shoulders. Wearing shawls was the rage in Paris and the Parisiennes had seen nothing to match these.

As a return for the courtesies showered on him, Dwarkanath Tagore hosted a reception to which the King and Queen and all the lords and ladies of the realm were invited. It was held in an enormous salon, the walls of which were draped with the most magnificent shawls the blue-eyed beauties had ever seen. Whenever their host caught one of them looking at a shawl with particular interest, he walked over to her and taking it off the wall, put it around her with the words, 'Receive this humble present, Milady, and make me the happiest man in the world.' By the time the guests left, the walls were reduced to their pristine starkness. Never had Paris witnessed a spectacle like that!

It was in France that Dwarkanath met Max Mueller. A young man—six years younger than his son, Debendranath—Max Mueller had obtained a Ph.D. from the University of Leipzig and was now in France, studying Sanskrit from Professor Burnoff. Dwarkanath knew Burnoff and enjoyed his company for, though his own knowledge of Sanskrit was elementary, he was fairly well versed in ancient Indian art and literature. Max Mueller was highly impressed with Dwarkanath's knowledge and visited him everyday, listening avidly to whatever the older man said. The young man's interest in India was truly phenomenal!

Dwarkanath and Max Mueller shared many interests, of which one was music. Dwarkanath had a fine ear and his voice was a rich, deep baritone. When he sang snatches from the Italian operas he loved, Max Mueller listened, enthralled. Sometimes he accompanied the prince on the piano.

One day, Max Mueller expressed a desire to hear a rendering of the classical music of India. The prince waived away his request with the words, 'Foreigners have no ear for it.'

However, on Max Mueller's insistence, he sang a piece and asked smiling, 'Well! Did that mean anything to you?'

'No,' was Max Mueller's frank confession. 'I could make nothing of it. It wasn't music to my ears.'

'That's the trouble with you Europeans!' Dwarkanath said angrily. 'You're incapable of accepting anything new. When I first heard Italian music I thought it sounded like the wailing of a cat. But with patience and perseverance I have learned to appreciate it. But you—you think our religion is nothing, our philosophy is nothing, our literature is nothing! Simply because you don't understand it.'

Max Mueller hung his head in silence. Dwarkanath was very short-tempered these days. The slightest delay in receiving his monthly remittance infuriated him. He dashed off angry letters to Debendranath, reprimanding him for neglecting the family business and estates. That, as a matter of fact, was true. After Dwarkanath's departure, Debendranath had turned away almost completely from his father's world. More and more he withdrew into his own, practising his new dharma and working for its proliferation. Already the initiates numbered more than five hundred and word of the new religion was spreading beyond the city limits and entering the villages.

One evening, as Debendranath sat in the outer room, reading the newspaper, the steward of the household, Rajendranath, rushed in weeping. 'Is there no redress in the land?' he cried out incoherently. 'This is gross injustice!' Debendranath folded his paper and said quietly, 'Dry your tears and tell me what has happened.' The story, as Rajendranath told it, was this. Last Sunday, as Rajendranath's wife and sister-in-law were on their way to a wedding celebration, his younger brother, Umesh, stopped their palki half-way and took his wife away by force to Reverend Duff's house. They were to be baptised in a few days. Umesh was fourteen years old and his wife, eleven. Rajendranath's father had gone to Duff Saheb and entreated him to send them home but the latter had refused. The old man had then appealed to the Supreme Court. The court had ruled that, though a minor, the boy had the right to decide what he wished to do. Following the verdict, Rajendranath and his father had approached Duff Saheb once again and begged him to postpone the baptism till the time a second appeal had been considered. But their entreaties had fallen on deaf ears. News had just arrived that Umesh and his wife had been converted to Christianity the previous evening.

Hearing this account, Debendranath was filled with fury. What was the country coming to? What was the worth of law in a land where the Supreme Court gave a ruling in favour of minors converting to another religion? He sent for his friend and employee, Akshay Datta, and commanded, 'Take up your pen and write a strong protest against the court ruling. Send it to all the papers. Our religion is in danger. We must act swiftly.' Next he sent for his carriage and visited all the important men of the city. 'The priests are converting our boys in large numbers,' he said. 'They do so by holding out hopes of free education. Something must be done to stop this menace. If we don't act now, there will be no Hindus left in our next generation.' Many of these men disliked Debendranath. He had hurt the sentiments of the conservative group by establishing the Dharma Sabha. But now, seeing his concern, they came forward to join hands with him. A few English-educated Hindus questioned the validity of the steps Debendranath proposed to take. 'Christianity is a great religion,' they argued. 'Why do you object to its proliferation? Besides, every man should be given the right to choose his own religion.'

'Christianity is a great religion,' Debendranath agreed. 'And every man should be given the right to choose his own religion. I admit both your arguments. The question, however, is different. Conversions are taking place among the very young; among those who have no knowledge of either religion—Hinduism or Christianity. They believe what the priests tell them—that our Vedas and Vedantas are primitive texts and our religion barbaric and ritual-ridden. That is why I call for a wider dissemination of Hindu philosophy. So that our boys know what they are leaving in favour of Christianity.' Impressed with his conviction and considered arguments, the city elders decided to open a Hindu seminary along the same lines as the Christian Mission schools. Here, boys would gain an education free of cost. There was talk of opening a girls' school as well but that was to come later. Money came pouring in. Forty thousand rupees were collected in one day at a meeting in Simulia. Debendranath's triumph was complete.

It was the month of Sravan.[20] Wearied by years of relentless pursuance of his goal, Debendranath decided to recover his health by taking the air of the Ganga. Hiring an enormous pinnace, he installed his wife, Sarada Devi, and his three sons, Dwijendra, Satyendra and Hemendra, in it. For himself he took a small boat. He travelled alone, keeping only Rajnarayan Basu with him. Rajnarayan had become a Brahmo a few months ago and was now Debendranath's boon companion and secretary. His English being extraordinarily good, he was given the responsibility of making drafts of Debendranath's views on current subjects and sending them to the English papers. In short, he did in English what Akshay Datta did in Bengali. Debendranath and Rajnarayan sat together all day, discussing a variety of subjects. In the evenings, Rajnarayan made his extracts, which, in turn, were discussed over a glass of wine just before the night meal.

A few days went by. The boats glided gracefully over the breast of the Ganga. Nabadweep and Patuli were left behind. His eyes on the declining sun, Debendranath said to Rajnarayan, 'It is time you made your notes for the day.' 'There's an hour or so of daylight left,' Rajnarayan answered, smiling, 'A great deal may happen in that time.' Even as he said this a small black cloud flew towards them from the west, as if on wings. The boatmen looked up in alarm. Seeing that a storm was imminent, Debendranath rose to his feet. 'Let us go to the pinnace,' he told Rajnarayan. 'The boat is not safe.' The boatmen proceeded to row the boat in the direction of the pinnace but before they could reach it the storm broke. Violent winds tore at the mast of the pinnace, snapping it in half. The broken mast, with one torn sail and festoons of rope, fell with a crash on the boat, pinning it down. Now the pinnace darted over the water with the speed of an arrow, pulling the rocking boat behind it. 'Fetch a chopper,' Debendranath shouted to the boatmen, 'and cut off the ropes.' But no chopper could be found in the confusion. Suddenly, an oar swung in his direction and hit Debendranath on the nose so hard that blood streamed from his

---

20 Mid-July—Mid-August.

nostrils. Debendranath looked on the heaving Ganga with eyes of despair as death stared him in the face.

In the meantime, someone found a knife and cut off the ropes. Released from the pinnace, the boat took a violent spin and was dashed against the sandy shore. The two men leaped out and were saved within an inch of their lives. The pinnace, with Debendra's wife and children in it, was carried away on the wings of the wind—no one knew where.

Suddenly, out of the dark, a dinghy appeared on the water and made straight for the shore where Debendranath stood with Rajnarayan. A man leaped out of the boat and handed a letter to Debendranath. It was Swarup—the khansama of the house of the Thakurs of Jorasanko. Debendranath read the letter by the flashes of lightning that burst from time to time out of a sky as black as pitch. 'We have just received the tragic news from England,' he read. 'Dwarkanath is no more.' Trembling violently, Debendranath would have fallen to the ground if Rajnarayan hadn't caught him in his arms. However, he pulled himself together in a few minutes and started planning his next move. He would go back home. He had heard, only the other day, that Dwarkanath's debts in the Calcutta markets had exceeded a crore. Creditors would be waiting to pounce on him. He had to be there to face them.

Debendranath left for Calcutta the next morning, braving the storm that raged on unabated. Reaching Palta he hired horses and drove them relentlessly through the night. The creditors hung like a pack of hungry wolves outside the house for the thirteen days of mandatory mourning, for Debendranath had told them that he would discuss no business till after the shraddha. But a storm awaited Debendranath at home as well. His uncle, Ramanath Thakur, said to him, 'The shraddha must be conducted according to Hindu rites. Dada was a great man and highly respected.'

'But I am a Brahmo,' Debendranath answered. 'I can't go against my own faith. I hold the Shalagramshila to be nothing more than a piece of stone. I shall perform the shraddha according to the Upanishads.'

'No, no,' Raja Radhakanta Deb intervened. 'You must not do anything Hindu law does not sanction. It is not seemly.

Besides, your father's soul will not be free till the appropriate rituals are conducted.'

Debendranath sent for his brother, Girindranath, and sought his opinion. Girindra was a Brahmo and his brother's follower. But now he advised caution. 'We will be cast out of our family and community if we insist on Brahmo rites,' he said. Debendra stared at him in surprise. What kind of country was this, he thought, in which religion and social commitment were treated as separate entities? Even Brahmo initiates feared social disapproval enough to compromise their faith. He withdrew into his own self and questioned his conscience over and over again. 'What shall I do? Shall I abandon my faith for fear of social disapproval?' One night he dreamed that his mother stood before him. 'I wanted to see you so much,' she said. 'You have risen above everybody. You have realized God. The family is blessed in a scion like you. Your mother is blessed in a son like you.' Debendranath woke up, trembling with joy.

On the day of the shraddha a huge atchala, a structure of bamboo and straw, was erected in the western court of the mansion in Jorasanko. Dwarkanath's sons were to perform Dan Sagar in his memory and the atchala was filled to overflowing with gold and silver. The priest sat in the centre, the Shalagramshila before him. At the appointed hour, Debendranath came in, his tall, fair form, wrapped in a silk shawl. He sat for a while, recited some shloks from the Upanishads, then rose and departed, ignoring the cries of his relatives. His brother, Girindranath, took his place before the sacrificial fire and the rites commenced. Debendranath had abandoned his birthright as the eldest son, to perform his father's shraddha. 'My clan and community may cast me out,' he said to himself. 'But God will receive me with all the more love.'

# Chapter XXII

All the nights in a man's life do not end with dawn. Occasionally, one of them may stop half-way at the command of time, which stands still and beckons . . .

Babu Ramkamal Singha lay in Kamala Sundari's arms in her house in Janbazar. A delicious languor crept over his limbs as, saturated with wine and love, he gazed deep into her eyes. Suddenly, he sat up with a shattering cry. 'I'm dying! O Kamal, I'm dying!' His arms flailed the bedclothes with the frenzy of a newly slaughtered goat. His spine arched into a bow and the saliva foamed at the corners of his mouth. Kamala screamed in terror and shook Ramkamal. '*O go*, Babu! What is to become of me? *O go*, to whom shall I turn? *O* Ma *go*!' On hearing her cries, her maids came running in. They were all young and pretty for Ramkamal hated wrinkles and grey hair in women. Some of them received his favours from time to time but these were passing fancies. He belonged heart and soul to Kamala Sundari. He had changed mistresses every year when he was younger but ever since he saw her, Kamala's dark beauty had held him in thrall. 'Kamal,' he often said in melting tones, 'you must come with me to Heaven when I die. I can't bear the thought of leaving you.' He had never doubted that he was going to Heaven. Alas! Who had ever thought to see him in this state?

Kamala stared wildly around her. Her musicians lay in a drunken stupor in the next room. Not all the cries in the world would awaken them. Unlike other prostitutes, Kamala had no mother and so, no one to depend upon for guidance and counsel. She looked with anxious eyes at her maid, Atar. Atarbala was very intelligent. She had wheedled a lot of money out of Ramkamal and was now the proud owner of a shack just outside the city, in which she carried on an independent business. Atar took in the situation in the twinkling of an eye and turning to Ramkamal's servant Dukhiram, who stood weeping helplessly, she cried, 'Oh, that a great man like him should die in a whorehouse! You oaf! You hulk! Is this the time for weeping? Take him home to his wife. Think of her humiliation if he dies here. And that of his sons.' Kamala was thoroughly alarmed at her words. Was Ramkamal dying? If so what would become of her? He hadn't made any provision for her as far as she knew. He said often enough that the house in Janbazar had been bought in her name. But where were the papers? She was a woman—helpless and dependent. What would she do if his sons threw her out? 'Stop, stop.' She ran after Dukhiram as he hastened out of the room. 'Stop a moment. My life is falling to pieces. Give me time to think. Babu is too ill to be moved. What if he dies in the carriage? Won't the blame fall on me?'

'So?' Atar snapped back. 'Shall a man of his standing die in the arms of a whore? Think of his prestige. Think of what the world will say.' At this moment, the tabla player, rudely woken out of a sweet slumber in which he dreamed that the dugi—the taller tabla—was his beloved, came in, rubbing his eyes. Taking in the situation, he cried, '*Arré! Arré!* Babu is sick to death and you haven't even sent for a doctor. Women's brains are always addled.' He ran out of the room to do the needful but, stumbling over the threshold, he fell in a heap and did not rise again.

A stone's throw away from Kamala Sundari's house stood the palatial mansion of Rajchandra Madh—one of the wealthiest men of the city. After his death his wife managed the estates, and so great was her wealth and power that people had dignified her with the title of Rani even though she was a Shudra by caste. Rani Rasmoni had a resident physician who, it was rumoured, was the divine physician, Dhanwantari, in human form. 'Go, fetch the kaviraj,' Kamala Sundari commanded her maids. 'If he refuses, fall at his feet and suck his toes. Do whatever he wants but don't come back without him.' The maids ran out of the room. Dukhiram left too. He had to go to Bidhusekhar. Only Ukil Babu would know what to do. Keeping to the darker lanes he ran on silent feet till he came to his destination. Once there he set up a howl that woke up the whole household. A light sleeper, Bidhusekhar was the first to come down. He heard Dukhiram's story from beginning to end, then sat still and thought for a while. Then, sending for the darwan, he ordered him to wake up the coachmen and get the stable doors open. Donning his clothes in a few minutes, he stepped into his phaeton and drove off in the direction of Janbazar. At the Chitpur crossing, he stopped the coachman with a sharp command. He looked for a few moments at the dark mass looming ahead of him. It was the Singha mansion. He wondered if he should give Bimbabati the news, then made up his mind and drove on. Arriving at Janbazar, Bidhusekhar walked straight into Kamala Sundari's chamber. Rani Rasmoni's kaviraj sat by the side of the bed, trying to feel the sick man's pulse without success, for Ramkamal threshed his limbs so violently that the old man had a hard time keeping his balance. Indeed, he was so old and frail that he seemed nearer Heaven than his patient. Now Bidhusekhar looked at Dukhiram and commanded in a loud voice, 'Hold the legs, Dukhi. I'll pin down the arms.' Then, without even turning his head towards the other occupants of the room, he ordered, 'Light a torch! This room is too dim.' Kamala Sundari gazed at Bidhusekhar with the eyes of a dumb animal. She knew everything about him even though she was seeing him for the first time. He was the supreme lord and master of the Singha household and soon he would hold her destiny too in the hollow of his hand. Bidhusekhar didn't even glance in her direction. His lip curled with disgust at being forced to enter this house of depravity and shame.

Putting down the wrist he had been holding, the kaviraj wagged his head from side to side. 'The end is near,' he murmured. 'The soul will leave its mortal frame in a few hours.' At these words, Kamala Sundari threw herself at the physician's feet. 'Save him, Kaviraj Moshai!' she cried wildly. 'I'll give you everything I have. All my money and jewels.' The old man withdrew his feet and said solemnly, 'I'm a physician. I heal the sick. I can't fight death.'

'Can I take him home, Moshai?' Bidhusekhar asked the old man. 'Will he survive the journey?'

The old man wagged his head again.

'Is there nothing you can do? To ease the pain?'

'No. He has been stricken with tetanus. Even Yama is fearful of this disease. His messengers are so nervous and hesitant that death is long drawn-out and painful. I can do nothing.'

'Can you bring him back to a conscious state? Even if it is for a few moments?'

'I can,' the kaviraj nodded, astonishing the room full of people. '*Suchikabharan* is easy. The rest is in God's hands.' The kaviraj touched something to the sick man's lips—something so potent that Ramkamal's limbs relaxed and his eyes opened almost instantly.

'Sri Hari! Durga! Sri Hari!' the old man chanted, with folded palms and closed eyes. Then, rising, he said, 'I'll leave now. I have nothing more to do here. Will someone show me out?'

Ramkamal murmured, 'Bidhu!' There was no sign of pain or suffering on his face. He glanced at the weeping Kamala and said tenderly, 'Don't be afraid, Kamala. Bidhu will look after you.' Then, turning to his friend, he said 'Bidhu! I'm leaving Kamala in your care. Don't abandon her.'

'I've come to take you home,' Bidhusekhar said. 'Bimbabati! Your sons, Ganga and Nabin! Don't you want to see them?'

Tears rolled down Ramkamal's cheeks. 'What day of the moon is it?' he asked.

'The eleventh.'

Ramkamal smiled. 'Bidhu,' he said. 'Do you remember what the astrologer said? The one in Kashi? He said I would go on Ekadasi.'

'Many Ekadasis will come and go. What is your hurry?'

'I've something to ask you. I may not get the time . . .'

Bidhusekhar raised his voice and commanded everyone to leave the room. 'Dukhi,' he called, glancing out of the corner of his eye at the weeping Kamala. 'Ask her to leave. I'm going to shut the door.'

'No,' Kamala raised a tear-streaked face. 'I won't go. I'm staying here.'

Bidhusekhar was so taken aback that, for the first time that evening, he looked directly into her face. Rage and revulsion swept through him. This woman, this low-born whore, had dispossessed Bimba! What did Ramkamal see in her? Her skin was as black as coal! As for her features, Bidhusekhar saw nothing extraordinary in them. She wasn't fit to be Bimba's slave. He glared at Kamala and she quailed under his glance. 'Leave the room,' he ordered severely. 'I want to be alone with my friend.' Not daring to disobey, Kamala Sundari left the room, shaking with sobs. Bidhusekhar placed a hand on

Ramkamal's forehead and said, 'Don't worry about anything. All will be well,'

'I knew death would come early in my life. I should have been prepared. But I'm not, Bidhu! I don't want to die. Life is too sweet.'

'You'll live, Ramkamal. Why do you say these things? Do you feel any pain?'

'The end is near, Bidhu, very near. There is something—something I must know before I die.'

'Do you want to make any changes in your will? The estates—'

'I leave all that to you.' Ramkamal's large, dark eyes rested on his friend's face. 'There is something else. It has been on my mind ever since . . . Tell me—my son, Nabin—I love him so! Is he mine?'

Bidhusekhar's heart quaked at these words. His face grew pale. He felt as if a roll of thunder had passed through his soul, shaking it down to its foundations. He opened his mouth to speak but only a hollow sound came through his lips.

'Who will light my funeral pyre, Bidhu?' Ramkamal whispered. 'Ganga? Or Nabin? Neither of them is mine—'

Now Bidhusekhar took hold of himself. 'What are you saying?' he cried. 'Nabin is the son of your seed. Bimbabati is the chastest and holiest of women. How can you doubt her?'

'Is he mine? Tell me the truth, Bidhu. Is he not your son?'

'*Chhi! Chhi!* Ramkamal. How can you even think such a thought?'

'I've been tortured by this fear all these years, Bidhu! There's a burning in my breast . . . All my life I've flitted from woman to woman but not one has carried my seed. Can it be possible that all—all of them were sterile? The fault must lie with me. Could Bimba—?'

'Take it as God's blessing that your only child was born out of your wife's womb; a wife as pure as Bimba—'

'Then Nabin is mine—not yours. Can you swear it?'

'I can. I'll put my hand on whatever you say—copper, tulsi or Gangajal—and swear that . . .'

'Put your hand on my head.'

'Here it is. Nabin is your son. Your blood flows through his veins. I have never touched Bimbabati except in blessing.'

'Ahh!' Ramkamal breathed a sigh of relief. 'My heart feels as light as a leaf. Bidhu, I long to see Nabin. I was a beast, an ingrate! I suspected Bimba and kept away from Nabin all these years.'

'I'll take you home.'

But the effect of the *suchikabharan* was over. Ramkamal's body contorted violently and his breath came in short guttural snarls. 'Tara! Tara! Brahmamayee!' Bidhusekhar chanted in the dying man's ears. He would have poured some Gangajal down the throat but where, in this whorehouse, would he find Gangajal? Ramkamal turned his face for the last time and resting his cheek on his friend's hand, died a peaceful death.

Now everyone came crowding into the room. Kamala Sundari flung herself on her protector's breast and set up a piercing wail. Her maids knocked their heads on the dead man's feet, weeping bitterly. Bidhusekhar looked around him, his nostrils flaring in disgust. He would take the body away without delay. No one must know that Ramkamal Singha had breathed his last in a harlot's bed. But rumours of a great man's death travel faster than men's thoughts. Within minutes, a crowd had collected outside Kamala Sundari's gate. Tottering above the other heads the human ladder, Raimohan Ghoshal. Bidhusekhar breathed a sigh of relief. He knew Raimohan to be a man capable of performing any task to perfection if it promised payment. Sending for him, Bidhusekhar said, 'Clear the room of these women. We must take Ramkamal home. The proper rites must be performed.' Raimohan's crocodile tears dried in an instant. He fell on the weeping women and dragged them out of the room.

Raimohan loved a house of death. Things lay scattered everywhere—an ideal situation for a man who lived by his wits. His greedy eyes darted here and there. Within minutes of his appearance on the scene, Kamala Sundari's chain of gold shells had left her neck and found its way into Raimohan's *jeb*. Elbowing everyone aside, Raimohan lifted Ramkamal's body and carried it to the carriage. Even as he did so, two large rings slid from the dead man's fingers and clinked merrily against Kamala's chain.

After all the rites were concluded, the house in Jorasanko truly became a house of death. Bidhusekhar had stood firm as a rock all these days. No one had seen a tear in his eye or any sign of weakness. He had made all the arrangements on the grandest scale the city of Calcutta had seen in many years. The newspapers had carried reports of the death and funeral for weeks and the Landholders Association had held a meeting of condolence. The whole city had been feasted. The effort had been too much even for Bidhusekhar. He had been taken ill and it was quite a few days before he came to Jorasanko again.

Bidhusekhar entered the house unannounced. As he walked down the verandah his eyes fell on Nabin, who sat playing in a corner with Dulal. The lines of his face softened and a little smile flickered on his lips. But he said nothing. He walked on till he came to the end of the verandah—to Bimbabati's room. Pausing at the door, he called softly, 'Bimba! Bimbabati!' The door opened and Chinta came out. Seeing Bidhusekhar, she bit her tongue and pulling the veil over her head, walked hastily away. Stepping into the room, Bidhusekhar's eyes fell on the newly widowed Bimbabati. His heart beat fast in shock and pity. The rippling river of silky black hair that had hung to her knees had disappeared, leaving a naked grey shell. Her arms, once weighed down with gold, were like carved marble, stark and pure, and the golden form, once draped in the finest muslins and balucharis, was wrapped in a white *than*. Bimba rose from the bed and came towards him. 'I'm an ill-fated, wretched woman,' she said. 'My son is an infant. I have no one to protect me.' Bidhusekhar took a step forward. 'I stayed away from you,' he said. 'I couldn't bear to see you like this. But you must know that, while I live, no harm can come to you.'

'You were unwell. I heard—'

'It was nothing. You must be strong, Bimba. You must take charge of the household. However, while I live—.'

'My son,' Bimba whispered, coming a little closer. 'He's the only light my dark life has known. He's everything to me. If anyone casts aspersions—'

'No one will ever know. Your husband believed what I told him and died in peace. The rest of the world will, too. Only you—you must be strong.'

Bimbabati's lips trembled and a shudder passed through her frame. She flung herself at Bidhusekhar's feet and wept, 'I can't. I'm weak—weak.'

'You can and will,' Bidhusekhar said firmly. 'I'll be with you, by your side, as long as I live. You are the jewel of my eyes, Bimba!' He raised Bimbabati from the ground and clasped her to his breast.

# Chapter XXIII

Goopi the goldsmith was a rich man now. He no longer sat working by lamplight far into the night. He had five or six craftsmen, whose work he supervised, sitting on a carpet and sucking at his *albola*. Goopi was monstrously fat and his skin shone with sugar and oil. The credit for it all went to Raimohan Ghoshal, who had got him contracts in rich men's houses.

Raimohan Ghoshal walked in, without banging his head. This shop was new and had a high ceiling. Belgian mirrors flashed from the walls and there was a tall iron gate. Goopi raised his vast bulk from the carpet in welcome. 'Come, come, Ghoshal Moshai,' he wheezed. '*O ré*, fetch the Brahmin's *albola*. And some paan. And take Goshal Moshai's shoes from him and keep them in a corner.' Raimohan crossed his legs comfortably and let out a loud belch. 'Send for some water, Goopi,' he commanded. 'My stomach is like a bag of wind from all the ghee I've been eating.'

'Who has been feeding you ghee, Ghoshal Moshai?'

'Rich men are dying like flies in the city. And the poor have to ruin their digestions with being fed at their funerals.'

'Why? Who's dead now?'

'Ramkamal Singhi. Weren't you invited to the shraddha?'

'Of course. He was a great man; a godly man. Understood good craftsmanship and was never one to haggle or drive a bargain.'

'True, true. He was the most generous man I've seen. Ever ready to give. Yet, the estates he left behind—'

'What else is going on in the city, Ghoshal Moshai?'

'All the young men are turning Christian. There won't be a Hindu left in the country. As for these Pirili Brahmins—they are worse than Christian priests. Deben Thakur says our gods and goddesses are nothing but pieces of stone. And our Vedas—'

'*Chhi! Chhi! Chhi*!'

'Did you know, Goopy, Dwarkanath Thakur—God rest his soul—lies buried in a foreign land? Thousands of *mlechhas* walk over him with shoes on—day and night. And Deben didn't even perform the proper rites over his father's body.'

*'Chhi! Chhi! Chhi!'*

'He says the caste system must go. Shudras should be allowed to read the Vedas and Brahmins and untouchables should eat together.'

A torrent of *chhis* issued from Goopy's lips. The shop assistants had stopped their work a long while back and now sat staring at Raimohan with round eyes, gobbling up his words. Raimohan turned to them. 'What are you doing here, my sons?' he enquired kindly, then added, 'Go home. Go home.' After they left, Goopi pulled down the shutters and settled down comfortably.

'Ghoshal Moshai!' he said. 'I saw the strangest sight today. A little creature, no bigger than a doll, with a yellow skin and a long plait, came into my shop. I don't know if it was a man or a woman. *Tuk tuk tuk*, it tottered on its tiny feet. And *ching chang chung*, it spoke in the drollest way you've ever heard.'

'That was a Chinaman, Goopy. Haven't you seen one before? There are quite a few in the city. They've set up a machine for making sugar.'

'This one was selling lanterns.'

'They've come from China—a faraway country beyond the Himalayas. They look exactly like one another—men and women. Each like another's twin. A country full of twins. Ha! Ha! Ha!'

'What a frightening thought! How did they come? Did they jump across?'

'No one can jump across the Himalayas. Lord Shiva and his attendants stand guard over them day and night. They come on ships. Rustomji's ships sail to China and back. So many people come to our city. The other day I saw one as black as a bat's wing. He was a Kafri. Then there are Greeks from Sikander Shah's country. Have you heard of Sikander Shah? No? You're a nitwit, Goopi! Greeks are even bigger and stronger than Mughals and Pathans. Everyone wants to come to Calcutta. Even the Russians.'

'Russians?'

'From Russia—where the best brandy is brewed. Someone

was talking about it the other day in Jagamohan Sarkar's house. Even the English are afraid of the Russians, he said.'

'Why?'

'It is rumoured that the Russians are going to fight the English and take over our country. The Russians are very brave. Even Nepo could not defeat them.'

'Who is Nepo?'

'Nepo was a Frenchman. Haven't you seen Frenchmen? In Chandannagar? Nepo was like a giant in size and he ate live human beings—skin, bones, hair and all. All the other sahebs feared him. But not the Russian sahebs.'

'Then they will be our new masters. What will become of us, Ghoshal Moshai?'

'Nothing, Goopi. We'll be exactly where we are. Kings may lose or win wars but the lot of the poor never changes. Now for business—'

'Have you brought anything?'

Raimohan took out his *jeb* and poured its contents into Goopi's palm—a chain of gold shells and two rings with large stones in them. Goopi turned them over in his hand and said, 'They look familiar. I fashioned the chain myself.'

'It's my grandmother's. I found it while rummaging among her things. How could you fashion it? You're getting short-sighted, Goopi.'

'The rings, too,' Goopi murmured, not daunted.

'They're my grandfather's,' Raimohan said firmly.

'But I recognize them. I set the stones myself. This stone, now—Palmerstone Company started selling these only two years ago.'

'*Arré*, Palmerstone was my grandfather's company. Didn't you know that? Come, don't waste time talking. Weigh them. Weigh them.'

This battle of wits went on for a little longer. Then, the deal concluded, Raimohan thrust his earnings for the day into his *jeb* and rose. The two left the shop together.

Like other rich men of the city, Goopi now kept a mistress in Rambagan. He longed to show her off to Raimohan and take his opinion, for Raimohan was an expert in these matters. At Goopi's request, Raimohan agreed to accompany him. Rambagan slept under the sun all day and stayed awake all night under the stars. With dusk the houses were flooded with light and the air resounded with strains of song, the tinkle of ankle bells and loud, raucous laughter. The house Goopi entered had an open drain in front of it, beside which lay a young man, sodden with liquor. Flies buzzed around his open mouth but he didn't twitch a muscle. Walking past him, Goopi entered the door and walked up the stairs where Chunni Bai alias Padmabala waited. She was fat and round and looked exactly like Goopi.

Padmabala poured brandy for the men and sang two passionate love songs. Her voice, Raimohan thought, was exactly like the bleating of a goat being led to the slaughterhouse. His mouth twitched in amusement. He hobnobbed with expensive, exclusive women—reared for the rich and powerful—and he had no use for such as this one. Goopi, for all his money, was a miser. This was as far as he could get. Nevertheless, Raimohan winked at Goopi in appreciation, as if to say, 'Not bad. Carry on, my son.' Tucking the bottle of brandy under his arm, he rose to leave. He would die if he had to hear another song. Whatever else may be said of him, Raimohan's taste in music was of the highest order.

Coming out of the house, he passed by the drunk who lay exactly in the same position. Raimohan tried to raise him to his feet but he was too heavy. Slapping him smartly on the cheeks, Raimohan shouted in his ear, '*Ei*! *Ei*! Get up.'

'Bu bu bu.' A froth, reeking of liquor, formed on the drunk's mouth. He rolled further away, almost to the edge of the drain. 'Want some brandy?' Raimohan shouted. This did the trick. The young man opened his eyes and crooking his fingers as if he held a glass, said clearly, 'Yes, give it.' Raimohan poured some neat brandy down his throat. The man sat up, coughing and wheezing, as some of the fiery liquid entered his windpipe. 'Where am I?' he asked. 'Come, brother,' Raimohan said kindly. 'Let me take you home.' The man heaved himself to his feet and leaning heavily on Raimohan's shoulder, started walking down the road.

'Give me more brandy,' he said. 'Here it is.' Raimohan put the bottle in his hand.

'Who are you? An angel?'

'Of course. Don't I took like one? What's your name?'

'Harachandra Samanta.' He continued in English, 'Your most obedient servant. Allow me to take the dust of your feet.'

'Hunh! You've got some learning in your belly, I see. What were you doing by the drain? If I hadn't picked you up, the jackals would have been gnawing at your flesh by now. Where do you live?'

'Nowhere.'

'What do you do?'

'Drink.'

Raimohan had a soft corner for young men like this one—homeless waifs, unloved and uncared for, wild and free. Men like Harachandra never hurt anybody. They only played fast and loose with their own lives.

Raimohan had been living in Heeremoni's house since the day he had found her lying on the floor in a death-like state. He had nursed her back to health and looked after her child. Now, after regaining her full measure of strength and beauty, Heeremoni had taken up her business once again. Though Raimohan had adopted her boy, Chandranath never called him 'father'. Heeremoni would not allow it.

An elegant carriage stood outside Heeremoni's door and sounds of music and laughter floated out of the windows. Harachandra paused at the threshold and asked, 'Whose house is this?'

'What is that to you? You need a roof above your head. I'm giving you one.'

'I don't step into strange houses. Why have you brought me here? To rob me? I've told you I have nothing—nothing. I'm as sucked out as a mango stone.'

'I knew that the moment I saw you.' Raimohan dragged the young man into a tiny room under the stairs. Raimohan had cleaned it out himself and used it as a hideout when Heeremoni had customers. Pushing Harachandra on the bed of wooden boards, he said, 'Rest here. I'll give you food if you want it. But don't make a sound.'

'I want more brandy.'

'I'll give it to you. But sleep for a while first.' He cocked a ear at the strains of music that came pouring down the stairs. A smile of pure happiness lit up Raimohan's face. Heeremoni was singing a song he had written and set to music. How rich and deep her voice was! And how chiselled her technique! Heeremoni was the finest singer in Calcutta these days and the most sought after. Her admirers had a new name for her—a name that suited her to perfection. Heera Bulbul!

# *Chapter XXIV*

Bidhusekhar sat in Bimbabati's chamber, reading out Ramkamal Singha's will to his widow and sons. Nabin was only six. He had little idea of what was going on. Nevertheless, he sat very quietly by his mother's side, his glittering eyes fixed on Bidhusekhar's face. Ganga sat on the floor, his chin resting on his knees and his back against the wall. Although the one-month mourning period was over, Ganga wore no shirt under his tussar uduni. Both the boys had shaven heads. Ganga's was bare while Nabin's was covered with a red velvet cap. Ganga looked away out of the window. He couldn't bear the sight of Bidhusekhar these days. All his love and respect for his father's friend had crumbled to dust.

Bidhusekhar cleared his throat in preparation and said, 'I have something important to communicate to you, Ganga. We have kept it a secret all these years. But you are an adult now and well educated. It is not right that your true parentage be kept from you any longer. You are not the son of Ramkamal's seed. You were not born out of Bimbabati's womb. Being childless at the time, they adopted you and reared you as their own. Nabin is their only child. It is he who bears the Singha blood in his veins—' Bidhusekhar shot a glance at Bimbabati but the veil was pulled down to her breast and he couldn't see her face. Ganga looked down at the floor. Bidhusekhar's communication had not come as a surprise. He had no memories of his own parents. He had known only Ramkamal and Bimbabati. But after Nabin Kumar's birth, his true parentage had been revealed to him through servants' gossip and the sympathetic anticipations of poor relations. The revelation had had little effect on him. Ramkamal and Bimbabati had continued to love him as much as ever and he had felt secure in their love.

'I'm making this communication today with a purpose,' Bidhusekhar continued ponderously. 'You must know that the bulk of a man's estate passes to his blood heirs even if there are adopted children. I'm preparing you for disappointment, Ganga. According to Ramkamal's will, your share in your father's property is much less than Nabin's.' Ganga looked up and said quietly, 'Nabin is my brother. Let him have it all—even my share. I don't mind in the least.'

'Ganga!' Bimbabati called, softly touching his arm.

'Ma!' Ganga put his hand on her feet.

Silence fell between them. Bidhusekhar sniffed. He disliked emotional scenes. He commenced reading the will as if there had been no interruption. The will was not long. Of Ramkamal's inherited property, one fifth went to his widowed sister-in-law, Hemangini Devi, and the rest to his successors. Out of his self-created assets, which included zamindari taluks in seven parganas, seven mansions in the city, quite a few bighas of land, three business houses, one ship, two collieries and ten lakh rupees worth of gold and gems, only one house and one pargana were left to Ganganarayan. All the rest, barring certain small sums of money left to the servants, was Nabin Kumar's. Ganga's eyes burned and hot tears sprang into them. His heart swelled with self-pity. He wondered why he felt like that. He had never cared for property and riches. He was well educated. He could earn all the money he needed. The British government had changed its policy and was now offering jobs to educated natives. Many of Ganga's friends were deputy collectors now. Why did he feel so shattered? Was Ramkamal's love for Ganga only a pretence, he thought? Was that why Ganga's share was just a little more than a servant's? It would have been far better for Ganga if his father had cut him off completely.

Little Nabin's bright eyes darted from this face to that. Though only an infant, he understood that he was to share something with Ganga. 'Who gets more?' he asked in his high, sweet voice. 'Dadamoni? Or I?'

'You,' Bidhusekhar answered gravely.

'I get more! I get more!' Nabin clapped his hands in delight. 'Dadamoni has lost. I've won.'

'Which will is this?' Bimbabati raised her eyes to Bidhusekhar's. 'It was different—'

'Ramkamal changed his will last month. He may have forgotten to tell you.'

Ganga's eyes blazed with indignation. He knew that

Bidhusekhar had engineered the change. He had a great deal of power over his father and he had used it against Ganga. Bidhusekhar had loved Ganga once but now he hated him. He was a hard, cruel man and he had devised this method of punishing Ganga! 'I challenge this will,' he was about to shout angrily but he checked himself in time. Bidhusekhar was an astute lawyer. He must have taken care of all the loopholes. Ganga knew he was no match for Bidhusekhar! He turned to his mother and said, 'Ma! Let Nabin have everything. I'll leave the house tomorrow.' Bimba clasped Ganga to her breast and wept. 'I'll die if you leave me, Ganga. I don't care what is written in the will. I have two sons and they will inherit equally. You are Nabin's elder brother. You should be his guardian.'

'Bouthan,' Bidhusekhar could hold himself no longer. 'Money and estates are not toys to be given away on a whim. We must respect Ramkamal's will. I suggest we give Ganganarayan his share and let him go.'

Bimbabati's head shot up angrily. For the first time in her life the gentle, soft-spoken Bimba found the courage to contradict Bidhusekhar. 'Ganga will stay in this house as long as I live. Nabin is a minor. Who will look after his property?'

'You and I,' Bidhusekhar answered. 'It is written in the will.'

'Ganga will represent me in everything. Prepare the papers accordingly.' Then, turning to Ganga, she said, 'I swear on my head, Ganga, that you and Nabin are equal in my eyes. You are both my sons; two halves of my heart. You must never forget that.'

Bidhusekhar looked on in sullen silence. This was a mess. Ganga had no legal rights over the property but, as a trustee, he could prove a thorn in Bidhusekhar's side. As for Ganga, he welcomed the turn of events. All his life he had squirmed under Bidhusekhar's power over him. He would do all he could to curb that power. Frustrating Bidhusekhar in all his endeavours would be Ganga's aim in life from now onwards. Bidhusekhar looked at Ganga with hatred in his eyes. 'Go out of the room, Ganga,' he said. 'And take your brother with you. I have something to say to Bouthan.'

After the boys left, Bidhusekhar and Bimbabati sat in silence for a while. Bidhusekhar's breast heaved with indignation. Bimbabati had humiliated him. She had flouted his command.

He could hardly believe it even now. 'You are being foolish, Bimba,' he began aggressively. 'Ramkamal's estate is worth a king's ransom. Even real brothers would quarrel over such a huge property. And Ganga is an outsider.'

'Don't say that. Ganga is my son. He loves Nabin.'

'People change. How can you be sure that he will continue to do so? I wanted to get him out of the way for Nabin's sake. Nabin is my son and—'

'You promised never to utter those words again. If someone overhears—'

'I won't, ever again. But—'

'It is not proper that we converse together in private. The boys are growing up.'

'Are you asking me to stop coming to the house?'

'No. I feel insecure in your absence. But it looks better if a third person is with us when we are together.'

'Bimba! Don't you love me any more?'

At this question, Bimba flung herself on the ground, weeping. Bidhusekhar raised her to her feet and said tenderly, 'You are so good and beautiful, Bimba! Ramkamal did not value you as he should have done. But I? I knew where your sorrow lay. You wanted a son. I gave you one. Was that a sin? I've never performed an immoral act in all my life except for what I did for your sake. But even that did not spring from lust or greed. It was my duty as a Brahmin. If a woman's husband is unable to give her a child, she is justified in seeking it from a Brahmin. Our traditions endorse such a coming together. We have not sinned, Bimba. Cast out all guilt and fear from your heart.' Bimba went on weeping unrestrainedly. 'I loved Ramkamal,' Bidhusekhar continued. 'He had many good qualities. But I can never forgive his treatment of you. He rejected you, my beautiful, golden Bimba, and gave himself up to a dust heap. I'll make that bitch pay for it. I'll drive the filthy whore out of the house, into the street. There is no mention of her in the will.'

Bimba wiped her tears and said huskily, 'Let her stay. It is only one house. We have so many.'

'What are you saying? Shall I give up a house for a common prostitute? She must have changed hands seven times before she came to Ramkamal.'

'Never mind. My husband was fond of her. He bought the

house for her. Besides, it was a dom's house—so I've heard. It will be of no use to me.'

'It wasn't a dom's house,' Bidhusekhar smiled. 'It belonged to a *firinghee* called Dom Antony. Anyway, we aren't planning to live there. It will fetch a good rent. That woman is a siren. She turns men into sheep. I'll drive her out this very week.'

Bidhusekhar had his first clash with Ganganarayan over this issue. Bidhusekhar's first move was to send four armed guards, led by Dibakar, to bully and frighten Kamala Sundari into leaving the house. 'You may expect a substantial reward,' he told the old retainer, 'once the task is accomplished.' At the mention of a reward Dibakar swung into action. Arriving at Janbazar, he pushed and pummelled the maids and swore at the musicians so viciously that they ran scurrying like rats into the streets. But he stopped short at the sight of Kamala Sundari. Kamala sat on a grass mat in the centre of the hall. She was wrapped in a white *than* and not a speck of gold adorned her person. She was the image of a newly widowed Hindu woman. Every line of her face proclaimed her loss.

'Who is it?' Kamala raised a tear-streaked face at the sound of footsteps. Dibakar stared. He couldn't believe his eyes. Kamala had always worn the most vibrant colours and her jewels had become heavier and more ostentatious with her increasing fame as a dancer. He had never heard of a whore turning herself into a widow on the death of a babu. They generally geared up to catch a new one even before the ashes had cooled.

'B-Bara[21] Babu sent me,' he stammered.

'Who is Bara Babu?'

'The gentleman who was here the other day. Our Babu's friend. He is our master now. He said . . .'

'I know only one master. And he has gone away from me. I know no other.'

'Our Babu—God rest his soul—has gone to heaven. Bidhu Mukherjee has taken his place. He commands you to leave the house immediately.'

'Leave the house? And go where? This is my house.'

---

21 Elder.

'There are no papers to prove it. Babu left you nothing in his will. You'll have to fend for yourself.'

'I won't go.'

'Don't be stubborn, girl. You don't know Bidhu Mukherjee. He can crush you like an ant.'

'My Babu died in this house. I will, too. You can have it after I'm dead.'

'Tchk! Tchk! Why do you talk of dying? Your whole life is before you. If you don't see reason, my girl, I'll have to use force.' He took a couple of steps into the room.

'Don't dare touch me!' Kamala stood up in a flash. Her eyes glittered like a wild cat's. 'I'll swallow poison and die in this house. But I won't walk out of the door. See there—' She pointed to a small packet, lying near the mat.

Dibakar was really frightened now. If she did as she threatened, he would be in deep trouble. Bidhusekhar would be the first to denounce him. He stood his ground, however, and said in a voice he strove to control, 'I give you two days to make your arrangements. I'll come again the day after tomorrow. You'll have to leave—whether you like it or not.'

Returning to Jorasanko, he found Bidhusekhar and Ganganarayan poring over a pile of old papers. Bidhusekhar heard Dibakar's account with attention and commented, 'You did well in not using force. We'll have to start legal proceedings. I'll send someone to the court tomorrow morning.'

'Why,' Ganga said angrily, 'she has no right to be there. Why should we bother ourselves with courts and lawyers? I'll drive her out myself.'

'No, no. You don't have to go there.'

'Why not? It is our house.'

'Let the slut leave first.'

But Ganga made it a point to disobey Bidhusekhar. He went to Janbazar that very evening—alone.

# Chapter XXV

Once again, Ramkamal Singha's carriage stood outside Kamala Sundari's house. From the day the house had been bought, four years ago, the enormous equipage, bearing the Singha crest, had rolled up there every evening and stood outside the gate. It was carved out of black mahogany and its brass fittings shone like gold. The horses were milk white and wore saddles, embossed with silver. Up on the box, reins in hand, sat the coachman in the splendid livery of a Mughal cavalryman while on the pedestal behind stood tall, turbaned footmen, ready to leap down and open the door for their master. Leaning heavily on their shoulders, Ramkamal would alight, his huge swaying figure resplendent in velvet and gold. From behind his thick moustaches, his sensual lips would smile benignly and his heavy feet walk in a measured tread.

But the figure that leaped out of the carriage that evening was young and slight; in a puckered dhoti and banian of China silk. The coachman yelled after him as he walked rapidly into the house, 'Babu's son, *go*! Babu's eldest son, *go*! Move away, everyone. Knock your heads on the ground! Babu's eldest son!' Ignoring the greetings of the people around him, Ganga ran nimbly up the stairs. It was the first time he had stepped into a house of ill repute and he felt sick with shame and disgust. Scions of wealthy families like himself kept mistresses as a rule, it being considered low and vulgar to sleep night after night with one's wife. But the boys of Hindu College had rejected this fashion and pledged themselves to a clean and austere mode of life. Ganga's friends shared his distaste for low women.

Ganga stepped into the audience hall. It looked curiously clean and bare—as if someone had scoured it out only a short while ago. A single couch stood in the middle of a neatly carpeted floor. All the paraphernalia of music and dance had vanished. So had the musicians. In fact, there was no sign of male occupation in the house. Three maids, young, fresh and prettily dressed, stood in various poses, as if waiting for Ganga.

They came forward at his entrance and exclaimed in one voice, 'What great good fortune is ours! You have graced our house with the dust of your feet!' Taking Ganga by the hand, they led him in and seated him on the couch. One knelt at his feet and loosened the laces of his shoes, another held a marble urn brimming with a creamy concoction to his lips.

'What is this?' Ganga asked, alarmed.

'Pistachio sherbet.' The girl flashed a dazzling smile at Ganga. 'You are tired and thirsty. A little—'

'I'm not thirsty.' Ganga waved it away. The third girl held out an *albola* whose long pipe was coiled in silver. 'I don't smoke,' Ganga said shortly. Then the three girls spoke again, as if with one voice, 'We are your slaves. Command us.' The prettiest of the three brought her lips to Ganganarayan's ear and whispered, 'Shall I open a bottle of champagne?' Ganga's ears flamed and he trembled with shame and fury. 'What is all this?' he said roughly. 'I've come to see your mistress. Send her to me.'

'Our mistress won't come. She locked herself in the minute she saw you.'

'Why won't she come?'

'You're her son. How can she come to you?' Ganga stood up. 'I have some business with her,' he said severely. 'Send her to me immediately.'

'Aha! Aha! Why do you lose your temper? We are weak women, Babu, and dependent on you for our support. Our hearts quake with fear when we see you angry. See for yourself. Put your hand here.' One of the women seized Ganga's hand and pressed it on her luxuriant breasts. 'If you frighten us like this, our hearts may stop beating altogether and we may drop down and die. Then the blame will fall on you.'

Ganga felt trapped. He wanted to run away out of the room, beyond the reach of these disgusting women. But he knew that if he did so, they would burst into peals of mocking laughter. Why should he, scion of the house of Singhas, make himself a laughing stock for these street women? Why should he run away from his own property? Turning to the coachman who stood at the door, he said gravely, 'Go find the mistress of the house, Karim Baksh, and send her to me.' Even as he said these words, a side door opened and Kamala Sundari stood in the room. She was wrapped in widow white and her arms and neck were bare. Her hair was open and streamed down her back, thick and black. Ganga stared at her. He had built up a mental image of her from what he had heard all these years. He had imagined her to be a portly, middle-aged woman, glittering with jewels, her eyes lined with kohl and lips stained with betel. He had hated her for the unhappiness caused to his mother. But this—this girl was even younger than himself. She was Bindu's age and in her widow's weeds she reminded him, with a stab of pain, of Bindu.

Kamala's eyes held Ganga's for a long while. 'You are Ganga,' she said softly, hesitantly. 'I've heard so much about you. What a great scholar you are! And so kind-hearted! I'm blessed that I've lived to see this day.' Ganga stood staring at her, speechless with amazement. 'I know I stand neck deep in sin,' she continued in that soft, sweet voice. 'Even hell is too good for me. But as God is my witness, I was as faithful to your father as few women in the world are to their wedded husbands. I looked on him as my sole lord and master. I knew no other.' Pausing to dash away the tears that poured down her cheeks, she continued, 'I'm a weak, defenceless woman—cursed by fate from the moment of my birth. Abandoned by my lord, floundering in this ocean of sorrow, to whom can I turn? He breathed his last here, in that room. "I'm going, Kamal", he said. "Don't leave the house. I'll watch over you from Heaven". I haven't crossed the threshold since that night. A storm rages in my breast day and night. Looking at you he comes back to me so vividly! The same eyes; the same expression!'

Ganga sighed. Many people said he resembled his father. They didn't know Ganga was only an adopted son. 'He died in this house,' Kamala continued. 'This house is, for me, the holiest of pilgrimages. This is my Kashi; this my Brindavan. I'll stay here to the end of my days, worshipping his memory.' Again, Ganga was reminded of Bindubasini. She had been sent away from the home she loved, only because she was young and helpless and couldn't fight her persecutor. Would Ganga ever see her again? 'The guards may hack my body to pieces,' Kamala Sundari went on. 'They may torture me in any way they please but they won't get me out.' Seeing that Ganga was still silent, she changed her tone. 'Do you want me to leave the house, Ganga?' she asked in a normal, everyday voice. 'Have you come to drive me out? You're embarrassed to say so, aren't you? And that is why you are silent. Say the word and I'll go, this instant, just as I am. None of you will ever see me again. I know I'm lower than a worm and God will strike me dead for saying this. I look on you as my son, Ganga. I can do whatever you command me. If you send me to hell—I'll go, willingly.'

Ganga stood up. 'Ma,' he said, his voice choking with emotion. 'You will stay where you are. No power on earth can drive you out.'

'Ma! You called me Ma!' Kamala laughed and wept hysterically. 'Oh! Sinner that I am, you called me Ma. Listen, everybody! My son called me Ma. I'm saved! I'm pure and whole again.' She wrung Ganga's hand with both hers. Tears of ecstasy ran down her cheeks.

Bidhusekhar and Ganganarayan sat together for a few hours every morning. Ganga had expressed a desire to learn the affairs of the estate and Bidhusekhar was instructing him. The discussions were practical and businesslike—love and respect having faded from both sides. 'Now that you have some idea of the extent and position of your father's estate,' Bidhusekhar remarked drily, 'you should see them with your own eyes. I suggest you begin with a tour of Ibrahimpur. The peasants there are an unruly lot. It might be a good idea to sell the indigo fields to the British. We'll never be able to compete with them.'

'Let me see. I'll decide when I get back.' Then, suddenly, abruptly, Ganga dropped the bombshell. 'We are surrendering the house in Janbazar,' he said quietly.

'The house in Janbazar! Which house? The one your father bought from Dom Antony?'

'Yes. It wasn't bought for us. My father left it to someone else.'

'Left it to someone else! There are no papers to prove it.'

'No, but he gave a verbal promise and that is enough for me.'

'Forget about verbal promises. No one gives up a valuable property like that for a whore to enjoy. Now, if it was donated to a religious institution—'

'I've given my word.'

'To whom?' Bidhusekhar's lips curled in derision. 'Are you visiting brothels these days?'

'Yes.' Ganga's eyes pierced Bidhusekhar's. 'I'm not forsworn in this respect—to you or to anyone else.' Ganga turned to leave the room.

'Come back,' Bidhusekhar commanded in a voice of thunder. 'You say you've given your word. On whose permission? What right have you over the property?'

'Ma gave her consent,' Ganga said in a voice that, though soft, was as firm as steel. 'She said we didn't need it. We are not so poor that we must squeeze the honey out of a bee's stomach.'

'Your mother always consults me before taking a decision.'

'Khuro Moshai, you know I never lie. You can ask her if you like.' He turned to leave the room.

'Wait. Even if your mother said that it was out of ignorance. I say that the property is ours and will remain so.'

'I, too, have a right to some decisions. At least, while my mother lives. That is the text of the document, is it not? If her feelings towards me change, if she loses faith in me I'll leave the house at once.'

Losing control, Bidhusekhar shouted, 'Insolent boy! You dare contradict me? Your mother will do as I say.'

'I'm not so sure. You may try to dissuade her.'

'The venomous snake! The filthy harlot!' Bidhusekhar muttered. 'Don't I know she's set herself up for sale already? That son of a pig, Jagamohan Sarkar, goes to her every night. Everything reaches my ears. Why should we give up a house for her? Never!'

Ganga stood silent. Kamala Sundari's form rose before his mind's eye—pure and chaste in her widow's than. That wasn't Kamala. That was Bindu!

'I've given my word. That house is hers.' Turning, he walked rapidly out of the room. His breast heaved with powerful feelings. A heady triumph was uppermost. He had fought Bidhusekhar and vanquished him. He had avenged Bindu's disgrace. He called for his carriage. He would go to Debendranath Thakur's house, where the Brahmos were to congregate that evening. His friend, Rajnarayan, had invited him to attend the meeting. Ganga liked the Brahmos. They were intellectuals, austere and high-principled and they involved themselves in many good works. Ganga was often tempted to join their ranks. But he couldn't. His mother, Bimbabati, would have no objection to his keeping a mistress but she would die of heartbreak were he to become a Brahmo. 'Brahmos are atheists,' she had said on one or two occasions. 'To have an atheist son is a fate worse than death.' When Ganga had attempted an explanation, she had covered up her ears with her hands and cried, 'No. No. Don't say a word. Even to listen to such blasphemy is a sin.' Ganga was powerless. He wouldn't, couldn't ever cause unhappiness to Bimbabati.

# Chapter XXVI

That great champion of female liberation, Jagamohan Sarkar, sat in Heeremoni's reception room, weeping copious tears. The night was far advanced as was the state of his inebriation. Heeremoni knew from experience that this was the second stage. The first was a series of thundering belches; the second of tears and self-recrimination. The third was at hand. In another half-hour, Jagamohan would pass out and she would be free.

'Heere!' Jagamohan's vast body rocked with grief and tears rolled down his chin. 'What a worthless creature I am! What have I done with my life? Nothing. Nothing.'

Heeremoni suppressed a yawn and said, 'You've made a lot of money. You've bought houses, carriages—'

Jagamohan wrung Heeremoni's hand and cried out in agony, 'What good will they do me? I bought a new house only last month. But it won't go with me to Heaven, will it?'

'You've given away large sums in charity—'

Jagamohan felt comforted. 'I've never stinted anyone, have I, Heere?' he asked, gathering her in his arms. 'Haven't I always given you whatever you've wanted?'

'That you have. My tongue will fall out if I deny it.'

'Only last week I gave you a pair of bracelets. Surodasi got a ring and Kamala a moon necklace.'

'You love Kamala more than me,' Heeremoni said, pouting and tossing her head.

'She's an arrogant wench. She's turned herself into a widow after Ramkamal Singha's death. Have you heard of anything so funny? A whore turned widow.'

Heeremoni gave him a little push in pretended indignation. 'If she's your favourite, why do you come to me?'

'*Arré, na na,*' Jagamohan drew her closer. 'Can Kamli sing like you? Is her skin like yours—all milk and vermilion? It is you I love. But I need Kamli. Do you know why? Because she's the most sought after whore in the city. All the great men are fighting over her. If I win—what a victory that will be! But she's a cunning bitch. She took the moon necklace as coolly as you please, then sent a couple of women, uglier than sin, to pleasure me. "Call Kamala", I said. "I want to see her". "She won't come today", one of the she demons simpered. "Today is Ekadasi". Have you heard of anything like it, Heere? Can you blame me if my blood boiled with fury?'

'*O go! Na na*. Ah! The wicked harlot! To humble a great man like you and send you away! Don't cry, Babu, don't cry. The bitch will be licking your feet in a couple of days. You wait and see.' Heere stroked Jagamohan's head and clicked her tongue in sympathy.

'Becha Mallik is after Kamli. Did you know that, Heere?' Jagamohan rubbed his face on Heeremoni's strong young breasts. 'Can I bear to lose her to a worthless fellow like that? A moneylender and a cheat! Who knows Becha Mallik? What does he have except his money? And I? I write articles in the newspaper. I'm opening a girl's school.'

'You're opening a school?' Heere's eyes shone with eagerness. 'Then take my son—' The words were out before she could stop them.

'Your son?' Jagamohan sat up with a jerk. His eyes grew round with surprise. 'I didn't know you had a son!'

Heeremoni had kept her motherhood a secret for it was considered improper for a prostitute to give birth to a male child. It was even more improper to admit it to one's customers. But Heere's maternal feelings were getting stronger every day. She thought of her child day and night. Even while sleeping with a babu, her son's face came before her eyes. He was such a beautiful boy and so clever! The young man Raimohan had brought into the house was drunk half the time. But he seemed to be well educated. *God mad sad*, he jabbered in English. He was teaching Chandranath. Heere's heart was fit to burst with pride when she saw her son sitting on his little mat and learning by rote. '*Sasha*—cucumber; *chasha*—ploughman; *cumra*—pumpkin.' '*O go*,' She would chide Raimohan from time to time. 'Chandu is so clever. Why don't you send him to school?' 'They'll ask his father's name. And you won't disclose it. What can I do?' Raimohan would shrug his shoulders in helpless resignation.

'How old is your son?' Jagamohan asked cautiously.

'Eight or nine.'

Jagamohan stared at Heeremoni, his drunken eyes taking in every line of her face and form. She wore a tight kanchuli and ghagra tonight, like the prostitutes of the west. Her skin shone like silk, her eyes were jewel bright and her breasts tilted upwards as if in arrogant defiance. The wine of youth coursed through her body. Looking at her no one would imagine that she was a mother.

'Where is your son?'

'In the room downstairs.'

'Doos! Of all the—! Lay my head on your bosom, Heere, and rock me to sleep.'

Heere did as she was commanded. Jagamohan's eyes closed in delicious languor but Heeremoni wouldn't let him off so easily. 'Why don't you take my son in your school?' she repeated, patting his head as one would a child's.

'Silly girl! What will your son do with an education? He's not going to raise a family.'

'He can be a babu in the saheb's office.'

'Heh! Heh! Heh! A whore's son a babu in an office! He'll never have the brains for it.'

'You don't know. He's very clever. He can write his own name.'

'That's quite enough for him. Let him train to be a wrestler or, better still, a tabla player.'

'Try him out, Babu.'

'*Arré*, my school is for girls. There are scores of boys' schools in the city. I have nothing to do with them.'

'For girls? Will girls walk down the road and go to school? They will lose caste—'

'No, no. Times are changing. Girls will come to my school in dozens. Little girls—soft and pretty as flowers. Fresh, sweet and fragrant. They'll laugh and sing and dance. I'll take them out of their dark ignorance and show them the light of knowledge. Ahaha! How I'll love them.'

Jagamohan pressed his face deep into Heeremoni's breasts and drooled with pleasure.

# Chapter XXVII

Bidhusekhar was up at dawn. He had been sleeping apart from his wife for the last few years for he liked his sleep undisturbed and her nights were restless from frequent urination and painful joints. The chamber was large and the bed faced the window to the east. The first light of the sun fell on Bidhusekhar's eyes and woke him up every morning at the same time—summer and winter. Though past fifty, he was strong and healthy. He sat up in bed with a quick movement, joined two palms in reverence to his family deity, then brought his left hand to his nostrils to examine his breath. Bidhusekhar believed that, on first waking, a man breathed through one nostril, either right or left. For some reason he preferred it to be the left. This morning his breath was falling from the right. Instinctively, he put out his left foot and stepped out of bed. Then, pressing each nostril in turn, he took short, vigorous breaths. This often proved a corrective as he knew from experience.

The clatter of his wooden clogs woke up the whole household. That, too, was a pattern set by Bidhusekhar himself. The servants could not be allowed to go on sleeping after the master was up. Scrambling out of bed they got ready for their morning duties.

On his way out, Bidhusekhar entered his wife's room. Sugar in the blood and severe rheumatism had crippled Soudamini and she was almost completely confined to bed these days. A maid, sleeping on the floor, started up at the master's entrance and crouched against the wall, her eyes anxious. Bidhusekhar approached the bedstead and gazed at his wife's sleeping face. Soudamini had been a plump, comfortable woman till quite lately. But now she was thin and her once fair, healthy skin hung in sallow folds from her bony frame. Bidhusekhar lifted her hand and examined the yellowing palm and bluish nails. Shaking his head he felt her pulse, then placing the hand gently back on her breast, he sighed. It was her fate! He had been a good husband to her. As a *kulin* Brahmin he could have had as many wives as he pleased. But he didn't marry again. Not even when Soudamini failed to give him a son. What use were five daughters to a man? They wouldn't carry on the family name. He thought of his friend and contemporary, Rajnarayan Datta. His son, Madhu, had turned Christian and left for distant Madras. Rajnarayan had disowned and disinherited him and was now taking one wife after another in the hope of a male heir. And Bidhusekhar? Soudamini had urged him herself, many times, to take another wife but he had refused. All was in God's hands. If it was God's will that he had a son, one wife would have been enough. Soudamini would have borne a male child in her womb.

The working of fate was indeed a mystery. Soudamini had been loved and cared for all her life. She had had a good life and never known a moment's anxiety. Yet, here she was, shattered in health and spirit. She would never get well again. Death was approaching slowly but surely and soon she would be claimed . . . And Bimbabati! Poor, deprived, rejected Bimbabati! She had never known a husband's love; a husband's faith. How she had suffered all these years! And, then, to be widowed so young! Yet she enjoyed superb health and radiant beauty. Pride and joy in having borne a male child shone in her eyes and gave her the grace and dignity of a queen.

Sighing once more, Bidhusekhar came out of the room and walked with measured steps down the stairs. It was his habit, on winter mornings, to clean his teeth, sitting in the garden at the back of the house. The servants had everything ready for him. A vast armchair stood in its appointed place in the sun. A servant waited beside it with a basket of neem twigs, out of which Bidhusekhar selected one after careful consideration. Cleaning his teeth, Bidhusekhar followed the train of thought already begun. No, he had not taken another wife. Neither had he adopted a son like his friend, Ramkamal. Bidhusekhar had been averse to the idea from the very beginning but Ramkamal hadn't taken his advice. And the consequence of that foolhardiness was—Ganganarayan. Thoo! Bidhusekhar shot a mouthful of spittle on the grass. The thought of Ganganarayan made his blood boil. Gone was the shy, gentle boy who had revered him like a god. The new Ganga was drunk with the wine of new manhood and it was his pride and pleasure to thwart and frustrate Bidhusekhar in all his endeavours. He had sent Ganga to the estate house in Ibrahimpur with precise instructions to lease the indigo fields to white growers. Indigo cultivation being very lucrative, the British were monopolizing it. Since no white man could be tried by a district court, they cared little for the law and oppressed the peasants shamelessly in their drive for higher profits. Natives were ruled by law, so competition was impossible. Bidhusekhar wanted the lands leased while the going was good and it was with that end in view that he had sent Ganga to Jessore. But Ganga had flouted his command. He had cancelled the contracts with the peasants and made fresh ones, allowing them to grow rice instead of indigo.

Bidhusekhar spat another mouthful of bitter spittle. He had no illusions about Ganga. Ganga might pretend that he disobeyed Bidhusekhar's command out of consideration for the peasants but Bidhusekhar knew better. Ganga was doing all he could to annoy Bidhusekhar and erode Nabin's inheritance. He didn't know that Bidhusekhar Mukherjee could crush him like a fly whenever he felt the need. If Bidhusekhar had wanted to, he could have had the whole of Ramkamal's property. He could have wiped out the Singhas of Jorasanko. But he loved Bimbabati and Nabin and he would guard their interests to the end of his days. When Nabin came of age he would take his place among the highest of the city's elite. Bidhusekhar would see to it. As for Ganga—he would break him; break him so ruthlessly that he would never be whole again. The wretch had returned Bidhusekhar's love and affection by trying to seduce his daughter. The venomous snake! Had they reared him all these years for this? To poison the existence of his benefactor? He didn't know that Bidhusekhar had the power to reduce him to a beggar; to crush him with his heel and fling him away.

Before his death he would leave instructions with Bimbabati that Nabin should perform his last rites.

Bidhusekhar threw the neem twig away and held out his right hand for the tongue scraper. A few brisk strokes, then he washed his mouth and got ready for his bath. There was a pond in the grounds but Bidhusekhar never bathed in it. Vast quantities of water frightened him so much that, conservative Hindu though he was, he had never bathed in the Ganga. A porcelain tub, filled with water was brought out each morning and left to warm in the sun. A mat was spread beside it. Bidhusekhar took off his clothes and donning a *tel* dhoti, worn for massage, lay on the mat, his limbs outstretched. Now three or four servants began massaging his body with large quantities of oil. This lasted a long time. Then, his muscles fully relaxed, Bidhusekhar stepped into the tub. He lay in the warmed water, eyes closed luxuriously, for a full half-hour while the servants scrubbed his limbs scrupulously clean. On his way back to the house he brought up his hand once more to his nose. The body was purified after a bath and breathing should be normal now. But no—his breath still came and went from the right nostril. Bidhusekhar frowned and, in that moment, he felt a quivering in the right eyeball. He was startled but chose to ignore it. He would not give way to fear. Wrapping a tussar dhoti around his freshly bathed body, he entered the puja room but even while chanting the Gayatri mantra, his hand came up inadvertently to his nose. The right nostril, still.

This was the same puja room in which Bindu spent her days before her banishment to Kashi. She used to have everything ready for his puja—the copper vessels filled with Gangajal, sandal paste, flowers and basil. This was the only time they met. He would ask her a question or two and she would answer briefly. He felt her presence overpoweringly in the room this morning. Not that he felt any guilt or fear. He believed her punishment to be a mild one, considering the enormity of her crime. She had sullied the purity of this room; she had insulted Janardan. Ganga had cast sinful eyes on her and touched her with sinful hands and Bindu, depraved creature that she was, had succumbed. She should have hanged herself or swallowed poison before allowing that to happen. He would have been proud of her then and put up a tablet in the Kali temple in her memory. Didn't she know that stoic renunciation was the brightest ornament for a Brahmin widow? That the more rigid the abstinence in this life, the greater the chances of everlasting wifehood in the next. He had told her all that often enough but she had chosen to ignore his advice. . .

Bidhusekhar rose from his asan. His mind was wandering and he couldn't concentrate on the mantras. There was no point in going on trying. He could resume his puja in the evening. He brought his hand up to his nose. The right nostril!

Breakfast was a spartan affair—a *sandesh,* an orange and a glass of buttermilk—after which he went up to his wife's room. Soudamini lay sprawled on the bed while the barber's wife applied vermilion on her feet. Early morning was hardly the time for an elaborate toilette but Soudamini had strange fancies these days and would weep and sulk like a child if they weren't gratified. One night she woke up crying bitterly. She had heard the drums and cymbals of Maha Astami, the eighth day of the Durga festival, in her sleep and seen her own body being borne away by pallbearers. If she died in the autumn she would miss the new molasses from the winter palms and the thought saddened her so much she set up a wail. She wanted to eat molasses balls that very moment. Unable to control her, the maid woke up Bidhusekhar's widowed eldest daughter, Narayani. Narayani, who had taken charge of the household from the time of her mother's illness, came into the room and tried to pacify her. It was only a dream, she said, but Soudamini wept and beat her breast. 'I have done so much for you all,' she cried. 'Can't you do this much for me?' It was two o'clock in the morning. Narayani hadn't disturbed her father. She had sent a servant to Posta to buy the molasses, then rolled the balls herself and fed them to her mother.

Bidhusekhar waited till the barber's wife had left the room. 'How do you feel this morning, Sodu?' he asked.

'Very well,' Soudamini pulled her veil a little longer. She was a good wife and would not worry her husband needlessly.

'How is the knee? Is it better?'

'There's hardly any pain. Kaviraj Moshai's medicine is very good.' Then, pausing a little, she added. 'Why don't you stop the medicines? It is better that I go now with the sindoor in my parting.'

'That's impossible.' Bidhusekhar smiled indulgently. 'My wife will live on after me—so my horoscope says. And my lifespan is to be eighty.'

'May it be much more! But it is not proper for women to live too long.'

Bidhusekhar placed a hand on Soudamini's brow. It was cold, too cold and clammy. He suppressed a sigh. 'You are much better,' he said.

'Has no letter come from Suhasini?'

'Not yet. They've only been gone five days.'

Bidhusekhar had sent his youngest daughter, Suhasini, and her husband to his ancestral home in Krishnanagar. It had been sadly neglected all these years and was about to fall apart. Bidhusekhar had given instructions to his son-in-law to repair the house and clear the grass of weeds and undergrowth. It would fetch a good rent. Rents were high now that the British had taken over the government. Besides, the change would be good for Suhasini. She had been suffering from dysentery and dyspepsia. The water of Krishnanagar was said to be good for these ailments.

'Aren't you going to the other house?' Soudamini asked her husband. The other house was the Singha mansion. 'I'm on my way.' Bidhusekhar brought his hand up to Soudamini's nose. Her breath was falling from the right nostril. This was strange indeed!

Bidhusekhar went down the steps, frowning a little. A knot of clients, agents and clerks waited for him in the hall below. A little apart from them, his arms crossed over his chest like a *garud*, stood Raimohan Ghoshal. Raimohan was here quite often now that Ramkamal Singha was dead, though what he expected from Bidhusekhar Mukherjee was a mystery. Bidhusekhar had neither time nor inclination for wine, women and toadies. The whole city knew it.

'Well,' Bidhusekhar addressed himself to Raimohan. 'What news?'

'I've come to hear good news from you, Karta.' Raimohan folded his long body almost double and grinned ingratiatingly. Bidhusekhar turned away, without deigning to make an answer. Ignoring everyone else he walked rapidly away, out of the house, past the saluting darwan and anxious coachman, down the streets till he reached Jorasanko. Dibakar stood at the gate, his face pale and tense. Bidhusekhar's heart missed a beat.

'What is wrong, Dibakar? Chhoto Khoka[22] . . . Nabin? Is he well?'

'Yes, Karta. Chhoto Babu is doing his lessons.'

'And your mistress?'

'She's gone for a dip in the Ganga.'

Bidhusekhar heaved a sigh of relief. All was well. There was nothing to worry about. The thought of Ganganarayan did not even enter his mind. 'Bara Babu,' the muscles of Dibakar's face twitched painfully. 'Is this to be my reward for all these years of service? Shall I and my children starve in the streets?'

'Why? What is the matter?'

'Ganga Dada has given me notice. The estate does not need me any more. I'm to leave as soon as I can.'

'Why?'

'I'm disloyal. I'm worthless. So he says.'

Bidhusekhar knew that Dibakar was neither disloyal nor worthless. He was a thief. But he was a reliable servant. If you wanted something done you had only to trust it to Dibakar. All servants stole and swindled these days. How many could deliver the goods?

'I've always taken my orders from you, Karta,' Dibakar mumbled. 'I've carried out your orders even before they left your lips.' Dibakar was as clever as a fox. He had sensed the tension between Bidhusekhar and Ganganarayan and knew that a severe clash was imminent. A man could not serve two masters. Nor could he maintain absolute neutrality. Dibakar had made his choice. He would serve Bidhusekhar. Ganga was only a hot-headed youth—no match for the powerful, astute Bidhusekhar.

'You'd better go out of the city for a while, Dibakar,' Bidhusekhar said with a wry smile. 'I have a mind to send you to Ibrahimpur. The ryots need to be taught a lesson. A few houses must go up in flames. You understand?'

'I can set hell on fire if you command me, Karta.'

At that moment, Bidhusekhar's servant, Raghunath, came running in. There was bad news from Krishnanagar. Suhasini was ill, dangerously ill. Bidhusekhar stood as if turned to stone.

---

22 Younger son.

He had been breathing through the right nostril all morning. He knew some evil would befall him but he never thought it could be this. Suhasini—his youngest, his best loved daughter. . .

Bidhusekhar willed himself back to action. He would leave for Krishnanagar at once. No effort must be spared to save Suhasini.

# Chapter XXVIII

Krishnanagar was a long way off. By road it took the best part of two days. By river one saved a few hours but Bidhusekhar was nervous of boats. His horoscope predicted a watery death. He took a quick decision. He would send Dibakar and two trusted servants ahead of him by the water route. He himself would travel by land with a band of armed guards for the area was infested with bandits. Ganganarayan offered to go with him but Bidhusekhar refused his company. It was more important, he said, for Ganga to stay back and look after the two families. The difficulty lay in breaking the news to Soudamini. Prolonged illness had made her so childish and wilful that she would never agree to his leaving her for such a long time. And if he were to tell her the true reason the grief and anxiety would kill her. He decided to take refuge in a lie. He had been sent for from the palace at Krishnanagar, he told her, to settle some legal dispute. He had accepted because it would give him the opportunity to meet Suhasini and see how far his son-in-law had progressed with the repairs of the house. His presence there would surely hasten the process and then he could bring them both with him when he returned to Calcutta. His reasoning appealed to Soudamini. 'Bring Suhasini back with you—repairs or no repairs,' she said. 'I want to see her face before I die.'

Getting her father's things together, Narayani asked softly, 'Shall I come with you, Baba?'

'No,' he answered. 'The management of the house is in your hands. It will fall to pieces without you, Ma.'

'Someone should be with her. Suhasini is pregnant.'

'What?' Bidhusekhar felt like tearing his hair. Why had no one told him that? He would never have sent Suhasini to Krishnanagar if he had known. Suhasini was his youngest; his best-loved daughter. He had always kept her with him; had wedded her to a poor boy who would live in his house so that she would never know the pain of parting with her parents. And now she was alone in a strange house, pregnant and dangerously ill. It was winter and cholera raged in the land. Was she afflicted with cholera? The bearer of the news had given no details.

Bidhusekhar sat in the carriage, tense with anxiety, while the horses cantered merrily down the road. Self-pity overwhelmed him. Fate had denied him the son who would carry the family name and keep it alive through his progeny. Five daughters had been born to him, of whom two were dead and two widowed. Suhasini would die too. He had hoped to teach her husband the business of the estate and nominate him as his heir. But what use would Durga Prasad be to him after Suhasini was gone? His last hope was Nabin Kumar. He would leave everything to him. In the eyes of the world, Nabin was Ramkamal's son, even as Arjuna was Pandu's. Arjuna had declared himself a Pandava—not a son of Indra. Nabin, too, would deny his true father. But Bidhusekhar did not mind. Gods and Brahmins impregnated and fulfilled women whose husbands were incapable. He had done his duty. He had done well. He had taken Bimbabati, not out of lust but out of a sense of his Brahminical obligations. He had, by his act, saved the Singhas from extinction, saved his friend the pain of the knowledge of his own sterility. What could be a purer, a more benevolent act? He had put an end to all sexual contact with Bimbabati after the child was born. And now she was a widow. She was vulnerable . . .

The horses' feet came to a halt. 'Why? What are you stopping for?' Bidhusekhar hollered to the coachman. 'I'm in a hurry—'

'A company brigade is marching down the road, Karta. We must make way for the soldiers.' He led the horses into a nearby field. Bidhusekhar raised the window and fixed his eyes on the advancing troops. Over a thousand soldiers marched or rode to the sound of bugles, not to war as might be assumed but with the intention of striking terror into the hearts of marauders, by a show of strength.

These soldiers were respected by the people for they represented security, unlike the Nawab's soldiers, who had raped and looted and had, therefore, been hated and feared by the villagers. Even as Bidhusekhar watched, his eyes shining with admiration, a cavalry officer came galloping up to the carriage. Raising his whip he brought it down viciously on the horse's back and barked a question. 'Who is within? Male or female?'

'I am, sir.' Bidhusekhar stuck his head out of the window.

The officer was a young Englishman. His face was red and angry. Brandishing his whip he cried, 'And what maharaja are you? How dare you sit at your ease while the Company Brigade marches! Step down this instant and stand at attention.'

The man's English was incomprehensible to Bidhusekhar. He couldn't understand quite what was required of him. Nevertheless, he scrambled down and saluted the officer in all humility.

'Who are you?'

'Bidhusekhar Mukherjee, sir. Lawyer, sir. Practice in civil court, sir.'

'Take off your turban, son of a bitch.'

Bidhusekhar was dressed in his lawyer's robes—a loose coat over trousers and an elaborate turban. He had never seen a Company Brigade and did not know the rules. Seeing that his own guards stood by the roadside, heads bare, weapons on the ground, he quickly took off his turban and salaamed. The officer turned his horse in an instant and galloped away in a cloud of dust. Bidhusekhar looked on with awe. 'What spirit! What valour!' he thought. 'Such men are born to rule.' The humiliating way in which he had been treated did not hurt or anger him. He admired strength. The English were strong. They were a nation of rulers. They had every right to command obedience from their subjects. It was only when they interfered with native religions and customs that Bidhusekhar was angered.

An hour and a half later, Bidhusekhar resumed his journey. Reaching Krishnanagar he found his daughter and son-in-law, lying side by side in the last throes of the deadly disease—kala-azar. Kala-azar had ravaged Khulna and Jessore and had now struck Krishnanagar. Bidhusekhar was crazed with grief and anxiety. He knew that death was the ultimate reality. Death had struck down his near and dear ones, one after another, and he had borne the assaults with stoic humility. But this—this was too much. He could not bear to see his youngest snatched away from his arms. He collected all the doctors of Krishnanagar at Suhasini's bedside—the physician from the royal palace, a Christian doctor renowned for his healing powers and a Muslim hakim. All three looked solemn. The disease was too far advanced, they said, but they would do their best.

The night passed. The morning brought no hope. Bidhusekhar sat by the bedside through the day, peering into each face by turn. Was the breathing a little easier? Would even one of them live? And then, at dusk, wearied by the long vigil, he fell asleep. It was only for a few moments but in that time he saw a vision or dreamed a dream—he didn't know which. The room was filled with light and an ethereal essence pervaded it. And then, little by little, a form materialized before his eyes—the radiant form of a celestial deity. Yama! Bidhusekhar thought. But no, it was not the lord of death. It was Janardan, lord of life; creator of the universe. In his four hands he held the wheel, the lotus, the club and the conch. His lips were parted in a smile. Bidhusekhar knocked his head on the ground and cried, 'Janardan! Friend of the poor and needy! Oh Benevolent One, give me a boon.'

'That is why I'm here,' a voice spoke, grave and tender. 'What is it you seek?'

'The life of my daughter. And that of her husband.'

'One.' A single finger rose from the hand that held the lotus.

Bidhusekhar did not understand. He stared at the dazzling form, eyes glazed in wonder. 'I grant you the life of one. Make your choice.' The celestial form flickered like a flame. Afraid that it might vanish, Bidhusekhar cried out in agony, 'Help me choose, Omniscient One! My son-in-law has taken the place of my unborn son. My daughter is the light of my eyes. I can't live without her. Her mother's heart will break—'

'One,' the voice repeated, deep, inexorable.

Bidhusekhar made up his mind. Suhasini was only thirteen. Long years of rigorous austerity lay before her if Durga Prasad died. If she succumbed to temptation and slipped from the path of virtue she would be cursed by God and scorned by men. She would suffer untold misery in all her lives to come. With a man it was different. After his wife's death, Durga Prasad could take up his life again. He was young, intelligent. The world had a lot to give him. For Suhasini there was nothing.

'Durga Prasad,' Bidhusekhar murmured.

The deity vanished. The light dimmed and the essence faded away. Bidhusekhar couldn't bear the agony of parting with Janardan. 'Lord! Lord!' he cried and ran across the room. Stumbling over the threshold he fell in a heap on the floor.

Durga Prasad died the next morning and Suhasini recovered—slowly at first, then so rapidly that the physicians were astonished. But she was weak and feeble for days afterwards and lay in bed, waiting for her strength to return. Bidhusekhar wondered why Janardan had saved Suhasini. He had asked Him for Durga Prasad's life. Had He misunderstood? But He was omniscient! He must have looked into Bidhusekhar's heart and seen what was there. Bidhusekhar's lips had asked for Durga Prasad but his heart had wanted Suhasini.

Even as she lay in bed, her legs too weak to support her weight, Suhasini's conch bangles were broken and the sindoor wiped away from her parting. Bidhusekhar's well-wishers had asked him to wait a little longer. The girl was still weak and the shock of her widowhood might kill her. But Bidhusekhar upheld the code of laws with rigid control over self and others. He would not allow any straying—whatever the cost. The shastras were written by ancient rishis, who knew what they were doing. Bidhusekhar would obey them to the letter. Suhasini bit her lips, too weak to cry aloud. Though only thirteen she knew what a widow's life was like. She had seen her sister, Bindu.

Bidhusekhar spent two and a half months in Krishnanagar, nursing Suhasini back to health. And then, one night, her labour pains came and she delivered her child—a fine, healthy boy. Bidhusekhar's heart leaped up in delight. This was the first male child in his family after fifty years. Looking on the child's face he shuddered and thought, 'And I had asked Janardan to take Suhasini even while this child pulsed in her womb!'

# Chapter XXIX

The slight bashful boy, whose voice was so soft as to be barely audible in the great house of the Singhas, had turned into a tall, strapping, vigorous youth with a strong personality. His fair cheeks were now covered with velvety down and his eyes were dark and fiery. From time to time he raised a hand and tried to twist a budding moustache.

Ganganarayan was now a very busy man. He who had idled his time away with friends and classfellows now spent several hours each morning in his office, apportioning the day's work to the stewards and other officials of the estate. Then, after a bath and meal he set off on his daily inspection of the three houses in which the Singha monies were lodged. He kept a large watch in his pocket, which he drew out every now and then for every minute was precious. The evenings were devoted to business discussions that went on far into the night. If Bidhusekhar was present (as he was sometimes), Ganga and he got invariably locked in an argument. But Ganga was still a romantic at heart. Tears sprang to his eyes when he read the poems of great masters. His wife, Lilavati, was still a child. She spent most of her time playing with her dolls. Every now and then she would weep for her mother and ask to be sent back to Bagbazar. Ganganarayan did not care in the least. He felt nothing at all for her. He spent night after night reading poetry—Sanskrit and English—by the light of the lamp. Sometimes, the erotic verses he read made his ears flame with embarrassment and something else—he didn't know what. At such times he shut his book, lay back on the pillows and thought of Bindubasini. A tremendous storm raged in his breast but he stifled it. He had sworn an oath and he had to keep it. He could never see Bindu again.

Ganga woke up every morning to the sound of Sanskrit hymns, sung in a sweet, childish treble. Nabin was only eight but his memory was phenomenal. He could remember and recite the most difficult shloks from the Mahabharat on hearing them once or twice. Bimbabati had not yet overcome her fears regarding her son. She refused to send him out of her sight, so Nabin did not go to school. He studied at home, taking lessons, by turns, from three tutors. Ganga had appointed them himself, choosing the three brightest students of Hindu College and Sanskrit College for the purpose. Also, seeing that Nabin had an excellent ear and sang the songs he heard from itinerant minstrels with the greatest of ease, Ganga had engaged an ustad to teach him the classical music of the north. The love and affection between the two brothers annoyed Bidhusekhar intensely for Nabin was the trump card with which he meant to foil Ganga's game when the time came.

One afternoon Bimbabati sent for Ganganarayan. 'A train of servants came from Bagbazar this morning, bearing gifts,' she said without preamble. 'Did you know that?' Somewhat dismayed, Ganga could only say, 'Oh!' Gifts were exchanged during certain seasons of the year between the Singhas of Jorasanko and the Bosus of Bagbazar. But it had nothing to do with him. He wondered why Bimbabati was telling him all this.

'Can you guess the reason?' Bimbabati probed.

'Reason?' Ganga laughed. 'Must there be a reason for sending gifts?'

'Of course, there must. People don't send gifts except on feast days. There's an intention behind this—'

'What intention?'

'Your mother-in-law is reminding me of my duties. Bouma[23] has been gone for six months. It is time we brought her back.'

'Oh!'

'They sent twelve headloads. I shall send sixteen. I've asked Debipada and Janardan to buy the best *sandesh* and the biggest carp in the city. Then, the day after tomorrow, you must go to Bagbazar and bring Bouma back with you.'

'I'm very busy, Ma. Send someone else.'

'That will look bad. You should visit your in-laws sometimes or Bouma will feel hurt.'

'I have no time. It's impossible—'

Bimbabati laid a hand on Ganga's back and stroked it

23 Daughter-in-law.

lovingly. 'Go just this once,' she pleaded. 'Bagbazar isn't too far off. How long will it take? Your father-in-law is a man of status. He won't send his daughter with anybody else. Of course, it is not good for a man to visit his in-laws too often. It lowers his prestige. My husband brought me from my father's house when I was nine and never let me go back. He didn't go himself, either. I haven't seen my parents since that time—' Memory of Ramkamal brought tears to Bimbabati's eyes. She lifted the edge of her than and wiped them away.

Ganga did not have the heart to disobey his mother. He went to Bagbazar as he had been commanded and brought Lilavati home. There was a change in her now. She was taller and her limbs were full and rounded. Her skin and hair shone like silk. The old childish wilfulness had given way before a shy reticence. Even Ganga noticed the change. Not that it altered his attitude towards her or made him more aware of her presence in the house.

One morning Nabin came complaining to Ganga. 'Bara Bouthan is a very bad pupil,' he said. 'I try so hard to teach her but she doesn't learn anything.'

'You are teaching your Bara Bouthan!' Ganga exclaimed in amusement. 'Very good. I must arrange to pay you your fees.'

'But she doesn't listen to a word I say. She only laughs and pinches my cheek.'

'That's very wrong of her—'

'I gave her a book to read and she's torn it to pieces. I ran after her to punish her but she hid behind Ma's back.'

'Tchk! Tchk!' Ganga laughed and ruffled Nabin's hair.

But the encounter with Nabin sparked off a train of thought that wove in and out of his head during his morning's duties. What if he tried to educate Lilavati? She was his wife. He would have to accept her sooner or later. Education would improve her mental powers and she might, in time, come to be a true wife—a wife he could respect and love. He would employ a European governess to give her lessons. Bimbabati wouldn't mind. Bidhusekhar might object but who cared for Bidhusekhar's objections? Ganga had endured the termination of Bindu's education without uttering a word. But with his own wife it would be different. He would not allow Bidhusekhar to dictate to him.

That night Ganga walked into his bedroom to find Lilavati awake and waiting for him. She wore a sari of a vividly patterned silk and a gold embroidered shawl hung from her shoulders. Ropes of jasmine were entwined in the rich knot of her hair and around her dazzling arms. Ganga looked at her in surprise. What was she doing, sitting up so late at night? And why was she dressed like that? Coming closer he saw tears in her eyes. 'Is anything wrong?' he asked with a smile. 'Are you missing your mother so much that you are all dressed and ready to leave for Bagbazar?'

Lilavati bent her head and said softly, 'No.'

'What is it then?'

Lilavati rose and stood facing her husband. 'You hardly ever talk to me,' she said, pushing out her lower lip. 'My Gangajal's[24] husband sits up all night, chatting with her.'

'I'm not mad that I must follow his example.'

'But everyone does! My Gangajal says—'

'Your Gangajal's husband must be a do-nothing. I work hard all day. I must sleep at night.'

'But they say you don't love me. They laugh—'

'Let them. Listen, Lilavati. Nabin tells me he is trying to teach you to read and write. Why don't you let him?'

'He's only a little boy. I don't like him bossing over me.'

'Then take lessons from someone else.'

'No.'

'Why not? I'll employ a memsaheb to come and teach you.'

'No. Book-learned women become widows.'

'Nonsense. Who told you that?'

'My mother.'

'She doesn't know.'

'Look at Suhasini. Her husband was teaching her to read and write.'

'Suhasini's husband died of kala-azar. Hundreds of men die of it. Are their wives all book-learned? Fetch me that book from the niche in the wall. I'll read out a passage from it.'

---

24 According to a Bengali tradition, women call their special friends by names culled from natural phenomena, as for instance, Kadamphal, Sagar, Makar, Gangajal, etc.

'Get it yourself.'

'Are you afraid I'll die if you touch a book?' Ganga laughed merrily. Then, fetching it, he opened it at a particular page and said, 'This is a dialogue between two women. Imagine that one of them is you and the other your Gangajal. The first woman says: "*O lo*! I hear women are learning to read and write. Do you think it a good thing? What is to become of them?" The other woman answers, "Only good can come of it, Didi. The women of our country are unlettered. All they have learned is domestic work. They lead mindless lives—like animals.

Q: Good. You are saying that educated women need not do any domestic work. Then who will do their work for them? Who will look after their husbands and children? Men?

A: I didn't say that. Women must see to their households. But if they can read a few books in their spare time they'll glean a little knowledge of the world. And this knowledge will save them from being fooled easily.

Q: Very good. I understand from what you say that education is a good thing. But our old women tell us that book-learned women become widows. Is that true? Because if it is I refuse to learn to read. Who knows what may happen!

A: No, sister. That is just idle talk. It is the stupid and lazy among us who have started this rumour. My grandmother says that nothing like that is written in the shastras. What about the women of the Puranas? Were they not book-learned? What about the memsahebs? Are they all widows?"'

'Stop, Stop,' cried Lilavati. 'I don't want to hear another word. This book has been written by a *mlechha firinghee*. I'm sure of it. All they want is to rob us of our caste and turn us Christian.'

'You're wrong. It has been written by a Brahmin pandit called Gourmohan Vidyalankar. Listen to a bit more—'

'When I was a child (I wasn't married then) I went to my brothers' Guru Moshai and said, "Teach me to read and write". As I sat with my palm leaf before me my Natun Pishi[25] came rushing in and pulling me up by the ear, dragged me away, crying, "Stubborn, disobedient girl! Are you a man that you sit reading with your brothers? Do you want to become a widow

25 Father's fifth sister.

and spend all your life like me—a wretched, miserable creature whom nobody loves?" My heart quakes when I remember those words.'

'This is not your father's house,' Ganganarayan said solemnly. 'In this house you will do as I say. You'll take lessons from an English governess from the first of next month.'

'But I have no brains!' Lilavati cried out in alarm. 'Lessons are hard. How shall I learn them?'

Ganga was so exasperated he felt like flinging the book away. She was really stupid. Would he ever be able to mould her into the woman he could love? Putting the book away he lay down and shut his eyes. A few minutes later he felt Lilavati creeping up close to his chest and clasping his neck with her arms. She had never done such a thing before. Not knowing how to react, Ganga lay motionless, pretending to sleep. 'Are you angry with me?' Lilavati whispered, bringing her mouth close to his ear. 'I'll learn to read if you teach me yourself. I'm scared of memsahebs.'

'Very well. Now go to sleep.'

'You don't love me one bit. My Gangajal says—'

'I'll hear what your Gangajal says tomorrow morning.'

'She says, "Doesn't your husband want to make you a mother? You should tell him—"'

'*Chhi*! I don't want to listen to such stuff.'

'Gangajal is a mother. So are Suhasini, Durgamoyee and Khemankari. Why can't I be a mother? They laugh at me. They say, "Your husband doesn't love you".'

'I want to sleep. I have a lot to do in the morning.'

Lilavati snuggled closer to her husband and rubbed her face against his chest. She was a simple girl and couldn't understand why her husband was so different from other men. Her friends had advised her to seduce him by making herself as beautiful as she could. Pretty clothes and jewels, together with a few tears, would do the trick, they told her. But poor Lilavati had tried both and failed!

Wearied by her efforts, Lilavati fell asleep, but Ganga lay awake, hour after hour, staring at the ceiling. A strange restlessness seized him—he didn't know why. After a long time he sat up and fixed his gaze on Lilavati. Her arms had slipped from his neck and the quilt lay crumpled at her feet. A stream of translucent light from the winter moon came in from the open window and bathed the sleeping form in molten silver. Ganga's heart beat rapidly. Why did he feel so strange? Was the moon playing tricks with his eyes? Or was Lilavati really so beautiful—so exquisitely beautiful? Why had he never noticed it before? 'Oh, she doth teach the torches to burn bright,' he murmured under his breath. Then, very gently, he placed his hand upon her brow. Looking at her face all the descriptions of female beauty he had read in his books came crowding into his mind. 'If I profane with my unworthiest hand this holy shrine,' he murmured, taking her hand in his, 'the gentle sin is this—' Ganga was not Ganga any more. He was a romantic hero! He was Romeo. 'Oh then; dear saint, let lips do what hands do. They pray. Grant thou lest faith turn to despair.' Ganga touched his lips to Lilavati's and kissed them passionately.

'Who? What?' Lilavati woke up with a start. Ganga went on murmuring as if in a dream: 'Sin from my lips? Oh trespass sweetly urged. Give me my sin again.' Ganga bent his head and planted another kiss on Lilavati's quivering mouth.

'How good it feels!' Lilavati said happily. 'My head goes round and round so deliciously! Now I can tell my Gangajal that my husband loves me. She thinks only hers—'

'Be still. Don't speak a word.' Then Ganga laid Lilavati gently on the bed and gazed, deeply and tenderly, into her face. A verse of Sanskrit poetry came to his mind. He recited it softly.

*Tanvi Shyama Shikhari—dashana pakka bimbodharosthti*
*Madhye Kshyama chakita harini prekshana nimnanabhi*
*Sronibharadalas—gamana stoknamra stanabhang*
*Ya tatra syad yuvati—vishaye srishti radyeb dhatu.*

'Are you reciting our marriage mantras?' Lilavati asked puzzled. 'But we are married already.'

'No. It's something else. You won't understand,' Ganga laughed.

'Explain it to me.'

'"She's slim and dark. Her teeth are like mountain peaks strung together. Her lips are as red as ripe berries. Her waist is small; her eyes dart about as bright as a gazelle's. Her navel is deep and her walk slow and languorous from the weight of her rounded hips and thrusting breasts. If you see such a woman you will know her to be the creator's model."'

'Do you know who wrote these lines? Kalidas. You are such a woman.'

'But I couldn't understand half of what you said!'

Then Ganga repeated the lines again, touching by turns Lilavati's lips, eyes, waist and navel as he explained. Placing a hand on her heaving breast he went on:

*Ghatayati sughana, Kuch—yuga gagana*
*Mriga mada suchi suchi te*
*Manisara Mamalang, taraka patalang*
*Nakha—pada—shashi—bhushite.*

'Can I tear these delicate breasts with my nails?' Ganga demanded, untying the knot of Lilavati's kanchuli and baring her breasts in the moonlight. 'Can I draw blood from them?' Ganga squeezed them with both hands. 'Does it hurt?' he asked.

'Ah! Ah! Ah!'

Then, Ganganarayan took off every particle of Lilavati's clothing in the exact order described in *Kumar Sambhava,* and began the process of mating. They were both young and inexperienced but their joy knew no bounds. Lilavati was happiest because now she could tell her Gangajal that her husband had made love to her. She was now every bit as good as her friends and might even become a mother, very soon. She wanted to share these thoughts with her husband but the moment she opened her mouth, he cried, 'Shh. Don't talk.' Then, possessing her wholly, he thought, 'This isn't Lilavati. This is Bindu. Bindu—whom I love.'

# Chapter XXX

On a fine April morning John Eliott Drinkwater Bethune set foot on Indian soil. At forty-seven, he was tall and strong in body and vigorous and alert in mind. A scion of a county family, he had studied law and mathematics at the University of Oxford, leaving it as senior wrangler. This was his first visit to Calcutta and the sight of the beautiful city, bathed in spring sunshine, filled his heart with joy.

Bethune had been interested in India since the time that, as a practising lawyer in London, he had been invited to participate in a law suit regarding sati—the Indian practice of burning widows on the funeral pyres of their husbands. The invitation had come from a group of Indian traditionalists, who had appealed to the privy council to revoke the ban on sati if it ever came to be passed by the British government in India. On making enquiries Bethune discovered that such a ban was under serious consideration, following appeals made by several enlightened Indians who considered sati to be a blot on their religion and culture. The discovery left him thunderstruck. He had read of sati in books but had thought it to be a custom practised so far back in history as to be almost a myth—on par with witch-hunting and the horrors of the Inquisition. That Indian culture, one of the oldest and finest in the world, could be so retrogressive that anyone could wish to perpetuate such a bizarre custom as burning to death a live human being, had come as a shock to him.

In John Bethune's own country, England, the Feminist movement was in full swing—women demanding equal rights with men. Bethune supported them for he believed women to be equal to men in everything—intellect, sensitivity and moral strength. God made no distinctions. Why should man? European women had been subjugated for centuries and were now raising their heads, slowly and painfully, and demanding equality. It saddened him to think that the same was not the case in India. Women there were still cruelly crushed, even burned to death at the will of men. He yearned to do something for them; to better their lot in any way he could. When the East India Company offered to send him out to India as law secretary, he accepted it gratefully. Having no ties to bind him in his own country, he looked forward to going to India where he could glean first-hand information of the country and her people.

On his arrival in Calcutta Bethune was appointed chairman of the Council of Education. This was a post that suited him. He had an ambition and that was to bring the light of reason to this great and ancient country. The concept of liberal humanism, that had already taken root in Europe and was growing vigorous and strong, had to be planted in India and it could only be done through education. Taking stock of the educational institutions of the city he found segregation on the basis of religion that surprised him greatly. The most illustrious of them all, the famed Hindu College where the students received an education on par with public schools of England, admitted Hindu students only, and those, too, from the upper class families of Calcutta. Muslim boys were denied the privilege of a western education, being forced to enrol in madrasas where they studied Arabic and Persian. There was a Sanskrit College, too, where boys from the poorer Hindu families studied Sanskrit. The boys were all Bengali but their mother tongue was conspicuous by its absence from the curricula. Was it possible to visualize English boys studying Greek and Latin and no English?

The citizens of Calcutta, as he discovered from his conversations with eminent Indians, were very proud of the fact that there was an institution like Hindu College in their city; an institution in which native boys were trained in the art of reciting Shakespeare and Homer and writing English like Englishmen. That they learned virtually no Bengali was a matter of pride rather than of shame. This state of affairs disturbed Bethune not a little. Education, he felt, was the key to an expansion of the mind and a strengthening of the character. Hindu College, in his opinion, was not an educational institution at all. It was a factory which churned out clerks for the British government in India, year after year. The products displayed a slavish devotion for the language and culture of the rulers and a disdainful superiority to their own. Coming from

England, where love of the motherland and pride in her institutions were instilled from childhood, Bethune found it hard to understand the psyche of the educated Indian. Till he discovered the truth! Education in India was geared to the purpose of creating a working force of devoted slaves. It was expedient, the rulers felt, to pick them out from among the Hindus for Hindus were weak and feeble and easy to brainwash. The Muslims were sleeping lions. It was best to leave them alone. Hence the policy of enrolling only Hindu boys in Hindu College.

One morning Bethune's khansama came into the library with the message that an Indian babu was outside, waiting to see him. On receiving permission he ushered in a young Bengali gentleman, impeccably attired in English clothes. This was an old student of Hindu College—Gourdas Basak by name. Pointing to an armchair, Bethune said, 'Pray sit down, sir, and tell me what I can do for you.'

'I have not come to seek anything for myself,' Gour answered. Then, unwrapping a book from a piece of waxed paper, he held it out to Bethune with the words, 'A friend of mine is the author of this volume of verse. You are a fine scholar and a lover of poetry. I've come to present you a copy.'

'Who is the author?'

'A childhood friend of mine. He would have come himself had he been here. He wrote to me from Madras, where he resides at present, requesting me to—'

'I'm sorry. I can't read Bengali.'

'It is written in English, sir. Very superior English.'

Bethune took the beautifully bound book and turned it over in his hands. It was entitled, *Captive Lady*, and the author was one Michael Madhusudan Dutt. He opened the book and read a page.

'My friend has been a poet from childhood.' Gour smiled at the Englishman. 'We have great hopes of him. He may attain the stature of Milton or Byron some day.'

Bethune shut the book with a sigh. 'Why does your friend write in English and not in Bengali?' he asked. 'I've never heard of poetry being written except in the mother tongue.'

'Madhusudan Dutt writes English like an Englishman. Many of your countrymen have admitted it.'

'Even so. I know Englishmen whose French is as good as

that of natives born to the soil of France. But when they write poetry they do so in English. Bengalis should write in Bengali.'

'But that's impossible, sir. The language is crude and low—meant for the vulgar masses. It is unfit for any kind of literary composition—least of all poetry.'

Bethune drew his brows together in displeasure. He hated the way the upper class Bengali reviled his own language. He remembered an incident that had taken place only a few days ago. He had been invited to preside at the annual day celebrations of Krishnanagar College. After the prize distribution was over, the students had recited poems for his entertainment which, to his surprise, were all in English. Turning to some eminent members of the board, he had asked, 'Are these boys not taught their mother tongue? Why do they not recite in Bengali?'

'Bengali is not worth learning,' one of the worthies had replied with a smile. 'It has very little written in it and whatever there is, is crude and coarse.'

'Five hundred years ago,' Bethune had retorted warmly, 'English was equally crude and coarse. But we didn't abandon it in favour of another language. Our ancestors worked hard to make it the language it is today. You should do the same for Bengali. If there is a dearth of good writing in Bengali you should commission translations of European classics. That will help to improve the language.'

Fixing his eyes on Gour's face, Bethune said, 'I'm of the opinion, sir, that young men of intelligence and education, like your friend, should take up the responsibility of refining the language. If Bengali is, indeed, as crude and shallow as you say, he should seize the opportunity of being the first to give it depth and character. This is a historic moment in your lives, young man. Take it and make the most of it. A fine harvest lies before the man who sows his seed on virgin soil. Why waste your labour on a field already ploughed by many?'

Gour felt some disappointment at Bethune's response. He had hoped to secure a letter of recommendation, which he would have posted to Madhu. Rising, he said with exaggerated politeness, 'Thank you for your advice, Mr Bethune. I shall pass it on to my friend.' On Gour's departure Bethune opened the book once again. He suppressed a sigh. The poet was tying himself in knots in his efforts to display his mastery of the English language. There was not a trace of lyrical beauty in the poem. The man didn't stand a chance of being numbered among the great poets of England. His countrymen were very proud of him on account of his English education but in Bethune's opinion he was no better than an ignorant rustic, for his soul still slept within him.

# Chapter XXXI

Thakomoni had found her place, at last, among the servants of the Singha household. Her rustic innocence was a thing of the past. She was now as fully trained in her duties as she was aware of her rights, and her voice, raised in shrill quarrel, could be heard quite frequently in the kitchen and courtyard. She had grown quite plump and her face shone with good living. Poets all over the world have lamented the fate of the caged bird in their verses. But a caged bird is not always unhappy. How long can it mourn the loss of its freedom? A time comes when it ceases to weep for the wide blue sky and leafy boughs and falls in love with its cage. Thakomoni was once the wife of a penurious peasant. She was now a servant in a wealthy household. She had mourned the loss of her old life for a long time, then, over the years, her memories had dimmed and she had come to terms with the new. She thought of her husband only rarely now, and when she did, it was with angry condemnation. The worthless lout must have run away on purpose, leaving her destitute. If he were still here looking for her, why did she never run across him? She went out of the house often enough. Only the other day she had walked with the other servants to Bagbazar, bearing a headload of gifts. Boudimoni's[26] mother had given her a sari and two silver rupees. Besides, the mistress always took her along when she went for her ritual dip in the Ganga. Thako knew the city well by now and was familiar with the streets.

Needless to say, Thakomoni had had to shed her chastity before a year was out. Chastity was a virtue maids in great households could not afford to cherish. A healthy young woman with no protector was the natural prey of men—masters and servants alike. Thako had resisted in the beginning out of the conviction that loose women went to hell.

26 Little mistress.

Then, seeing that making oneself available to men was the rule in her new world and that Heaven and Hell were both right here, she had surrendered. Having done so she found the experience pleasant enough and was, in consequence, quickly assimilated into the life around her.

Servants in great houses lived precariously. The most trusted of them might be sacked; even banished from the city at a moment's notice. The mistress's favourite maid, Chintamoni, was turned out of the house only the other day for some trifling error—no one knew what. Thako had heard that Chinta was never to show her face again within seven miles of the city. Only Sohagbala still reigned supreme, queening it over all the other servants. She was older now and monstrously obese. She had given up walking for her legs couldn't support her weight. She was carried out each morning by half a dozen maids and seated on her marble block in the courtyard. Cramming betel into her mouth from the box she held in her hands, she screamed instructions at the servants and sent them scurrying around her. She was always very hot and rivulets of sweat cascaded over the heavy bolsters of her breasts and formed pools between the rolls of her stomach. From time to time she dug her banana-like fingers under her breasts and scratching vigorously at the rashes of prickly heat, called in a voice that had lost none of its old thunder, 'Duryodhan! Where are the fish heads, you old thief?' or, 'Gopali, you worthless wench! Are you bathing in ghee these days that the tin is empty? Didn't I fill it only the day before yesterday?'

Sohagbala and Dibakar had milked the Singhas so steadily in their career as steward and stewardess that they were very wealthy now. Dibakar had built a temple in his ancestral village and had a pond dug. He was also the proud owner of two brick houses and several orchards of jackfruit and mango. He often urged Sohagbala to give up city life and retire with him to the village, where they could enjoy the fruits of their labours. They were old and childless. Wasn't it time they thought of their souls? But Sohagbala was not ready to leave. Would she have so many servants under her in the village? Would she enjoy the power she had here? There she would have to pinch and scrape for the money she spent would be her own. Here she could swim in oil and treacle if she wished. She could roll down mountains of sugar and rice. Of course, she was much too fat and inert now for rolling and swimming. She also suffered acutely from joint pains and was often confined to bed.

It didn't take Thako long to discover that Sohagbala's authority was supreme in the servants' quarters of the Singha mansion. Sohagbala might be as cruel and unjust as she pleased—there was no redressing of grievances. The inmates of the upper floors lived lives totally insulated from the goings-on below them. Once when in the middle of a quarrel, one of the cooks had thrown a burning faggot at another's head, it was Dibakar who had dispensed justice. Supporting the aggressor, he had sacked the one who was badly burned. The family had not even come to know. One of Sohagbala's favourite punishments for disobedient maids was branding their backs with red hot spuds. The maid might writhe and moan in agony but she dared not cry out.

From time to time Sohagbala would take a fancy to one or other of the twenty-two maids under her. If a maid received a command to press Sohagbala's legs for an evening, everyone knew that her troubles were over. Her star was in the ascendant. Thako, of course, had no hopes of reaching that exalted position. Sohagbala hated her from the first and even more so now that Dulal was Nabin Kumar's personal servant and playmate. Thako hardly ever saw Dulal these days. He, too, was learning his duties and learning them fast. He knew already that whatever abuse and humiliation his young master heaped on his head, he must grin and bear it.

Sometimes, during a mock battle, Dulal would fling himself to the ground, feigning defeat. Then, lying spread-eagled, he would allow Nabin to sit on his chest and twist the point of his wooden sword into his neck, laughing all the while in pretended delight though the pain was excruciating. The louder Dulal laughed, the more fiercely Nabin twisted. He carried on this cruel game till the tears gushed out of Dulal's eyes and his face crumpled up in spite of himself. Then, satisfied, Nabin jumped up and bade his adversary rise. But for all his cruelty, Nabin loved Dulal. He not only gave him a share of all the good foods he ate, he even lent him his books. Under Nabin's tutelage Dulal had learned to read and write. He could even read a difficult book like *Data Karna*.

One evening, at dusk, as Thakomoni sat alone in her room, the door opened noiselessly and Nakur walked in. He was high on hemp. His eyes were fire red and he had the strength of ten demons in his body. Thako sprang up in alarm.

'Why starve yourself, dearie?' he whispered in honeyed tones. 'Make me a chillum with your soft hands tonight. I yearn for a pull.'

'O Ma! O Ma!' Thako cried helplessly as Nakur swayed towards her and laid his hot trembling hands on her body.

Nakur had recently been promoted to the position of a purchasing clerk. He was now superior to the other servants and was called Nokro Dada in consequence. He was much richer, too, for he made a lot of money on the side. He bought fish at eight annas a seer and billed it at ten. Since eight to ten seers were bought every day, he made sixteen to twenty annas per day on fish alone.

Thako managed to escape Nakur that first day. Wriggling out of his grasp she ran out of the door as fast as her legs would carry her. Instinct told her that the only person who could protect her was Sohagbala. Even Nakur was powerless before her. 'O Ma!' Sohagbala exclaimed, staring at Thako's frightened face and heaving breast. 'Why are you puffing and panting like a street whore? What's the matter?'

Thako made no answer. She knew that a complaint against Nakur would get her nowhere. Men were above the law in her new world. Whatever happened, it was the woman's fault and it was she who had to be punished.

'Have you seen a ghost?' Sohagbala probed. 'Why is your face all crumpled up like a slice of dry mango?' This was safer ground. 'Yes,' Thako nodded vigorously. 'I saw something slip away—like a shadow.'

'Was it near the lavatory pits?' Sohagbala whispered, her eyes rolling in her fat face. 'I've told you and told you not to wander about in unwashed clothes. But will you girls listen? Wait till it grabs you by the neck and snaps your head off—'

Nakur didn't follow her that first day. He sat on Thako's bed, smoking and grinning to himself for over an hour. She would come back! It was only a matter of time.

Then, one day, Thako really saw a ghost and it was right inside the house. One of her duties being the lighting of the lamps on the ground floor, she went from room to room at dusk, a flaming sulphur stick in one hand and a tin of oil in the other. That evening, as she bent over the niche in the front verandah, a shadowy form glided from behind a pillar and stood before her. It was Dibakar. Pushing the hall door open he said quietly, 'Come.' Thako was so startled she couldn't even cry out. She had seen Sohagbala in the back verandah only a few minutes ago. And here was Dibakar, propositioning her within a few yards of where his wife was sitting. Dibakar was nearly sixty—years older than her father. Besides, for all practical purposes, he was her master.

'Come,' Dibakar repeated. 'Why do you stare like that? Have you seen a ghost?' Then, grinning amorously, he added, 'You've grown quite plump and luscious, Thako. Like a ripe fruit—'

With a stifled cry, Thako fled down the dark passages till she came to where Sohagbala was sitting. Trembling violently, she sank to her knees, not daring to utter a sound. Sohagbala's eyes raked her form in the dark. 'Death be on your head, you foolish girl!' she scolded. 'You'll burst your lungs one of these days from running in the dark. Ghosts! She sees ghosts swarming all over the house? Don't we have our Narayanshila in the puja room, guarding us all? Let me tell you, girl, that a ghost dare not show his face here, this house is so holy . . . '

That night Thako kept awake till dawn, clutching the sleeping Dulal tightly to her bosom. Tears of helplessness poured down her cheeks as she saw her future clearly before her. The sky above her head was dark with kites and vultures, ready to ravish her in one fell swoop. She had eaten so well in the last few months that a soft layer of fat had crept over her bones. She was warm and voluptuous now—so changed in her looks that she could hardly recognize herself in the mirror. The thought of two men being attracted to her sent little shivers of delight down her spine, which was pleasurable enough. But triumph was submerged in the terror that she might end up like Matu. There was another maid, Bhava, who had become pregnant and had been forced to abort. She hadn't died like Matu but, once it was all over she had fallen into a decline, and now crept about the house like a broken bird—a handful of skin and bones and hair. No man bothered to look at her now.

Thako could have walked out of the house that very night,

holding her son by the hand. No one would have stopped her. But alas! She was used to her cage and afraid of the world outside it. Her son was given a share of all the delicacies his young master ate. She herself sat down twice a day to a basin of white rice and fish curry. Where, except in this house, would they be fed so well? The outside world was strange; frightening. She dared not leave . . . .

And then, one day, Sohagbala sent for her. Sohagbala's rheumatism had worsened with the onset of winter and she was now almost completely confined to her bed. She had grown quite fond of Thako in the last few months, so it was natural that she should send for the girl to wait on her. Dulal was still upstairs with Nabin. He wouldn't come down for a couple of hours. Thako wrapped a fresh sari around her and made her way to Sohagbala's room. As she did so she noticed the other maids tittering and exchanging meaningful glances.

Sohagbala lay sprawled on a vast bedstead in one of the three rooms allotted to Dibakar. The mattress on her bed was very high for the heavier Sohagbala got, the softer and deeper her bed had to be. Thako pulled the veil low over her face and seating herself at Sohagbala's feet, started pressing her legs, which, though they looked more like Bhim's clubs than human legs, were surprisingly soft to the touch. Sohagbala allowed Thako to carry on her ministrations for half an hour, then said abruptly, 'That will do, girl. Come over here to me. Let me see your face.'

Thakomoni lifted her veil and raised her eyes to the older woman's. There was something in them that she couldn't fathom. Sohagbala's eyes, voice, manner—all had changed.

'Go to the other room,' Sohagbala said, after gazing long and earnestly at Thako's face. 'Your Gomosta Babu is lying there, sick of a fever. Look after him. Stroke his forehead. Press his legs if he wants you to.'

Thako's body stiffened at these words. Sohagbala was sending her to Dibakar's room! Dibakar, who had tried to seduce her only the other day. It was obvious that Sohagbala didn't know the truth of her husband's character. Should she tell her? Thako stopped herself just in time. It would be useless. No woman liked to hear of her husband's infidelities. Thako shivered involuntarily. She wished the earth would open and swallow her up.

'Don't be afraid,' Sohagbala said in a voice of command. 'Go.'

Thako dared not disobey. Turning, she walked mechanically in the direction of Dibakar's room. The bed was empty. Dibakar stood behind the door. He had heard Sohagbala's words and was waiting with mounting impatience. The moment Thako stepped in he pounced on her and dragged her towards the bed. His body burned but with no ordinary fever. He suffered from a fever of lust.

'Save me, Babu! Have mercy on me!' Thako wept piteously.

'Quiet,' Dibakar roared. 'Another sound from you and I'll wring your neck.'

Thako was still sobbing like a child when she came out of the room a couple of hours later. Sohagbala lay where she was, her face turned to her husband's door. Beckoning to the girl to come to her, she pointed to a niche in the wall and said, 'Bring me the basket you see there. Why do you stare at me like that? Do as I tell you.'

Thako wiped her eyes and obeyed. Sohagbala dug her fingers into the basket and brought out a little bunch of dried roots. Handing them to Thako, she said, 'Grind these with water and swallow the paste as quickly as you can. Don't be afraid. No harm will come to you. I've kept my man under my control these thirty-three years. Not one night has he spent except under this roof. It hasn't been easy, I can tell you. Particularly for a woman like me, whom God has cursed with sterility. Obey me in everything and all will be well.' Lifting her pillow she pulled out a Santipuri sari from beneath it. It was new and crisp. Handing it to Thako, she said, 'Wear this the next time I send for you. Be sure to bathe first. Now, go.'

Strangely, even after this incident Thakomoni did not leave the house. She shed some bitter tears but only for a few nights. And, strangest of all, when on the next occasion Sohagbala sent for another maid instead of her, something like envy and resentment rose in her breast. These emotions were short-lived. Her turn came the very next week and after that, every other day.

And then, one evening, Nakur came to her again. Looking

at her out of his bloodshot eyes he slurred, 'So you've shed your precious chastity, haven't you, dearie? Why couldn't it have been for me? I'm obliged to have you second-hand. But it doesn't matter.' Springing on her he felled her to the ground and mounted her with all the ferocity of a wild animal. Thako lay under him like a washed-out rag. She had no strength left—either of body or of will.

As time passed Thako got used to her situation. The two men took turns with her and she surrendered meekly to both. She even came to enjoy it—especially with Nakur. Dibakar was old and his breath smelled foul from his missing teeth. Nakur was young and strong like an ox—full of sap and sperm. The months rolled away. Thako's personality changed slowly but perceptibly. She became proud and self-confident. She had an air of dignity. She had realized her full potential; the full worth of herself—as a woman.

Dulal had been ill and confined to bed. Nabin Kumar had missed him so much that he had made his way down to Thako's quarters to look in on him. This was unheard of. Masters did not visit servants even when they lay dying. But nothing and no one could stop Nabin once he had made up his mind. Thako had been distracted with worry. Her child, her only link with the past, was ill; perhaps dying. What could she do? How could she live without him? In her terror she had turned to Sohagbala. Sohagbala had been a great help. She had sent for the kaviraj and earned Thako's undying gratitude. Dulal was much better now and would be completely cured in a few days.

One night, as mother and son lay sleeping side by side, a tap on the door woke them up. Thako knew what it meant. Dibakar had sent for her. She rose and went for her bath. Then, returning, she proceeded to change into her new sari.

'Where are you going Ma?' Dulal piped in a weak, fretful voice.

'Nowhere in particular,' Thako said awkwardly. 'Ginni Ma has sent for me, perhaps. I'll go and see—'

'Don't go.' Dulal set up a wail. 'Stay with me.'

Thako petted and cajoled him and promised to come back soon but Dulal's wails rose higher and higher. He was sick and he wanted his mother. Thako got desperate. She was getting late and Sohagbala would be annoyed! Suddenly, she lost her temper—violently and completely. Seizing her sick child by the hair, she slapped him hard on both cheeks. 'Die,' she muttered between clenched teeth. 'You burden on my back! Die and give my bones a rest.'

# Chapter XXXII

The city of Calcutta was rocked by an incident that occurred in the girls' school at Barasat. At the annual prize distribution ceremony, the chief guest, an Englishman, had shown his appreciation for a little girl's performance by lovingly pinching her cheeks. His action had had a violently disruptive effect on the audience. There was a great clamour in which some shouted that the girl and her family had lost caste by this physical contact with a *mlechha* foreigner; others that the girl had been violated. Things got so bad that the school had to be shut down. The teachers were ostracized by their friends and families and were even beaten up by goons hired by the local zamindar. All the newspapers of the city carried the sensational news.

The Englishman responsible for the trouble was aghast. But John Bethune was even more so. He wondered what he could achieve in a country where people were so irrational, where minds were so closed. As it was he was having difficulties persuading the government to accept his proposals for opening a school for girls. The British government in India favoured English education for the male but was wary when it came to the female. Women's education, for some strange reason, went against the spirit of native religions and was a sensitive area. Indians were indifferent to material losses but brooked no interference with their religion and culture.

It was at David Hare's death anniversary that Bethune found a way of realizing his cherished dream. Hare Saheb had been dead these six years but he lived on in the memory of the people. The day of his death was commemorated every year by the educated elite of Calcutta. Speeches extolling his greatness, his passionate devotion to native causes, were read out in English and Bengali. Bethune saw, with some surprise, tears standing in the eyes of many among the audience. 'A strange people,' he thought. 'The touch of one Englishman robs them of their caste while they weep and mourn for another.'

It was here, at David Hare's sixth death anniversary, that he met Ramgopal Ghosh and his cronies—followers of Derozio and members of the erstwhile Young Bengal movement. These men were among the first to receive an English education and held liberal views. On hearing that they met from time to time and discussed important issues, Bethune had an idea. He invited Ramgopal Ghosh and his friends over to his house to tea one afternoon. The guests arrived with English punctuality in flawless English suits. With one exception—a man in a dhoti and vest and wooden clogs on his feet. An enormous *shikha* sprang out of his shaven head. He was none other than Ishwar Chandra Vidyasagar's old friend—Madanmohan Tarkalankar.

After some preliminary small talk, the discussion veered to the subject of education for girls. 'You are the education secretary, Mr Bethune,' Ramgopal Ghosh said. 'Can't you do something?'

'But the people of this country are against it,' Bethune laughed. 'Haven't you heard of the incident in Barasat?'

'We were discussing it just before we came,' Ramgopal smiled. 'But should a stray incident like that frighten us away from a good cause?'

'Even the government is against it,' Bethune sighed. 'I, though education secretary, can do nothing by myself. Hobhouse, president of the board of control, laughed my proposals away. But I didn't give up. I had taken a vow before coming to this country that I would open a girls' school here even if I had to do it with my own money. I am a single man and my needs are few. It was a foolish dream.' Bethune shook his head sadly. 'The Barasat incident has opened my eyes. This country doesn't want education for its women.'

'We'll help you realize your dream.' Dakshinaranjan shot up from his chair in great excitement. 'We'll do everything we can—'

'My daughters, Bhavamala and Kundamala, will be your first students,' Madanmohan said. 'And I'll persuade others. You can leave that part to me. But you must look for a woman of high moral character to teach in the school.'

'You are a Brahmin and you propose to send your daughters out of the house to attend school! Won't your fellow Brahmins ostracize you?'

'Why should they? Education for Brahmin maidens is

nothing new. Our women have been educated through the ages. If a few idiots choose to spit on me I shall simply ignore them.'

'Your women have been educated through the ages!' Bethune echoed in surprise. 'I didn't know that.'

'Women in ancient India received equal education with men. I'll give you a few examples. Maharishi Valmiki's daughter, Atreyi, was enrolled in Agastya Rishi's ashram. Gargi and Maitreyi took lessons in Brahma Vidya from Rishi Yagna Valkya. The Mahabharat records that Rukmini, daughter of King Vidarbha, wrote a letter to Lord Krishna. Leelavati, daughter of Udayanacharya, was learned enough to preside over the debates between Shankaracharya and Mandan Misra. The wife of our great poet, Kalidas, was a learned woman, as was Vishwadevi, authoress of *Gangavakyavali.* A woman named Kshana was such a fine astrologer that her predictions are honoured to this day. How many more examples shall I give? And why only in ancient India? Even now, a woman by the name of Hoti Vidyalankar runs a *tol* in Varanasi very successfully. Everyone has heard of her.'

'You should make the public aware of these facts. Why don't you?'

'I will—most certainly. And I will prepare the textbooks for the school myself—'

'If you are ready to start, Mr Bethune,' Dakshinaranjan interrupted, 'I can donate the school building. I have a house lying vacant in Mirzapur.'

'Excellent! Let's go see the house. The earlier the better.'

In a few minutes, a carriage clattered down the streets of Calcutta in the direction of outer Simulia and stopped before a handsome mansion in Mirzapur. It was built in the old style, with domes and arches, and was surrounded by beautiful old gardens of fruits and flowers. Wishing to extend them even further, Dakshinaranjan had acquired the adjoining land, another five and a half bighas, at the cost of nine thousand rupees. The house alone could have fetched a rent of a hundred rupees a month but Dakshinaranjan made the entire property over to Bethune without a moment's hesitation. Madanmohan was pleased with what he saw. 'We must employ a couple of armed men to guard the gate,' he said. 'And I must get my friend, Ishwar Chandra, to join us. We need someone like him. Stern and upright.'

The next thing to find was a name for the school. 'If we name it after the Queen,' Bethune said, 'we might get the government to give us a grant.'

'Victoria Girls School!' Madanmohan exclaimed. 'A fine choice. Our school will be named after the most powerful woman in the world!'

'My sister is acquainted with the Queen. I'll write to her to secure Her Majesty's permission. It will be granted—I think.'

The school opened on a Monday morning. The schoolmistress, a genteel, learned lady by the name of Miss Readsdale, stood at the gate, welcoming the little girls. Handing over his daughters to her care, Madanmohan looked around him with appreciation. His face beamed with satisfaction and his *shikha* fluttered gaily in the wind.

There were twenty-one children on the first day. But though no fees were charged and books and writing materials distributed free, the number started dwindling. Within a couple of months it had come down to seven. A few eminent men had applauded the new venture but the bulk of the Calcutta citizens were against it. The newspapers were full of gossipy columns, describing the school as a kind of brothel although the girls who studied in it were all under the age of six. 'There can be only one relationship between a male and a female,' an elderly editor wrote. 'The one between a lion and a lamb. One devours—the other is devoured.' But criticism and malicious comments failed to daunt the founders. Although the school expenses ran to eight hundred rupees a month and the students were only seven in number, Bethune continued to nurture his dream of this little school growing into a mighty institution where hundreds of native girls received an education, and to this end, bought up all the surrounding land he could lay his hands on.

But negative propaganda was not the only reason for the sad state of affairs, as well-wishers pointed out. Mirzapur was out of the way, on the outskirts of the city. Parents found it difficult to send their daughters so far away from home. Bethune saw the logic of the argument and decided to move his school to a more central area. Having made his decision, Bethune submitted a proposal to the government. He would make over the house in Mirzapur, along with all its surrounding land, in exchange for the marshy tract that lay on the west bank of the lake at Hedua. The government had no objection and within a year and a half, a splendid mansion rose from out of a wilderness of palmyra and rank weed. The school building cost Bethune eighty-four thousand rupees, of which over forty thousand came from his own savings. The rest was donated by Dakshinaranjan and several others. The most liberal contribution came from the education enthusiast, Raja Joykrishna Mukherjee of Uttarpara.

But one school was not enough for Bethune. He wanted to open several more in the city. He was also closely involved with the spread and development of the Bengali language. He believed that it was only through the mother tongue that true education could be received. But Bengali was lacking in texts of excellence. To remedy this he set up a society for commissioning translations from English to Bengali and picked out the best scholars and writers for the purpose. 'Write in Bengali,' he advised them. 'Help to improve the language.' And, wherever he went, he pleaded with the people to work for the uplift of women.

Bethune's zeal for native causes and his constant association with Indians proved to be a source of embarrassment and annoyance to his countrymen in India. In consequence, he became the butt of ridicule among his own people. Not content with belittling his efforts, his fellow officials reprimanded him sharply for trying to secure Queen Victoria's name for his school, without seeking permission from the British government in India. The Queen was advised to withhold her consent. Hurt and angry, Bethune wrote to the governor-general, Lord Dalhousie, requesting him to intervene. But to no avail.

Returning from a school inspection in Jonai a few days before the inauguration of his new institution, Bethune got caught in a violent shower of rain. He returned to Calcutta, drenched to the bone, and developed a fever immediately afterwards, from which he never recovered. For a full day he lay unconscious, then opened his eyes painfully. Rows of friends and admirers, both Indian and European, stood at his bedside. 'Has the painting been completed?' he asked. 'What does the school look like?' Tears rushed into the eyes of those who heard him. 'It looks beautiful, sir,' someone answered, his voice quivering with emotion. 'Get well soon and see it for yourself.' Bethune sighed and was silent for a while. Then he said quietly, 'We English are not afraid of death. Nor do we believe in the hereafter as you do. For us everything ends with our dying breath. But the school mustn't die. Look after it, gentlemen, and keep it alive after I've gone.' Then, Bethune beckoned to a lawyer who stood on one side and made known his last will and testament. All his assets, moveable and immovable, were to go to the school. His personal carriage was to stand by the gate, ready to bring or take back the girls as and when necessary.

The problem of the school's name was solved with Bethune's death. 'Bethune Saheb's School' it came to be called by popular usage and then, over the years, it became Bethune School.

# Chapter XXXIII

The radiance of the night; the ash heap of the day—the old adage fitted in perfectly with Heeremoni's lifestyle. At night her house was flooded with light from the thirty lamps in her crystal chandeliers and sounds of sweet singing and the tinkling of ankle bells floated from her windows. The lanes and alleys around her house resounded to the clatter of carriages, the clip-clop of horses' hooves and drunken voices raised in laughter and quarrel. But with dawn all was dark and silent. The only sound that could be heard was a little boy's voice, learning his lessons by rote. Heeremoni had become the most famous courtesan in Calcutta and the most sought after—Kamala Sundari running a close second. Her voice was so melodious that to hear it once was to remember it forever. She had given up prostituting her body and was now a professional singer. Invitations to perform at births, marriages and religious festivals poured in from the houses of eminent and wealthy men. She had a new name now. Bulbul—Heera Bulbul. A tribute from the city's elite to her magnificent voice!

Affluence had come with recognition. She could afford every luxury in the world these days but her tastes were amazingly simple. Seeing her in the mornings, a duré sari of coarse striped cotton, wrapped loosely around her, no one would imagine her to be the same woman whose silks and jewels had dazzled so many eyes only the night before. And she, who could afford to eat pearls and drink molten gold, loved nothing better than a tasty hot *chacchari* of *pui* greens and shrimps and a bowl of khesari *dal*, which she ate with a mound of rice, eagerly and with relish, sitting on the floor, legs stretched out before her. She turned up her nose at expensive fish like carp and hated mutton, which, she said, had a disagreeable stink. She loved shrimps and tiddlers and the coarsest of vegetables and greens. But, despite the poor food she ate, she grew in beauty every day, shining out with a radiance that dazzled the eyes of the beholder.

Heeremoni had to have a bath the moment she awoke for her head felt as if on fire till half a dozen pitchers of water had been poured on it. That morning, as she approached the well in the courtyard, she saw that the rope had been torn from the pulley and the bell metal pitcher had vanished. Heeremoni flew into a violent rage and started berating the servants with the filthiest abuse in her stock. Then, weary of raining recriminations on passive, bowed heads, she turned the full force of her anger on Raimohan. 'Where is that wretched, do-nothing bastard?' she screamed shrilly. 'Warming his crumbling bones in bed, I warrant! While I stand here with my head flaming like a coal and my things disappearing from right under my nose. Oh! God, why do I suffer so? Thieves! Thieves! I'm surrounded by thieves. Each one bigger than the other.'

Startled out of his bed, Harachandra, the drunk Raimohan had picked up from the gutter, rushed to the well, where a strange sight met his eyes. Heeremoni stood by the pulley, half-naked—the scanty *gamchha* she had wrapped around her middle revealing more of her golden body than it hid. Her eyes rolled and her mouth foamed as streams of ribald curses poured from it. From time to time she gesticulated so violently that the *gamchha* threatened to burst open and expose her voluptuous body altogether.

'O Didi,' Harachandra said timidly, his eyes large with panic. 'Shall I go buy another pitcher?'

'Didi!' Heeremoni mocked in a rasping voice that belied her name of Bulbul. 'Since when have I become your Didi, you worthless parasite? He sticks to me like a leech and eats my rice,' she appealed to the world at large, 'because everyone else has kicked him out! And he dares to call me Didi. Oh! Oh! How my body burns!'

'It will burn more if you don't have a bath,' Harachandra said. 'I'll run to the market and buy—'

'Shut your mouth! Why, where's he? That vulture-faced, crocodile-skinned son of a pig? Why don't you send for him? Can't he jump into the well and find my pitcher for me? Eating mountains of rice and snoring in bed all day long! What use is he to me?'

Now, Heeremoni could have bought twenty pitchers had she wished but she was convinced that someone had stolen her pitcher and hidden it in the well. And whose duty was it but Raimohan's to find it for her? One of the servants having shaken him awake in the meantime, Raimohan came on the scene, rubbing his eyes. 'Why?' he cried, his eyes starting out of his head. 'What ails you so early in the morning?'

'What ails me? He asks what ails me. Oh, my God! Am I not standing naked here for the last two hours, waiting for my pitcher? But my sufferings, of course, are nothing to him! As long as he has his bottle and his bed he doesn't—'

Raimohan took in the situation in an instant. 'Bell metal is expensive, Heere,' he said peaceably. 'That's why your pitcher gets stolen every other day. What you need is a bucket. A strong iron bucket which no one will steal. I've told you and told you—'

'Iron!' Heeramoni leaped into the air as though stung by a hornet. 'You want me to bathe out of an iron vessel? What if my body breaks out in boils? What if the flesh comes off my bones like rotten fish? Oh! The base ingrate! Oh! To think I've fed this snake on milk and kept him in my house all these years! If you truly loved me, you would have bought a gold pitcher and filled it with rose-water for my bath.'

Raimohan crinkled his eyes and laughed. 'Abuse me all you can, Heere. Your curses fall on my ears as sweetly as dewdrops on flowers.' Then, seeing that the *gamchha* was loose and threatened to slip off Heeremoni's waist any moment, he turned to the servants and abused them roundly. 'Get out,' he hollered. 'Have you nothing better to do than to stand gaping here all day? Can't you fetch water from the tank by the mosque?'

But Heeremoni would not bathe in tank water. She would have water from her own well, drawn by her own pitcher. There was nothing now for Raimohan but to go to the bazaar and get hold of a 'Get things out of your wells, *go*!' But though that particular cry was uttered often enough to burst people's eardrums on other days, not one of the tribe was in evidence that morning. As is usually the case. When you want a barber, scores of cobblers will pass you by. And when you need puffed rice, you'll be besieged by curd-sellers. Raimohan waited in vain for a long time, then bought a new pitcher and a length of thick, strong rope, and came home to find Heeremoni sitting on the well's parapet, a hand on one flushed cheek. Seeing the pitcher, she jumped up and would have resumed her curses but Raimohan stopped her with a gesture. 'Wait! Wait!' he said. 'Not one of those rascals is around this morning. So I've decided to jump into the well myself. It is the least I can do for you.' Then, sitting by her side, he took her hand in his. 'Heere,' he said, making his voice deep and tender, 'I thought I would drown in the deep pools of your eyes. But I'll do what you wish. I go to meet my death in your well.' He fastened one end of the rope firmly to the pulley and brought the other end around his waist.

*'Illo!'* Heeremoni gave a snort of contempt. 'If it was so easy to die, you'd be dead long ago. Who stopped you?'

'I am dead, Heere,' Raimohan put one leg across. 'Killed by the darts from your lovely eyes. But one death is not enough for me. I could die over and over again for love of you.' He put the other leg across and said in the voice of a tragic hero, 'Goodbye, my bulbul. May we meet in the other world.'

Now Heere screamed in alarm. *'O go!* Don't, don't,' she cried, rushing forward. 'I don't want my pitcher. I don't want anything. Who'll look after me when you're gone? The vultures out there will tear me to pieces—'

'Keep a darwan,' Raimohan called back, placing a foot gingerly on the first niche. 'With a gun.'

By now the inmates of the household had come crowding around the well and were pushing and jostling each other to get a better view. 'Jump, Dada, jump!' Harachandra cried out encouragingly. 'Do or die.' Heere grabbed Raimohan by the hair and screamed, 'Don't jump. Don't! I'll knock my head on these stones and die. I swear I will. I won't live for a day after you've gone.'

After a few minutes more of this play-acting, Raimohan climbed out of the well. Needless to say, he had no intention of embracing a watery death. He knew Heeremoni. Now Heere wept and sobbed while Raimohan poured water over her and bathed her as tenderly as he would a child. Then, cooled in body and spirit, she sat down to her music and all was as it had been. Raimohan was a fixture in Heeremoni's house these days for she depended on him for everything—particularly for protection against her former clients, who made demands on her body. Raimohan had found a novel way of keeping them away. Ferreting out their deepest, darkest sins, he composed verses about them, which he set to music and taught Heeremoni. 'The time is at hand, Heere,' he said enthusiastically, 'when you won't even need to sing for a living. Rumours and threats will earn you all the money you want. All the bigwigs of the city will come running to you, begging you to spare them. And they won't come empty-handed either. They'll cover your feet with gold. Just wait and see. We'll catch them one by one!'

Heeremoni's son, Chandranath, was a shy, gentle youth of fourteen, with a handsome face and pleasing manners. His milk had been laced with opium all through his infancy for a wailing child was a distinct liability in Heeremoni's profession. But though Raimohan had had the practice stopped the moment he had come to know of it, some of its effect had remained. Chandranath slept heavily from early evening till dawn, oblivious of everything that went on in the house. There was a curious detachment about him, too, that worried Heeremoni at times. He was old enough now to know what his mother did for a living but he never betrayed his knowledge by a word or glance. He was very keen on his lessons and very quick to learn. Harachandra had taught him all he knew but it wasn't much. The time had come to send him to school but no school would enrol a boy whose paternity was unknown. Raimohan had pleaded with Heeremoni often in the past to allow him to adopt the boy and give him his name. Raimohan Ghoshal had pure Brahmin blood in his veins, even if he hung around with drunks and prostitutes, and his name commanded respect. But Heeremoni was adamant. Chandranath was hers—only hers. God had given him to her. Alas! All men are God's children but society does not recognize the fact. It demands a human father.

One afternoon, as Raimohan sat eating his midday meal, he said suddenly, 'If you wish it, Heere, we can send Chandu to Hindu College—the best and most famous school in Calcutta. Only you must be ready to do a few things.'

'I?' Heeremoni looked up in amazement. 'I can't tell one letter from another. What do I know of schools?'

'You don't have to know anything. Listen carefully. There's a mujra at the house of the Dattas day after tomorrow, at which you will be singing. I've made enquiries. All the big men of the city—sahebs and babus—are to come and wine is to flow freely. Men in their cups get sentimental and guilt-ridden when they hear God's name. Sing songs of bhakti and you'll have them weeping and throwing purses of gold at your feet. Then, choosing an opportune moment, go up to the five members of the school board one by one—I'll give your their names—and say, "I'm a lowly woman—unfit to receive these riches. But if you truly wish to reward me, grant me a boon. Take my son into your school and give him an education." Make your face sad and tearful and be sure to touch their feet first.'

But Raimohan's plan proved to be extremely ill-advised. Heeremoni came home that evening in a flaring temper. She had never been so humiliated in her life. On hearing one of the five uttering exclamations of praise over and over again, she had picked up courage and walking over to him, had bent down to touch his feet prior to making her request. But the great man had recoiled from her touch as if she were a snake and had screamed abuse. How dare a prostitute pollute him with her touch? Did she not know who he was? What kind of a house was this where street whores could take such liberties?

Raimohan's jaw tightened and a queer light came into his eyes as he heard Heeremoni's account. He had spent years fawning on the wealthy and pimping for them, and now they inspired nothing in him but hatred. 'Don't cry, Bulbul,' he said, a smile of cruel amusement lifting one side of his face. 'I'll send your son to Hindu College—yet. But I'll see all these whoresons in hell first. Scoundrels and hypocrites! Too pure for a prostitute to touch them during the day! What about the nights, when they grovel at your feet, begging for favours? I'll trumpet all their doings in the streets—the bastards!'

Then, one morning, Raimohan called for a hackney coach and taking Heere and Chandranath with him, journeyed towards Hindu College. He had dressed the boy with his own hands in a fine dhoti and muslin kurta. A raw silk uduni hung from his shoulders and shoes of polished English leather encased his feet. Heeremoni had followed Raimohan's instructions and was resplendent in brocade pyjamas and shirt. A scarf of the finest Cashmere wool covered her breasts and her feet glittered in gold embroidered *nagras*. Her fingers were loaded with rings and her mouth was crimson with betel. This was the way Heeremoni dressed when she went out on her nocturnal trysts with the most eminent of the city's men. When the coach stopped at the Pataldanga crossing, in full view of the great institution of learning, Raimohan said, 'Take the boy by the hand and walk straight in. Keep your chin high and your eyes steady. Do exactly what I've told you. Now, go.'

'Why don't you come with us? I'm afraid—'

'There's nothing to be afraid of. There's a board meeting going on. Don't you see the carriages? Go straight into the room and say, "Gentlemen, you all know me—Heera Bulbul. This is my son, Chandranath. I want you to take him into your school." Then, when they ask you for his father's name, look full into their faces and ask, "Shall I?" Be sure to smile and wink meaningfully before adding "Will that be proper? Isn't it much better for you all if I say his father's name is God?"'

# *Chapter XXXIV*

Vidyasagar stood on an upper verandah of Sanskrit College, watching the commotion outside the great gates of the adjacent building. A young woman of a striking, arrogant beauty and glittering in brocade and jewels had just stepped out of a carriage, holding a young boy by the hand. But as she made her way into the college she was surrounded by a group of students who tried to bar her entry with cries of *'Arré! Arré*! What's this? What's this?' For no woman had ever entered the sacred portals of Hindu College before. There were others, boys from the first families of Calcutta, who stood by and watched but took no part. Among them Vidyasagar recognized Ramkamal Sen's grandson, Keshab, Dwarkanath's grandson, Satyendranath, Mahendralal Sarkar, Deenabandhu Mitra and Pratap Chandra Majumdar. The boy whose hand the woman held was about the same age as these boys. His ears flamed with embarrassment and his eyes were fixed on the ground.

Heera Bulbul looked neither left nor right. Chin high, head held erect, she swept past the boys and entered the hall. As she approached the staircase she heard voices from a room just beyond it and knew that Raimohan's information was correct. A meeting was going on in that room. Heeremoni took a deep breath and walked in. The members looked up, startled at her entry and she had the satisfaction of seeing quite a few jaws hang in dismay. 'You know me gentlemen,' she began, repeating parrot-like what Raimohan had taught her, but before she could complete her prepared speech, a member of the board, a native, cried hastily, *'Arré! Arré*! Who let her in? Where are the darwans? Ramtahal! Brijwasi!'

'My name is Heera Bulbul,' Heeremoni flashed a smile at the gaping faces. 'Can a darwan lay hands on me with so many gentlemen present?'

'Let us hear what she has to say,' an Englishman said peaceably. 'Please take a seat, madam.'

'Are you suggesting, sir,' another native member, an

exceedingly eminent personage, asked coldly, 'that a woman as low and depraved as this one should dare to sit down before us? Is it not enough that she pollutes the air of this venerable institution with her presence?' Heeremoni fixed her gaze on him and held his eyes for a long time. Her lips smiled but her glance conveyed the clear threat that if she wanted to she could burst into speech any moment. She could exclaim, '*O go*, Babu! Don't you know me? Have you forgotten the nights we've spent together, cuddling in my bed?' The man bit his lip and lowered his eyes. But Heeremoni did not say a word. She turned the same glance to the faces of the other four, one by one, and an enigmatic smile lifted the corners of her mouth. The Englishmen on the board perceived the dilemma of their native compatriots and found it diverting.

'We don't understand your attitude,' they said as if with one voice. 'The woman is a Hindu. Why should her son be denied admission?'

'A prostitute's son! What religion or caste can he claim? Who knows who the father is?'

'I know,' Heeremoni said. Her eyes rested on the five faces, turn by turn. She flashed a smile at each and gave a conspiratorial wink. 'Shall I give his name?' she asked softly. 'Will that be proper under the circumstances? But I will if you press me to. Think about it and let me know.'

All five faces turned pale with horror. 'Who knows what the she-devil has in mind?' each one of them thought. 'What if she utters a name—my name? A whore's story goes down well with the public. Even newspaper reporters lap it up. I'll be ruined. I'll become the laughing stock of the city.' They rose, as if in one body, and left the room, their jowls quivering in protest.

On examining Chandranath, the English sahebs were pleasantly surprised. He was exceedingly bright; far brighter than average and very keen to learn. Deeming him fit to study in Class III, they sent for the teacher and handed him over. Heeremoni stepped out of the building with the air of a conquering queen and took her place in the carriage. One look at her face and Raimohan knew that the mission planned by him and executed by her had been successful. He bared his teeth in a grin and pirouetted with joy. 'Wasn't I right, Heere?' he cried. 'We've taught the bastards a lesson they won't forget in a hurry.

You should have seen them squealing and running to their carriages. Like jackals with their tails between their legs.'

That evening all the boys of Class III went home to find their parents in a state of agitation. Their clothes were ripped from their bodies and thrown out into the streets and they were made to bathe in Gangajal. Meetings were held in Raja Radhakanta Deb's palace in Shobha Bazaar, Debendranath Thakur's mansion in Jorasanko and Rajendranath Datta's house in Taltala to discuss the issue and seek redress. What was the country coming to? If boys from the first families of the land had to rub shoulders with the sons of pimps and prostitutes, what would the future hold for them? This college, set up by eminent Hindus, was now in the grip of the sahebs and they were dictating terms. It was intolerable.

The next day the college wore a deserted air. There was only one student in Class III and that was Chandranath. The Hindu teachers declined to teach him but the English authorities were steadfast in their resolution. The boy had been admitted into the school and he would be taught. Those who had refused to do so would be dealt with. As Chandranath sat huddled over his books in one corner of the classroom, a teacher, an Englishman, approached him. 'Come, my boy,' he said. 'We shall read poetry today. Have you heard of Byron?' Chandranath rose to his feet and recited softly—

Oh talk not to me of a name great in story,
The days of our youth and the days of our glory.

The Englishman listened, enraptured.

The outcome of the meetings was that a strongly worded letter was lodged with the authorities, protesting against their decision to enrol Heera Bulbul's son in Hindu College. But the latter stood firm. Prostitutes were not born, they argued. They had been created by this very society and been nurtured for ages because they fulfilled a social need. Yet, they were rejected by the very people who couldn't do without them and this rejection went beyond them and extended to their children. There were prostitutes in England, too, but their children were not denied education. Why should Indian prostitutes be treated so unfairly?

Sitting in his office on the first floor of Sanskrit College, Ishwar Chandra Vidyasagar heard what was going on next door. But it did not concern him for, barring the English lessons he took from some of its teachers, he had nothing to do with Hindu College. That night, as he walked down Sukia Street on his way back home, he found himself being followed by a young woman. It was well past midnight and a mild rain was falling. He walked away from her as fast as he could but the woman was desperate. Running after him she clutched his arm. Vidyasagar shook her off and walked on but after a few yards he stopped and turned back. She stood where she was. She was very young and frail with a tense, anxious face.

'What are you doing here so late at night?' he asked. 'Go home.' The girl sighed. She could see his face now. He was only a poor Brahmin—a cook, perhaps, in some rich household. She cursed her luck. She had wandered in the streets, half the night in the falling rain, only for this! 'What else can I do, Thakur?' she asked. 'I haven't had a single customer tonight. I have no money. What shall I eat?'

Vidyasagar lowered his eyes. What right had he to sit in judgement on the girl for what she did for a living? This society denied education to its women and forced them into marriage when they were mere infants. Then, if a woman was unfortunate enough to lose her husband, all the pleasures of life were denied her. She was cheated of her husband's property by grasping in-laws and treated like a servant in the family. She might even be turned out of the house. Then, when she was reduced to selling her body in order to feed herself, the brand mark of shame and rejection was stamped on her forehead. Heera Bulbul's encounter with the authorities of Hindu College had exposed much of the rot that society hid so cleverly. Her son's father was one of the very men who had denied him the right to study in the college.

Tears rolled down Vidyasagar's cheeks. This tendency to weep was getting to be a nuisance. He rebuked himself for his weakness. Taking out all the money he was carrying he handed it to the girl with the words, 'Don't walk about in the rain any more, child. Go home.' Then turning, he walked away as fast as he could.

'O Thakur!' the girl called after him. 'Why do you give me

money for nothing? Come to my room and I'll pleasure you well. O Thakur!'

Vidyasagar covered up his ears with his hands and started running down the road.

One day, on his way back from college, Chandranath was set upon by three or four lathi-wielding men and beaten so badly that he fell to the ground unconscious. A dog came and sniffed the bleeding boy but no one else came near him. And as luck would have it, that very day Raimohan and Harachandra had got hold of a bottle of liquor and were drunk before dusk. The usual hour of Chandranath's return being long past, Heeremoni became worried and anxious. Twice she expressed her fears to Raimohan but he laughed them away. Chandranath was not a child that he would lose his way, Raimohan explained. It was far more likely that the sahebs, thrilled to find a pupil of Chandranath's intelligence, were giving him extra lessons. It was only when Heere, in her desperation, snatched up a broomstick and laid it about their heads and shoulders that the two ran out of the house to look for the boy. Their arms twined about each other's necks, the two drunks walked out into the moonlight, calling out to the passers-by in slurred voices, 'O Moshai! Have you seen Chandu?' When they reached Hindu College they found the gates locked and the building dark and deserted. 'There's no one here,' Raimohan said. 'Chandu must have reached home by now. Let's go.'

On their way back they discovered Chandranath by accident. The liquor fumes clouding their brains were dispelled in an instant and they cried out aloud in frightened voices. Raimohan flung himself to the ground beside the unconscious boy and raved and cursed the great men of the city, taking each one's name by turn. His cries drew the attention of the great physician, Durgacharan Bandopadhyaya, who was passing by in his palki. Poking his head out of the window, Durgacharan saw a strange sight. A young boy, fair as a flower, lay on the ground, still and inert as if in death, and two drunks, sprawling beside him in the dust, shrieked and cursed and knocked their heads on the ground. Durgacharan stepped down and examined the boy. He wasn't dead. He had fainted from the loss of blood caused by a great wound on the head.

'Who did this to him?' Durgacharan addressed the two sternly. 'Was it one of you?'

'No,' Raimohan screamed like one possessed. 'It was you. You and all those others,' he pointed with a trembling finger at the handsome mansions of the rich. 'You have beaten him and killed him.'

'Quiet!' Durgacharan roared. 'Stop screaming like a mad jackal and help me lift the boy into the palki. He's badly hurt but not dead. I must attend to his wounds.'

'Look, Moshai!' Raimohan roared back. 'You'd better hear who he is before you decide to touch him. He's a prostitute's son.'

'He's a pupil of Hindu College,' Harachandra said in English. 'His mother's name is Heera Bulbul.'

Now all was clear to Durgacharan. He had heard the story of Heera Bulbul's encounter with the members of the board and was aware of the mood of the city's elite. 'I'm a doctor,' he said gruffly. 'I don't lose caste that easily. Lift him quickly into the palki. He needs immediate attention.'

Chandranath recovered completely in a few days and insisted on going to college although a great white bandage was still wrapped around his head. Heere was against it but Raimohan backed him up. 'That's the spirit,' he exclaimed. 'Show the bastards that you're not afraid. Don't worry, Heere. I'll take him to college myself and bring him back from now on. But we must have our own carriage. We'll keep our own guards if necessary. As for you,' he turned to Harachandra. 'If you dare pump me with liquor ever again before Chandu comes home, I'll break your neck.'

People were boycotting Hindu College and the number of students dwindled every day. But no one could prevent Chandranath from getting an education. The sahebs stood firm in their support. Finally, in their desperation, the important men of the city decided to open another college. The Hindu Metropolitan College was established practically overnight by Rajendranath Datta with help from others—the most substantial contribution of ten thousand rupees coming from Rani Rasmoni. Captain Richardson, sacked by the authorities of

Hindu College for immoral behaviour, was brought in as principal. Raimohan's victory was complete.

That evening, Raimohan was in an amorous mood. 'Let tonight be our night together, Heere,' he said. 'Only you and I, with no one between us. I'll lie back against the cushions and you'll hold the glass of wine to my lips. You'll wear your finest silks and jewels and line your eyes with kohl—only for me. The chandeliers will blaze with light and the air hang heavy with attar—only for me. And you'll sing—'

'Ah! Ha, ha, ha.' Heera laughed derisively. 'What hopes! A two-cowrie babu like you! Why don't you go to Rambagan? You'll find plenty of women to suit your purse.'

'Heere!' Raimohan's eyes looked steadfastly into hers. 'You ask me to go to another woman. You! Don't you know I haven't looked at anyone else ever since I came to you?'

'My sarangiwala will be here in a few minutes. It's time for my practice. You'd better clear out.'

'You kick and spurn me like a dog,' Raimohan said without a trace of pain in his voice. 'But it doesn't touch me. All I want is to be near you. You can't get rid of me tonight, Heere. I must be king to your queen.'

They argued a little longer, then Heeremoni had to give in. Dismissing her sarangiwala, she dressed herself as if for a mujra. All the lamps were lit in the crystal chandeliers. Champagne sparkled in cut glass goblets. Raimohan lay against the cushions and Heeremoni sang one song after another. From time to time the sound of carriage wheels came to their ears but every time that happened, Raimohan drew her closer to him and whispered, 'No one, Heere. No one but you and I. The world is ours—only ours. I'll pour my soul in lyrics for you to sing in that divine voice of yours. And then, one day, we'll leave everything behind us and walk out into the world, hand in hand, singing as we go along. And just like that, hand in hand, singing together, we'll walk into Heaven. Don't shake your head, Heere. Don't doubt my words. I'll make a place for you in Heaven. I swear I will.'

# Chapter XXXV

A number of tutors had been employed for Nabin Kumar—a pandit to teach him Sanskrit and Bengali, a saheb by the name of Mr Kirkpatrick for English and a skilled professional for music and wrestling. But none of Nabin Kumar's tutors lasted for long. Though very bright and quick to learn, Nabin was a difficult pupil—haughty, capricious and excessively spoiled. The fault lay with Bimbabati. She made no effort to discipline him or teach him obedience and humility. If Nabin wanted the moon he was to have it. Such was Bimba's attitude to her son.

At twelve Nabin was an extremely handsome lad. His finely cut features glowed with spirit and intelligence and his eyes sparkled like jewels. That he was no ordinary boy was stamped on his mien. But looking at him no one could imagine the viciousness and cruelty he was capable of. His mother had employed seven servants, solely to serve him. Nabin would never sit down to a meal. He ate when and where the whim took him. To see a servant following him about with a *thala* heaped high with food from the roof to the garden, from the balcony to the bedroom, was a common sight. Every time Nabin beckoned imperiously, the servant would dart forward. Nabin might or might not take a spoonful but the slightest inattention or delay and he would kick the *thala* so viciously that it would crash to the ground. If the temperature of his bath water was not to his liking he would curse and abuse the servants bathing him and even slap their cheeks. Once Ganganarayan saw Nabin sprawled on the sofa, his legs stuck out in front of him while a servant tied the laces of his shoes. Ganga was appalled. His education in Hindu College had enlightened him to a great extent. He had read Rousseau and believed in the equality of men.

'*Arré,* Chhotku,' he said smiling, 'don't you know how to tie a shoe-lace?'

'No,' Nabin answered, lifting his chin proudly.

'But it is so easy. If Baharu can do it surely you can.'

'Can Baharu recite Sanskrit shloks? I can. Tying my shoe-laces is his job. Not mine.'

'We must all learn to do our own work. Come, I'll teach you—'

'Shoes have dust on them. My hands will get dirty if I touch them. Ma has forbidden it.'

Ganga sighed. Bimbabati was blind and deaf where her son was concerned. If he wanted someone's head he was to have it. Ganga had tried remonstrating with her on several occasions and drawn a blank each time. Ganga was often worried about his little brother. Nabin reminded him, uncannily, of his friend, Madhu. Madhu's parents had indulged him beyond reasonable limits and turned him into an arrogant, selfish egotist. And, as was to be expected, they were the ones at whom Madhu had struck the cruellest blow. His mother had wept herself into the other world. And his hurt and angry father had cast him out and taken one wife after another in the hope of begetting another son. But all his efforts had been frustrated and he had died bitter and unhappy to the end. Nabin was like Madhu—brilliant, arrogant and wilful. But there was one difference. Madhu was *firinghee* in his tastes and disdained the native languages and Nabin loved Sanskrit and Bengali above all other subjects.

On Ganga's return from a tour of the estates, his wife, Lilavati, told him in a series of whispers that in his absence, Nabin had committed the unspeakable offence of cutting off a Brahmin's *shikha*.

Every year, on the last day of Poush,[27] Bimbabati performed certain religious ceremonies with great pomp and extravagance. Gifts of gold, cloth and rice were made to several Brahmins and one of them even received a cow. This year, the Brahmin singled out for the honour had led the plump white calf from the gates of the Singha mansion straight to the abattoir in Kolutola and sold him to one of the butchers. Quite by accident, he was caught in the act by two servants of the Singha

27 15th December—15th January.

household, who ran back to inform their mistress. When Nabin heard the story he ordered that the Brahmin be brought before him.

'Cut off his *tiki*,' Nabin commanded. 'I'll frame it in glass as a warning to others like him.' Bimbabati tried to remonstrate; to tell him that cutting off a Brahmin's *shikha* was a grievous sin. But Nabin was not to be overruled. 'The cow should be as a mother to a Brahmin,' the twelve-year-old announced ponderously. 'Why else do we call her *gomata*? A Brahmin such as this one has forfeited his right to the insignia of Brahminhood.' Then, abandoning his gravity, he commenced whining and sobbing. 'I want to cut off his *tiki*, Ma! I must and I will.' 'Don't cry, my child,' his mother hastened to comfort him. 'Don't cry.' The consequence was that four able-bodied servants held down the quaking old man by force and Nabin, cackling with laughter, snipped off his *shikha* with a pair of scissors.

Ganga was stunned when he heard the story. He himself had little respect for the illiterate hypocrites who called themselves Brahmins these days. But he understood their constraints and sympathized. Most Brahmins were poor and had to make a living out of the alms they received. By gifting a cow—(always a male of the species, never a female) the rich bought up mansions for themselves in Heaven, but what use was such a gift to a poor Brahmin, who had no land and thus no plough to yoke him to? The calf would grow into a sturdy bullock and eat the poor man out of house and home!

That afternoon, Ganga called Nabin to his room. Placing a hand on the child's head, he asked gently, 'What is this I hear, Chhotku? People say you've cut off a Brahmin's *shikha*?'

'Yes, Ganga Dada.' Nabin's face broke into an ecstatic smile. 'I've framed it and hung it in my room. You're the only one who hasn't seen it. It was such fun! You should have seen the old man leaping into the air and screaming, "*Hai* Ram! My *chaitan chutki's* lost! *Hai* Ram".' Nabin rolled all over the bed in mirth. Ganga smiled with him, but inwardly, he felt uncomfortable.

'You're a crazy boy, Chhotku,' he said. 'What if no one agrees to teach you after hearing what you've done? I've engaged a very renowned pandit this time—'

'I know. I've threatened him already. I've said, "If you refuse to teach me, I'll set my guards on you and snip—they'll cut off your *tiki*".'

'How terrible of you!' Ganga exclaimed. 'And what did Pandit Moshai say?'

'He said I was right in what I did. There are thousands of fake Brahmins these days and they deserve to be punished.'

'People will talk about us. The story will be out in the newspaper.'

'You can buy off the newspaper. Come, let me show you the essay I've written. I wrote it especially for you to read since you weren't here. It's entitled "A Brahmin is a Chandal". Nabin ran out of the room and came back with a sheaf of loose papers. Ganga took them in his hands and was charmed at the beauty of the handwriting. The letters were as neat and rounded as pearls. Reading the essay he was even more charmed with the ideas and sentiments. Also, he found it hard to believe that a boy of twelve had such a great mastery of the language.

'Excellent, Chhotku!' he exclaimed. 'Even I can't write so well. Did you write it by yourself or did Pandit Moshai help you?'

'I wrote it by myself. I've written many more. No one has seen them except Dulal. Ganga Dada, I can write songs and set them to music. Shall I sing one to you?'

Ganga was amazed. Was Nabin destined to be a poet and author like Madhu? Were all poets wild and indisciplined from childhood? He would show Nabin's essay to Vidyasagar Moshai and take his opinion.

Nabin's English tutor, Mr Kirkpatrick, advised Ganga to send Nabin to school. The discipline would do him good, he said, and being with boys of his own age would give him a more balanced view of life. Ganga had considered it already for he was keen to see his brother receive a public school education. The difficulty lay in tackling Bimbabati. She refused to let Nabin out of her sight for a moment. However, the problem was solved for him by Nabin himself.

'Ganga Dada,' the boy said one day. 'Every morning I look out of my window and see boys going to college with their books under their arms. I want to go to college like them. I'm tired of home tutors.' For Nabin to want something was to have it. He wept and screamed and caused such a havoc that

Bimbabati was forced to change her mind. 'You'd better do as he says,' she told her elder son. 'Seeing that he's so keen—'

Many of the old teachers of Hindu College remembered Ganga and some of his contemporaries were teaching there now. He had no difficulty whatsoever in getting his brother admitted. Preparations were made for this new phase in Nabin's life. English suits were ordered at the tailor master's. A carriage with two attendants was set aside solely to take Nabin to college and bring him back. But the day before Nabin was to join, Bidhusekhar came to Jorasanko. Meeting Ganga on his way up the stairs, he said coldly, 'I hear you are sending Nabin to Hindu College. You didn't even consider it necessary to inform me?' Then, without waiting for an answer, he went up and entered Bimbabati's room.

'Nabin is not going to Hindu College,' he said briefly. 'He will continue to study at home as he has been doing.'

'But he's very keen to go,' Bimba said in faltering tones. 'He will cry himself sick if we stop him.'

'Let him cry. He'll get over it in a few days. Hindu College has become a den of shame and iniquity. Shall a scion of the Singha family sit in the same room with the son of a prostitute? It was Ganga's idea, was it not? Has he no sense of propriety, of family honour?' Pausing a little he fixed his eyes on Bimba's face. 'Is the boy's future only your concern?' he asked softly, but his voice had a hint of steel in it. 'Is my opinion worth nothing?'

'No, no.' A shudder ran through Bimba's frame. 'All will be done as you wish it.'

On his way down, a little later, Bidhusekhar sent for Ganga. 'Nabin is not going to college,' he announced in a voice of finality. 'He will be thirteen next month. I've arranged a marriage for him.'

# Chapter XXXVI

The splendour of Nabin Kumar's wedding arrangements took the city by storm. Nothing like it had ever been seen before though there was no dearth of wealthy families in Calcutta. Everyone admitted that Ramkamal Singha's widow had put the Malliks, Dattas, Devs, Shils, Ghoshals and Sarkars to shame. Expensive gifts were sent out with the wedding cards—Cashmere or Benaras shawls for the men; brass vessels and conches, bound in silver, for the women. For seven days the guests ate and drank and were entertained by dancing and singing girls. All the newspapers carried detailed reports. Of course, it had all been arranged by Bidhusekhar Mukherjee, who had proved himself a true and trusty friend. Usually, after a man's death, his close friends and relatives robbed the poor widow of her property. But Bidhusekhar had not only guarded it closely, he had, by judicious management, increased it four-fold.

On the wedding night, crowds of people lined the streets from Jorasanko to Bagbazar to watch the procession go by. The groom, in a dazzling costume sewn with emeralds, rubies and diamonds, rode a white horse. With a brocade turban on his head and a sword in a gold embossed scabbard at his waist, the thirteen-year-old boy looked like a prince from a fairy tale.

In all this Ganga had no part to play. Bidhusekhar dealt with every detail himself and did not care to take Ganga's opinion on any point. His personal humiliation apart, Ganga was not happy for he was opposed to child marriage. He considered it a social evil and responsible for a great deal of unhappiness. He himself had been forced into marriage before he was ready for it and he was determined to save Nabin from the same fate. Nabin was to study, attain wisdom and maturity, and marry only when he understood what marriage meant. Ganga tried to speak to his mother but she ignored his pleas. Mukherjee Moshai, she said, knew best. Surely he wouldn't want any harm to come to Nabin. Ganga couldn't understand his mother's attitude. She, who couldn't bear to see her child crying for a minute, had endured his tears for two whole days and stood firm against his entreaties to be allowed to go to college, simply because Bidhusekhar had forbidden it. He couldn't understand why Bidhusekhar was forcing his opinion on the Singhas. And why Bimbabati was allowing him to do so.

Ganga trembled with rage every time he remembered the old man's curt dismissal of his plans for Nabin. Bidhusekhar's cold, harsh words had fallen upon his ears like burning lava and seared his soul with humiliation. That night, Ganga swore a solemn oath. He would break the old man's arrogance if it was the last thing he did. Bimbabati might try to stop him but Nabin would take his side. Nabin was his brother and he loved and honoured him. Besides, Nabin was not afraid of Bidhusekhar.

But the strangest thing happened. Nabin wept and stormed for two whole days but the moment he heard that he was to be married his mood changed. His disappointment at being kept away from college was dispelled by his enthusiasm for his approaching nuptials.

'Chhotku,' Ganga said to him one day. 'You are too young to know anything of marriage. Don't you think you should wait a few more years?'

'No, Ganga Dada,' Nabin answered solemnly. 'I would like to get married. I'm going to marry Radha.'

'Radha?' Ganga was surprised. 'Who is Radha?'

'I'm Lord Krishna. So Radha must be my wife. We'll have such fun. We'll play hide and seek in the garden. Do you know, Ganga Dada, that I can play the flute?'

A few days after the wedding, Ganganarayan left Calcutta for another tour of the estates. The indigo planters were getting more cruel and rapacious every day and the peasants groaned under their yoke. They had represented their case several times and begged their zamindar to intervene. Ganga had tried his best but all his efforts had drawn a blank. The government decree, barring mofussil courts from putting an Englishman on trial, stood unshaken. Flushed with triumph, the sahebs redoubled their oppression. Rape and arson, whippings and killings became everyday affairs. A planter without a whip in his hand was the strangest of sights. Ganga had no hopes of being able to improve the situation. Yet he couldn't ignore it either. If someone didn't register his presence from time to time, the family would lose the estates. Since Bidhusekhar never left Calcutta if he could help it, the responsibility fell on Ganga.

Ganga didn't mind in the least. In fact, he was glad to escape the house, which was still crammed with wedding guests. He felt an alien in his own home and his heart was heavy within him. The country was awakening to a new dawn but his own near and dear ones still slept the sleep of ignorance and superstition and refused to see the light. A child marriage had taken place within these very walls and he had been powerless to stop it. He felt frustrated and utterly humiliated.

The moment Ganga's boat touched Ibrahimpur Ghat, the peasants crowded around him with their tales of woe. The situation at Ibrahimpur was a complicated one. Years ago, when Ramkamal Singha was still alive, the Singhas grew indigo in Ibrahimpur and had even set up a kuthi. But the indigo business being very lucrative, the local British planters were straining every nerve to make it their monopoly by creating trouble wherever they could. Weary of the tension engendered by an unfair competition, Ganga had taken Bidhusekhar's advice and leased half his fields to the sahebs. But the action had disastrous consequences. The ryots were bonded for life on the payment of two rupees as contract money. A ryot who refused to set his thumb to the contract was carried away to the kuthi by the guards, where he was whipped and tortured till he obeyed. Appalled at the plight of the peasants, Ganga had wanted to put an end to the lease and, instead, farm rice on those fields. But Bidhusekhar had advised him against it. Bidhusekhar believed in the principle that if you lived in water you couldn't afford to quarrel with the crocodile. The sahebs were the masters. They were ruling the country. The sight of waving fields of golden grain would hardly be a soothing sight to eyes greedy for gain. On the contrary, they might turn themselves into Chinese dragons and, breathing fire from their nostrils, set the fields ablaze.

One saheb in particular, a Mr MacGregor, was a veritable demon. He carried a whip which the locals had named Shyamchand. One lash from Shyamchand had the power to break a rebel ryot's spine. The rains had failed this year and the indigo harvest was poor. But MacGregor would not admit it.

He was convinced that the ryots had deliberately neglected the fields and manipulated a scanty harvest as a form of revenge. Wild with fury, he decided to teach the ryots a lesson. Lashings and kidnappings became more frequent than ever and houses were burned in scores. The frightened ryots fled to the neighbouring villages but there was no escaping the MacGregor eye. MacGregor didn't believe in confining his activities to his own land but rode out as far as his horse would go and hunted down his victims like animals.

Ganga heard the peasants out but could not commit himself to help them. They looked upon their zamindar as a kind of God, stern and just, but also merciful where mercy was sought. They didn't know how powerless Ganga was. He had leased his lands to the British planters and, in doing so, had handed over the lives of his subjects. He couldn't change the situation. His brain reeled with the tales he had just heard—of crimes perpetrated by MacGregor and that devil incarnate associate of his—Golak Das. Among them, the one that affected him most was that of the disappearance of Hanifa Bibi, the comely young wife of Jamaluddin Sheikh. Convinced that his wife had been kidnapped by Golak Das and handed over to his master, Jamaluddin had gone to the kuthi to make enquiries and hadn't returned. This was some days ago. The villagers believed that Jamaluddin was either being kept prisoner in the kuthi's cellar or had been killed outright. Ganga remembered Jamaluddin Sheikh—a fine, manly, broad-chested youth, strong as a bull. His voice and manner were rough but inside, he was as simple as a child. 'I'm your slave, Raja Babu,' Jamaluddin's old father quavered. His eyes were scaled over with cataract and his hands trembled before him like a blind man's. 'Give my boy back to me.'

'Have you informed the magistrate?' Ganga asked. 'Only he can help you.' But the peasants shook their heads. Majestar Saheb, they said, was a relative of MacGorgor Saheb's. The former stayed at the kuthi whenever he was here and the two went shooting together. MacGorgor kept an elephant and two hounds the size of tigers. Majestar Saheb would turn a deaf ear to any complaint about MacGorgor.

'I'll go,' Ganga announced suddenly and prepared to step out of the boat, but Akshay Sen, the local steward, rushed towards him, exclaiming, 'Where are you going, Babu? You haven't had a bath and meal yet. Besides, you are the zamindar. The Sahebs are your tenants. They must come to you. Send MacGregor a message—'

'What if he disregards my message?' Ganga asked. 'From what I've heard of him he might—quite easily.'

'Then it is better for you not to see him. You must not compromise your dignity because your subjects demand it. You must think of the honour of your family.'

'Sen Moshai!' Ganga replied with a calmness he was far from feeling. 'If at this minute I were to see a deadly snake wriggling at my feet, I would scream and leap into the air, would I not? That wouldn't be dignified conduct for a zamindar. But could I help it? Situations arise sometimes when one is forced to put one's dignity at stake.'

'Then send word to MacGregor that you propose to visit him this evening. We must give him some time to prepare for your reception. Besides, you need a meal and some rest.' Ganga was forced to agree. But, as it turned out, it would have been much better for him had he disregarded Akshay Sen's advice. Ushered into the Englishman's presence, Ganga found him lying on a camp chair in the garden, a large hat shielding his face from the sun. His shirt front was stained with curry and a sickening stench of liquor rose from his person and the empty bottles that rolled about his feet. One of the servants ran inside to fetch a chair for Ganga while another whispered something in MacGregor's ear. Raising the hat a few inches, MacGregor turned a pair of bloodshot eyes on Ganga. 'Hallo, Zamindar!' he slurred. 'Nice seeing you. Come on, sit down.' Then, pulling the hat down again, he prepared to go to sleep.

'Good evening, Mr MacGregor,' Ganga cleared his throat and began. 'How are you? I trust you find the climate of our little district conducive to your health and spirits. I have come to discuss a matter that is of interest to us both—'

MacGregor's reply was a loud snore. Ganga was shocked. He had met many Englishmen in his life but not one like this fellow. The man was a barbarian. Ganga turned to the servant who had announced his arrival—a short, round dumpling of a man—and said sternly, 'The fields leased to your master extend only as far as Sonamura. All the land beyond falls within my demesne. Your guards have no right to enter it and terrorize the villagers. They are my subjects—not ryots of the kuthi.'

'Huzoor,' the man wrung his hands in abject humility. 'We wouldn't dream of harassing your subjects. Our own ryots run away from us and hide in your territory. We give them two annas per day as wages and a seer and a quarter of rice. My master is that generous! Even then—'

'Two of my sugarcane fields were burned down just before harvest. And the sugar factory had to be closed down because you threatened—'

'Don't believe everything you hear, Huzoor,' the man interrupted. 'The wretches fight amongst themselves and set fire to each other's houses. Who knows but your own subjects set your fields ablaze!'

Ganga was about to make a sharp retort but he stopped himself. He felt humiliated at being forced to express his grievances before a servant. This man, for all he knew, might be the infamous Golak Das.

'Is there no other Englishman in the kuthi?' he asked. 'I had something important to discuss.'

'No, Huzoor. The sahebs have gone out pigsticking. MacGregor Saheb stayed behind because you were coming.'

'A peasant called Jamal-ud-din came to the kuthi a few days back. He didn't return—'

'So many people come here—' The man shrugged his shoulders.

'Those buggers!' MacGregor mumbled, suddenly from beneath his hat. 'They all look alike.' He recommenced his snoring.

Ganga's nostrils dilated and his ears blazed with fury. The man was awake and listening to every word. 'Wake up your master,' he thundered. 'I wish to speak to him.'

'I wouldn't dare,' the man bit his tongue and shook his head. 'Gregor Saheb hates being disturbed in his sleep. He wakes up, roaring like a fire, and vents his anger on the first person he sees.'

Ganga stood up trembling. He felt like dashing his fist into the snoring red nose beneath the hat but he had never indulged in violence before and could not begin now. Was this creature really an Englishman? A member of the same race that had produced Shakespeare and Milton? Suddenly, his mind went blank. He stood like a figure of stone, his eyes glazed, not knowing where he was or why he had come. And all the while, the lowly reptile went on hissing into his ear: 'You see that kadamba tree, Huzoor? That's where the subjects wait when they come to see the master. You, of course, are an important person and that is why you were allowed into the kuthi! But your Suja-ud-din or Gaja-ud-din, whatever his name is, how could he come here? He would need seven heads on his shoulders to get up the guts to confront MacGregor Saheb.' Ganga's head was swimming. A black mist swirled around him. 'Huzoor has no objections to eating in a saheb's house, I presume,' the whining noise went on. 'Shall I send for some refreshments?' Mercifully, Ganga heard nothing. He stumbled and would have fallen if his servants hadn't caught him. And then—the mist cleared. He looked about him and said in a faraway voice, 'What is the matter? Why do you hold me?'

'Do you feel unwell, Huzoor?' one of them asked.

'No,' Ganga sighed. 'Let's go.' He walked with slow, measured steps out of the kuthi.

# Chapter XXXVII

Stepping into the palki, Ganga fell against the cushions in a dead faint. The frightened bearers, not knowing what to do, carried him as fast as their legs would go to the river, where Ganga's bajra waited. While some of his attendants took him up to his bedchamber, others made haste to inform Akshay Sen.

Akshay Sen sat by Ganga's side and felt his pulse. Though descended from a family of vaidyas and possessing some knowledge of herbs himself, he decided to take the boat back to Calcutta, where English doctors were available. However, before he could give the order, he found himself in the middle of a tremendous uproar. A large band of men pushed their way into Ganga's room, yelling and brandishing lathis.

'Death be on your heads, you scoundrels!' Akshay Sen hissed between clenched teeth. 'How dare you come up here and make this commotion? Don't you know Raja Babu is sick and needs rest and quiet?'

'The sahebs have beaten our Raja Babu,' the men shouted. 'We've sworn we'll take revenge. We'll fight them till the Neel Kuthi runs red with our blood!'

'Get out of the room, you bastards. How dare you force your way into the Raja's presence? You think to fight the sahebs with your pitiful lathis? Don't you know, you fools, that with one signal, the sahebs can marshal a whole army with guns and cannon?'

At this moment, Ganga opened his eyes and addressed the mob. 'Who told you I was beaten? No one laid hands on me. Go back home and attend to your work.'

A hush fell on the crowd. Seizing this opportunity, Akshay Sen turned on the men and pushed them out of the room as roughly as if they were animals. Then, turning to Ganga, he said, 'You shouldn't have gone to the kuthi, Huzoor. You laid yourself open to insult simply because an ignorant hulk of a peasant was deprived of a wife. Does it really matter? Has the world come to an end? Take my advice, Huzoor. Lease the rest of your lands to the sahebs and go back to Calcutta. That's the only way you can get some peace.'

'But Jamal-ud-din Sheikh and his wife have been kidnapped by the kuthi guards. I must find out where they are. What if they've been murdered?'

'Can you stop the sahebs from murdering anyone they please? Why should you stick your neck out? Jamal-ud-din Sheikh is a fool. He should have known better than to confront the sahebs. What's one wife, after all? He could have had ten if he had stayed at home.'

'You shock me, Sen Moshai! Doesn't a man owe his wife some protection? Wasn't he doing his duty in trying to save her?'

'Duty!' Akshay Sen shrugged his shoulders. 'Had he saved his own life he could have married another beautiful girl and sent her to the kuthi for the Saheb's enjoyment.'

'I don't like your tone, Sen Moshai. This is not a joke.'

'Forgive me, Huzoor. I wasn't joking. If the sahebs could steal our beautiful country from under our very noses, what is one woman? Women are meant to be enjoyed. It is written in the shastras—'

'Leave the shastras alone for the present and tell the villagers that I propose to see the magistrate tomorrow morning.'

Sitting down to a meal, Ganga experienced a complete lack of appetite. The arrangements were on a princely scale for Bimbabati took care to send a retinue of cooks and servants with him whenever he left Calcutta. A huge silver *thala*, with a mound of rice in the centre, as white and fragrant as jasmine petals, was placed before him. Surrounding the *thala* were a dozen silver bowls, brimming over with delicious curries. But Ganga could eat nothing—neither the kalbosh fish, caught fresh from the river and boiled into a tasty soup, nor the enormous lobster, dipped in batter and fried to a golden crispness. Not even the jackfruit savoury that was Duryodhan's speciality. Even the warmed milk with which he habitually ended his meal smelled strange and he put down the bowl in disgust. He knew there was nothing wrong with the food. The trouble lay within himself.

Lying in bed, he stared out of the porthole for a long time, watching the moon roll about on the wavelets like a child at play. He tried to sleep but sleep wouldn't come. His eyes burned as though in a fever and his mind went round and round in circles. His subjects were suffering untold tyranny and oppression. He had promised to help them. But could he keep his promise? Everyone had warned him that the magistrate was as rough and uncultured as MacGregor, and he had seen for himself what MacGregor was like. A slow fire rose in his limbs. Drums and cymbals beat in his brain. What was happening to him? He had felt just so when he sat facing the snoring MacGregor in the garden of the kuthi. After that, he had lost consciousness.

He rose from bed and poured water down his head and neck. Then, leaving the room, he climbed up the stairs till he stood on the roof of the bajra. The fresh air revived him a little. He walked up and down, breathing in great gulps of the cool night air, and then, suddenly, without warning, everything blacked out before his eyes—the river, the sky full of stars, the little pinnace with its sleeping guards. He lost all sense of time and place. He didn't know who he was, where he was or why. From time to time memories flashed into his brain with the suddenness of lightning but they were strange and terrifying. Ganga—an infant, lying on an unknown mother's lap; Ganga—a child, tearing a garland to pieces; Ganga—in the robes of a prince, floundering, sinking in the sea of time, waves curling around him, his hands above the water; Ganga—lying naked on the floor of a temple. He looked up at the sky, where a bright moon swam in and out of fleecy clouds. And gazing on that vast expanse of midnight blue, he experienced the eternal; the infinite. His breath came in heavy gasps. His face glowed with an ethereal light.

A sound of splashing water brought him out of his reverie. He glanced towards the bank and saw a group of men and women washing themselves and talking to each other in low voices. He turned away from them and fixed his thirsting eyes once again on the great sky with its glittering orbs. Suddenly, without knowing why, he climbed down the steps and came to the stern of the boat. One leap and he was standing on the bank. Then, with resolute steps, he walked over to where the figures he had seen now sat in a circle. In the centre of the ring was a huge vessel, heaped with soaked *chiré* and molasses. An old man mixed the two and passed the preparation around in large handfuls. Ganga sat down and stretched his hand out with the others. Without a word the man put a ball of the mixture on Ganga's outstretched palm. He ate it and found that it tasted of nectar. Greedy for more he put out his hand again.

'Who are you, son?' The man asked. Ganga made no answer. Putting another lump on Ganga's palm, the man said, 'Eat as much as you want for a guest is akin to God. But we are poor pilgrims. We have nothing of value with us.'

Finishing their meal they arose and resumed their journey. Pilgrims didn't usually walk by night. But the indigo district was notorious for its lawlessness and they wanted to put it behind them before daybreak. Ganga walked with them, away from the bajra, the river, his subjects and the land he had come to inspect. The pilgrims, convinced that he was a robber, though unarmed, thought it best not to ask any questions. But looking on him in the first light of dawn they were filled with wonder. This man was no ordinary man. He looked like a prince—his graceful physique and large, dark eyes proclaiming his noble lineage. He wore a sherwani over a kurta of fine silk and a long mob chain of delicately wrought gold hung from his neck. Five rings, set with precious stones, glittered on his fingers. But his face was sad and his eyes shadowed and far away.

'Where are you going, Moshai?' The leader of the group addressed him. 'Where is your home? We are poor pilgrims. Why do you follow us?'

'Let me walk with you,' Ganga said simply. 'I do not know the way.'

Was Ganga a coward? Was he trying to run away from the promise he had made to his subjects? Ganga remembered nothing; felt nothing. All the ties that had bound him had melted away and he was free.

After many days of walking, the pilgrims reached their destination—the meeting place of three rivers, Ganga, Jamuna and Saraswati at Prayag—where they were to bathe in the holy waters. Ganga rose with the others in the early dawn and came to the river. As he dipped his head into the water, the lifeblood flowed back into his veins. The mists cleared from his brain and he felt whole again. He looked up at the sky and remembered that Kashi was only a short distance away from Prayag. Bindu was in Kashi. He had to go to her. Taking leave of his fellow pilgrims, he turned his steps towards Kashi.

# Chapter XXXVIII

The month of April was drawing to a close and the summer vacations had begun. But for the principal of Sanskrit College there was no rest. Braving the pitiless sun, Vidyasagar went from village to village with the persistence of a top that couldn't stop itself from spinning.

Bethune Saheb had been dead these many years but his spirit lived on in the diminutive Brahmin, whose dhoti wouldn't fall below his knees and whose coarse uduni barely covered his chest. Bethune had declared that true knowledge could only be imparted through the mother tongue. Vidyasagar had taken this advice to heart. He believed that though the study of Sanskrit served very well for those who wished to pursue a scholastic career, the average Bengali child should be instructed through the vernacular. It was important to open schools, thousands of them, not only in towns and cities but in villages and suburbs. And who could bear the expense of such an ambitious project but the Company's government? A great deal might be achieved if the rulers could be persuaded to part with a mere fragment of the profits they shipped out to England, year after year. Putting his proposals on paper, Vidyasagar placed them before the authorities. Luckily for him, Frederick Halliday was appointed lieutenant governor a few months after the submission. Halliday had been a member of the Council of Education and was Vidyasagar's close associate. Approving the proposals, he placed them before the viceroy and was successful in obtaining a legal sanction.

The next step was to find a man who could be given the responsibility of identifying areas where education was most needed, establish institutions and see to their running. Vidyasagar proposed his own name. He would take up this responsibility in addition to the one he had already—the principalship of Sanskrit College. And he sought no honorarium either. The authorities had no doubts about his ability and gave their ready consent.

And thus, Vidyasagar began his long career of walking the length and breadth of Bengal. Starting with Shirja Khola, Radhanagar and Krishnanagar, he walked through Kheerpai, Chandrakona, Sripur, Kamarpukur, Ramjivanpur, Mayapur, Malaipur and Keshavpur. His method was simple. He entered a village, sought out its elders and told them of the government's plan of opening a school in their village. The response was favourable everywhere he went. Someone or the other came forward to donate land—others cane, bamboo and coconut fronds to build the schoolroom. No fees were charged for all other expenses were borne by the government. But Vidyasagar had one difficulty to contend with. People refused to believe that the man who stood before them, looking more like a palki-bearer than a Brahmin, was the great Vidyasagar of whom they had heard so much. It was only after a great deal of effort that they could be persuaded to accept the truth.

But Vidyasagar's task did not end here. He had also to see to the running of the schools once the initial work was done. Walking did not tire him. Meals posed no problem. A handful of rice and lentils, which he boiled himself over a couple of faggots, was enough for him. For sleep he sought out the shade of a tree. The fierce rays of the sun, the pouring rain—nothing had the power to deter him.

One afternoon, as he sat resting outside the schoolroom in Ramjivanpur, he felt a desire to examine the pupils. Walking in he found the boys sitting on a mat on the floor and repeating their tables loud enough to burst his eardrums. It saddened him to see them. Their upper bodies were bare for the most part and tattered *gamchhas* or rags covered their loins. Their teacher was in an equally sorry state. Pandit Moshai's dhoti was ancient, the great rents in it brought together in knots, presumably because, as a conservative Brahmin, he wouldn't wear cloth that had been stitched together. The only thing on his person that was clean and whole was his *poité,* the sacred thread which hung thick and white on his hairy chest. Pandit Moshai brought a pillow and a palm leaf fan with him from home every morning and went to sleep immediately afterwards, stretching himself out at the door so that the boys couldn't run away. The pupils took turns to fan him, not without hope of a reward—whoever managed to do so without hitting his head was allowed to go home an hour earlier. Pandit Moshai started up at Vidyasagar's entry.

'I've come to see your pupils,' Vidyasagar said, sitting down by the venerable instructor. 'How do they fare? Well, I hope!'

'Very well,' the pandit cried, covering his anxiety with a forced hilarity. 'I'll lose my job if they don't, won't I? That's why I force the lessons down their throat. Ask them if I don't—'

Examining the boys, Vidyasagar found that the pandit's claim was not without foundation for they had learned the rudiments of arithmetic and simple Bengali. But there was more, much more, that they had to know. '*O ré*,' he said, addressing one of them. 'Can you tell me how day and night are born?' The pupils stared. What a question! Even their mothers and grandmothers knew the answer to that one. 'Day is born when the sun rises and night when it sets and the moon appears in the sky,' the boy answered.

'But how does the sun rise?' Vidyasagar persisted. 'And how does it set?'

Afraid that his pupils would appear at a disadvantage before this peculiar Brahmin, Pandit Moshai answered quickly for them, 'Why, day breaks when the Sun God takes his seat in the seven-horse chariot. And it comes to an end when he has concluded his journey over the sky from east to west.'

'That is a myth from the Puranas,' Vidyasagar smiled. 'Haven't you heard of rotation and revolution?' The pandit shook his head. 'The sun does not move,' Vidyasagar continued. 'It is fixed in the sky. The earth moves around the sun.'

'The earth moves! What are you saying, Moshai? You're not joking, are you?'

'No, I'm not joking. The earth moves in two ways.'

'Well, if you say so—' the pandit muttered sullenly. 'How can I contradict you?' Then, brightening a little, he added, 'It is possible that the earth moves in towns and cities. Not here, Moshai. Believe me, I haven't felt it move even once. It's as fixed as fixed can be.'

Vidysagar burst out laughing. Then he proceeded to give the boys a lesson in geography. He told them about rotation and revolution, of the lengthening and shortening of days and nights and the vernal and autumnal equinoxes. The pandit listened in solemn silence, ejaculating from time to time. 'The earth moves! It has moved for centuries! Let it move as much as it will. Who cares?' That afternoon Vidyasagar discovered a profound truth. It was not enough to open schools for the education of children. Teachers had to be educated first. He had to open a normal school, which would turn out men capable of imparting instruction. He would discuss this with Akshay Kumar Datta, the editor of *Tatwabodhini*, and request him to take on the responsibility. Akshay Kumar Datta was a man of liberal views and would be ideal for the job.

The vacations were coming to an end and Vidyasagar had to return to Calcutta. But he wanted to see his parents first, and with that end in view, he turned his steps towards Birsingha village.

Thakurdas Bandopadhyaya and his wife, Bhagwati, had seen dark days but those were over now. Their eldest son, Ishwar, earned one hundred and fifty rupees a month, apart from what he made out of his books. Their second son was earning, too. They had repaired the house and added extra rooms. Their paddy bin brimmed over with golden grain and big fish leaped and danced in their pond. A plump milch cow stood tethered to her post in the courtyard. Their affluence had made life easier not only for them but for many in the village for they were charitable by nature and ready to extend a helping hand to the poor and needy.

Ishwar Chandra entered the house shortly before dusk. The next day was Ekadasi—the eleventh day of the lunar cycle—when Hindu widows undertook twenty-four hours of rigorous fasting. He remembered the time, years ago, when he had come home on just such an evening to hear that his childhood playmate, Khetramoni, had been married and widowed in the three months of his absence. She was only thirteen. Ishwar had wept bitterly and flung his *thala* of rice away. He couldn't bear the thought of putting food in his mouth when Khetramoni was being denied even a drop of water. Was it her fault that her husband had died before her?

Khetramoni had been dead these many years but Ishwar experienced an identical pain every time he heard that a young girl had met with the same fate. And that was often for one or two girls were widowed each year in the village. This time, too, he entered the house to receive the news that his old tutor, Kalikanta Chattopadhyaya, had died, leaving six widows behind him, the youngest of whom was only nine years old. Besides them there was another—the eleven-year-old Satyabhama who lived next door. Ishwar's eyes burned; he felt a tightness in his chest. A great wave of hatred welled up in him for his fellow caste Brahmins who, in following a meaningless tradition, married off their suckling infants to decrepit old men, then condemned them to a living hell after they became widowed.

In the evening, as Ishwar sat talking to his father, Bhagwati Devi entered the room. '*O ré*,' she cried. 'I can't bear to look on the girl's face. I've seen her from birth and carried her about in my arms. To think that she's a widow! The poor girl is weeping her eyes out.'

'Who are you speaking of? Satyabhama?' Thakurdas clicked his tongue in sympathy. 'The child is very dear to me. I can't bear to look on her face either.'

'I told them over and over again not to marry her off to that old widower—'

'Ishwar,' his father turned to him. 'You've studied the shastras very carefully. Do they all enjoin us to treat our widows so harshly? Can't widows be given better lives?'

'Of course, they can,' Ishwar replied, his face red with suppressed agitation. 'They can even remarry.'

'Remarry! What are you saying?'

'There are three options which widows may choose from. They may burn with their husbands; live lives of abstinence and piety; or remarry—as they will.'

'Can you prove it?'

Ishwar's eyes blazed. He looked straight into his father's eyes and said, 'You know that once I set my mind to a task I don't leave off until it is accomplished. I'll wring the shastras dry till I come upon the proof. I've wanted to do it for some time now. If you give me your blessings—'

'Why not? Why should I withhold my blessings? Besides, you must do as you think best even if we try to stop you. Even if the whole world goes against you.'

'What do you say, Ma?' Ishwar glanced towards his mother.

'Are you sure that the shastras allow widow remarriage? Is your interpretation of the shloks correct?'

'It is. I'm going to write a book about it and get a law passed in its favour. I'll offend a lot of people. I know that. But I don't care. Only you mustn't be offended.'

'Do all you can, my son. If you succeed not only I but millions of unhappy women will raise their hands to you in blessing.'

Returning to Calcutta, Ishwar Chandra immersed himself in a sea of Sanskrit scriptures. Instinct told him that there was nothing immoral or unethical in widow remarriage. No code of laws would force a life of abstinence on a girl who was widowed even before she knew the true meaning of marriage. And if it did, it was erroneous and must be rejected. A society must move towards the light. But how was he to achieve his goal? The people of this country preferred to live in a primeval world of traditions and superstitions. They had bound their eyes against the light. From where would he get the power to break those bonds? Besides, he had to get a law passed by rulers who were wary of hurting the religious sentiments of their subjects. The only way to tackle the problem was by quoting shloks from the shastras themselves, justifying his proposition. Ishwar flung himself into the task with the single-minded fervour that was characteristic of him. He stopped going home after his day's work; renounced food and sleep and spent the night poring over a pile of texts in the college library.

'Ishwar,' his friend, Rajkrishna Bandopadhyaya, said to him one day. 'You are working hard enough to kill yourself. But it will avail you nothing. People have advocated widow remarriage before and have tried to find justification for it in the shastras. But nothing came of it.'

'I know,' Ishwar Chandra replied. 'Raja Rajballabh Sen of Dhaka was the first. He was followed by many others, including Derozio's pupils. They did not succeed because their conviction was not strong enough. But you know me. I'm as stubborn as a mule. I'll achieve my goal simply because I'll know no peace till I do.'

Sitting up night after night, reading by the light of an oil lamp, Ishwar's brain got heated and confused. Whenever that happened, he went out and took a walk, breathing in the cool, fresh air in great lungfuls. One morning, in the early dawn, he stopped short in his tracks and muttered, 'I've got it.' Then, striding down the deserted highway, he murmured a few shloks and raising his fingers to an imaginary audience said, 'With these I start my debate. Let me see how many pandits there are among you who can prove me wrong.'

# Chapter XXXIX

Hindu College was in a bad way. The boys were leaving in large numbers and swelling the ranks of the newly established Metropolitan College. There were not more than three or four left in each class and class III had only one—Chandranath. Alarmed at the state of affairs, the principal announced a reduction in the fees but even that proved useless. Finally, the authorities had to face the fact that if Chandranath continued to study in the college, he would soon be its only student. Chandranath's exit from Hindu College was as simple and unceremonious as his entrance had been complicated and eventful. One morning, as he sat in his classroom, taking lessons from his English teacher, the principal walked into the room and raising an admonitory finger, said curtly, 'Get out of this room and out of this college. And don't come back—ever.'

Teacher and student rose to their feet in alarm. 'Am I not to come here any more, sir?' Chandranath asked in a trembling voice.

'No.'

'Then where shall I go for my lessons?'

'You may go to hell if you like. But don't set foot on these grounds again. This college has nothing to do with you any more.'

The English youth, who was the boy's teacher, opened his mouth as if to say something but was quickly silenced by the older man. Seeing that Chandranath stood motionless as if rooted to the ground, the principal called in the darwans and ordered them to throw him out of the building. The darwans obeyed with alacrity for their loathing for the 'whoreson' was no less than that of their caste superiors.

Standing outside the college, the midday sun raining its fierce beams on his head, Chandranath wondered what had happened. He was no fool. He knew that his presence was responsible for the sorry state the college was in. He realized that the authorities would have to do something to bring the boys back. He had thought that some special arrangement would be made for him. But, loving his lessons as passionately as he did, he did not dream that that something would be his dismissal. He looked around him in bewilderment. What should he do now? Where should he go? Raimohan wouldn't come for him till evening. He couldn't stand here in this hot sun all day. He took a step forward and thought, 'What if the goons are lying in wait for me like that other day?' Then, squaring his shoulders, he said emphatically to the world in general, 'Let them beat me. I'm not afraid.'

Dragging his feet he walked in the direction of Gol Dighi. There, sitting by the water, he buried his face between his knees and burst into tears. He cried for a long time, his body shaking with sobs and his heart thumping painfully against his ribs. There were people around him, sitting by the water or resting under the trees—pedlars and middlemen, tramps and loafers—but no one came near him or asked him what the matter was. At last, exhausted with weeping, he raised his head and saw his face reflected in the water. People said he was good-looking but he had not seen a face more loathsome and ugly as the one that stared back at him, for it was the face of an outcaste, an untouchable. He had read the Ramayan and the Mahabharat; he had read Shakespeare, Milton and Byron. He knew the characters well and loved them as if they were his own people. He identified with them but they didn't identify with him. No one did. No one loved him or wanted him. Why had he come into this cruel world? He hadn't asked to be born.

Picking up a book from the pile beside him, he tore out a page and set it afloat on the water. Then, feverishly, like one possessed, he tore page after page into tiny fragments and blew them about him till the air was thick with the floating flakes. His books exhausted, he took off his shirt. He ripped and tore, using nails and teeth, and his eyes gloated and glittered like a madman's. Then, rising to his feet, he started walking once again, where or why he did not know.

He wandered about the streets till dusk. At last, weary and footsore, he flung himself in the dark shadow of an ashwatha tree and rested the limbs that quivered with exhaustion. And then, for the first time he remembered his mother. His mother served him his meal with her own hands when he got back in the evenings. It was well past evening now. What was she doing? Was she sitting in a rich babu's carriage and saying to Raimohan Dada, 'I've given my word. I must go. Send me a message when Chandu gets back.' Or was she ripping the brocades and jewels off her body and weeping and beating her breast? 'If I were to die tonight,' Chandu thought whimsically, 'will my mother go to her mujra tomorrow?' No, he decided. She wouldn't. She would weep for him; for weeks, months and years till she grew old and ugly. She would give up her life of sin. 'I'll die,' he thought. 'I'll jump into the river and drown.' Drowning in the Ganga was a good death. It cleansed you of all your sins. She was everyone's mother, Ma Ganga was, and drew everyone to her bosom, not caring for caste or social status. He rose to his feet. He had to find the river.

Chandranath walked and ran by turns till he reached Bagbazar, where the rich elite of Calcutta lived. Stopping to rest awhile, he noticed a crowd of people pushing and jostling just outside the iron gates of a splendid mansion. There was obviously a feast going on within for servants hurried out with baskets of soiled banana leaves and clay tumblers, which they threw out with a great clatter on the footpath. The people waiting outside were destitutes, who were to be fed after the guests had eaten. A sickening wrench in his insides brought Chandranath to an awareness of how hungry he was and he remembered he had eaten nothing since morning. Limping painfully, he made his way towards the gate and took his place among the destitutes. He forgot his misery. He forgot that he was on his way to the river where he was to meet a watery death. He forgot everything except how hungry and thirsty he was. A raging fire burned in his stomach; his throat and breast were crackling with thirst.

'Sit down in a row, all of you,' a man called out to the destitutes. 'Don't push. There's enough for you all. Mutton curry, sweetmeats—you'll get everything—' He proceeded to dispense *luchis* from a vast wicker basket. The destitutes scrambled to find places for themselves and the leader shouted, '*Jai* to the Bara Babu! The most generous babu in the world!' And the others shouted after him. Chandranath sank down on his haunches in the dust, making a strange contrast to the others for he was fair and well formed and his dhoti was clean and new. Hitherto, all the delicacies that appeared on rich men's *thalas* had been his for the asking. But he felt no qualms about sitting by the road, wolfing down *luchis* and pumpkin stew with a crowd of beggars. He licked his fingers and waited eagerly for the mutton curry for his hunger had increased manifold after the first few mouthfuls. And then, Lady Destiny played another trick on him. The man who was serving the mutton stopped short and stared long and hard at Chandranath's face. In that sea of dark ugly faces, the boy's looked like that of an angel's from Heaven. 'Who are you?' he asked. 'Why are you sitting here?' And, that very moment, a boy came out of the house and, catching sight of Chandranath, screamed shrilly, 'Why! That's him. That's the whoreson. Chhoto Kaka[28], come quick.'

There was a stunned silence. The serving men froze in their places and even the destitutes stopped eating and craned their necks to get a good look for a 'whoreson' was not to be seen every day. 'That's the one who is studying in our college,' the young worthy went on inexorably. 'His whore mother brought him along. Everyone saw her.' There was a ripple in the crowd. The destitutes rose up in a body as if at a signal. Even they would not eat in the same row with the son of a whore. The serving men came back to life. With a muttered oath, the boy stepped forward and kicked Chandranath's leaf away. 'How dare you come into our house and eat our food?' he screamed. His uncle, who had hastened to the scene, grabbed Chandranath by the ear and hauled him to his feet. 'Get out, you bastard,' he yelled. Now the servants fell on Chandranath and dragging him across the street, flung him into a ditch. Chandranath didn't say a word. He didn't even feel any pain. He gathered himself together slowly and purposefully and, looking this way and that, picked up a large stone. Then, running forward like one possessed, he threw the stone, aiming it at the head of one of the men who had dragged him across the asphalt. *'Baap ré,'* the man yelled and fell to the ground with a tremendous thud. Picking up the same stone, Chandranath threw it again, this time in the other direction. Then, turning, he ran down the street as fast as he could. He could hear footsteps

---

28 Younger Uncle.

behind him and knew that the guards were running after him. But they couldn't catch him.

A couple of hours later, Chandranath reached the river. But he didn't jump in. He didn't want to die. Not any more. His hand felt sticky. He thought it was from the pumpkin stew he had been eating and he stooped to wash it. But just then, the moon floated out from behind some clouds and in its light he saw what it was. It was blood—human blood. He felt a sudden elation and his eyes burned in the dark. This was a beginning; a new beginning.

# Chapter XXXX

One afternoon, Nabin returned from college to find Krishnabhamini playing with another little girl in his bedroom. They were exactly like the dolls they played with—English dolls made of vulcanite—except in the way they were dressed. Both girls wore rich silk saris and rows of gold bangles on their arms. The moment she saw him enter, the stranger pulled her veil lower and turned her back to Nabin.

'*O go,*' Nabin addressed his wife. 'Who is she?'

'My Miteni.[29] You've seen her before. She was sitting next to me all the time when we got married.'

'What is your Miteni doing in this neighbourhood?'

'Her in-laws live in Hatkhola. Her mother-in-law sent her over in a palki to play with me.' Then, taking her friend by the shoulders, Krishnabhamini forced her to turn around. 'You don't have to cover your face before my husband, you silly,' she said, pulling the veil away from her face. 'You can be his Miteni, too.' Nabin stared in wonder at the girl's face. He had never seen anything so beautiful. Krishnabhamini was fair, too, but this girl's skin was like a rose petal and her eyes, blue as a rainwashed sky. Nabin threw his uduni on the bed and seated himself on the floor. 'What is your name, *go*, Miteni?' he asked, sidling up to the two girls. Krishnabhamini gave her friend a little push and whispered, 'Tell him your name.' Then, seeing that the girl's face was pink with embarrassment, she said, 'I forget what it is. I've always called her Miteni. Oh! Yes. It is Kusum. Your name is Kusum, isn't it?'

Now, the girl lifted her face a little. 'My name is Kusum Kumari,' she said.

'Kusum Kumari!' Nabin burst out laughing. 'A silly name. It doesn't suit you one bit.'

'Why do you say that?' Krishnabhamini was peeved at this

29 Girl-friend.

insult to her friend. 'Everyone says her name is very pretty. Even prettier than mine.'

Kusum rose to her feet and gathered her sari around her. 'It is nearly evening,' she said. 'I must go home now. Ma must be getting ready for her puja.' Nabin put out a hand and took hers in it. 'Don't be angry with me,' he said. 'It's not your fault if your name doesn't suit you. I'll give you a beautiful one in a minute.'

'Why don't you go to your mother?' Krishnabhamini pouted her red lips at him. 'We're playing in this room. My son is about to marry her daughter.'

'Why can't I play with you? I'd like to. Do let me.'

'We aren't allowed to play with boys,' Kusum Kumari said. 'Ma will scold me if she finds out.'

'Very well then. I'll turn myself into a girl.' And, pulling a sari from his wife's cupboard, he draped it around himself with a few quick movements. Then, simpering and sucking his little finger, he walked towards the girls with swaying hips and downcast eyes. 'Dear Miteni!' he said in a high, squeaky voice. 'Are you angry with me?' Krishnabhamini looked sternly at him but Kusum Kumari gave a little giggle. 'Good,' Nabin said, dropping down beside her. 'I'm forgiven then. May the three of us play together, dear Miteni? But I must give you a name first. Your name is Vanajyotsna.' 'O Ma!' Krishnabhamini cried out in surprise. 'What sort of a name is that? I've never heard such a name in my seven lives.'

'Seven lives are nothing. Seven sevens are forty-nine. Women had names like Vanajyotsna in your forty-ninth incarnation from this one.'

'It is the name of a flowering creeper,' Kusum Kumari said, suddenly. 'How can it be my name?'

'Oh!' Nabin was startled at her knowledge. 'How did you know?'

'It was in a story called *Shakuntala.* I heard Pon Moshai read it out to my brothers. I used to sit by them when they did their lessons. It is a sad story.'

'Do you see how learned your Miteni is?' Nabin turned to his wife, his brows dancing with pleasure. 'And you—'

'Do I have a brother by whom I could sit when he did his lessons?'

'*O go*, Miteni,' Nabin gushed romantically. 'You are as

beautiful as a flowering creeper! That is why your parents called you Kusum Kumari. And that is why I call you Vanajyotsna!'

'Are we only going to talk? Aren't we going to play?' Krishnabhamini cried out in an imperious tone.

'Yes. Let's begin our game. Let me see. You are two mothers getting your children married. What are their names, by the way?' The two girls exchanged glances. They hadn't thought of names.

'All right then, we'll call the girl Shakuntala and the boy Dushman.'

'No, Bhai Miteni. I'm not playing any more,' Kusum stood up frowning. 'Your husband is using bad language. The king's name was Dushyanta, not Dushman.'

'You remember that!' Nabin gave a delighted laugh. 'Very well, then. We'll call him Dushyanta.'

'I don't like that name. And the story is very sad.'

'It has a happy ending.'

'You're being too troublesome,' Krishnabhamini said severely and putting her hand into the basket, she brought out another doll. 'Come, Miteni. Let's get the wedding over and done with. Here's the priest—'

'We don't need a priest,' Nabin interrupted. 'This marriage is being solemnized in the woods. They will marry each other without help from a priest.'

'That's no way to get married,' Krishnabhamini cried out in alarm. 'I won't allow it.'

The game went on, Nabin taking a lively part. Looking at him no one could guess that he was the star student of Hindu College. He put words in the mouths of the dolls and, with his flair for imitation, changed his parts in quick succession. Now he was the bride, now her mother, then priest, bridegroom, servant and widowed aunt, all in a matter of minutes. And after the wedding, when the *sandesh* was brought out for the feast, he turned himself into a greedy guest and grabbing large handfuls, crammed them into his mouth.

The game over, Kusum Kumari rose to leave. Four palki-bearers had come with her and two maids. But, seeing that dusk was about to set in, Nabin sent two guards along as escort. Krishnabhamini embraced her friend tenderly at parting. 'When will you come again?' she begged. 'Tomorrow? The day after?' Kusum twisted her pretty lips and rolled her eyes. 'A ha ha,' she said. 'Why should I come day after day? Can't you come and see me?' Krishnabhamini glanced at her husband. And Nabin answered for her: 'Of course she can and will. But what about me? Am I not your Miten[30]? Can't I come, too?' Kusum Kumari raised her innocent blue eyes to his but said nothing. There were two dolls in her arms—she was taking her daughter and son-in-law to spend a few days with her—and she climbed into the palki with some difficulty.

Kusum Kumari was ten and a half—eighteen months older than Krishnabhamini, who was barely nine. They had been friends from childhood for their fathers' houses stood side by side in Bagbazar. They loved each other dearly and couldn't bear to be parted for long. Kusum's husband, Aghornath, was a good deal older than her and suffered from some form of paranoia. It was rumoured that he had wanted to become a Brahmo on the death of his first wife but couldn't because his mother threatened to slit her throat with the fish *bonti* if he did. Not wishing to commit matricide, he had given up the idea but had fallen into a severe depression from that time onwards. He gradually withdrew from the world, took no interest in the family business and estates and was completely oblivious of his beautiful second wife.

On Kusum Kumari's departure, husband and wife went back to their bedroom. 'If you had a son and your Miteni had a daughter,' Nabin remarked as they went up the stairs, 'you could have a real wedding. That would be fun, wouldn't it?'

'Yes,' Krishnabhamini nodded, without a trace of embarrassment. 'That's what I have planned.'

Nabin shot a glance at his child bride's face. He had read lots of books and knew a great deal but he hadn't a clue to the mysterious link that connected marriage and childbirth. One thing was certain. Children were born only to married couples—not to widows, widowers or bachelors. But why this was so he had no idea. He felt consumed with curiosity and wondered if Krishnabhamini was better informed than him. But, overcome with shame, he could not ask.

---

30 Boy-friend.

Back in their bedroom, Krishnabhamini got busy putting away her dolls, till she discovered to her dismay that one of them was missing. 'You must have hidden it,' she accused her husband. 'Where is it?'

'I don't know what you're talking about! I haven't seen your doll,' Nabin answered, his eyes shining with innocence.

'Where can it be then?' Krishnabhamini bit her lip, trying hard not to cry. 'My mother brought it from Kalighat. It was my best doll.'

'Your Miteni must have stolen it and taken it away with her.'

'What! You call my Miteni a thief?' And beside herself with fury, Krishnabhamini slapped her husband smartly on the cheek. Now, Nabin grabbed her by the hair and cried, '*Ré*! *Ré*! Hapless woman! To what depths art thou fallen that thou durst strike thy lord and master? Let me send thee to hell for hell alone is a fitting abode for females such as thee that gossip, display greed and belabour their husbands.' Krishnabhamini struggled in his grasp for a few minutes. Then he released her with a laugh and gave her the doll, which he had concealed behind the couch.

One afternoon, a few days later, Nabin said to his wife, 'What news of your Miteni? She's walked off with our son and shows no sign of returning him. How much longer must the boy stay under his father-in-law's roof? That's not the way in the Singha family. Our daughters-in-law come to us—not the other way around.' But Kusum Kumari did not come and Nabin got more and more restive. 'Write to your Miteni,' he kept pestering his wife, then weary of begging Krishnabhamini, he composed a letter himself in his pearly hand and sent it along with the customary gifts of a large carp and a tray of *sandesh*. Still, Kusum Kumari did not come. She sent back the dolls the next day, with two trays of *sandesh* and a larger fish. There was a letter, too, in a neat, round hand. 'I am unable to accept your kind invitation due to unavoidable circumstances,' she wrote. 'Since my coming to you is fraught with uncertainty, I send the children. May the Lord keep them well and happy. Yours Kusum Kumari Vanajyotsna Miteni.'

Nabin read the epistle, then knitting his eyebrows he asked, 'Who wrote this letter for her? Her husband?'

'My Miteni can read and write,' Krishnabhamini said proudly. 'She knows everything.'

'She's a stupid, arrogant girl,' Nabin said spitefully, 'and her handwriting is terrible.'

After this Nabin's desire to meet Kusum Kumari again grew greater than ever. And he was filled with curiosity about her husband. Swallowing his pride he wrote another letter—this time to her husband, Aghornath. He loaded his letter with flowery courtesies, then, at its conclusion, begged them both to come and have a meal at Jorasanko. The answer came a few days later—from Kusum Kumari. She sent her regrets for declining the invitation but requested them to come and pay her a visit instead. In normal circumstances, Nabin would never have accepted an invitation that had not been extended by the man of the house. But he was in no mood to stand on ceremony. 'Come,' he said to his wife. 'We'll go see your Miteni's house. Be sure to take your dolls along.'

Nabin had never been more insulted in his life than he was at the house in Hatkhola.

# Chapter XXXXI

The Malliks of Hatkhola were a noveau riche family, who could trace their wealth only as far back as two generations. Jagai Mallik, Kusum Kumari's grandfather-in-law and the founder of the family fortunes, was said to have begun his career by selling parched gram outside the temple of Chitteswari in Peneti. It was rumoured that the Goddess had appeared to him in a dream and directed him to help himself to a jar of gold that lay buried in the middle of a stagnant pond behind the temple. There was another story, too, to account for his sudden prosperity. This was that a notorious dacoit had taken shelter in Jagai Mallik's house while fleeing from justice and had died of cholera the same day. Within hours of the event, Jagai Mallik had disposed of the body and fled to Calcutta, taking the dacoit's stores of gold and jewels with him. In his anxiety to cover his tracks, he had even abandoned his first wife and children in Peneti and started another family in the new city. However, it is only fair to add that rumours of this sort were rife about nearly all the rich families of Calcutta.

Jagai Mallik had three sons by this second marriage. The eldest, Chittaprasad—a man of keen business acumen—had increased his father's wealth several times over. It was he, too, who had founded this stately family mansion in Hatkhola. With his sudden death, the business and estates had passed into the hands of his second brother, Kaliprasad, the youngest, Chandikaprasad, and his son, Aghornath, being minors at the time.

Once in possession of the properties, Kaliprasad displayed a greater knack for throwing money around than earning it. The stigma of being 'that parched gram-peddling Jagai Mallik's son', sat heavily on him and he sought to dispel it by lavish living and heavy donations to charities. No one who came to him for help—be it for a daughter's wedding or a father's funeral, the establishing of a school or the digging of a well—went back disappointed for he had learned fairly early in life that earning money was not good enough; one had to earn a reputation. So, he made it a point to find out who the other benefactors were and whose was the largest contribution. Then, adding one rupee to that, he said carelessly, 'Go to my khazanchi and collect the money. I believe in doling out cash—not promises.' But this was not all. Kaliprasad was equally lavish in his entertainments. Only the year before, he had had a vast pavilion erected on Chhoto Babu's grounds and got a hundred nautch girls to perform before an immense crowd of spectators. The tunes were so catchy—'From the serpent's head the gem you stole. And lost your life on alien shores!'—they still lingered in the ears.

Kaliprasad's younger brother, Chandikaprasad, was his ardent admirer and followed closely in his footsteps. With one difference. Whereas Kaliprasad favoured the *firinghee* style in dress and manners, Chandika fell back on the older nawabi tradition of Muslim India. He wore elaborately embroidered Lucknow pyjamas, with a vast shirt whose brocade panels were held at the waist with a fine silken sash. Gold encrusted slippers on his feet and a magnificent turban covering one ear completed the ensemble. A kerchief of scarlet silk dangling from his fingers added a final touch. And being partial to strong smells—leeks and onions and attar of roses—he preferred Muslim prostitutes to their less odorous Hindu counterparts. Chandikaprasad knew nothing of the family business and cared even less. He was encouraged in this attitude by his elder brother, who preferred to keep him out of all the important affairs of the estate. But he didn't stint him in the least. Chandikaprasad received a princely sum as allowance each month—a sum large enough to purchase a small taluk—and had his hands full trying to spend it. The brothers were united in their contempt for their low-born father and worked hard to wipe out his memory from the minds of the public. And the only way they knew how was to outbabu the richest babus of the land.

Their tragedy was that that ancient patriarch, Jagai Mallik, was still alive! No one quite knew how old he was but according to his own calculations, he was born the year Nawab Siraj-ud-dullah had led his troops in battle against the *firinghee*, Clive, in the fields of Plassey. That made him ninety-one years old. He had been deaf for the last ten years and having lost all his teeth, his gift of speech as well, for no one understood what he said. But his limbs were intact and he moved around without much difficulty. He pottered about in the house all day in a coarse homespun dhoti and soiled vest, and every evening he sat in the temple of Chitteswari, watching the *arati*. But whereas only a few years ago he had walked there, he was now carried in a palki.

Kusum Kumari's husband, Aghornath, was a different type altogether. Physically, he resembled neither his father nor his uncles (the Malliks had the coarse, blunt features of shopkeepers) but got his good looks from his exquisitely beautiful mother—a penniless girl whom Chittaprasad had taken as his third wife, the earlier two having failed to give him a son. Lost and lonely in the great house of the Malliks, Aghornath's mother had lavished all her care and attention on her only child and managed to keep him free of its influences. Thus, Aghornath grew up in the shadow of his mother's love—tall, strong and handsome in form and mien and alert and intelligent in mind. A brilliant student of Hindu College, he soon came under the spell of Deben Thakur of Jorasanko. The rest of his history we know already.

Nabin Kumar stepped out of the carriage and looked around him eagerly. He had expected a grand reception; had even visualized a scene in which all the male members of the household stood in a row—hands folded in respectful greeting. He was Ramkamal Singha's son and sole inheritor of his father's vast estates. He knew what was owing to him. And his wife was not to be trifled with either. She had been born in the famous Bosu family of Bagbazar and was now his wife.

But there was no sign of anyone at the gates of the Mallik mansion, barring a darwan, who gazed on them with some curiosity and scratched idly behind one ear. Nabin wondered if he had mistaken the date. But no—Kusum Kumari had asked them to come on Saturday and today was Saturday. Had she forgotten? How could she! Even as he stood, a carved box of dolls on one arm, a serving maid came tripping up to them and said, 'Natun Bouthan[31] is waiting for you.' The two followed

31 New sister-in-law.

the veiled figure down a pebbled pathway, Krishnabhamini walking with difficulty in her heavy brocade sari, till they came to a verandah where two men servants stood waiting. Nabin looked at them with distaste. They had the startled, furtive looks of men who had been discovered plotting something no good. And there was little deference in the manner in which one of them opened a door and bid them step in. Once inside, the maid led Krishnabhamini by the hand into a room beyond, shutting the door noiselessly behind her.

Nabin Kumar lifted the finely frilled edge of his dhoti carefully with one hand and sat down on one of the padded chairs with which the room was strewn. A large *chowki*, covered with white sheets, stood at one end and English landscapes (clearly bought in one lot from a sale) covered the walls. Nabin pulled out his watch by its gold chain and looked at the time. It was six o'clock. And, at that very moment, the cannon from the fort fired six shots in confirmation. Kusum Kumari had asked them to come at six o'clock.

But no one came to him. Nabin rocked his knees for a while, walked about the room and sat down again. 'Don't these people have any manners?' he thought, knitting his brows in irritation. 'Why do they keep me waiting as if I've come to ask for a job?' He hadn't dreamed of being treated like this. In upper class families, a daughter-in-law's friends and relatives were shown the utmost deference and courtesy. After a while, Nabin couldn't bear it any more. He cleared his throat, hoping to attract the attention of the servants, but getting no response, he walked over to the door and said sharply, '*Ei*! Where's your master?' The servants grinned and nudged one another. Nabin's grim severity sat oddly on one of his years—more so, because of the box of dolls he held in his hands.

'Which master?' one of the men asked carelessly, raising his eyes boldly to Nabin's.

'If it is Mejo Babu[32] you want,' the other butted in, 'we don't know when he will return. And if it is Chhoto Babu—he might not return at all.'

---

32 Second Master.

'I'm speaking of Aghornath Babu,' Nabin said angrily. He was not used to servants speaking to him in that tone of voice.

The two yokels stared at one another for a few minutes, then the first one said with a snigger, 'He's upstairs!'

'Go tell him Nabin Kumar Singha is here to see him.'

'We have our duties and carrying messages is not one of them,' the man announced coldly, then shot a blob of spit neatly across the verandah.

Nabin's face turned red with fury. If this had been his house, he would have had the man whipped till the blood ran down his back. But here he could do nothing. Fuming with anger he returned to the room and paced up and down, thinking furiously. What should he do? He could leave the house but how was he to inform Krishnabhamini?

After half an hour or so, a servant entered the room, bearing a glass of sherbet in one hand and a stone platter, piled with sweets and fruits, in the other. Placing them on a small table, he said, 'Natun Bouthan requests you to refresh yourself.' Nabin trembled with fury. Was he to eat all by himself in this ugly room? He, who had to be coaxed a hundred times before he touched a morsel to his mouth? How could they treat him like this? 'Take it away,' he said, trying hard to control the tremor in his voice, 'And tell them upstairs I'm leaving.' Brushing the man aside he strode out into the verandah and proceeded to walk over to his carriage. He would wait for Krishnabhamini out on the road but not within these hateful walls! But before he could step down from the verandah, he caught sight of a palki being lowered at the gates, followed, almost immediately afterwards, by a phaeton. The bearers bent down and pulled someone out of the palki. It was a little old man—a mere handful of bones, covered over with fold upon fold of wrinkled, grey skin. The eyes were blurred and opaque. Two servants held him under the arms and led him into the house, his little bird body swaying from side to side like a toddler's. 'Jedo! Medho!' an imperious voice slurred from within the phaeton and the two servants on the verandah were galvanized into action. 'Huzoor!' they yelled and ran as fast as their legs could carry them. Chandikaprasad stepped out of the phaeton, dead drunk. His nawabi costume was in utter disarray and splotched with wine and betel juice. He walked a few steps without help, then spun around like a top and would have fallen to the ground if the servants hadn't caught him in time. Nabin looked on in astonishment as father and son were led into the house, one behind another.

Chandikaprasad was in a hurry. He had come home for some money and was anxious to get back to his amusements. Catching up with his father in a few minutes, he said in a wondering voice, 'Eh! Who are you, son?' Then, lifting the old man's chin and peering into his face, he burst into peals of drunken laughter. 'Baba!' he exclaimed, at last. 'My own Baba! You're still alive! Whenever I come home I find you're still alive. Is that fair of you, Baba? You might die once in a while!' Jagai Mallik's jaws worked furiously and the flaps of loose skin that were his cheeks fluttered wildly. But, 'm-m—m—mm,' was all he could say. Chandika gave the bald pate a smart little tap and made soft clucking noises with his mouth. 'Live all you want, Baba,' he said indulgently. 'Live till we're all dead and gone.' Then, suddenly losing his temper, he shouted, 'I've been planning such a grand shraddha for you, you bastard, and you refuse to die! Can a man be denied the right to perform his own father's shraddha? Do you want to do it yourself, you gram-peddling skinflint?' At this point, the palki-bearers tried to save the old man by attempting to lead him away. But Chandika wouldn't let them. '*Haramzada*!' he yelled, grabbing one of them by the shoulder. 'How dare you take him away? I'm talking to my father. What's that to yours? I'll tear your mouth to pieces with my shoe!' And, stooping to pull off his shoe, he tumbled out of the servants' hands and falling prostrate at his father's feet, burst into tears. 'Baba!' he howled piteously, knocking his head in the dirt, 'I'm your unworthy son—unfit even to perform your shraddha. Oof!'

By now, the servants had managed to separate the two. Jagai Mallik's led him away and Chandika's hauled him to his feet. The sobbing fit over, Chandika burst into song: '*Paréro monéro bhavo*,' he sang in a tuneless bass, '*Bujhité na paaré paré*,' and gesticulating wildly, prepared to climb up the steps to the verandah. Nabin slipped behind a pillar but couldn't escape the bloodshot eyes. 'Who are you, boy?' Chandika asked, peering into his face. 'You're quite a dandy, you know.' Then, considering him unworthy of any further attention, Chandika walked away, his great body heaving and rolling like a ship at sea. Nabin wrinkled his nose at the reek that came from him. The man was drunk. He knew that, though he had no direct experience of drunkenness. Ramkamal Singha had never touched liquor when at home. Besides, he had died when Nabin Kumar was still a child. Bidhusekhar didn't drink; neither did Ganga. Some of his fellow students in Hindu College drank, of course. But that only prompted a mild curiosity in him—never a desire to emulate. But today, all feelings were swamped in the wave of revulsion that the drunken boor had let loose in him. Nabin took a vow. He wouldn't touch liquor. No—not as long as he lived.

Nabin sat waiting in the carriage for half an hour before Krishnabhamini came. He was so overwrought by his troubles by then that he felt like grabbing his young wife by the hair and slapping her hard on both cheeks. But before he could say or do anything, Krishnabhamini whispered agitatedly, '*O go!* My Miteni is so unfortunate—my heart breaks for her! Her husband is mad! How could her parents marry her off to a madman?'

'Mad!' Nabin burst out indignantly. 'He's not mad in the least. He's a coarse, arrogant boor with no manners.'

'*Na go,*' Krishnabhamini persisted. 'He is mad. Stark raving mad. He doesn't go out anywhere. He keeps sitting before a portrait and talks gibberish to himself. Or he does not speak a word. He didn't open his mouth once all the time I was upstairs. Miteni and her mother-in-law weep all day long.'

'Have you brought our son and daughter-in-law?'

'I didn't get the chance—'

'Forget them. Let them stay in that hell-hole. We shouldn't have gone there in the first place.'

'But my Miteni begged me to come again. She wouldn't let go of my hand till I promised.'

'No,' Nabin thundered.

Krishnabhamini never went to Hatkhola again. She was struck with cholera within ten days of the unfortunate visit. All the great doctors of the city attended on her but no one could save her. She died within a few hours and escaped into another world, leaving her boy husband and her box of dolls behind her.

# *Chapter XXXXII*

Leaving Mughalsarai behind, Ganga came to Varanasi, a beautiful city which stretched out in a half moon on the left bank of the Ganga. Dusk was falling but rows of lamps lit up the river ghats and the roofs and cornices of houses and shops. It was the night of Dipawali! Ganga's heart quivered with anticipation. The time was at hand for his meeting with Bindu.

But Ganga didn't enter the city just then. He had something to wrestle with and knock down before he could stake his claim. And that was his conscience. Many years ago, when he was little more than a boy, Bidhusekhar had taken him to the temple of Kali in Bowbazar and made him swear an oath. And Ganga had obeyed. He had held the Goddess's feet in his hands and sworn never to see Bindu again. Bindu knew about it. What if she turned away from him in disgust? No one respected the violator of a solemn oath. Ganga didn't either. But, he argued with himself, he was too young at that time to know what was best for him or for Bindu. He had been prompted by his fear of Bidhusekhar as well as his assurance that if he obeyed, no harm would come to Bindu. But Bidhusekhar hadn't kept his promise. He had banished Bindu to Varanasi and then forgotten her.

Even as he stood thinking these thoughts, a wave of exhaustion swept over Ganga. He was hungry, thirsty and footsore from his long journey and his body craved rest and refreshment. He could have gone into one of the inns (he had sold two rings on the way and had a good supply of money) but he wouldn't enter the city just then. Seeing a tree near at hand, he dragged himself across and collapsing under it, shut his eyes. The moment he did so, an image flashed before his inward eye; of a face, black as night, with slivers of glittering gold for eyes and rows of sharp stone teeth, through which a gleaming gold tongue hung to her breast. It was She before whom he had taken his vow. Ganga trembled though not with fear. His faith in the powers of the supernatural had been considerably eroded since his years in college. This was a different emotion—one that he couldn't fathom. Shutting his eyes tight, he tried to bring Bindu's features to mind. But he couldn't. That dark, cruel face wouldn't let him. Ganga strained his memory for a long time. Beads of perspiration appeared on his forehead and his breath came in painful gasps. Then, suddenly, he murmured to himself, 'I denounce you! I denounce all false deities—dolls of clay, wood, stone and metal—with which my fellow Hindus play their unending games. From this day onwards I set myself apart.' Then, kneeling in the dust, he raised his hands in the air and chanted, *'Om tat sat shristi-sthiti-pralaya.* The Lord is the Truth. The one and only Truth. He is knowledge. He is light. He is eternity. He is Param Brahma, from which all life springs. I dedicate myself to His worship. He and no other shall be my God.'

Thus, Ganga became a Brahmo, with only his conscience as witness. He tried to recall Bindu's face once more but failed again. The same gold eyes and glittering tongue swam into his view. But he didn't care any more. He felt as though a weight had been lifted from his heart and he was free. He was not bound by his vow for he was no longer a Hindu.

Ganga rose and walked through the vast iron gates into the city. Passing the police station, he came upon the main thoroughfare, swarming with carriages and bullocks-carts and lined with shops and stalls. Torches blazed everywhere; there was hectic buying and selling. Ganga entered one of the shops and bought a new outfit for himself, the one he wore being travel-stained and dirty. Then, sitting outside a sweetmeat stall, he had a hearty meal of *kachauris* and *malai*. Now, he had to find an inn in which he could spend the night. Tomorrow, he would start looking for Bindu.

Walking through the city the next morning, he was amazed at what he saw. He knew Varanasi to be an ancient city and a place of Hindu pilgrimage but he wasn't prepared for its size and the variety of its people, which seemed to him to outstrip the city of Calcutta. Varanasi was indeed the holiest of holy cities—so ancient that Shiva was supposed to have come here to beg alms of Annapurna. Originally a Hindu principality, it had been leased to the Nawab of Ayodhya, who had passed its administration over to the British. Thus, Varanasi had a conglomeration of cultures that was rarely to be seen anywhere. Every lane and alley had a temple and a mosque standing cheek by jowl and pilgrims, Hindu and Muslim, swarmed over the streets and waterfronts. Fiery English officers galloped through crowds of pedestrians and laughed to see them scatter under the horses' hooves and sedate Muslim aristocrats cantered gently by, the bells on their horses' hooves ringing with a melodious sound. Sometimes, whole streets were blocked by processions—weddings and funerals—and the movements of sadhus and maharajas.

Ganga knew that his father had a house in Varanasi, in which he had spent a few months each year in the company of Kamala Sundari. He also knew that Bidhusekhar owned no property except in Calcutta. It was highly likely, therefore, that Bindu was being kept in the Singha house. The house was situated near Dasashwamedha Ghat (Ganga had seen the address in the family documents and noted it down). There were eighty ghats in Varanasi, of which five, the Pancha Tirtha, were holier then the others. Dasashwamedha was one of these, so everyone knew it. Ganga made his way thither, asking for directions as he went.

After an hour or so of brisk walking, he saw a temple in the distance which held his attention for its peak glittered like gold. Stopping a passer-by, he asked, 'What temple is that, brother? What metal is it covered with?' The man stared in astonishment. What sinner was this, he thought, who stood on the holy soil of Varanasi and did not know the temple of Baba Vishwanath? Talking to the people around him, Ganga came to know that the temple was so old that no one knew its age. It had been razed to the ground during the reign of Emperor Aurangzeb and had been rebuilt by Rani Ahilyabai, the gold for the roof being donated by Maharaja Ranjit Singh. One of the men took Ganga's hand and said, 'Come, I'll take you there,' but Ganga pulled it away. He would not bow his head before a graven image. He was a Brahmo!

He found the house quite easily. It was a stone mansion, three storeys high, with a marble plaque bearing the inscription, Singha Manzil, in Devnagri on one of its columns. But the doors and windows were barred and there was no sign of life within. Outside, on the porch, some activity went on, which struck an discordant note. Five or six men sat oiling and sunning themselves and wrestling with one another in play. Ganga watched them for a while and wondered what to do. Taking a decision, he walked up to them and said, 'I've come from Calcutta to meet a lady—a relative of mine—who lives in this house. I wish to go inside and see her.' The men stared. 'But this house is the property of Raja Chait Singh,' they said. 'It is empty. There is no lady within.' Explaining that they were the Raja's bodyguards, who had been sent on ahead (their master being expected in a few days), they suggested that Ganga had come to the wrong house. But Ganga shook his head. Pointing to the plaque, he said, 'This house belongs to my father, Ramkamal Singha.' The men glanced at one another and shrugged. They were simple, ignorant folk, they said, and had no knowledge of such things. Raja Saheb would be here within a week. It would be better for the Bengali Babu to talk to him. Besides, Singha Manzil could be named after Raja Chait Singh, too—could it not? Ganga couldn't deny the logic of that argument. Was there another house, then, of the same name on Dasashwamedha Ghat? The men shook their heads. If there was, they hadn't heard of it. But Mansaram Chhadiwala would know. Mansaram made a living by applying sandal paste on the foreheads of pilgrims on Dasashwamedha Ghat. He had lived in Varanasi all his life and knew the city like the back of his hand.

Mansaram Chhadiwala sat under a canopy of woven reeds, on the bank. He was long and thin like a rope and seemed to be a hundred years old. But his memory hadn't dimmed in the least and his voice was strong and clear. Yes, he said, he remembered Babu Ramkamal Singha—a great babu of Calcutta, who came every year with his mistress and spent his evenings on the river. Such music and dancing went on in the bajra! Such feasting and merrymaking! But Babu Ramkamal was no ordinary debauch. He was a very religious man and had a heart of gold. Every month, on the night of the full moon, he feasted the Brahmins and *pandas* of the city. Yes, Singha Manzil was the name of the house in which he stayed when he was here. On Ganga's asking him how it came to be in the possession of Raja Chait Singh, Mansaram said that the house had been sold five or six years ago. Raja Chait Singh had bought it for twelve hundred rupees—a real bargain, for Babu Ramkamal had paid twice that sum for it. But that was the way of the world! When a great man died, his property and estates fell into a decline. Mansaram had seen many cases like this one.

Ganga walked away from Mansaram's shed, agitated beyond description. What would he do now? Where, in this great city, could he even begin looking for Bindu? Had Bidhusekhar really sent her here? Or had he spread such a rumour in the hope that Ganga would think her lost to him? Ganga didn't trust the wily Brahmin. For all he knew, Bindu was still in her father's house—a prisoner. Or she may have been dispatched to their ancestral mansion in Krishnanagar. But, thinking it over, Ganga dismissed the idea. Bidhusekhar wouldn't take such a risk. He had sent her to Kashi and here she must be if she hadn't been robbed and murdered on the way. He had to find her. He had lost everything for her sake. There was no going back.

Ganga spent the next few days roaming about the streets and lanes of Kashi, his senses alert for the slightest trace of Bindu. Dawn and dusk saw him at the ghats, pacing up and down and peering into the faces of the women bathers. The sight of a girl in a white than sent his pulses racing. He would rush towards her and then turn away with a murmured apology. At such times people stared at him as though at a madman. But he was oblivious of everything and everyone. Only one thought haunted him like a passion, day and night, and that was to find Bindu.

A month went by. One evening, as Ganga sat on the steps of Dasashwamedha Ghat, gazing into the water with listless eyes, Mansaram Chhadiwala came and stood beside him. 'You are the young man who was looking for Babu Ramkamal Singha's house,' he said. 'Are you related to him?'

'Yes,' replied Ganga. 'I am his son.'

'What are you doing all by yourself here in Kashi?'

'I'm looking for a woman—a sort of relative of mine. People tell me you know everyone in Kashi. Do you know her? A young Bengali widow called Bindubasini?'

'I've heard about her,' Mansaram said grimly. 'She was the daughter of Babu Ramkamal Singha's best friend—the lawyer,

Bidhu Mukherjee. She did live here for a while. But you won't find her now. She's dead.'

'Dead! That's impossible. When did she die? Of what malady?'

'What is the use of all these questions? Hearing the details will only increase your pain. Go back where you came from—to your home and family. Kashi is no place for a young man like you. Believe me, I say all this for your own good.'

Something in his manner of speaking puzzled Ganga. He was convinced that Mansaram was hiding something from him. Bindu wasn't dead. Of that he was sure. He wouldn't go back. He would stick to Mansaram and ferret out the truth.

## Chapter XXXXIII

Bidhusekhar was recovering from a diabetic stroke that had left one side of his body in a state of paralysis. He was better though even now his speech came out thick and slurred and he could breathe only through one nostril. His left arm and leg had been dead for a long time and he had to suffer the indignity of being supported by his servants and seeking help for all his physical needs. But it hadn't been for long. He could walk short distances now, with the help of a stout walking stick. He tired easily and dragged his leg painfully. But he wouldn't give up. He was a man of immense will power and accepted the changed circumstances without fuss.

Bidhusekhar's wife had died some years ago and his widowed, eldest daughter, Narayani, had the care of her ailing father and the two small children of the house, one being her own youngest daughter and the other, Suhasini's five-year-old son. Bidhusekhar doted on the latter for he was the only male of the family; the one who would don his mantle after his death. Bidhusekhar had named him Pran Gopal. 'Gopal! Gopal!' he called for him day and night, all through his illness. As if Gopal were indeed his Janardan in human form! Peace flooded his soul at the sight of the little face and he yearned to press the warm softness of his body against his tired old flesh.

Pran Gopal's paternal grandfather, Shiblochan Bandopadhyaya, was still alive and wished to rear him in his own house for, as he explained to Bidhusekhar, the child was a member of his line and would carry his family name. The proposal left Bidhusekhar quivering with rage. How dare the beggarly Brahmin attempt to take his grandson away? He had sold his own son to Bidhusekhar and taken good money for him. Bidhusekhar had brought the boy over to his house, fed and clothed and educated him. Fate had denied Durga Prasad the opportunity of inheriting his father-in-law's vast estates. But his son would do so. Bidhusekhar would not give him up. Why should he?

But Shiblochan was very persistent. He turned up at the house every day. He couldn't live without seeing his grandson, he said. His wife was breaking her heart over her son's death and only the sight of her grandchild would console her. But Bidhusekhar dismissed his pleas with the contempt they deserved. Shiblochan hadn't enquired after Durga Prasad even once after passing him over to Bidhusekhar, and after his death, had shown no consideration at all for Suhasini. And now, the beggar was shedding crocodile tears over his grandson! Bidhusekhar knew the motive behind this struggle for possession of the boy. A male child was a great asset in a *kulin* household. Shiblochan would turn him into a professional bridegroom as soon as his thread ceremony was over. He would fill his coffers over and over again with dowry.

That morning, as Bidhusekhar sat in the reception room, reading the English paper and pulling gently at his *albola*, Munshi Amir Ali was ushered in. Bidhusekhar looked up in surprise. Amil Ali was a Muslim aristocrat of noble lineage and a reputed lawyer of the civil court. What could such a man want of him? Amir Ali entered the room, murmuring a polite adab. He was a fine, distinguished looking man in a gold embroidered black kurta. A tall fez sat atop his silver-streaked head. Inviting him to take a seat, Bidhusekhar commanded the servant to fetch another *albola*. He then commenced conversing with his guest in flawless Persian.

Munshi Amir Ali lowered his bulk into an armchair and recited a couplet from Hafiz, to the effect that his heart was quivering like a reed at the thought of the beloved's illness and possible departure from the world. Bidhusekhar replied with another couplet which ran thus: 'There is nothing in the world worth living for except the love of good friends. It is only for this that a man desires a long life.' Then, Amir Ali (who also spoke fluent Bengali) enquired after his friend's health and informed him that his prolonged absence from the court had rendered it akin to a forest without the lion king. Bidhusekhar made a polite rejoinder to the effect that when spring breezes blew and the cuckoo sang, who cared to hear the roar of a lion? Amir Ali was the lord of the cuckoos and his sweet melodies echoed in and out of the courtroom.

These preliminary courtesies over, Amir Ali came to the

point. 'By Khodatallah's blessings and the good wishes of sincere friends like yourself,' he began, 'I have been enabled to acquire a humble cottage, standing on a strip of land in Janbazar. I had cherished great hopes of entertaining you there but your illness—' Bidhusekhar scanned Amir Ali's face closely as he spoke. He knew him to be an immensely wealthy man. It was obvious that he had bought another large property in Janbazar. But he hadn't come here to offer him flowery compliments and invitations. There was something else.

'From whom did you buy the property?' he asked.

'From the Thakurs of Jorasanko.'

Bidhusekhar nodded. He knew that the Thakur family was in a bad way. Deben Thakur was being forced to sell off land, houses and taluks, to pay off his father's debts.

'The house is small,' Amir Ali went on, 'but the garden around it is exquisitely beautiful, with every kind of flower and fruit growing in it. It has been neglected for many years but can be redeemed and turned into one of the loveliest pleasure gardens in the city. But the woman who lives on the adjoining property is creating difficulties. She has been enjoying it all these years and won't keep off it. Her servants help themselves to my fruits and her cows wander in and out of the flower beds.' The matter was clear to Bidhusekhar. Amir Ali had an eye on the woman's property. He wanted to acquire it for himself. But why come to him?

'The woman is a prostitute,' Amir Ali said, watching the expression on Bidhusekhar's face.

'Oh!'

'I've decided to start legal proceedings against her. I've come to you for advice.'

'To me?' Bidhusekhar gave a mirthless little laugh. 'You are the most astute lawyer I know. What advice can I give you?'

*'Toba! Toba!'* Amir Ali touched his ears in exaggerated deference. 'What am I before you? The tiniest fragment of counsel from you is enough to disentangle the most complicated lawsuits. Besides—' And here, Amir Ali lowered his voice. 'I've made enquiries. The property isn't hers. It belongs to the late Ramkamal Singha, of whose will you are a trustee.'

Bidhusekhar remembered everything in a flash. That whore,

Kamli! Yes, it was in her house that Ramkamal had breathed his last. She had been occupying it all these years. Bidhusekhar had tried to get rid of her but had failed because of Ganga. An opportunity had come round again—a golden opportunity. He wouldn't miss it. He would sell off the property to Amir Ali and leave it to him to evict her.

Bidhusekhar felt enthused for the first time that morning. Discussing the matter for some minutes more, he told Amir Ali that he would take a decision after consulting Ramkamal Singha's widow. After Amir Ali's departure, Bidhusekhar leaned back against his cushion with a sigh. He had resigned from the court but the court was loath to let go of him.

That evening, Bidhusekhar went out for the first time after his illness. As he stepped out of his carriage at the gates of Singha mansion, the servants and officials of the estate came running out to meet him. He had aged considerably in these few months. His face had thinned and one eye had marbled over. 'Come in, Bara Babu!' Dibakar welcomed him, hands folded in respectful greeting. 'Your absence from this house has left us orphaned. We have no one to turn to.' Bidhusekhar stood for a few minutes in the hall, talking to the men—a sharp word of command here; a rebuke there! A great deal was amiss. He was sure of that. He had to take charge once again. Bimbabati and Nabin depended on him. He had to see that no harm came to them. 'Get the books ready,' he ordered Dibakar. 'I'll inspect them tomorrow morning. And send word to your mistress that I wish to see her.' He hauled himself up the stairs, dragging the lifeless leg after him. Half-way up he stopped to catch his breath. The effort had exhausted him. As he stood leaning heavily on his stick, Nabin came tearing down. He dashed past Bidhusekhar without a glance. 'Chhotku,' Bidhusekhar cried, shocked beyond belief. Nabin looked up from the bottom of the stairs. 'Jetha[33] Babu!' he said coolly. 'I didn't see you. Please wait upstairs. I'll be back in a few minutes.' Bidhusekhar stood as if turned to stone. He had come to the house after months yet Chhotku had not bent down to touch his feet. He had been sick to the point of death yet Chhotku had not cared to enquire after

---

33 Father's elder brother.

his health. He hadn't come to see him once during his illness. Bimbabati had—twice or thrice. She had stood at a distance, the veil pulled over her face. She hadn't spoken a word. She never did except in the privacy of her chamber. Bidhusekhar sighed. He felt a stab of pain at the thought that Chhotku did not return his love. Yet the boy was all he truly had. By right, he was the one who would perform the last rites over Bidhusekhar's body! Suddenly, he felt a wave of resentment sweep over him. Why was he being punished in this way? Would his limbs ever recover their full strength? Would he ever be able to stride up and down on smartly shod feet as he had done before? Kaviraj Moshai assured him he would. But who knew?

Bidhusekhar took a deep breath and resumed his climb. Crossing the landing he stopped short in amazement. Ramkamal's reception room, kept locked ever since his death, was open. Though the doorway Bidhusekhar caught a glimpse of new furnishings—thick Persian carpets and crystal chandeliers. Bidhusekhar knitted his brow. He wondered who had given orders for opening up this room and why.

Walking down the gallery toward Bimbabati's room, Bidhusekhar noticed that many of the cages that still hung from the ceiling were empty. The birds were either dead or had flown away. Bimbabati's interest in them had obviously waned. The old myna was there—the one who greeted passers-by with the words, 'Myna! Say *Jai* Radha! *Jai* Krishna!' But today, it merely turned a red eye in Bidhusekhar's direction, then tucked its head under one wing. It was old and tired and had lost its speech.

Bidhusekhar stood outside the door and called, 'Bimba!' A maid came hurrying out. 'Ginni Ma is waiting for you,' she said, then escorted him in. Bidhusekhar frowned. The maid was new. The women who had served Bimbabati in the past knew that Bidhusekhar did not like them to be present when he was alone with her.

Bimba stood at the foot of a life-sized portrait of her late husband. She wore spotless widow white and her head was covered to the brow. But her youth and beauty were undimmed and shone out with a radiance that belied her forty-two years. Bidhusekhar dragged himself to the bedstead and gripped a corner post with one hand. 'Bring paan,' he ordered the maid. 'And then leave the room.'

Now, Bimbabati came forward and, bending low, touched Bidhusekhar's feet. Bidhusekhar placed his hands on her shoulders and raised her gently from the ground. 'How are you, Bimba?' he asked. Tears ran down Bimbabati's face. She was too overcome to reply. 'I had given up hope,' Bidhusekhar continued, 'of our ever meeting again—just you and I—like this.' Bimba's tears fell faster and she sobbed audibly. Now Bidhusekhar seated himself on the bed and, lifting Bimbabati's chin, gazed long and ardently into her face. 'Why do you weep?' he asked tenderly. 'I'm here with you now. Am I not?' Bimbabati wiped her cheeks with the palm of her hand. 'I prayed for your recovery day and night,' she said huskily. 'I would have killed myself if anything had happened to you.'

'Nothing will happen to me. I'll live for many more years to come. All will be as before.'

'Everything's going wrong for me. Everything.'

'Why do you say that?'

'This was a happy house. Full of people, full of laughter. But now it is empty and desolate. I feel I can't breathe in it any more.'

The maid brought the paan. Bimba served Bidhusekhar, then seated herself on a small stool at his feet. 'Where was Chhotku rushing off to in such a hurry?' Bidhusekhar asked. 'He didn't stop even on seeing me.' 'I don't know,' Bimba replied. 'He has many friends. He had clamped up completely after Bouma's death. He wouldn't talk to anyone; he didn't shed a tear. I tried to take him in my arms; to make him weep but he wouldn't respond. It is only now, for the last week or so, that he's going out with his friends. I don't stop him.'

'We'll find another bride for him. Then all will be well.'

'And my Ganga! No one cared to find out what happened to him.'

Bidhusekhar knew that Bimba would bring up the subject of Ganga. She always did, even though she knew that Bidhusekhar did not relish it in the least. 'Ganga is not a child,' he said sharply. 'If a strapping young man leaves home and goes off somewhere, no one can stop him. Dibakar did all he could to trace him.'

'I have an idea.'

'What is it?'

'He may be in Kashi. I feel it in my bones.'

'Why Kashi?'

'You kept the facts from me at the time. But I know what happened. Bindu is in Kashi. He may have gone there to look for her.'

'If he has, he won't find her. My Janardan has saved me once again. Bindu isn't in Kashi.'

'What do you mean?'

'Bindu is dead.'

'Dead!' Bimba's voice choked with tears. 'How can that be? O Bindu, my darling child!'

'I used to send money for her upkeep every six months. Last year it was returned to me along with a message that she was dead.'

'But someone from the family should have gone to her; should have nursed her in her illness and seen that the funeral rites were decently performed.'

'Who was to go? You know I don't like travelling. And there's no other male in my house. Sethji, in whose care I left her, is an old client of mine—a good, God-fearing man. He must have done all there was to do.' Bimba wept unrestrainedly. Bidhusekhar allowed her to do so for a few minutes, then focussing his one clear eye on both hers, he murmured unemotionally, 'Fate! Fate ordained widowhood for Bindu! An early death was her destiny! Janardan wrote this with his own hand upon her brow. What can you and I do? Be grateful that she died with her chastity intact. Your loving son did his best to despoil her—' Bimba went on weeping. Bidhusekhar changed the subject. 'While coming up the stairs, I noticed that the reception room has been opened up. That portrait of Ramkamal's used to hang there, if I remember rightly. Who brought it here?'

'Chhotku,' Bimba spoke through her tears. 'He and his friends meet every Saturday evening in the reception room. They call themselves members of the Vidyotsahini Sabha. They've even set up a theatre—'

'A theatre!' Bidhusekhar couldn't believe his ears. It took a little while for this information to sink in, then he burst out angrily, 'Is your son a low-born player that he should paint his face and prance about on a stage? *Chhi! Chhi! Chhi*! That a scion of the Singha family should stoop to this! Tighten the reins, Bimba. You're far too indulgent.' Then, taking a deep breath, he continued, 'All this is owing to my own negligence. I must take him in hand myself. I'll be here every morning from tomorrow and the house will run according to my dictates. We must find a bride for him as soon as we can. He mustn't be allowed to run loose or he'll turn into another Ramkamal. Don't weep, Bimba. I'm here to look after him. All will be well.' And, with these words, Bidhusekhar lifted his still healthy right leg and placed it on Bimbabati's lap.

# Chapter XXXXIV

Everyone agreed that Rasmoni, the widowed daughter-in-law of the immensely wealthy Preetiram Marh of Janbazar, displayed remarkable acumen and insight in the management of her business and estates. Born of poor Mahisya parents, she had no learning and hardly knew one letter from another. But her knowledge of the world was phenomenal and she was as spirited as she was intelligent. Her husband was no raja but his name being Rajchandra, she was dignified by the title of Rani by her subjects. Rani Rasmoni was a name to reckon with—one that commanded instant respect.

It was her beauty, however, that had attracted the attention of the young Rajchandra when, sailing on the breast of the Ganga on a pilgrimage to Kashi, he had seen the eleven-year-old girl bathing at the ghat near Halisahar. He was suffering from a broken heart (his second wife had died a few months ago) and thought all the tender emotions to be dead within him. But the sight of the fair maiden brought the blood rushing back and he felt his heart whole again. Making enquiries his friends found out that a marriage was possible—the girl's caste being the same as his. Returning to Calcutta they apprised his father of the events and Preetiram, glad that his son was ready to take up a normal life again, brought the girl of his choice home as daughter-in-law. The new bride brought luck with her. The family fortunes waxed and swelled with her coming till the Marhs were numbered among the wealthiest in the land.

Rani Rasmoni's name was relatively obscure during her husband's lifetime. It was after his death, when the rituals of the shraddha were taking place, that people came to realize the extent of her benevolence and generosity. Money was distributed to the poor in fistfuls, for two whole days in succession at the Rani's command. No one was to be turned away. Then, on the third day, she had had herself weighed against silver rupees—six thousand and thirteen of them—which were then distributed among Brahmins and pandits.

There was another side to the Rani's nature. She delighted in multiplying her assets. The family business flourished under her guidance and taluk after taluk was added to the estates. But though she was so ready to spend, it was never on herself. Unlike many other heads of great houses, she led a very spartan life, even sleeping on the bare floor on certain days of the month. In this she could be compared only to Debendranath Thakur, who had renounced all worldly pleasures in the pursuance of his new religion. But the two were in keen opposition on basic beliefs. Debendranath denounced idols and advocated the worship of a formless Brahma. Rani Rasmoni's devotion to all the gods and goddesses of the Hindu pantheon was unwavering. She had one burning ambition. And that was to preserve Hinduism from the onslaughts of the Christians and Brahmos and spread the message of her glory throughout the land.

Rani Rasmoni celebrated Hindu festivals with great pomp and ceremony. Her Dol and Durga festivals were famous and the citizens of Calcutta thronged to her mansion in Janbazar to witness them. Equally famous was her Rath. An enormous silver chariot, fashioned like a palace, was brought out into the streets. The procession was over a mile long, kirtaniyas singing all the way till the skies resounded to the beat of drums, the clash of cymbals and cries of *'Hari Bol.'*

There were many stories about Rasmoni and the intelligence and spirit with which she outwitted the toughest English sahebs. One of them centred around her Durga Puja celebrations. One early Saptami morning, the seventh day of the Durga festival, an Englishman's sweet slumber was rudely shattered by a procession of Brahmins. The saheb looked out of the window and was amazed and infuriated by what he saw. A mob of half-naked men leaped and pranced about, beating drums and cymbals and shrieking wildly, their *shikhas* dancing above their black faces. He knew that the natives had many bizarre customs but this was too much. To wake up the whole city at the crack of dawn, shrieking like devils let loose from hell! It was intolerable! He roared a command to them to stop their infernal din but the men turned a deaf ear and passed on.

Wild with fury he sent a message to the police station, requesting the police to stop the procession on its way back from the river. A few of the men had hastened back, in the meantime, to report the event to their mistress. Now, Rasmoni had quite a temper of her own, which flared up whenever she saw intolerance or injustice. 'We are Hindus,' she cried, her face flaming. 'How dare the sahebs interfere with our religious rituals? Do we stop them when they disturb our sleep with their drunken revels during their own festivals? Go back. Beat the drums harder and make more noise. And do it all day long, up and down the street on which that red-faced boor lives.' A few policemen tried to stop the procession without success for the leaders answered defiantly, 'Our Rani says that this street is ours. We may make as much noise as we please.' The saheb paced about like a wounded lion in his lair. His eardrums were fit to burst.

The following day, the saheb filed a legal suit against Rani Rasmoni. The verdict went against her as was usual in such cases—judge and plaintiff both being British—and she was ordered to pay a fine of fifty rupees. Rasmoni decided to teach the sahebs a lesson. She paid the fine without a murmur but gave orders, the very next day, to seal off the road from Janbazar to Babughat with stout trunks of mangrove. 'I built this road,' she declared. 'No one will walk over it without my consent.' All the traffic of the city came to a halt. The municipal authorities were in a quandary. Finally, after frantic consultations, an apology was sent and her fifty rupees returned. It was a tremendous victory for Rani Rasmoni and the native population of Calcutta rejoiced at her triumph.

On another occasion, Rani Rasmoni put the Company Bahadur quite out of countenance. The facts of the case were as follows. From early Magh[34] to late Ashwin,[35] the breast of the Ganga was dotted with fishing boats for hilsa fish swarmed in the waters. But the presence of so many dinghies restricted the movements of the ships coming into harbour. In consequence, the Company decided to clear the river by levying a tax on every dinghy, calculating, quite correctly, that very few fishermen

---

34 Mid-January—Mid-February.
35 Mid-September—Mid-October.

would be able to pay it. Threatened with the loss of their livelihood, the fisherfolk went weeping to Rani Rasmoni and begged her to help them. Rasmoni had a brilliant idea. The Company was levying a tax on fishing. Very good! She would pay the tax but lease the waters for herself. Handing over ten thousand rupees to the Company's treasury, she gave orders that the whole stretch of the Ganga, from Ghusuri to Metiaburj, be cordoned off with thick ropes. Then, addressing the fishing community, she said, 'Fish all you want. No one can stop you.' This proved a disaster for the British. Their ships were stuck midstream and the life of the city was well nigh paralysed. The natives were thrilled. One of their members had outwitted the sahebs once again! People crowded to the river to watch the fun. It was indeed a strange sight. Rows of ships stood on one side of the cordon, the sailors staring at the cables in bewilderment while the dinghies of the fisherfolk flitted about on the water like thousands of moths. Among the crowd of spectators stood the young Nabin Kumar. 'Look, look,' he cried out to Dulal. 'The zamindarin of Janbazar has rubbed the Company's face in the dirt!' He had heard the phrase, uttered by adults, and liked the sound of it.

An alarmed Company Bahadur demanded an explanation. Rasmoni's answer was simple. She had leased the stretch of water from the officials of the Company, paying good money for it. What she did with it was her business. She could not allow ships to pass since they would disturb her fish. The Company had no right to demand it. Surely it knew that once one leased out a stretch of land or water, one surrendered one's rights over it. The officials of the Company were forced to admit the justice of her statement and make a deal. They would allow the fishermen to ply their boats as always and, in return, the Rani would have the restricting cordon removed.

Rani Rasmoni was sixty years old but her health and strength were phenomenal. So was the strength of her will. Once she set her mind to something, she brooked no hindrance. But on one occasion, the Rani came perilously close to defeat. And that was by her own countrymen.

Rani Rasmoni went on a pilgrimage every two or three years. One year, she was filled with a desire to visit Kashi and offer prayers at the temple of Vishwanath and Annapurna.

Kashi was a great way off and there was a danger of pirates on the river. But they held no terrors for the indomitable Rani. She had decided to go to Kashi and go she would. She took the necessary precautions, however. Twenty-five bajras would sail with her, filled to overflowing with members of her family, servants, maids and armed guards. A stock of provisions, calculated to last the retinue six months, was to be taken. But on the night of her departure, something happened that changed the course of history and flung her in the midst of a long and arduous struggle.

The party was to set sail at midnight. The Rani entered her private bajra shortly after dusk and, wearied with the long preparations, fell into a deep and restful sleep. Then, an hour or so before dawn, she had a dream. Ma Kali, Mother of the world, stood at the foot of her bed. 'Where are you going?' the Goddess cried out to her in a voice of reproach. 'Your sons and daughters are starving. Serve them and you will serve me. Build a temple for me, here on the bank of the Ganga. You need not go to Kashi.' The vision faded and Rasmoni woke up, sweating and trembling all over. This was no dream. She was sure of it. Ma Kali had appeared to her in person and commanded her to build a temple by the river. She ran out on the deck, crying wildly, 'Stop! Stop the bajra!'

At daybreak, the Rani distributed all the provisions the boats were carrying among the local poor and returned to the city. She told no one the reason for her sudden change of plan but, immediately on entering her palace, she sent for her son-in-law, Mathur. Rasmoni had four daughters but no son. She had wedded her third daughter to Mathur. Then, on the girl's untimely death, wedded him to her fourth and youngest. Mathur lived in the house and was so intelligent and capable that Rasmoni had come to depend on him for everything. 'Look for a piece of land on the bank of the Ganga,' she told him without preamble. 'I wish to build a temple.'

Efforts were made, at first, to find a stretch of land to the west of the river for, as the saying went, 'The western bank of the Ganga equals Varanasi in holiness.' But land could not be found here except in small lots. On the other hand, a large tract of good land was available in the village of Dakshineswar on the eastern bank. An abandoned graveyard, the shrine of a

Muslim *pir* and an enormous kuthi, belonging to the Supreme Court attorney, Hasty Saheb, stood on fifty-four and a half bighas of land and could be had for forty-two thousand and five hundred rupees. The land was bought and the construction began. Vast embankments were built on the river and an enormous ghat, whose stone steps led down to the deepest waters. Then, above them, a whole complex of temples rose—the Shiv Mandir, the Nat Mandir, the Vishnu Mandir. The Kali Mandir was the most gorgeous of them all—its peak glittering with gold and *navaratna*.

The temple of Dakshineswar took several years to build. To ward off any evil influences that might hinder the process, the Rani practised the severest austerities. She bathed thrice a day, ate nothing but boiled rice and ghee, slept on the bare floor and prayed day and night. She sent for Mathur from time to time and even visited the site to keep herself informed about the progress of the work. Then, when the end was almost in sight, Mathur brought the bad news. The Brahmins of the city had decreed that the temple built by Rasmoni Dasi in Dakshineswar could not be used for worship. She was a Shudra woman and deities did not accept offerings from the hands of Shudras. It would go against the shastras.

Rasmoni stared at her son-in-law, shocked beyond belief. How could her work go against the shastras? She had undertaken it at the behest of Ma Kali herself! She had drained herself of her wealth, expecting no return. Was her birth in a Shudra family her sole identity? Did her faith, her dedication, her life of purity and abstinence amount to nothing? Did not her royal seal carry the insignia, 'Kalipada Abhilashi Srimati Rasmoni Dasi?' And now, when the Goddess had appeared to her and commanded her to build a temple, the Brahmins were taking away her right to worship? What priest would agree to perform puja if the Brahmins passed a decree against it?

Rasmoni threw herself on the floor, weeping bitterly. The blow was harder to bear because it came from her own countrymen, whom she loved; from Brahmins, whom she revered like gods. But, within a few minutes, she sat up and wiped her eyes. 'I've never accepted defeat,' she told her son-in-law. 'I can't begin now. The decree of the Calcutta pandits is not the last word. Send messengers to Varanasi and the land of the Marathas. There are great pandits there—well versed in the scriptures. Seek their opinion.'

But, opinion was unanimous everywhere. The lower castes had no right to establish religious institutions. The Calcutta pandits started a movement against her, openly declaring that they would not tolerate her arrogance. She thought she could buy everything and everyone with the power of money. But not all the wealth in the world could change the shastras. How could she dare to presume that the gods would accept rice offerings from her hands?

Rasmoni had fought many battles with the British and won them, but what weapons could she use against the Brahmins who represented the religion she loved and sought to preserve? She felt utterly defeated. She spent her days lying on the floor, weeping. From time to time, she raised her head and cried out aloud, 'Ma! Why am I being denied the right to serve you? Is it my fault that I was born of Shudra parents? Oh! Mother of the world! Are we Shudras not your children?'

One day, Mathur came into her room and said, 'I have good news for you, Ma. It is possible that our troubles are at an end.' Rasmoni did not even look up. This was another of Mathur's periodic attempts at consolation, she thought. 'What is it?' she asked bitterly.

'You must sit up first. I have a lot to tell you.'

Rasmoni did as she was bid but there was not a trace of enthusiasm in the voice that said, 'You say our troubles are at an end. Pray explain yourself.'

'A renowned scholar of the Vedas has decreed that if the temple property is gifted to a Brahmin before the images are installed, the stigma of Shudra worship will be wiped away. The shastras will condone it.'

'That is quite easy,' Rasmoni said, her face brightening. 'I'll make it over to my Gurudev. I shall be his servant.'

'An excellent idea!' Mathur agreed, smiling.

'But will the other Brahmins accept his decree?'

'Of course they will. He is a renowned pandit and commands a great deal of respect. He quoted an extract from the shastras in support of his decree. What Brahmin will dare to refute the scriptures?'

'Who is this pandit? Where does he live?'

'His name is Ramkumar Bhattacharya. His ancestral home is in Kamarpukur village on the Hoogly river. But he has a *tol* in Calcutta, in Jhamapukur, and that is where he lives with his younger brother—a boy of seventeen by the name of Gadadhar. The boy has an excellent singing voice.'

# Chapter XXXXV

Raimohan and his party found Chandranath at the *samshan* ghat in Nimtala. The boy sat crouching over a *chulli*, poking it with a pole, longer than himself. His upper body was bare, and only a tattered, filthy piece of cloth covered his loins. His face and chest were coated in ash and grime and his hair stood up on end in streaky strands. Raimohan didn't see him at first. But Chandranath gave himself away. As the men came towards him, he flung the pole away and ran as fast as his legs could carry him. It was Harachandra who recognized him. 'Why!' he cried out, startled. 'That's Chandu!'

Then a frantic chase began, Raimohan running with difficulty for he was getting old and his joints creaked with rheumatism. Harachandra was not much of a sprinter either, being soft and sodden with years of hard drinking. However, some other fellows took up the chase. They were social outcastes, who hung around the *samshan* and made a living out of it. They slept most of the time or played Bagh Bandi with bits of stone and brick. But the moment they heard the chant, '*Bolo* Hari. Hari *bol*,' they sprang to their feet and went sniffing up to the corpse to see what they could get out of it. This, however, was no corpse. It was a live boy. He was probably a thief. With the excitement that the pursuit of a thief generates in the lower classes, these *samshan* parasites ran after Chandu, screaming instructions to one another. 'Catch the boy! Grab him! Hold him tight!' Chandu ran this way and that like a frenzied rat, then, in a desperate bid to elude his pursuers, jumped into the river. But, not knowing how to swim, he threshed his arms and legs wildly in the water and was about to drown when some of the men dived in and brought him up, kicking and screaming, on to the bank. These men were wonderful swimmers for they were used to plunging into the deepest waters to retrieve the copper coins thrown in by funeral parties.

Raimohan pushed and jostled his way through the crowd and took the dripping boy in his arms. 'Chandu! Chandu, my son!' he cried in a voice, cracking with emotion, 'My heart breaks to look at you! What do you eat here? Where do you sleep? Your golden skin is as black as soot. Come home, son. Come home to your mother. She weeps so—she'll turn blind with grief.' Chandranath's face puckered up with hatred. He shut his eyes tight and screamed, 'Get away from me. I won't go back. I don't know you.'

Then, Raimohan, Harachandra and two others simply lifted the boy off his feet and carried him to a hackney coach that stood waiting outside the *samshan*. 'Go as swiftly as you can,' Raimohan urged the driver. 'We'll pay you good money.' He sat, his back to the door, his tall body hiding Chandranath from view.

Heeremoni lay face down on the floor of the bedroom, a coarse white than wrapped around her. She hadn't eaten for three days and had wept and wept till her lovely egg-shaped face had assumed the size and dimensions of a shaddock. Raimohan entered the room, crying, 'O Heere! Open your eyes and see what I've brought you.' Heere raised her face and seeing Chandu, sprang up and fluttered over to him like a mother bird shielding her fledgling with her wings. But Chandranath would have none of her caresses. Mother love meant nothing to him any more. He pushed her away so hard that she fell against the wall, striking her head with a thud. 'You're not my mother, you demon!' Chandranath hissed at her like an angry cat. 'Why did you carry me in your womb? And, even if you did, why didn't you strangle me to death at birth?' Chandranath's manner of speaking had changed in these few days. He spoke in the voice and language of an adult.

Heeremoni wept as if her heart would break. 'Don't cry, Heere,' Raimohan comforted her. 'It is such a happy day for us. Your son has come home to you. Quarrels between mother and son break out all the time. The boy didn't mean to hurt you. You mustn't mind his words.' Then, turning to Chandu, he said, 'Don't speak so harshly, son. Don't break our hearts. We have shared your humiliation and suffered with you. Your mother has been in torment ever since the day you left us. Don't pour salt on open wounds, my son.'

'Don't call me "son". Are you my father? Since when have

you become my father? And how? How dare you bring me here?'

'I'll answer all your questions. But first you must have a meal and some rest. You look hot and tired. Wash your face and hands and have something to eat. Then—'

'No.' Chandranath spat out the word, his eyes rolling like a trapped animal's.

*'O ré,* Chandu!' Heere broke in, sobbing piteously. 'I deserve all your reproaches. I'll give up my life of sin—I promise it. I'll do penance. We'll go on a pilgrimage together—you and I. I'll send for the goldsmith this very afternoon and order a gold crown for Lord Jagannath of Puri and a gold flute for Lord Krishna of Brindavan. Won't my sins be washed away, then?'

'Die!' Chandranath muttered between clenched teeth. 'Die a hundred deaths. I don't care what you do. I'm none of yours.'

Now, Raimohan and Haran took hold of Chandranath and led him to his room. This proved even worse. For Chandranath fell upon his books and papers and tearing them into shreds, scattered them all over the room. Next, he lifted the *thala* of food that waited invitingly for him and flung it against the wall with a crash. After these destructive acts, he sat crouching on the floor like an angry porcupine, its quills raised—ready for attack. His look and manner were so alarming that no one dared go near him.

Next day, at early dawn, Chandranath ran away again. Raimohan and his search party looked everywhere, even among the derelicts at Kalighat and the beggars at Pathuriaghat, but there was no sign of the boy. It was only on the fifth day Raimohan found him, sealing a pond in Metiaburj with about fifty other labourers. This time Chandu made no effort to run away. He picked up a crowbar and aiming it at Raimohan's head, hurled it with all his strength. Raimohan saved his head with a quick movement but the crowbar hit his shoulder before falling about ten yards away. Raimohan did not even cry out. He ran to the boy and clasped him in his arms. 'No more running away, son,' he cried. 'I won't leave you alone for a second. I'll hold you like this, to my breast, for the rest of my life.'

The English contractor, who was getting the work done, came up to them and asked, 'What is the matter?'

'My child, sir,' Raimohan answered in his colourful English. 'Very mad, sir. Mad dog bited him, sir. Since then, head troublesome, sir.'

The Englishman waved his hand twice as if to say, 'Clear out and take the bugger with you.' Chandranath was lifted off his feet, once again, and taken home. This time he was pushed into his room and the latch was raised so that he couldn't escape.

'I say, Heere,' Raimohan said that very afternoon as they sat down to their midday meal. 'Let's leave this neighbourhood and go live somewhere else. You've been wanting to quit sleeping with the babus for some time now. Why must we go on living in this house, then? Lets leave the city and go to Khidirpur. Or we could even go to Rasa Pagla, where they're cutting down trees and building houses. We could take one of those and live like husband and wife. No one need ever know the truth. The boy's brain is heated and agitated. He needs looking after. Regular doses of *makaradhwaj*, mixed with basil and honey, is the treatment for such ailments. He will soon be well—'

'Uhun!' Heere shook her head. 'I want to go on a pilgrimage. I must make atonement for my sins.'

'What sins? Can a woman sin by herself? Where are the men who were partners in your sin? Are they going on pilgrimages? It is those bastards who are responsible for what's happened to Chandu. They'll have to pay for it. I'm not letting them off so easily. If I do, you may name the red-bottomed monkey after me.'

'I've heard enough of your tall tales. My son is all I have and—'

'All you have?' Raimohan echoed sadly. 'Am I nothing to you? Haven't I grovelled at your feet all these years like a faithful dog?'

'O Ma! I didn't mean that. Let's all three go together then, on a pilgrimage to some distant country. I don't want to come back—ever. I'm sick to death of this city.'

'Why should we run away? We haven't done any harm.'

'You stay then. I'm going.'

'Where will you go?'

'Wherever my two eyes lead me.'

'Just like a woman!' Raimohan cried out impatiently. '*O ré*!

These things are easier said than done. You have a body, brimming over with the sap of youth, and a face like a moon in spring. There'll be wolves and wild cats lurking at every bend of the road, ready to spring out at you and tear you to bits.'

'That is why I want you to come with us. You can protect us from harm.'

Raimohan looked down at his ageing body and sighed. 'I don't have the strength. Besides, I've never so much as held a lathi or a gun in my hands. My power lies here.' And he tapped his forehead twice. 'That is why I say, we'll stay here. Stay here and fight.'

'But Chandu! How can we save Chandu? The police may be looking for him even now. You said yourself that Chandu threw a stone at a babu and cracked his skull.'

'We won't keep him in this house. Let me think. Yes, there is a place where the police won't dream of looking. Why didn't I think of it before?'

'Where is that?'

'We can hide him in Kamala's house. She's rather fond of me and—'

'Whose house? What name did you take?'

'Kamala Sundari of Janbazar.'

'Kamli!' Heeremoni screamed, rearing her head like a wounded snake. She and Kamala were the two most famed courtesans of Calcutta and close competitors, each being peerless in her own field—Heeremoni in song and Kamala in dance. 'That low-born whore, who strips herself naked before a crowd of men! You worm-eating bastard! How dare you suggest such a thing? Just because I've fallen on evil days! If Kamli is so dear to you, why don't you go sleep in her bed, you pimp? What are you doing in my house, eating my rice from heaped up *thalas*? Oh! To think I've nurtured this viper in my bosom!' Raimohan waved his hands helplessly before her, begging her to stop and listen, but Heeremoni had gone beyond reason by now. A stream of abuses, each one filthier than the last, issued from her lovely lips till Raimohan was forced to clamp his hand over her mouth. 'You little fool!' he scolded tenderly. 'Kamli's house is safest for Chandu because the whole world knows you and she are sworn enemies. The police will never think of looking for him there. And Chandu will find it difficult to run away for I'll stand guard over him myself.' Heeremoni strained and bit her mouth free from the restricting hand and cried, 'You've got worms feeding on your brain, you bag of bones, if you think Kamli will keep my son all safe and snug under her roof. The first thing the whore will do is call in the police.'

'No, she won't do that. Just think what you would do in her place? Would you send her son to prison if she sought your protection for him? People don't treat their caste fellows that way.'

'Caste! Are you suggesting that we are of the same caste? She carries the blood of scavengers! I can take my oath on it. Have you seen her colour? Charcoal would blush for shame.'

'*Arré*! *Arré*! I didn't mean that. I meant caste in the sense of profession Like you, she has enjoyed the company of some of the greatest babus of the land. Her mind must have broadened a bit—'

After a lot of coaxing and cajoling, Heeremoni was brought around to admitting that, in the present circumstances, Kamala's house was the best place for her son.

There was a grand gathering that night in the house in Janbazar. Kamala Sundari was older now and layers of fat had crept over the slim, lissom figure of yesteryears. But her limbs were still supple enough and her dancing had lost none of its vigour. In her brocade ghagra and kanchuli, Kamala Sundari still had the power to hold her audience in thrall. She was so drunk that she couldn't understand what Raimohan was saying at first. 'Whose son?' she kept asking, straining to keep her eyes open. 'Heere's son? Who's the father? Only Heere's son! Heh! Heh! That's funny. What has he done? Robbed or swindled? Well, well, stay my dear. Stay as long as you like. Who am I to say "no"? But where have you been all these years, beloved? I've longed and longed to see your sweet face.'

Raimohan led Chandranath up to the attic and seated himself on the floor, his legs stretching out across the threshold. 'Here I am,' he announced. 'I'll lie here all day and all night. You can't get out without killing me first.'

'How long can you do that?'

'Say, ten or twelve days. The uproar will die down by then and you can go where you like. I won't stop you.'

'I won't stay here for a minute. I can't bear the sight of your face.'

'Then I'll sit with my back to you. You needn't look at me.'

'Get out! I hate you.'

'Look, Chandu,' Raimohan began with gentle persuasion. 'Don't let your circumstances get you down. People are not responsible for their birth. Karna said that in the Mahabharat. Don't you remember? We, who love you couldn't change that but we did try to help you attain a position of respectability. We did our best. Only our best wasn't good enough. But—'

'Quiet!' Chandranath roared at Raimohan. 'Shut up. I hate you.'

'I know you do. And you hate your mother. But, whatever we may be, we've kept you protected from life's impurities and—'

Chandranath could bear it no longer. He spat venomously into Raimohan's face. The blob of spittle hit Raimohan's face and slid down his neck. But Raimohan did not even wipe it away. Tears gathered in his eyes, wise and sad like a wizened old monkey's, and rolled down his gaunt cheeks. Chandranath stared back at him, his eyes hard and dry. No one's sorrow had the power to move him.

Sleep claimed the pair after a while. Chandu was the first. Raimohan kept awake for a long time, watching the boy's head lolling against the wall. Then, towards dawn, he fell asleep, his long body stretched across the threshold. The sun was high above the horizon when he awoke. Sitting up hurriedly, he shot a quick glance at the other end of the room. The boy was gone.

Raimohan sighed. This was the end. Chandranath was gone forever. Looking for him was useless. Raimohan remembered that even as a child, Chandu had never betrayed any signs of love and affection—not even for his mother. And now, he had stepped over Raimohan (no man ever stepped over another) and walked out of the room. He had burst asunder all the ties that bound him! Raimohan had known a lot of suffering. Injury and insult were his daily companions, even now. But he couldn't plumb the depths of Chandranath's suffering. Why the boy had changed so drastically was a mystery to him.

Raimohan walked over to the garden at the back of the house, his heart heavy within him. The worst was yet to come.

It was he who would have to break the news to Heeremoni. Heeremoni would lay the blame for her son's disappearance on Raimohan for bringing the boy here had been his idea. Intent on his own thoughts, Raimohan did not see the two men who watched him from the adjoining garden till one of them called out: '*O hé*! Come over here for a moment.' Looking up, he saw an aristocratic looking Muslim in a fez, standing beside a man in a dhoti and shawl. He recognized the latter, though with a sense of shock. Was this thin, dried up old man, leaning heavily on his stick, the redoubtable Bidhusekhar Mukherjee? And why was he wearing a black patch over one eye?

'Aren't you called Raimohan Ghoshal?' Bidhusekhar addressed him first.

'*Pronam,* Mukherjee Moshai!' Raimohan folded his hands and bent his long body ingratiatingly. 'It is so many years since we met but you recognized me instantly! Your memory is as phenomenal as ever, I see.'

'What are you doing there?' Bidhusekhar fixed his one eye on Raimohan's face with a piercing look.

'You know me, sir,' Raimohan answered lightly. 'I'm a tame pigeon. I flit from cage to cage, pecking at whatever grain I can get.'

'Well! Whose grain are you pecking at, now?'

'I can't say for sure. I eat what I find, asking no questions. What does it matter whose it is? I was Ramkamal Singha's protégé for many years but he died, leaving me orphaned. I won't find another patron like him if I live a hundred years.'

'Look here!' Bidhusekhar looked at him sternly out of his one eye. 'You must have seen ants crawling away from a tottering old house just before a storm. Well, learn to emulate them. Crawl away, as fast as you can, from where you're standing. I propose to evict the whore very shortly. The case is already in the court.'

'What bird is that?' Amir Ali asked his friend, in Persian.

'I doubt if you've seen it before. It's a *garud*. This bird is mentioned in our scriptures—'

At this moment, Raimohan took a decision. He would revive his old profession of conning rich men. Not this old man, though. He had been sucked dry and was nothing but fibre! Raimohan would seek out younger men. He had to avenge

Chandranath. Leaping across the hedge, Raimohan came and stood in Amir Ali's garden. 'Huzoor!' he said. 'You've decided to get rid of Kamli. Well! You're powerful enough for that. I need a roof above my head. It doesn't matter whose it is.' He stooped and touched Bidhusekhar's feet. 'Huzoor!' he went on, 'I'm your servant. Command me and you'll get instant obedience. If you wish me to, I'll whip the whore's buttocks with nettles and drive her out of the country. But I must have your blessings first.'

# Chapter XXXXVI

Ganga sat on the steps of Dasashwamedha Ghat, lost in thought. Six months had passed since that fateful day on which he had taken a vow to abjure all idols. He had changed a great deal since then. When he closed his eyes, as he did now, he no longer saw the dark, beautiful face with gold eyes and glittering tongue that had haunted him all these years. Gods and goddesses had lost their power over him. As far as he was concerned, they were nothing more then bits of stone and clay!

He stayed on in Kashi though his search for Bindu had drawn a blank. He had managed to track down the Seth who had had the caring of her and to whom Bidhusekhar had sent money at regular intervals. But his replies to Ganga's questions had been as evasive as Mansaram's. Bindu was dead. There was no point in looking for her. What she had died of and when, he had not cared to reveal. Ganga didn't believe either of them. Bindu was not dead. He felt it in his bones.

That afternoon, Ganga took a boat and crossed over to Ramnagar on the other bank. Unlike Kashi, Ramnagar was largely rural still, with vast stretches of open land, dotted with the pleasure houses of the rich—the Maharaja of Varanasi's palace among them. Ganga walked up and down the bank and his thoughts went back, as they often did these days, to Calcutta. He suffered a pang every time he thought of his mother. She was the only one from his old life whom he missed. He felt a supreme indifference for everyone else—even his wife. Lilavati, he realized, would never be anything more than a bedfellow. But he needed a soulmate; someone who could take Bindu's place in his heart. He had tried to mould her to his tastes and aspirations and had failed miserably. He had failed in every way.

Suddenly, he thought of his friends—Madhu, Bhudev, Rajnarayan, Banku, Gour. They were successful men, each in his own way. But Ganga! Ganga had frittered his life away and gathered only frustration and despair. He couldn't even go back for how would he explain his disappearance from Ibrahimpur, where he had gone to see to his estates and improve the lot of his tenants?

Dusk was setting in. Ganga started on his walk back to the ferry, keeping as close to the bank as possible. Soft breezes blew up from the river and the first rays from the rising moon bathed the sky in a haze of silvery light. Crossing a ghat that fell on the way, he caught sight of a woman rising from the river. Her wet sari clung to her limbs, outlining her immaculate form, and her rich hair fell in clusters over her back and shoulders. Her eyes were shut. Ganga's heart missed a beat. Without stopping to think, he cried, 'Bindu!' and started running towards her. Two serving women stood on the ghat, holding a piece of red broadcloth to shield their mistress from curious eyes. Seeing Ganga run towards her, they shrieked a string of sentences in an unintelligible tongue, at which two huge, hefty men sprang out of the shadows and made a rush at Ganga. Pinioning his arms, they thundered, 'Fool! Shameless dog!' in harsh, cracked voices. Ganga tried to wrench himself free from their grasp, crying, 'Bindu! Bindu!' But a sharp shove in the groin and another on his neck dashed the breath out of his lungs in a great gasp. But, even so, he noticed a tanjam a little way off, with six or seven guards squatting beside it with spears in their hands. Some of them came forward and helped the other two to drag him away, kicking and cursing all the while. It was well for Ganga that he hadn't shaved or trimmed his hair for several days. For, as he was, the guards took him to be a half-crazed lout and decided to spare his life. Flinging him in the middle of a clump of thorn bushes, they went back to the waiting tanjam.

Ganga stared at the departing men, his eyes dazed, not so much with pain as with wonder. The woman he had seen was Bindu. He was sure of it. But why did she have so many guards with her? He had called out to her. Why hadn't she looked up or answered?

After a while he heard the 'Hum! Hum!' of the bearers as they swung along the path behind two men who ran ahead, holding flaming torches above their heads. Ganga gathered himself together, though every movement was agonising and walked, reeling and stumbling, towards the approaching tanjam. Desperate by now, Ganga rushed forward before anyone could stop him and, parting the curtains, cried out in a passionate voice, 'Bindu! I'm Ganga. Don't you recognize me? Where are you going?' A split second and the guards sprang on him and flung him headlong in the dust. Then, stepping over him as if he were some inanimate object, the, men walked away, taking Bindu with them. Ganga's body was a mass of bruised flesh and splintered bones but his mind was clear. He was not mistaken. The woman in the tanjam was Bindu; a new Bindu—more beautiful then ever before and as majestic as a queen. Priceless jewels glittered on her arms and neck and flashed from out of the masses of her hair. But Bindu's eyes had held not even a flicker of recognition. She had sat in the tanjam, her face set and expressionless, and stared straight before her with a fixed, unflinching gaze. Ganga trembled when he remembered that face. A wave of fear swept over him. 'Which Bindu is this?' he thought.

Mansaram Chhadiwala had swept the ghat clear of discarded flowers, tulsi and bel leaves and was preparing to go home when Ganga arrived like a whirlwind and grabbing him by the shoulder, asked fiercely, 'Why did you lie to me?' His hair and beard were matted with blood and dust and his clothes were torn and dirty. Mansaram was startled. He looked about him with furtive eyes and said, 'Come to my house, Babuji, and I'll tell you the whole story.'

'No,' Ganga shouted hoarsely. 'First tell me why you lied to me. Why you made such a fool of me.'

Mansaram folded his hands before Ganga and said in a pained voice, 'I'll answer all your questions, Babuji. But not here. It is too dangerous. Come with me.' Grasping Ganga by the hand, he dragged him across the ghat to a stone mansion that stood a furlong away. Mansaram lived in two dark, damp little rooms on the ground floor, with two wives and three children. He was very poor and barely managed to make a living for himself and his family. He washed Ganga's wounds with a rag dipped in water and handing him a new unbleached dhoti, said, 'Change into this, Babuji.' The room was damp and close, the only light in it coming from an oil lamp flickering in a corner. The two wives appeared at the door and stared at the stranger with curious eyes. Mansaram shooed them away. 'Go, go!' he scolded. 'Bring some water for Babuji and a pot of curds with some salt in it.' Then, turning to Ganga, he said gently, 'Have some curds. It will cool your body. And spend the night here in my humble dwelling.' Ganga looked at him with eyes blazing with scorn and fury. Mansaram trembled before that glance and muttered, 'What could I do? Can a rabbit pit himself against a lion? Everyone in this *mohalla* fears Devi Singh like the very devil. He is a man of enormous wealth and keeps an army of lathi-wielding guards. I'm a poor man but even you would be powerless before him. That is why I advised you to go back to your own city.'

'Why did you tell me the girl was dead? I saw her today with my own eyes.'

'I told you the truth, Babuji. When a Hindu girl is taken by a man other than her husband she is as good as dead. There is no going back for her.'

'Oh! What a stone-hearted villain you are! To think that she was alive all the time. Even her own father believes her dead. That Lalaji is as big a liar as you—'

'Siyaram! Siyaram! Lalaji is a devout old man. Most holy and pious! He wanted to save your family the shame and dishonour that would have fallen if the truth were known. Bidhu Babu is a Brahmin. And his daughter is a widow. If the news of her desecration were made public, his whole clan would have lost its place in the Brahminical order and suffered humiliation for generations to come. I've heard of many Brahmins in Bengal losing caste in that way—'

'Tell me what happened. Tell me that truth.'

'It was nothing new, Babuji. It happens all the time. When a wealthy, powerful man sees a beautiful woman, he is consumed with lust and burns to possess her. If he can seduce her with money and jewels—well and good. If not, he abducts her. His guards carry her away in broad daylight in front of crowds of people. And no one can do anything. I was present at the ghat, myself, the day Bidhu Babu's daughter was taken but I could do nothing. Neither could anyone else.'

'What about the police? Is there no law in this city? I'll report the matter to the police station myself tomorrow morning. I'll bring her back.'

'This is Ravana's city, Babuji. There is no sign of Ramji as yet. The police won't help you. Even they are afraid of Devi Singh. It is a terrible thing but women are being bought and sold by the gross here in Varanasi. You Bengalis send your widows here and then forget about them. You have no idea of how many of them end up in rich men's harems. Some are even taken to Surat and shipped off to Arabia.'

'Did Bindu's abductors sell her?'

'You've guessed rightly.'

'Do you expect me to respect the sale?'

'What else can you do?'

'I can free her from Devi Singh's clutches. The Company has imposed a rule of law over the whole country. People can't break it with impunity. The law is on my side. I'll see that Devi Singh is brought to justice.'

'Go to sleep, Babuji. Your brain is fevered and restless. Tomorrow, when you are calmer, you will see the futility of what you propose. There is a Sanskrit shloka that runs, *Lekhani, pustika, bharya par hastang gata gatah,* meaning, "Once a pen, a book or a wife fall into another's hands they are gone forever". Even if you manage to get her out of Devi Singh's zenana, what will you do with her?'

'I'll take her back with me to Calcutta.'

'You don't understand. Who knows how many times those beasts ravished her after her abduction? And Devi Singh—well, one hears he keeps twenty to thirty women. Who will take such a woman under his roof? Will you? Will her father? And even if you wish to, will the society in which you live let you do so? Such women have only one place waiting for them, Babuji. And that is the whorehouse. Forget her and go your own way. Why do you ruin your life for a fallen woman?'

Ganga remembered that his khazanchi in Ibrahimpur had given him similar advice when he had declared that he would bring Hanifa Bibi back from the Neel Kuthi. Men were all the same. They spoke of women as if they were objects of glass. A touch from a strange hand and they broke and became useless! Ganga's eyes burned and tears fell from them in large drops. Bindu had never permitted him to touch her. Her refinement and delicate sensibility had stood in the way. And because she couldn't give herself to him, she had embraced a life of rigorous abstinence. To think that Bindu—his pure, chaste, honourable Bindu, had been set upon by some animals in human form and . . . He couldn't think any more. It was too painful!

'It would be better for such women if they were to die,' Mansaram went on calmly. 'Even the *Angrez* police do nothing to bring them back because no one will take them back.' Even as he spoke, he saw that Ganga had fainted. His head jerked backwards and would have hit the floor if Mansaram hadn't caught him in time. Laying him down on the bed, Mansaram shook his head sorrowfully. The boy came from a good family. That was obvious. Wealth and distinction were stamped on every line of his face and form. But he was young and his heart was soft. The assaults of the world were too much for him.

Ganga lay ill in Mansaram's house for a week—the wives taking turns in nursing him. They were strange women for though they shared the same man, they never quarrelled over him but lived in amity like two sisters or two friends.

When Ganga was well enough to leave, Mansaram pleaded with him once more to leave Varanasi and go back to Calcutta. It was dangerous to stay on. If Devi Singh came to know that Ganga had raised his eyes to his woman, retribution was sure to follow. Ganga nodded but in his heart he knew he would not leave Varanasi. Walking away from Mansaram's house, he went straight to a sadhu's *akhara* and started living there among the other disciples. He joined his voice to theirs during the morning and evening kirtan and even learned to take a few puffs of ganja. And, quite often, at dusk, he slipped quietly away and took a boat to Ramnagar.

And then, on the night of the full moon, he saw her again.

Each year, on the night of Vaisakhi Purnima, Varanasi was transformed from the holiest of pilgrimages to a city of joy, throbbing with music and dance and quivering with the pleasures of the flesh. Thousands of bajras floated on the waters like flocks of proud-breasted swans, their sails gleaming pearly white in the light of the moon. And from the decks above, lit by rows of bright lamps, the sweet strains of sarangis, the soft tapping of tablas and the tinkling of ankle bells floated out over the waters. The wealthy aristocrats of the city vied with each other in their entertainments. Singing and dancing girls thronged the bajras. *Bhang* was churned in enormous pots, with cooled milk, almonds and essence of roses, and the choicest wines and liquors flowed like water. The revels were meant to last all night but hours before dawn, the decks could be seen strewn with the bodies of the revellers, lolling about in a drunken stupor.

Devi Singh's four bajras stood together, bobbing up and down with the waves. Devi Singh was fifty and as fair as a *gora*. Enormous pepper-coloured whiskers waved out of a face as bright and fierce as a tiger's. His huge form swayed with the music as he danced in the moonlight, his feet nimble like those of his dancers. But it was well past midnight and he was very drunk. His eyes were clouding over and his dhoti threatened to slip down his waist. Then, when all was still and silent under the waning moon, a small dinghy came creeping up the river. A figure leapt out of it and running to one of the cabins, called through the porthole, 'Bindu!'

Bindubasini lay on her bed, in a pool of moonlight. Folds of heavy silk, tinted a rich blood red and encrusted with gold and gems, wrapped her slender form. A garland of jasmine, swaying upon her breast, sent eddies of perfume into the soft, warm air. She opened her eyes on hearing Ganga's voice; bloodshot eyes, drowsy with *bhang*, and smiled. 'Who is that? Ganga?' she asked softly. The, sitting up with a rustle of silk and a tinkling of jewels, she stretched out her arms towards him. 'Come, Ganga,' she said in a normal, everyday voice. As if the years separating them had rolled away; as if destiny hadn't played a cruel trick on her. A tremor ran through Ganga's frame. Leaping into the room, he clasped her in his arms. Bindu clung to him, her fingers digging into his back as if she would never let him go. Not a word was spoken. Not a sound was heard except the soft murmur of the water. Aeons passed. Then, Ganga spoke, his voice fevered and urgent. 'We must hurry. I have a boat with me. Come, Bindu.' A smile, as luminous as a ray of moonlight, flickered over Bindu's face. 'Where?' she asked simply.

'We'll go away together. To some far away place; very far away—where no one knows us.'

'Where is that?'

'We'll have to look for it. In some deep forest perhaps; by the bank of some river. We'll build a little hut. Only you and I—'

'Is there such a place?' Bindu sat up excitedly. 'Let's go.'

'Come. Take my hand.'

'O Ma! My jewels!' Bindu cried suddenly. 'I forgot to bring my jewel box. We'll have to go back to Ramnagar.'

'We don't need your jewels.'

'Don't we? But I have so many. I can't leave them behind.'

'How can you think of your jewels at a time like this?' Ganga said in a hurt voice. He did not know that Bindu was not herself; she had been heavily drugged with *bhang*. Bindu looked at Ganga with glazed eyes and giggled. 'Are you really Ganga? My childhood playmate? No, I must be dreaming. I hate these dreams—'

'Bindu!' Ganga cried out in anxiety. 'There's not another moment to lose. Someone may wake up and see us.'

'Ma *go*! That is true. But how did you get here? If Devi Singh's men catch you, they'll tear you to pieces. Go back as fast as you can.'

'You must come with me. Not another moment in this den of sin!'

'What about my son?'

'Your son?'

Ganga and Bindu stared at one another for a long time. Then, Bindu laid her head upon his breast and sobbed uncontrollably. 'Ask me why I'm still alive,' she cried. 'Why I didn't die.'

'We must get away fast—'

'Can you give my son back to me?'

'You're talking in riddles, Bindu. I don't understand you.'

'Ma *go*! They've got me so drunk I can't see your face. But you're different somehow. You're thin and worn.'

'We mustn't delay. If they catch us—'

'Listen, Ganga. I could have died—quite easily. But they wouldn't let me. I screamed for help the day they took me. "Ma! Ma *go*", I cried. But no one came near me. I was pure and untouched but even so, the gods abandoned me. They tied me up and poured milk down my throat. They abused my body in a thousand ways. I prayed for death and do you know what was sent to me? A child. Can a woman kill herself if she has a child in her womb?' She giggled a little and continued. 'How did you know me, Ganga? Am I not changed? I was a widow and look at me now—the bright colours I wear; my dazzling jewels. My maids massage my limbs each day with turmeric and cream.'

'You had a son?' Ganga asked, his voice flat and toneless.

'Yes. A lovely little boy. As fair as a prince. Just think, Ganga. I asked for death and God gave me a son. Then—he was taken away.'

'Who took him away?'

'They. They snatched him from my breast. He was only three months old. I begged them to give him back to me. I keep begging them even now, I obey them in everything. I drink *bhang*, I dance when they command me to. I never knew what it is to be a mother. They joy of it! The pain!'

Ganga sighed. He felt himself to be a doomed creature, destined to fail in everything he attempted. He had rowed himself across the swirling waters—a dangerous attempt for one who had no experience. He had risked his life but it had availed him nothing. 'Go back, Ganga,' Bindu murmured. 'I'm a fallen woman. My body is impure; worm-eaten. I'm not the Bindu you knew. I'm a whore of Kashi. Oh! How my head aches! Will you stroke it a little?' But the moment Ganga laid a hand upon her brow, she pushed him away. 'No, no!' she cried. 'I'm talking like a mad woman. You must go. Go quickly.' The insistence in Bindu's voice decided Ganga. He rose to depart. Bindu wouldn't go away with him. He understood that clearly now and sympathized. What mother would abandon her child? Fruit of sin though it was, it had ripened in her womb.

Taking his place in the dinghy, Ganga looked up for a moment and saw Bindu's face, framed in the porthole. It was pale and the eyes were drunk and staring.

'You are going away, Ganga? she cried, her voice unnaturally high. 'You're leaving me behind?'

'Come, then.' Ganga put out a hand. Bindu took it without a moment's hesitation and climbed into the boat.

'Sit still and keep your head bowed,' Ganga cautioned. 'No one must see you.'

When the dinghy had moved a hundred yards or so away from the bajra, Bindu splashed some water on her head and stood up. Her hair was open; her jewels glittered in the moonlight. She looked around her and murmured, 'Beautiful! How beautiful the world is!' 'Sit down. Someone may see you,'

Ganga cried out a warning. But Bindu did not heed it. Grasping her throat tightly with both her hands, she let out a piercing wail. 'Oh! Oh! Oh! No one gave me . . . No one.' Then, calming herself she continued, 'The gods are in the sky above. Ma Ganga flows beneath. They stand witness to my vow. If another birth is granted me; if there is such a thing—I shall claim you for my own. Everything went wrong in this life. Everything was withheld from me. I got nothing—nothing!' Then, even as Ganga stretched out his hand towards her, she gave a spring and became a swirling red mass in the fast flowing water. Ganga stared with dazed eyes for a few moments, then sprang out of the wildly rocking dinghy.

The moon shone in the sky, washing the earth with silver. The river flowed on like a wide path, leading to some destination unknown. Then, after some time, the storm broke. There was a violent swaying of bajras and the earth was misted over with rain and lashing winds.

# Book II

# Chapter I

Winter had ended that year but summer was taking her time in making an appearance. It was springtime—a season of sweet winds and sunshine as smooth and caressing as a web of gossamer; of languorous long days and soft balmy nights, when flowers yielded their perfume into the warmed air and birds sang unceasingly. A season of beauty; of fragrance; of nostalgia.

In Chhatu Babu's park, rows of tents had sprung up overnight and all that could be seen from morning till night was a sea of human heads, which broke from time to time, waved and rippled with the excited cry: '*Dhyo Mara*! *Dhyo Mara*!' Outside the tents the giant-sized cages were crammed with bulbulis of every shape and hue. Coal-black birds with flaming tails and underbellies; soft brown fledgelings, dappled white with maturity, their bright, beady eyes darting menacingly; small, brown-winged creatures with red-streaked heads and tall black tufts like sepoys' turbans. Lal bulbulis, Shah bulbulis, Sepoy bulbulis! Warrior birds—trained to fight till death overcame them, by skilled and patient khalifas.

The birds were kept starving for a full twenty-four hours before they were taken to the pit, two by two. A handful of soaked gram was flung to the ground and the birds released. Violent clashings of beaks and wings followed, the spectators yelling encouragement: '*Dhyo Mara*! *Dhyo Mara*!'

Nabin Kumar, scion of the famed Singha family of Jorasanko, stood a little apart from the crowd. He was a fine, handsome youth of fifteen, with sensitive features and flashing dark eyes. He was dressed in English clothes—a coat of yellow China silk over white trousers and black leather boots. An enormous diamond gleamed on the first finger of his left hand and a heavy gold watch hung from its guard in his breast pocket. Dulal Chandra, his servant and constant companion, stood by his side. Dulal had changed a great deal in the last few years. He was tall and burly now, with broad shoulders, heavy wrists and a head of flowing hair atop a short, squat neck. He wore his dhoti tucked tight between his legs, like a wrestler, and a quilted vest over it. His voice, deep and manly, was a startling contrast to Nabin's childish treble.

'I've had enough of this game,' Nabin declared suddenly. 'I'm going home. You may stay if you like.'

'I'll come with you,' Dulal said hastily, though he was actually enjoying himself enormously.

'It is not surprising,' Nabin said loftily as they walked back to the carriage, 'that commonplace people like you should get excited over a birdfight. What fills me with wonder is that great men from great families enjoy this paltry game. Their skulls must be crammed with cow dung. If you were to turn them around, Dulal, you'd find tails springing up from their behinds.' Dulal kept a discreet silence. He couldn't quite catch the drift of his master's speech. 'This country is swarming with monkeys,' Nabin went on ponderously. 'The clever, powerful British race is taking full advantage of it and bleeding us dry. A birdfight! *Chho*! Playing at dolls with little girls is better sport.' Leaving the throng of spectators behind, Nabin pointed a finger. 'Let's go there,' he said.

'But the carriage is on the other side.'

'I know that. Come along.' A little smile flickered on Nabin's lips.

Every year, from the first day of the bulbuli festival, Chhatu Babu's park was tranformed into a fairground, with rows of stalls in which edibles like *moa*, *mudki*, *papad* and fritters were sold in enormous quantities together with earthen pots, clay dolls, *gamchhas* and bulbulis. This last item was the biggest draw—bird-buyers outnumbering the prostitutes who flocked to the fairground from the red-light district, Rambagan. 'Come, buy! Come, buy!' The bird-sellers hawked their wares unceasingly, each one claiming that his birds were trained by khalifas more experienced than those of his neighbours'. Names like Jamir Sheikh of Khidirpur and Hossain Shah of Posta were bandied about though everyone knew that the birds were newly-caught fledgelings, with little or no training.

Halting before a stall piled high with bird-filled cages, Nabin said, 'Ask how much they cost, Dulal. I wish to buy some birds.' But Dulal almost fainted when he was told the price. Four rupees a pair for these tiny slips of feathers! A milch cow could be had for seven. Dulal was convinced that these men had got wind of the fact that his master was an enormously wealthy man and were trying to rob him in consequence. 'This is daylight robbery,' he cried indignantly. 'What are you thinking of, you scoundrels?' A hard bargain was driven, following which the price was reduced to two rupees a pair.

'Pull out that one,' Nabin commanded, pointing to the largest cage. 'Count the birds in it.' Then, finding it to contain fifty birds, he slipped his hand carelessly into his pocket and taking out a hundred silver rupees, flung them with a merry jingle on the floor of the stall. Opening the door of the cage, he thumped upon it, crying exultantly, 'Fly away, little wings! As quick as you can.' Everyone turned to stare as the bulbulis tumbled out joyfully and became a cloud of flapping wings above their heads. In a few minutes the cage was empty. Nabin bought another, then another. He had had no idea that setting birds free was such an enjoyable sport. After the third he stopped and bit his lip. He had no money left. But he had his ring—a large solitaire diamond. Slipping it off his finger, he handed it to Dulal. 'Go to the nearest jeweller and sell it,' he commanded, but Dulal shook his head tearfully. 'No, Babu. I can't do that. Karta Ma will kill me. That is your father's ring.'

'Then go back home and bring some money.'

'You come, too. It is getting late.'

Nabin was in no mood to argue with Dulal. Besides, he didn't have the time. Pulling out another cage he fumbled with the door, but this time the owner came hurrying out.

'What do you do, sir? What do you do?'

Nabin threw a brief glance in his direction and said, 'Collect your money from my steward tomorrow morning. My word is worth a lakh of rupees.'

When all the cages were empty, Nabin walked over to his carriage, pushing his way through the crowd of spectators who had abandoned the desultory battle of birds in the pit to enjoy the new game. On approaching it, however, he found a man lying across his path; a madman of about fifty, his grey head and beard matted with dust and grime. He started up on seeing Nabin and cupping his hands together, said quietly, 'Can you give me a little water, Babu? I'm looking for some water to soak my *chiré*.' Nabin hated and feared drunks and lunatics and called out to Dulal in panic. Dulal came forward and pushed the man aside with a cruel thrust of his arm. Nabin took his place in the carriage but even as it rolled away, he heard the madman call after him: 'A little water, Babu, to soak my *chiré*. I haven't eaten all day.' The coachmen laughed, nudged one another and said, 'A well-to-do beggar! He has the *chiré*. All he wants is water.'

But the poor fool went doggedly on, from one man to another, uttering parrot-like the same words over and over again. The sun, sinking in the west, dappled the trees with gold; bulbulis sang merrily out of leafy branches. The crowds dispersed. The shopmen shut their stalls and dusk fell on Chhatu Babu's park. The madman looked up at the sky, now slowly filling with stars. Long ago, on a night like this, he had gone out in search of water and lost his whole world. He had to find it again. Leaving the deserted park, he ambled along the street, muttering to himself. From time to time he peered into the faces of passers-by and said very quietly, very reasonably, 'Can you give me some water, Babu?' But no one understood his need. 'Death be on your head,' they cried, moving back in alarm. 'Get away. Shoo! Scram!'

## Chapter II

Ishwar Chandra's book, *A Discourse on the Necessity of Introducing Widow Remarriage in Society*, let loose a storm of controversy. Scores of pandits took up their pens in protest but Ishwar Chandra was ready with his counter-arguments and these were amply supported with quotations from ancient texts. What was so sinful about widow remarriage, he questioned in article after article. Was it not a way out of social abuses like adultery, abortion and abandoning infants? Were these not consequent in a situation in which human beings were condemned to live lives of abstinence for no fault of their own? But logic and reason rarely make a dent in crude self-interest and narrow chauvinism. Hindu males felt threatened by this dimunitive Brahmin and his razor-sharp pen and tried to harm him in many ways. Walking out on the street, Ishwar Chandra would suddenly find himself pelted by a shower of stones, or see six hefty men advancing on him menacingly. Nothing daunted, he would stare full into their eyes till they were lowered in shame. Already, rich men's toadies were advising their masters to take a short cut. 'Huzoor!' they said, 'why not put a knife into the rogue of a Brahmin one night? It would save us all a deal of trouble.'

That old worthy, Jagamohan Sarkar of Simulia, had turned over a new leaf since we saw him last. He had given up his flirtation with female education and had become a rabid Hindu fundamentalist. The change had come over him after he was caught dallying with two little girls in a pleasure garden—the girls naked and he and his toadies high on liquor. The neighbours had heard a commotion and come to investigate. 'We aren't doing any harm,' Jagamohan had tried to explain. 'We are teaching the girls to read. My contribution to the cause of female education is well known.' But the neighbours had ignored his protestations and beaten him and his toadies black and blue.

Jagamohan had had to lie low for a while for the press had

played up the incident, reporting it with a great deal of zest. 'Citizens of Bengal,' one newspaper cautioned, 'look around you and see what is being done in the name of education for women. Our reformer Babus have invented a new game. They strip young girls naked and romp and dance with them to the rhythm of C-A-T Cat and B-A-T Bat. A book in one hand—a glass of wine in the other! Hurrah for the glories of Female Emancipation!'

But now Jagamohan was back in full though metamorphosed form. Following his disgrace, he had suffered a bad bout of liver pain and had had to give up alcohol. He had set up a Society for the Prohibition of Intoxicating Beverages and had even written a book entitled *Drinking Wine or Drinking Poison*? He was also working day and night for the preservation of Hindu ideals and traditions—this last taking the form of a slander campaign against Vidyasagar.

'The English allow their widows to remarry!' Jagamohan ejaculated indignantly one evening as he sat surrounded by his toadies. 'Are we bootlickers that we must follow their example?'

'Huzoor!' one of the toadies sidled up to him. 'Have you noticed the airs the sluts are giving themselves? And it is all owing to that whoreson, Vidyasagar. Even tottering old widows are clamouring to get married—'

'Tottering old widows!' another echoed. 'My own Pishi (she's eighty-five if she's a day) was widowed at the age of six or was it seven? Anyhow, ever since then, she has lived contentedly in our house, cooking for the family and praying in her spare time. Ah! Her cooking is a treat! Her *shukto* of raw bananas and melt-in-the-mouth lentil puffs! Aha—ha! And her gourd curry with a splutter of fenugreek seeds—'

'Shut up croaking about lentil puffs and fenugreek seeds,' Jagamohan scolded. 'Tell us about your Pishi.'

'That is just what I'm telling you, Huzoor. She says, "I can't be bothered cooking for you any more. I've ground my bones to dust all these years. I must have a bit of fun like the rest of you. Raimoni and Neerobala were saying the other day that a great pandit called Vidyasagar has decreed that widows may remarry. Start looking for a groom. I want to get married."'

*'Arré!'* Jagamohan cried out startled. 'An old woman of eighty-five, did you say?'

'Yes, Huzoor. Every day there's a scene. She refuses to go into the kitchen. "I won't cook any more," she says. "I want to get married today. I must have my fun while I can."'

'Fun! A creaking old widow out to have her fun!' Jagamohan gave a scream of laughter and thumped the storyteller heartily on the back. *'Wah! Wah!* A good story.'

Not to be outdone, the first one began, 'Have you read Ishwar Gupta's latest poem, Huzoor? The one about ruptured hymens?'

'What about them?'

'A lot of people are saying that widows may remarry on one condition. That is—if their hymens are intact.'

'But who is to inspect their hymens and find out if they're lying?' Jagamohan asked with a great cackle of mirth.

'The government must employ inspectors,' the wit replied. 'Thousands of men will apply for the job.'

A storm of laughter and applause greeted this last sally. Indeed, it must be said for Vidyasagar that he had given his compatriots scope for much erotic conversation with his fixations, whether it be women's education or widow remarriage.

But Vidyasagar was not without support. The Brahmos and the leaders of the Young Bengal movement welcomed his efforts. Resistance came mainly from the new, rich mercantile class and its Brahmin protégés. Vidyasagar realized that to win the former over he would have to seek the patronage of the leader of the community—Raja Radhakanta Deb.

Radhakanta Deb's grandson, Ananda Chandra Basu, was a friend of Vidyasagar and had tutored him in Shakespeare at one time. Vidyasagar sought his help, saying, 'Your grandfather is one of the most respected men of the city. He can change the destinies of our widows if he so wishes. Why don't you talk to him and get him on our side?' But Ananda Chandra shook his head. He stood in great awe of his grandfather—a man of towering personality—and was afraid that such talk would be dismissed as impertinence. 'Send him a copy of your book,' Ananda Chandra advised his friend, 'and ask for his opinion.'

Radhakanta Deb praised the book but refrained from

passing an opinion. 'I'm an ordinary man,' he told Vidyasagar. 'What do I know of such lofty matters? The only way I can help you is by calling a meeting of the greatest pandits in the land. An exchange of views will be beneficial to all.' Vidyasagar agreed and a fierce debate was sparked off, in which Radhakanta Deb took no part. In fact, to demonstrate his neutrality, he presented a shawl each to the two main contestants, Ishwar Chandra Vidyasagar and Brajanath Vidyaratna of Nabadweep. But Vidyasagar was not content with merely displaying his knowledge of the shastras. His was a practical proposition and he was determined to make it see the light of day. Putting up a petition for a new law sanctioning widow remarriage, he started collecting signatures from many eminent men. Thirty-two signatures were taken—the last on the list being Vidyasagar's himself.

Radhakanta Deb flared up when he heard of the petition. Intellectual enquiry and debate was one thing. But getting a law passed to overthrow centuries of tradition was quite another. The rulers were aliens, who knew nothing about Hindu culture. What right had they to interfere? Change, if it came at all, would come from within—by a process of evolution. He had opposed the Anti-Sati Act for this very reason and now he set himself resolutely against widow remarriage.

The evening before the petition was to be submitted an incident occurred, which some people were to remember all their lives. It had been a long and gruelling day for Vidyasagar and he was weary to the bone by the time he walked back home with his trusty guard, Srimanta. It was very late at night and the streets were deserted. Approaching Thanthan, he noticed a group of men lurking in the shadows.

'Chhiré!' he called. 'Are you there?'

'Yes,' Srimanta replied. 'Keep going. I'll take care of the bastards.' And with that, he sprang forward, brandishing his lathi so fiercely that the men turned tail and ran. Vidyasagar recognized one of them. He had seen him somewhere, lolling about by some babu's side. He stopped in his tracks for a few moments, then making up his mind, walked resolutely in the direction of Simulia till he came to Jagamohan Sarkar's house. Ordering Srimanta to wait outside, he walked in, straight into the presence of the master of the house. 'You sent your men to beat me up, did you not?' he asked a startled Jagamohan. 'Well, here I am, standing before you. Beat me up all you can.'

## *Chapter III*

One winter morning, the *Bentinck* sailed from Madras Presidency and docked at Calcutta harbour. Among the passengers who stepped out of it was a dark gentleman in a flawless English suit. A long, white cylindrical object dangled from his lips. This was the first time that a cigarette was seen in the streets of Calcutta.

This native saheb was Madhusudan—only son of the deceased lawyer, Rajnarayan Datta. But he bore little resemblance to the old Madhu, the wild, arrogant egotist with the heart of gold and mind of surpassing brilliance, who had taken the city by storm in his turbulent youth. This was a portly middle-aged man of thirty-two, with a sagging face and tired eyes. Looking about him for a familiar face in vain, Madhusudan sighed and hailed a hackney cab. 'To the ferry ghat,' he commanded. He would go to Bishop's College to Rev. Krishnamohan Bandopadhyaya's house. He could think of no other place where he could ask for a night's shelter.

Madhusudan looked eagerly on as the cab swayed and rattled down the street. The city was changed, much changed, since he had left it eight years ago. What hopes he had cherished of returning one day—a rich and famous man! But nothing had happened the way he had imagined it. He had embraced Christianity in the belief that it was the stepping-stone to the country of his dreams—England. But the opportunity to go there was denied him. He was a native and the stigma remained despite his change of religion. For the same reason, his efforts to secure a prestigious post in some renowned English concern had come to naught—the only job deemed fit for him, that of a petty schoolmaster. His verses, composed in imitation of Milton, had brought him little recognition and his marriage to the daughter of an indigo-planter had broken down. He had always believed European women to be superior to their native counterparts. But Rebecca had left him and taken the children with her. Madhusudan was now living with a French girl named Henrietta.

His ties with the city of his youth had slackened over the years. His friends had forgotten him. Many believed him to be dead. Only Gour remembered him and wrote to him regularly though he seldom bothered to reply. Gour scanned the pages of all the journals published from Madras for anything written by him. Madhusudan used pseudonyms freely these days but Gour made no mistake. He knew his friend's distinctive style and identified it at a glance. Madhusudan's mother, Jahnavi Devi, had passed her last days in terrible suffering and was now no more. Added to her grief at losing her only son was the humiliation of co-wives being brought into the house. Crazed with pain and anger, Rajnarayan had married Shivsundari, Prasannamayee and Harakamini, three beautiful, high-born maidens, in the hope of acquiring another son and heir. But not one of them had fulfilled this hope. Jahnavi Devi had cursed him with the words, 'If I have been a true and chaste wife, no seed of yours will ever take root in another woman's womb.' Rajnarayan, too, had spent his last days in grievous mental affliction, then passed away into another world. Madhusudan had had no knowledge of his father's death for nearly a year. Rajnarayan's brothers were fighting over the estate, as following Madhusudan's conversion, they were the next of kin according to Hindu law. However, a new bill had recently been passed, dissolving the law, and Gour, determined that Madhu should take advantage of it, had written to him to come and claim his inheritance.

Aware of his father's extravagant lifestyle, Madhusudan was not sure of what or how much he had left behind. But the poverty in which he was passing his days was too pressing to be borne. Even if he got the house in Khidirpur, he reasoned with himself, he could sell it and use the money to buy a few comforts. It was for this that he had responded to Gour's call and was now here in Calcutta.

'Why, Gaure?' Madhusudan had drawled in his pukka saheb English when Gour made an appearance that evening. 'You're as handsome as ever!' Gour had done well for himself. Like many other bright students of Hindu College, he was a deputy magistrate now and looked sleek and prosperous. Only his eyes were sad for he had lost two wives in quick succession.

'But you?' Gour stared aghast at the ageing, flabby face with dark pouches under the eyes. 'What has happened to you?' A vision rose before his eyes of a figure, lithe and slim as a reed, with a glowing dark skin and eyes flashing with spirit and intelligence.

'Come, Gaure. Let's go out for a while.' Madhusudan shifted his feet restlessly. He hadn't had a drink for hours now. His host was a teetotaller and would not tolerate drinking under his roof.

'I have a carriage waiting outside,' Gour said. 'We'll go to Khidirpur—to your old house.'

'Will they let me in?'

'Why not? I went there a couple of days ago and told P. Babu and B. Babu to expect you.'

'I wish you hadn't spread the news of my coming. I thought to have remained incognito for a while.'

'Why? Don't you want to meet our old friends?'

'The prospect embarrasses me, Gaure. I lived here in this city like a king. Now I come as a beggar.'

'What nonsense! You're no beggar. You are our old, dear Madhu. Our pride and joy. But why do you speak in English with me? And why do you call me Gaure? Have you forgotten Bengali altogether?'

'Sorry. I am profusely sorry,' Madhusudan replied, still in English. 'Tell me about our old friends. How is Ganganarayan—that shy, introverted fellow? I was very fond of him.'

'Ganga has gone away from Calcutta. No one knows where he is.'

As the carriage approached Rajnarayan Datta's mansion in Khidirpur, Madhusudan grasped Gour by the hand and said, 'Let's go back. I can't bear the thought of entering that house. My mother's dead. The house is empty, empty—' His voice cracked and large tears rolled down his cheeks. 'I'm guilty. Guilty as hell. It was I who killed her.'

'You've realized it rather late, haven't you?' There was an edge to Gour's voice. 'You didn't care to come to her even as she lay dying.'

The carriage stopped. The house was dark and silent and the

gate unguarded. In the old days five servants would have come running forward with smiles and salaams, ready to serve their young master. Suppressing a sigh, Madhusudan made his way up the stairs. Why were the rooms so dark? Where were all the chandeliers that had blazed with light every evening? The wooden steps creaked under his feet and the bannisters rocked precariously. Everything was coming apart. The house was a ruin. It might even be haunted.

'Is anyone there?' Gour shouted up the stairs. No one answered. 'Let's go back,' Gour said a little uneasily. 'We'll come back tomorrow morning.'

'I want to see my bedroom before I go.'

'You won't be able to see anything. It is too dark.'

'I'll feel the walls with my hands and ask them if they remember me.'

Madhusudan pushed the door of his bedroom open. It was not as dark as the rooms downstairs. A shaft of light entering through the window from the next house shed a dim glow over the bare walls. All the furniture had gone. His books, pictures, writing materials, even his clothes had vanished. Madhusudan laid his head on Gour's shoulder and sobbed like a child. 'How things are changed, Gour!' he cried in a broken voice. 'The days of our past—our beautiful past—where are they? Do you remember the bed in which you slept with me one night? I loved you so passionately, so madly. Never have I loved a woman as I've loved you.'

'Who is that?' Gour cried out startled. A figure had come creeping up to the door. It was a young woman in widow white but, standing in the shadows, she gave the impression of something ethereal; insubstantial. Gour took a few steps towards her and said in a voice that sounded relieved, 'Oh! It's you. Why is the house so dark?'

'Who is she? Who is she, Gour?' Madhusudan asked agitatedly in a voice that trembled a little.

'She is your mother. Her name is Harakamini Devi.'

'How can she be my mother? I've never seen her in my life,' Madhusudan said sharply. 'And why does she stand there, silent, like a ghost?'

'She's your father's fourth wife. Grief and affliction have taken their toll on her.'

Then, turning to the figure, he said gently, 'Why are you here all alone, Ma? Is there no one else in the house? And why is it all so dark?'

'There is only one servant left,' the woman spoke in a voice so low that it was almost a whisper. 'I've sent him to the market. I'll bring you a light.'

The shadowy figure moved away and returned in a few minutes, bearing a lamp by whose light they saw that she was only a girl of about sixteen. Her head was shorn and her face pale and sad.

'Who are you?' she whispered. 'Where do you come from?'

'This is your son, Madhu,' Gour said, pointing to his friend. 'You must have heard about him.'

Harakamini trembled a little at these words and walking slowly over to Madhusudan, she raised the lamp and scanned his face for a few seconds. Then, in a soft moaning voice, she said, 'You're Madhu! You've come too late, son. Everything is finished.'

Suddenly, her control gave way and she burst into loud, frightened sobs. '*O go!* Where shall I go? I have no one to turn to. No one.' Madhusudan stepped back hastily. He could not bear to see anyone weep, particularly a woman. 'Tell the lady,' he instructed Gour in English, 'that I have no intention of driving her away. She may stay as long as she likes.' Harakamini looked around her with wild, dazed eyes. She didn't understand a word of what Madhusudan was saying and in her desperation, she clung to him, sobbing bitterly.

'Have you even forgotten the word "Ma?"' Gour cried out angrily. 'Can't you tell her yourself, "Ma. This is your house?"'

Though greatly embarrassed, Madhusudan obeyed Gour and addressing a woman half his age as Mother, he assured her that she could live in the house for as long as she liked. The two friends then left the house.

Madhusudan had to stay on in Calcutta much longer than he had expected, for the property being sub judice he was not likely to get any of it in a hurry. But he needed a job and a place to stay. Miraculously, both came his way quite soon and through the same source. Pyarichand Mitra's brother, Kishori, offered to keep him in his house in Dumdum—a stately mansion, surrounded with beautiful gardens—and also promised to secure a job for him in the police court. Madhusudan was rather peeved for the post was that of a clerk. His breast heaved with indignation. How dare this man make such a proposal? Could one who wrote like Scott and Byron be expected to push files for a living? But he needed money desperately. He was already in debt. Swallowing his humiliation, he smiled acquiescence. 'I am very grateful to you, Kishori Babu,' he said.

Kishorichand's house in Dumdum attracted hosts of intellectuals and scholars, who dropped in every now and then for spirited discussions on a variety of subjects, interspersed with lavish imbibings of food and wine. Madhusudan knew many of them already. Ramgopal Ghosh, Dakshinaranjan Mukhopadhyaya, Ramtanu Lahiri and Pyarichand Mitra were his seniors in Hindu College and among the first to adopt western ways. But now, Madhusudan saw to his surprise that they had given up their English suits and were dressed like native babus in dhotis, jackets and shawls. And although they spoke excellent English, they were more concerned with the rise and spread of Bengali. Another favourite subject of discussion was widow remarriage. He gathered from their talk that one Ishwar Chandra Vidyasagar was promoting it and that Raja Radhakanta Deb was opposing it. Madhusudan did not believe widow remarriage to be possible in the social conditions that persisted. His heart was saddened whenever he thought of his young stepmother. Her life was ruined. Could any of these men lead her to a better existence?

One day Madhusudan and Pyarichand entered into a duel of words, which flared up into a quarrel. Pyarichand and his friend, Radhanath Sikdar, had started a journal called *Masik Patrika,* copies of which they had been distributing among their friends. It had been conceived with a view to entertain the partially educated sections of society—mainly the women—and for this reason, the articles were all written in colloquial Bengali prose. Among the contributions appearing in serial form was a novel by Pyarichand Mitra, *Alal 'er ghar 'er Dulal*, which had taken the city by storm. Madhusudan read a few lines and put it aside. He considered the language vulgar in the extreme; crude and unaesthetic. Unable to contain himself, he burst out, 'What trash you are writing these days,

Pyarichand Babu! You are sullying the exalted realms of literature with language used by servants!'

Pyarichand looked up, surprised at this outburst. Then, with a superior smile, he said, 'We are speaking of Bengali, Mr Dutt. You know nothing of it.'

'I know enough to understand that the language of fishermen and farmers, oil crushers and weavers cannot be used for literature. Bengali is such a language. It needs large doses of Sanskrit injected into it to make it worthy of a literary medium.'

'The days of Sanskrit are over, Mr Dutt. The language in which I've written my novel is simple, earthy Bengali as the people of our country speak it. It is the language of the future. Mark my words, Mr Dutt. One day everyone in this country will write as I do.'

'Impossible!' Madhusudan interrupted arrogantly. 'Literature is the finest of all the arts and you treat it as child's play. If Bengali is to be the medium of the future, it must be improved first. I'll do it. I'll create a language that will live forever.'

'What language? Greek, Latin, Tamil?'

'Bengali.'

There was a roar of laughter. A man who couldn't write a word of Bengali, couldn't even speak it properly, had made the arrogant claim that he would mould the language anew and make it immortal!

'When do you propose to embark on the project?' Pyarichand asked, his lip curling in derision. 'In Satyayug?'

Madhusudan did not reply. He sat looking into his wine glass—lost in thought.

# Chapter IV

No one had ever heard before that obesity was a disease which could eventually lead to death. But that was exactly what was happening to Sohagbala. She grew fatter every day, even as she lay helpless in her bed. Her arms had swollen to a great size, each one resembling the trunk of a full-grown man, and her legs had the weight and volume of Bhim's clubs. In fact, it was doubtful whether even Bhim had the strength to lift them. The more she swelled, the fairer her skin grew, stretching thinner and whiter everyday, except in places where the blood vessels had ruptured, forming patches of red and blue. The space between her thighs had disappeared and any attempt to move them caused trickles of blood and pus to flow upon the sheets. One sari was no longer enough; two had to be stitched together to cover her bulk. But though the material was of the finest, softest cotton and wrapped very loosely, she could not bear the weight of it. Pushing it away from her, she would cry fretfully, '*O go*, Ma *go*, my limbs are burning. I'm burning all over.'

Dibakar had done everything he could for her. He had called in the best doctors and vaidyas but not one could diagnose her disease, let alone cure it. The maids took time off to nurse her and serve Dibakar for Dibakar, though over sixty, was a man and needed to satisfy the lusts of his body. Of all the maids, Dibakar liked Thakomoni best and so did Sohagbala. There was no need for subterfuge now. Dibakar and Thakomoni made love in Sohagbala's presence, even lying on her bed, while Sohagbala's round eyes darted from one to the other—the only moving things in that mountain of inert though breathing flesh. Sohagbala never forgot her duty to her husband. She made it a point to question Thakomoni every day. 'Have you served him well? Did you bathe and change your clothes when you went to him? Go, touch your forehead to Babu's feet and seek his forgiveness for any lapse on your part.' Then, turning to Dibakar, she would ask eagerly, 'Are you well and happy? Did she pleasure you as you wished? *O go!* Whenever you need anything just ask it of me. Whatever you want shall be yours. Oh! If only I could go now with the sindoor in the parting of my hair! God has blessed me with the best of husbands. What more can I want?' And she would burst into tears.

When Sohagbala died, taking her body to the burning ghat posed a problem. Four pall-bearers not being enough, extra bamboos were strapped to the bier and it was carried by ten men. Hers was a glorious death indeed! Everyone who saw it envied her fate. Even the mistress of the house had come to see her as she lay dying, and pouring Gangajal down her throat had said, 'She was a chaste and faithful wife. She's going to Heaven.' Later, Bimbabati had sent an expensive silk sari to cover the corpse.

After Sohagbala's death, Thakomoni stepped into her place as a matter of course. It was she who sat now on the marble block in the courtyard and ordered the servants about. She occupied a special position in the hierarchy. She was Dibakar's favourite and enjoyed his patronage. She was also Dulal's mother. Dulal could hardly be called a servant these days. He was Chhoto Babu's companion and spent all his time on the upper floors. He had received some education and considered himself superior to the other servants.

Thako's youth and beauty were on the wane but her new air of authority sat well on her. She had gained considerable poise and experience in the last few years. She knew what herbs prevented conception and what roots brought on a miscarriage. She occasionally took a night off from her duties to Dibakar, sending a newly appointed maid in her place. She had wedded her son three years ago but had not managed to make her home with him. Dulal hated and scorned his mother for being a servant and a loose woman. His wife ignored her mother-in-law and did not encourage her visits to the house in which the couple lived with their little son. Thako swallowed her hurt and humiliation as well as she could but sometimes she lost control. 'Son!' she would mutter on such occasions, thrusting out her lower lip to express disdain. 'If I waited for my son to feed me I'd be waiting forever. I can look after myself and need be beholden to no one. Money is all one needs and I have enough by the grace of God.' And that was true. Thako was a rich woman now. Her wages had been raised to six rupees a month and she got her cut out of everything that was bought for the household, from the fish, milk and spices that came into the kitchen to the gram that was fed to the horses. The servants feared and respected her exactly as they had feared and respected Sohagbala. She was Dulal's mother and Dulal was well on his way to taking Dibakar's place.

Thako kept all her money spread out under the mattress in her bed and sat up nights, counting it. There was nothing she enjoyed more. There was a time when she didn't know that two and two made four but that phase of her life was over. She hardly remembered any of it. Sometimes, as if in a dream, an image swam before her eyes—of a small hut, thatched with straw, standing between two sturdy fan palm trees. And then, one day, the zamindar's men had set it on fire. But the fire had burned itself out in her mind and could trouble her no more.

Lying on all that money, Thako dreamed a different dream these days. She would buy land in some other village, build her house and have a pond of her own. Dibakar hadn't discarded her yet but Thako knew that he would, before long. And she had seen how maids were treated in the house once they lost their health and strength. They were humiliated by one and all, blamed for others' lapses and pushed out of the house at the first opportunity. Thako had seen many elderly maids pick up their bundles of ragged clothing and walk out of the gates, weeping bitterly. She wondered where they went. Cows were sent to the abattoir when they grew old and useless. Was there such a place for human beings?

Thakomoni had money but no idea of how to put it to use. Till only a short while ago, all her dreams of the future had centred around Dulal. She had seen, in her mind's eye, a small house of mud and brick in some unknown village; a yard, neat and smooth with cow- dung, with a shaddock growing in one corner and little Dulal playing in it—his hands and hair coated with dust. But Dulal didn't belong to her any more. He lived in a different world; a world in which she had no place.

Sometimes, in the afternoons, when all her work was done, Thako walked timidly up to her son's door. 'Bouma[1]! O Bouma!'

---

1 Daughter-in-law.

she called softly. 'Is my little darling asleep? Open the door, O Bouma!' Dulal's wife, Subala, always made her wait outside for a long time before opening the door a crack and saying carelessly, 'Oh! It's you. The child's asleep.' The truth was that she didn't care to have her afternoon nap disturbed. And she knew that her husband would never reprove her for being rude to his mother.

'Let me come in for a moment, ' Thako begged. 'I long for a glimpse of his dear little face. I won't wake him up.'

'Can't you come some other time? I've just put him to sleep. He was playing all this while.'

'I'm so busy in the mornings—I don't know if I'm standing on my head or my feet. And I'll have to go back within the hour. The spices have to be ground; the lamps filled with oil and the dough kneaded for the *luchis*.' Then, although she knew Dulal was never home at this hour, she asked 'Where is Dulal, Bouma?'

'He's gone out with Chhoto Babu,' Subala replied, making no effort to move away from the door. Thako fixed her eyes on Subala's face and wondered at her courage. She was only fourteen and the daughter of a poor, shiftless carpenter. Only three years ago, she had been a shy, timid little bride with a twinkling nosedrop. She had shed her nosedrop and with it her fear and respect for her mother-in-law. She looked so different now—Thako hardly knew her. Her skin shone with oil and good living and her eyes were bold and black. She wore her sari pleated and could easily pass for a babu's concubine. Thakomoni stood in awe of her. But that didn't prevent her from slipping into the room the moment Subala moved away. Seating herself by the sleeping infant, she stroked its head and drooled, 'Oh, my jewel! Oh, my lump of gold! What beautiful eyes my moonface has! Look, Bouma—just like Dulal's.' But Thako's Bouma responded by making a rush at her mother-in-law and pushing her hand away. '*Arré*! *Arré*!' she cried. 'Don't touch him. He'll wake up and scream till the roof comes down.' Thako bit her lip, trying hard to control its trembling. As if she hadn't borne a son and reared him to maturity! But there was nothing she could do to retaliate. In an attempt to restore her lost dignity, she said faintly, 'Put his arms down by the side, Bouma. It is not right for a male child to sleep with his hands on his chest.' But her heart burned within her. She thought of all the hopes she had nurtured of Dulal growing to manhood, of a demure, dutiful daughter-in-law and healthy grandchildren—all living within the shadow of her protection and tender care. But all her dreams had come to naught. Subala would not share her husband and child with her.

Sometimes, by a lucky chance, she found Dulal at home. On such occasions she longed to sit by his side, stroke his face and head and ask, 'How are you, Dule? *O ré*, can't you see how my heart yearns for you?' But she was never given the chance. Dulal's face hardened the moment he saw her and his voice became harsh and impatient. Sometimes he feigned sleep, snoring louder than was natural. Thakomoni looked on with sad eyes. '*O ré*, why do you hate me so?' she pleaded wordlessly with her son. 'What have I done? If I gave up my chastity it was for your sake alone. You were so little; so vulnerable. I wanted you to live; to grow into a man . . .'

One day, Dulal was home and awake for a change. 'O Dule!' Thako cried eagerly. 'I have something to say to you. Bouma, you come, too.'

'What is it?' Dulal said with an impatient gesture. 'I'm in a hurry. I'm going out with Chhoto Babu.'

'I have saved quite a lot of money,' Thako said, her face bright with hope. 'What do you say to our building a house of our own in some village? We could have our own pond and—'

'Build a house in a village? What for?'

'It will be our own house. Our very own.'

'But who'll live in it?'

'We'll all live in it. You and I and Bouma and Khoka.'

'And what shall we eat? Our thumbs?'

'Just listen to me. I've thought of everything. I've saved enough money to buy a few acres of farmland. We can grow our own rice and breed our own fish. We could even keep a cow. Bouma and I will do all the work of the house. And you can take charge of the fields and—'

'Rubbish!' Dulal turned angry red eyes on his mother and rose to leave. 'You've gone mad. Am I to turn peasant and yoke myself to a plow? What's wrong with my life here? Chhoto Babu needs me and depends on me. I'm not leaving the city to rot in some mosquito-ridden village. You can go if you like.'

# Chapter V

One morning, just as dawn was breaking, Chandikaprasad Mallik of Hatkhola was carried into the house in a dead faint. Bubbles of froth streamed from his lips and his limbs twitched painfully. He had been spending the night in the company of a Muslim prostitute and had fallen to the ground while dancing with her. His brother, Kaliprasad, sent for the best doctors and vaidyas of the city but no one could bring him back to consciousness. Days passed and his condition did not change. It seemed highly unlikely now that he would ever be able to carry out his soul's ambition of performing his father's shraddha. On the contrary, judging from the vigour with which Jagai Mallik rocked back and forth from the balcony rails and called out 'M-m-m-m-m-m' to the passers-by, the situation could well be reversed.

Chandika's wife, Durgamoni, was only a few years older than her niece-in-law, Kusum Kumari, and the two were great friends. Durgamoni was Chandikaprasad's third wife. There was an unwritten law—one that scions of great houses followed religiously. This was, that notwithstanding the number of mistresses a man may keep for his pleasure, he had to have a wife. If one died—another; and another . . . A man's enjoyment of other women lacked spice and wasn't quite complete if he didn't have a wife weeping and tearing her hair in the zenana. The lucky man loses his wife; the unlucky his horse. The old adage was justified for with the death of a wife, a new bride was brought into the house, together with a new dowry. But the death of a horse spelled financial loss and a gap in the stables.

Chandika was a lucky man. His first wife died during childbirth within two years of the marriage; his second committed suicide within one. But his luck gave way at this point. Durgamoni was far from being the soft, submissive, adoring wife she might have been. She was a woman of considerable beauty and great force of character. She had tried hard, in the beginning, to change her husband's ways but, having failed, had turned away completely from him. She didn't care now if she didn't see his face from month's end to month's end.

One afternoon, Kusum Kumari came to Durgamoni's room to enquire after her uncle-in-law. Durgamoni looked up from her embroidery. 'Come,' she said. 'Sit.'

'How is he?' Kusum Kumari pointed a finger at the adjoining room.

'Just the same,' Durgamoni answered indifferently.

'What do the doctors say?'

'I don't understand doctor's jargon. Neither will you. He will live if his destiny favours him.'

'His destiny? Or yours?'

'I'm not worried in the least. I don't relish meat and fish—as you know. It matters little to me if he lives or dies.'

'O Ma!' Kusum Kumari cried out in alarm. 'How can you say such a thing, Khuri? Aren't you afraid of what people will say?'

Durgamoni shrugged a careless shoulder. She was not the weeping, sulking, clinging wife that men of Chandikaprasad's type love to possess. She gave as good as she got. Chandikaprasad beat her often but her retaliation was immediate and ruthless. Kusum had seen, with her own eyes, Durgamoni deliver several stinging slaps on her drunken husband's cheeks. Durgamoni had done something else that called for supreme courage. She had written a letter to Vidyasagar, which read, 'Innumerable *pronams* to you! May your efforts in the cause of the unfortunate widows of our land meet with success! I pray that God grants you the boon of immortality!' And slipping off a thick gold bangle from her wrist, she had it sent along with the letter.

'Why are you so interested in widow remarriage, Khuri?' Kusum Kumari asked her one day.

'Have you heard of the phrase, death in life? It applies to me. I'm a widow though I have a living husband. And so are you.'

Kusum Kumari grew pale at the mention of her husband and her lip trembled like a child's.

'How is he?' Durgamoni threw her a sidelong glance.

'He's been sleeping all day.'

Durga watched her face closely. 'I'm afraid for you,' she said.

'I'm afraid you'll go mad too, one of these days. It happens when one spends all one's time with a lunatic.'

'Don't, Khuri!' Kusum Kumari shuddered and clung to her aunt-in-law. 'You're frightening me.'

'That is exactly my intention. I want to frighten you.'

Suddenly, a loud thud was heard from the next room. The women looked up, startled, and then hurried over to see what had happened. Chandikaprasad lay sprawled on the thick Persian carpet.

'O Ma!' Kusum Kumari cried out in panic. 'Khuro Thakur[2] has fallen from the bed. He must be badly hurt. Come quick. Let's lift him and—'

'Wait,' Durgamoni's voice was cold and hard. 'Don't touch him. He's a filthy man. He sleeps with hundreds of low-caste women. The thought of touching him makes me puke.'

Kusum Kumari's blood froze in her veins when she heard these words. She stared at Durgamoni, her eyes wide and scared. But Durgamoni didn't even glance in her direction. Turning away she called out to her maid, Chandan Bilasi, to fetch her husband's servants, Jedo and Medho. 'Babu has fallen from the bed,' she said briefly. 'He has to be picked up.' The two worthies, Jedo and Medho, were at the gate, smoking their afternoon ganja. It took Chandan Bilasi a long time to find them and even longer to persuade them to come to their master's assistance. And all that while, Chandikaprasad lay alone and helpless on the floor, his wife having settled down to her embroidery in the next room, without giving him a second glance.

However, despite Durgamoni's indifference to her husband, Chandikaprasad improved every day and was soon able to sit up. But it was a trying time for a man like him. He had never stayed home in his wife's company for so long at a stretch and was first shocked, then enraged at her negligence of him. 'Wait and see, you bitch,' he snarled from time to time. 'Just let me get back on my feet. I'll get me another wife.' On the twelfth day of his convalescence, Jedo and Medho managed to smuggle a bottle of wine into the sick room. And as the first few drops hit

---

2 Father's younger brother.

his stomach, Chandikaprasad came into his own. Roaring like a lion, he called out to the servants to bring him his clothes. He would go out that very day. Dressed like a medieval courtier in wide pyjamas, cummerbund and turban, Chandika tottered down the stairs, waving his red kerchief and singing *Paréro monéro bhabo bujhité no paaré paré,* as he went. He reached the gate just as his father was being brought in. Resisting the impulse to slap the tiny bald pate, Chandika rolled his eyes at him and shouted, 'You thought you'd outlive me, you malicious old gnome! But you'll have no such luck. I'll enjoy your shraddha yet.'

A few days later another incident rocked the house in Hatkhola. Kusum Kumari's husband, Aghornath, burst out of his chains and went on a rampage. He was a terrible figure to behold, with his tangled hair and beard and immense body, naked except for a strip of loin cloth. The servants and darwans ran after him, not daring to touch him as he broke vases and statues, one after another, and roared and rolled his eyes. Aghornath's mother wept and beat her breast while Kaliprasad's sons, Shibprasad and Ambikaprasad, screamed instructions from the upper verandah. Finally, under their able directions, Aghornath was pushed into the courtyard by the Bhojpuri darwans and beaten with heavy lathis till he fell to the ground. Everyone heaved a sigh of relief as his shackles were fitted on him once again. Only his mother wept on and on, muttering at intervals, '*O ré,* why did I stop you from becoming a Brahmo? O Aghor! Oh, my darling boy! Do what you like. Be a Brahmo; a Christian—whatever pleases you. Only look at me with sane eyes. Only call me Ma but once.' Kusum Kumari stood by her side like a figure of stone. Then, suddenly coming to life, she ran to her husband and knocked her head on his shackled feet, crying wildly, 'Get well! Get well! God! Make him well.' Aghornath looked on, surprised, for a few seconds, then jerked his feet so violently that Kusum Kumari was thrown against the wall with tremendous force. A trickle of blood streamed down her cheek from a cut in her head and the world grew dark around her.

On regaining consciousness she felt soft hands stroking her face and hair, and opening her eyes, found herself lying on Durgamoni's bed. Durgamoni rose from where she was sitting and locked the door. Turning to the girl, she demanded fiercely, 'Why did you fall at his feet?' Kusum Kumari was startled by the passion in her voice and could make no answer. 'Why don't you speak?' Durgamoni went on inexorably. 'Answer me. Why did you do such a thing?'

'I don't know, Khuri,' Kusum Kumari muttered helplessly. 'Something burst in my head and—'

'I knew it. Living with a madman day and night you'll go mad, too. Listen to me. I want you to do something.'

'What is it?'

'Poison his food. I have some poison hidden away in my coffer. I can give it to you.'

'What are you saying, Khuri?'

'Only what is right and just. I want you to become a widow. Then I'll get you married again. I wrote to Sagar for your sake. I'm an old woman at twenty. You are young—'

'Khuri!'

'Take courage, Kusum! Learn to live with dignity. Why should we spend our lives with drunks and madmen? Don't we have a right to happiness? Can you do what I say? Answer me!'

Kusum turned on her side and burying her face in Durgamoni's lap, burst into tears, 'Don't say such things, Khuri. Even to hear them is sin.'

# Chapter VI

Chandranath had never known suffering or hardship. In his mother's house he had been indulged from morning till night, been fed on cream and butter and dressed in the finest of garments. He was a different person now in the *samshan* at Neemtala. His soft, plump little body had stretched and hardened into a rope of steel and tufts of wiry black hair sprang aggressively from his head and chin. His name had changed, too. His new compatriots and followers called him Chandu or Chendo.

Chandu had had to prove his worth before he was accepted by the creatures who skulked about the *samshan*, picking up a living from the remains of the dead. About a year ago, Chandu had got into a fight with the leader, Fakir. Pinning him down with one hand, Chandu had twisted his arm so viciously with the other that it had broken with a snap. Following this incident Chandu was hailed as the new leader while Fakir went about with a disconsolate face, his broken arm dangling by his side—lifeless and useless. These days Chandu wore a flaming red rag around his head and a murderous looking knife at his waist. The moment a funeral party arrived he leapt into the fray, brandishing an immense lathi which he spun into the air with a swishing sound. It was Chandu who decided if the wood used for burning would be sandal or ordinary mangrove; how much ghee would be poured on the pyre and how many cakes of camphor; if the burning should stretch to four hours or six. He laid claim to everything, from the clothes the corpse wore to the bedstead on which it lay. No one dared oppose him, not even the chandals whose caste vocation it was to make a living out of the dead.

Of all the parts of the body the skull takes longest to burn. To hasten the process, the dom is required to hammer it with his lathi till it cracks open. Of all the duties of the dom Chandu liked this one the best and appropriated it for himself with jealous pleasure. To see him in action was a sight indeed!

Leaping high into the air, he crashed his lathi down with tremendous force, over and over again till the fragments flew about and the brain gushed out in a hissing torrent. At this, a smile of pure joy irradiated his face and his eyes, bloodshot with ganja, gleamed and sparkled. No one could imagine, seeing him like that, that the same head had brimmed over with the verses of Byron and Kalidas not so long ago.

There were two chandals in the *samshan*. One was called Tarhu, the other Jhinia. Tarhu was married and lived with his wife, Motia, in a little leaf hut. Jhinia was much older than Tarhu and drunk all the time on toddy or drugged on ganja. No one knew where he came from. He spoke an alien dialect—a strange jumble of Hindi and Bengali. Chandu and his followers loved poking fun at Jhinia and thought of all kinds of tricks to play on him. One of them snatched away his pot of toddy or funnel of ganja right from out of his mouth and ran away as fast as he could while another stole up from behind and gave a sharp tug at his loin cloth. Then, as he stood, stark naked, wailing and cursing and flailing his arms, cacophonous laughter, loud enough to rouse the dead, would echo and re-echo from the *samshan* ghat.

Tarhu was a different type altogether. He was a man in his prime, about forty years old, with a coal-black skin and hair shining with oil. Though plump and sleek and as unlike a chandal as anyone could be, he was very professional about his job. Chandu and his gang got on well with Tarhu though they often wondered how he had managed to marry Motia in the first place and how he had got her to live with him in the *samshan* in the second. For Motia was a city girl and had held the enviable post of a Sahebpara scavenger before her marriage. Occasionally, terrible fights broke out between Motia and Jhinia. Jhinia was desperately jealous of Tarhu. Tarhu had a wife and he didn't and he felt the deprivation keenly. Sometimes, when he was drunk to overflowing, he couldn't bear it any more and would force his way into Tarhu's hut, to be pushed out vigorously by Motia, with the aid of loud curses and swishes from her broomstick. Chandu and company would form a ring around the two, laughing and shouting encouragement. Then, at a signal from Chandu, some of the boys would lift the old man bodily and fling him into the river. They knew that Jhinia would find his way back. Like a turtle, he took a lot of killing.

All in all, Chandu was enjoying his life in the *samshan*.

One night, when the moon was pouring out her rays in tumultuous torrents and a wild, sweet wind danced in and out of leafy branches, a strange thing happened. Four men bearing a corpse on a bier entered the *samshan* and depositing their burden in an isolated spot, ran away as fast as their legs could carry them. Chandu, whose eyes were as sharp as needles, caught sight of them first. '*Arré! Arré*!' he cried. 'Run after the buggers. Quick!' The members of his gang jumped up and ran in different directions but couldn't catch even one. It looked as though four hefty, hulking men had been spirited away by the ghosts who were sure to be abroad on a night like this.

Giving up the search, Chandu and his party approached the bier and stood staring at it, speechless with shock and horror. For upon it lay a young woman of surpassing beauty. Her face, clearly visible in the moonlight, was as fair as a flower and the long, dark strands of hair surrounding it hung over the edges. Her eyes, wide open and vibrant with life, stared compellingly into Chandu's. Chandu stood petrified for a few moments, then putting out a hand he gave a tug at the sheet that covered her. And, then, he got another shock for the creamy white body under it was stark naked, except for one spot between the breasts, where the hilt of a knife gleamed wickedly in the moonlight. Masses of clotted blood surrounded it and blood had streamed over the fair breasts in dark, evil streaks. Though seeing and handling corpses was their daily vocation, Chandu's followers became hysterical with terror. 'Murder! Murder!' one shrieked. 'A girl from a great family!' 'Whore! Whore!' another screamed while a third voice rose above theirs—'She's alive! She's still alive!' Chandu took the girl's head in his hands and shook it from side to side but it was cold and lifeless. 'She's dead! Dead!' he shouted but before he could do anything, Nyara had jumped on her and clasped her in his arms. Gurgling with pleasure, he rubbed his face, over and over again, on her naked thighs till Chandu kicked him forcefully aside. But two others took his place and, falling on the corpse, commenced kissing and caressing the dead limbs with moans of ecstasy. Chandu tried to pull them away with kicks and curses but found his authority gone. Nyara gathered himself up from the ground where he had fallen and said roughly, 'Don't interfere, Ustad. Clear out if you don't want any part in it.' The others had been waifs from infancy and had no memories of a home or decent living. Chandu was not like them. He was horrified at what they were doing and went on trying to stop them even though he knew that mutiny had broken out in his ranks and he was one against many. Pulling out the knife from his waist, he held it against Nyara's throat. 'I'll kill you, you dirty dog,' he shrieked in his desperation. 'I'll kill the whole pack of you.' But while Nyara struggled in Chandu's grip, another of the gang plucked out the knife from the woman's breast and advanced menacingly on him. But what was a knife to Chandu? Within seconds he had felled his opponent to the ground and stood with his back to the corpse, shielding it. 'Come on, you sons of bitches,' he roared, 'and touch her if you dare.'

Within a few minutes the rebellion was crushed and peace restored. 'Let's take her to the river,' Chandu said, 'and set her afloat on the water.'

'What if she's still alive?' one of the boys asked feebly.

'Ma Ganga will take care of her.'

Watching the fair body float away, Nyara burst into tears. No one had ever seen Nyara weep before. No one knew who the woman was; where she had come from or why she had been murdered so cruelly. No one knew if anybody had mourned her death. But here, in the *samshan* ghat at least, there was one who was shedding tears over her.

Another strange thing happened one night. A sound like that of the mewling of a kitten, mingled with agonized moans, came floating out of Tarhu's hut, drowning the sound of the pouring rain. Nyara heard it first and shook Chandu awake. 'Ustad! Ustad!' he called. 'An argala has got into Tarhu's hut. It is attacking Motia.' Everyone woke up at the urgency in his voice and ran towards the little leaf hut. Nyara was the first one to enter. But he was out in a second, his tongue between his teeth. '*Arré*! *Shabash*!' he cried gleefully. 'There's a baby in Motia's bed.'

# Chapter VII

No one quite knew to which race this country belonged. The Hindus believed India to be theirs for they bore Aryan blood in their veins. They had lived in this beautiful land, girdled by blue-green oceans and crowned with glittering mountain peaks, from time immemorial. Their religion, their culture, their way of life sprang from this very soil. Muslims, though here for six hundred years, were outsiders. They were different in every way. Theirs was a desert culture and they fell back on their Arabic roots for sustenance. They turned to the west, to Mecca and Medina, when saying their prayers—not to the east from where the sun rises. Even though the Muslims had conquered India and kept the Hindus under their domination for four hundred years, Hindus looked down upon them, considering them savage and uncivilized and unworthy of social intercourse.

The Muslims argued that if they were outsiders, so were the Hindus, for the Aryans were also an alien race. Indian Muslims were converts for the most part, coming from those castes and classes of Hindu society that had faced the severest discrimination over the years. Impressed with the egalitarian principles of Islam, they had embraced the religion in large numbers. There were people, of course, who could claim descent from the Mughals and Pathans, but after the passing of so many centuries, they too had come to think of the land as their own. Muslims had ruled the country for four centuries, then suddenly found their authority gone. They hated the British for it and looked upon them as usurpers. They lived sullen, resentful lives, licking their wounds in private and lamenting their fate in each other's company. The British, on the other hand, scorned the Muslims and mocked them openly. Rulers who couldn't protect their kingdoms even when they had mighty armies at their command were not worthy of that name, they argued, laughing at the ease with which the British had overcome them.

The British treated the country like a fruit plucked off the branch of a tree. They had found it. It was theirs and they could do what they liked with it. They could bite into it, chew it or swallow it, as they pleased. Or they could suck it dry till it was reduced to stone and fibre. They avoided the Muslims, getting on better with the Hindus, not without a return of preference.

Even two decades ago, Persian had been the language of the courts and offices. Educated Hindus spoke and wrote fluent Persian and Urdu. But now, English had replaced Persian everywhere and Hindus had come forward in large numbers to learn the new language. Muslims, jealously guarding their traditions and lost prestige, had abstained, and had consequently found no place in the huge workforce that was being created for the purpose of running the government. The number of Muslim clerks, doctors, teachers and lawyers could be counted on the fingers of one hand. Robbed of their rule, robbed of their language, the Muslims became weaker than ever before and in their vulnerability clung to each other, shutting out the rest of the world.

The Muslims had caste professions of their own. They were masons and carpenters for the most part, with a sizeable section of tailors and embroiderers. The latter were so deft with their needles that their Hindu counterparts couldn't compete and were slowly edged out of the business. Muslim tailors and *zardoz* workers now held the monopoly for all the fine garments that city men wore. Calcutta was full of Muslims, but socially, the community was sharply polarized. The rich were very rich indeed, and the poor, exceedingly poor.

One rich Muslim of Calcutta was Janab Abdul Latif Khan. His two-storeyed mansion at Khidirpur was built like a fort and even looked like one. Such strict purdah was observed in the zenana that its inmates had never felt the sun on their bodies or the wind in their faces. Latif Khan had Pathan blood in his veins but his family had lived here for three generations and he looked upon the land as his own. He had taken a Hindu woman for a second wife and spoke fluent Bengali. A wealthy man with extensive estates in Murshidabad, he had rendered himself even wealthier by purchasing part ownership in a sugar factory. Sugar was like gold. It yielded returns at the rate of a hundred per cent. The house, built by his father, had been in use only part of the year when the old man was alive. He had preferred living in his ancestral mansion in Murshidabad, coming up to Calcutta only now and then for relaxation and entertainment. Latif Saheb was a city bird and preferred to make his home here. There was another calculation behind the move. Latif Khan believed that a non-resident zamindar raked in higher rents, the officials of the estate taking their responsibilities more seriously if they didn't have a zamindar at their beck and call. The presence of a zamindar also encouraged defaulters to fall at his feet and beg for mercy. Latif Khan hated scenes of this sort. He was a soft-hearted man and couldn't stand tears.

One evening as Latif Khan sat in the outer room, smoking his *albola,* the sound of shrill weeping came from the slum that lay a little beyond the mansion wall. Latif Khan started up and called out imperiously, 'Mirza! Mirza!' Mirza Khushbakht was Latif Khan's personal guard and stood just outside the door in full regalia, which included a sword in his belt.

'Huzoor!' Khushbakht rushed in at the sound of his master's voice.

'Who cries? Is someone crying or am I dreaming?'

'No, Huzoor. You are not dreaming. Someone is crying in the bustee. It must be a child. The little bastards have nothing better to do.'

'Go give him a few licks and he'll stop.'

'Children are very peculiar, Huzoor! They cry louder when they're beaten. The boy is crying because he is hungry.'

'Then why doesn't he eat his rice?'

'Who knows?' Mirza shrugged an indifferent shoulder. 'The men in that bustee are very poor. They go out every morning in search of work. Most days they don't find it. Then they come back empty-handed and beat their children if they ask for rice. That's when the children cry.'

'Don't say such things, Mirza. You know how they pain me. Why do poor men come to the city? They should stay in their villages. Go to the bustee, Mirza, and make the child stop crying. I hate tears.'

Mirza bowed himself out of the room and, strangely enough, the crying stopped after a few minutes. He came back a little later, bringing Munshi Amir Ali with him. There was a little smile on his face for he knew his master would be pleased.

Munshi Amir Ali was a lawyer of the Diwani Adalat—the only Muslim lawyer of the city—and, as such, he commanded a great deal of respect from the members of his community. He had a devious, cunning brain, which he kept successfully hidden under a mild, unassuming exterior. His conversation, earthy, even verging on the erotic, sat oddly on a man of his years and position. To look at Munshi Amir Ali was to remember the Urdu proverb, *'Budhapé mé insan ki kuwate shah wani zaban mein a jaya karti hai* (When a man is old his lusts and desires find their way to the tip of his tongue)'. This evening, however, Munshi Amir Ali's usual joviality was in abeyance. Greeting his friend with a preoccupied *'Salaam Alaikum'*, he stood gazing at him, hurt and anger in his eyes.

'Is anything the matter?' Latif Khan hastened up to him. 'Have I said or done anything to offend you?'

'Today is a day of mourning for the sons of Islam,' Amir Ali began harshly. 'And you sit here, smoking your *albola* without a care in the world!'

'Why? Why?' Latif Khan spluttered, alarmed at his tone. 'What's today?'

'Nawab Wajed Ali Shah is coming to Calcutta. Didn't you know that?'

'Which Wajed Ali Shah? Badshah of Avadh? How can that be? Why should he leave Lucknow and come to Calcutta? Are we not living under British rule?'

Munshi Amir Ali smiled bitterly and quoted a couplet: *'Chale wahan se daman uthati hui, Karhe se karhe ko bajati hui* (She walks away from thence the protecting veil whipped away from her face while her chains clank one against another)'. Latif Khan still didn't understand. 'Take your seat, Janab[3],' he said anxiously, 'and tell me what has happened. Why should the Nawab of Avadh come here? He is our last hope.' Amir Ali sighed and dropped his bulk into a chair. Then, taking a few puffs from the *albola*, he said, 'The British annexed Avadh at the beginning of the year. Don't you even know that? The devils have betrayed the Nawab. Not a shot was fired. Not a drop of blood was shed. Our soldiers refused to fight. The British took

3 Sir.

the Nawab's crown as easily as could be. Our last pride; our last hope is gone. What is left for us?'

Latif Saheb understood. His head reeled from the shock. He felt as bereft as if he had just received the news of the loss of his own estate. He couldn't speak for a few minutes, then he asked with a catch in his voice, 'But why is he coming here? So far away from—'

'He's coming as a prisoner,' Amir Ali burst out angrily. 'Can't you see that? He'll be dragged through the streets in fetters. The Emperor of Hindustan has been robbed of all his powers. He's a prisoner in his fort in Delhi. The Nawab of Avadh has fared even worse. He's been exiled from his own land.'

'But I don't understand,' Latif Khan persisted. 'Nawab Wajed Ali Shah had large armies at his command. I've even heard you mention a female battalion. Why didn't they fight? Have they turned weak and cowardly—like Hindus?'

Amir Ali sighed and shook his head. 'No, friend,' he said gently. 'The soldiers haven't forgotten how to fight. The truth is that the Nawab had lost interest in matters of state. He spent all his time composing verses and in music and dance. And that Dalhousie, with his hunger of a thousand devils—he took advantage of it. He's been gnawing at our country for many years now and won't rest till he has swallowed the whole of it.'

'Where will the Nawab stay?' Latif Khan asked hoarsely, his eyes moist with tears.

'In Metiaburj. I'm told that the British have very kindly allowed him a house and some land—'

'*Hai Allah! Hai Allah*!' Latif Khan beat his forehead with his fist. 'To be forced to give up Kaiser Bagh and Badshah Manzil in that jewel among cities, Lucknow, in exchange for a marshy tract of land so far away—' His voice cracked with emotion. 'Ah, what a cursed fate has brought him to this pass!'

The two men talked a little while longer, then decided to go out and witness the Nawab's entry into Calcutta. Leaving Khidirpur behind, they came to the outskirts of the city, where surging crowds were massing on either side of the road along which the Nawab's cavalcade was to pass. Soldiers and policemen rushed about, cursing and brandishing lathis in an effort to control the mob. Amir Ali and Latif Khan stepped out of the carriage and came out and stood at the crossroads, their bodyguards taking up positions close behind them. Both Hindus and Muslims had turned out in large numbers for the Nawab's entry into the city was a historic event. Amir Ali scanned the faces around him. The Muslims looked uniformly sad and dispirited—the Hindus surprised and amused.

With the approach of the carriages, it became evident that Amir Ali's apprehensions that the Nawab would be dragged through the streets in fetters was totally without foundation. The Nawab was entering the city with a vast retinue of queens, mistresses, servants, dancers and musicians. As a matter of fact, he had chosen to come to Calcutta of his own accord for the Supreme Court was here, and he wanted to sue the Company for illegal annexation. If he lost here he would go to London and move the Privy Council; even seek audience with the Queen. He would ask Her Majesty to define the law by which the Company had robbed him of his kingdom.

A shout went up from the crowd as the first carriage, full of musicians and their intruments, rolled by. Carriage after carriage followed, carrying all kinds of birds and animals. There were peacocks, mynahs, pigeons and swans. There was a whole cage of turtles and another of deer and one of leopards. Three cages, with a variety of monkeys and baboons in it, came next and after them camels, giraffes and elephants. These walked alongside the cages, being too large to be put into them. Another shout went up as the Nawab's gold-embossed tanjam, borne by four negroes in splendid livery, went past. His four queens came after him, each in her own covered palki, followed by those of her servants and maids.

The Nawab's tanjam was hung with fine muslin curtains through which a dim shape could be seen, leaning forward a little, with head bent low. He looked as though he was intoxicated—the spectators were convinced that he was so—but that was far from the truth. Wajed Ali Shah had never touched wine, opium or *bhang* in his life. His addictions were different. They were music, dance and women and he was drunk to overflowing on these every hour of the day. The figure sat immobile even as the torches on either side of the road flashed their light into his face and shouts of welcome and wails of despair rent the air around him. He was oblivious of his surroundings for he had just composed a verse and was setting it to music. The city he was entering held no charms for him and he felt no curiosity. *'Babul mora,'* he hummed to himself, *'naihar chhut hi jai.'*

Latif Khan's eyes grew moist at the sight. *'Khuda Nawab Sahib ko salamat aur Begum Sahiba ko kayam rakhe,'* he called out in a voice cracking with emotion and made a rush towards the tanjam. Amir Ali ran after him and dragged him back. He was older in years and more in control of his emotions. He knew the *gora* police to be no respecters of persons. They wouldn't think twice before hitting out with lathis at anyone who broke the rules. But his heart was heavy within him. The Nawab of Avadh was entering Calcutta without an official welcome. Not one shot had been fired in his honour.

Sitting in the carriage, on his way back home, Latif Khan burst into tears. Amir Ali's face worked painfully as he patted Latif's hand and said, 'Dry your tears, Latif, and take a vow. We, the Muslims of Hindustan will not forget this insult. There are lakhs of soldiers in this country, simmering with discontent. They'll avenge the treachery of the British. A mutiny is brewing and we must all be a part of it. Remember that and take comfort in the thought.'

# Chapter VIII

Following Ishwar Chandra's petition to the government, Raja Radhakanta Deb sent another, protesting against it. The signatures on Ishwar Chandras's petition numbered less than a thousand—the ones on the Raja's crossed thirty-three thousand. In addition, letters in support of the latter poured in every day from Bombay, Poona, Tripura, Dhaka and many other cities. It was evident that those in favour of widow remarriage constituted a minute fraction of the population. It was not that Ishwar Chandra's opponents had arguments at their command to disprove his. Their contention was simple. The problem of Hindu widows was their problem and they would solve it in their own way and in their own good time. An alien government had no right to interfere.

The British government chose to ignore the mandate, overwhelming though it was, and passed a bill, legalizing the remarriage of widows. Not content with that it passed another, decreeing that a widow's children by her second husband would have full legal claim to their father's property. It was agreed in council that social reform was always started by a few courageous men and gradually snowballed into a movement if helped along the way. This was a universal truth and could not be dismissed as irrelevant in India. The new law was hailed as a great victory for Ishwar Chandra's followers till they discovered that the mountain, for all its labour pains, had given birth to a mouse and that they stood exactly where they had been all these centuries. Now it was their opponents' turn to celebrate and they did so with wild jubilation. To Jagamohan Sarkar and his toadies, Ishwar Chandra's discomfiture was too good a joke to be allowed to exhaust itself easily. For not one young man had come forward to marry a widow—not even from among those who had written burning articles in newspapers and shed copious tears over the lot of widows.

'*Ki hé,* Phatikchand!' Jagamohan laughed throatily between puffs from his *albola.* 'What does your Vidyasagar say, now that he's made himself the laughing stock of the city? *Arré chha! Chha*! After all the fine promises his bootlickers made not one of them is ready to marry a widow! From what I hear they've run away from him, with their tails in the air. Why doesn't he set them an example and marry one himself? Then we could all have some fun.'

'The wily Brahmin has got himself a wife already, Huzoor! So have his followers. The moral, you understand, is this: "Let others practise what we preach."'

'So what if he's got a wife already? He can take another. *Arré* Baba! A widow, after all, is a second-hand woman. A number two—'

'Hé! Hé! Hé!,' the toadies cackled. 'That's a fine phrase, Huzoor. A second-hand woman. There should be a shop, selling them along with other second-hand goods.'

'With widows going so cheap, no one need spend money on mistresses any more. We can each have a wife at home and as many widows outside it as we please. All for a few rupees to a Brahmin for reciting a little *'Ong bong khong'*. It will be as good as living in an *akhara*, where a Vaishnavi can be had for a string of basil.'

'Have you heard what Sreesh Chandra has done, Huzoor?'

'Who is Srisha Chandra? What has he done?'

'Sreesh Chandra is a follower of Vidyasagar's. He's no ordinary man, Huzoor. He's a pandit in the judge's court in Murshidabad and has been honoured by the title of Nyayaratna. He's been saying, "I'll marry a widow the day the Bill is passed," for several years now. Just as if he's the reformer of the century! And now people are calling him Chhi Chhi Chandra.'

'Why? Why?'

'Because, in anticipation of the event, he has already run off with a widow from Shantipur.'

'Aaaah!' Jagamohan screeched in horror and anguish. 'What kind of a widow? Is she from a decent family? Where is he keeping her?'

'Somewhere here in this city. I don't know exactly—'

*'A molo ja!'* Jagamohan cried out in exasperation. 'I'm sick to death of the pack of you. I feed you on the choicest delicacies and spend money like water on your entertainment and all you

bring me is half-baked news. Now move your behinds a bit and set your noses on the trail. I want to know where this Shreesh Chandra is keeping the woman.' Then, sighing and shaking his head mournfully, he added, 'What is the world coming to? Tender little girls are being dragged out of their homes and set up as whores in the bazaar! Are we all dead that we allow such things to happen? That bastard, Vidyasagar, ought to be whipped from head to foot!' Snorting with fury, Jagamohan continued, 'I must take this matter to Raja Radhakanta Deb at once. We'll teach the pair of ill-begotten Brahmins the lesson of their lives. I'll not rest till I see them turning the millstones in jail.'

Around this time, Ishwar Chandra Vidyasagar fell seriously ill. For years he had worked beyond his strength walking miles in the hot sun during the day and poring over ancient texts through the night, and now his body rebelled and broke down altogether. Lying on the vast bedstead in his friend, Rajkrishna Bandopadhyaya's house in Sukia Street, he tossed restlessly from side to side and groaned in agony. 'Ma! Ma *go*!' Rajkrishna sent for the best doctors in the city but nothing seemed to help for, to tell the truth, Ishwar's sickness was not of the body but of the spirit. Disappointed beyond his wildest imaginings at the turn of events, he was particularly wounded by Shreesh Chandra's behaviour. He had always believed Shreesh to be a young man of courage and idealism and had taken it for granted that his would be the first widow remarriage. Shreesh had given him his word and had even found a child widow for the purpose—an eleven-year-old girl from Shantipur called Kalimati. Everything had been arranged. The young Bengal group had spoken to the girl's mother, Lakshimoni, and managed to convince her to agree. And then, Shreesh had backed out on the plea that his mother had threatened to commit suicide if he married a widow. Vidyasagar's blood had boiled when he heard the news. What sort of a young man was this who sacrificed his principles so easily? That it was emotional blackmail was obvious. For which mother worthy of the name would actually carry out such a threat? It was the duty of every young man to stick to his ideals and to flout his parents' wishes if he considered them unworthy.

Raja Radhakanta Deb was quick to seize advantage from this

setback in Vidyasagar's fortunes and sent another petition to the government. He pointed out that since events had proved the implementation of the Bill to be an impossibility, the rulers would do well to withdraw it. Otherwise, they were liable to become the laughing-stock of the country. Another development took place around the same time. A group of diehards met Lakshimoni and persuaded her to bring a suit against Shreesh Chandra for breach of promise. He was either to marry her daughter at once or pay a penalty of forty thousand rupees.

'Serves him right,' Vidyasagar said grimly, when the news was brought to him, and turned his face to the wall.

'Don't break down so easily, Ishwar,' Rajkrishna exhorted him. 'We may have failed once. We won't fail every time.'

'Nonsense!' Ishwar exclaimed irritably. 'Don't hold out false hopes. I'm sick to death of all this hypocrisy.'

'We're straining every nerve to make your dream come true,' another man, a journalist, said. 'We're bound to succeed. Only you must pull yourself together and be our leader once more.'

'Don't expect anything of me. I've learned my lesson.'

'Don't say that. You are our general. You must lead us to victory.'

'Your general is a sick, broken man. It is time you found yourselves another.'

'We'll take our orders from your sickbed. Only, don't leave the city.'

'You talk of cities,' Vidyasagar answered with a bitter smile. 'The time has come for me to leave the world.'

A couple of days later, as Vidyasagar lay sleeping in the afternoon, a shadow crept across the room and stood at the foot of the bed.

'Who is that?' Vidyasagar started up as a pair of hands fumbled at his feet.

'It's me. Shreesh Chandra.'

Vidyasagar withdrew his feet and said in voice choking with emotion, 'I'm a dying man, Shreesh. Have you come to finish me off altogether?'

'I came to seek your forgiveness.'

'Who am I to forgive you? The court will decide what to do with you.'

'The case has been withdrawn. I'm a free man. But it is you I have wronged the most. I shall know no peace till I obtain your forgiveness.'

'Get out of my sight.'

'The wedding arrangements are complete. I've come to you for your blessings.'

'Ah!' Vidyasagar drawled in derison. 'So you decided to marry after all. Why? Was it from fear of losing your job? Or was it the forty thousand rupees?'

'Don't think so poorly of me,' Shreesh burst out passionately. 'If you lose faith in me I'll turn ascetic and abandon the world altogether. You've known me for so many years. Am I the man to break a solemn vow? My mother was opposing the marriage; she was being unreasonable. But I'm her son. I didn't have the heart to hurt her. All these days I've been by her side constantly, reasoning with her, trying to persuade her to change her mind. And I've succeeded. She gave her consent this morning. So I've come rushing to you to give you the news.'

'Why do you come to me? Go to the bride's mother and ask her to forgive you.'

'She has done that already. I've been sending messages every day, assuring her that the wedding, though delayed, will take place. She knew it and trusted me. But some enemies of ours worked on her and blackmailed her into filing a case. She has seen the truth now and withdrawn it. If you don't believe me, see this—' He drew out a piece of paper from his pocket and held it out to Vidyasagar. It was the draft of an invitation. It read:

> Sri Sri Lakshmimoni Devya humbly presents
> On Sunday, the 23rd Agrahayan, my daughter's nuptials will be solemnized at House No.12, Sukia Street in the Simulia area of East Calcutta. I request you, Sirs, to grace the occasion with your presence. Invitation by letter is regretted.
> 21st Agrahayan.

Ishwar Chandra read the letter through twice, then handed

it back with the comment, 'Why does she write, "my daughter's nuptials?" Ask her to change it to "my widow daughter's nuptials". I don't like prevarication. Whoever comes to the wedding must know it is a widow's.'

'I'll get it changed.'

'The letter says the marriage will take place in this house. Have you taken Rajkrishna's permission?'

'I have. He has given his consent most willingly.'

A fortnight later, the city of Calcutta witnessed the first widow remarriage, from the highest stratum of the Hindu caste hierarchy. Ishwar Chandra, though still weak in body, stood as though welded to his post and saw the ceremony through from beginning to end. Over two thousand guests were invited—all from the highest families of the land. Vidyasagar, his ill health notwithstanding, visited a number of people in person and invited them to attend. At one place he got a rude shock. Rammohan Roy's son declined with the muttered apology, 'Leave me out of it. My absence will not stand in the way of the marriage.' Vidyasagar's face turned pale. Ramprasad Roy had often spoken in favour of widow remarriage and had signed the petition. Why was he wavering now? What sort of response was this from the son of the man lion who had spent his life fighting the curse of sati? He turned his eyes upon the portrait of the late Raja that hung upon the wall and said, 'What is that portrait doing in your house, sir? Why don't you pull it down and fling it to the ground? You're right. Your absence won't make a dent in the proceedings.'

Kalimati and her mother were brought to Rajkrishna Babu's house a few days before the wedding. The bridegroom was to come from the house of Ramgopal Ghosh. To guard against any untoward incident, policemen were stationed every few yards along the stretch of road between the two houses. The bridegroom was to arrive by dusk though the ceremony was to take place after midnight. The street was bursting with people and slogans, both appreciative and condemning, were flung into the air as the carriage bearing the bridegroom and his party rolled slowly by. Suddenly there was a loud explosion, like the bursting of a cracker. Shreesh clutched Ramgopal's hand in fear but Ramgopal laughed. 'Do not be afraid,' he said. 'There are policemen everywhere. Our enemies can do nothing.' Then, signalling to his friends, he leaped out of the carriage. Forming a human wall around it, Ramgopal and his compatriots walked all the way to Sukia Street, daring anyone to come near. And thus, Shreesh Chandra was brought to the wedding pavilion.

The ceremony was conducted in all solemnity by two erudite pandits. Among the guests were Vidyasagar's colleagues from Sanskrit College, the Young Bengal group and members of the wealthy elite, from Raja Digambar Mitra to Nabin Kumar Singha. Even Ramprasad Roy, shamed by Vidyasagar's comparison, had decided to put in an appearance. And there were many, many women. No detail was overlooked. The recitation of the mantras; the giving away of the bride, with the customary gifts of clothes, jewellery and vessels of bronze and silver; the Stri Achar, the women's rituals, with its fun and frolic, such as the tweaking of the bridegroom's nose and the binding of his hands—all were carried out with scrupulous adherence to convention. And, finally, came the grand wedding dinner—a sixteen-course meal, of which the guests ate their fill.

Weary to the bone but intensely happy, Vidyasagar stood at the gate, taking leave of his guests. Suddenly, one of them stooped and touched his feet.

'Who are you, son?' Vidyasagar asked the young man, 'Have I seen you before?'

'My name is Nabin Kumar Singha. I have a favour to ask of you.'

'Yes, what is it?'

'I want to help you in the work you are doing. You have spent a great deal of your own money on this occasion. For every future widow remarriage, I would like to contribute a sum of one thousand rupees.'

Ishwar Chandra stood staring in amazement at the boy's departing back.

# Chapter IX

Ganganarayan had been given the responsibility of looking after the guests at Suhasini's wedding. Now, at her son's Upanayan, the thread ceremony, the duty fell on Nabin Kumar. Watching him darting about, giving orders, Suhasini was reminded with a pang of Ganga. Ganga had been of about the same age then but there was a world of difference between the two. Ganga had been a shy, gentle lad, modest and retiring. Nabin was bold and confident, even brash. His voice was loud and domineering when addressing people from a lower social stratum and his orders curt and commanding. Suhasini watched him as he stood at the door, holding the elegantly frilled pleats of his dhoti in one hand. How Chhotku has grown, she thought! Only the other day he had been a child and now he spoke and behaved like an equal with the most distinguished of the guests and looked straight into their eyes without a trace of nervousness.

With recollections of Ganga, the memory of Bindu crept in although Suhasini tried her best to ward it off. Sejdi was an ill-fated woman, cursed by God. Even a child had been denied her. And she had sullied her widowhood by running off with Ganga. Everyone knew that. Her death had come as a blessed release to her and to everyone else. No one in this house took her name any more. And, on an auspicious day like this one, even thinking of her was sin.

Bidhusekhar sat on a high-backed chair in the garden. He was too old and enfeebled now to rush around, supervising the arrangements. The sugar was running thick in his blood again and his vision was growing dimmer and dimmer. One eye was blinded altogether and he saw very faintly with the other. He knew everything was being looked after, there being no dearth of servants and poor relatives in the house. Yet he kept sending for Nabin Kumar and asking how things were going.

The feasting of the guests and the distribution of gifts to Brahmins went on all day, coming to a close only at ten o' clock at night, with the firing of the cannon from the fort. Then, when everything was over, Bidhusekhar's eldest daughter, Narayani, sent for Nabin. She had his meal ready for him on a vast silver *thala*, surrounded by rows of silver bowls. Fatigued with the exertions of the day, Nabin had lost his appetite. Forcing himself to eat a few mouthfuls, he dropped his hand into his glass of water and attempted to rise.

'Chhotku!' Narayani cried. 'You've eaten nothing. Have some *kheer* at least.'

'That's the way he eats,' Bimbabati said with a sigh. 'Like a bird.'

'I'm very tired,' Nabin rose to his feet. 'My back aches from standing around all day. I must go home and get some sleep. But I'll have a look at Gopal first.'

The women stared at one another in dismay, then Bimbabati said, 'You can't see Gopal tonight—'

'Why not? I want to give him a pat on his little shaven head before I go.'

'Gopal is sleeping,' Narayani said shortly.

'But he was awake only a little while ago. I saw him sitting counting his money.'

The women exchanged glances in embarrassed silence. The shastras decreed that a newly initiated Brahmin should spend three days and three nights in isolation, away from the polluting influence of women and non-Brahmins. Bimbabati took upon herself the task of answering her son. 'Go home,' she told Nabin. 'Gopal is not supposed to see anyone tonight.'

Even as she said these words, a young man, a poor relative of Bidhusekhar's, came bustling into the room. 'Gopal wants his milk,' he said to Narayani. 'Can I give him some?' Nabin was puzzled for a few minutes, then realizing that something was being kept from him, he looked straight into Narayani's eyes and asked sharply, 'Why do you forbid me? If he can go to Gopal, why can't I?'

'He's a Brahmin,' Narayani murmured. Nabin's face grew pale. He understood, for the first time in his life, that as a non-Brahmin, he, Nabin Kumar Singha, was inferior in some way. By virtue of his birthright, even the illiterate peasant who stood before him, goggling in amazement, was his superior. Nabin's heart swelled with fury. He, who had worked so hard for Gopal's Upanayan, had no right to see him! Little Gopal, whom he loved so much and who had whispered in his ear only that morning, 'Chhotku Mama,[4] I hope you are giving me the walking elephant you promised!' He had always thought of himself as a son of the house. Now he knew he wasn't and would never be. He stormed out of the room, his breast heaving with indignation. He hated Brahmins; low, despicable creatures who lived on charity. He remembered with fierce triumph the incident in his childhood when he had snipped off a Brahmin's *shikha*. He decided he wouldn't stay here one moment longer. He would go home and never set foot in this house again.

At the gate he came upon an aged Brahmin, cringing before the darwans and begging something of them. Nabin had never seen Pran Gopal's grandfather, Shiblochan, and did not know him. Shiblochan had been forbidden the house by Bidhusekhar but had come, notwithstanding, to bless his grandson on the day of his Upanayan. Nabin did not know that the old man was simply asking to be taken to his grandson. He thought he had come to claim his share of gifts and felt all the force of his anger directed against him.

'What does the old man want?' he asked the darwans in a loud, commanding voice. 'Haven't you told him that the almsgiving is over?' Shiblochan turned to him in humble supplication. 'I only want to—'

'Get rid of the old fool,' Nabin thundered 'Give him some *luchi* and sweetmeats and turn him out!'

Then, with quick angry footsteps, he walked away from Bidhusekhar's house.

'Didi!' Suhasini burst into tears. 'How could we do this to Chhotku? He's so angry—he has left the house.'

'Don't upset yourself, child.' Bimbabati stroked Suhasini's back with a comforting hand. 'Chhotku has been like that from childhood. He flares up one moment and cools down in another. He'll be himself by tomorrow .'

'Chotto Ma!'[5] Suhasini laid her head on Bimbabati's shoulder. 'What harm was there in allowing him to see Gopal?'

---

4 Maternal uncle.

5 Younger mother.

'O Ma! How can we go against the shastras? Besides, it is only for three days—after that Chhotku can see Gopal all he wants.'

'Chottku is my little brother; my only brother. I've never known any other. What difference does it make if he isn't a Brahmin?'

'It does make a difference, child.'

'Stop fretting, Suhas,' Narayani said with the authority of an older sister. 'I'll send for Chhotku tomorrow and explain everything to him. Let's go finish our work. There's the larder to be locked up and heaps of other things to do.'

But, as it turned out, bringing Nabin around wasn't as easy as the women had thought. Bimbabati wept and remonstrated but Nabin was steadfast in his refusal to set foot in Bidhusekhar's house. 'Don't ask me to do what I cannot, Ma,' he said with astonishing firmness. 'Why should I go to a house where I must watch my steps all the time? I remember now that as a child I once stepped into their puja room and Jethima[6] reprimanded me for doing so.'

'You astonish me, Chhotku! Don't you know that Brahmins are far above us? Can we claim to be their equals?'

'I don't know. I don't want to argue with you. But don't ask me to go to Jetha Babu's[7] house, either.'

'How can you say such a thing? They are our family. They do so much for us. It is only during religious ceremonies that a little . . . At other times you can move about the house as freely as you like.'

'Excepting the puja room, of course—'

The matter was reported to Bidhusekhar in due time. Though decrepit in body, he was still alert in mind and the news had a powerful impact on him. He sat hunched up in his chair for hours, lost in thought. His daughters had followed the ruling of the shashtras in forbidding Nabin to look upon the face of a newly initiated Brahmin. So far so good. But Nabin was a Brahmin. Just as the Sutaputra Karna in Mahabharat was, in reality, a Kshatriya. Chhotku had said he wouldn't step into the

6 Elder paternal uncle's wife.
7 Elder paternal uncle.

house again. He was young and hot-headed. He would cool down and all would be as it had always been. What would he do without Chhotku? Chhotku was sole heir to his vast fortune! In whose hands would he leave Pran Gopal after his death? He would have to reveal the truth some day. If only he hadn't promised Bimbabati . . .

# *Chapter X*

After some months of working as a clerk, Madhusudan was promoted to the post of interpreter in the police court, with a substantial increase in salary. He now started thinking seriously of moving out of Kishorichand Mitra's house. Kishorichand and his wife were extremely hospitable and looked after his needs with scrupulous attention. But Madhusudan felt ill at ease. One was never totally at home in someone else's house. The slightest mistake—even a clumsy movement, resulting in a broken glass, filled one with guilty feelings and the assurances of the host that it was nothing to worry about brought little comfort. There was something else that troubled Madhusudan. Kishorichand left home early each morning for the journey from Dumdum to Lalbazar was a long one and, being a punctual man, he made it a point to reach office by ten o' clock. But he was delayed every now and then by his guest who went with him. Madhusudan drank heavily all evening and found it difficult to wake up early enough in the mornings to keep time with his host. The sight of Madhusudan dashing into the carriage, unbathed and unshaven, half an hour after the appointed time, was a common one as was that of his host, waiting with a pained smile on his face and an eye on his watch. To Madhusudan's profuse apologies, Kishorichand would reply. 'It's all right, Mr Dutt. It's perfectly all right,' making him feel even worse.

In addition, Madhusudan found the company that assembled in the evenings not quite to his taste. He was like a child—always demanding attention—and it was rarely given to him in Kishorichand's house. Kishorichand's elder brother, Pyarichand Mitra, and his cronies were eternally discussing the driest of subjects—social reforms, women's uplift, the freedom of the country. Madhusudan sat with them, evening after evening, feeling bored and resentful. What sort of men were these? How prosaic their minds were! Why didn't they ever speak of poetry? Didn't the resounding lines of Milton and

Byron mean anything to them? He also noticed something else. Whenever he tried to enter into their discussions, they shrugged off his comments with little ceremony. He was convinced they looked down on him for being a Christian and a hanger-on in Kishorichand's house. Little did they know that Madhusudan Datta, petty clerk in the police court and living on charity as he now was, was the son of one of the wealthiest men in the city and had once commanded the attention of their betters.

One day Madhusudan broached the subject of his moving out to his host and hostess. To their shocked exclamations and anxious queries, he replied that their house, though very comfortable, was at a great distance from his place of work and being a habitual late riser, he was having trouble reaching office on time. If he wanted to keep his job, he would have to rent a house close enough to the court to enable him to reach it punctually even if he overslept. Kishorichand and his wife could not deny the soundness of his reasoning and had to agree. A few days later, Madhusudan took up residence at No. 6 Lower Circular Road, a small double-storeyed house within a hundred yards of the police court. Now he could sleep with a clear conscience for as soon as the court was in session, a bailiff would be dispatched to wake him up and bring him to his desk.

Weary of living alone and missing her husband very much, Henrietta, Madhusudan's second wife, set sail from Madras as soon as she heard that he had moved into a house of his own. Madhusudan was still desperately poor. Rajnarayan Datta's vast properties, from the ancestral mansion in Sagardari to the plantations in Sundarban and the houses in the city, had all passed into the clutches of his brothers. Not content with appropriating everything, they had embroiled their nephew in a legal suit that was draining him of whatever he earned and forcing him to incur vast debts besides. Madhu realized that one needed money—a lot of it—to live a life of grace and dignity and that the amount he earned as interpreter was merely a drop in the ocean of his needs. He had spent lavishly all his life and never learned to economize. Poverty depressed him and robbed him of his self-esteem. His experience at court had shown him that lawyers with a command over the English language had huge practices and earned in thousands. He decided to turn over a new leaf; to cut out drinking and address himself to the task of making money in all seriousness. He started studying law and in his spare time took lessons in Sanskrit from an eminent pandit.

One morning, Gourdas came to see his friend. Brushing past the liveried attendant who stood at the gate, he entered the house and was appalled by what he saw. Henrietta sat in one of the rooms upstairs, sobbing uncontrollably, and in another, Madhusudan lay in a drunken stupor. His lower limbs trailed on the ground from the sagging sofa on which the upper half of his body, strangely contorted, rested. Empty beer bottles rolled about all over the floor and a small towel, stained with gravy, hung from his neck. That he hadn't passed out altogether was obvious from the burning cigarette that dangled from his fingers. Gour was shocked. It was barely eleven o' clock.

How could Madhu get drunk so early in the day?

'Madhu!' Gour called, placing a hand on his friend's arm.

'Gour!' Madhu turned to look at him. 'Hello, my boy!'

'What's wrong with you? Why are you in this state?'

'Can you do me a favour, Gour? Ask that woman to stop crying. Please!'

'Tell me what is wrong. Today is Tuesday. Why aren't you at work?'

'What do you think of me?' Madhu roared suddenly, violently angry. 'I was not born to be a damned interpreter in that damned police court.'

A rustling of skirts made Gour look up. Henerietta stood in the doorway. She was thin and frail, as delicate as a stem of ivy, and her face was flushed and swollen with weeping. Madhu jumped up from the sofa the moment he saw her and kneeling at her feet, said in impassioned tones, 'Henrietta, beloved! It breaks my heart to see you weep.'

'Won't you introduce me to your wife, Madhu?'

'Of course, of course. Henrietta! This is my friend, Gour, of whom I speak so often. The self-same Gour who holds my life in his hands. You know him well though you've never met him before, don't you, Henrietta?' So saying, Madhusudan picked up a beer bottle and took a deep draught.

'Why do you weep, madame?' Gour said gently. 'All will be well now that you are here. You must be strong or else, how will you control this wild husband of yours?'

'Dear friend,' Henrietta replied in a voice, choking with tears. 'I am new to this city and know no one here. My husband doesn't listen to a word I say. He is ruining his health with excessive drinking. We have so little money. I find it impossible to run the house. I feel so helpless; so lost.'

'The man downstairs—is he a creditor?' Gour asked, his face paling at the thought.

'He has come from the court to call my husband. But he refuses to go—'

'The magistrate, Mr Rye, is a damned slow coach,' Madhu said, removing the beer bottle from his mouth. 'I refuse to waste my time interpreting for him.'

'You mean you're giving up your job? You can't do that, Madhu. What will you live on? And how will you support your wife?'

Madhu flung the beer bottle angrily at the wall opposite, smashing it, then rising unsteadily to his feet, he said, 'If making me do the work of a damned clerk makes the two of you happy, I'll do it. Call the attendant. I'll go with him.' Walking across the room, Madhu stumbled over the sofa and fell. Then, gathering himself together, he said, 'Yes, I'll go. I'll make a slave of myself since that is what you want.'

'Madhu!' Gour put out a hand and stopped him. 'You can't go to court in this state. Your eyes are bloodshot. Your breath is reeking of liquor. Send a letter through the attendant, asking for leave of absence for today.'

'Letter? Who'll write the letter? I've forgotten how to write. I'm dead. I'm a walking ghost.'

'You're crazy! All right, I'll write the letter. But you must sign it.'

Madhusudan was so pleased by Gour's suggestion that he clasped him in his arms and planted a passionate kiss on his cheek. 'Henrietta !' he called out to his wife. 'My saviour is here. We need not worry any more. Do you have any money with you, Gour? Send out for some bottles of beer. Don't weep, Henrietta. Have some beer and all your troubles will be over.'

After dispatching the letter Gour sent for the servants and ordered them to clean the room and help their master take a bath. Henrietta was young and inexperienced. Besides, she didn't know the language and so had no control over her servants.

Lunch was served. At Madhu's insistence, Gour ate with them and prepared to depart. But Madhu would not let him go. Holding him tightly by the hand, he said, 'Sleep in my bed, Gour. It is ages since we slept together.' Lying side by side the two friends talked of many things, good and bad, that had happened to them since they were boys together. Madhu was sober again by this time but his spirit was oppressed and he felt lost and alienated.

'Madhu!' Gour asked after a while. 'What happened to Rebecca and her children?'

'That damned planter's daughter? Don't remind me of her. She made life hell for me.'

'But your children? I've heard there were four—'

'Gour! Gour! Please don't speak of them. I want to forget them. I want to erase them from my memory. Didn't you like Henrietta? She's a Frenchwoman, real French—not Eurasian.'

'You're really amazing, Madhu! Fancy marrying a Frenchwoman. You must be the first native in the land to do so.'

'I should have been the first native in the land to do many things. But I've ending up pushing files in a damned police court. I shall die like a common man, Gour!'

'Don't say that. Your life isn't over. We have great hopes of you yet. Didn't you tell Pyarichand Mitra that if you tried, you could write better Bengali than him?'

'Bengali! Pooh!'

'You did, didn't you?'

'I'm worried to death about money. And all you can talk about is writing in Bengali. Absurd nonsense.'

'Why did you stop writing? Try writing in Bengali.'

'I need money, Gour. There must be more money. I've got to get hold of my father's property.'

'You will—some day. Kishori Babu is doing his best to help you. But that doesn't mean you should give up writing. Why don't you contribute an article to Pyari Babu's journal?'

'Good God! What do you take me for? Pyarichand and company are horribly prosaic. The stuff they write is disgusting. How can you bear to read it?'

'Have you read Ishwar Chandra Vidyasagar? His language is excellent. Full of vitality and ringing with melody.'

'That is prose too. And Bengali prose at that. *Chha*!'

'Why do you scorn Bengali so? A number of brilliant men are taking an interest in the language and writing in it.'

'Write me off!' Madhu cried, pounding his fist on the pillow. 'Don't expect anything of me. I'm a failure. Forget I ever existed.'

'Have you taken leave of your senses?'

'Sorry. I'm sorry, Gour.'

'Pull yourself together, Madhu. You were the brightest star in our galaxy. We used to call you Jupiter—don't you remember? But you've hidden your light from the view of people who matter. You must shine out again in full glory.'

'How can I do that? The people you speak of are wealthy, eminent men. I'm only a miserable clerk. I'm a raven among the peacocks. Ha! Ha! Ha!'

'You're no raven. You're a poet.'

'What about my colour? A jackdaw is fairer than I.' Sitting up he lit a cigarette and offered one to Gour. 'No, Madhu,' Gour declined it with a laugh. 'The thought of smoking tobacco through a twist of paper puts me off. I prefer my *albola*. Of course, there's no such thing in your house.' Then, growing serious again, he said,' Listen, Madhu, things have changed since we were boys. The men in the forefront of affairs now are not all wealthy men. They are men with visions of a better world. So much is happening all around us. Schools are being opened for the education of the masses. Widow remarriage has become a reality, thanks to Vidyasagar Moshai's courage and perseverance. The Young Bengal group is actively helping him. But not one from our batch in Hindu College has done anything to distinguish himself. Don't you think we ought to do something?'

'What can we do?'

'The least we can do is stand by Vidyasagar Moshai. Listen, Madhu. He has arranged a marriage for a young Kayastha widow. It is to take place tonight. Let's go there. He needs all the support he can get.'

'A widow remarriage!' Madhu burst out laughing. 'Am I to

waste my time in such useless things? *Chho*! Do you think me such an ordinary man, Gour?'

# Chapter XI

Nabin Kumar kept his promise to Vidyasagar by donating one thousand rupees for every widow remarriage that took place in the land. Though still a minor, Nabin was never at a loss for money. It came to him as easily as the air he breathed. His adoring mother denied him nothing. Even Bidhusekhar, though strict and calculating as a rule, allowed him to indulge this whim without a murmur. But, astute man of the world that he was, he took one precaution. He sent for Raimohan Ghoshal and ordered him to watch over the boy. Nabin was too young and trusting and might be led astray.

The news spread like wild fire and petitioners started coming to him nearly every day in twos and threes. Nabin gave each one the promised sum till Vidyasagar advised him against it. 'Many of the men who come to you are cheats and swindlers,' he warned the boy. 'Some simply make off with the money. Others go through a mock ceremony, then abandon the girl. Make proper enquiries and be sure your money is going into deserving hands before parting with it.'

One morning, Raimohan Ghoshal was ushered into Nabin Kumar's presence. He had someone with him; a square-faced, bullet-headed man of about thirty, in a soiled dhoti and vest. 'Huzoor!' Raimohan grinned from ear to ear. 'I've come to complete my fiftieth.' Nabin didn't understand. He looked questioningly at Raimohan but the companion took over. Bowing low he touched Nabin's feet and said, 'Huzoor is a great man! I'm in great trouble and only your compassion can save me.' 'English!' Raimohan snapped. 'Speak in English, you dolt.' Then, turning to Nabin he continued, 'He's a greatly reformed man, Huzoor. He speaks English.'

'Most noble sir,' the greatly reformed man began. 'Me a very humble man. I pray to your benevolence.'

'What is it you want?' Nabin asked, both puzzled and amused.

'Huzoor!' Raimohan answered for him. 'His heart is pained

by the sad lot of widows. He has vowed not to marry if it is not to a widow. His parents are giving no support. So I said to him, "I'll take you to Huzoor and he'll find a way out."'

'You wish to marry a widow? Very good. Who is the girl? And where is she?'

'Girl ready, sir,' the man replied. 'Our neighbour's daughter, sir. At Jaynagar Majilpur. My birthplace, sir!'

'Your heart will burn with grief if you hear the whole story, Huzoor,' Raimohan intervened. 'She was married at the age of three and widowed within six months. The poor girl has no memories at all of her husband.'

'It has got to stop,' Nabin muttered below his breath. 'Child marriage must be abolished first. It is more important to do that than to arrange widow remarriages.' He said aloud, 'Very well. I'll speak to Vidyasagar Moshai about it. He can go there this evening.'

'Vidyasagar Moshai is out of the city,' Dulal told his master. 'He has gone to Midnapore.'

'Then let us wait a while,' Nabin advised the duo. 'Let him come back.'

'That's not possible, Huzoor!' Raimohan brought a piece of paper out of his pocket and handed it to Nabin Kumar. 'The invitation cards have been sent out already. If the marriage is not solemnized on the due date, the girl will be ruined. Her father will have no option but to send her to Kashi.'

'But how can the marriage be arranged without Vidyasagar Moshai?'

'That is why we have come to you, Huzoor. You must take his place. We want you to have the full credit for sponsoring the fiftieth widow remarriage in the country.'

'What do you mean?'

'I've kept a close count, Huzoor. Forty-nine widows have been married so far. This will be the fiftieth. Just think, Huzoor! Your name will be in all the newspapers! And how pleased Sagar will be when he returns from Midnapore and hears of it! How he will bless you for it!'

A wave of enthusiasm swept through Nabin Kumar at these words. He was young and adulation had just started coming his way. It was a fine idea, he thought. Jubilees were the fashion these days. To think that he would stand sole sponsor at such a great event as the golden jubilee of widow remarriage in India. His heart swelled with pride and triumph. He took up the card and scanned it eagerly.

A few days later, Bidhusekhar sent for Raimohan.

'I'd like to whip you till the skin and flesh fall off your back in strips,' he said without preamble.

Raimohan did not appear to be startled in the least. A small smile hovered about his mouth as he announced insouciantly, 'Do you see skin and flesh on me, Huzoor? People tell me I am a bag of bones. You won't get any satisfaction out of whipping me.'

'I'll set a pack of hounds on you. They like bones. They'll grind yours to powder.'

'Are you keeping hounds these days, Huzoor? I had no idea they made good domestic pets! But I've heard hounds have the appetites of demons. These few poor bones of mine couldn't fill a corner of their bellies.'

'You're a cheat and a swindler! You take twenty rupees from me every month, only to stab me in the back!'

'I never stab my benefactors in the back. I sing their praises all day long.'

'I pay you to keep an eye on Chhotku and you take advantage of his youth and innocence and swindle him.'

'But, Huzoor. You said yourself that you had nothing against widow remarriage.'

'Does that mean you bring petitioners in dozens? And make Chhotku pay? Chhotku is a child. He believes whatever you tell him. But I'm up to all your tricks. How much are you pocketing per case? Don't try to lie. I can drag the truth from your belly at the point of my cane.'

'Not a paisa, Huzoor. Believe me. I swear by Ma Kali—'

'*Chup*! You rascal! What about the wedding in Barahnagar?'

'I've worked like a demon for it, Huzoor. And all for the glorification of Chhoto Huzoor! What a great event that was! Even Vidyasagar Moshai sent his blessings.'

'You cheated both of them.' Bidhusekhar turned an eye, sightless but staring balefully, on him. 'And, hardened sinner that you are, you didn't suffer a twinge of conscience. Was that a marriage? The bride is a whore's daughter. God only knows how many times you've used her for a similar purpose. The groom is a notorious drunk you keep in your own house. Tear the *poite*' from your neck, you scum of a Brahmin, and go pimping for your pleasures like the pimp you are.'

Raimohan stared at Bidhusekhar, his eyes shining with admiration. What a man he was! Even at this age, enfeebled by so many diseases and robbed of his sight, his brain was more agile and his ability to collect information sounder than many others, far younger and stronger than him. Here was a man who deserved respect. Raimohan fell to the floor and clasped his benefactor's feet with both his hands. 'You are right, Huzoor!' he cried, 'I'm a stray dog; a pariah. A whore's daughter or a scavenger's son—they are all the same to me. We share a common caste—the caste to which all the unhappy and deprived of the world belong. They are what you say. But they love each other really and truly. And I helped them to come together.'

'Let go of my feet, you rogue,' Bidhusekhar thundered. 'What right does a whore have to a formal marriage? Many such women live out their lives with the men they love. To think that you made such a mockery of the Vedic mantra. Oof! Is our religion to be held in such contempt?'

'They wanted a proper marriage, Huzoor. Not just a—'

'Get out of my sight. It makes me sick to look at you. Do you know why I don't hand you over to the police? Because, if the truth comes out, Vidyasagar Moshai will be put to shame. And Chhotku will feel hurt and humiliated. I can deal with you myself. Rub your nose on the floor right from that door to my feet here. And keep on doing it till I tell you to stop.'

Raimohan did as he was bid, five times, without a murmur. Bidhusekhar watched him closely, then fixing a stern eye on him, he said, 'If I ever catch you at your tricks again it will be the end of you. Another thing. I've had enough of this widow remarriage nonsense. I want you to divert Chhotku's attention.'

'Would you like me to stop it altogether, Huzoor?'

'You won't be able to do that—'

'Try me. I'll show you what I can do.'

Within a few days, a strange rumour spread all over the city, startling its inhabitants out of their accustomed placidity. It was being said that a famous pandit from Nadiya, by the name of

Ram Sharma, had declared the fifteenth of Kartik[8] to be 'the day of the returning dead'. He had said that a wedding had been arranged in Heaven that day and as part of the celebrations, all the men who had died in the last ten years were being sent back to the earth much in the same way as prisoners are released in the event of a great national rejoicing.

No one knew who started this rumour or where it had its genesis but by the time the fifteenth of Kartik came, it had spread to every lane and alley of the city. People could talk of nothing else. Grieving wives and mothers waited with fluttering hearts and bated breaths for their darlings to return. Only the men were being released, it was heard, not the women. This might be because no one wanted their women back and the gods were in a mood to please the denizens of the earth. Nabin had a good laugh when the news reached his ears. But Raimohan cautioned him in a whisper. 'Don't laugh, Huzoor! Your guru, Vidyasagar's reputation is at stake.'

'Why? What has Vidyasagar Moshai to do with this?'

'Don't you see? A number of men have married widows on Vidyasagar's request. If the husbands return—'

'What if they do?'

'Can a woman have two husbands? There'll be such a to do! The very foundation of our religion will crumble to dust.'

'Nonsense! How can the dead come back? They've been burned to ashes.'

'You're the only one who doubts the pandit's word. What if they do come back? What will the living husbands do then?'

'What if my aunt grows moustaches? What will my uncle do then?'

'Huzoor! You'd better take care when you move about the city. Everyone knows you to be a great champion of widow remarriage. People are in a dangerous mood. Don't be surprised if you find stones hurled at you.'

However, the fifteenth of Kartik went by like any other day. A few practical jokers crept about, pretending to have returned from the dead. Cries of joy— 'He's back! He's back!' —accompanied by frenzied blowing of conches were heard

8 15th October—15th November.

from time to time. But they invariably gave way to angry threats and cackles of shameless laughter. Not one dead husband actually came back to the world to claim his wife and embarrass his co-husband.

A few days later, Nabin Kumar fell seriously ill.

Winter was slow in coming that year. Though the month of Agrahayan wanted only a few days, the rays of the sun pelted down with all the ferocity of Bhadra.[9] Worse followed. The freak weather let loose a flood of ailments, a particularly bad type of enteric fever among them, which spread through the city with the rapidity and virulence of an epidemic. People started dying like flies in slums and tenements and even the middle classes in their houses and the rich in their mansions were afflicted. One of them was Nabin Kumar. He suffered excruciating abdominal pain for three days and three nights and vomited incessantly. Bidhusekhar sent for the best doctors of the city and even moved into the house, occupying the room adjoining Bimbabati's. He wanted to keep a round-the-clock watch on the boy's condition and it was not possible to do that from his own house. Besides, he was the only one who could console Bimbabati and give her courage and support.

On the fourth night, Nabin opened his eyes to see his child bride, Sarojini, sitting by the side of his bed. Two maids dozed uneasily, their backs to the wall, and a young doctor from the Medical College kept vigil sitting in a chair on the verandah. Nabin's throat and chest were so parched and cracked with thirst that he couldn't utter a sound. Raising his head from the pillow, he pointed to the crystal jar of candy water that stood on a little table. Sarojini started up and pouring some of it into a marble urn, held it to his lips. Nabin took a few cautious sips, then waited apprehensively for the familiar symptoms that invariably followed any passage of food and drink down his throat. But, miraculously, he didn't retch or vomit though the pain in his belly continued unabated. He drank the rest and, his throat moistened, was able to speak.

'Go to bed,' he told Sarojini. 'How much longer can you keep awake?'

---

9 15th August-15th September.

'I'm not sleepy. How do you feel now?'

'There's a terrible pain here.' He laid a hand on his stomach.

'Shall I stroke it for you?' Sarojini put out a soft little hand and began stroking Nabin's stomach. But the pain was so great that it brought little relief. Nabin groaned in his agony, then, suddenly clutching the little fingers, he said feverishly, 'Give me your word, Sarojini—'

'Yes, what is it?'

'I have a favour to ask of you. You must grant it. Will you?'

'Of course, I will.'

'Swear it. Touch me and swear—'

'Yes, here I am holding your hand.'

'That if I die you'll marry again. That you will not live your life out as a widow. Swear it. I'll know no peace, even in Heaven, if you don't.'

# Chapter XII

The crisis passed and Nabin recovered. His appetite returned in a few days and his limbs slowly regained their strength. But his head felt strangely empty and his hearing had grown extremely faint. Sounds came to him as if from a great distance and were laden with echoes, and that made him impatient and angry. He ate, drank, slept and took walks on the terrace in the evenings. But he felt that the world was passing him by and that added to his frustration. The only light in his life was Sarojini. She was by his side day and night.

One afternoon Nabin had a visitor. The midday meal over, he lay stretched out on his bed, turning the leaves of a book with an idle hand. From time to time his eyes flitted to the door through which Sarojini would come. Then, overcome with the warmth of the afternoon and the food he had eaten, he drifted away into a light slumber.

'Look who is here!' Nabin felt Sarojini's soft lips at his ear and opening his eyes saw a form standing by the door. It was that of a young girl, slim and shapely. But he couldn't see her face. It was heavily veiled. 'Who is she?' Nabin's brows came together in concentration.

'Kusum Didi!' Sarojini called out in a gay voice. 'Why don't you come forward? Don't pretend you don't know my husband.' Then, taking the newcomer by the hand, she led her to Nabin's bedside and pulled the veil away from her face. 'Look!' She cried. 'It's Kusum Didi—my sister's Miteni. Don't you remember her?' Kusum Kumari raised her large blue eyes to his and said in a voice as sweet as the sound of cascading water, 'How are you, Miten? I was told you were ill. So I came to see you.'

'He doesn't hear very well,' Sarojini hastened to inform her guest. 'The doctors say it is only for a few days. Then he'll hear better than ever before.'

'Who is the girl?' Nabin asked curiously, a blank look in his eyes. 'I don't think I've seen that face before.'

'My name is Vanajyotsna. Don't you remember me?'

'She says her name is Vanajyotsna,' Sarojini said, bringing her mouth close to her husband's ear. 'Do you recognize her now?' Nabin shook his head. Kusum's eyes filled with tears. Her mouth trembled and she turned and ran out of the room, the end of her sari trailing on the floor behind her. Sarojini ran after her and Nabin went back to his book.

Returning a while later, Sarojini said sadly, '*Chhi! Chhi!* How could you treat Kusum Didi so! She came to see you and you made her cry.' Nabin went on reading his book. He had heard nothing. Now, Sarojini came forward and, coiling her arms around her husband's neck, spoke into his ear. 'You don't remember Kusum Didi?' she asked anxiously. 'You don't—really and truly?'

'I think I've seen her somewhere. Did she come alone? Where is her husband?'

'Her husband is mad. Stark raving mad. You went to their house. Don't you remember?'

'I went to their house! When was that?' A shadow passed over Nabin's face. 'Why can't I remember? I remember nothing—nothing.'

Sarojini was frightened by the intensity in her husband's voice. She bit her lip and tried to fight back her tears. But in a few days it became obvious to everyone that Nabin's illness had robbed him of more than just his hearing. His memory was damaged. There were large areas of his life of which he had no recollection. His eyes grew blank at the mention of the Vidyotsahini Sabha or of widow remarriage. And he didn't remember people. He had even forgotten Vidyasagar.

Once again, Bidhusekhar sent for the best physicians of the city. But they were unanimous in their opinion that medication would not bring back the patient's hearing or revive his memory. Only time could do that. The boy was young and would regain his faculties. But he needed a change of scene. Bimbabati was against sending him away. She couldn't bear to part with her child but Bidhusekhar prevailed upon her. It was imperative for Chhotku's health, he told her, that he be sent away from the city to a place where the air and water were pure and invigorating.

After a few days of deliberation, it was decided to send

Nabin on a cruise of the Ganga. Winter was approaching and the river air was cold and bracing. It would put new life in the boy. And the fish, caught fresh from the river, and the vegetables and greens that grew on its banks would be excellent for his digestion. Three bajras and four pinnaces were fitted up for the purpose and staffed with serving men and maids, lathi-wielding guards and gun-toting sepoys. A couple of doctors, an allopath and a kaviraj, made up the party. Two old and trusty servants, Dibakar and Dulal, were to supervise the arrangements and see to the comfort of their young master and mistress. For Sarojini was to go with Nabin. She was not only his wife. She was his only link with the world of sound.

An auspicious day was chosen and the fleet set sail from Nimtala Ghat. As it floated on the breast of the Ganga, the cannon from the fort boomed the noon day hour as if in salutation to the great scion of the Singhas. Nabin was thrilled. He had never left the city before and the prospect of the long pleasure cruise ahead excited and delighted him.

These feelings, however, were short-lived. Within two or three days, Nabin had had his fill of river scenery and the old frustration returned. He sat staring at the water for hours, his face drawn and weary. Birds wheeled about the boat, crying as they circled, but he couldn't hear their cries. He could see the boatmen's lips move as they plied their oars but he could not hear their song. When the bajra stopped at a village *haat* and the tradesmen came running up to sell their wares, he couldn't hear what they were saying. The world of sound was lost to him and with the dimming of his memory, even the world of sight was robbed of its colour and light. Sarojini tried hard to pull him out of his apathy. 'What bird is that?' she would ask him, or, 'Why is the colour of the water different there?' But he simply shrugged and said, 'I don't know.' Sarojini tried to entertain him by putting her lips close to his ear and singing the few songs she knew. Her voice was sweet and Nabin loved music but here, on the boat, everything seemed drab and uninspiring. Even Sarojini's touch failed to evoke an answering delight.

After a month or so, Nabin became aware of the world of sound, stirring slowly, very slowly, into life. One day he noticed some faint sounds floating into his ears and saw that they matched the movements of the boatmen's lips. Then, one night, he heard the soft splash of the water outside his window. And with his newly revived hearing, he made a discovery. He realised that all the varied sounds around him made up a universal symphony, within which lay the germ of life, throbbing and pulsing with power and beauty. And with this realization came a sense of fulfilment, the like of which he had never known in all his life of pampered indulgence.

One evening in Magh, Nabin came down from the roof of the bajra. Dusk was falling and the wind over the river had turned as chilly as ice. As he entered his cabin, he saw Sarojini standing by the window, her eyes fixed on the sheet of water beyond it. 'These sweet new stirrings within me,' she sang softly. 'I know not what they are. I die of shame, dear friend. Why does my heart yearn so?' Nabin felt a shudder run through his limbs as he gazed on her. The white silk of her sari shimmered in the lamplight and her dark hair hung to her waist, as soft and billowy as a monsoon cloud. He could not see her face but he knew what was in her heart in an instant and his blood leaped up in response. Walking softly over to where she stood, he placed a hand on her back. 'Saroj!' he cried, in a voice choking with emotion. 'You—you are beautiful. I feel as if I've never seen you before.' Sarojini turned to face him. Her eyes were full of tears.'

'You're crying, Saroj!'

'I'm afraid. Terribly afraid! You say such strange things. You forget people. I'm afraid you'll forget me, too, some day.'

'Silly girl! How can I forget you?'

'But you said just now—'

'What did I say?'

'That you've never seen me before.'

'I meant it differently. I've never seen you the way I see you now. You're beautiful!'

'Swear it,' Sarojini burst into tears. 'Swear it on my head. Swear that you'll never, never forget me.'

Nabin laughed and drew her close, right to his breast. That night, seventeen-year-old Nabin took his twelve-year-old wife to him and possessed her wholly. And, next morning at dawn, he woke her up with the words,' I dreamed a strange and lovely dream. The sweetness of it lingers still. Life is so beautiful, Saroj!'

# *Chapter XIII*

The vast arm of the company's forces, that stretched from Calcutta to Peshawar, was called the Bengal Army though it had hardly any Bengalis in it. Made up of professional soldiers from every race and colour of the Indian subcontinent, it had had a recent addition. A sizeable section of the royal forces of Great Britain was now stationed in India.

Oudh had fallen without a trace of bloodshed and peace reigned supreme in the north and the east. The soldiers sat idle for the best part of the day, exchanging jokes and passing on information, the collection of which was made possible by those two wonders of wonders—the rail and the telegraph. But for all their camaraderie during parade hour and at gossip sessions, the soldiers observed the distinctions due to each caste with a fastidiousness that the new recruits from England found inscrutable and irrational. The sight of a risaldar or hawaldar knocking his head at the feet of a common jamadar when out of uniform was not an unusual one. And the reason? The jamadar was a Brahmin and the other a goala or milkman. A Hindu sepoy might make the meekest, most obedient servant to his Muslim master but he would not tolerate his touch. If so much as the latter's shadow fell on his food, he would consider it polluted and throw it away in disgust. The white soldiers had one common kitchen but innumerable kitchens had to be set up for the natives. They could not understand it and considered their tolerance of native ways a weakness in their superior officers. It would be far better, they felt, to recruit Christian soldiers from the Middle East, Malaya, China or even Latin America for the Company's army in India.

It was peace time now and the soldiers had plenty of leisure, most of which they spent in idle gossip and speculation. The air was thick with rumours. Every day someone had something new to report. In some barrack, somewhere or the other, a Muslim soldier had been served the remnants of a meal eaten by a Hindu. Chapatis made of meal with powdered beef bones mixed in it were being fed to Hindu sepoys in Kanpur. Was not the loose cover of the new cartridge—the one that had to be pulled open with the teeth—filled with a sticky grease made of beef and pork fat? Sepoys fighting in foreign lands received a commission of four rupees over and above their salaries of eight rupees a month. But it ceased the moment the war was won and the territory occupied. Was that fair on the part of the British masters? Why should the sepoy fight with all his strength, only to lose his commission the moment his efforts had borne fruit? The British bastards thought only of themselves. Even after a hundred years in the country, they didn't give a thought to their subjects. It was exactly a hundred years, was it not, since the Battle of Plassey had been fought and won? How much longer would the white race go on ruling the country? '*Arré* Bhai, have you heard what happened in the barracks at Dumduma? A low-caste lascar had poured himself a drink of water from the pitcher of a Brahmin sepoy. The infuriated Brahmin had kicked the son of a pig in the face and sent him reeling to the ground. But the lascar had raised his head and lashed out at the Brahmin. "Give over your high caste pretensions, you humbug!" he had cried. "You've been putting your teeth to the new cartridge just like the rest of us. Don't you know that makes us all equal? We're all polluted. Every son of a Hindu and a Muslim. We're all equal now."'

On one bank of the Ganga, a short distance away from Calcutta, a vast tract of forest land had been cleared and a cantonment set up by the East India Company. The villagers had never seen so many barracks all in one place before and, in consequence, started referring to it as Barrackpore. The name gained currency over the years and came to be accepted by the rulers. It even started appearing in their dispatches and memos.

One morning, towards the end of March, Sergeant Major Hewson of the 34th Infantry, stationed in Barrackpore, sat down to his chhota hazri. He had barely begun eating when the sound of a high, cracked voice shrieking some strange slogans came to his ears. The sounds seemed to come from the Parade Ground. Hewson knitted his brows in anger. He had observed a change in the mood of his sepoys in the last few days. From time to time he came upon little knots of native soldiers whispering to each other, then looking up with bland faces the moment they saw him. But what was all this noise about so early in the morning? If it was a lunatic who was screaming like this, why were the other soldiers not stopping him?

He got his answer in a few minutes. A native officer, accompanied by an orderly, came running in with news that sent Hewson dashing out of the breakfast room, his meal uneaten. Approaching the Parade Ground he saw a strange sight.

About twenty uniformed sepoys and their native officer stood together, so quiet and motionless that they seemed rooted to the ground. In front of them a musket-bearing sepoy leaped up and down as if on springs and screamed some words, over and over again, in Hindustani. Hewson's jaw tightened as he approached the group. The man with the musket saw him first and ran in the direction of the cannon. Then, from behind it, he cried the same words in the same high cracked voice. 'Brothers!' he shrieked. 'Kill the *firinghee*! Destroy the traitor enemy.'

'Who is that bugger?' Hewson thundered, his eyes on the native officer, Ishwari Pande. 'Why is he shouting?'

Ishwari Pande brought his heels together in a salute but made no answer.

'Capture him,' Hewson shouted.

The man behind the cannon was a sepoy named Mangal Pande. He looked at Hewson with red, frenzied eyes and his limbs trembled with hate. Raising his musket he took aim and fired point-blank at his white officer. Hewson dropped to the ground in a flash and the bullet whizzed over his prostrate form. His face was contorted with shock. He couldn't believe his eyes. A mad sepoy from his own regiment had tried to shoot him and twenty others had stood passively. His native officer had disregarded his express command. He rolled away in an attempt to escape the lunatic, who had raised his musket once again. This time, Mangal Pande fired at Lieutenant Baw, who had just come riding into the Parade Ground. For the second time Mangal Pande missed his target for the bullet hit the horse instead and animal and rider fell crashing to the ground. But Baw was up in a moment, sword in hand. Mangal Pande, who had also drawn his, ran towards him and struck him twice on the head. For the first time in the history of the country, a native had struck a white man. A violent clashing of swords commenced between the two Englishmen on one side and a lone native sepoy on the other. 'Brothers!' Mangal Pande shrieked between blows. 'Kill the *firinghees* before they kill you. Snatch their arms away before they disarm you.' And Hewson and Baw shouted till they were hoarse, 'Guard! Capture him. Disarm him.' But no one responded. Mangal Pande's pleas and the commands of the Englishmen went equally unheeded. At last, seeing that the whites were getting the worst of it, a native sepoy by the name of Sheikh Pant came to their rescue. Mangal Pande stepped nimbly back to his place behind the cannon. Sheikh Pant made no effort to capture him.

By this time a number of English officers had come running up to the Parade Ground. But no one dared to go near the cannon. Then old General Hearsay came galloping in and rode straight towards Mangal Pande.

'Careful, sir. He has a musket!' someone cried.

'Damn his musket!' Looking around him Hearsay cried out in a terrible voice, 'He who disobeys my command is a dead soldier! Follow me and capture the lunatic.'

There was a slight ripple now in the group that had stood all this while as motionless as stone. Submission to their white officer was in their blood and had been bred into them over generations. The sight of that indomitable figure, and the sound of his voice raised in command did something to them. They moved forward as if mesmerized. A groan, as if of pain, came from the direction of the cannon. A shot was heard and a cloud of smoke rose into the air. There was a thud as of a body falling. But it wasn't the general's. Mangal Pande had held the musket to his breast and pressed the trigger.

The twenty soldiers were disarmed in the twinkling of an eye. Mangal Pande, grievously injured but not dead, was chained to a horse and dragged across the Parade Ground till his body was cut to ribbons. But still he did not die. In course of time, the court marshal verdict was announced. Mangal Pande was to hang by the neck till he was dead. So was Ishwari Pande. The others were spared the death sentence but were imprisoned for life.

Mangal Pande died on the gallows, cursing the English with his dying breath. 'Brothers!' he cried till death drowned his voice. 'Kill the *firinghee*! Destroy the *Angrez*! Brothers! Sepoys!'

Mangal Pande died but his ghost lived on. It hovered about in the cantonment of Barrackpore, making the sepoys restless and their masters uneasy. The 34th Infantry was disbanded and sent to the north of India. And the sepoys were made to swear new oaths of allegiance. But the British had become suspicious and wary. They looked at the faces of their soldiers and found that each one bore an uncanny resemblance to that of Mangal Pande's. They saw or thought they saw the sepoys' lips curl with derision as they looked at their white masters. Many of them had seen Mangal Pande fencing swords single-handedly with two English officers and overcoming them. Was the native belief in the invincibility of the white race under assault? Were these black bastards thinking traitorous thoughts? Damn these Asiatics! Their faces were so bland; their eyes so hooded. One never knew what went on in their heads.

Doubts and fears such as these grew and could no longer be contained within the mind. People started talking. The Company's dominions had become too extensive; too unwieldy. There was no question of holding them without the help of native troops. But could natives be trusted? The name, Mangal Pande, shortened to Pande and mispronounced Pandee, became a symbol of terror to English men and women. He was dead but there might be other Pandees. Who knew if they were all Pandees?

The reaction of the native civilians of Calcutta was a mixed one. Some were shocked and frightened by the event. Others dismissed it as of little consequence. The man had either been drunk or was a lunatic. No one in his senses would do what he had done. But doubts nagged and worried. Why did the other soldiers not stop him? Why did the native officer disobey his white superior? And it was a fact that the incident had occurred exactly a hundred years after the Battle of Plassey. Was that significant in some way?

# Chapter XIV

Exactly forty-nine days after Mangal Pande's execution, a fire broke out, not in Barrackpore but in the military base at Ambala, many miles away. And it wasn't one fire. It was the beginning of a series. No sooner was one put out than another started raging. Gradually a pattern was observed. Only those camps where sepoys were using the new grease-coated cartridges, were being thus affected.

A strange restlessness took hold of the north and rumours ran rife in all its cities. One morning, a petition from the Shah of Iran, exhorting the Muslims of India to join him in a Jehad against the infidel British, was seen hanging from a wall of the Jama Masjid in Delhi. It couldn't have come from Iran. But from where had it come? General Simon Fraser had ripped it off the wall and torn it to pieces before a gaping crowd. And the very next day an identical paper was seen hanging from a wall of the Red Fort. Another titled, 'Islam under Stress', purporting to have come from Dost Mohammed of Afghanistan, appeared a few days later. He, too, would join the Shah, it was rumoured. And the Russians might strike any day. Could the British withstand the Russians? Hadn't they sustained a terrible defeat in Crimea only the other day?

At Bithoor, Nana Saheb bided his time—bitter and angry. He was the adopted son of Peshwa Baji Rao II of Poona. But the British had derecognized him, robbed him of his lands and titles and stopped his pension of eight lakh rupees a year. In the city of Lucknow, able-bodied men roamed the streets in search of employment. They were soldiers from the disbanded armies of Nawab Wajed Ali Shah. They had been soldiers for generations and the humiliations they had suffered made their hearts burn with hate and their fingers itch to hold weapons with which to avenge themselves. The Mughal Empire was gone. Akbar and Shah Jehan were gone but their blood still throbbed in the veins of their descendant, Bahadur Shah—a flame, feeble and flickering. But could it not be fanned into life? Was it impossible to restore the old glories of Islam?

Maulvi Ahmad-ul-lah went from city to city, exhorting people to rise—Hindu and Muslim alike for both religions were under assault. The time was at hand to strike at the *firinghee*. Delay could be fatal.

Another strange thing was happening. Chapatis were being circulated from village to village and from one army camp to another. He who received one would make five and pass them on. Not a line of writing went with them. They carried their own secret message.

The second incident took place in Meerut. Mangal Pande's revolt had shaken the British so badly that several army commanders had advocated a rejection of the new Enfield with its grease-coated cartridge. But their pleas went disregarded. It was a sign of weakness, their superiors felt, to revoke an order because of a silly rumour. The thing to do was to remove all doubts and suspicions by means of a practical exercise. Ninety hand-picked sepoys from the trusted 3rd Light Cavalry of Meerut would demonstrate before the others that it was perfectly possible to tear the cartridge open with the hands. There was no need to put it in the mouth.

On a hot morning in the month of May, the sepoys chosen to perform the exercise stood waiting on the Parade Ground before a huge crowd of spectators. But when the cartridges were brought to them, only five put out their hands. The others declared solemnly that they would not touch the polluted stuff. The eighty-five sepoys were courtmartialled the next day and the verdict announced to the entire camp. The majority would be shipped off to the Andamans for life. Only a few were given ten years. All eighty-five were stripped of their uniforms and made to stand, practically naked, in the blistering sun for several hours. But not one begged for mercy or admitted his guilt. When they were being led away, their feet in shackles, one of them hurled a shoe at his captors and cried out in a strangled voice, 'Go to hell, *firinghee*! May your kingdom perish!' Immediately, as if rehearsed beforehand, eighty-four other voices rose in unison and repeated the same words.

The next two days passed peacefully enough and no disturbance was reported. But on Sunday evening, when the

English officers, just returned from church with their families, were settling down to drinks in the coolness of their verandahs, mutiny broke out in Meerut cantonment. A row of flames appeared on the darkening horizon and sounds of shots rent the tranquil air. The sepoys, fully armed, came out of the camp and freeing their imprisoned fellows, opened fire on the white officers, their wives and children. Many were killed; others escaped with their lives. But by next morning, Meerut was cleared of all its *firinghees*. Not only the cantonment, the whole town passed into the hands of the sepoys.

The next thing to do was to march to Delhi; to the Red Fort, where the last relic of India's glorious past, Bahadur Shah, still held court. Bahadur Shah was eighty-two—a slight, stooping midget of a man with lacklustre eyes. Though enfeebled by his years and misfortunes, he was the obvious rallying point, and Delhi, the obvious capital of a free India. Bahadur Shah was king without a kingdom but within the Fort, he felt like one and pretended that all was as it had been. Every morning at the appointed hour, the soft tapping of his stick would be heard outside the Durbar Hall. Every morning, he sat on the Peacock throne, dim and dusty with neglect though it was, and administered, or thought he administered, justice to his subjects. He would hear accounts of rape and arson, of thefts and forcible occupations, and turning solemnly to his waiting ministers and generals, give orders for redress. '*Jo hukum, Jahanpanah*!' the official addressed would reply—though he knew as did his master, that he could do nothing. Sometimes, the king dispensed non-existing taluks and jagirs. It was a game that the old man played day in and day out and everyone joined in out of the love they held for him in their hearts. From time to time, the king broke into song in a high quavering voice, a verse perhaps from a newly composed ghazal, amidst murmurs of appreciation from his courtiers. Then, he was no longer king of Hindustan. He was Zafar the poet and the patron of poets. The famous Zauk was court poet and young Mirza Ghalib his protégé. Ghalib was writing an account of the glories of the Mughal Empire but he was poet, first and foremost. Bahadur Shah loved Ghalib's verses. One line in particular—'*Main hun apni shikast ki awaaz* (I am the sound of my own defeat)'—

haunted him and he hummed it under his breath every now and then.

One day there was great excitement in the city. An army of cavalry men was espied from a distance, riding into Shahjahanabad, the horses' hooves raising a cloud of dust. Men, women and children ran out into the streets and climbed up on roofs and terraces to get a better view. There was fear and wonder in every face. Delhi had seen so many invasions; so much plunder. There were those who hadn't forgotten Nadir Shah's hordes. Who were these soldiers? And what were their intentions?

But when the cavalcade drew near a shout of joy arose from the people, for these were their own sepoys of the 3rd Light Cavalry of Meerut. Racing ahead of them, the citizens flung open the gates of the Red Fort and the soldiers galloped up the path with joyful cries of 'Badshah Bahadur of Hindustan! The *firinghee* has been driven out. Our land is free!' Hearing the commotion, Bahadur Shah appeared on the balcony, leaning heavily on his stick. His heart quaked with a mixture of hope and trepidation. The sepoys wanted to restore the monarchy and put him back on the throne. But was it possible? The British were still here. They had cannons and ammunition that could mow down these sword-wielding youths and grind them into the dust. The soldiers looked at their king and their hearts sank. 'So old! So feeble!' they murmured. 'What kind of a leader will he make?' But they roused their flagging spirits with the thought that he was, after all, the descendant of emperors and the blood of the Great Mughals ran in his veins. His name and lineage would make a good enough rallying point.

Bahadur Shah raised a hand, commanding silence. But no one obeyed. Drunk with victory, the sepoys yelled and shouted. Some leaped off their horses' backs and started dancing in a frenzy of joy. The old man begged them to keep calm, to disperse, to send a representation. But his appeals went unheeded.

Bahadur Shah sent for Captain Douglas, the officer commanding his personal troop of security guards. But seeing his own troops join hands with the sepoys, the latter tried to escape by scaling the walls of the fort. His effort was in vain for he fell heavily, twisting his foot, and a shrieking sepoy rushed forward and cut off his head.

And from that moment the killings started. The Europeans and native Christians of the city were sought out and killed with a ruthlessness that the sepoys did not even know they possessed. Within a few hours the walled city was free of the *firinghee* and Bahadur Shah discovered, to his surprise, that he was King of Hindustan—a real king with an army at his command. He could, if he wished now, levy taxes on his subjects. Happy and enthused at this turn of events, he composed a number of verses.

It was a Saturday evening. Lights blazed from the windows of the Singha mansion of Jorasanko and carriages and palanquins thronged the gates. Nabin Kumar Singha was home again, fully recovered from his illness and with his strength and faculties regained. He had got the Vidyotsahini Sabha going from the day he stepped into the city and this evening the members were to perform *Vikramvarshi*, a play written by the great poet, Kalidas, and translated by young Nabin himself during his pleasure cruise over the Ganga. Nabin was to do the role of Raja Pururba—an ideal choice for he looked extemely handsome in his princely robes and his singing voice was sweet and clear. He had been taking riding lessons of late for in one scene he had to appear on horseback. There were a few hours to go before the performance and a dress rehearsal was in progress behind the curtain of the stage, set up in the courtyard. Pururba was in the middle of a declaration of undying love to Urvashi when Jadupati Ganguly burst in on the company of actors, crying excitedly, 'Are you in your senses, Nabin? The country is in the throes of a revolution and you waste your time play-acting?'

'A revolution!' Pururba dropped his romantic attitude and turned to face his friend. 'What do you mean, Jadupati?'

'Haven't you heard the news? The Mughals are back on the throne of Delhi. The British are being driven out in thousands.'

'What did you say, Jadupati?' Nabin leaped down from the stage and cried out in a shocked voice. 'The Mughals are back! Oh, no!'

# Chapter XV

The summer was a specially scorching one that year and Janab Latif Khan Bahadur's household was in the middle of hectic preparations. This year too as in all others, Latif Khan was to spend the hot months in Murshidabad in his ancestral mansion on the banks of the Ganga, where a sweet wind blew up from the river and orchards full of ripe mangoes and jackfruits awaited his pleasure. Latif Khan loved the good things of life.

One evening, a few days before his departure, as Latif Khan sat pulling at his albola and giving last-minute instructions to his personal servant, Mirza Khushbakht, a visitor was ushered into his presence. This was none other than our old friend, Munshi Amir Ali. But Amir Ali's face was hot and distressed and the hand that held his silver-headed cane was tightly clenched.

'I knew you to be a simple, unassuming man, Latif Saheb,' he said angrily. 'But I didn't realize you were such a big fool!'

'Why? What?' Latif cried, his fat face collapsing like a balloon. 'What have I done?'

'What have you done? You're off to Murshidabad to gorge yourself on mangoes. Have you any idea of the state the country is in?'

'The country! What have I to do with the country? I must visit my estates, musn't I, to keep them in order?'

'I didn't call you a fool for nothing,' Amir Ali sighed. 'There's a revolution going on. A revolution! Do you understand the word? The English and the Muslims are fighting each other and the Muslims are winning. The *firinghees* have been driven out of Delhi and Emperor Bahadur Shah Zafar now sits on the throne in the Red Fort—'

'The Muslims are winning! Are you saying that we will rule over India once again?'

'That's exactly what I'm saying. The British are frightened to death. They are surrendering everywhere. Haven't you heard of what happened in Barrackpore and in Meerut?'

'No, I haven't. Do tell me .'

Munshi Amir Ali placed his stick on his knees and proceeded to give an account, duly interspersed with expansions and explanations, of the events of the last few months. Latif Khan's eyes brightened as he heard the lawyer's story. He said emotionally, 'Are the sepoys coming to Calcutta? I'll go to the masjid myself as soon as it is dark and pray—'

'Prayer will not be enough, Latif Saheb. They'll need our help. And we'll have to give it.'

'Will the Hindus of the city join us?'

'The ones who've read a few pages of English won't. They'll lick the boots of the *firinghee* till their dying day. But who cares if they don't join us? Have the Hindus ever learned to hold a weapon? All they can do is stuff their stomachs and wag their tongues. We needn't worry about them.'

'But they outnumber us by thousands and hold the highest positions in the Company's government. Besides, though bad fighters, they are good schemers. What if they join the English and plot and plan against us?'

'They'll find themselves in trouble if they do. But it is highly unlikely. Many Hindus have had their fill of the British. Don't forget it was a Hindu who shot a *firinghee* in Barrackpore. Dhundu Pant Nana Saheb of Bithoor is actively supporting the rebel sepoys. After all, Hindustan is the country of Hindu and Muslim alike. The *firinghee* is our common enemy and must be driven out. And once the country is free, Bahadur Shah will be our new king. He will usher in a new era of glory for Islam.'

'*Inshallah*! When are the sepoys coming from Delhi, Munshi Saheb?'

'Why should they come? Don't we have sepoys of our own? Barrackpore is full of them, seething with anger. The tiniest spark will set them aflame. What we need now is a general under whose banner they can fight the *firinghee*.'

'Can you think of anyone?'

'The thirteenth of June is drawing near. Do you know what happened on that day a hundred years ago? The British wrested the throne of Bengal from Nawab Siraj-ud-doulah in a battle, fought on the field of Plassey near Murshidabad. Would it not be a fitting answer to that insult if the Nawab of Murshidabad were to lead the troops to victory and drive the *firinghee* out of the land?'

'That would be ideal! Ideal!'

'The proposal was sent to him. But that worthless coward refused. He's afraid to go against the British.'

'Isn't there anyone else?'

'There is one who can command the highest honour and respect. The deposed Nawab of Awadh—Wajed Ali Shah.'

Calcutta had turned into a city of desolation. Streets which used to be so crammed with people that Brahmin and scavenger had perforce to rub shoulders; where Allah's bulls chewed garlands of marigolds and pariah dogs sniffed and whined outside butcher shops, were now stark and empty. Shops and buildings which had hummed with activity till late into the night were shuttered even during the day and only dim faces, pale and ghostly, appeared at the windows. Not a soul was in sight except for the *gora* soldiers stationed at strategic spots to beat back the sepoys should they ever attack the city. Every day more soldiers were coming in from the presidencies of Madras and Bombay; from Burma and Ceylon. For Calcutta was the capital of British India. Calcutta had to be protected at all cost.

The newspapers were heavily censored as they carried articles that inflamed the public. But the consequence was disastrous for the rulers. Rumour and speculation, like the genie in the bottle of Sinbad's story, assumed enormous proportions and grew more threatening with every passing day. But rumours apart, it was true that the whites were shaking in their shoes. Many had escaped to England; others were ready to leave at a moment's notice. The British were being defeated everywhere. Their attempt to recapture Delhi had proved abortive. They had set fire to one armoury but the other, the larger one, was in the hands of the sepoys.

Ramgopal Ghosh had been ailing for some months—the consequence, no doubt, of excessive drinking. His friends had come to see him. Radhanath and Pyarichand were frequent visitors but Dakshinaranjan had come after a long time and so had Ramtanu from Krishnanagar. They were in the middle of a heated argument—Ramgopal sitting up in bed and the others in comfortable chairs surrounding him—on the subject that was on everyone's lips these days. Ramgopal supported the rebel sepoys and was convinced that the end of the British Empire was in sight.

'What are you saying, Ramgopal?' Radhanath burst out in a shocked voice. He was a stern critic of the British at other times but now the full battery of his wrath and scorn was turned on the sepoys. 'The fever has addled your brains. These fellows are no stronger than palm leaves waving in the wind. How can they bring about the collapse of the British Empire? I've travelled a lot and met all kinds of Englishmen. And I can tell you this. They're made of a different metal altogether. The sepoys have laid hands on their women and killed their children. They don't know what a terrible retribution awaits them! White men think nothing of sacrificing their lives to protect their women's honour.'

'But my dear Radhu,' Ramgopal cried. 'The British are waging an immoral war. They are choking the voice of an awakening nation. And the sepoys are fighting for the freedom of their country. Isn't there a difference? I've heard that in many places peasants have joined hands with the soldiers. This is a revolution—not a mutiny. And it is bound to succeed. Think of the war of American Independence—'

'You talk nonsense, Ramgopal. That was a war between white races. Can natives sustain a war with sahebs?'

'Radhu,' Ramgopal said with a wry smile. 'The Americans are natives in their own country. And so are the English. If I go to England I'll be the saheb among natives.'

'But Ramgopal,' Pyarichand intervened. 'Have you considered the implications of British defeat? Do you visualize any good coming out of it? What sort of ruler will old Bahadur Shah make? And his sons are even worse from what I hear. Weak and depraved and sunk in the pleasures of the flesh. Perpetuating their dynasty will be terribly retrogressive for a country that has just started receiving the benefits of western civilization. Consider the reigns of the later Mughals. Was not that a Dark Age with poverty, illiteracy, superstition, injustice and oppression all but tearing the country into shreds? What have we ever received from Muslim rule? Did a single ruler open schools and colleges for the welfare of his subjects? As for the nawabs, can one good word be said for them? The country was sunk in a cesspool of vice and ignorance and would have continued to do so if the British hadn't come and saved us. You may not agree with me, Ramgopal, but I consider the British our saviours.'

'A revolution ushers in a new age,' Ramgopal replied solemnly. 'This is an age of science, of advancement, of knowledge. When freedom comes to us our country will move towards the light. There is no question of going back to the days of the Muslims.'

'Ramgopal!' Radhanath gave a bellow of laughter. 'Even the ideas you mouth so glibly have been gleaned from English books.'

'Knowledge is universal. No race can claim a book as its personal property.'

'But the sepoys are not book-learned,' Pyarichand said. 'Neither, is Dhundu Pant. If they win they'll take us back to the Middle Ages.'

'Win! *Chhaa*!' Radhanath gave a snort of contempt. 'How you talk!'

'If saddens me,' Ramgopal said, clicking his tongue gently, 'that, though disciples of the great Derozio, you have no yearning for freedom in your hearts. How can a man be happy under alien rule? Barring a few Englishmen like Hare and Bethune, the others look upon us as slaves—don't they?

'But we Hindus were slaves even under the Mughals,' Pyarichand pointed out. 'If we have to have a foot on our necks, isn't it better to have one that is clean and fair?'

'Bhai Pyari.' Dakshinaranjan spoke for the first time that evening. 'You are forgetting a very important aspect of British rule. Before the British came, India was a flourishing country with industries and markets of her own. The story is quite different now. Her industries are being crushed and her raw materials taken out and sold in European markets. English cloth is like sacking compared to the fine textiles of Dhaka and Farashdanga. But we are being compelled to use the former. Is not this exploitation of the worst kind? The foot of the Englishman may be clean and fair but it is twenty times heavier than that of the Muslim. The Mughals were bad rulers. I'm not denying that. But they lived here and considered this their country. They didn't scrape the country's treasures together and ship them off to Persia or Arabia. And they didn't turn planter and rob the peasant of his land. Look at what the indigo planters are doing! They are snatching the food from the mouths of the peasants by forcing them to grow indigo instead of rice. The Mughals were hot-headed; chauvinistic. But they were not hypocrites. The British mouth high-sounding words like justice and fair play for all. But, in effect, they are very deftly and skilfully starving the nation to a point of no resistance.'

'You're right, Dakshinaranjan,' Ramgopal said.

'I agree with what you've just said.' Ramtanu spoke for the first time. 'But I'll still say I would like the English to stay on for a little longer. The country is not yet ready for self-rule.'

'If the sepoys come to Calcutta,' Ramgopal said excitedly, 'I shall go out and meet them personally and wish them luck.'

'The sepoys will chop you into little pieces,' Pyarichand teased.

'Why do you say that? The sepoys haven't turned on their own people—as far as I know.'

'They hate the Bengali Babu. They are attacking everyone wearing western clothes. You'd better stop going out in pantaloons.' After a pause Pyarichand continued, 'I went to see Vidyasagar Moshai a couple of days ago. He looked very grim. I think he's afraid—'

'Afraid of what? He doesn't wear pantaloons.'

'No. But he was the man behind the Widow Remarriage Act and the sepoys dislike him for it. They consider the ban on sati and the Widow Remarriage Act to be cutting at the roots of the Hindu religion. And they believe that we Bengalis are instigating the British. I hear Vidyasagar is thinking of requesting the government to repeal the Act.'

'Impossible!' Ramgopal cried. 'That must never be. It is a humane act and should not be repealed at any cost. These rumours are being floated by some unworthy sepoys—blind and rooted in tradition. I have not a doubt of it!'

'So you see, Ramgopal. The moment the British go these humane acts will go with them. We'll be back where we were.'

'We're disciples of Derozio,' Ramgopal said, glancing towards Dakshinaranjan. 'We won't let the country retrogress. We'll protest. Have we no voice?'

'We must fight for our rights,' Dakshinaranjan replied. 'We must try to win our freedom. But at this moment, when the atmosphere is so volatile, wisdom lies in maintaining a neutral stance. Don't go against the English so openly, Ramgopal!'

# Chapter XVI

One afternoon Munshi Amir Ali brought a couple of strangers to Janab Abdul Latif's house in Khidirpur. One was a young, good-looking man in snowy leggings and a handsome sherwani. On his head sat the tall peaked cap called alam pasand. A rope of pearls hung from his neck. His name was Agha Ali Hassan Khan and his manner and mien marked him out to be what he actually was—an aristocrat from Lucknow. The other was a middle-aged man in a dhoti, green banian and fez. He was rough and ready in speech and manner and his name was Muhammed Garib-ul-lah.

It was obvious from the hushed voices in which the men spoke and the way the doors and windows were bolted from within that a secret conference was going on in the room. Agha Ali Hassan Khan had brought a message from the sepoys. In order to drive the *firinghee* from the country it was imperative that Calcutta be taken. The sepoys wanted to know what the natives of the city were doing about it.

'Don't expect anything from the Hindu Bengali,' Amir Ali said with an edge to his voice. 'They're boot-licking traitors and have reduced the country to half a *tanka's* worth. Forget about them. It is we Muslims who must take the fight into our own hands. We need aristocrats like Abdul Latif on our side.'

'I'm ready,' Abdul Latif said without a moment's hesitation. 'I don't mind giving up all my worldly goods if it helps to reinstate the Muslim in his rightful position.'

'From where I come,' Agha Ali said, 'Hindus and Muslims are fighting shoulder to shoulder. Lucknow has many Hindu jagirdars with private armies. These armies have joined the sepoys. We've put a ban on cow-slaughter to please the Hindus.'

'I don't know about Lucknow,' Amir Ali said with a touch of impatience. 'But the Hindus of this city are a set of scoundrels.'

Garib-ul-lah gave a little cough and said, 'May I speak a word?'

'Certainly, certainly.' Amir Ali introduced him to the others. 'This is Janab Garib-ul-lah from Dhaka. He's a disciple of Dudu Mian—the Ferrazi. He speaks a rustic dialect which will be of great use to us for the fight must start from our villages.'

'You must have heard,' Garib-ul-lah said in his quaint dialect, 'that the English whoresons have arrested Dudu Mian and are keeping him in a Calcutta jail. We'll get him out if we have to break the jail down. We have twenty-five thousand *lathyals* ready for the job.' Munshi Amir Ali translated the speech for the benefit of Agha Ali, adding, 'The Muslims of Bengal have revolted twice in recent years—once against their local zamindars and once against the rulers. These were peasants from Nadiya and Barasat and they fought under the banner of the famous Wahabi leader, Titu Mir, disciple of Sayyad Ahmed. You've heard of Sayyad Ahmed, haven't you, Agha Saheb?'

'He's a Sunni,' was Agha Ali's cryptic comment.

'The Muslims of Bengal are mostly Sunni,' Amir Ali said drily. 'Please don't confuse the issue with talk of Shia and Sunni. Dudu Mian's disciples are ready to fight the British. Am I right, Garib-ul-lah Saheb?'

Garib-ul-lah nodded. 'Dudu Mian has written a letter to his son-in-law. He says that if we could only get him out of prison he'll have the English whoresons out of the country in a week. By the way, you said just now that you wished to exclude the Hindus. I don't agree. There are many Hindus among the Ferrazis. We Ferrazis believe that the poor are all equally victimized. Why should we leave the Hindus out? The zamindar, be he Hindu or Muslim, is our oppressor and it is him we have to fight.'

Janab Abdul Latif stared at Garib-ul-lah in amazement. What sort of talk was this? Amir Ali's face was flushed with embarrassment as he said quickly, 'Certainly, certainly. We don't mind using a few Hindu *lathyals* if they are on our side. But we mustn't lose sight of the real issue. We must drive the British out and establish Mughal rule in the land.'

'We don't want Mughal rule in Lucknow,' Agha Ali said. 'The Mughals are Sunni. In Avadh we follow the

Shia-isna-asiri—the only true religion of Islam. The Mughals may rule Delhi if they will but we won't let them come to Avadh.'

Amir Ali was really alarmed by now. 'Don't say that, Agha Saheb,' he begged. 'The Mughals are Muslim even if they are Sunni and their triumph will be the triumph of Islam! Besides, your own nawab, Wajed Ali Shah never made any distinction between the two sects. Let's not talk about Shia and Sunni. Tell us about the state of affairs in Lucknow.'

'Lucknow is free from *firinghee* rule. Rebel sepoys from Allahabad and Faizabad have driven the British out and put Nawab Wajed Ali Shah's ten-year-old son, Birjis Qadru, on the throne.'

'A ten-year-old on the throne!' Abdul Latif exclaimed.

'Well. It had to be someone from the Shahi dynasty. The boy's mother, Begum Hazrat Mahal, is Regent.'

'But a mere boy! And a woman!' Amir Ali exclaimed. 'How long do they hope to sustain their government? And who is leading the sepoys?'

'That's where the trouble lies. The sepoys refuse to cooperate. Ahmed-ul-lah, leader of the rebels from Faizabad, presides over a durbar as if he is nawab of the realm. He flouts Begum Hazrat Mahal's authority and issues orders of his own. That's why I am here in Calcutta. The rebellion started in Suba Bengal. But it died out almost immediately afterwards. It has to be reactivated. The sepoys of Bengal must rise and fight the British. And Nawab Wajed Ali Shah must lead them to victory. Then he can return in glory to his own kingdom.'

'That idea has already occurred to me, Janab,' Amir Ali said drily. 'Latif Saheb and I went to see him but—'

'He didn't agree?'

'We couldn't get to him. His courtiers take care to keep him out of reach. It is a terrible thing to say, Agha Saheb, but the Nawab flouts the tenets of Islam by indulging in wine and women, music and dance all day long. *Tobah*! *Tobah*! *Chhiya*! *Chhiya*! '

'We must get him out of it,' Agha Ali said urgently. 'We must go to him at once, Munshi Saheb.'

'But how? The company's soldiers stand guard at the gate. You'll be caught the moment you try to enter. The British encourage him in his vices because it keeps him out of mischief, in their opinion. Besides, the sooner he exhausts his wealth the better it is for them.'

'Our Badshah's wealth is inexhaustible.'

'You call Wajed Ali Shah "Badshah". But for us there is only one Badshah—Bahadur Shah Zafar of Hindustan. Anyway, the point, Agha Saheb, is this. We can only reach the Nawab if we go disguised as singing and dancing girls. It may be possible for you—you have a pretty face and manner—but how can it be possible for me?'

'Don't waste time on trivial jokes, Munshi Saheb!' Agha Ali exclaimed. 'There's no dearth of singing and dancing girls in the city of Calcutta. I've heard that the courtesans of Calcutta beat the houris of Paradise. We can hire a few and go with them as their musician and drummer.'

'Can an aristocrat like you sustain such a role?'

'I can do anything to drive out the British.'

The next two days were spent in scouring the city to find women of their choice. Finally, a brothel was discovered near the tomb of Maulah Ali, which housed some of the most exquisitely beautiful and accomplished prostitutes of the city. A deal was struck with the mistress, Chand Bibi, and two girls, whose beauty and charm were calculated to make heads reel, were picked out. The two men now set about assuming their disguises. They donned loose pyjamas and cheap, shiny silk banians. Red kerchiefs waved from their necks and caps, gay with tawdry gold embroidery sat on their heads at jaunty angles. Their mouths were full of betel and bright red spit ran down their unshaven chins. Munshi Amir Ali hadn't touched liquor in his life but his eyes were red and drowsy with imagined fumes as he shuffled along with his companions to where the white soldiers stood on guard. Clutching his sarangi with one hand, he held out the other. It had a letter in it—a faked invitation from the Nawab. The English soldiers didn't even glance at it. They crinkled their eyes to get a better view of the two females who followed—their faces covered with fine gauze veils, embroidered in gold and silver. Then, smiling and nudging one another, they waved their hands and said, 'Go.'

Crossing the deuri, Agha Ali and Amir Ali breathed a sigh of relief. The worst was over. There was nothing to fear now.

But there were so many wings, courts and gardens within that they looked around them in dismay. From where would they begin looking for the Nawab? On making enquiries they found (though not before doling out substantial bribes) that he was in Surses Manzil—a mansion bright with lights and surrounded by beautiful gardens. Once inside Surses Manzil, the next step was to find out in which room he was. Once again bribes were sought and given to two servants. With the third, Agha Ali lost his temper. Clutching him by the throat, he waved a knife in his face and said, 'I'll tear the heart out of your body if you don't tell me where he is.' The servant's eyes rolled in terror as he pointed to a room. Agha Ali released him and turning to the dancing girls, said, 'Your work is done. You may go now—wherever you like. But don't dare breathe a word about tonight to anyone.'

Agha Ali slipped the knife back into his cummerbund, yanked the kerchief off his neck and moved towards the room indicated. Then, anticipating resistance, he pushed the door open. He got a shock, for inside the Nawab knelt on his prayer carpet along with five of his courtiers. It was the hour between dusk and twilight and Wajed Ali Shah was offering namaz. Agha Ali waited at the door, head bowed, cap in hand. When the Nawab had risen to his feet, he came forward five steps and knelt and touched his master's jewel-studded *nagras* in salutation. 'Long live our Badshah!' he cried in Persian. 'Your humble slave, Agha Ali Hassan Khan, is in your presence. You remember me, do you not, Huzoor?'

The Nawab was dressed in a long, loose robe of fine white silk, through which a vest of pale blue satin glimmered like moonlight. Beads of perspiration dotted his brow. His eyes, large and sombre, were fixed on Agha Ali's face. Munshi Amir Ali had, in the excitement of the moment, forgotten to doff his cap and kerchief. He did so quickly and bowed, over and over again, in humble apology.

'Be seated,' the Nawab said at last.

'I have something to say to you in private, Huzoor,' Agha Ali said agitatedly. But the Nawab neither moved nor nodded. Neither did he ask anyone to leave. Agha Ali glared at the Nawab's companions. They recognized him, perhaps, and went out of the room.

'You must remember me, Huzoor-e-alam!' Agha Ali said. 'I'm Masiha-ud-din's nephew; Masiha-ud-din, whom you sent with a petition to England. Huzoor-e-alam has seen me many a time.'

The Nawab made no answer. Agha Ali went on to tell him about the changed situation in Lucknow. Birjis Qadru was on the throne. Coins were being minted in his name and his subjects were paying him taxes. Everyone was happy now. Everyone wanted him back. The Muslims of Bengal were preparing to rise against the British. All they needed was a call from Huzoor-e-alam. Under his leadership victory would surely be theirs. Then Amir Ali took up the tale and told him about the Wahabis and Ferrazis and their efforts to vanquish the *firinghee*. The Nawab heard the two men out but didn't say a word. His face was immobile. Not a muscle twitched.

'Say something, Huzoor,' Agha Ali begged at last.

The Nawab rose and went into the next room. There, turning his face to a whitewashed wall, he burst into a fit of loud weeping. Amir Ali and Agha Ali were shocked. They stared at one another in amazement. The Nawab clung to the wall and wept till his chest was damp with falling tears. At last he turned his face and fixing his gaze on the courtiers and servants who had crowded at the door, murmured huskily, '*Khwab tha jo kuchh bhi dekha, jo suna afsana tha* (What I saw was a dream; what I heard was a tale).' Then, sending for his scribe he dictated a note. Addressing the Company Bahadur, he declared that the rebels were instigating him against the British. He had no intention of joining them. He hadn't fought the British when they deposed him. He wasn't going to fight them now. But he needed protection. The letter ended with a plea to house him in the fort.

Amir Ali and Agha Ali were apprehended instantly and sent to military prison. A few days later, Nawab Wajed Ali Shah was moved to Fort William. Among the personal effects that came with him were seventeen pillows. The Nawab had pillows even for the ears.

Lying in bed with his pillows around him, Wajed Ali Shah breathed a sigh of relief. He had nothing to worry about now. He could go back to his pleasures. But he would compose a poem first—a paean of praise to the lofty ideals and humanitarian principles of Lord Canning—governor-general of India.

## *Chapter XVII*

Heere Bulbul's desire to go on a pilgrimage grew in intensity day by day. Irate and impatient with Raimohan's dithering and laziness, she decided to make the arrangements herself. The first thing she did was to go to Goopi the goldsmith and sell some of her jewellery, of which, thanks to the babus of Calcutta, she had a goodly store. The next was to hire a bajra, fit it up with the essentials of a long journey and get hold of some boatmen, servants and guards. She would go to Puri, to the temple of Jagannath. Jagannath was the saviour of lost souls. Would he not save her, sinner though she was?

Raimohan was appalled when he heard of what she had done. This was not the time for travel, he reasoned with her. The sepoys had risen against the rulers and there was chaos in the country. Killings, arson and rape were being reported every day. But Heeremoni turned a deaf ear to his pleas. She was going on a pilgrimage, she said, and God would protect her. At last, worn down by her resistance, Raimohan agreed. But he wouldn't let her go alone. He insisted on accompanying her.

On the eve of their departure, Heeremoni said to Raimohan, 'I don't know why you are tagging along after me. I'm telling you quite clearly. I may not return—ever. If God so wills it, I'll spend the rest of my life at his feet.'

'Silly girl,' Raimohan smiled indulgently. 'Who do you think you are? Chaitanya Mahaprabhu? We'll go to Puri, visit the temple, bathe in the sea, enjoy ourselves and come home—'

'What! You're going on a pilgrimage to enjoy yourself! Don't dare utter those foul words again or I'll pull your tongue out.'

'*Arré! Arré*! Why do you lose your temper? I don't propose to enjoy myself with anyone else, my Heeremoni. Only you and I . . . Besides, the shastras exhort us to visit places of worship. There's no merit in making one's home in them.'

'I refuse to listen to a word you say. If I don't feel like coming back to this garbage dump, I won't. You're free to do as you wish.'

'Can you bear to part with me? Won't your heart be wrung—?'

'Ha, ha, ha!' A peal of ugly laughter issued from Heeremoni's pretty lips. 'My limbs burn at the sight of you, you cadaver! Sitting on my chest like a demon and eating and drinking on my money. A whore's keep! *Thoo*! *Thoo*!' and Heeremoni spat viciously in Raimohan's direction.

'Honey! Honey! Honey!' Raimohan sang, skipping nimbly aside. 'What rivers of honey flow from your lips, my sweet. What streams of pearls and rubies! A little more. Just a little more. Let me feast my eyes and ears—'

'You've cut off your ears and nose, you shameless bastard. All you have left are those dead fish eyes of yours. Oh! if I could only dig my nails in and claw them out!'

Raimohan swayed and sang:

Oh! My life! I'm robbed of life.
My nose is gone; my ears are gone.
What little's left is yours, my life.
I die of shame! My life is gone.

'Do you remember the song, Heeremoni? Do sing a few lines—'

'*Chup*! Remember what I said. Don't blame me if I don't return.'

'Oh, my sweet Heeremoni! Can I have the heart to blame you? But why do you say, "I?" Say, "we." You know I can't bear to live away from you.'

'Very well, then. Don't change your mind.'

There was an excellent overland route to Puri, Raja Sukhomoy Roy having built a road from Ulubere to Cuttack for the convenience of pilgrims. But Heere and Raimohan preferred the boat to the palki. They had been on pleasure cruises on the Ganga before and enjoyed the freedom and luxury that a big bajra afforded. Raimohan got over his initial reluctance quickly enough and even started looking forward to the journey. This was as good as going with a babu! It was even better for he would be the babu. He would wear finely pleated dhotis and yellow silk banians. He would stick little balls of cotton, dabbed with attar of roses, behind his ears and his eyes would be bright with antimony. And he would lie on a silk carpet on the roof of the bajra, with Heere by his side. Heere, in midnight blue silk, spangled all over with silver stars, her fair forehead marked with sandal paste! The moon would shower her beams upon them and the air would be heavy with the scent of jasmine from the garlands around their necks. He would pour wine from the crystal decanter and hold the goblet to her lips. And Heere would sing for him, her mellifluous voice rippling like a cascade over three octaves. And springing up from the cushions, he would cry, '*Meri jaan*! *Meri jaan*!' and fling gold coins at her feet.

But Raimohan's dream remained a dream. Heeremoni did not allow the smallest particle of it to take shape. She wore cheap duré saris and neglected even to braid and put up her hair. Far from singing herself, she snapped at Raimohan if he ventured to hum a tune. And one day she seized the brandy bottle from his hand and flung it into the river. Raimohan fixed his eyes on her—not in anger but in sorrow. Heere! His Heere! He remembered a time not so long ago when two or three sips of wine were enough to bring out the best in her. Her voice gained in strength and clarity; her limbs in power and grace. Eyes closed he could see her, even now, swaying her hips as she sang, the jug of wine poised aloft on her head. Her lips swelled with ecstasy and her eyes flashed like twin knives of Baghdad. At some point or other in her song, she would fling her odhna away and her magnificent bosom would be exposed to view.

This was only a few years ago. But now Heeremoni was so changed he hardly knew her. She sat silent, sunk in gloom all day, and when she spoke, if at all, it was of Jagannath. 'Won't Jagannath give my son back to me?' she asked Raimohan over and over again. 'If I slit my breast and offer its blood on a gold bel leaf? Not even then? Won't my heart's darling, my Chandu, ever come back to me?' 'Of course, he will,' Raimohan consoled her but in his heart of hearts, he doubted it. They had spent the last two and a half years looking for Chandranath but all efforts had drawn a blank. Raimohan was convinced that Chandranath had left the city. Who knew where his destiny had taken him!

Two nights before they were to reach Cuttack, a gang of dacoits came silently across the water in fast moving boats and attacked the bajra. The armed guards were killed in their sleep. Of the people who manned the ship, many lost their lives and several jumped into the river in a desperate bid to save themselves. Rudely awoken from their sleep, Heere and Raimohan started up to find three or four men at the door of their chamber—their faces gleaming dark and ugly like those of demons in the light of the torches they carried in their hands. One of them hit out at Raimohan and he fell across the bed in a dead faint. Heere screamed—a long-drawn-out piercing scream that shattered the silence of the night.

Raimohan must have had the proverbial nine lives of the cat for he survived the blow on his head. He recovered consciousness the next morning to see the bajra, battered and broken, floating aimlessly on the breast of the Mahanadi river. The deck was littered with the dead and the dying. Two men sat at the stern in a state of shock. There was no sign of Heeremoni.

Raimohan's head felt like a stone and his neck and shoulders were caked with dried blood. His mouth felt foul with stale vomit. But he managed to crawl up to the two men and say, 'Try and take the boat to the shore, boys, or we'll all sicken and die.' And then he fainted once again.

Heere Bulbul was found by some woodcutters two days later in a dense jungle on the bank of the Mahanadi. There was not a stitch of clothing on her body and it was torn and bleeding, as if mauled by wild beasts. Except that there were no fierce animals in the jungle—so the woodcutters said. Raimohan heard the news and made his way to the village to which she had been brought. A wave of relief passed through him when he saw her. 'You're alive, Heere!' he cried, his voice choking with emotion. 'Thank God! Thank God!' But Heere sat immobile, eyes glazed and expressionless. Raimohan tried over and over again. 'What had to happen has happened,' he cried. 'Forget it. You're alive. Thank God for that.' But Heere neither spoke nor moved.

Then, Raimohan could bear it no longer. Cradling her broken body in his arms, he burst into tears. 'Speak, Heere,' he cried. 'Look at me. *O ré*, all is not lost because a few animals have clawed and torn your golden limbs. Forget them. Forget everything. I'm here by your side. I'll take you on fifty pilgrimages.' But there was not the slightest quiver of response from Heeremoni.

Raimohan decided to return to Calcutta and hired a palki for the purpose. But taking Heeremoni along was like carrying a sack of potatoes. She went unresisting, but with no awareness of self or surroundings. People stared at her as Raimohan dragged her in and out of rest houses, her eyes stark and staring and her limbs as heavy as stone. Sometimes, her sari slipped from her shoulder and her breasts—two vast, shimmering moons—were open to view.

On the fifth day at dawn, something curious happened. Raimohan was fast asleep when a loud shriek assailed his ears. He started up in alarm to see Heeremoni sitting on the bed in the old familiar pose—an elbow on one knee, a hand at her ear. And she was singing in a voice that seemed sweeter and more penetrating than ever. Raimohan's heart gave a terrific leap and tears rushed to his eyes. He leaned forward and patted her thigh. 'Sing, Heere! Sing another song!' he encouraged. Docile as a child, Heere obeyed. Unable to contain himself, Raimohan clasped her to his breast and cried, 'Thank God! Thank God! You've got your voice back. Now I have nothing to fear—' Instantly, a change came over Heeremoni. Her body stiffened and two angry flames sprang up in her eyes. Her voice became harsh and metallic like a cockatoo's voice. 'Who are you?' she cried shrilly. 'How dare you touch me, son of a whore? Dog turd! Bastard! Get out of my sight.' And rising to her feet, she kicked him violently on the stomach. Raimohan fell off the bed under the impact of the blow and Heeremoni leaped on top of him. Sitting on his chest she pulled and clawed at his face and hair. Raimohan tried to stop her; to hold her flailing arms, then failing, he yelled for the palki-bearers and with their help bound her hands and feet.

Heere had sworn that she wouldn't return to the city. She didn't. Raimohan had sworn he would bring her back and he did. It was indeed one of life's little ironies.

From that day onwards, Heeremoni assumed a dual personality. She would remain silent and withdrawn for days. Raimohan would coax and cajole her; try to make her eat and speak but she turned away from him, her face as lifeless and colourless as if carved out of marble. Then, suddenly, she would burst into song, her voice richer and more resonant than ever. At such times Raimohan dared not go near her for at some point or other in her song, her second personality would assert itself. Then her face would grow dark and ugly, her eyes roll in frenzy and her voice become harsh and grating. And all the force of her rage and hate would be turned on Raimohan. She would go for him with whatever weapon she could find—a pestle, a fishknife or even her nails and teeth. At such times she would roam all over the house, pick up whatever food she could find and cram it into her mouth. And drooling and dribbling, she would laugh loud and long like a maniac. Raimohan was at his wit's end. He tried one doctor after another but no one could do anything. There was also a serious dearth of money. All the money and jewels they had taken with them had been stolen by the pirates. He didn't know if Heere had anything else. There was no way of knowing either.

One evening, Raimohan left Heere in Harachandra's charge and came to Goopi's shop. You could hardly call it a shop now. It was a seven-roomed mansion with iron doors and walls lined with Venetian mirrors. And where Goopi used to sit, huddled over his lamp, were rows of craftsmen, working at his command. Goopi himself leaned against piles of cushions, one hand on the cash box and another holding the tube of his *albola*. No one called Goopi a goldsmith these days. He was Sri Gopimohan Sarkar—Jeweller. And the more wealth he accumulated, the more amorous he became, changing mistresses every six months. It was even rumoured that he had lured his current favourite, Rangi, from Kaliprasad Datta's clutches. Raimohan was struck dumb at first but he quickly recovered his old composure. '*Ki ré*, Goopi!' he called in the sneering tone he always used for him. 'Your tummy's grown so fat—it'll burst like a bomb one of these days.' Goopi made a slight movement but did not rise. 'Ghoshal Moshai!' he said formally. 'Be pleased to come in and take a seat. It is many years since you have graced this poor man's shop with the dust of your feet.'

'Poor man! ' Raimohan echoed, looking around him with interest. 'If you are poor, Raja Digambar Mitra and Nabin Singha are paupers. Well, how are things?'

'As well as they can be in the circumstances. Business is

slack; very slack. The sahebs and mems have either run away or hidden themselves. And the big men of the city are so scared of the sepoys, not a single wedding has been arranged this year.'

'Tchu! Tchu! Tchu! ' Raimohan made soothing noises at Goopi. 'Don't worry, Goopi. Old times are coming back. The *firinghees* have broken the backs of the sepoys and are now busy grinding them to powder. To get to the point. I've come to you for something—'

'Yes. What is it?'

'I'm in a spot of trouble. I need a hundred rupees.'

'Of course, of course. My money is yours for the asking. You know that.' Then, seeing that Raimohan made no move on his own, he added, 'Can I see what you have brought?'

'You must lend me the money.'

Goopi looked fat and foolish but he was as cunning as a fox. He also kept himself very well informed. 'Your—ahem!' he coughed delicately. 'Heere Bulbul's turned lunatic—from what I hear. She had a lot of jewels. Sets and sets of diamonds and pearls. Why don't you get hold of some before others do?'

'We'll talk about that later,' Raimohan said quietly. 'Give me the money first.'

'You're doing business with someone else, are you not?' Goopi said suddenly, his lips pulled back from his teeth in a suggestion of a snarl. 'You pass on your jewels to Jagu Sarkar and come to me empty-handed for a loan. Is this fair, Ghoshal Moshai?'

'I don't have any jewels to pass on to anybody,' Raimohan said wearily. 'Give me the money. I'll return it. I swear I will.'

Goopi looked full into Raimohan's face. It was loose and slack and the once bright eyes, flashing with wit and intelligence, were sunk deep in their sockets. The man was old and a wreck and would drop down dead any moment. Goopi had no scruples about discarding people like him. 'Impossible!' he said quietly. 'I can't lend so much money. Take five. It is only for old times sake that I give it.' Raimohan's heart swelled with powerful feelings. What a base ingrate Goopi was! He had forgotten that it was he, Raimohan, who had taken him around to great men's houses. If it weren't for Raimohan, Goopi would still be sitting in his old shack, sweating by his smoking lamp. But he controlled himself. Anger would do him no good—not now, when Goopi was rich and powerful and he, old and decrepit and at his mercy.

After a lot of coaxing and pleading, Goopi agreed to raise the amount to ten. Handing the coins to Raimohan, he said in a tight voice, 'I must ask you to leave, now, Ghoshal Moshai. I've got to count the cash and wind up for the day. It is late enough already.' Raimohan had a sudden urge to fling the coins in Goopi's face. But it lasted only a few seconds. He remembered that ten rupees would feed them for a fortnight. Besides, he dicovered to his dismay, that he was too old and weary for an act of violence. Swallowing his hurt and humiliation, he walked out of the shop, cursing and muttering to himself.

A few days later, Heere Bulbul's madness entered a third phase. For the first time since the assault on her, she beat her breast and wept loud and long. So piteous was her weeping that passers-by stopped in their tracks and paused by her window, wondering what went on. She didn't rave any more. Neither did she sing. She kept talking of old times and sobbing her heart out. Raimohan wept with her but he felt relieved. The fumes of rage and hate that had poisoned her brain were being washed away by her tears. Now it would grow whole again; healthy again.

But within three days, all was over with Heeremoni. Her body was discovered floating in the well that stood in her own courtyard. Whether it was an accident or whether she had jumped in on purpose, no one could say.

The early dusk of a winter afternoon was setting in when Raimohan and Harachandra carried the body to the *samshan* ghat with the help of a few boys of the neighbourhood. Both pyres were burning and they had to wait. To while away the time, Harachandra and the boys went off to a shack close by, where a few puffs of ganja could be had on payment. Raimohan waited alone, his hand on Heere's breast. He hadn't wept a single tear. If he felt anything at all—it was relief. There was nothing more for him to worry about. He was free.

Suddenly, a group of wild young men burst in from the shadows, demanding the clothes of the deceased and the bedstead on which she had been brought. It was all theirs,they claimed, as was the money for the wood. Raimohan gazed, trembling, at the face of the leader. A fierce black beard and a red rag wound around his head rendered it unrecognizable but he knew the voice. Leaping to his feet he grasped the boy's wrist and called out in a strangled voice, 'Chandu!'

'Heh! Heh! Heh!' The boy laughed a sneering laugh. 'What have you done, you old Brahmin? You've touched a chandal! Go home, eat dung and purify yourself—'

'Look, Chandu. It's your mother.' Raimohan turned the sheet with a quick movement of his hand and Heeremoni's face was exposed to view. In the light of the flaming pyres on either side, Chandu saw it clearly. The eyes were open and stared upwards into his own. Chandu was shocked into silence for a moment. He looked around him wildly—at Raimohan; at the other chandals crowding around. Suddenly, in a high, clear voice and with perfect enunciation he recited a stanza from a poem of John Keats—

To sorrow
I bade good morrow
And thought to leave her far behind.
But cheerly cheerly
She loves me dearly
She is so constant to me and so kind . . .

Then, with a swift movement, he wrenched his wrist free of Raimohan's grasp and dashed off in the opposite direction.

'Wait, Chandu, wait,' Raimohan called after him, his voice cracked and quavering. 'You are her son. You must perform her last rites. She has suffered much in this life. She deserves some peace in the next. For her soul's sake, Chandu—'

But Chandu turned a deaf ear. He ran, swift as an arrow, away from Raimohan; away from the gang and away from the *samshan* ghat.

# Chapter XVIII

If there be on Earth a Paradise of bliss
It is this; it is this; it is this.

These lines etched in Persian, on the walls of the Diwan-e-Khas were rudely mocked that morning of 20 September when English soldiers came marching into it on roughshod feet and went on a rampage. Searching the fort and finding it empty of humans, they took out their anger on the exquisite panels and statuary of the Diwan-e-Khas. The dome cracked under the impact of their guns and pieces of carving, richly enamelled and sparkling with gems, fell to the ground. The Union Jack was flown in the courtyard and a prayer of thanksgiving offered to Jesus the Merciful for leading the Christian to victory against the pagan infidel.

Bahadur Shah and his family had abandoned the fort months earlier and had taken up residence in the palace adjoining the tomb of his ancestor, Humayun, only four miles away from Shahjahanabad. Some of his counsellors advised him to flee to Lucknow and join the sepoys; others advocated a plea for forgiveness. But Bahadur Shah did neither. Dazed and broken he bided his time, waiting for the inevitable.

It came in the shape of General Hodson and a small band of fifty soldiers. Hodson had strict instructions to capture the Emperor alive. So, though his fingers itched for action, he could do nothing but send a message of reconciliation. After three hours of waiting in the hot sun, during which the Emperor's soldiers could easily have overcome his paltry band of fifty, a palanquin was seen emerging from the palace. A small, frail, wizened old man lay within it, his hair and beard and face of an equally snowy white hue. A tiny, shrivelled hand gripped the tube of an *albola*. He spoke not a word.

Bahadur Shah was kept a prisoner in a tiny room of the Red Fort on an allowance of two annas a day. But still the king said nothing. From time to time he murmured a few lines of poetry:

*'Hindustaniyon mein kuchh dost, kuchh shagird, kuchh aziz, kuchh masuk woh sab khakh mein mil gaye . . .* (My friends, my pupils, my relations and all the people I loved in Hindustan have turned to dust and ashes).' Not content with keeping the Emperor prisoner, Hodson stripped his sons of their fine robes and jewels and shot them like dogs in the streets, leaving the carcasses to rot as a warning to the people of the city. The heads were placed on silver platters and presented to their nonagenarian father. Next, he gave orders to the soldiers to loot and kill at their pleasure. Delhi, the fine old city of seven kingdoms, became a living hell. The streets were littered with corpses and howls of woe and despair rent the air. There were so many rapes that a whole new generation of bastards was born within a year—a hybrid race, neither white nor black but seeking slavish identification with the ruling race. Governor-General Lord Canning tried his best to stop the madness but could do nothing. He was a man of justice and principle and sought to defuse the situation by pleas and threats. But they only added fuel to the fire and earned him the nickname of Clemency Canning. Killings, arson and rape continued till long after the sepoy mutiny was crushed and the rajas subdued and humiliated.

This vindictiveness shocked the educated elite of Calcutta. They had refrained from joining the sepoys, believing British rule to be just and fair and good for the country. But they found to their dismay that they were being treated on par with the rebels. Was it for this that they had endured the mockery and contempt of the northerners? Had submitted to being called parasites and bootlickers? A slave acknowledges his master's right to cuff and kick him into submission if he commits an act of revolt. But what if he finds himself victimized in return for loyal service and absolute subservience? Bengalis were frightened at first, then unhappy and resentful, they decided to do something about it. Many of them had enough English at their command to make appeals in the newspapers. They pleaded for mercy, assuring the rulers that they had supported them against the traitorous sepoys through the unfortunate war that had devastated the country. Stories appeared in the papers of fleeing Englishwomen finding refuge in the homes of ordinary peasants and being looked after as tenderly as mothers and sisters. Bengali papers followed suit for many Englishmen knew Bengali. The jewel in the crown among the poets of Bengal, Ishwar Chandra Gupta, wrote a hilarious article on the fate of the thousands of widows of North India whose husbands had been erstwhile sepoys. 'Oh! If they only had another Ishwar Chandra Vidyasagar at hand,' he wrote, 'they could have eaten and drunk and slept with new husbands as merry as could be.' He even wrote a poem in which he compared the sepoys to ants who grow wings, only to dash against the light and turn to ashes; the Rani of Jhansi to a broken-beaked she-crow and Nana Saheb to a husking pedal. The Maharaja of Bardhaman called a meeting of his peers in which a letter of congratulation was composed and sent to Lord Canning. The epistle bore two thousand five hundred signatures, Raja Radhakanta Deb's among them.

A similar meeting was held in the mansion of Jorasanko. The English papers had been clamouring for the removal of Bengalis from important positions; for taking away the right to keep armed guards from wealthy natives. Something had to be done about it. The intellectuals of the city—Jadupati Ganguly, Nabin Kumar Singha, Kishorichand Mitra, Krishna Kamal Bhattacharya among others—decided to send a message of goodwill to the governor-general. But even as they composed the letter of thanksgiving for the victory of the rulers, their faces were pained and anxious and they spoke little to one another. The letter was passed around and signatures obtained. When Nabin's turn came he said quietly, 'I sign this because you ask me to but my heart tells me otherwise.' Fixing his eyes on Jadupati, he continued, 'I've condemned the sepoys but I tell you frankly, brother, during those months when Delhi was rid of the *firinghee*, I experienced a sense of freedom for the first time in my life. The British are an alien race. Living under their rule is like carrying a mountain on one's chest, is it not?'

'I told you that right in the beginning but you wouldn't listen,' Jadupati cried.

'It was Harish. He influenced me—'

Harish Mukherjee, editor ot the *Hindu Patriot*, looked crestfallen. 'I apologize, Nabin,' he said. 'I didn't know the British race then as I do now. We may flatter them and plead with them all we can but it will avail us nothing. A realization has just dawned on me. The eyes of history will view the sepoy war in a very different light from what we do today. Mark my words. Things are going to change very soon, within the span of our own lives perhaps. Another thing. I take an oath today in your presence. I'll never write another word of praise for the English as long as I live. If I do, I'm lower than the lowest whore in the city.' Then, digging his hand into the pocket of his kurta, he brought out a brandy bottle and poured the liquid fire down his throat.

Harish Mukherjee was a self-made man. He had received no support from childhood upwards and had, in consequence, learned to do without it. He hardly knew his own father for his mother was one of three wives that her *kulin* husband had taken and she had never known the privilege of making a home with him. Like many other *kulin* girls she was permanently lodged in her father's house, much to the annoyance of her brothers who, being *kulins*, too, had wives and children of their own to fend for. His uncles having made it clear that they could not pay for his education, Harish applied for a free ship in a local school and being a brilliant pupil was granted it readily. But it lasted only a few years. As soon as he reached the age of fourteen, he was told by his uncles that it was time he found a job and assumed charge of his own family. His brother, though older than him, was a worthless fellow and had complicated matters even further by taking a wife, which, being a *kulin*, he could do quite easily.

But where was Harish to find a job? He was only fourteen and hadn't even completed his schooling. He decided to sit outside the post office and offer to fill money order forms and write letters and applications in return for a small tip. People came to him for his handwriting was good and his English flawless. After several years of this his talents were discovered by an auctioneer, who offered him the post of a secretary in his office at a salary of ten rupees a month. Harish accepted the offer but his heart swelled with pain and indignation. The whole world, it seemed to him, had conspired against him; had forced him into the role of a petty clerk. He vowed he would overcome his fate. He would educate himself; he would master the English language and then money and prestige would come to him.

Every evening, after the day's work was done, Harish went to the public library and read whatever he could lay his hands on—newspapers and journals in particular. He read a few issues of the *Edinburgh Chronicle* over and over again, even learning it by rote for this, he was convinced, was the best method of learning English. Once he had mastered the language sufficiently, he started reading books on history, economics and philosophy. And the more he read the more fascinated he was by the written word. Soon it became such a passion with him that he couldn't resist the temptation of buying books even when there wasn't enough rice at home to feed them all. Ten rupees was really too little! He decided to ask the auctioneer for a raise. But not only was his request turned down, he was abused and humiliated at which, being of a fiery temperament, Harish threw up his job and returned to his seat outside the post office, pen and ink before him.

Life became harder than ever. He never had enough to eat. But his passion for learning grew and grew as did his hatred for the society which kept him enslaved, overworked and underfed. He vowed he would take revenge and waited eagerly for his day to come.

One day his eyes fell on an advertisement in the newspaper. A clerk's post was vacant at the military auditor general's office and the selection was to be made on the basis of a written examination. The salary was good—twenty-five rupees a month. Harish sat for it, stood first and got the job. With more money coming in, a certain amount of stability came into his life. But domestic peace was denied him. His first wife had died within a few months of the marriage and at his mother's insistence he had taken another. But mother-in-law and daughter-in-law fought incessantly and Harish found himself caught in the crossfire. Being a good son he didn't have the heart to reprimand his mother and he could not, in justice, blame his wife. Unable to resolve his family problems he started withdrawing from them and living in a world of his own.

Judging that the time had come to put his knowledge of English to the test, Harish wrote some articles and sent them to the *Hindu Intelligentsia.* To his surprise they were all accepted.

But this recognition was not enough for him. The editor, Kaliprasad Ghosh, was a well known English scholar but he was, after all, a native. Emboldened by his success, Harish sent an article to the famous paper, *Englishman*. The article was not only accepted and published, it even got a mention in the editorial. The editor, Mr Cobb Harry, wondered who the native writer was whose English was as good as that of a thoroughbred Englishman's. Harish Mukherjee's heart swelled with triumph. He had arrived at last. No one dared look down on him any more.

Harish had devoured English books and journals from the time he learned to read. As a result, he had gleaned a great deal of information about the history of the British and their social and political ideas. And now he discovered something that, admirer of the race though he was, disturbed him not a little. This was that while the British valued independence above all things for themselves, they had no scruples about denying it to other races. They instilled a passion for freedom in their own children and taught them to guard it closely but regarded self-respect and patriotism as vices in the people they ruled. Harish decided to use his pen with a purpose. He would rouse the sleeping rabble who were his countrymen to an awareness of their subjugated status. Fate played into his hands. He was offered the sole editorship of a paper called *Hindu Patriot*. Now, Harish came into his own. His pen became like a living flame, seeming to sear the paper it wrote on.

Harish was now at the top of the social ladder. He received a salary of four hundred rupees in the same office in which he would have been grateful to work for twenty-five. And the *Hindu Patriot* grew more and more popular every day. The governor-general, Lord Canning, himself sent for copies in advance for they were sold out the minute they hit the stalls. Harish was now a member of the British India Association, in which only the richest and the most famous Indians of the land had the privilege of enrolling themselves. He also developed a new passion. He started studying law.

One evening Nabin Kumar came to see Harish at the office of the *Hindu Patriot* and was appalled by what he saw. Harish sat huddled over his papers before a rickety table, on which a lamp burned with a dull, low flame. Beside it stood a brandy bottle and glass. 'Give me a few minutes, Nabin,' Harish said, his pen racing over the paper as if it had a life and volition of its own. Sheet after sheet he filled with his neat pearly hand, pausing now and then to take a deep draught from the brandy bottle.

'Nabin,' he said, looking up suddenly. 'I'm surely the worst host in the world. I haven't offered you anything. You'll have some brandy? Let me fetch another glass.'

'No, friend,' Nabin said. 'I don't drink. And you shouldn't either. Only last month you had such a bad attack of—'

'Don't,' Harish interrupted, waving his left hand impatiently. 'Don't lecture me like the prim old aunt you are. If you don't want to drink—that's your business. Leave mine to me.' Pushing his papers away, he rose to his feet. 'Enough for today,' he said. 'Come, let's go.'

'Where?' Nabin stared at his friend. 'Are you going home?'

'Home?' Harish echoed. 'Do I have one? Must I go back to that cauldron of boiling oil?' A little smile flickered on his lips and his eyes narrowed with liquor fumes. 'I'm going to Rambagan. There's a young woman there—newly arrived. Wonderful stuff! Her name is Harimati. You're a big boy now. Let me take you.'

*'Chhi'* Nabin pulled his hand away from his friend's grasp. 'Forgive me.'

'What!' Harish exclaimed in amazement. 'What did you say? Don't you know that men of genius must have plenty of sex or their brains rust and decay? Come with me. Give it a try. It won't kill you.'

'No,' Nabin replied, turning away.

# Chapter XIX

Bimbabati lay on her bed, weeping into her pillow. Chhotku was away in Bardhaman for Sarojini's sister was to be wed and after his father-in-law's death he was the head of the family. The house was empty and still. A great wave of loneliness swept over Bimbabati. She couldn't understand it. Chhotku was the best of sons and Sarojini the best of daughters-in-law. Why, then, did she feel so lost? So unhappy?

'Bimba!'

Bimbabati started up. Bidhusekhar stood at the door. Bimba wiped her eyes, then pulling the veil over her head came forward to where he stood and, kneeling at his feet touched her head to the floor.

'May you live long.' Bidhusekhar touched her head in blessing. 'May you be happy!' Then, peering into her face, he added, 'Why do you weep, Bimba?'

'I don't know.' Bimbabati shook her head as fresh tears poured down her cheeks. Bidhusekhar limped into the room, tapping his stick before him. Seating himself on the bed, he said, 'Have you ever seen me weep, Bimba? I've believed in battle—not in tears. But of late, I don't know why it is, I catch myself quite often with tears in my eyes. I must be turning senile.'

'Is your health better?'

'Much better. I feel so well that I'm afraid it is the last flicker before the flame goes out. How are you, Bimba?'

'I'm well'

'Then why do you weep? You have nothing to fear while I live. I'll look after you and Chhotku. You know, don't you, that I could have had all this'—his hand swept across the room—'if I had wanted to. Everything that Ramkamal possessed could have been mine. This very bed—' Suddenly, Bidhusekhar started laughing, peal after peal of excited laughter. Bimbabati stared at him in amazement. She had never heard him laugh like that. 'This is another odd thing that is happening to me,'

Bidhusekhar said, checking himself. 'I find myself laughing for no reason—' He sat for a few minutes, sunk in thought, and then said, 'I've something to say to you, Bimba. That is why I'm here. Chhotku is becoming a problem.'

'Why? What has he done?'

'He's sold seven bighas of land. Prime land in Kolutola, right in the heart of the city. Land there is more valuable than gold. Do you know why he did it?'

'No. He has said nothing to me.'

'He wanted to snub me. He wanted to show the world that he was his own master and could do without my guidance or counsel. Ganga offended me too and I punished him. I couldn't forgive him. He dared to raise lustful eyes to my widowed daughter. But Chhotku! How can I punish Chhotku? He's the light of my eyes!'

'Chhotku has never done anything like that.'

'But he considers me his enemy. He humiliates me and hurts my feelings. How can I bear it? And with whom can I share my sorrow but you?' Tears poured down Bidhusekhar's face. He wiped them away and said, 'Do you know why I laughed just now? See here.' And he took a document out of his pocket and held it out to Bimbabati. It was the sale deed of the seven bighas of land in Kolutola. 'I bought it back,' he said. 'Funny, isn't it?' And he laughed again—a high-pitched cackle— 'Heh! Heh! Heh!'

'What would we do without you?' Bimba said in utter humility. 'You must continue to look after my son. You musn't let any harm come to him.'

'I'll do that. But I ask something in return.'

'What is it?'

'I'm like the flame that bursts into life at the very end. I'm consumed with lust for your golden body, Bimba! I must make you my own once again. I want you. I must have you.'

Bimbabati's face turned as white as chalk. She tried to speak but couldn't utter a sound. She threw an agonized glance at the door.

'I have strange desires these days. Strange fancies. I imagine myself stretched out on Ramkamal's bed, with you by my side, my handmaiden, ready to serve me at my command.'

'No!'

'Bimba!'

'Have pity on me. You promised—'

'No one keeps promises these days. It is a dissolute age and I'll be as dissolute as I choose. Come, Bimba. Come to me and lay your head on my breast.'

'Forgive me.' Bimbabati burst into loud frightened sobs. 'The old Bimba is no more. She's dead.'

Bidhusekhar's jaw tightened. 'Do what you are told,' he said gravely. 'Come and sit here by my side. But bolt the door first. Go.'

# Chapter XX

Calcutta was agog with excitement over *Vikramvarshi*—translated from Sanskrit to Bengali by young Nabin Kumar Singha and staged by the Vidyotsahini Sabha. It was a brilliant play and so well performed that even the sahebs and mems of the city came to see it. The English papers were fulsome in its praise. The prominent citizens of Calcutta saw that this was, indeed, a novel way of attracting the attention of the rulers. In consequence, the staging of Bengali plays became the fashion—a fashion that spread like wildfire through the length and breadth of the city.

Raja Pratap Chandra Singha of Paikpara and his brother, Ishwar Chandra Singha, two aristocrats of Calcutta, had acquired the villa of Belgachhia, belonging to the late Dwarkanath Thakur, and established a centre for vocal and instrumental music that went by the name of Our Own Club. The success of *Vikramvarshi* kindled the imagination of its members(some of the most distinguished men of the city) and set it flaring in a new direction. They decided to stage a play and invite some prominent Europeans to see it. Since none of them had enough knowledge of Bengali or Sanskrit to translate a play, they chose one that was there already—the famous playwright, Ramnarayan Tarkalankar's *Ratnavali*. Rehearsals commenced and went on with great enthusiasm till one of the members voiced a doubt. Would the sahebs understand anything of the play? *Vikramvarshi* had gone down well on the strength of its sets and costumes. But would *Ratnavali*? A heated discussion followed during which Ramgopal Ghosh came up with an idea. How would it be if an English translation of the play was prepared and distributed to the foreign section of the audience well in advance? The sahebs would then have no diffficulty in following the twists and turns of the plot. The idea was a good one and acceptable to all but the question was—who had enough knowledge of English to take up this formidable task? Ramgopal Ghosh was the obvious choice but he declined it firmly. He had enough English, he said, to translate a few fiery pamphlets but he couldn't dream of touching a poetic drama. It would be an act of the most unbridled arrogance. Gourdas Basak came up with another name. 'I have a friend,' he said, 'who can do this quite easily. I could speak to him if you wish me to.'

'Who is this gentleman?' Ishwar Chandra asked.

'His name is Madhusudan Datta. His father was the famous lawyer, Rajnarayan Datta. You may have heard of him.'

'Yes, yes, I recollect. Madhusudan was a brilliant student. He converted to Christianity and took on a new name—Michael or something like that—did he not?'

'That is the man.'

'I've heard of him, too,' Ramgopal Ghosh said. 'He stayed in Kishori's house for a while. But he, I've heard, is a pukka saheb. What does he know of Bengali?'

'He knows it well enough. Conversing in English is a kind of style with him. Besides, he has been studying Sanskrit of late. He'll have no difficulty in understanding the play.'

'Let's try him out,' Pratap Chandra said. 'Why don't you sound him, Gour Bhaya? Bring him to one of our rehearsals. Then we can all meet him.'

'Et tu, Brute,' Madhu drawled on seeing Gour. 'Even you've forgotten me, Gour! You don't give a damn if I'm dead or alive.'

'What about you?' Gour laughed. 'Have you ever cared to find out if I'm dead or alive?'

'How can I? I'm a poor clerk. Who'll pay my cab fare? And don't forget, my dear Gour, I'm a Christian now. I can't walk into your house as and when I please.'

'You've come often enough in the past. My mother has fed you with her own hands. Has your being a Christian ever stood in the way?'

'Ah! Your mother's cooking! It's pure nectar. My tongue is like a piece of leather from the beef and pork I eat all day long. My soul yearns for her cauliflower curry. I ate it one day with hot *roti*. It tasted so divine that the flavour still lingers in my mouth.'

'Why don't you come then?'

'The trouble, dear Gour, is this. I don't drink water. I drink only beer. And I can't do that in your house.'

'You don't drink any water? Why?'

'You want me to die of cholera? All the water of this city is contaminated.'

'How are the rest of us alive then?'

'You're used to it. Besides, I haven't been well lately. Last month I had a terrible attack of abdominal pain. *Baap ré*! I felt as if my liver, spleen and kidneys were being torn to pieces.'

'You should have seen a doctor. I know a kaviraj who has an excellent potion for abdominal pain. Shall I—?'

'Kaviraj! How horrible! They're quacks. Don't forget I belong to the race of rulers. I can't be so uncivilized.'

'Suit yourself. I see nothing civilized about nurturing diseases and—'

'Forget it. Tell me about yourself. Where have you been hiding, like the fig flower you are, all these days?'

'I've acquired a new passion. I'm acting in a play with the Rajas of Paikpara.'

'What play? I heard the other day that some group or other was putting up *Merchant of Venice*.'

'Our play is in Bengali.'

'Bengali! Don't call it a play then. Call it a *jatra*. What's wrong with you? Why are you getting mixed up in a *jatra*?'

'It isn't a *jatra*. We'll have a proper stage, curtain, footlights, proscenium—all in European style. Like you've seen in Sans Souci. And what's more—we need your help. You must translate the play for us into English.'

'You're crazy.'

'Why? Isn't your English good enough for the sahebs?'

'Of course it is. But that is not the point. Why should I waste my time on something so trivial?'

'The play is a good one. I've brought you a copy. Take a look at it, at least.'

Madhusudan took the book and read the first few lines. With a grimace of distaste, he handed it back. 'Prose,' he said, shrugging his shoulders. 'I can't stand Bengali prose, whether it is Pyarichand Mitra's or Vidyasagar's. Their compositions are all equally insipid. My stomach can't digest it. Forgive me, Gour. I beseech you—'

Gour rose to his feet. 'I'll take my leave then, Madhu,' he said. 'I had hoped you would agree. The Rajas are offering an honorarium of five hundred rupees.'

'What!' Madhu exclaimed. 'What did you say? How much?'

'Five hundred.'

'Wait a minute. Wait a minute. That makes a big difference. Five hundred rupees! That's four months' salary. And I can finish this damn thing in four days. Money is particularly tight just now. My creditors are tearing me to pieces.'

'Then, you will do it?'

'Like hell I will. But what if I don't know the meaning of all the words?'

'I'll help you all I can. Why don't you come to our rehearsal one day? When you hear the actors speaking their lines, you'll find them easier to understand.'

Madhusudan sprang to his feet and clasped Gour in his arms. Kissing him on both cheeks with loud smacking sounds he exclaimed, 'Hooray! Hooray! Henrietta, dear. What great news! I'm earning five hundred rupees. I'll buy you a French gown.' Turning to Gour, he said sombrely, 'You're a true friend, Gour. You're always there when I need you. Five hundred rupees! And, like a fool, I was refusing it. The work is wretched, of course.' He continued, a hint of arrogance creeping back into his voice, 'But great writers have done hack-writing before. I needn't be ashamed. Besides,' and his voice changed again, became soft, humble, 'I'm not a great writer. I'm not a writer at all. I'm nothing but a rake. Am I not, Gour?'

Madhusudan came to the rehearsal the very next day and regularly after that. And he was appalled at the amount of money the Rajas were spending. What a waste it was! The play was as weak as weak could be. Its sentiments were trite and shallow; its language dull and arid. He expressed his opinion energetically and often, adding, 'If I wrote a play it would be a thousand times better than this one.' One day, Gour took him up. 'Why don't you, Madhu?' he said with a mocking smile. 'If anyone can do it, you can. Only—I don't know if your Bengali can stand the test.'

Madhusudan made no answer but the suggestion seemed more attractive to him every time he thought of it. Eventually, he set himself in earnest to the task. Selecting an episode from the Mahabharat—the story of Sharmistha and Devyani—he started writing a play. He showed the first few pages to Gour, who was so charmed by what he read that he passed them on to Prasanna Kumar Thakur's adopted son, Jatindramohan, for his comments. Jatindramohan was a very fine man and a great scholar, with a genuine love of literature. He found the language so forceful and dynamic, the concepts so new and so orginal that he declared he had read nothing like it before. Jatindramohan's first meeting with Madhusudan in Belgachhia led to many others. Jatindramohan invited him often to his own pleasure villa, Emerald Bower, and soon the aquaintance deepened into a friendship. Madhusudan's play thrived under Jatindramohan's patronage and the members of Our Own Club decided to stage it after *Ratnavali*.

One day, during a discussion of Bengali poetry, Madhusudan declared that good, strong, vigorous poetry could be written in Bengali but only in blank verse. Jatindramohan disagreed. Bengali, in his opinion, was too weak a language to stand the strain of blank verse. Madhusudan, arrogant as ever, retorted, 'It can be done but, naturally, not by everybody. Only I can do it.' And within days of this declaration, he embarked on his second venture—an epic poem in blank verse by the name of *Tilottama Sambhava*.

The scheduled date for the performance of *Ratnavali* drew near. Among those who eagerly awaited it was Madhusudan. His turn was about to come. After *Ratnavali*, Our Own Club would begin rehearsing *Sharmistha*.

On the day of the dress rehearsal, Madhu came dressed in his best clothes. He had taken care not to drink too much. He looked and felt on top of the world. But after a while he noticed that the Rajas of Paikpara were paying him much less attention than usual; that they were almost totally preoccupied with someone else—a man of about forty, with a shaven crown, wearing a coarse dhoti and uduni of homespun and slippers on his feet.

'Who is that man, Gour?' he asked his friend.

'Don't you know him?' Gour asked in a startled voice. 'He is Vidyasagar Moshai. The famous—'

'Oh! The saviour of widows! Well, well. What a handsome

man! Adonis would hang his head in shame. I tell you truly, Gour. I thought a palki-bearer had wandered in by mistake—'

'You haven't seen his eyes. They burn brighter and fiercer than a lion's. And he is a lion at heart. The lion of Birsingha! Come, I'll introduce you to him.'

With these words, Gour dragged the protesting Madhusudan over to where Vidyasagar sat. 'This is my friend, Michael Madhusudan Datta,' he said. 'He's a poet and a playwright.' Madhusudan put out his hand as was his custom but Vidyasagar did not take it. Fixing his eyes on the other's face, he brought his own together and touching them to his brow said, '*Namaskar*.'

# *Chapter XXI*

The success of *Vikramvarshi* had a strange effect on Nabin Kumar. He did not, as everyone had anticipated, translate more plays. In fact, he turned away from the theatre altogether. Too many people were caught up in it. He had no intention of following the herd. He had to do something different. He decided to write prose narratives out of his own experience and imagination. No more translating someone else's books. He would write his own, each one better than the last, and the world would resound with his praises. In the matter of writing, as in everything else, Nabin was not the slow, diligent, painstaking type. His pen flew over the paper once he set his hand to it and a book a week was an easy target. And being haughty and impatient by nature, he couldn't dream of waiting outside publishers' offices. He decided to buy a printing press and publish his books himself.

But the glory of being a writer was short-lived. He got bored with adulation and realized that it came to him not because his work was outstanding but because he was Nabin Kumar Singha. It was true that the newspapers, both English and Bengali, had praised his style, but somehow, even that had left him cold. The only person who brought a breath of fresh air into his life was Harish. Nabin left a copy of every book of his with Harish and begged him for his comments, but Harish never found the time to even glance through them. 'Brother Nabin,' he said. 'My head is weighed down with real problems. I neither have the time nor, forgive me, the patience to read the unrealistic yarns you writers delight in spinning.'

One day, Nabin forced him to listen to an extract from his latest book. But, after a few pages, Harish covered up his ears with a muttered ejaculation. 'Stop! Stop!' he cried. 'My head is beginning to reel! What kind of language is this? Why don't you write the way you speak. Plain, simple, no-nonsense Bengali?' Then, pausing to catch his breath, he added, 'Do you know why I've never tried my hand at Bengali? Because it's a hybrid language—a bastard of Sanskrit. And it stinks of morality. English has no such pretensions.'

'Friend!' Nabin sounded crestfallen. 'Why do others praise my work then?'

'Don't you understand?' Harish laughed. 'You're a tender young lamb and you're covered with a golden fleece. Toadies swarm around you and eat *luchi* and sweetmeats at your expense. Naturally, they'll sing your praises. Now I'm a poor Brahmin who's never lived off anybody. I can afford to speak the truth. Your Bengali is like that of a pandit's from a village *tol*. I can't stomach it.'

'But even Vidyasagar Moshai praised—'

'I respect Vidyasagar,' Harish interrupted, bringing his hands together in reverence. 'I don't wish to comment on the quality of his writing. But I'll tell you what I've found worth reading in Bengali lately. Pyaribabu's *Alale'r Ghare'r Dulal*, for which he assumed the pseudonym, Tekchand Thakur, is a brilliant piece of writing. Simple, lucid prose which anyone can understand.'

As the days went by, Nabin found himself more and more attracted to Harish Mukherjee. Harish was a strange character, a compound of contradictions, as passionate and fiery as he was gentle and tender. When enraged, he could be as foul-mouthed as the lowest gutter wench. But the language he wrote rang like a bell for clarity and sweetness. He was a practising Brahmo and preached the doctrine at the Brahmo Mandir at Bhabanipur with unfailing regularity. Yet, every evening he drank himself into a stupor and spent most of his nights in some low class brothel. He loved his countrymen but there was no one who cursed them more bitterly than he.

Nabin couldn't make him out. Once he said to him, 'Friend! You're a devout Brahmo. You attend every prayer meeting and listen to the hymns, your eyes closed in reverence. Yet you drink so much!'

'What does drink have to do with revering the Lord? I see no contradiction in the two.'

'I've seen a lot of Brahmos and I can say this for them. Though a greedy lot—as much for attention as for sweetmeats—they live clean, pure lives on the whole. They don't touch liquor.'

'Rammohan Roy used to drink. And Ramgopal Ghosh and Ramtanu Lahiri—'

'But you go to bad women!'

'There's no such thing as a bad woman, you epitome of morality! A woman is a gem that sparkles all the brighter for use. Do you know that the great philosophers of Greece and Rome spent their evenings in houses of ill repute and discussed their ideas with bad women, as you call them? Can there be anything more aesthetic in the world than a woman—young, healthy, beautiful and free?'

Another trait in Harish Mukherjee's character that puzzled Nabin Kumar was his weakness for that old scoundrel, Raimohan Ghoshal. Raimohan came to the office of the *Hindu Patriot* every evening, looking a ghost of his former self. His dhoti and uduni were stained and shabby and hung from his emaciated frame, and his eyes, filmed over and opaque, looked out of a face that seemed more dead than alive. Though he would be sodden with liquor already, he was always greedy for more. '*Koi*, Mukhujjay Moshai!' he would call out the instant he arrived. 'Where's the golden brew? My throat and chest are as dry as dust.' Harish would leave his work, however important it was, and taking the bottle out of the closet, hand it over to him.

Raimohan was changed in other ways too. He didn't cringe before Nabin or flatter him any more. He sat drinking in silence, ignoring him for the most part, and if he spoke at all, it was with an acid edge to his voice. 'Chhoto Babu,' he would shake his head at Nabin at such times. 'You've brought your family prestige so low—you've mixed it in the dust. What's the use of amassing wealth if you don't spend it? If you don't nurture a few toadies and keep a few mistresses? What a babu your father, Ramkamal Singha, was! So large-hearted! So generous! Wine would flow like water at his gatherings and drunks and bottles would roll about on the floor in dozens.' Nabin never took him up; only looked at him with hate and scorn in his eyes. Raimohan would turn to Harish. 'O Mukhujjay Moshai!' he would say with a great cackle of laughter. 'Send the suckling infant home to his mother and let us make our way to our place of pilgrimage. Shall we go to Kamli tonight? She's selling her wares all over again. I'm going there.' Harish would laugh with him and put away his papers.

One day Harish was very rude to Nabin. He had been in a foul mood all day; had cut out every line he had written and drunk himself into a state of acute irritation. When, Raimohan came and demanded the bottle, Harish handed it over to him as usual. Raimohan was stone-drunk already and he proceeded to sing in a high, cracked voice as he drank. He made such a disgusting spectacle that Nabin lost his temper and cried out to Harish, 'How you can stand that man is beyond my understanding. Why don't you throw him out?' Harish was suddenly, violently angry. 'Why should I throw him out?' he roared, his eyes blazing with anger. 'What do you know of him, you pampered spawn of a feudal system that should have died out centuries ago? I understand his suffering because I suffer too like him. You scorn people who drink. You look upon yourself as an epitome of virtue! But what virtue can you claim when you've never put yourself to the test? If you have courage, taste first and abstain afterwards.'

Nabin was so shocked by this outburst that he could not speak a word. Rising to his feet he said gravely, 'I'm going.'

'Very well. Good night,' pat came the answer.

Nabin's face grew pale. He had never been treated in such a cavalier fashion in his life. Anger surged through him, making his blood boil. How dare Harish and Raimohan humiliate him like this? His first impulse was to send for his *lathyals* and have the two men beaten to a pulp. Then, sobering a little, he realized that that was not the way to prove himself. He had to beat these two at their own game. 'Friend,' he addressed Harish. 'Is drinking really a test of courage and greatness? If so—give me some.' And he stretched out his hand. Harish filled a glass instantly and put it in his hand. Nabin poured the liquid fire down his throat in one draught and said, 'So! What now?'

'One glassful is just about enough to get the taste of milk out of your mouth,' Raimohan cackled in high glee. 'True, true.' Harish gave a great burst of laughter. 'Have another.' And, pouring out another drink, he handed it over with the words, 'This is wonderful stuff, newly arrived from France. My tongue feels like sandpaper from the brandy I drink all day. This is called cognac. Each drop is as life-giving as a pint of blood.'

Nabin snatched the bottle from Harish's hand and put it to his mouth. Harish and Raimohan exchanged glances. Raimohan winked and his sunken cheeks contorted themselves in a malicious smile. 'Friend,' Harish cried, laughing. 'I was initiated into this divine passion by the great Ramgopal Ghosh. Yours today by one as brilliant and famous as myself is no less glorious. This day will go down as a red-letter day in your life.'

Nabin poured the cognac down his throat but could not keep it there. A violent fit of hiccups seized him. Tears gushed out of his eyes as he vomited all over the floor.

Nabin opened his eyes painfully and wondered where he was. The ceiling was not moulded like the ones at home. It was criss-crossed with wooden beams and the windows had green shutters. One of them was open and Nabin caught a glimpse of blue sky and floating clouds. He couldn't see the sky from his own bedchamber—the room he shared with Sarojini.

The sound of the cannon booming the seventh hour startled him. He had never heard it quite so loud before. The fort must be near at hand, he thought. He sat up with a quick movement, the bed of wooden boards on which he had slept creaking in protest, and glanced around the room. Raimohan lay sleeping on the floor, his long body turned on one side, his bony knees pulled up to his chest. Another man lay on his back in one corner of the room. Saliva dripped from his mouth on to the sheets. Large blue flies buzzed angrily above his face and swarmed thick on the plate of half-eaten kebabs that lay beside him. An odhna of cheap red silk, covered with tinsel, trailed on the floor. Nabin rubbed his eyes in astonishment. Had he spent the night here? In this sordid room, with these low-class people? Why? What had happened to him? His head felt soft and fuzzy and he couldn't remember. He swung his legs to the floor and stood up gingerly. His memory came back in flashes. He had drunk a whole bottle of wine. And then . . . and then . . . he had sat on a couch, watching a woman dance. She had smiled at him and swirled her skirts as she danced, revealing her legs and thighs. And then . . . someone had come for Harish and he had left. He could remember no more.

Nabin stumbled out of the room. His legs shook under him and his head felt as light as air. In the corridor outside, Dulal sat with his back to a wall, his face sunk between his knees. He was fast asleep but he awoke the instant Nabin called him. Hastening to his master, Dulal led him to the carriage which stood outside the gate.

History repeated itself as the carriage with the Singha crest rolled in, at dawn, through the gate of the mansion at Jorasanko. Thus had Ramkamal Singha arrived, day after day, years ago, after spending the night with Kamala Sundari.

Sarojini entered the room and kneeling at Nabin's feet, pulled off his shoes. 'Your bathwater is ready,' she said softly, 'Shall I send Jadu to give you a massage?'

'Hunh.'

'I'll tell the cook to get your breakfast.' Sarojini went out of the room. Nabin kept on sitting where he was, his head in a whirl. He found Sarojini's attitude bewildering. Why hadn't she asked him where he had been all night? Why wasn't there even a shadow of disappointment on her face? He raised his head and found himself looking into his own face in the mirror on the opposite wall. It seemed to have aged considerably. The faint down on his upper lip had darkened. And it was blotched and bloated with mosquito bites and quite unrecognizable.

'Why! You haven't gone for your bath?' Sarojini exclaimed, coming into the room once again. 'Thakur[10] is frying *luchis* for your breakfast. They'll get cold.'

'I'm just going.'

After a good oil massage and bath, Nabin sat down to the first meal of the day. But he had no appetite. Glancing out of the corner of his eye at Sarojini, who sat fanning him, he asked, 'Does Ma know I didn't come home last night?'

'Yes.'

'Send word through her maid that I would like to see her.'

Bimbabati sat waiting for her son. She had prepared a sherbet for him with her own hands—a blend of curd, honey and lime juice. It cooled and soothed the body after a sleepless night. She used to make it for her husband when he was alive. Putting the silver glass in her son's hand she said, 'Come. Drink it up quickly.'

Nabin seated himself on a couch and looked across at his

---

10 Brahmin cook.

mother. 'How are you, Ma?' he asked gravely. 'I haven't enquired after your health for many days now.' Bimbabati was overwhelmed by her son's consideration. 'When you are well and happy,' she answered instantly, 'what can be wrong with me? My daughter-in-law is chaste and virtuous as becomes a woman of her high birth and lineage. And she is kind and generous and dutiful. She looks after me very well.' Like father, like son, she thought. Her husband had been exactly like that. Kinder, more considerate than ever after a night or two out of the house. With his wife, especially, he had been very tender. And now her son! She floated on a sea of bliss.

But Nabin's reaction was just the opposite. He felt a dull rage simmer within him. And a sense of humiliation. Didn't his mother understand why he had gone to see her? Did it mean nothing to her that her son hadn't come home all night? She hadn't said a word. He didn't expect a reprimand, of course. But a gentle query? A word or two of advice? Surely it was her duty to see that her son did not fall into loose and licentious ways. Had she taken it for granted that he would follow in his father's footsteps?

Nabin went out with Harish again that night. And the next. And every night after that. He started drinking heavily and occupying the most prominent place in *mehfils*. Slinking behind him like a jackal behind a tiger, Raimohan followed unfailingly. And as time went on, others joined him—professional toadies who sniffed at his golden fleece and licked the droppings. These fellows devised new amusements every hour of the day for Nabin's benefit and their own. But there was something that puzzled Nabin. And that was Raimohan's oft-repeated reference to a woman called Kamala Sundari. 'You've become quite a connoisseur of music and dance, Chhoto Babu,' he said over and over again, 'but you still haven't seen the best. What a ravishing beauty Kamala Sundari is! What a face and form! What skill and grace in her dance! The babus of the city are mad for her.' Nabin ignored him most of the time but one day, when he was in the first flush of drink and the whole world seemed rosy and beautiful, he said suddenly, 'Why don't you fetch her here? How much money does the wench take as a rule? Hold it to her nose like a carrot to a donkey's and—'

'*Baap ré*!' Raimohan bit his tongue and tweaked his ears. 'She is not on call. He who wishes to see her dance must come to her. I've heard that the Nawab of Lucknow sent for her and she refused.'

'Why?' Nabin's brows came together. 'What call has she to be so arrogant? She may dance till her limbs drop off, but at the end of it all she's only a common prostitute.'

'She's not like the others. That is why I'm so keen that you see her. She's like a goddess, wrought out of black marble. Time cannot touch her. Age dare not cast its shadow on her peerless form. Rajas and maharajas vie with each other to possess her. But she turns everyone away. No one can possess her any more. In fact, if she knows who you are she won't let you in.'

'Why? Is she afraid I'll gobble her up? Am I a demon?'

'That's a dark secret. I mustn't tell you—' Nabin rose from his seat and grabbed Raimohan by his throat. 'You old scoundrel!' he shouted. 'What are hiding from me? You keep talking about this woman. You keep tempting me. And now you say she won't let me in.'

The others came forward and, parting the two, said amicably, 'Aha ha! Why waste time on words? Why don't we go there and find out for ourselves?'

'Yes, let's go. Tonight. This very minute.'

The darwans outside Kamala Sundari's house recognized the Singha crest and leaped up to open the gates for the carriage to pass. But they were not swift enough for Raimohan. 'Are your eyes sunk in your heads, you rabbits?' he scolded. 'Can't you see it is the young master? Babu Ramkamal Singha's youngest son. Open up quickly.'

'Whose house is this?' Nabin glanced up at it in surprise.

'Kamala Sundari's.' Raimohan gave a crooked smile. 'It is yours, too—in a sense.'

'Why did you say they wouldn't let us in?' One of the toadies gaped at Raimohan. 'Chhoto Babu's name was like a password. They opened the gates in a flash.'

*'Chup.'* Raimohan rolled his eyes at him, then turning to Nabin Kumar, said, 'Come, Babu.'

'Where's the woman? Send her word that I've come to see her dance.'

'You'll see her dance—in course of time. But come upstairs first.'

'Bibisaheba[11]!' he called as they made their way up the stairs. Three young women came and stood on the stair landing. They had obviously been taken unawares for their hair was loose and their clothes in a state of disarray. 'Who are you?' one of them asked in a surprised voice. 'Why do you come so late at night?'

'*Chup*, Beti,' Raimohan snapped at her. 'Do you know who's here? The master of the house in which you live. Himself—in person. Where's Kamli?'

'She's gone to bed.'

'I've come to see her dance,' Nabin Kumar said, the words slurring in his mouth. 'Where's the dance? My throat is as dry as . . . as dry as . . .' Raimohan handed him a bottle. 'Have a few sips, Chhoto Babu,' he said tenderly. 'How can you enjoy the dance with your throat as dry as dust?' Then walking up, to Kamala Sundari's door, he banged on it with both hands. 'Open up, Kamli,' he cried. 'Look who's here.' There was a click and the door opened. Kamala Sundari stood within it like a picture in a frame. A long, low cut gown of Jewish brocade clung shimmering to her voluptuous form and a string of emeralds rested on her deep breast. Her hair was open and fell below her waist, covering her hips like a satin sheath.

'*O ré*, Kamli!' Raimohan cried on seeing her. 'Blow the conches. Send offerings to the gods. Do you know who has come to you tonight? Bara Babu's son.'

'Who is Bara Babu?' Kamala's arched brows came together.

'Your Bara Babu, you little fool! Babu Ramkamal Singha, who died in your arms! Who turned you into a widow. Don't you remember? His son is mad with love for you—'

'Dance!' Nabin said, his head wobbling on his chest. 'Dance,' he repeated, raising it with difficulty. 'I'm falling asleep.' Kamala Sundari gazed at him with tears in her eyes. Then, turning to Raimohan, she said, 'How can you torture me so? Don't you have any human feelings? I know I'm a sinner but—'

'Wait, wait,' Raimohan cried, his eyes gleaming with triumph. 'Don't give up sinning so soon. The bowl is still to brim

---

11 Mistress.

over. Go braid your hair and put on your anklets. You must dance for the young master tonight.'

'I must lie down,' Nabin said. 'I'm falling asleep. She can dance on the bed. I'll watch her from my pillow.'

*'Wah! Wah!!'* Raimohan roared in appreciation. 'A novel idea! That's what you must do, Kamli. Dance on the bed. We humble folk will stand outside the door.'

'I'll break a broomstick on your mouth, you wretch! I'll make the darwans whip you till the flesh flies.' A torrent of foul abuse broke from the lovely mouth. 'Give me a bed to lie on. I'm falling.' And Nabin would have fallen if Kamala Sundari hadn't rushed up and caught him in her arms. *'A ha re'*!' she cried, clicking her tongue in sympathy. 'What have these scoundrels done to you, my precious! My darling! My jewel of a thousand kingdoms! Go home, Babu. This is no place for you.'

'A bed! They've given me too much to drink.'

'I can give you a bed as soft and white as the foam of milk. I can press your limbs and fan you all night. But it wouldn't be proper for you to stay here. This is an evil place; a den of sin.'

'Stop nattering, you whore,' Raimohan cried out sharply. 'Lay him down on your bed. And do what he says. Dance!' Then, addressing Nabin, he added, 'You'd like that—wouldn't you, Chhoto Babu?'

'Yes! yes. A bed . . . and dance . . . '

'Don't say that son,' Kamala Sundari stroked Nabin's brow. 'I'm like your mother.'

'No, you aren't. My mother is like a goddess. The colour of gold.'

'That she is. But I'm like your mother, too. Your father used to grace my home with the dust of his feet. This humble slave had his love and protection.'

'So what?' Raimohan screeched. 'Can't father and son buy goods from the same shop? You've set yourself up for sale. You've no business to choose customers.'

'May your mouth rot, you old cadaver! May worms crawl out of your eyes! May jackals tear at your lungs and liver!'

Raimohan turned a deaf ear to these abuses and let loose a string of his own. 'You dirty harlot! Bitch!' he ground his teeth at her; then cackling with laughter, he mimicked her cruelly: '"Mother! I'm like your mother!" Don't you know, you slime from the gutter, that whores can never be mothers. Nor sisters; nor daughters. A whore is a whore for all time to come. Take Chhoto Babu to bed. Come, Chhoto Babu.'

'Where am I?' Nabin gazed around him with bewildered eyes.

'In bed. You'll watch her dance as you fall asleep.' He gave Nabin a little shove, pushing him on to the bed. Then darting out of the room, he closed the door and pulled up the latch. His face contorted in a wicked grin as he skipped and danced around the amazed spectators, clapping his hands and crying, 'What fun! What fun!'

After a while he stopped and stood for a few moments, deep in thought. There was something else that he had to do. He had to go now, this very minute, to Bidhusekhar's house and give him the news. And if Bidhusekhar so wished, escort him here and let him see the truth with his own eyes.

# Chapter XXII

On the steps of the river ghat in the market town of Birahimpur in Ibrahimpur pargana, a stranger sat gazing across the sheet of water. He had a tall, bronzed, muscular body, bare from the waist upwards, and a fraying dhoti was wrapped around the lower limbs like a lungi. His hair was long and matted and a veritable jungle of growth covered his cheeks and chin. It was a cold morning, with a bitter wind, but he seemed unaware of it. From his looks he could have been a sanyasi or a dervish but he made no effort to attract anyone's attention.

The community at Birahimpur was Muslim-dominated, with a few Hindu families. But Hindu or Muslim they were all equally poor. Going to and fro from the ghat, men, women and children eyed the stranger and muttered among themselves. 'He must be a fakir,' they whispered to one another, 'for he wears no saffron or rudraksha.' Finally, one man took courage and called out in a loud voice, '*Salam Alaikum,* Fakir Saheb! Don't sit out there in the cold. Come into the village.' The man raised his head. His eyes were quiet and gentle but there was a force in them that communicated itself instantly. But the words he spoke were unexpected. 'Do you know Sheikh Jamal-ud-din?' he asked in a sombre voice. 'Can you show me his house?' Even as he said these words a shudder passed through his frame. Perhaps he felt the cold at last.

Sheikh Jamal-ud-din! The man knew him, of course. Everyone did. But he couldn't understand what this stranger, obviously a city man, speaking a cultivated tongue, could want with one so insignificant. What was Jamal-ud-din's worth outside his own family? Was his fate changing at last? Was this stranger an angel sent by Allahtala to open the gates of fortune for the poor wretch? A wave of enthusiasm surged through the people at the ghat as they rushed forward to escort the stranger to the little hut in which Jamal-ud-din lived.

Jamal-ud-din looked up from the coir rope he was twisting and a look of alarm came into his eyes. What were all these people doing outside his house? What did they want? Jumping up, he ran and hid behind the cowshed, ignoring the calls that came to his ears. 'O Jamal! O Jamalya! Come out and see who's here.' Several of the men darted in and looking here and there, pounced upon him and dragged him out of his hiding place. The stranger looked at him in surprise. He saw a young man of about twenty-five, thin and frail as a bird and trembling like a leaf in a high wind. He was naked, save for a tattered loin cloth, and every rib was outlined on his bare, emaciated chest.

'You . . . your name is Sheikh Jamal-ud-din?' the stranger asked in a puzzled voice.

'Yes, Huzoor.' The man wrung his hands in supplication. 'I've never done anything wrong; never disobeyed the sahebs.'

'Has your wife returned?' the stranger asked; then seeing Jamal-ud-din's stare of surprise, he added, 'Your wife, Hanifa Bibi? The sahebs took her away—'

'No, Huzoor. My wife's name was Fatima. She died last year, leaving three children.'

'Fatima! Have I got the name wrong? But . . . Jamal-ud-din Sheikh! He looked different somehow . . . And as far as I remember his wife's name was Hanifa. She was taken away to the Neel Kuthi.'

Now everyone understood whom he sought. True, there had been another with the same name in the village, whose wife, Hanifa, had been carried away by the Neel Kuthi's steward, Golok Das. Jamal-ud-din, a strapping, hot-headed youngster, had ignored everyone's advice and gone after her. Neither had returned. But that was many years ago. Jamal-ud-din's father was still alive though broken by his son's disappearance and blind in both eyes. If the gentleman wanted to see the old man, they could take him to his hut.

'My name is Ganganarayan Singha,' the stranger said, kneeling before the old man. 'I gave you my word I'd look for your son. But I couldn't keep it. I got confused and was led away from my path. But I've come back.' The old man understood little of what was being said to him. He clawed the other's hand with skinny fingers and whimpered like a child. The stranger rose to his feet, muttering, 'I must stay here.' Then, addressing the men who accompanied him, he said, 'I'm thirsty. Can you give me some water? And can I stay here with you all?' The men exchanged glances. Ganganarayan Singha was a Hindu name. 'You're a Hindu,' one of them said. 'How can you stay with us?' The stranger stood still for a while, his brow furrowed in thought. Then, he said suddenly, 'There was someone here . . . by the name of—what was it? Bhujanga! Yes, Bhujanga. He was our nayeb. Is he still here?' At this a loud murmur rose from the crowd. Yes, everyone knew Bhujanga. He was the zamindar's nayeb and lived in the kuthi a little distance away. They would take the stranger to him.

Bhujanga narrowed his eyes and scanned the face before him. 'Who are you?' he asked.

'I'm your master. Don't you recognize me?'

'My master! Heh! Heh! Heh! I thought ghosts walked only at night. It's the middle of the day.'

'I'm Ganganarayan Singha.' the stranger stepped forward. 'Have you forgotten me, Bhujanga? I was in the boat. And then, one night, something came over me and I went away. Get a room prepared for me. I propose to stay here for a while.'

'Stay here? What audacity. Is this your father's zamindari?'

'That is exactly what it is. My father's zamindari. I'm Ramkamal Singha's son.'

'If you are Ramkamal Singha's son, I'm Siraj-ud-doulah's grandson. Ganganarayan Singha has been dead these many years. Even his funeral rites are concluded.'

'I didn't die, Bhujanga. I became a sanyasi. Why do you waste time in idle words? Get a room prepared.'

'If you're really Ganganarayan Singha, why don't you go to Calcutta and move the courts for your rightful share of the property?'

'I don't need to move any court. All I need to do is to write a letter to my mother. She's still alive, I hope.'

But Bhujanga was a tough nut to crack. He went on resisting Ganga and would not be convinced. Then, disgusted by it all, Ganga sent for a barber. Once the growth on his face was shaved off, his true features would be revealed and Bhujanga would recognize him! And that is exactly what happened. A roar of applause rose from the crowd as Ganga's face emerged in its pristine form. Not only did the people present recognize their young master, they also found sufficient resemblance in his face to that of the late Ramkamal Singha's. This was undoubtedly his son. He had his father's brow and his eyes. Bhujanga was struck dumb at the spectacle. He gaped at Ganga with round eyes, then falling to the ground, folded his hands before him and begged forgiveness. Ganganarayan rose from among his shorn locks and, ignoring Bhujanga, walked in the direction of the kuthi.

Ganga had leapt into the water after Bindubasini but the night was dark and not being an expert swimmer, he had lost track of her. Within a few minutes he had lost consciousness. Regaining it, he had found himself lying on a bank in the centre of a small copse, coated with mud from head to foot. How he came to be there he did not know. The desire to live was gone but the god of death had shown him no mercy. He had gone back to Varanasi and lived there for a while, hiding himself carefully from the public eye. Then weary of such an existence, he had travelled down the bank of the river till he reached Patna. Once there he had turned back. He had no wish to return to his native Bengal. Setting his face towards the west, he had travelled across Rishikesh and Lachhmanjhula till he reached Gangotri. He had thought, then, that he would spend the rest of his life in the heart of the Himalayas. Strange to say, the memory of Bindu evoked no pain; no suffering. All passion, all yearning was dead within him. Bindu had been laid to rest in the waters of the Ganga. That, it seemed to him, was a desired end to a life such as hers had been.

One night Ganga had a strange dream. He saw an old, bearded Muslim weeping bitterly before him and he, Ganganarayan, was consoling him with the words, 'I'll look for your son. I'll do all I can. I promise you.' The next night he had the same dream. And the next. It left him feeling drained and wretched. Very slowly, a faint memory rose within him of a dark night; of his rising from a deep sleep; stepping out of a bajra and joining a group of pilgrims; walking with them like a sleepwalker—like one possessed. And only after reaching Prayag and bathing in the Ganga had he woken to a sense of his surroundings. He remembered something else. He had promised an old peasant he would look for his son. It had been in a place called . . . Ibrahimpur. The dream troubled him. It wouldn't let him rest. And that was why he was back in Ibrahimpur. He had come to redeem his promise.

While staying at the kuthi in Birahimpur, Ganga came across an issue of the *Hindu Patriot* and read it from beginning to end. The editor was one Harish Mukherjee and he seemed to have a pen of fire. Only a student of Hindu College could write English as chiselled as this, he thought, and cast his mind back to his college days. But try as he would, he could not remember anyone of that name. Though the paper was called *Hindu Patriot*, it dealt with great sensitivity and at great length with the miseries of the Muslim peasant.

It was from this paper that Ganga learned of the court order, issued by the magistrate at Barasat, upholding the right of the peasant to sow whatever crops he pleased on his own land. A copy of the order had been forwarded to the police, with orders to stop the harassment of peasants by indigo planters. The news thrilled Ganganarayan. He had failed Jamal-ud-din Sheikh and Hanifa but he would not fail the others. He would see that such an incident never recurred. He would work for the welfare of the ryot and, with the police on his side, he would succeed. The fields of Bengal would be rid of the pernicious indigo and paddy, the colour of ripe gold, would wave in the breeze.

His first impulse was to muster the peasants together and initiate a revolt. Then he thought better of it. It was too soon. A certain amount of preparation was needed. The ryots were too weak; too broken spirited to even think of resistance. They had to be inflamed by degrees; to be brought to a state of resentment which would enable them to break out openly against their masters. He decided to go to the village the next morning and gauge the mood of the ryots. He would also visit the nearest police station, situated at a distance of ten miles from Birahimpur, and assess the situation for himself.

The next morning, after a breakfast of fruit and milk, Ganganarayan set off for the village. Crossing a shallow pond, he saw a man standing by it in the shade of an asthwatha tree. He wore a striped lungi and his bare chest was covered with such a thick mat of hair that it appeared to be a garment. His body must have been strong and muscular once but now the skin hung in loose folds over a rusted cage of bones. His eyes glittered strangely. Ganga had seen the man before and knew his name to be Tohrab. He remembered him specially because, unlike the other villagers, Tohrab never bothered to greet Ganga with the customary 'Babu, salaam.' In fact, he looked away whenever he saw him and broke into song in a harsh unmusical voice. Ganga walked towards the ashwatha tree, straining his ears to catch the words:

My house was robbed by the zamindar,
My faith by the priest, with the cross in his hand.
But the precious rice was snatched from my mouth
By the blue-faced monkey of indigo land.

A shade of embarrassment came over Ganga's face. People here made it a point to remind him that he was a zamindar's son. 'When did the zamindar rob your house?' he asked softly. Tohrab gave a roar of laughter. 'It is only a song I sing, Babu Saheb. It was composed by my father, Bashir-ud-din Sheikh. I had five bighas of land, all of which the Neel Kuthi sahebs marked with the blue line. I gave up farming in disgust. I even sold my plough and bullock but the mother fuckers won't leave me alone.'

'Listen, Tohrab,' Ganga said excitedly. 'Sow paddy instead of indigo. I'll help you.' But, even as he said these words, a loud commotion could be heard from the direction of the village and men, women and children ran out of their houses, shrieking in terror. Galloping wildly after them were three horsemen, followed by the guards, officials and *lathyals* of the Neel Kuthi. The sahebs always did everything in an organized manner. In the twinkling of an eye, the three horsemen formed parties and went off in three different directions. And immediately afterwards, a loud wailing could be heard from the direction of the mango grove.

Ganga looked around him and found that Tohrab had disappeared. Walking towards the mango grove, he saw a scene that made his blood boil with rage and frustration. An Englishman on horse back, three *lathyals* behind him, towered over a half-naked ryot, who clung to his boot, crying. 'Don't mark that land, O Saheb, that lies just by the pond. My women folk bathe there and draw water for the household. All the villagers use my pond, O Saheb!' The Englishman kept kicking the man away but he came back on the instant, clutching the shod foot and repeating the same words over and over again.

Ganga couldn't bear it. Coming forward he called out angrily, 'Stop this. Listen. Do you know of the recent order passed by the government?' The Englishman had lived in Bengal nearly all his life and had picked up the local language, particularly the abuses. Fixing his eyes on Ganga, he asked, 'Who's this sister fucker?' Ganga stared back at him. The mists rolled away and he recognized him. This was MacGregor—the man who had insulted him so cruelly that day in the Neel Kuthi.

'He's our zamindar,' some of the peasants said.

'What kind of a fool is he? One lick from my Shyamchand will fix him. Watch—all of you.' And, lifting his whip, he brought it viciously down on Ganga's back. Ganga's shirt was drenched in blood within seconds but he did not move an inch. He stood straight as an arrow and looked into MacGregor's eyes. 'There's a new law,' he said in a voice of thunder. 'You dare not disobey it. I'll get you arrested for trespassing on this man's land. I swear an oath before all these men that I'll see you in prison before I'm finished with you.'

'You bloody nigger!' MacGregor roared. 'How dare you teach me the law?' And he lifted his whip again. But this time Ganga snatched it from his hand and, unable to control himself, struck a blow full on MacGregor's mouth. Then, another and another till MacGregor fell from his horse in a bloody heap on the ground. After this, a small revolt took place. The sight of the white body rolling in the dust sent a thrill of triumph through the ryots and filled their hearts with hope and courage. '*Khabardar*!' they shouted as the *lathyals* moved towards Ganga. 'Don't dare lay hands on our zamindar.' Suddenly Tohrab appeared on the scene, an enormous lathi in his hand. Now the crowd fell on the *lathyals* and beat them to a pulp.

That night a fire broke out in the village. Tongues of flames could be seen licking the thatched roofs of the houses and the first to burn to ashes was the zamindar's kuthi.

# Chapter XXIII

Along with his efforts to implement the Widow Remarriage Act, Vidyasagar was straining every nerve to spread the cause of women's education in the land, when resistance came suddenly and from an unexpected quarter. The department of education sent for him and demanded an explanation. 'You are opening one school after another,' the secretary said to him. 'Who do you think is going to fund them?' Vidyasagar was stunned. The British made so many impassioned speeches about the backwardness of India and the importance of spreading the light of knowledge in the land. Now, when it came to spending a little money, they were changing their stance without a twinge of conscience. The sum total of the expenditure for the thirty-five schools already started was eight hundred and forty-five rupees a month—a mere pittance; a drop in the ocean of funds, contained in the imperial treasury. Truly speaking, the rulers' decision to educate the native had been born out of the pragmatic consideration of creating a workforce of clerks and lower officials to run the administration. Women's education, as they saw it, was a total waste. Women, however well educated, would never take up careers or go out of their homes. Vidyasagar was at his wits' end. The government was freezing its grants one by one and the teachers' salaries were going from his own pockets. How long could he sustain the situation?

But this was not all. Something else happened that Vidyasagar found intolerable. The post of inspector of schools having fallen vacant, everyone assumed that Vidyasagar would be the next incumbent—there being no one more experienced in the field than he. However, his candidature was passed over in favour of another, an Englishman, whose qualifications were nowhere near his, there being levels above which a native, however worthy, might not be raised. The injustice and humiliation of it enraged the lion of Birsingha and he sent in his resignation. But though the loss of five hundred rupees a month didn't impoverish Vidyasagar (he made enough money out of the sale of his books), his spirit was assailed by a sense of defeat. And it wasn't this incident alone that was responsible. There were several others.

Some years ago, on a visit to his friend, Pyaricharan Sarkar, Vidyasagar had found himself attracted to a proposal that the latter had put forward. Pyaricharan was the headmaster of Hindu School and a fine English scholar. He had recently published an English primer called *First Book*. 'Ishwar,' he said. 'Why don't you write a similar book in Bengali?' Then, seeing that Vidyasagar made no reply, he added, 'Are you visualizing a loss of prestige if a great Sanskrit scholar like you writes a book for infants? Look at it this way. A child's learning must be founded on rock, musn't it? Who, better than a great scholar like you, can provide that foundation? Come, let us work together, I in English and you in Bengali.'

Vidyasagar found himself enthused by the idea. In the palki on his way back home, he wrote some simple phrases in his notebook. 'The bird is flying. The leaf is moving. The cow is grazing. Water is falling. The flower is hanging. Gopal is a good boy. He loves his little brothers and sisters'. And he marvelled at the purity and simplicity the Bengali language was capable of. He realized for the first time that there was no need for Bengali to stand in the shadow of Sanskrit. It was complete in itself.

A few days later he published his *Barna Parichay* (*Know Your Letters*). It was obvious from the sales, which ran into thousands, that it served a real need, there being nothing like it in existence. The success of this volume encouraged Vidyasagar to write a sequel—*Barna Parichay Part II*. Then, in quick succession, he wrote several other text books, which sold equally well. Money came pouring into his coffers for he was publisher as well as author. But his expenditure exceeded his income for he had to finance all the widow remarriages himself—the great babus of Calcutta having conveniently forgotten their promises of help. All his difficulties notwithstanding, Vidyasagar decided to keep the schools going, with or without the help of the government. If all else failed, he thought, he would start a door-to-door collection. But, to his surprise, the attempt met with a very feeble response. The ones who had been loudest in their praise for Vidyasagar's efforts were the first to take a negative stance. Even Madanmohan Tarkalankar, his friend and contemporary, for whom he had done so much, openly expressed his disapproval. It was a cruel blow but Vidyasagar overcame it with his customary resilience. 'It is time I turned my mind to something else,' he said to himself. 'Something so difficult, so engrossing that all other thoughts will be driven out of my head.' And, thinking thus, he began translating the Mahabharat.

One day, a young man came to see him. He looked pale and haggard and his eyes were set deep in their sockets. And though he wore a dhoti and kurta of expensive silk, his feet were bare and coated with dust. There was something familiar about him but Vidyasagar could not recall having seen him before. 'Who are you?' he asked. 'You've forgotten me, Gurudev?' came the reply. 'I'm Nabin Kumar Singha.' Vidyasagar knitted his brow. He felt a mixture of wrath and disdain. He hated these pampered darlings of rich houses. They had no stability or consistency. Nabin Kumar had promised to contribute one thousand rupees for each widow remarriage. He had kept his word at first; had even attended the ceremonies. But his interest had petered out suddenly and without warning. And now, from what Vidyasagar had heard, he was following in the footsteps of his illustrious ancestors! He had believed himself to be an idealist and spoken fine phrases, but the lechery of his forefathers, lurking in his blood, had expressed itself at last. Wine and women! Sons of zamindars had to succumb to them sooner or later.

'You've changed beyond recognition,' Vidyasagar said with disapproval in his voice. 'I remember the name, of course. But since when have I become your guru, may I ask? A couple of disciples like you and I'll be famous throughout the land.'

'I'm not fit to be your disciple. I know that. But worthless as I am, may I touch your feet in reverence?'

'You may—if you feel such reverence is due to a Brahmin.' He attempted to rise but before he could do so, Nabin had flung himself at his feet, weeping bitterly. 'I'm impure,' he cried again and again between sobs. 'I'm a sinner.' Vidyasagar hated scenes of this kind. He invariably burst into tears himself and felt foolish afterwards. And he was in no mood to go through the process for Nabin—a youth for whom he felt little affection. 'Get up, my boy,' he said, averting his face. 'Calm yourself and tell me what you've come to say. No human being is impure, in my opinion. Besides, words like sin and impurity are not for scions of wealthy families like you. Only poor folk like us need bother about them.' But Nabin continued to weep. The fact is that he couldn't forget the night he had spent in Kamala Sundari's bed. The harder he tried to forget the experience, the more sharply was he assailed by it. He had only to close his eyes and he relived it all over again. Kamala Sundari's heavy, voluptuous body in his arms; she, straining to pull away, crying, '*O go*! Don't touch me. I'm like your mother.' And himself, sodden with brandy, crying in a slurred voice, 'Dance. I want to see you dance.' He shivered every time he thought of the scene. He had slept in the polluted bed of an ageing whore—a woman who(as he came to know later) had been his father's mistress.

'Get up, son.' Vidyasagar raised him to his feet. 'And tell me what you've done.' Nabin struggled to control himself but his lips trembled and his breath came in spasms. 'I've no one to guide me,' he said at last. 'No one to tell me what I should or should not do. Or punish me for doing wrong. And I've done something very wrong. I lost control over myself and—' Vidyasagar was amused by this confession. Young men from Nabin Singha's background were always losing control. It was expected of them. What was so new about it?

'You should be able to control yourself if you're a man,' he said severely. 'But why come to me? How can I help you?'

'Does a boy like me deserve to live? I could kill myself if you ask me to.'

'If I ask you to? What a terrible thought! But what have you done that you should kill yourself? A strapping young man like you, with everything to live for! It is strange that you should contemplate suicide! Very strange, indeed!'

'I have loathed the drinking of liquor from childhood upwards. Yet, one day, I started to drink. I hate promiscuity but I find myself visiting brothels and spending the nights with low women. I don't know why or how I am so changed. I only know that I must find release from this vile existence. Save me! Help me to find my old self again.'

'I'm no spiritual guide. I have neither tantra nor mantra at my command to effect a transformation. No one can help you but yourself.'

'How? I tell you I've lost control over myself.'

'You can regain it. You are young and you strayed away from the path of virtue and duty. But you can find it once again if you truly yearn for it. You have money. Spend some of it on the poor and needy. The very act will awaken your soul and give you strength to fight your weakness.'

'Are you telling me to go on living? Is my life of any worth?'

'Every life is worth living if some good is attached to it. Why don't you take up writing once again? You used to write at one time.'

'Yes, I could do that. But of a different kind. I've been thinking. Muslims do penance by copying the Quran. Wouldn't my sins be forgiven if I undertook to translate the Mahabharat?'

Vidyasagar was startled. What was the boy saying? 'Translate the Mahabharat!' he exclaimed. 'Or copy it?'

'I could rewrite it in Bengali prose.'

'Have you any idea of the vastness of the work?'

'I've been reading it from childhood. Not Kashidas's book. The one written by Mahatma Vyas Dev. I read it again, from cover to cover, a few months ago. It is an arduous task I'm undertaking. I know that. But it's the only way I know of atoning for my sins.'

Vidyasagar sat silent for a few minutes, sunk in thought. He had started translating the Mahabharat himself as an antidote to the tensions and frustrations of his life. The boy before him had a similar idea though his purpose was different. Making up his mind, he said firmly, 'Come back to me within a week with a sample of your work. It will enable me to assess the genuineness of your intentions.'

Nabin took his leave and reappeared within a few days with three sheets of paper in his hand. Vidyasagar took them from him and studied the writing closely. 'You're a wonderful young man,' he said at last, rolling up the sheaf. 'Your Sanskrit is faulty, of course. The true meanings of the shloks have eluded you in a few places. But your Bengali is astonishingly good. I've read a lot of Bengali prose but I've never come across anything so spontaneous and lucid. It has an in-built cadence too! But think once again. Can you sustain the effort?'

'I swear an oath before you. I can and I will.' And he bowed low and touched Vidyasagar's feet.

'Very well, then. But the work is too extensive for one man to tackle single-handedly. Take a word of advice. Employ a couple of Sanskrit pandits to explain the meanings to you.'

'I'll do everything you say.'

'Then get started at once. I'll abandon mine—'

'You mean you were translating the Mahabharat?' Nabin asked in a startled voice. 'Then I shouldn't—'

'It is no matter. I've done very little. In fact, I'm relieved in a way. I can turn my mind to other things. I'll keep track of your progress and help you all I can.'

Within days of the historic meeting, the mansion at Jorasanko started humming with activity. Famous pandits, picked out with great care by Vidyasagar himself, took up their quarters in the Singha household and were looked after like princes by their young host. A servant was allotted to each to minister to his personal needs and rows of Brahmin cooks sat in a specially appointed kitchen, turning out every delicacy the palate craved. The printing press, idle and rusting with disuse, was set in motion once again and reams of fine paper were bought and stacked in the adjoining room so high that they reached the ceiling. Money was being spent like water and all the servants of the household and estate were caught up in their young master's new venture. Nabin had never been happier in his life. All the melancholy and depression that had overtaken him in the last few months had vanished and he was once again the keen, bright-eyed boy that he had been. All morning the pandits sat in the outer room, rendering the Sanskrit shloks of the eighteen-volume Mahabharat into literal Bengali and Nabin, like one riding a storm, spent day and night working on them, polishing the phrases, adding colour and life till they were metamorphosed into elegant prose of astonishing beauty. His friends and co-members of the Vidyotsahini Sabha were delighted at the change in him. Jadupati Ganguly came to see him quite often and was warmly welcomed. Harish Mukherjee sent for him once on the plea that they hadn't met for a long time but Nabin ignored his summons.

One day his mother sent for him. It was a particularly busy morning and he felt a touch of irritation at this interruption. He put his pen down, however, and made his way into the inner quarters. Bimbabati was waiting for him in her own room. She sat cross-legged on a deerskin, a new white *than* wrapped around her. 'Why Ma!' he cried. 'What have you done to yourself?' For, Bimbabati's head was shorn of its long silky locks and her forehead marked with sandal paste. A string of rudraksha beads hung from her neck and tears rolled down her cheeks. 'Why Ma!' he cried again, flinging himself at her feet. But she shrank from him with a shudder. '*O ré*,' she cried. 'Don't touch me.' Nabin's blood froze in his veins. Why was his mother avoiding his touch? She had always been so warm; so affectionate. She had only to see him and she put her arms around him with the words, 'Chhotku! My precious child! The sight of you soothes my eyes like nothing else can. My heart is filled with peace when I clasp you to my breast.'

'Why do you ask me not to touch you?' he asked in a bewildered voice. 'Is it because I've sinned?'

'Sinned! You?' Bimbabati cried out in astonishment. 'You're my darling boy. The most precious thing in my life. I ask you to keep away because I've turned ascetic, as you can see. And you're coming from the outer rooms—'

'But why have you turned ascetic? And what makes you weep? Have I hurt you in any way?'

'No, son. Why should you hurt me? You're the best of sons. I was crying from happiness. God has called me to him. I shall spend the rest of my life at his feet.'

'I don't understand.'

'My guru,' she said, bringing her palms together and touching them to her brow. 'Jagatguru Eknathji has commanded me to renounce the world and spend the rest of my life in his ashram at Hardwar. I'm leaving tomorrow.'

'Tomorrow! Do you have any idea of how far away it is?'

'I've made all the arrangements,' she said. 'My bags are packed and ready. Gurudev is leaving tomorrow and I'm going with him. You can send me a few rupees each month if you like. And even if you don't—it is no matter. God will look after me.'

Nabin begged and pleaded but all in vain. Finally, realizing that her decision was final, he made elaborate arrangements for her journey and stay in Hardwar. Seven maids and serving men were to accompany her. A steward of the household was dispatched ahead of them, with sufficient money to build a brick house for her in the ashram premises. The whole household was in turmoil for the mistress was leaving for the first time since she had stepped across the threshold—a little bride of seven—and she was never coming back.

The next thing to do was to take leave of Bidhusekhar. Nabin was with his mother when she broke the news to him. Bidusekhar was not inclined to take her seriously at first. But Bimbabati fixed her clear, limpid gaze on his face and gave one answer to his many questions. 'I must go. There is no other way.' Her head was unveiled and her face open to view. Bidhusekhar had never seen her like that. After some time, Bidhusekhar turned to Nabin and said, 'Leave us for a while, Chhotku. I must persuade your mother to change her mind.'

'No,' Bimbabati said firmly. 'Chhotku will stay where he is.' Then, bursting into tears, she cried, 'He has promised not to disobey you. You love him. Promise me you'll look after him.'

'Of course I will. Is he not dearer to me than anyone else in the world? We may disagree on certain matters but we love and understand one another. Do we not, Chhotku?' Nabin nodded his assent. Bidhusekhar placed a hand on his shoulder and said, 'I wish to speak to your mother in private.' And, as Chhotku rose to his feet, he added, 'See that no one comes in and disturbs us.'

As soon as the door closed behind Nabin, Bidhusekhar turned his eyes on Bimbabati's averted face. The expression in them was like that of a lion looking at a lamb. 'Are you running away from your son?' he asked sternly. 'Or from me?'

'God has called me to him,' Bimbabati said, as she had so many times that evening. 'I must go.'

'What you say is strange,' Bidhusekhar said with a mirthless laugh. 'God has never asked a woman to renounce the world. A woman's place is in the home.'

'He called Mirabai to him.'

'Hunh!' Bidhusekhar said grimly. 'You've learned to give quick answers, I see. Who has taught you these words of wisdom? That scoundrel, Eknathji? How dare that son of a Vaishnav play guru to a daughter-in-law of a Shakta house? And why did you go to him without taking my permission?' He tapped the floor angrily with his stick.

'Forgive me,' Bimbabati cried, struggling to control the tears that ran down her cheeks. 'Have pity on me. Give me your blessing and let me go.'

'Why do you make me suffer so, Bimba?' Bidhusekhar cried back. 'Why do you play with my deepest feelings? The desire that has lain dormant within me for so many years is rearing its head, ready to erupt. I'm old and enfeebled, lame in one leg and blinded in one eye. But I'm consumed with lust for you. Come to me, Bimba. Put your head on my breast and let us weep together.'

Bimbabati gazed on Bidhusekhar with wonder in her eyes. How he was changed! He who had been a pillar of rectitude, austere and high-principled, had lost all control. He was utterly oblivious to the proprieties. He came to her room whenever he felt like it and shut the door in total disregard of the servants milling around. Nabin came rarely to this wing but Sarojini did. She might be wondering what went on between the two. Bimba had shaved her head and turned herself into a sanyasini in an effort to destroy her beauty and curb Bidhusekhar's lust. But it had had the opposite effect. His desire for her had grown in intensity and threatened to engulf her. 'I've made a will,' Bidhusekhar continued, 'leaving all I possess to Chhotku. Give me something in return. Don't leave me, Bimba. I yearn for the service of your soft hands in the few years left to me.' But Bimbabati was not moved by his plea. She sat, face averted, motionless as an image carved out of marble. Now, Bidhusekhar lost his temper completely and violently. '*Haramzadi*!' he screeched, grinding his teeth at her. 'Come to me as I command you.'

'No,' Bimbabati answered, gently but firmly. 'I shan't sin any more.' She raised clear, dark eyes to his. They were unflinching; unafraid.

'I'll put chains on you, you slut, and keep you as my bondmaid. The whole world shall hear of your conduct. How you came to my bed, time and time again, even when your husband was alive. All because of your greed for a son! It is too late now for you to play the chaste and holy widow. Adulteress! You think you can escape me?'

'Yes,' Bimbabati answered in a voice that did not waver. 'I'll go away from you. You can't stop me. No one can.'

Bidhusekhar rose to his feet and came towards her, leaning heavily on his stick. 'Then, let the truth come out,' he cried out shrilly 'Now. This very minute. I'll proclaim before the world, before your precious son, that you are Bidhusekhar Mukherjee's whore.' Bimbabati rose too, and shrinking against the wall, cried out in an agonized voice, 'Don't touch me. You're polluted. Everything here is polluted.' And lifting her left hand, she showed him a ring. 'There's poison in it,' she said. 'I'll put it to my lips if you try to pollute me.'

'Then do so,' Bidhusekhar snarled at her. 'Die here at my feet, writhing in agony. I'll watch you die with pleasure.' Bimbabati lifted the cover of the ring and raised it to her lips. But, quick as a flash, Bidhusekhar brought his stick down on the ringed hand and the poison was dashed to the ground. *'Na jatu kamaha kamanam upabhogen sammati,'* Bidhusekhar murmured with a sigh. 'Lust will not drive out lust. Forcing oneself on a woman is conduct worthy of an animal. I know that. The one thing I didn't know is that man can never claim control over his passions. Go, Bimba. Go to Hardwar and be at peace. I'll live a life of torment here without you. And don't be afraid. Your son is safe from me. I'll never allow any harm to come to him. I give you my word.'

Within a week of Bimbabati's departure, two messengers arrived with letters from Ibrahimpur. One was from the nayeb of the estate, Bhujanga Bhattacharya, and the other from the police. Both contained news of Ganganarayan.

# Chapter XXIV

*Sharmistha* was performed with great fanfare on the stage in Belgachhia. The lieutenant governor of Bengal, Sir John Peter Grant, and the chief justice of the Supreme Court were among the audience, as were several other high officials of the city. Madhusudan had prepared an English translation of the play and distributed it well in advance. In consequence, the British section of the audience enjoyed the performance as much as the native. It was agreed by one and all that a play such as this one had never been written in the Bengali language.

A great change had come over Madhusudan in the last few months. He had been a glum, unhappy man, sodden with beer and hating his job. He was now a workaholic, tense and alert to everthing that pertained to his writing. And he had got back his confidence. Once, during a rehearsal of *Sharmistha*, the Rajas expressed a regret that there were no comedies in the Bengali language and urged him to try his hand at one. Within a few days, Madhusudan came up with not one but two—*Ekei ki Bale Sabhyata?* (*Is This What We Call Civilization?*) and *Burho Shalikher Ghare Rou* (*The Old Thrush is Growing Down on His Neck*), leaving his readers stunned for the second time. He who had been unable to speak a full sentence in Bengali only a short while ago, had used the vernacular so brilliantly—it was as if he had done so all his life. The authenticity of the dialect and sharpness of the satire were of a kind that had never been seen before. And the speed with which he wrote was like magic.

After the two burlesques, Madhusudan started writing *Padmavati*—a play derived from Greek drama. But even as he wrote it, a wave of regret swept over him. What was he doing? In setting himself up as a playwright, he was turning himself into a writer of prose. He had abandoned poetry—his first love! How could he have done that? He would go back to it. He would write poetic drama of an excellence that no one had ever dreamed of, leave alone seen. But though he abandoned *Padmavati* midway and sought frantically for a subject, he was hard put to find one. And, in consequence, he started drinking heavily all over again.

One day Gourdas said to him, 'Have you heard the news, Madhu? Our Ganga is back again in Calcutta.'

'Ganga?' Madhu frowned in an effort at remembrance. 'Which Ganga?'

'Don't you remember Ganganarayan? Of the Singha family? He was very shy and quiet. An introvert type.' But Madhu didn't remember. He hadn't seen Ganga for seventeen years and couldn't recall him. But, within a few days, Gour brought Ganga to see him, and though Ganga had changed a great deal, Madhu recognized him at once. 'By Jove,' he cried, embracing his friend with a warmth that brought tears to Ganga's eyes. 'This is, indeed, our old goody goody Ganga! The silent philosopher of Hindu College! Did you know that I, too, returned like you to Calcutta just a few years ago? I was weary of playing the prodigal son and had to come back. But how you are changed! You were a zamindar's son. And now you look like a sadhu!'

Madhu opened a bottle of champagne to celebrate Ganga's return but Ganga did not touch it. Neither did Rajnarayan, who was also present. 'Do you know what our Ganga has been doing, Madhu?' he said, addressing his host. 'Hiding in the jungles and building up an army to fight the indigo planters. He's a hero now. Everyone has heard of him. The peasants of Bengal sing a song about him.' And Rajnarayan sang in a high unmusical voice:

Take care blue monkeys of indigo land
Ganga Singhi has jumped into the fray.
He'll set your sheets afire and your tails aflame
And turn your blue faces all ashen and grey.

Ganga laughed with the others and shook his head. 'I've done nothing much,' he said. 'But I've seen the plight of the peasants. It was a horrifying experience. Harish Mukherjee has taken up the cause in the *Hindu Patriot*. He's a man I truly admire.'

'I've heard he's as big a drunkard as myself,' Madhu said. 'You agree, then, that drink is not necessarily an evil thing.'

'Tell us about your experiences, Ganga,' Gour cut in. 'Tell us what you've seen and done from the very beginning.'

In the middle of Ganga's narration, a stranger walked into the room. He was a young man about thirty years old. 'You must be Michael,' he said, looking at Madhu. 'May I join your group?' Madhu was annoyed at this intrusion. 'I'm in the middle of an important discussion,' he said. 'May I enquire as to what I owe this visit?' 'I wanted to see you,' the stranger said simply. 'I've been wanting to see you for a very long time. You're a great poet and playwright—the greatest on the scene today. Your *Sharmistha* is a wonderful piece of writing. Is it not strange that Ma Saraswati should have chosen to guide the pen of a Christian?'

Adulation, at whatever time or place, was like the water of life to Madhu. Unlike Ganga, he took it as his due and felt no embarrassment. 'What do you do for a living, sir?' he asked with a serene smile. 'And what is your name?'

'I work in the postal department of the British government,' the stranger replied. 'And my name is Deenabandhu Mitra.'

Deenabandhu had no claim to fame. Born of simple rural folk hailing from Nadiya, he had had his early education in the village *pathshala*, and then found employment in the local zamindar's office. But young Deenabandhu had hated his job and chafed against the narrow confines of his village. Unable to resist the beckoning hand of the larger world beyond, he had run away to Calcutta, where he had managed to enrol himself in Reverend Long's free school. 'Look here, boy,' Reverend Long had said to him. 'I'm giving you a chance. But you must prove yourself. If your performance is not excellent you'll have to leave.' Deenabandhu had proved himself. He had stood first in every examination and moved up to the Kolutola Branch School and from there to Hindu School. But, while in Hindu School, he had a few misgivings. He was so much older than his compatriots. Young men of his age were already in service. Reasoning thus, he gave up his studies and found employment in the postal department. While studying in Hindu School, he committed another act of rebellion. Discarding the name Gandharvanarayan given by his father, he started calling himself Deenabandhu.

After the initial courtesies had been exchanged,

Deenabandhu said to his host, 'I have a request to make to you if you allow me—'

'Of course,' Madhusudan answered. 'Only make it brief.'

'I'll do that. Listen, Mr Dutt. You write fine poetry and your *Sharmistha* is an excellent piece of writing. But your burlesques are, to use one word, peerless among your creations. I've never heard such living dialogue in all my life. And the dialect is extraordinarily authentic. How did you come by it?'

'My native village is in Jessore. I've visited it often in my childhood. The dialect I heard then must have lain dormant in my memory all these years and has now sprung to life.'

'That's why I've come to you. You've written about the oppressions of the zamindar and the evil effects of drink. Now, write a similar play on the plight of the ryots.'

'Plight of the—?'

'Ryots. I've travelled extensively in Nadiya and Jessore and I've seen the victimization of the peasant by the indigo planter. I'm convinced, after reading your plays, that the only way to bring the atrocities to light is to write about them.'

'A strange coincidence!' Madhu murmured. 'My friend here was just telling us about the indigo menace. He's a zamindar's son but he has lived among the ploughmen and organized a rebellion.'

'You must be Ganganarayan Singha,' Deenabandhu exclaimed. 'I've heard so much about you. The peasants of Nadiya look upon you as a god.'

'No, no, ' Ganga muttered, blushing to the roots of his hair. 'I've done nothing to deserve such praise.'

'It seems, Ganga,' Madhu laughed, 'that you're more famous than me.'

'Mr Dutt.' Deenabandhu turned to him. 'You've heard your friend's account. Bring it to life in your drama. You have a pen of fire. Use it. You're the only one who can do it.'

'I don't wish to write any more prose. Only poetry! Poetry is the breath of life to me at present. Meghnad shall be the hero of my next poem. I'll show the world that Ram was a petty trickster and fought an immoral war. I'll destroy Ram as he destroyed Meghnad.' Turning to Deenabandhu, he said, 'Why don't you try your hand at it?'

'I? What do I know about writing drama?'

'Everything has a beginning,' Madhu said kindly, patting his shoulder. 'Besides, you are the one who has the first-hand experience. And it was your idea that it might make a good play. This is what we poets call inspiration. Be guided by your inspiration and all will be well. Only get down to it as soon as you can.' Madhusudan's touch sent a thrill of excitement down Deenabandhu's spine. And for a long time after he had taken leave of his host, his last words kept ringing in his ears.

*Neel Darpan* (*Indigo Mirror*) was written within three weeks of Deenabandhu's meeting with Madhusudan. But even as he handed over the manuscript to the printer, Ram Bhowmick, his heart beat heavily within him. The rulers were bound to find it offensive. And he might even lose his job. And though his name appeared nowhere in the book, the uneasiness remained. He decided to go to his erstwhile tutor and guide, Reverend Long, and seek his advice. Reverend Long was official translator for the government and knew the language well. Besides, having lived in Bengal for many years, he had learned to love its people. Reverend Long looked thoughtful and disturbed as Deenabandhu read out his play and then, as the end came near, agitated and angry. 'Get it translated at once,' he cried. 'I would have done it myself if the dialect hadn't been so obscure. Entrust the work to someone you think fit. I'll bear the cost of the printing myself and place it before the Indigo Commission.' The first name that came to Deenabandhu's mind was Madhusudan's. But he had refused to write the play on the plea that he had turned completely to poetry. Would he agree to do a translation? Fortunately for Deenabandhu, his request found favour with many of the poet's friends and Madhu had to agree. But he insisted on absolute anonymity, for he, too, was a government servant.

The translation was done in a single night in a house in Jhhamapukur. Madhu had two conditions. He had to have a dozen bottles of beer and Ganganarayan had to be with him to explain the difficult passages. As the night wore on and more and more empty bottles rolled about on the floor, Madhu's eyes grew as heavy as stones. 'Let's go to bed,' Ganga said. 'We'll do the rest tomorrow.' But Madhu wouldn't listen. Opening his eyes with great difficulty, he took another draught from the bottle in his hand and said, 'No. I'll finish this damn thing tonight. I must say the postmaster has done a good job. It's a brilliant play.'

'Don't drink any more, Madhu.' Ganga sounded a bit worried.

'Shut up, my boy,' Madhu replied. 'You do your work and I'll do mine.'

When they came to the fifth act, Madhu roared with laughter. 'Oh dear! Oh dear!' he cried. 'He's killing everybody off. Even *Hamlet* can't boast of so many corpses. The postmaster has out-Shakespeared Shakespeare right in his first play. Ha! Ha! Ha! This girl, Aduri, is a fine character. I like her. But Bindu Madhav's Sanskrit is too jaw-breaking for me. *Baap ré*!'

As soon as the last line was written, Madhusudan sank on the table before him in a heap—dead drunk.

# Chapter XXV

Aghornath of the Malliks of Hatkhola was dead and Kusum Kumari was now a widow. She had been brought back to her parental home in a dead faint, from a vicious bite on the shoulder by her mad husband. Aghornath had been chained and beaten and had succumbed to his injuries ten days later. Unlike others of their generation, her parents had not pushed her into the puja room and told her that God was her husband. Overcome with guilt and remorse at her plight, they did all they could to comfort their daughter and make a new life for her. She was given a room furnished with all the luxuries a young woman of her station was accustomed to, and a maid was employed for the sole purpose of serving her.

Kusum Kumari's father had four brothers and they all lived together in a vast extended household. But the values of this family were somewhat different from those of many other rich families of Calcutta. The sons of the house went to school and college and indulged in innocent pastimes like kite and pigeon flying. Wine and women were banned within the house though music was patronized, a style of Dhrupad music in particular, which Kusum Kumari's father loved. An austere, highly religious man, Krishnanath spent vast sums of money on religious rituals and encouraged activities such as amateur theatricals, which the boys of the house performed with great enjoyment. This year, Kusum Kumari's brothers were to put up Nabin Kumar Singha's *Vikramvarshi.* Kusum Kumari sat watching the rehearsals from morning to night. There was no question of her participating in the actual performance but she was able to give her brothers some good tips, which were well received.

One day, Kusum Kumari received a letter from Durgamoni. 'My dearest, most treasured Kusum darling,' she wrote. 'It is six months since I've seen you but those beautiful blue eyes, shining out of that flower-like face, haunt me day and night. I know you'll never come back to this house. Why should you?

You're free now and Heaven and Earth are yours. I'm a hapless creature, born to suffer; born to smoulder to ashes in this living Hell. *O ré*, Kusum! You don't know how fortunate you are. To be an independent widow is a thousand times better than to be chained to a mad, vicious brute of a husband. Ah! If only Destiny had dealt with me as it has dealt with you! But even so, our lives are worlds apart. You are young and beautiful; so beautiful that I, though a woman, am half in love with you. Hundreds of young men will sigh their souls out for a glimpse of your sweet face and graceful form. If I were a man, I would have carried you off to a far country and we could have lived happily for the rest of our lives. But I'm a woman—a plain, middle-aged, barren woman, neglected by her husband and despised by all who know her. There's no future for me. But your future is assured. You must marry again—a young, handsome, rich, brilliant boy, who will value you as you deserve to be valued. Don't resist him, sweet Kusum. I end this letter with love and blessings.

Your loving aunt
Durgamoni'

Kusum read the letter again and again, laughing and crying by turns. Then, tearing it into pieces, she flung it out of the window. 'Khurima is mad to write what she did,' she thought. 'Remarriage! *Chhi*!'

Kusum had no idea that the question of her remarriage was being seriously considered by her family. Her eldest brother, Nripendranath, had frequent discussions about the state of the country and community with Jadupati Ganguly, who tutored his two sons. Jadupati was a disciple of Vidyasagar's and had sought financial assistance from Nripendranath for several widow remarriages that had taken place in the city. 'You are a man of liberal views,' he said one day. 'Why don't you get your sister married again?'

'It isn't for me to take the decision,' Nripendranath replied cautiously. 'My father is the head of the house.'

'Then put it to him. I've heard that he's a friend of Ramgopal Ghosh and Ramtanu Lahiri. You must know that they are both ardent compaigners for widow remarriage.'

'I'll think about it,' Nripendranath replied. He was not quite sure of what he wanted to do. It was too bold a step. His father might welcome it. Or he might fume with rage. He hadn't the courage to approach him. He consulted his two younger brothers and found that they were not averse to the idea. Only, who would bell the cat? One of the brothers made a suggestion. They would go to Ramtanu Lahiri and request him to speak to their father. Ramtanu Babu was in Krishnanagar at present. They would approach him as soon as he returned.

One day, Nabin Kumar came to the house. He had been invited by the boys of the family to see one of their rehearsals and give them his advice. Handsomely dressed in a pleated dhoti and blue velvet banian, and twirling a silver-knobbed cane in his hand, Nabin Kumar stood in the middle of the courtyard and looked around him with an air of self-importance. 'How is it going?' he asked condescendingly. 'Is Surendra Babu to play the part of Pururba?' Kusum, who had been sitting with her brothers, rose at his entrance and walked away. She hadn't forgotten the day she had gone to see him and he had failed to recognize her. Nabin carried on talking to the boys, not deigning to cast a glance at the *than*-clad figure.

The next day Sarojini came to see Kusum. Taking the latter's hands tenderly in her own, Sarojini said, 'Kusum Didi, I've come to take you home. My Aryaputra wants to see you.'

'Your what?'

'My Aryaputra. My husband says that is how a wife must refer to her husband.'

'It sounds very funny,' Kusum giggled. 'Like a dialogue in a *jatra*. But what does your husband want with me?'

'He wants to talk to you. He didn't know that you've become a widow. He was very upset when I told him.'

'It is not proper for a widow to go to other people's houses,' Kusum said primly, not wanting to face Nabin Kumar.

'How could you say that?' Sarojini exclaimed indignantly. 'Are we other people?' Sarojini still spoke and behaved like a child. She pouted her full lips at Kusum and angry tears glittered in her eyes. Kusum resisted her for a while but had to give in at the end.

'Look who's here!' Sarojini cried triumphantly, dragging

Kusum into her husband's presence. Kusum was heavily veiled and her face was averted. 'Do you recognize me, Miteni?' Nabin asked, smiling, but there was no answer.

'Won't your Miteni talk to me?' Nabin glanced at his wife.

'You've forgotten. She was my sister's Miteni—not mine. O Kusum Didi! What makes you so shy? Is it because you've become a widow?'

'*He*' Devi!' Nabin sprang to his feet and folded his hands with a theatrical gesture. 'Unveil your face before me and loosen your tongue. Am I not your brother-in-law? Do you not know that the widowed Kunti spoke freely before her brother-in-law, Vidhur?' Even as he said these words, Sarojini pulled the veil away and Kusum's face was exposed to view. Her eyes were shut and her lips quivered with emotion. Nabin was startled. A great deal had happened to him in the last few years and he had forgotten the face that had made such in impression on him at one time. Now, seeing her again, he remembered. 'You're—you're Vanajyotsna!' he cried.

Kusum opened her deep blue eyes and looked full into his face.

'I must find a husband for your Kusum Didi,' Nabin said to his wife the next morning. Sarojini looked up startled. Her husband had a new whim every day and she was used to them. But what kind of talk was this?

'Are you in your senses?' she exclaimed. 'Kusum Didi was married years ago and she's now a widow Didn't you notice that she wore a *than* and there was no sindoor on her parting?'

'I did. And precisely for that reason I must find a husband for her.'

'Widows are remarried only among the lower classes. Not in families like ours.'

'That's the trouble with us. We talk about progress but act only when it affects others. Vidyasagar Moshai says that the push should come from within. Widow remarriage should become prevalent in the upper classes. It's a pity there are no widows in our house. If you were a widow I would have arranged a grand wedding for you.'

'Don't talk like that,' Sarojini said tearfully. 'It frightens me. See how hard my heart is beating.'

'Why?' Nabin laughed. 'Is it because I must die before you

become a widow? Well, I don't mind dying for such a good cause.'

*'O go!'* Sarojini set up a wail. 'What is to become of me?' Nabin clasped her in his arms and said, laughing, 'You're a silly girl. Can't you take a joke?' Sobering down, he continued, 'That's why I say girls must educate themselves. I bring you so many books and journals but you never bother to read them. If you were educated you would see that what I said was for your Kusum Didi's own good. Do you want her to suffer the deprivations of a widow's life forever?'

'It is her fate. Who are we to comment on it?'

'I can change her fate. I'll talk to her father tomorrow morning.'

Nabin did not talk to Kusum's father the following morning but the idea remained in his head. The fact is that he was too busy to pursue it. He spent eight to ten hours each day on his Mahabharat, of which one volume was out already and another in the press. The intellectuals of the city were dumbfounded by the quality of the translation and declared that they had never seen anything like it before. But Nabin, though determined to abide by his promise to Vidyasagar, was beginning to weary of the task, and he found a novel way of refreshing himself. Whenever the jaw-breaking Sanskrit shloks became unbearable to his ears, he took out a little bound copy book he kept for the purpose and jotted down a few sentences in everyday colloquial Bengali. These were in the nature of a commentary on the life of the city. Gradually, this new style of writing took such a hold of Nabin Kumar that its pages became covered with these jottings.

Nabin was tempted to publish them in the form of a book but was wary of putting his own name to it. What if people refused to believe that the translator of the Mahabharat could write such stuff? What if they were disgusted? He decided to use a pseudonym and started looking around for one. He had an idea. Birds, particularly crows and owls, flew all over the city and watched the goings-on with unblinking eyes. He would call his book *Hutom Pyanchar Naksha* (*The Etchings of Hutom the Owl*).

Busy as he was, he did not forget Kusum Kumari. The beautiful girl's deep blue eyes came before his own every now and then. He felt, though why no one could say, that he had to do something for her; that he couldn't let her down. Her father was away from Calcutta. Nabin decided to see him as soon as he returned and persuade him to find another husband for his daughter.

One morning, Ganganarayan accosted him just as he was leaving the house. 'I've been looking for you, Chhotku,' he said. 'I want a few copies of your Mahabharat. It's a brilliant piece of work. I gave my copy to a friend of mine. He was all praise for it and has sent you his latest book in return.'

And he handed Nabin a volume of verse.

'Who is this friend of yours?' Nabin asked.

'He's a well-known poet and dramatist. You may have heard of him. His name is Michael Madhusudan Dutt.'

Stepping into the carriage, Nabin opened the book. It was called *Meghnad Badh Kavya*. He had heard of Michael Madhusudan Dutt—the paid playwright of the Rajas of Paikpara. His lips curled a little. His *Vikramvarshi* had set off a spate of imitations. He had no opinion of them or their creators. But reading a few verses he sat up in astonishment. This was poetry of a totally different kind from anything he had read before. It was blank verse; there were no rhyming ends but the verses rang with melody and rhythm, like the grandest of orchestras. His lips started moving as he read and before he knew what he was doing, he started declaiming the lines in a sonorous voice. Dulal, who rode behind as footman, jumped down, startled, and running up to the window, poked his head in and asked, 'Did you say something, Chhoto Babu?' Nabin waved him away and continued his reading.

Nabin spent the next four days in a fever of excitement. He was consumed with curiosity about the *firinghee* poet who was his brother's friend. Weary of answering his many questions Ganga asked one day, 'Would you like to meet Madhu? I can easily bring him home.'

But Madhusudan was not destined to visit the Singha mansion in such an ordinary way. At a reception organized by his students for Mr Richardson, Nabin remarked, 'We are a strange race. We confer honour on outsiders; never on our own people.'

'You are right, Nabin,' Jadupati Ganguly agreed instantly.

'For our own people we have only brickbats. We gang up on them and carp and criticize. We should have given Vidyasagar Moshai a public reception years ago. Why don't you do something about it?'

'I don't think he will agree. He might even be annoyed if we propose it. I have another idea. Why don't we organize a reception for that new star rising on the horizon of letters—Michael Madhusudan Dutt?'

Nabin Kumar was not one to let grass grow under his feet. A grand reception was arranged in his own house and conducted under the auspices of the Vidyotsahini Sabha. The poet was to be honoured not only with a citation but with the gift—chosen by Nabin himself with much care and thought—of a beautifully embossed silver wine flask.

Madhusudan arrived at the Singha mansion in a state of considerable trepidation, but once there he enjoyed it all—the gift, the compliments and Nabin Kumar's unconcealed admiration. On their way back home, Gour, who was riding in the same carriage, remarked, 'I didn't see Harish Mukherjee. I wonder why he didn't come.' Madhusudan's brow furrowed at his words and he said, 'There was someone else I expected to see. Your Vidyasagar. Why wasn't he there? He must be a very proud man. If you meet him, tell him that M.S. Dutt does not give a damn for arrogant pandits like him.'

# Chapter XXVI

At a prayer meeting of the Brahmos, the *kulin* Brahmin, Jadupati Ganguly, announced that he had made a solemn resolve to cast off his sacred thread. He even mentioned a date. It was not too far off—only eleven days away. The news spread like wildfire and the Brahmins of the city, shocked beyond belief, denounced the act with all the passion they were capable of. Groups of people could be seen outside Jadupati's house at all times of the day, shouting threats and abuses, while larger numbers flocked to Raja Radhakanta Deb, begging him to do something. For wasn't it true that while all men had only one birth, the Brahmin was twice born and the symbol of that second birth was the sacred thread? The Brahmin was the custodian of the Hindu faith. Would not the skies fall down and the world be destroyed if such an act of blasphemy were committed?

But Jadupati did not care in the least. He was a widower, without chick or child, and he acted exactly as he thought best. Nor did he have an authoritarian father or a tearful mother at hand who would try to dissuade him. What Jadupati could not understand was why Brahmos, who had given up idol worship, still clung to caste distinctions in everyday life. Brahmins among them wore sacred threads and marriages were arranged with due deference to caste and *gotra*. Jadupati found this hypocritical and meaningless and vowed to do something to change it. His friends and well-wishers advised him against it. Even Debendranath Tagore sent for him one day and told him there was no need to do such a thing. The dissemination of the Brahmo faith had just about begun. Hostility from the Hindu camp would retard the process. But Jadupati had a one-track mind. He didn't believe in compromise. He wanted to make it clear, once and for all, that the Brahmo Dharma could not and would not contain caste distinctions. In this he was supported by the younger group—Keshav Chandra Sen and others.

On the appointed day, Jadupati came and stood on the balcony and listened to the insults and abuses flung at him by the crowd standing below, with an impassive face. Turning to a friend who stood by him, he said, 'Alas, Hinduism! Such are your custodians!' Returning to the room, he took off the thread and holding it within his cupped hands, he addressed his long dead father. 'Pitah!' he said. 'I seek your forgiveness. You taught me, as a child, to value the promptings of my own conscience above all other things. In doing what I do today I only follow your own instruction.' Then, kneeling on the floor, he touched his forehead to the ground and addressed his mother who lived in Bankura. 'Have faith in me, Ma,' he said. 'Ignore what others say. I'll never do anything to bring you sorrow or shame.' Then, holding the thread aloft in the air, he said, 'Farewell! I'm free of my bonds at last.'

Thousands of people lined up on either side of the street as Jadupati walked towards the Ganga, thread in hand. Jeers and comments assailed his ears but he paid no heed to them. With a passive, serene face he flung the thread into the swirling waters. A few days later Jadupati met Nabin Kumar. 'You're one up on me,' Nabin said. 'I wish I had a *poité*, which I could cast off and win public acclaim. But tell me, was there any need to immerse it in the Ganga? Does it not indicate a belief in the holiness of the Ganga? And in the sanctity of the *poité*?'

'It's not like that,' Jadupati murmured with some embarrassment. 'I could even have thrown it in the lavatory pit. My idea was to set an example. In carrying it to the Ganga, I made sure that thousands of people were watching me.'

'That you did.' Nabin laughed snidely. 'What's the point of giving up anything if you get no credit for it?'

But credit was not the only thing Jadupati was looking for. He had another motive behind discarding his thread and Nabin came to hear of it from Sarojini a few days later.

'You were quite right. What you said has come to pass,' Sarojini said that night as she settled herself cosily at his feet.

'Quite right about what? What have I said?'

Sarojini was dressed for the night in a fine cotton sari of the deepest blue and her lips were bright red with betel juice. Running her fingers through her hair, she said, 'About Kusum Didi getting married again. A widow to sleep with a strange man. *Chhi! Chhi!*' And she shuddered with the shame of it.

'Who told you she's getting married again?' Nabin asked in a suspicious tone.

'Everyone is talking about it. My mother burst into tears when she heard of it and cried, "The gods preserve us from harm! Heaven knows what destiny has in store for us with such unholy goings-on next door. Poor Kusum! She'll rot in hell forever."'

'I'm not interested in hearing what your mother said,' Nabin cried out angrily. 'Tell me what you've heard.'

What Sarojini had heard was the truth. Ramtanu Lahiri, at the request of the sons of the house, had broached the subject to Kusum Kumari's father, Krishnanath Rai. Krishnanath had profound respect for Ramtanu Babu and so gave the proposal due and serious consideration. Krishnanath was a man of the world and valued the traditions of his forefathers. But he was not a die-hard conservative. He was open to reason and willing to admit change. He had given Ramtanu Lahiri a patient hearing and said, 'I see the justice of your proposal. Kusum means the world to me and I want her to be happy. I have only myself to blame for her marriage to a madman. I would like her to have a second chance if such a marriage is endorsed by the shastras. But her mother must agree. I am powerless to do anything if she withholds her consent.'

But Kusum's mother, Punyaprabha's consent had been obtained easily. Wiping the tears from her eyes, she had told her sons, '*O ré*!' I was the first to bless Vidyasagar Moshai when he arranged the remarriages of child widows. Shall I draw back now when it comes to my own daughter? My poor, suffering child still shudders in terror when she remembers her mad husband!'

Hearing all this from Sarojini's lips, Nabin sat up in excitement. 'This is excellent news,' he said, fondling Sarojini's chin lovingly. 'I must arrange a grand wedding for her.'

'O Ma! Why should you arrange her wedding? She has parents, doesn't she? Besides, my mother said we're none of us to go to the wedding. I beg you not to get involved in this act of sin.'

'Saroj!' Nabin said sternly. 'Don't ever use such language again. There's no sin in a widow's remarriage. A second husband is also a husband in every sense of the word.'

'If you say so—' Sarojini began in a frightened voice.

'Several pandits have given their sanction to widow remarriage. Some have married widows and lived happily with them.'

'Is Kusum Didi to marry a pandit? Hemu said—'

'By pandit I mean a learned man—not one who's teaching in a *tol*. Why should your Kusum Didi marry a pandit? We'll find a handsome, well-educated youth from a rich and noble family. She's a daughter of the Rais of Bagbazar. This will be the widow remarriage Vidyasagar Moshai has dreamed about all these years. What a triumph it will be for him! I'll start looking for a suitable boy from tomorrow.'

'But Hemu said that a pandit wants to marry her. It is that friend of yours who doffed his *poité* and turned himself into a chandal.'

'Ha! Ha!' Nabin laughed heartily. 'So that was why Jadupati cast off his *poité*! What a joke!'

Next day, Jadupati Ganguly appeared in person—his face wan and sad. He had offered himself for Kusum but had been rejected. Nripendranath had told him that being a Kayastha family, they couldn't consider a Brahmin for their daughter. And, what was worse, he had even lost his job. A suitor of the daughter of the house could hardly be retained as tutor.

'People are strange, Nabin,' he said, after unburdening himself. 'I've cast off my *poité* but I still carry the stigma of Brahminhood. Our country is hopeless.'

'So that was why you made such a public spectacle of discarding it?' Nabin asked, smiling.

'Believe me, Nabin.' Jadupati gripped his hand. 'I have never seen the girl. Her nephews used to talk about her—her virtues and accomplishments. And that was what made me—'

'If only hearing about her has got you in this state, seeing her would cause your death. She's as beautiful as the Goddess Saraswati.'

'Will you put in a word for me? They are your father-in-law's neighbours.' Jadupati squeezed Nabin's hand in his desperation. 'Believe me. There's no lust or evil desire in me. I want to prove to the world that caste distinctions mean nothing to me. That is why I'm so keen on this girl.'

'Let me see.'

But Nabin knew that Jadupati did not stand a chance. The Rais of Bagbazar were an old and wealthy family and, in choosing a mate for their daughter, would seek him out of their own class. Jadupati was a fine scholar but he came from a poor family and had a rural background. The search was on and this time Kusum's father and brothers were scrutinizing the parties with great care and deliberation. They had made a mistake once. They wouldn't do it a second time. Nabin Kumar, too, was trying his best. Time passed. Kusum Kumari grew in age and beauty. But the right mate for her eluded them all.

One night Nabin woke up in a sweat. He had been restless all night and dreamed strange dreams. 'How wonderful!' he said to himself. 'There's such a simple solution. Why didn't I think of it before? Who could be a more fitting bridegroom for Kusum? I must fix this thing in a day or two.' And thinking thus, he sank into a deep and untroubled sleep.

Next morning Nabin went to see Vidyasagar at his house in Badurbagan.

'I've got good news for you,' he said.

'Really?' Vidyasagar smiled. 'Out with it, then. Good news comes rarely my way these days.'

'Do you know Krishnanath Rai of Bagbazar?'

'I've heard of him. He's an aristocrat and a man of considerable wealth.'

'He's the dewan of the kingdom of Tripura and holds an important position in Hindu society. A daughter of his has been widowed lately and he's looking for a match for her.'

'That is indeed good news.'

'The girl is talented as well as beautiful. But he's hard put to find a suitable groom. Jadupati offered himself but he's a Brahmin and a Brahmo. Krishnanath Babu did not agree. He's looking for a boy from his own caste.'

'It was very wrong of Jadupati. People are not yet ready for widow remarriage and he's trying to break caste barriers! He's a foolish boy and will land us in trouble.'

'I've found a match for her from her own caste and class. I've come to seek your permission.'

'Who is the young man?'

'Myself.'

'You?'

'Yes. I've known the girl from childhood. She was my late wife's friend and our caste and *gotra* match to a nicety. This marriage will be suitable in every way.'

Vidyasagar could hardly believe his ears. Could it be possible that a scion of the famous Singha family and sole heir to vast properties and estates was agreeing to marry a widow? If a marriage like this came about it would be a tremendous victory. The whole of India would hear of it.

'You!' he exclaimed staring at Nabin. 'Can you do it? Will your family let you? I've heard Radhakanta Deb is a relation of yours.'

'I don't care for anyone's opinion. Only yours. I can do anything with your blessings. You're my guru. I vowed long ago to follow the path you show.'

Vidyasagar was truly happy. The boy was a marvel—quite unlike other boys of his class. Nabin came home, brimming over with excitement. What a piece of luck it was that the idea had occurred to him in time. What a fool he was to have thought of giving Kusum away to strangers. She would come to his home now. She would be his—only his.

Nabin did not discuss the proposal with anyone else. He took it for granted that everybody would be as thrilled by it as he was. Sarojini was away at her father's house. He would go to her in the evening and give her the good news. Then he would speak to Kusum's father. Standing before the tall mirror in his bedroom, he murmured to himself, 'You'll be mine, Vanajyotsna! I'll be the sturdy tree to which you'll cling like a flowering vine; I, the stretch of calm water on whose breast you'll bloom like a lotus!' But, even as he was getting ready to go to Sarojini, Jadupati arrived with a message from Vidyasagar.

'He wants to see you at once,' Jadupati said.

'Why? What's the matter?'

'He didn't tell me. But he seemed very agitated. What have you been saying to him about me? He pounced on me as soon as he saw me and scolded me heartily.'

Vidysagar burst like a bomb at the sight of Nabin. 'So this was your little plan, was it?' he thundered. 'And you dared to make me a party to it. I should have known better than to have trusted you. You sons of rich men—you're all the same! Lechery and lust run in your blood.' Nabin stared at him in amazement. He had never been spoken to in such a manner before. 'I—I don't know why you're saying all this,' he stammered, his lips quivering and eyes close to tears.

'You don't know? You're a clever rogue. Didn't you tell me a deliberate lie? You have more money than you know what to do with. You can satisfy your lust in any way you please. Who is to stop you? But that you should stoop so low as to take advantage of an innocent widow—'

'You call it lust? That is unjust. What is wrong with wanting to marry a widow? I have told you no lie.'

'Didn't you tell me that the girl was a friend of your late wife's? Was that not a lie? Your wife is alive—'

'It wasn't a lie. The girl was indeed a friend of my late wife's. But I've married again. My present wife is my second.'

'And now you want to marry a third—a widow?'

'What is wrong with that? Our scriptures sanction polygamy for a man and our society endorses it.'

'When I proposed widow remarriage, I visualized a true marriage; a marriage of dignity and permanence. I didn't see the wretched girls occupying a second or third or fourth place—like concubines. Do what you please but get out of my sight. I'm sick to death of you.'

'You mistake my intention. I didn't mean to hurt anybody. I didn't realize that keeping more than one wife was wrong.'

'You should have realized it. For your wife's sake, at least. What justice is there in wrecking the life of one woman to build up another's?'

'My wife would have given her consent. She loves the girl and the two would have lived happily together like sisters.'

'Do women in families like yours have any rights? Is it for them to give or withhold their consent to anything? Do you ever care for their feelings? When you keep mistresses, when you come home drunk from visits to brothels, your wives receive you with due deference and see to your comfort. But aren't their hearts bursting with humiliation? You're not such a child that you can't see that. Anyway, as I've said before, you may do whatever you like. Only keep away from me. I have nothing to do with you in future. In fact, I shall oppose this marriage of yours with all the strength I can muster.'

'My wife is barren,' Nabin began in a halting voice. 'We have no children. If she fails to give me an heir—'

'Stop! Stop!' Vidyasagar roared, covering up his ears with both hands. 'Oof! Your words set my limbs on fire! How old is your wife that you label her barren? How old are you? At what age did your father beget you? Go away, Nabin, I can't bear to be in the same room with you any longer.'

Nabin went out of the room, his head bowed in shame. His chest felt tight and his eyes burned with unshed tears. A tremendous sense of loss assailed him. Vidyasagar Moshai, whom he respected above all other men, had ceased to trust him. He couldn't bear the shame of it. Suddenly, he turned in his tracks and went back to the room he had just left. Looking the older man straight in the eyes, he said, 'I can't bear to lose your love or be deprived of your blessings. Certainly not for a woman's sake. I give you my word. No one has heard of my plan as you called it. And no one shall.'

'You mean you won't marry her?'

'I'll never marry again as long as I live. Allow me to touch your feet and pledge my oath. I kept my promise about translating the Mahabharat, didn't I?'

Vidyasagar's face crumpled with remorse. 'You boys will be the death of me,' he said. 'You make me speak the harshest words. Don't you realize that people are out to discredit my actions? All they're waiting for is an excuse.' The tears he was fighting to control now ran down his cheeks.

Walking out of Vidyasagar's house, Nabin paused for a moment. Where should he go now? To Sarojini in Bagbazar? No—he couldn't face her tonight. He felt as if a volcano was about to erupt within him. His breast heaved with indignation and a wave of self-pity welled up in him. Biting his lips to control his feelings, he commanded Dulal to drive him to Bhawanipur. But the office of the *Hindu Patriot* was closed for the night and there was no sign of Harish. Nabin drove on to their old haunt in Janbazar. 'Why brother!' Harish drawled from his place at the centre of a knot of drunken men. 'You've come back. Are you by any chance a trifle weary of art and culture and good works? Not to mention playing disciple to Vidyasagar? Drinking and whoring are not the things for good boys like you.' He rose to his feet, reeling a little, a brandy bottle in his hand. Nabin took it from him and put it to his lips. Pausing for breath, he said, 'I've pledged two solemn oaths and I'll keep them while there's breath in my body. But I'm my own master in everything else. From tonight I shall live as I wish.'

# Chapter XXVII

Madam Destiny loves taking people by surprise. At a wave of her hand a king may turn into a fakir and a cowherd win a princess and half a kingdom. The Singha family of Jorasanko had borne their share of the lady's caprice, and no one more so than Ganganarayan. Reverend Long was serving a sentence of one month's rigorous imprisonment for his involvement with the English translation of *Neel Darpan* and Ganga felt overwhelmed with guilt for it was at his request that Madhu had agreed to translate it. Ganga's wife, Lilavati, had been living in her father's house when Ganga left for Ibrahimpur. She had never returned. Deprived of her husband, the poor girl had lived the life of a widow till her death eight months ago. There was something odd about her death, and the fact that a cousin of hers had hanged himself two days later lent credence to the rumours that floated about. Ganga had accepted the news with stoic calm. But Madam Destiny had yet another shock waiting for him.

One day, Ramgopal Ghosh came to see him. 'I've heard about you from Harish,' he said. 'You're a marvel. It's wonderful to think that one so modest, so soft-spoken could have toted a gun and led a revolt against those bloodhound planters.'

'Harish tends to exaggerate,' Ganga replied, bowing his head humbly before the older man. 'It is true that I held a gun in my hands. But I fired only once.'

After a few minutes of general talk, Ramgopal came to the point. 'I come to you with a request,' he said in his forthright manner. 'You have heard of Krishnanath Rai of Bagbazar? I appeal to you to consider marrying his widowed daughter, Kusum Kumari.'

Like Ganganarayan, Kusum Kumari had also become a living legend. Her beauty, her father's wealth, his decision to arrange a second marriage for her and his fastidiousness in choosing the groom were being discussed avidly in the elite circles of Calcutta. The ones who favoured widow remarriage saw this as a watershed event in the cause. The ones who didn't were shocked and agitated. They had watched the decline in widow remarriage with smug satisfaction and were appalled at its revival—doubly so because it was taking place in a family like that of the Rais of Bagbazar. Had Krishnanath, the pious, conservative, austere Krishnanath, lost his mind? The horrified traditionalists thronged Raja Radhakanta Deb's durbar, begging him to intervene. The upholders of widow remarriage had their own anxieties. Krishnanath was taking too long in making up his mind. What if he were to change it? What if he succumbed to pressure from the other camp? They joined the search for a suitable groom though many of them hadn't even seen Kusum Kumari. Ramgopal Ghosh was one of the latter group of a hundred important men of the city. They had discussed various possibilities and come to the conclusion that Ganganarayan Singha was the ideal husband for Kusum Kumari. He was young and handsome, a widower, and came from a rich and important family. Krishnanath could have no objections to him.

'You may be surprised at my coming to you,' Ramgopal went on. 'And quite justifiably so. You see, I'm not here at the request of the girl's family. In fact,' he smiled, 'I'm of the bridegroom's party. If you agree I shall put the proposal before Krishnanath Babu.' Ganga raised his head and fixed his frank, direct gaze on the older man's face. 'You've made a wrong choice,' he said quietly. 'I don't wish to marry again.'

'Why not? You've left the jungles behind you and are now in the city of Calcutta. Why should you not lead a normal life?'

'There are many among us who prefer to remain single. I'm one of them, Mr Ghosh.'

'This is no ordinary marriage. It is a responsibility that you must take up in the interest of your country and community.'

'I've imbibed a touch of saffron in the last few years. I'm in no mood now for a wife and family.'

'Your mood will change. Look at the mood of the country. Is it not changing?'

The exchange went on for a little while longer, Ramgopal pleading his case and Ganga declining it. When Ramgopal left, it was with a plea to Ganga to reconsider his decision. But the follower of Derozio did not leave it at that. He continued to mobilize opinion in favour of the match. In consequence, Ganga was flooded with requests. Harish Mukherjee was a keen enthusiast of the cause and so were Ganga's friends from Hindu College.

'*O re*' Ganga!' Rajnarayan said with his usual humour. 'All our votes are yours. We elect you bridegroom unanimously.'

'Did I submit any nomination papers that you elect me?'

'Did Cromwell submit nomination papers before he was elected?'

'You want me to go the way Cromwell did?'

'Well. Marrying is hanging oneself, is it not? Why are you so afraid of it, brother? Look at us. Gour, Madhu and I have been through it twice. Take Ma Durga's name and jump into the fray.'

'Stop nagging me.'

'Are you hesitating because you must marry a widow?' Rajnarayan probed. 'I would have taken a widow as my second wife if I wasn't married already when Vidyasagar started his movement. So I did the next best thing. I got my two younger brothers married to widows. At least, two young girls have escaped the rigours of widowhood. You can imagine my plight. Living in a village, as I do, I am continually assailed by threats—of my house being burned down; of my head being broken. But I'm not afraid. I go about with a stout stick in my hand and no one dares come near me. We'll look after you if anything happens. Don't worry.'

Ganga shook his head impatiently. Public opinion was the last thing on his mind. The truth was that he was thinking of Bindubasini a great deal these days. He had never seen Kusum Kumari but he knew how old she was. Bindu had been exactly the same age when she was banished to Kashi. He felt a constriction in his chest and his nerves screamed with pain. Why were people so cruel? Why were they reviving the agony he had believed was dead within him?

One night, Ganga saw Bindu in a dream—not as he had seen her last—a ravishingly beautiful woman, shimmering in silks and jewels—but as the little child widow with whom he did his lessons. She stood before him, her brow furrowed in indignation and cried, 'You promised you'd read *Meghdoot* with me. You're a liar. You didn't keep your word. You never do.'

Ganga woke up, trembling all over. Tears poured from his eyes, drenching his pillow.

One evening, Harish Mukherjee accosted Nabin. 'Has your brother come to a decision?' he asked. 'I have no idea,' Nabin said, averting his face. Harish was his mentor once again and he was following in his footsteps. He worked hard all day at his Mahabharat and drank himself into a stupor every evening. But unlike Harish he had no interest in women or in drunken revelry. He had matured in the last few months and was more serious and withdrawn.

'Didn't you speak to your brother?' Harish probed. 'Ganganarayan is the pride of Bengal. He and I have many plans together. We'll launch movement after movement and have the English at our feet in a decade.'

'Would it be wise of him to marry then? Are not a wife and family obstacles to social work?

'No, no. It is imperative that he marries the girl. It will be like the lash of a whip in the face of this sleeping country. If a man like Ganganarayan Singha marries a widow, many will follow him.'

'I have a feeling this marriage won't take place.'

'Why not?'

'My mother is alive even if she is in Hardwar. She will weep her eyes out at the news. I know my brother. He won't hurt her feelings for anything in the world.'

Harish put his glass down and cried out excitedly, 'You, Nabin? Do I hear *you* say such a thing? Have you forgotten the days when you donated a thousand rupees to every widow remarriage? Are you not a self-proclaimed disciple of Vidyasagar's? Now, because it involves your own family, you sing a different tune. You're all the same—hypocrites to the last. Look at me. I'm neck-deep in lawsuits with the British. Do I do all this with my mother's permission? If your brother declines this offer, I'll never speak to him as long as I live.' Nabin made no reply. Finishing his brandy in a slow, leisurely draught, he stretched himself out on the carpet and shut his eyes.

'Why don't you say something?'

'Please don't disturb me.'

'I know your type. When you're defeated in an argument you fall asleep. A typical Indian. Heh! Heh!'

The wedding was arranged within ten days of this conversation. Ganganarayan could not hold out for long against pressure from his own friends and well-wishers. He was too gentle, too refined. Besides, his mood had changed after his dream. He felt, in some strange way, that in refusing Kusum Kumari, he was failing in his duty to Bindu. He was pushing another innocent child widow into a life of torture and humiliation. If he married Kusum and gave her the status and dignity of a wife, Bindu's soul would rest in peace.

On the appointed day, Ganga drove down in a flower bedecked carriage to the mansion of the Rais in Bagbazar and the nuptials were concluded with much pomp and ceremony. Only Nabin was missing. He had seen the procession off and rushed over to Harish's house as word had reached him that Harish was seriously ill and had been vomiting blood for a whole day and night. Nabin took two English doctors with him and one native—Dr Durgacharan Bandopadhyaya. But all their combined efforts could not save his friend. Harish passed away in the early hours of the morning. There were many who wept for him; many who regretted that he had left so much undone.

In the crowd that had collected outside the gates stood Raimohan—an old, bent, dishevelled Raimohan—looking like a street lunatic. When news came from within that all was over, he suddenly burst into song in a high, quavering, unmusical voice.

Our golden land is ravaged
By the blue monkey I've heard tell.
Harish dies before his time
And Long rots in his cell.
What will the poor ryot do now?

# Chapter XXVIII

One day, soon after the funeral rites were concluded, Nabin entered the office of the *Hindu Patriot* with slow, measured steps. Looking around him he felt a stab of pain below the ribs and a weakness in the limbs. He had lost the only friend he had and felt totally cut off from the world. Turning to the young man who sat there with a dejected hang-dog expression, he asked, 'Is it necessary to wind up the paper?' The young man's name was Shombhu Chandra and he had been co-editing with Harish for some years now.

'I see no other way,' he replied. 'I doubt if we can even keep the press. The indigo planters have brought a defamation suit against Harish. His death will make no difference. They'll auction the press and claim the proceeds.'

'Can they do that?'

'The sahebs can do anything. If the press is lost, the family will starve.'

Nabin thought for a while. 'What if someone were to buy the press and the licence before the verdict?' he asked. 'What then?'

'Both can be saved.'

'How much do you think the press will fetch?'

'The machines are old but it should fetch between a thousand and twelve hundred.'

'Inform Harish's wife and mother that I'll buy it for five thousand rupees. The interest from the sum should keep them in reasonable comfort, should it not?'

'You'll pay five thousand for something worth one?' Shombhu Chandra exclaimed. 'I've never heard of this kind of haggling before. If all the great men of Calcutta had your generosity—'

Nabin waved his effusions away and said, 'Make all the arrangements. I'll bring the money tomorrow and complete the formalities. Another thing. I shall be the owner of the paper only in name. You'll have to shoulder the entire responsibility of running it.'

'I?'

'Yes, you. If you can't do it by yourself, send for Girish Ghosh. He has a lot of experience in this field. We can't afford to let the paper die out.'

From that day onwards, Nabin was a changed man. He plunged himself into a sea of work to overcome his grief. His evening expeditions were a thing of the past. He didn't touch a drop of liquor. Nor did he leave the house.

About this time Nabin published *Hutom Pyanchar Naksha*, startling the readers of Calcutta beyond their wildest expectations. 'Who is this new writer,' people asked one another, 'whose pen is sharper, wittier and more rooted in reality than even Tekchand Thakur's?' No one dreamed that it was Nabin Kumar Singha, who was even now penning the sonorous verses of the Mahabharat. Every evening Sarojini came into her husband's room, dressed in her best saris and jewels, her limbs perfumed with sandal paste. One day, standing by the door, she watched him as he bent over his papers by the light of a silver-meshed English lamp. Then, with a sigh, she walked softly over and stood by his side. 'It is very late,' she said stiffly. 'Won't you come to bed?'

'I have some work to finish,' Nabin answered as usual without looking up. 'You go on and sleep.'

'How much longer will you be?'

'I can't say.'

Sarojini stood uncertainly for a little while, then tiptoed to her own room. Her heart felt fit to burst. Tearing the garlands of scented flowers from her neck and arms, she threw herself on the bed in a fit of angry tears. This was happening night after night. She couldn't understand the change that had come over her husband. He had always been a busy man but he had found the time to tease and scold her; to love and pamper her. Now, he had lost all interest in her. Her mother and sisters were appalled at her news. 'It's the strangest thing I've ever heard,' her mother exclaimed. 'He doesn't keep a mistress or spend nights in brothels. He's at home all the time and takes no interest in his wife! He's mourning the loss of his friend. I can understand that. But for how long? Besides, in times like these, men cling to their wives more closely than ever.' Sarojini's mother and sisters felt that she was to blame in some way. '*O re*' Saro!' her sisters advised. 'Don't let him slip through your fingers. Hold on tight. Fall at his feet if necessary. Marriage bonds loosen very easily.'

Sarojini took their advice and one night she rushed into Nabin's room and flung herself at his feet.

'Why? What's this?' Nabin gave a startled cry.

Sarojini was looking very beautiful. A rich sari of Benares brocade covered her limbs and exquisite jewels sparkled from her hair, neck and arms. But her eyes were full of tears. 'Tell me,' she knocked her head on her husband's feet. 'You must tell me why you are so changed. What have I done? Am I an insect that you take no notice of me. Shall I jump into the fire and kill myself?'

Nabin was sitting at a table with several large sheets of newsprint spread out in front of him. Withdrawing his feet he said angrily, 'What is all this? Don't you see I'm busy? Don't disturb me at work, Saroj. You're too childish.'

Sarojini wiped her tears and rose to her feet. 'No. I won't disturb you any more,' she said quietly. 'But my mother wanted to know what it is you do night after night. It is bad for your health.'

'I'm bringing out a daily newspaper in Bengali. It is called *Paridarshak*.'

'What?'

'I knew you wouldn't understand. The sahebs have a daily paper in English, which they read first thing in the morning. I'm bringing out something similar in Bengali.'

Nabin tried to explain the nature of the work he was doing, without much success, to Sarojini, when she interrupted him suddenly. 'I want to ask you something,' she said.

'What is it?'

'You were so keen that Kusum Didi be married again. Now that she is married and in our own house, you don't speak a word to her.'

Nabin was not prepared for this accusation. He felt his breath stop and his eyes flash as he said, 'Your Kusum Didi needed a good husband. She has got one. We're all very happy for her.'

'But why don't you talk to her? She's right here with us.'

'I'm too busy to talk to anyone.' Then he added quickly, 'I don't even have the time to talk to you.'

'Kusum Didi wanted to know how she was to address you—Thakurpo[12] or Miten as she used to.'

'She can address me as she pleases.'

'You aren't coming to bed then. Shall I go?'

'Go.'

After Sarojini's departure, Nabin put down his pen and sat quietly staring at the wall opposite. His eyes were unnaturally bright in a very pale face. Then, a trembling seized him like that of a man in a high fever. Unable to control himself, he rose from the chair and lay down on the floor. A sound escaped him, pushing up from deep within his lungs—a cry of agony.

Bimbabati's abandoned wing was now occupied by Ganga and Kusum Kumari. Cages full of birds still hung from the ceiling of the long gallery, but many of them were rusted and their inmates dead from want of proper care. Kusum Kumari took on the responsibility of looking after the ones which had survived. She gave them their gram and water and spoke to each bird every morning, as her mother-in-law had done. In time she came to take the latter's place in many other things.

Kusum was lonely at first. Sarojini loved her but she was spending most of her time in her father's house in Bagbazar. Of the other women who lived in the house, not one came near her. Kusum, of course, had enough intelligence to understand it. She had even expected it. Widow remarriage, she knew, was even less acceptable to the boy's family than to the girl's. She had brought two maids with her from home, called Toru and Neeru, and they were her only friends and companions. Kusum found herself thinking of Durgamoni a great deal these days. Durgamoni must have heard of her marriage and rejoiced at it. Kusum Kumari had hoped for a letter from her and had been disappointed. She would have written herself, only she wasn't sure of the repercussions. Would Ganganarayan like her to renew her ties with her first husband's family? Besides, Kusum

12 Husband's younger brother.

herself was keen to wipe out that phase of her life from her memory.

Ganganarayan was a very busy man these days. Nabin Kumar took no interest in the properties and estates and Bidhusekhar was too old. Consequently, Ganga was forced to shoulder the entire responsibility. And he had to take all the decisions for discussion with Nabin yielded no result. 'Do as you think best, Dadamoni[13],' he invariably said before turning to his literary pursuits. Ganga felt trapped for he had planned to return to Ibrahimpur and take up the work he had only begun. Chhotku was completely unapproachable. Harish was dead. The cloud of depression that swamped him these days lifted only at the thought of Kusum Kumari. He spent the whole day in hard, soulless work, and lived only for the night, when he would be with her. But, though three months had passed since their marriage, they had not come together in a sexual union.

Discussing the next day's schedule with lawyers, attorneys and officials of the estate took up a large part of the evening and was often carried far into the night. But no matter how late the hour at which he entered his chamber, Ganga's eyes fell on a familiar scene—that of Kusum Kumari lying on the floor, reading a book by the light of the lamp. The book was familiar, too—Nabin's Mahabharat. He always stood in the doorway, not liking to disturb the reader, but she would sense his presence within a few minutes and sit up in haste. She would get busy in serving him his frugal meal of sweetmeats and fruits—a legacy of the days he had spent in the mountains—neatly and tastefully arranged on a silver *thala*. Pointing to some particular sweet, she would say, 'Ma made these herself and sent them over. Shall I give you some more?' Kusum Kumari always waited for Ganga to finish his meal before she sat down to her own. 'Times are changing,' Ganga said to her often enough, 'and many of the old traditions are dying out. Can't this be one of them?' 'That which is good should not be allowed to die out,' she would answer. Ganga would look at her in amazement. She was so young, yet she had such clear ideas of right and wrong.

---

13 Dear elder brother.

And she could articulate her thoughts so precisely. At such times he was invariably reminded of Lilavati. Lilavati could only react to purely domestic issues. Her part in any other conversation was restricted to 'O Ma!' or 'Really?' or, at the most, 'How can you say such things?'

One night, her meal over, Kusum came and stood by her husband, where he sat turning the pages of the book she had just been reading. 'You've read quite a lot, I see,' Ganga said. 'Do you like it?'

'Very much,' Kusum cried, her face shining with enthusiasm. 'I don't feel like putting it down for even a minute.'

'Do you understand it all? Is it not difficult in places?'

'Not at all. Well, maybe a word or two. But it is a beautiful book. I've read Kashidas but this is so much better!'

'Our Chhotku is a genius. He's so young—fourteen years younger than me—but look at the work he is doing! Have you made friends with him yet?' Kusum's blue eyes glowed like lamps and her lips curved in a smile as she answered with a charming tilt of her head, 'No. But I've seen him before. He was married to my Miteni—'

On another night, Kusum Kumari said to her husband, 'I have a favour to ask of you. Only don't be angry with me.'

'A favour?' Ganga looked up surprised. 'What is it? I couldn't be angry with you—not if I was the greatest villain on this earth.'

'Will you teach me to read Sanskrit? I've wanted it for so long. I was afraid to ask you because you work so hard and are so tired and worn out when you come up at night.' At her words, a wave of exultation passed through Ganga's frame and Bindu's voice echoed in his ears: 'You promised you'd read *Meghdoot* with me. You didn't keep your promise.' It was the same voice. 'Come and sit by me, Kusum,' he said. 'I'll read *Meghdoot* to you.'

'*Meghdoot*? I haven't heard of it before. I'd like to hear *Shakuntala*.'

'Why *Shakuntala*? Don't you care for *Meghdoot*?'

'I know nothing of either,' Kusum said with a timid laugh. 'I've heard the story of *Shakuntala* from my brother's tutor. Only Pon Moshai didn't finish it. I'm dying to know the end.'

'We'll read *Meghdoot* first and then *Shakuntala*.'

Ganga blew out the lamp and taking Kusum by the hand, led her to the window. The autumn moon shone amidst masses of white clouds and enveloped them in a flood of silver light. 'That is Meghdoot—the messenger cloud,' Ganga said, pointing to the sky. 'As Nal used a swan to carry his letters to Damayanti, so a Yaksha, exiled in Ramgiri, engaged a cloud to take a message to his beloved.'

'Where is Ramgiri?'

'Kalidas anticipated your question and began his poem with the words, *"Janakatanayasnan Punyodakeshu/ Snigdhachhaya-tarushu basatin."* Janakatanayu is Sita. Ram and Sita spent some years of their banishment from Ayodhya in Ramgiri. The waters of Ramgiri turned holy after Sita bathed in them. It is in this Ramgiri that the Yaksha—'

'What is the name of the Yaksha?'

'That's a good question. He has no name. Kalidas didn't give his hero a name because he didn't see him as a person. He saw him as the symbol of all thwarted lovers. If I were forced to live apart from you, I would express my agony in exactly the same voice.'

'Go on.'

'The exiled Yaksha sat on the mountain, mourning his separation from his beloved. Eight months passed and he grew thin and worn out with longing. Then, on the first day of Asadh,[14] he saw a cloud rising from behind the mountain. It had the shape and colour of an elephant and it heaved from side to side in a drunken dance. Calling the cloud to him he said—'

'Can a cloud hear a human voice?'

'A cry from the soul can be heard by all created beings—animate and inanimate. The poet says—' And Ganga recited the verses in a sonorous voice. He knew the whole of *Meghdoot* by heart. Kusum listened in silence for a while. Then she said softly, 'Shall we go up to the roof?'

'Why? Are you bored with *Meghdoot*?'

'I feel dazed with happiness.' Kusum laid her cheek on Ganga's arm. 'I'll die if you stop now. We can see the whole sky from the roof and the clouds will float right above our heads.'

---

14 15th June-15th July.

The house was dark and silent as the two tiptoed out of their room and up the stairs. It was a lovely night, with the moon pouring out her beams and a soft, sweet breeze rustling in the branches of the trees. A light dew fell on them as they sat side by side, their backs resting against a large earthen pitcher, a row of such vessels standing against the parapet. 'Somewhere along the river the champak blooms,' Ganga recited, his face turned up to the sky and his voice throbbing with emotion. 'Somewhere the earth smells fresh and sweet and the dappled deer runs across it in ecstasy . . . ' Ganga recited the whole of *Purba Megh* and fell silent.

'Why do you stop?'

'It is enough for one night. Good things should be taken in small doses. I'll recite *Uttar Megh* to you tomorrow night.'

'The sky is so beautiful. I don't feel like going back.'

'Very well. We'll sit here—'

'What if I ask to stay all night? Will you stay with me?'

'Crazy girl! Of course I will.'

'I'm happy! So happy it hurts. Here.' And she placed a hand upon her breast. 'Look at the moon. Does it not seem as if she is staring at us?'

'Not at us. At you. She is jealous of you.'

'She might well be. The moon is very lonely.'

They sat in silence for a while. Then Ganga said, 'Is there a reason behind the lives we are given? Do you know the answer, Kusum?'

'No. I've never thought about it.'

'There's a Supreme Being who created us all. There must be some reason for it. "I gave you a human life," he might say when I'm called to his side. "Have you put it to good use?" What answer shall I make then?'

'I don't know, but I'd like to find out. We'll do it together from this day onwards. Together! Promise me you'll never go away from me.' Kusum placed a hand on Ganga's feet.

'I promise.'

Ganga gazed on that lovely face, turned up to his like a new-blown flower. It was fresh and dewy and bathed in moonbeams. No, this was not Bindu's face. It was another woman's. But before that face, Bindu's dissolved in a mist and faded away. The past was dead. The present was too compelling. 'Come,' Ganga stood up and raised Kusum to her feet. Clasping her to his breast, he said, 'I've been very lonely, Kusum. Very lonely. Comfort me. Make me whole again.' And lifting her up in his arms, he made his way down the stairs.

# Chapter XXIX

Like Sohagbala before her, Thakomoni grew in size day by day. The marble block in the centre of the courtyard must have had something to do with it for whoever sat on it swelled like a summer gourd. And authority passed automatically into her hands. Thako's face and form, once smooth and firm as if cut out of black marble, were bloated and overblown. There were three chins to her neck now and even her hands and feet were puffed up like overripe fruits. Thako had been very ill in the last few months; so ill she could barely move her limbs. Everyone had thought she would die and Manada had already taken possession of the marble block. But, quite miraculously, Thako had recovered and her first act on getting out of bed was to dispossess Manada and take her seat on her throne once again. It was after her illness that she had started running to fat. She often wondered if she would end up like Sohagbala and her heart quaked at the thought.

A strange lethargy had taken possession of Thakomoni these days. She sat watching Nakur and Duryodhan cutting up the fish with lacklustre eyes, and even when she caught Nakur slip a hunk of carp under the scales and innards she hadn't the energy to reprimand him. She knew he would sell it later in the day. She could have demanded half the proceeds as her legitimate share but did not care to any longer. What would she do with the money? She had enough already, bundles and bundles of notes spread out below the mattress of her bed, and she had little use for it. Nakur and Duryodhan were puzzled at the change in her. Did she have a darker, deeper intention? Was this seeming carelessness only a trap to catch them in a more grievous offence? Thako enjoyed greater authority than Sohagbala even. For she was not only Dibakar's mistress; she was Dulal's mother.

Every night, after the day's work was done, Nakur came and stood outside Thako's door, calling softly, 'Are you asleep, Thako Didi?' Thako slept within the house these days, in one of the rooms downstairs, and Nakur, who had once been her paramour, called her Thako Didi. Thako remembered the night he had forced his way into her palm leaf hut and raped her in the presence of her sleeping boy. Now he stood outside her door, meekly awaiting permission to enter. Her mouth curled in derision. Nakur had ceased to be her paramour. He was now her humble slave.

'Come in,' she called. 'I'm still awake.'

Nakur entered the room, and unhooking a pouch from a niche in the wall, poured out its contents on the floor. Taking up a funnel he packed it with ganja and puffed it alight before handing it respectfully to Thako. This was the best hour of Thako's day and she lived only for it. Grasping it greedily with both hands, she brought it to her mouth and gave a long vigorous pull. Phut! Phut! Phut! The seeds crackled and burst and the pernicious smoke curled deep into her lungs. She sat rocking from side to side, her eyes shut in ecstasy. The funnel passed from her hand to Nakur's and then back again till Thako had had her fill.

Brimming over with dope, Thako lay sprawled on her bed. 'Do you feel a pain in your knee, Thako Didi?' Nakur asked tenderly, before putting out his hands and starting to press her legs. Thako watched him out of eyes red and glazed with ganja. It was good to have a man at her feet; a strong, young, thick-necked bull of a man like Nakur. Her body heaved luxuriously. Placing a foot on Nakur's chest she gave him a sharp shove. 'Go,' she commanded in the voice of a queen. 'Go back to your work.'

Nakur rose obediently and tiptoed out of the room, closing the door softly behind him. Thako never asked for her share of the money he made out of the Singha household. All she wanted as compensation was to kick him on the chest once at the end of the day. It was her right and it was not his place to protest.

But after Nakur left the room, Thako began to weep, softly at first, then with greater intensity as the hours passed. Her pillow drenched with tears, she sank into a drugged sleep. And in that sleep she never failed to dream the same dream. She was back again in Bhinkuri, not in her old hut but in a neat brick house by the canal. She had her own pond, brimming over with clear water at the back of the house, and rice fields beyond it.

Her son and daughter-in-law were with her, and with them her adored grandchild. And she reigned over her new kingdom with all the glory of a queen.

One night, the dream possessed her so wholly that she climbed out of bed and ran all the way to Dulal's house. Rapping wildly at the door, she called out in a high, unnatural voice, 'Let's go back to the village, O Dulal! Let's be mother and son again together. We'll be so happy. I'll treat your wife like a queen. O Dulal! Let's go this very minute.' Shocked out of his sleep, Dulal stumbled out of bed and opened the door. At the sight of his mother, her hair blowing wildly about her face and her sari slipping from her breasts, a terrible fury took possession of him. 'Get out of my house, you shameless whore,' he cried, grinding his teeth at her. 'It makes me sick to see your face. If you ever, ever—' And with these words he kicked her viciously on the breast; the same breast that had suckled him in infancy and kept him alive.

Next morning, Thako was not to be found in the Singha household or anywhere near it. Running away from her son like a hunted animal, she reached the Ganga and found refuge in its merciful waters. But before that she had asked everyone who passed by, 'Can you tell me the way to Bhinkuri?' Some had turned away, taking her to be a demented woman. Others, kinder and more patient, had enquired the name of the district and pargana. But she could tell them nothing. There were two villages by the side of a canal—Bhinkuri and Dhankuri. That was all she could remember. Shaking their heads and clicking their tongues, the passers-by walked on.

# Chapter XXX

With Keshab Sen's initiation, a new wave appeared in the stagnating waters of the Brahmo faith. Feuds and tensions had eroded its vitality of late and rendered it dull and lifeless. Ishwar Chandra Vidyasagar was still editor of *Tatwabodhini*, but God's name was rarely to be heard from his lips. Debendranath was old and his once rebellious spirit had turned conservative. He had admitted, under pressure from certain sections, that the Vedas were neither sacred nor inviolable. Yet the idea of non-Brahmins preaching from the pulpit of the Brahmo Sabha was distasteful to him. Again, though he upheld widow remarriage, dissolution of caste distinctions and renouncing of the sacred thread in theory, he was against drastic change in practice. He was the leader of the Brahmos, but Durga Puja was still celebrated in his house. He never graced the occasion with his presence but neither did he prevent it. The famous Ramkamal Sen's grandson and his own second son, Satyendranath's classfellow Keshab, was a spirited young man with a fanatical zeal for the truth. In him Debendranath saw the symbol of a new era. Keshab, he was convinced, would be a fit guardian of the faith after he was gone.

Keshab was an ardent believer in dissemination. 'Just a thousand or two members!' he exclaimed from time to time. 'What good will that do? We must carry the new faith to the ends of the country and even beyond it. Our God is a living God. The world is His temple and nature His priest. All human beings, be they high or low, rich or poor, learned or illiterate, have a right to His worship.' At times like these Debendranath felt a little uneasy. Keshab was too rash, he thought. He wanted to initiate people from all castes and classes. Was that wise? But, as time passed, Debendranath got over his hesitation. Keshab was gold—true unalloyed gold. If he wanted a universal brotherhood of Brahmos, he must be right and Debendranath would not stand in his way.

Debendranath's love for Keshab increased day by day and,

with the passing of time, this youth became more to him than his own sons. Keshab's influence over Debendranath was great. When, at Keshab's instigation, the Brahmins from the young group of Brahmo Sabha members decided to renounce their threads, Debendranath glanced at his own and said, 'Why keep this then?' And taking it from his neck, he dropped it on a table beside him. Conscious of the Pirali taint in his blood, Debendranath refrained from sitting on the dais at Brahmo Sabha meetings for only Brahmins of the purest strain were sanctioned by tradition to do so. Even when he addressed the members, as he did from time to time, he did it standing. But when Keshab urged him to put a stop to this practice, he could not refuse him. 'You are higher in our eyes than the highest of Brahmins,' Keshab cried. 'You are Maharshi! What do these Brahmin pandits know of our religion?' Debendranath hesitated a little but gave in eventually, breaking a convention hallowed by time and usage.

A few months later, while making the arrangements for his second daughter, Sukumari's wedding, he took another, bolder step. 'Why should the leader of the Brahmo Samaj give his daughter away in marriage in accordance with Hindu tenets?' the young Brahmo group demanded. For though Brahmos had rejected idol worship, they still fell back on the Narayanshila and yagna when conducting marriages, having no rites of their own. Acknowledging their demand as a reasonable one Debendranath announced that he would marry off his daughter according to Brahmo rites. Discarding the essentials of a Hindu marriage—the Brahmin priest, the Narayanshila and the yagna—he retained the peripherals. Conches were blown and the women ululated. Garlands were exchanged and the nuptial knot tied. The bridegroom was received by Debendranath himself, with the customary gifts, and the dowry was set out in the traditional manner. The only visual difference was that prayer and sermon took the place of mantras and elderly Brahmos the place of the priests. This was the first Brahmo marriage in the land and word of it spread far and wide. The English newspaper, *All the Year Round,* carried a report in its celebrated columns.

While the more zealous among the Brahmos regretted the presence of so much Hindu ritual in a Brahmo marriage, the

Hindus were horrified. They had believed the new dharma to be only a little ripple in the great stretch of water that was Hinduism—a slight stirring by a few eccentric aristocrats and some unruly college students—and were confident that it would soon die out. The rejection of the Vedas by the Thakurs of Jorasanko and the solemnizing of marriage vows in the absence of the Narayanshila and Vedic mantras came as a terrible shock. It was not to be borne. The Hindu community got ready for battle. Aggression and violence against Brahmos started taking the place of taunts and insults. The Brahmos were in a mood to retaliate. But they needed a general who could lead them to victory. Who was it to be? Who else but Keshab? Debendranath was helped in his decision by a vision in which the Lord stood by his side and commanded him to appoint Keshab Acharya of the Sabha. But Debendranath's well-wishers advised him against it. Keshab was too young, only twenty-three, and he was a Vaidya. Would it be wise to place him above so many elderly Brahmins? 'All he has to say for himself,' they commented, 'is "Perhaps" and "I'll try." How much work can be got out of him?'

'Perhaps' and 'I'll try' were indeed Keshab's favourite expressions. The fact was that he had such a fanatical zeal for the truth that he never committed himself to anything. People made fun of him behind his back, saying that he would sit down to a meal with the words, 'I'll try to eat my meal,' and rise with the words, 'Perhaps I've eaten.' But Debendranath turned a deaf ear to all the appeals and proceeded to put his plan into action. On the eve of the first of Baisakh[15]—the day Keshab was to become Acharya—Satyendranath said to his friend, 'Won't you bring your wife? It is but right that she should witness this great event.'

'This is excellent advice,' Keshab replied. 'Perhaps I ought to bring her.'

Keshab's family had tolerated a great deal from him. But they drew the line at this. A daughter-in-law of theirs would never set foot in the house of blaspheming *mlecchas* like the Thakurs of Jorosanko. If Keshab took his wife away, it would

---

15 15th April-15th May.

have to be forever. Neither of them would be allowed to step across the threshold ever again. And Keshab would be disinherited. But these threats failed to move Keshab. He stormed about the house, looking for his wife, but she was nowhere to be found.

That evening, Keshab left his ancestral home and came to his father-in-law's house in Bali. Standing outside, he sent a message for his wife. He wouldn't enter the house but she could come to him if she wished to do so. On Jaganmohini's appearing a few minutes later, he said to her, 'Listen to me carefully and think well before taking a decision. You have me on one side, and clan, family, religion, wealth and prestige on the other. From today it has to be one or the other. If you choose me you lose everything else. Am I worth so great a sacrifice?' Making no reply, Jaganmohini walked steadily towards him.

The next day the two stood outside the deuri of the Thakur mansion at dawn, Debendranath was waiting for them. Clasping Keshab to his breast, he exclaimed, 'Come, Brahmananda! My home is your home. Live here and be happy.'

# *Chapter XXXI*

One afternoon in Agrahayan, Nabin Kumar drove up to the office of *Paridarshak,* which was housed in a mansion in Chitpur. The founders of *Paridarshak,* Madanmohan Goswami and Jaganmohan Tarkalankar, escorted him up the stairs to the editor's room with due ceremony, for he was to assume charge from that day onwards. 'I have a few words to say to you all,' Nabin addressed the gathering, coming to the point in his forthright manner. 'All the people working on the paper, including Goswami Moshai and Tarkalankar Moshai, shall continue working with me.' At these words, cries of 'Excellent! Excellent!' rose from the assembly and tears glistened in the eyes of the two old Brahmins. This offer of Nabin's went far beyond their hopes and they were overwhelmed with relief. 'Start looking around for men of ability.' Nabin turned his eyes on them. 'We'll need more workers. I intend to make this paper a daily of four pages.' He noted the look of surprise on every face and continued, 'It is my intention to make *Paridarshak* as good as an English paper in every way. All the Bengali papers that have appeared so far have been weak imitations. Some of them offer stale news and others poor-quality translations. We'll have qualified reporters on the job. They will move around the city and suburbs, keep an eye on the markets and observe the proceedings of the High Court. They'll also interview important people of the realm and present objective reports. Another thing. A lot of news that is printed in English papers is of no use to us. Take, for instance, the notices of the arrival of ships from England. We'll leave all that out and concentrate on what affects our countrymen most. We must all take a pledge, here and now, to work for the welfare of the masses; to adhere to the truth, no matter how unpalatable; and observe the strictest impartiality in our columns. Do you agree?'

'Singha Moshai!' Madanmohan Goswami voiced the sentiments of the gathering. 'What you say is true, absolutely true. It seems strange to us that we have not thought on these lines before. Your words have aroused our deepest feelings.'

'Come, then. Let us take the pledge together.'

The circulation of *Paridarshak* commenced within a few days of taking the pledge. The Calcutta intellectuals were amazed at the size and quality of the paper and did not refrain from expressing their opinions. However, though Nabin Kumar worked day and night, he was unable to get it going the way he had envisaged. There were some who read a paper for its erotica and there was nothing of the sort in *Paridarshak*. Still others preferred to buy an English daily for that was a status symbol. Sales fell sharply within a few months but Nabin was undaunted. He reduced the price to one paisa and increased the matter to six pages. All this involved money—a great deal of money. Seeing no other means of raising funds, he decided to sell off that portion of the family property which housed the Bengal Club.

One morning, Ganganarayan sent for Nabin. 'What is this I hear, Chhotku?' he asked in a worried voice. 'That property is worth its weight in gold. The sahebs are buying up all the land beyond the Esplanade. Prices are rising every day.'

'What else can I do, Dadamoni? You have no more to give me and I need vast amounts.'

'You've spent nearly a lakh of rupees in the last five months.'

'I need more. The country has forgotten Harish but I haven't. I took a pledge to continue the work he had begun. Do you ask me to back out now? Why don't you proceed on a tour of the estates and see if you can bring back some money?'

But before Ganganarayan could do anything, *Paridarshak* crumbled altogether. For months it had been tottering on its last legs, despite the vast sums Nabin pumped into it every day. Its readership had declined to forty and even those were free copies. Stacks of unsold newspapers touched the ceilings of the office in Chitpur and the prestige of the paper dwindled to zero. There came a time when even the workers laughed snidely behind their proprietor's back. For what was the worth of a paper which people didn't want even when it was free?

Nabin could never take failure in a philosophical spirit. It filled him not with frustration but with anger, and in the throes of that anger, it was himself he sought to damage. Once again he flung caution to the winds. He began drinking excessively and took to roaming the streets in an aimless manner. He who had been up to his ears in work had nothing to do now. *Paridarshak* had closed down. Two of the pandits had passed away and the translation of the Mahabharat was at a standstill. Nabin spent his days in bed, reading or staring blankly at the ceiling. At sunset he rose and dressed himself and went for a drive in the carriage. He took no one with him. He hated toadies and hangers-on. His only companion was his brandy bottle, which he put to his lips every now and then. Sometimes he tottered out of the carriage and stood on the bank of the river and gazed at the infinite expanse of sky and water. Then, clambering back, he lolled against the cushions and wept like a child.

These nocturnal wanderings and indiscriminate drinking took their toll and he fell grievously ill, declining, within a week, almost to the point of death. The best doctors of the city were sent for but they shook their heads in dismay. The case was too confusing. Two English doctors and a kaviraj treated him for a while but there was no improvement. Dr Durgacharan Bandopadhyaya discerned symptoms similar to those that he had seen in Harish but he couldn't square them with Nabin's age. He was too young—only twenty-three against Harish's thirty-seven. The most renowned native doctor of the city was Surya Kumar Chakravarti. He was one of the two protégés of Dwarkanath Tagore who had had their medical training in England at their patron's expense. Once there, he had converted to Christianity and taken the name of Goodeve. This Goodeve Chakravarti took Ganga aside and said, 'Mr Singha, it is time I told you a plain truth. The will to live is the most important instrument in the hands of the physician. No matter how effective the medicine or how skilled the therapy, they lose their power if the patient has lost his grip on life. Your brother has given up the fight. He is so morose—I can't get him to even speak a word.'

'The weakness . . . perhaps—'

'He is not so weak that he cannot speak. And he certainly hasn't lost his hearing. His refusal to respond is deliberate.'

'You must do something about it.' Ganga clutched the doctor's hands in desperation.

'This young fellow is another victim of intemperance. That much is clear. Such is the sad state of affairs in our country that bright young men get infatuated with western ways and . . . Anyway, let's forget all that. The facts are that he is young and his liver is not damaged beyond repair. There's no reason why we cannot get him back to his feet again. My only worry is his depression. He has everything in the world to live for but he has lost the will to live. There was a disease in ancient Greece called melancholia. It afflicted people from the uppermost strata of society; people who had too much wealth and lived lives of excessive luxury and intemperance.'

'My brother is not like other young men of our class. He's a great scholar and is held in high esteem by one and all.'

'Nevertheless, this is a classic case of melancholia. You may consult my respected senior colleague, Durgacharan Babu, and take his opinion.'

That Nabin Kumar's lack of response was deliberate was true enough for he did give answers to the innumerable questions showered on him once in a while. Though the answers were invariably confined to 'yes' and 'no,' there was no doubt that he could speak and hear. The only alarming symptom, apart from his withdrawal, was an excess of vomiting that no medicine could control. Whatever he ate or drank came up within seconds and left him drained and exhausted. The flesh gradually crept away from his bones, leaving him looking like a skeleton with huge, unnaturally brilliant eyes. Ganga couldn't bear to see his adored younger brother waste away like this. 'What's wrong with you, Chhotku?' he begged over and over again. 'Tell me the truth.'

'Nothing.'

'Do you feel like eating anything? Or seeing anyone? Shall I call some ustads? You may like to hear some music?'

'No.'

'Why do you keep saying "no" to everything? What is worrying you? Tell me—my sweetest, dearest brother . . .'

'Nothing.'

One evening, Durgacharan Bandopadhyaya said to Nabin, 'You've eaten nothing all day. This won't do, you know. You must have something. A drop of buttermilk perhaps?

'No.'

'Why not? What ails you, son?' Leaning over him to stroke his head in affection, Durgacharan Babu recoiled in horror. Nabin's mouth was reeking of liquor. 'Why! What's this?' he asked sternly. 'You've been drinking brandy!' Nabin made no response. Durgacharan Babu peered under the bed and pulled out a bottle of French cognac. He looked around him with searching eyes. There was neither water nor a glass in the room. Nabin had obviously been drinking the brandy neat. 'What's all this?' he cried out angrily. 'Who's been giving the boy this pernicious stuff? Is it a plot to poison him?' Trembling with shock and anger, Ganga summoned all the servants and proceeded to cross-question them. It didn't take long to identify the culprit. Who could or would do such a thing but Nabin's favoured servant, Dulal? And who other than Dulal had the opportunity for was it not Dulal who stood guard outside his Chhoto Babu's bedroom day and night? Dulal admitted his guilt, adding that he was only a servant and dared not flout his master. Chhoto Babu had asked him to get the brandy and he had obeyed. 'If you dare do such a thing again,' Ganga thundered, 'I'll have you whipped and turned away from the house.'

The next day passed in the same way. All efforts to pour nourishing fluids down Nabin's throat ended in disaster. He brought everything up and sank back on the bed each time in greater exhaustion. Finally, in utter frustration, Dr Goodeve Chakravarti said to his patient, 'Give me just one answer. Tell me the truth. Do you not wish to live?' Nabin was silent for a while, his brow furrowed in thought. Then, he answered softly, 'I do.'

That night at about ten o'clock, Dulal came tiptoeing into the room, a bottle of brandy tucked under his uduni. 'Chhoto Babu,' he whispered though Nabin was alone. 'I've got it.' And at that moment, two women entered from adjacent doors, as if from two wings of a set in a play. They were Sarojini and Kusum Kumari.

'Give that to me,' Kusum said in a tone of command.

'Scoundrel! ' Sarojini screamed at the top of her voice. 'Get out of my sight.'

Dulal set the bottle on the floor and withdrew hastily. 'Come, Saroj,' Kusum said, dropping down on the floor by the side of the bed. 'We two sisters will sit here all night.' She turned to Nabin Kumar. 'If you don't eat, we won't either.' Kusum's eyes fell on the bottle and, as if in a dream, a long-forgotten phase of her life swam back into her consciousness. Drink was an evil thing. It had ruined Durgamoni's life. Her heart was wrung with pain at the thought of her aunt-in-law. She would move Heaven and Earth to save Sarojini the same suffering. 'Call a maid,' she commanded her sister-in-law. 'And tell her to throw that bottle into the rubbish dump.'

'Saroj!' Nabin spoke for the first time since their appearance. His voice was clear and his enunciation perfect. 'Give me the bottle.' 'O Didi!' Sarojini threw an agonized glance at Kusum Kumari. Nabin turned over on his side and looked piercingly into his wife's face. 'Give it to me,' he said sternly. Kusum rose and stood by the side of the bed. '*Chhi*!' she said gently, fixing her clear blue eyes upon his face. 'Why are you killing yourself? You musn't—' 'It is very late. Go back to your room, Bouthan.' With these words Nabin pushed away the sheet that covered him and tried to rise from the bed. 'What are you doing?' Kusum Kumari called out in alarm while Saroj gave a piercing shriek. '*O go!* Ma *go!*' she cried as Nabin made a desperate effort to stand on his own feet. At the sound of their voices, the entire household came rushing into the room. Ganga clasped his brother in his arms and cried, 'What's the matter, Chhotku? What do you want?'

'Let go of me,' Nabin said roughly. 'Tell everyone to go out of the room or I'll go out myself.'

Ganga forced Nabin down on the bed. Ordering all the curious onlookers to leave the room, he gestured to Kusum Kumari to shut the door. Then, leaning over Nabin, he said in a pleading voice, 'Chhotku, please be reasonable. The doctors—'

'Give me the bottle.'

'No. You'll die if you drink that stuff on an empty stomach. Don't be childish, Chhotku.'

'Give it to me.' Nabin held out his hand imperiously. Though thin and frail in body, his voice held the authority of his position. There was no mistaking the fact that he was the head of the Singha family and its principal male member. Ignoring Ganga's pleas, he said once again, 'Give it to me.'

Ganga bent down and picked the bottle from the floor. 'You're giving it to him?' Kusum Kumari cried out in an anguished voice. Ganga did not reply. He handed over the bottle in silence. Nabin took it, his hand trembling with weakness and exhaustion, but before he could put it to his lips, it slipped from his grasp and fell crashing to the floor. An overpowering reek of expensive liquor filled the whole room.

# Chapter XXXII

Kusum Kumari sat poring over her books in a tiny room adjoining the terrace. It was her little hideout and she loved it and spent most of her day in it. It was very quiet here—far away from the noise and bustle of the main house—and she could do her lessons in peace. Ganganarayan was a stern taskmaster and she had to work hard to come up to his expectations. He had been tutoring her in English of late and she was already quite advanced. Ganga's method of instruction was novel. He would read out a poem and make her repeat it after him till she was word perfect. Then he would explain it line by line in Bengali. After this she would be required to make a Bengali translation and copy it out in a beautifully bound exercise book that he had given her for the purpose.

That afternoon Kusum was working on Shelley's *The Indian Serenade*. She remembered what Ganga had said to her while explaining the poem. 'As our own poet, Kalidas, was inspired by a cloud, so the great English poet, Percy Bysshe Shelley, wrote an immortal lyric inspired by the Indian air. The strange thing is that Shelley had never seen India. Yet he loved her gentle breezes and wrote this supremely beautiful poem.

The wandering airs they faint
On the dark, the silent stream—
The champak odours fail
Like sweet thoughts in a dream;
The nightingale's complaint,
It dies upon her heart;
As I must on thine
Oh, beloved as thou art.

'Did you mark the word, champak? It is our Indian flower, the champa—

Let thy love in kisses rain
On my lips and eyelids pale.

'Do you understand the phrase, 'Kisses rain? You don't? I'll show you.' And, jumping up from his seat, he had kissed her feverishly on her lips, eyes and throat.

Boom! Boom! Kusum Kumari was startled out of her thoughts by what sounded like a roll of drums just above her head. Shutting her book with a snap, she ran to the door and looked up, amazed. An enormous black cloud was rising swiftly over the southern horizon. It looked like a pack of bears, massed tightly together. Even as she stood watching, it raced across the sky, letting out a blood-curdling rumble. A shaft of jagged lightning tore its way through the sky, nearly blinding the girl, and a gust of wind almost swept her off her feet. Frightened, Kusum tried to run back to the safety of her own room, but before she could reach the stairs, the storm had taken possession of her. Her slender body was spun round and round, the folds of her sari whipping frenziedly against her legs. Her hair streamed out in the wind as if torn from the cloud that swung menacingly above her head. And then the rain came, quick warm drops drenching her face and form within seconds, and in the sheer delight of that sensation, Kusum gave up the struggle and surrendered herself to the elements. 'Wonderful! Ah! How wonderful!' she murmured, her face lifted to the pelting rain. Deafening explosions rent the air all around her and the lightning flashed trails of gold in the blue-black sky above her head. 'I'm so happy! So happy! Who knew life could be so sweet!' After a while, Kusum ran to the stair landing and called, 'Saroj! Saroj!'

'What is it? Why, Didi, you're all wet!'

'Come up quickly. Let's bathe in the rain together.'

'Bathe in the rain!' Sarojini shrank from the idea. 'Are you mad? We'll die of *sannipatik*[16] if—'

'Why are you such a coward, Saroj? If we die—we'll die. That's all. Come up this minute.'

'If someone sees us—'

---

16 Typhus fever.

'Who can see us here? The walls are so high. You should have come up half an hour ago and seen the storm. It was magnificent! The clouds looked like wild elephants on a rampage.'

The two young women bathed in the rain for nearly an hour—Kusum in ecstatic delight and Saroj a little withdrawn; a little hesitant. Then, shivering with cold, they ran downstairs to change and dry their hair. Kusum sent a maid down to the kitchen to prepare a special brew of ginger, cardamom and cinnamon. 'Drink this up while it's still hot,' Kusum said, handing her sister-in-law a cup full of the pungent liquid, 'and *sannipatik* won't dare come near you.'

Towards evening the rain stopped and the thunder with it. But the sky remained overcast and seemed to hang lower in the heavens. Lightning flashed from time to time and an eerie silence descended on the earth. A tremendous depression overtook Kusum. She had never felt so desolate before, so lonely. She was used to a lot of people around her and here, in this great mansion, she had no one but her husband. Saroj loved her but Saroj was changed of late. She seemed sad and preoccupied most of the time and all Kusum's efforts to cheer her up drew a blank.

After dusk the rain started falling again, first in a fine drizzle and then as a pelting torrent. The wind rose and a roar, as of waves in the sea, could be heard even through the closed doors and windows. The floors vibrated to the sound and the walls shook slightly. At this point, a maid entered with the news that all the palm leaf huts which housed the servants had been blown away and that the Ganga had risen above her banks and was flooding the area around the fort. The gale was so strong it was uprooting all the old trees of the city and buildings were collapsing. One wing of the Thakur mansion at Pathuriaghat had been reduced to a heap of rubble.

Kusum felt stifled within the four walls of her room. Why didn't Ganganarayan come? It was past ten o' clock and she was frantic with worry. Whom could she turn to at this time of night? From whom could she seek advice? Even as she stood uncertainly, a fierce gust of wind blew one of the windows open, shattering the glass and sending the splinters flying about the room. Kusum watched in horror, as a tree was blown away by the wind. It was there one moment and gone the next. Kusum shivered and ran out of the room, down the gallery to Sarojini's room. 'Saroj! Saroj!' she cried, banging on the door with both her fists.

'Why Didi!' Saroj stared at her. 'What's happening? Is the world coming to an end? I'm frightened! Terribly frightened!'

'Where's Chhoto Babu? Is he at home?'

'Yes. He's been here all day.'

'Call him. I'm afraid all is over with me.' Then, seeing Sarojini hesitate, she cried out with feverish urgency, 'Why don't you go? My husband hasn't come home and I—'

'Hasn't come home?' A terrible pallor spread over Sarojini's face. 'Where is he?'

'How do I know? Call Chhoto Babu. I have no one else—' And pushing the pale, trembling girl aside, she ran to Nabin's door herself and banged on it with all her might. 'Open the door, Chhoto Babu!' she called. 'I'm in terrible trouble.'

'Bouthan!' Nabin stared at his sister-in-law. 'What is the matter?'

'Your brother hasn't returned. And this dreadful storm—'

'What storm?'

'Haven't you noticed what's happening outside?'

'Calm down, Bouthan. Don't be afraid. Where is Dadamoni?'

'I don't know.'

Nabin thought for a few moments, then walked across and opened a window. A gust of wind blew into the room, nearly knocking him down. 'Yes,' he said quietly, shutting the window, 'there's quite a strong gale.' Raising his voice, he called, 'Dulal! Dibakar! Tell the coachman to bring the carriage around. I'm going out.' Ignoring the presence of the two women, he picked up a bottle of brandy and poured its contents down his throat. After which he took up his stick and strode out of the room with the words, 'Don't be afraid, Bouthan. I'll bring Dadamoni back from wherever he is.' Sarojini could hold herself in no longer. '*O go!*' she let out a piercing wail 'Don't go out in this terrible storm. Please don't.' Nabin didn't even bother to reply. Addressing Dulal, who stood by the door, he said, 'Is the carriage ready? Come then. Let's not waste any more time.' But, for the first time during all his years in the

Singha mansion, Dulal contradicted his master. 'We can't go out, Chhoto Babu,' he cried out in astonishment. 'You have no idea of what's happening outside. The horses won't take a step.'

'Then we'll walk.'

'O Didi!' Sarojini cried out in an agonized voice.

Kusum felt very guilty. In her anxiety for her own husband, she was endangering Sarojini's husband's life. 'Don't go.' She ran after him. 'You're not well. Don't take this terrible risk. Send a servant if you must.' But Nabin ignored her pleas and walked down the steps and out of the house. Dulal was right. On such a night as this the horses would not have taken a step forward. The sky was pitch-dark and the streets littered with straw, bamboo and pieces of masonry. Nabin inched his way painfully along, stumbling over heaps of rubble and fallen trunks. Fortunately, he didn't have to go far. Within a hundred yards of the house, he heard Ganganarayan's voice. Ganga had been caught by the storm on his way back from Dakshineswar. His carriage had toppled over and though both horses were dead he had escaped unhurt.

That night a wall of the mansion crumbled to the ground with a deafening crash. The inmates of the house heard the sound but could do nothing about it. Leaving the house was dangerous but remaining within it was equally so. Who knew when the roof would collapse above their heads?

The storm abated towards dawn but the rain kept falling in a steady downpour. From afternoon onwards reports started coming in of the damage the city had suffered. No one had seen anything like it before. An oil crusher declared that he had not only seen trees and animals flying through the air, he had even seen a boat. It was true. Several boats had been wrenched away from their moorings in Armenian Ghat and blown to Ultadanga, justifying its name. A young woman who made a living by vending vegetables howled out her story. Her four-year-old son had been blown away by the wind. The milkman, the gram seller, the fisherwoman—all had tales of woe. Their houses were gone, their cows were dead and many had lost members of their families. Crowds of homeless destitutes braved the rain and gathered outside the gates of the Singha mansion, for Nabin Kumar's generosity was well known.

'What do you say, Chhotku?' Ganga asked his brother. 'Should we do something for them?'

'You understand these things better than me, Dadamoni. Do what you think right.'

'There are thirty to forty people at the gate. We must give them something or the reputation of the house will suffer. I think ten rupees per head is a reasonable amount. What do you say?'

'I agree.'

'Another thing. The coachman, Kalim-ud-din, has just brought the news. Bindu's— I mean, Jetha Babu's house has been badly affected. The roof has caved in. We must go there—'

'You go if you like.'

'Won't you?'

'No.'

'That will look bad. Jetha Babu will think you don't care about his welfare.'

'Why don't you send a servant and find out the real extent of the damage first?'

'You're right. I'll do that.' Ganga turned to go but Nabin stopped him with the words, 'Listen, Dadamoni. About those people at the gate. Don't give them ten rupees.'

'How much shall I give them then? Five?'

'Give them one hundred rupees each.'

'One hundred! Are you mad? There are thirty to forty there just now. Who knows how many more will come! Ten rupees is a good sum. With five they can rebuild their shacks and another five will feed them for a month.

'It is hardly generous. You mentioned our family reputation a little while ago.'

'But more and more people will come crowding as soon as the word spreads.'

'Don't deny anyone. Give a hundred rupees to each.'

Ganga stared at his brother. What was the boy saying? They would have the whole city at their doorstep at this rate! Nabin looked his brother in the eye and said quietly, 'Why did you ask me for my opinion, Dadamoni? You could have taken any decision you pleased. I wouldn't have stopped you.'

'But the treasury will get exhausted!'

'Stop the distribution when that happens.' There was

something in Nabin's tone that unnerved Ganganarayan. 'Well, if that's what you want,' he mumbled and rose to leave. Halfway across he paused and turning around, asked softly, 'Will you take charge of the distribution, Chhotku?'

'No. If you find it inconvenient give the responsibility to Dibakar.

But that was hardly a solution. Though the handling of money was intensely distasteful to Ganga, he couldn't entrust the work to Dibakar. He knew Dibakar to be in the habit of taking a cut on every deal he made and who knew how big that cut might be? Ganga ordered the petitioners to be brought into the hall and the gates locked. Then he proceeded to take down their names and addresses in a register. Securing their thumb impressions he handed them over to Dibakar, who doled out the money from the cash box. But Ganga took one precaution. He set Dulal on guard. With Dulal around Dibakar wouldn't dare play any tricks.

This done, Ganga made his way to Bidhusekhar's house. Though the property had suffered extensive damage, no one was hurt or dead. Several fine old trees had been uprooted, one falling on the cowshed, killing two cows. The roof of the room adjoining Bidhusekhar's had collapsed and a great gaping hole had appeared in the ceiling. But Ganga was struck with admiration at the sight of Bidhusekhar. He who had been almost confined to bed was moving around his property, supervising its reconstruction—his old indomitable spirit intact. 'What news do you bring?' he asked, fixing his one eye on Ganga. 'I was leaving for your house in a few minutes.'

The morning papers were full of news. The English dailies carried detailed reports of the losses sustained by the Europeans of the city—of the ships they had lost, the gardens that were ruined and the property that had been destroyed. There was no mention of native losses. It seemed the country belonged to the whites alone and it was only they who mattered. The Bengali papers doled out information in a half-hearted, lackadaisical way. Mixed with it was lot of blurred sentiment and foolish prognosis. Bengali editors had no edge to their pens and no feel for analysis.

Nabin flung the papers on the floor with an impatient gesture. It was amazing to him that news of this sort had a wide circulation and that the readers of Calcutta had rejected his *Paridarshak* in favour of this. If only Harish were alive; he would have shown everyone what real reporting was. A man like Harish was the need of the hour.

But the storm did something else for Nabin Kumar. It shook him out of the stupor he had fallen into in the last few months, when he lay on his bed, hour after hour, the brandy bottle at his lips. He felt a strong stirring within him and his body and mind were galvanized into activity. 'Dulal,' he called out imperiously, 'tell the coachman to prepare the horses. I'm going out in a few minutes.'

'But the streets are littered with rubble and fallen trunks,' Dulal answered. 'No vehicles are moving.'

'Then we'll walk.'

'Where do you wish to go?'

'To Barahnagar. I must get back to my Mahabharat.'

'Walk to Barahnagar! From Jorasanko?'

'Why not? Aren't other people walking this distance every day?'

Ignoring Dulal's pleas, he ran down the steps and out into the road. People stared as the scion of the Singhas walked rapidly down the road, his dhoti tucked between his legs and his elegant black pumps coated with mud and slime. But his eyes shone in a face bright and flushed with energy, and the stick in his hand swung jauntily. His keen glance shot this way and that as he stepped over heaps of fallen bricks and skipped over puddles. He beheld destruction all around him but felt no remorse. In fact, a fierce joy welled up in his breast. All that was old and decaying had been knocked away. A new city would rise on the ruins of the old; a bright, beautiful city—a city of joy and hope.

# Chapter XXXIII

Among the buildings destroyed by the storm was the one in which the Brahmo Samaj assemblies were held—a fine old mansion established by Rammohan Roy. But, now, one wing had crumbled to the ground and the roof swung dangerously low. The storm seemed to have hit the institution as well. A chasm appeared among the members, one so deep and fundamental, that the Brahmo Samaj was riven forever in two.

Despite his love for Keshab, Debendranath had always found some of his ideas unacceptable. As, for instance, his intense love of Christ and the Bible. For Debendranath hated the British and disliked Christianity. It was not that he was closed to other doctrines. He had studied Persian and had a high regard for Sufism. But the Brahmo Dharma, as he envisioned it, was a branch of Hinduism. Hinduism accommodated idol worship, it was true. But the very basis of Hindu philosophy rested on the doctrine of monotheism. As Debendranath saw it, the Brahmo Dharma was Hinduism in a renovated form. It embraced the true spirit of Hinduism, discarding the peripheral. There was no need, therefore, to break away from time-honoured Hindu traditions, especially in so far as they related to clan and family. But the young Brahmos led by Keshab did not share his opinion. Keshab had studied the Bible, Quran and Avestan and found all of them to be flawed. There was truth in them all but none contained the whole truth. He believed that if the Brahmo Dharma ceased to be the exclusive preserve of high-caste Hindus and became a universal religion, composed of the best in all these existing faiths, it would come to be the most widely accepted religion of the world and the best for mankind.

The immediate target of attack by Keshab and his group were the Brahmins of the old school, who still wore their sacred threads. If Brahmos rejected the caste system, they argued, why carry its symbol? They clamoured for their dismissal. But, though Debendranath had cast off his own *poité*, he was reluctant to force others to do the same. If a Brahmin wanted to keep his out of deference to tradition, why not allow him to do so? Debendranath was in favour of change but not revolution. He disapproved of the inter-caste marriages that the Keshab group was organizing in large numbers. And in his heart of hearts, he found the idea of widow remarriage unacceptable. But not wishing to strike a dissenting note, he went along with the others. And then came the storm.

It had been decided that while the building was under repair, the weekly assemblies would be held at Debendranath's house in Jorasanko. On the Wednesday following the storm, Keshab and his group arrived to find Ayodhyanath Pakrasi conducting the assembly. An uproar followed, Keshab's group demanding that he be asked to step down in favour of Bijoykrishna Goswami, for the former was one of the Brahmins who had refused to give up his sacred thread. Shocked at such unruly behaviour, Debendranath rose from his seat and announced that it being his house, he had the right to choose the Acharya. At this, the clamour intensified. The assemblies, the rival group declared, were organized by the institution and not by an individual. The place of worship was of no consequence whatsoever. As a last effort to save the situation, Debendranath offered a compromise. Let Bijoykrishna sit on the dais by Pakrasi Moshai's side and conduct the assembly as second Acharya.

But the very idea of compromise was unacceptable. The question was of principle, the Keshab group declared. What was the sense in having a conservative, caste-ridden fossil of a Brahmin and an enlightened, forward looking, prejudice-free young man on the same dais? 'Is Debendranath Babu the Pope?' Bijoykrishna's voice was heard loud in comment, 'That we must all be governed by his whims and fancies?' Now Debendranath's face hardened. 'Yes,' he said grimly. 'My word is the last word—here. I will not ask Pakrasi Moshai to step down. If anyone has objections to his presence, they are at liberty to leave.' Keshab and his party rose and left the assembly. That same evening they held a separate Brahmo Sabha on the terrace of a friend's house.

Keshab's desertion was a cruel blow to Debendranath but he took it with his usual stoic calm. Coolly, unemotionally,he removed Keshab and his followers from the board of trustees and appointed his eldest son, Dwijendranath, secretary of the Brahmo Samaj. Ayodhyanath Pakrasi was made joint secretary. The editorship of the *Indian Mirror*, hitherto held by Keshab, passed overnight into other hands. Keshab's group was totally unprepared for such an outcome. How could Debendranath Babu be so vindictive, they exclaimed in shock and anger. Was the Brahmo Samaj his personal property? And if the Samaj was to be split in two, its funds should be divided equally. But all their agitation was wasted. They raved and ranted against the Maharishi but could do nothing more. The Maharishi, with the dignity of his breeding, uttered not a word of protest.

However, a loneliness assailed him such as he had never known before. His own followers outstripped Keshab's by a large margin in numbers, but he felt a strange withdrawal both from them and from the Samaj. It seemed as though the boy he had loved above his own sons had taken away with him all the energy and inspiration he possessed. He sensed within himself a draining away of life. His sight grew dim and his hearing faded. Though only forty-seven, he felt the end of his life to be near; very near. Soon, the sun would set.

Debendranath spent hour after hour sitting in his armchair on the balcony. And every few minutes, Keshab's face floated before his mind's eye—a bright young face, burning with energy. 'May victory be his,' he murmured to himself. 'May his soul hold a candle to the world. And his name spread through all the countries of the earth and even beyond it.'

# Chapter XXXIV

To travel across the great ocean to 'Albion's distant shore' had been Madhusudan's boyhood dream—one that had haunted him all his life. Now, at the peak of his life and career, when Fortune was showering her blessings on him, he decided to make it a reality. After years of litigation he was, at last, in possession of his father's money and estates. Fame had come hand in hand with wealth and he was now looked upon as the greatest poet of Bengal. Yet, this was the time he chose to go to England and study law at the Bar. His friends and well-wishers pointed out to him the foolishness of leaving the country just when he was emerging as its leading man of letters and being dignified by the titles of 'new Kalidas' and 'Milton of Bengal'. But Madhusudan turned a deaf ear. 'This is just the right moment,' he argued. 'I came, I wrote, I conquered. I gave Bengali poetry her first blank verse. Had I failed I would have stayed. Now I go a hero.' But within a few months of his departure, letters started arriving with the rapidity of falling leaves at the onset of winter. They were invariably appeals for financial assistance and were primarily addressed to Vidyasagar.

Madhusudan had left his property in the care of his childhood friend, Raja Digambar Mitra, with the stipulation that a certain amount be sent to him every month. But the latter had proved unworthy of the trust. He had appropriated everything, ruining Madhusudan for life. He had not only not sent any money—he had left every letter unacknowledged. It was to this same Digambar Mitra that Madhusudan had dedicated his *Meghnadbadh Kavya*.

Betrayed by his friend and penniless in a foreign land, Madhusudan now found himself in dire straits. Having heard that France was a cheaper country to live in, he had moved from London to Paris, but with no income, starvation stared him in the face even here, and he who had once thrown money about with both hands was reduced to begging from societies. His household goods had to be sold or pawned one by one. Even the silver cup presented by Nabin Kumar Singha—one of his most treasured possessions and to which he had clung to the last—had to be taken to the pawnbrokers. The money it brought had fed his children for a week.

Madhusudan had appealed to many people for help, and drawing a blank everywhere, had decided to write to Vidyasagar. The man, he had heard, was not only an 'ocean of learning' but also 'an ocean of mercy'. And, quite unexpectedly, the money had arrived. Madhusudan marvelled at the fact that of all his countrymen, many of whom were wealthy landowners and industrialists, only this poor Brahmin who depended on his books for a living, had offered to help him. After that it became a habit with Madhusudan to write to Vidyasagar whenever he needed money. His famous pen was now being used solely for the composition of letters to Vidyasagar.

One morning Henrietta came crying to Madhusudan as he sat working at his desk. 'I can't bear it any more,' she sobbed. 'How much longer must we live like this?' Madhusudan looked up from his books in surprise. 'The children are clamouring to go to the fair,' Henrietta explained. 'All the children of the neighbourhood are going. But all I have is three francs. It won't even buy their tickets.' Madhusudan's heart was wrung with pain and guilt at the thought that it was out of his power to give his children even this simple pleasure. He sat in grim silence for a few minutes, then said suddenly, 'Wait a little longer. Vidyasagar has sent some money. It will arrive today. I'm sure of it.' And by some strange coincidence, the money arrived within the hour. A sum of fifteen hundred rupees.

Vidyasagar was in a quandary. He had developed a reputation as a philanthropist and now it threatened to engulf him. He knew that many of the petitions he received were not genuine. People took money from him pleading sickness and deaths of parents and children and spent it on wine and women. Many of the destitute women who received allowances from him practised prostitution on the sly. But he had no means of judging. Unable to separate the wheat from the chaff, he gave to everyone who asked. And all he got for his pains was criticism and slander. The burden of receiving is heavy and people lighten it by abusing the giver. Vidyasagar realized that it was a common human failing and forgave his slanderers, but it hurt him and he was assailed by a weariness such as he had never known. Another thing that upset him was his own growing distrust of his fellow men. He shrank from praise, believing it to be a preamble to a petition for money. And thus, he grew sadder and lonelier day by day.

But that didn't stop him from continuing his work for the welfare of widows. It struck him that prevention was better than cure; that hitting out at polygamy, sanctioned by Hindu law for males, would be more effective than widow remarriage, for it was the former that was responsible for the creation of innumerable child widows. Another thing to work for was the education of women.

Around this time an elderly lady called Mary Carpenter arrived from England. She was actively engaged in the cause of women's education in her own country and wanted to extend it to the ends of the Empire. She had heard of Debendranath Thakur and Vidyasagar and was keen to meet them. But Debendranath did not return the compliment. Disliking the white race in general, he escaped to the mofussils to avoid meeting her. The young Brahmos, led by Keshab, held a large meeting in her honour, to which Vidyasagar was invited. At this meeting Mary Carpenter said that the concept of women's education in India could never be properly implemented as long as teachers were recruited only from the European community. It was important to build up a workforce of native women teachers. The suggestion was received with great enthusiasm and a committee proposed for the purpose, with Vidyasagar heading it. But Vidyasagar declined the honour. He was disgusted at the way his countrymen flocked to a foreigner's banner. Could they do nothing on their own? However, Mary Carpenter would not let him off so easily. She insisted on his accompanying her on an inspection tour of the girls' schools of Bengal and Vidyasagar had to agree.

Returning from a trip from Uttarpara Balika Vidyalaya, in company with the inspector of schools, Mr Woodrow, and the director, Mr Atkinson, Vidyasagar met with an accident. While negotiating a sharp bend in the road, the driver lost control over the horse. The carriage overturned and Vidyasagar was thrown out, sustaining considerable injury to his head and spine. It was evening and the road was full of people. A crowd collected instantly but no one came forward to help him up or carry him out of the reach of the nervous rearing horse. It was his great good fortune that the second carriage, carrying the white passengers, drew up in a few moments. Displaying great courage, Woodrow and Atkinson sprang out and gripping the bridle in a flash, mastered the pawing horse. Mary Carpenter knelt on the ground and took Vidyasagar's head on her lap. The tears poured down her cheeks.

# Chapter XXXV

It was the Brahma muhurta—the auspicious moment—at dawn. Nabin stood in the Ganga at Nimtala ghat and immersed his head thrice in her holy waters. The sky above his head was the vivid blue of late autumn; the breeze was mild and sweet. 'Ahh!' he sighed in deep contentment. Then, bringing his hands together, he murmured an invocation to the sun. *'Om Jabakusum Sankasang Kashyapeyang Mahadyutum.'* A burden had fallen off Nabin's back. The seventeenth and last volume of his Mahabharat was to emerge from the press that afternoon. He had redeemed his promise to Vidyasagar. He was free.

He had completed the mammoth task in less than eight years. He had shown the world what he was capable of. The Maharaja of Bardhaman had tried to compete with him. He was much wealthier and had far more manpower at his command. But it was Nabin who had completed his work first. 'Dulal,' he cried out in a burst of generosity. 'Do you want anything of me? I've turned myself into a wishing tree. Ask for whatever you wish and I will grant it.'

'I have everything, Huzoor.' Dulal wrung his hands in humility. 'You have given me more than I know what to do with.'

'Ask for something. I command you to.'

'I have your love and protection. What else can I ask for?'

'You're a fool. I'll give you the house in Barahnagar.'

'Oh no, Chhoto Babu. If Bara Babu hears of it—'

'*Chup*! That house is your son's from this day onwards. I'll draw up the papers as soon as I get home. Aren't you glad? Come on. Show me your teeth. Good. That's settled then.'

'Get out of your wet clothes, Chhoto Babu.'

But Nabin was in no hurry to change. He sat on the bank and gazed out on the watery expanse, dotted with large boats and dinghies. He felt light as a bird winging its way towards the sky and peace flooded his soul. 'The world is beautiful. Is it not, Dulal?' he asked.

'Yes, Chhoto Babu.'

'Time flows on like a river. We are, each of us, travellers in time.'

'Yes, Chhoto Babu.'

'We don't know where we come from. We don't know where we are going. We are aware only of the present. But even that is beautiful; surprisingly beautiful—is it not, Dulal?'

'Yes, Chhoto Babu.'

'Why do you keep repeating "Yes, Chhoto Babu" like a parrot? Don't you have an opinion of your own? Do you like fried fish?'

'Yes, Chhoto Babu.'

'And horse's egg? You're worthless, Dulal. You're completely insensitive.'

'Shall I say something, Chhoto Babu?'

'I've been trying to get you to say something all along.'

'You seem in good spirits after a long time. And that makes me happy.'

'Excellent. So you have a thought or two in your head, after all. Now do something for me. Collect all the destitutes you can find by the riverside and give them ten rupees each. There's a purse full of money in the carriage.'

'Why don't you distribute the money with your own hands? God blesses the giver—'

'I have neither the desire nor the intention of storing riches in Heaven. I give because I enjoy giving.'

While Dulal was distributing the money, Nabin continued gazing at the Ganga, rapt in his surroundings. Suddenly, he thought of Bimbabati. She was in Hardwar, a city on the bank of this same river. It was so long since he had seen her!

Reaching home he changed and had a meal. Then taking up a copy from the pile that had just come out of the press, he proceeded to Badurbagan to Vidyasagar's house. A meeting was to be held that evening in Jorasanko to celebrate the conclusion of the Mahabharat, but Vidyasagar would not be able to attend. He had been badly injured by the fall and was still confined to bed.

At Badurbagan Nabin was informed by Vidyasagar's friend, Rajkrishna Babu, that the patient lay in a stupor from a high fever and that the physicians had advised absolute rest and quiet. 'I won't speak a word,' Nabin pleaded. 'I only wish to see him once for a few minutes.' Although Rajkrishna and his brother, Shombhu Chandra, had turned away many visitors, they couldn't refuse Nabin Kumar Singha.

Vidyasagar lay on a plain wooden cot. He was covered with a white cotton sheet. It was a bare, austere room, with no other furniture. There was only a large clock that ticked loudly from one wall. The sick man's eyes were closed but his brows were knitted and his lips pursed as if some secret worry nagged him even in his sleep. Nabin stood gazing at his face for a few moments. 'I took an oath before you,' he said to himself. 'I've kept that oath. As of today I'm free.' Then, gently, reverently, he placed the volume he had brought next to the pillow. As he did so, a wave of self-pity washed over him. 'You were unjust and unkind to me,' he murmured half-audibly. 'You read my work but didn't care to examine my heart. Farewell, Gurudev.'

The evening's function was a thundering success. A great many eminent men spoke at the meeting, lavishing fulsome praise on the young scholar's rendering of the Mahabharat and requesting him to take up the Ramayan next. Nabin Kumar assured them that he would do so, and after the Ramayan the *Harivansh Madbhagavat Gita*. The pandits received gifts of brass pitchers, shawls and gold coins. The meeting came to an end only after the cannon from the fort had boomed the seventh hour. Nabin had not been so happy and excited in many years.

But after the guests had departed, a deep depression took hold of him. He felt lonely; terribly lonely. His home was no home, he thought, his wife no wife. He had tried hard to mould her into a friend and companion but had failed miserably. Sarojini did not share a single thought of his. She had turned religious of late and, convinced that she was barren and disliked by her husband in consequence, she was filling the house with pandits and astrologers, knowing fully well that her husband hated them and considered them charlatans.

Nabin spent hours tossing and turning in his solitary bed for he slept apart from his wife these days. Then, towards midnight, he felt he couldn't bear the pain that ravaged his soul for one moment more. Rising, he walked over to Sarojini's room and banged at the door with both his hands. 'Saroj! Saroj!' he cried out of his great desolation. Sarojini tumbled out of bed and ran to the door. She could hardly believe her ears. Her husband; her famous, learned husband, was calling out to her after years of neglect. 'Saroj.' Nabin's voice throbbed with anguish. 'I'm unhappy; very unhappy. I don't know why I feel like this. What shall I do, Saroj?'

Sarojini was startled. A look of alarm sprang into her eyes. Was the old malady taking hold of her husband again? 'Do you feel unwell?' she asked agitatedly. 'Does your head ache? Shall I send for a doctor? Dulal—'

'No. No. I'm well enough in body. But my mind—I feel something, someone, is holding it in hands like pincers and slowly squeezing the life out. I feel like a strangled kitten being dragged along—'

'Ma *go!* How terrible! Would you like some syrup? They say it cures the troubles of the mind and makes it happy again. Shall I fetch the bottle from your room?'

'No. It won't do any good.'

'Shall I press your head? Or your legs?'

'Can you restore my mind, Saroj? I feel thousands of thorns pricking into me. Thousands of thorns—' Nabin fell with a thud on Sarojini's bed. Sleep was claiming him at last, but before he surrendered himself, he thought suddenly, 'I must go to Hardwar as soon as I can. Tomorrow if I can manage it. I must go to my mother.'

Nabin Kumar did not get out of bed for the next four days. He lay as if in a drugged stupor. The physicians who attended him were puzzled for he was perfectly healthy in body. On the fifth day he opened his eyes and commanded Dulal to fetch Ganganarayan. Ganga was at home at that time and he came rushing over to his brother's wing. 'I wish to leave the city in a day or two,' Nabin said, coming straight to the point. 'I don't know when I'll return. I shall go to Hardwar first and spend a few days with Ma. Then I intend to travel a bit and see new lands.'

'That's an excellent plan,' Ganga agreed enthusiastically. 'You've grown very thin and weak in the past few months. The air of the west is cool and dry. It will do you good. I have been thinking of visiting Ma myself for some time now. But we can't both leave together.'

'You may go to her after I return. I've been dreaming of Ma often in the last few days. I think she's calling out to me.'

Preparations for the journey were started from that very day. Nabin's signature was obtained on all important documents for he would be away for an unspecified period. Three bajras packed with cooks, maids, guards and serving men were to accompany his pinnace. At this point, Dulal struck a discordant note. His wife was pregnant for the second time and he was loath to leave her. He begged to be spared but Nabin wouldn't hear of it. He couldn't dream of going anywhere without Dulal. Finally it was decided that Dulal would accompany him as far as Hardwar and then return to Calcutta.

One morning, within a fortnight of Nabin's departure, a young sanyasi came to the gate of Singha Mansion and asked for Ganganarayan Singha or his younger brother, Nabin Kumar Singha. Ganga was not at home, so the servants bid him enter the house and wait. But the stranger stood where he was for a full morning and afternoon. He would not, he said, step inside the home of a householder. He never did. When Ganganarayan returned in the evening, the sanyasi put a small bundle in his hands, explaining in his unintelligible Hindi that he had been commanded by his guru to deliver it personally to one of the sons of Ramkamal Singha. Opening the bundle, Ganga found a neatly folded *namabali*, a string of rudraksha beads and a gold ring. He recognized them instantly. They were Bimbabati's. Looking up he met the stranger's calm, clear gaze. Bimbabati was dead, he said. She had died over two months ago.

# Chapter XXXVI

Ganga's first thought was of Chhotku. How was he to reach him? Nabin Kumar was to travel up the river to Allahabad, then proceed by slow stages to Hardwar. Who knew where he was at this point of time? Ganga thought of going after him in person but then changed his mind. There was too much for him to do here. He decided to send Nakur and Duryodhan for that trusted old retainer, Dibakar, was stricken with rheumatism and had lost the use of his limbs. It was these two who ran the household in his place.

Kusum sat in her room, crocheting a lace table cover when Ganga burst in on her. 'Kusum,' he said in a trembling voice, 'Ma is no more.' Kusum Kumari looked up, startled. Ganga's face was pale and drained and an anguish such as she had never seen before was stamped on it. And, indeed, Ganga was overcome with guilt and remorse. He had not only neglected his mother—he hadn't been to see her once after she left home—he had married against her wishes. He knew that being a conservative Hindu woman, she wouldn't accept the idea of his marrying a widow. The wedding had been arranged in a hurry and he hadn't had the time to secure her permission. Later, of course, he had written to her and she had replied. But being unlettered, someone else had penned the epistle for her. It had been addressed to no one in particular. She had merely sent her blessings to all in the house and informed them that she was well and happy. She had made no mention of Ganga's marriage. Nor had she sent a present for her new daughter-in-law. Ganga had meant to go to her, to ask for her forgiveness, but had been caught up with other things. It was too late now.

Seeing her husband in such a state, Kusum burst into tears. There was no guilt on her side for her widowhood had been forgotten long since and she thought of herself now only as Ganga's wife. That seemed to her to be her sole identity. But she remembered Bimbabati from the days of her visits to Krishnabhamini—her beauty, her warmth and affection.

Husband and wife wept in silence for a while. Then Ganga pulled himself together. He had a great deal to do. Weeping was a luxury he could ill afford.

The first task that awaited him was to inform Bidhusekhar. But how? It would not be proper to send a servant. On the other hand, he shrank from facing the old man and breaking the shattering news in person. But seeing no way out, Ganga steeled himself and went to Bidhusekhar's house. It was fairly late in the night and Ganga expected Bidhusekhar to have retired for the night. He even hoped for it in his heart of hearts. Entering, the first person he saw was Pran Gopal. Pran Gopal had grown into a handsome youth, with a well-cut face, high nose and large bright eyes. Looking at him, Ganga was suddenly reminded of Nabin. Nabin had looked a lot like him at his age. But Pran Gopal's manner was quite different. He was shy and reserved and spoke in a gentle voice.

On being informed of his arrival, Suhasini came running in. 'Why, Ganga Dada!' she exclaimed, a stricken look in her eyes. 'What is the matter? Has a letter arrived from Hardwar? Is Karta Ma all right?' Ganga was startled. A woman's instinct, he thought, was amazing. He hadn't guessed the truth even on seeing the sanyasi. Her fears confirmed, Suhasini sank on the floor, weeping. 'Sinners flourish in the world and are granted long lives,' she sobbed. 'The good, the pious are taken away. Dear Karta Ma! So generous, so chaste and holy! *O go*, she was more to me than my own mother.'

Ganga placed a gentle hand on her head. 'Stop crying, Sushi, and give me your advice. How do I break the news to Bara Babu? He's so old and frail. Can he sustain the shock? If I keep it from him—well, the truth will come out some day and the—'

Bidhusekhar was in the habit of taking his night meal punctually at nine o' clock. Ganga decided to wait and give him the news after he had eaten. But fate willed otherwise. Bidhusekhar had seen Ganga enter the house from an upstairs window and was expecting him. As soon as the cannon from the fort boomed the ninth hour, Bidhusekhar's stick came tapping down the gallery to the room in which his meal was laid. Allowing Suhasini to lead him to the velvet asan, he sat down and pouring water over his hand, made the customary ritualistic offerings to the five deities. Then, looking up with a furrowed brow, he said, 'I thought I saw Ganganarayan come into the house—'

'Yes,' Suhasini said in a voice she strove to control. 'Ganga Dada is here.'

'Why?' Bidhusekhar fixed his one clear eye on his daughter's face. 'Why is he here so late at night?'

'I don't know. He has something to say to you.'

'Send for him.'

'Have your meal first, Baba,' Suhasini pleaded. 'There's no hurry. Ganga Dada will wait.'

'*O ré*!' Bidhusekhar raised his voice in command to the servants. 'Tell Ganga Babu to come up here.'

Ganga, who was sitting with Pran Gopal only two rooms away, heard Bidhusekhar's voice and rose to obey. He came to the room but did not enter it. He knew that the lower castes were forbidden by the shastras to enter a room in which a Brahmin sat eating his meal. Bidhusekhar turned his head. His eyes rested on Ganga's face for a few minutes. 'Who has expired?' he asked. Ganga hesitated, not knowing what to say. But Suhasini burst out weeping and the truth was revealed. Ganga watched, amazed, as Bidhusekhar went on eating as calmly as if Bimbabati's death was an everyday occurrence. Picking up a small bowl of *dal*, he asked dispassionately, 'Has a letter arrived from Hardwar?'

Ganga had to tell him about the arrival of the sanyasi and the message he had brought. Bidhusekhar heard the account with close attention and said, 'Well! She had renounced the world of her own free will. Now God has claimed her. There's no need to mourn her death.' But not one word that he said entered Ganga's ears. His attention was fully taken up by the quantity and quality of the food that had been placed before the old man. A mound of rice, as white and fragrant as jasmine petals, sat in the middle of a vast silver *thala*. Surrounding it were sixteen silver bowls, filled to the brim with fried and curried fish and vegetables. Actually, Bidhusekhar ate only a dab of cottage cheese and a piece of stewed magur fish at night. And, occasionally, flouting the doctor's orders, a bowl of masur *dal*, cooked into a thin soup. But it was his whim to sit before an elaborate meal each night. He knew he couldn't eat fried lobster head or poppy seed curry ever again in his life. But why deny himself the pleasure of looking at these dishes and inhaling their aromas? Smelling was half-eating—so the shastras said.

Bidhusekhar drank the *dal* from his bowl in one draught and said in a calm, detached voice, 'Your mother expired two months ago from what I gather. I advise you two boys to perform the shraddha as soon as possible. Tomorrow, if you can. Keep it simple. Grand shraddha ceremonies are unseemly for those who renounce the world. Another thing. See that Chhotku makes the rice offering. You don't need to—'

'But Chhotku isn't here!'

'Isn't here? Why? Where is he?' Bidhusekhar seemed more agitated at the news of Chhotku's absence than that of Bimbabati's death. 'He left Calcutta without seeing me!' Then, a note of hopelessness creeping into his voice, he added, 'He doesn't come any more. He hasn't—for a long time now.' Turning to Suhasini, he said, 'Haven't you made *kheer*? I'll have some tonight. My mouth feels bitter . . .'

Ganganarayan performed the shraddha the very next day. Whatever Bidhusekhar might say or hint, Ganga had always looked on Bimbabati as his own mother and he was unwilling to wait till Nabin's return. But he dispatched Nakur and Duryodhan immediately afterwards, with the express command to bring Nabin back from wherever he was, be it the furthest end of the country. After that he waited in a fever of impatience. A whole week passed and no one returned. Ganga became moody and despondent. Bimbabati's memory haunted him day and night. He found traces of her presence everywhere. The servants still referred to the room she had slept in as 'Karta Ma's room'; the birds that flitted in their cages as 'Karta Ma's birds' and the palki she had used as 'Karta Ma's palki'. Bimbabati had her own money and estates. Ganga had looked after them all these years on the strength of a legal document she had made out in his name. Now, with her death, everything of hers passed to Nabin Kumar. Bidhusekhar came over one day and told him so without mincing words. He was to leave everything exactly as it was till Nabin's return.

Pacing up and down on the terrace at night, Ganga looked up at the star-studded sky. He had been told as a child that with the passing of every soul from this world a star is born. Was that star in the east that was shining down on him with such benign radiance, Bimbabati? He would have liked to believe it. He hadn't been conceived in her womb in this life. Perhaps, in the next . . . ? Who was it who had said something about a next birth? A shudder passed through him as he remembered. Varanasi! The Ganga! Bindu had said they would be together again in their next birth. And he? He had forgotten her—as completely as if she had never existed. Even when he went to her father's house the other day, he hadn't remembered . . . Life was so strange!

'What are doing here out in the cold?'

Ganga turned around. Kusum Kumari had come to call him. The fair face that was raised to his was as lustrous as the stars above his head. He suppressed a sigh. There was no such thing as another birth. The present was all there was. Poor Bindu! Poor, unhappy, deprived Bindu! She had lost everything including himself.

A few days later, a murder was reported in the newspapers—a murder so monstrous and bizarre that it shook the city out of its complacence. A high-born Hindu woman, a daughter-in-law of one of the wealthiest families of Calcutta, had killed her husband. She had walked out of the house after the deed, her face unveiled, her clothes and hair splattered with blood. 'I've killed my husband,' she had said. 'I'm glad I did it.'

The news spread like wildfire, getting more exaggerated and distorted as it went along. Some said that the woman had killed the two sepoys who had been sent to arrest her and that she would be hanged on the gallows in the middle of the maidan for everyone to see, as Raja Nanda Kumar had been. Others said no, she had surrendered of her own volition. She hadn't even engaged a lawyer but had pleaded her case herself. She had told the judge that she had suffered the torments of Hell in her life with her husband and had killed him as a means of escape. Did the court, which had allowed her sinful debauch of a husband to torture her day and night, have any right to indict her? Some feared for the Hindu religion if women, who were its custodians, flouted its traditions so shockingly. Others said it was something to rejoice about. If more women of the country could strike their evil brutes of husbands dead, it would be a better place to live in.

All this was rumour, of course. The truth was that one night,

Durgamoni, wife of Chandikaprasad of the Malliks of Hatkhola, had hacked her husband's neck to pieces with a falchion. She had tried to kill herself afterwards but hadn't succeeded. She was alive even now and in police custody. The moment Kusum heard this, she fell with a thud at Ganga's feet. She had fainted.

# Chapter XXXVII

Nabin awoke each day before dawn and felt his heart overflowing with happiness. Rising from bed, he came and stood by the window and gazed at the expanse of bank and river, dim and shadowy against a pearl grey sky. Peace flooded his soul at the thought that the world was all his—his to see and hear, to touch and smell and taste. He had never felt like this before and wondered whether this heightened sensitivity came naturally with age or was the consequence of his renunciation of alcohol. For Nabin hadn't touched a drop since he had stepped into the boat. He felt light in body and free of soul. He almost felt as if he had been granted a new birth.

Having gazed his fill, Nabin wrapped a shawl around himself and came to the roof of the bajra, where he stretched out on a reclining chair and watched the dawn break over the horizon. He sat like this every morning at the same hour. Soon, Dulal would come with a pot of frothing sap, freshly collected from the winter palms. Filling a marble urn to the brim, he would hand it to his master, who would drink it eagerly, even greedily. Three urnfuls he would drink, thinking all the while, 'Why did palm juice never taste like this before?' After an hour or two, Dulal would bring up tender coconuts he had gathered from the palms that grew thick and lush on both sides of the river. Slicing the top off one giant green egg with his knife, he would nick a hole in it and offer it to Nabin. Nabin would seize it with both hands and pouring the sweet milky water down his throat, murmur below his breath, 'Nothing can match this. No, not the most expensive wines of France.'

One day Dulal brought a bunch of bananas, freshly cut from a clump growing by the bank. The fruits had ripened to perfection. The powdery pollen still clung to their skins, stretched taut and golden over plump, healthy bodies. Peeling one, Dulal handed it to Nabin. Biting into it, Nabin felt as if he had tasted nectar from Heaven. 'God is the king of all cooks,' he thought whimsically. 'And the earth is his kitchen. So many dishes are cooked every day, with so many different tastes and aromas! The palate-burning sharpness of the chilli! The sticky, overpowering sweetness of the mango and jackfruit! The pleasant bitterness of palta greens and neem! The acid bite of lime and tamarind! And some with mixed flavours, like the bel and rose apple—defying description.'

On this journey Nabin became aware that solitude was a state of mind, independent of environment. Here on this bajra, though surrounded by people, he was alone, truly alone for the first time in his life. Another realization that dawned on him was that solitude sharpened a man's perception of the world and heightened his sensibilities. As he sat in the boat, watching the world go by, the present became mixed with the past, memory was blended with imagination. So much that had long been forgotten swam into view and took on a new meaning. And continually haunting him was a face—a face he strove to forget; to deny. Why was surrender so difficult? He had worked all his life to achieve, to appropriate. He had used all his strength, not stinting himself. And he had succeeded. But now, when his efforts were strained towards renunciation, not possession, he found that strength to be insufficient.

Nabin and his entourage were at Nadiya when Nakur and Duryodhan caught up with them. Nabin received the news of his mother's death very calmly. It was as though he was expecting something like it and had prepared himself. But Dulal, who stood outside the door, set up a loud wail. He worshipped Bimbabati. He had never forgotten that were it not for her, his mother and he would have starved to death on the streets. Nabin let him weep for a while and then commanded Nakur to bring him into his presence. 'Chhoto Babu,' Dulal cried, hoarsely dabbing at his flowing eyes, 'Karta Ma has left us . . .'

'Tell the boatmen to cast anchor by some big village on the waterfront,' Nabin said, his face calm and eyes dry. 'We must get hold of a Brahmin priest and make all the arrangements. I wish to perform the rites here, on the bank of the Ganga.'

'Will you not return to Calcutta?' Nakur asked with folded hands. 'Bara Babu has given express commands—'

'No, I shan't return just yet. You two get back to your duties.'

Dulal, who was eager to return, pointed out that performing

his mother's shraddha on someone else's land did not become a zamindar with the wealth and importance of Nabin Kumar Singha. It would involve a loss of prestige. His reasoning seemed fair enough. The rituals could have been conducted on the deck of the bajra but the shastras forbade worship of the Narayanshila on water. The only thing to do was to buy a house. As soon as the idea occurred to him, Nabin ordered Dulal to look for a house with a few bighas of land adjoining it immediately. He would make the rice offering to the departed soul the very next day.

The fleet of boats came to a halt by the bustling town of Raspur a little way up the river and the party descended. Some of the men were immediately dispatched to find a house and others to collect the articles listed by the priest. The ritualistic 'sixteen gifts' to the departed soul had to be of the best quality. So some trusted servants were sent on horseback to Nabadweep to procure them.

The shraddha was conducted with due ceremony. Nabin had his head shaved, bathed in the Ganga and sat down to perform the rites in the newly bought house, surrounded by eleven bighas of land, just a mile above the river from Raspur. A hundred Brahmins were feasted on the first day—fortunately, the area swarmed with Brahmins—and given ten silver rupees, a brass pitcher and a pair of dhotis each. The Brishotsarga—the freeing of four bulls—was performed with due deference to the status of the deceased and nearly three thousand destitutes were fed, Nabin serving the first batch with his own hands.

After it was all over and the guests had departed, Nabin sat in the shade of an ashwatha tree on the bank and gazed out on the river. He had not wept a single tear since he heard the news, marvelling at his own self-control. But now the hard, dry eyes softened and hot, stinging tears coursed down his cheeks. 'Ma,' he murmured hoarsely, 'I've pained you over and over again. But you've forgiven me. I know it. I feel it in my heart.'

Even as Nabin ruminated thus, a boat sailed up to the bank where he was sitting and a middle-aged man, plump and sleek in a bright red dhoti and muga shawl, stepped out. Bringing his palms together, he touched them to his brow and said. 'Namaskar, Chhoto Babu!' Seating himself a little distance away the stranger said, 'I received the news this morning. But now,' and here he glanced meaningfully at Nabin's shaven head and continued, 'I see I've come too late.'

'Who are you and where do you come from? '

'I'm Bhujangadhar Sharma and I come from Ibrahimpur. You had estates there, if you remember.'

'Had estates? Don't we now?'

'In a sense you do. In a sense you don't.'

'Stop talking in riddles,' Nabin cried out angrily, irritated at the man's familiarity. 'If you require anything of me come out with it or else—take yourself off.'

Bhujanga Bhattacharya grinned from ear to ear, obviously enjoying the situation. 'I'll talk plain then,' he said. 'I used to be your nayeb but now I've become the zamindar. I've pretended to be a zamindar for so long that the pretence has now turned into reality.'

'Our nayeb turned zamindar! What can you mean?'

'Exactly what I say. It's been six years since a member of your family has set foot on the zamindari or collected the rents. Six years is a long time. It is natural, in the circumstances, that someone will misappropriate it. It is mine now. I'm all in all.'

'You've filched our zamindari!' Nabin cried, his cheeks flaming. 'And you dare to brag about it to my face?'

'They are still in your name. As per the terms of the Permanent Settlement a zamindari can change hands only after a sale. What all clever nayebs do in a situation like this is to suck the zamindari dry. And that is what I've done.'

Nabin was puzzled by the man's manner. But, for some reason, he also felt vaguely attracted to him. He had never met anyone like him. 'I still don't understand,' he said, 'why you've come to me.'

'The air is thick with rumours that the great Ramkamal Singha's son, the jewel of Karta Ma's eyes, Nabin Kumar Singha, is so impoverished that he is going to perform his mother's shraddha on land that does not belong to him. I couldn't allow that to happen, could I? That is why I came rushing over. But the rites are concluded—as I see now. Even so, you must come to Ibrahimpur where you belong. I've built a new kuthi. You'll be very comfortable there.'

'You've come to take me to Ibrahimpur?'

'Yes.'

'That's strange. What if I try to regain my zamindari?'

'It is up to you. If you wish to have them back, who can stop you?'

'What if I send you to jail for robbing me all these years? Not paying me a single paisa as rent?'

'That you can't, Chhoto Babu. I've got my books and ledgers in perfect order. I've shown no income at all—only debts and losses. You can't touch me.'

'I can sack you. And employ another nayeb. After all, I am the zamindar if only in name.'

'You can do that but it will avail you nothing. Your new nayeb will turn tail and run before you reach the city. The peasants acknowledge me as their master. They'll obey no one else.' A great burst of laughter issued from Bhujanga's deep chest, making him rock to and fro. Then, controlling himself, he said, 'How's your elder brother? He's a great man, a godly man. I've heard he has married again. But I wasn't even invited. Who has ever heard of a zamindar not inviting his nayeb to his wedding! How can you expect to keep your zamindari if you're so careless? Where's the steward, Dibakar? Hasn't he come with you? He knows me.'

On hearing that Dibakar was too old and enfeebled to leave the house, Bhujanga sighed and shook his head sagely. 'Now I know why things have come to such a pass. Old heads are better than young ones. The youngsters of today are a worthless lot. Look at the way they've allowed the zamindar to sit on the bare ground like a destitute! Come, Chhoto Babu. Order your servants to pack up and get ready. I'm taking you with me to Ibrahimpur. It's not too far—only three hours' journey by boat.'

# Chapter XXXVIII

The new kuthi, a fine, handsome mansion, reared its head proudly to the sky. A little distance away the old one huddled shamefacedly—a little heap of straw and rubble, covered all over with weeds and creepers. Pointing to it Bhujanga said, 'That's the old kuthi. That's where I lived with my family till the night the indigo sahebs set it on fire and I ran out of it like a chased rat with my wife and children.'

'How are the planters behaving now?' Nabin asked.

'I'll tell you everything. But have a wash first and something to eat. People say my Brahmani is a wonderful cook. If you permit me I'll arrange for your meals to be served from my kitchen.' Then, opening a door, he led Nabin into a large, comfortable looking room, furnished expensively and tastefully. 'I'm ready to receive you as you can see,' he continued. 'I've kept this room exactly like this for the last five years. But neither you nor your brother deigned to set foot on our humble soil.'

After the servants had dusted the room and set out his things, Nabin sat back on the couch and surveyed the scene. It was indeed a beautiful room, fitted with every luxury he was used to, from the high carved bedstead to the punkah that swung from the ceiling. Bhujanga hadn't omitted a single detail. Seating himself on the floor at Nabin's feet, Bhujanga said in his usual mock-serious way, 'I may be a swindler but I'm not an ingrate. I wouldn't have kept this room waiting for you if I was. I haven't forgotten that I've eaten of your salt all these years. Your brother, Ganganarayan Singha, was the last to visit the kuthi and it was he who inflamed the ryots against the sahebs. Had he come with you he could have seen the results with his own eyes.'

'What are the results?'

'MacGregor—the dreaded one, whose name made the stoutest hearts quake—committed suicide a couple of years ago. There was a liaison with the district magistrate's wife but that's none of our concern. He's been punished as he deserves and that's all we need to know. The Neel Kuthi was burned down immediately afterwards and the sahebs ran away—their tails between their legs. We don't grow indigo any more. Paddy, bright golden paddy, waves from every field.'

'I'm very glad to hear it. My brother risked his life to help the ryots. It makes my heart rejoice to know that his struggle and sacrifice have borne fruit.'

'But he never came back. He returned to the city and became a non-functioning zamindar like the rest of you.'

'My brother is a very busy man. But do you mean to tell me that no one from the family has visited the estate in all these years?'

'Not from the family. Servants have been sent from time to time. Your steward, Dibakar, came thrice. But I shooed him away. "You rascal," I said to him. "Next time I catch you skulking here I'll break your legs."'

'But he came as our representative! May I know what right you had to treat him like that?'

'You may. I treated him the way I did because I wanted to. Listen, listen, don't flare up. That's the trouble with you zamindars. You're too hot-headed. Hear me out, Chhoto Babu. If I'm a fox, Dibakar is a crocodile. I may have swindled you but I've worked for what I've got. Dibakar would have pocketed what I gave, if I gave him anything, and you wouldn't have got a paisa. So I thought—why give him a share? It is not as though the money is too much for me.'

'What you mean is that your business as our nayeb has been to rob us systematically.'

'Why not? Did you spare a single thought for me when I was out on the streets with my wife and children? Did you ever care to enquire where I was living and what I was eating when my house and possessions were burned down in a single night? Did you even know that your tenants were dying like flies of the famine that was raging in these parts? How do you expect me, then, to wash your steward's feet, feast him like a king and hand him bags of gold coins?'

'Do you mean to tell me that other zamindars visit their estates in person?'

'Those who don't lose them. Your grandfather made regular

trips to Ibrahimpur. So did your father—at least for many years. When he couldn't come himself he sent your brother. Then, when Ganga Babu stopped coming, your zamindari started running dry—'

'Suppose I sell off my lands?'

'You can if you wish to. But you'll get nothing for them. Who wants a zamindari as drained as an empty river bed?'

'Why didn't you write to us about the famine?'

'I wrote at least seven letters. But I didn't get one reply. Your brother was away and you were too busy translating your Mahabharat to have time for your petty peasants. It is a great piece of work and I revere you for it. If I weren't a Brahmin, I would have touched your feet and invoked your blessings. But though you're a great man, you're a worthless zamindar. You spend lakhs of rupees on widow remarriages in the city but not a handful of copper coins for keeping your tenants from starvation.'

'Is there anything wrong in promoting widow remarriage?'

'There's nothing wrong. But there's a contradiction. Don't you realize that your negligence of your duties as a zamindar has been responsible for the creation of innumerable widows in our villages? But of course, you didn't care to cast your eyes in this direction.' Suddenly, Bhujanga remembered himself. Starting up he touched his ears and bit his tongue. '*Arré!* Ram, Ram,' he said. 'I've quite forgotten that you've had a long journey and are tired and hungry. Rest a while, Chhoto Babu, while I see to your meal.'

A couple of days later, Nabin, yielding to Bhujanga's persuasion, set off on an inspection tour of his estates. He travelled in a palki, accompanied by his nayeb, his trusted servant, Dulal, and a number of armed guards. Wherever he went, he found the villagers in a state of near starvation and wondered why things were so bad even after the planters had gone. At one village he found over a thousand men waiting outside the court house, where he was to have a meal and rest. 'Hear me, subjects of the estate,' Bhujanga addressed the gathering. 'Our revered zamindar, Sreel Srijukta Nabin Kumar Singha Mahashai, is in our midst. He is a very busy man and can't visit us as often as he would like to. So many of you have never seen him. But you've seen his brother and remember his efforts on your behalf; his struggle and sacrifice. Babu Ganganarayan's younger brother is cast in the same mould. His heart bleeds for your sufferings. And having heard of the famine that has devastated these parts, he has of his own volition offered to exempt his ryots from paying tax for the next two years.'

There was a stunned silence for a few minutes, and then the crowd went wild with joy and shouts of applause rent the air. Nudging his master, Bhujanga whispered, 'Make the announcement in person, Chhoto Babu.' But Nabin, who was as taken aback as his tenants, said angrily, 'Why this farce? You know as well as I do that I don't receive a copper coin as tax. What is the sense of my announcing an exemption?' Bhujanga brushed this reasoning aside with exemplary calm. 'Chhoto Babu,' he said, 'what you receive is between you and me. I know the ryots are in a bad way and I shan't press them for the taxes. But for them their zamindar is like a god and they won't rest easy in their beds if they feel they've cheated him of his dues. If you announce the exemption, that anxiety will be relieved.' Raising his hands for silence, Bhujanga continued, 'Chhoto Babu wishes to speak to you. Be quiet and listen to what he says.'

'I exempt you from paying taxes,' Nabin said to the gathering.

'For two years,' Bhujanga prompted.

'No. For all time to come. I declare my lands to be freehold from this day onwards.'

At these words, the crowd surged forward with cries of jubilation, so loud and excited that Nabin's eardrums were fit to burst. Some, wondering if their ears had deceived them, kept questioning each other in voices that rose higher and higher as the clamour increased in intensity. Was it possible that a peasant could till his master's land without ever paying tax? Not only in his own lifetime but in that of the coming generations? Did it make sense? Others, quicker to comprehend and seize their opportunity, pushed and jostled to reach their master's feet, nearly knocking him down. The situation got so out of control that Bhujanga was forced to take Nabin's arm and drag him into the court house, out of the reach of the crowding men. Now, Nabin Kumar turned to Bhujanga. 'Nayeb Moshai!' he said with a triumphant smile. 'What do you have to say now?'

'Of all the childish—!' Bhujanga spluttered in shock and bewilderment . 'How could you make such an announcement, Chhoto Babu? Exempting the taxes for— Who has ever heard of such a thing?'

'You thought you'd batten on the fat of our land. I've put an end to it.'

'What about the annual tax you pay the goverment? From where will you find the money?'

'We'll see about that.'

But Bhujanga Bhattacharya was not the only one who was affected by Nabin's sudden decision. Nabin hadn't dreamed that it would boomerang on him the way it did. From that day onwards he was practically in a state of siege. Crowds of peasants from the other villages of Ibrahimpur flocked to the court house, morning, noon and night. They had heard that the zamindar had declared an exemption. But they weren't sure of who had been granted the privilege and who hadn't. Each wanted to hear of his own fate from the master's lips. Nabin was given no time to eat or rest. His mouth hurt from repeating the same words over and over again. He ordered a drummer to make the announcement in all the villages but the men kept on coming. The situation became so desperate that Nabin was forced to leave Ibrahimpur and set sail once again. But this time he took Bhujanga with him. His obsession with nature had given way to an obsession with humanity. He wanted to know more about the common people—their struggles and hardships— and only Bhujanga could tell him. 'We are still the zamindars of Ibrahimpur,' he told Bhujanga, 'and you are our nayeb. You'll be on our payroll from now on and receive a salary every month. You'll have to work for your salary though—a different kind of work. I want schools to be started—one for every two villages on my estate. And one more thing. No ryot of mine will ever suffer the pangs of hunger again. You must see to that.'

'You'll forget all these resolutions the moment you reach Calcutta. Besides, Bidhu Mukherjee is still alive, I'm told. He'll take care to turn you around.'

Within a few days of Nabin's sailing away from Ibrahimpur, the mast of his bajra came down and had to be repaired, forcing the boatmen to cast anchor. Two little villages stood side by side on the bank, their names making a pretty jingle—Bhinkuri and Dhankuri. Nabin, whose limbs felt cramped from the long hours of confinement, stepped out of the bajra with the intention of taking a little walk and Dulal and Bhujanga accompanied him. It had rained the night before and the air was fresh and soft, and the foliage and undergrowth a bright, luxuriant green. Talking animatedly to his companions as he walked, Nabin did not notice the crowd of curious villagers that had collected behind him—their numbers swelling every minute. Suddenly, Nabin stopped in his tracks, cocking a ear. He had heard a strange sound and it seemed to come from a burned down hut, grown over with ferns and creepers. A singed fan palm stood as if on guard just outside it. The sound came again—a harsh, guttural groan—and something crept out of the hut. At first Nabin thought it to be a wild animal. But the creature stood up and it became apparent that he was a man. He hadn't a stitch of clothing on him. A bough of green leaves, dangling from a thread around his middle, hid his genitals and tufts of wild grey hair, matted with earth, covered his face and body. Advancing a few steps, he fixed a pair of unblinking eyes on Nabin.

'Careful, Babu,' someone warned from behind. 'Don't go near him.'

'Who is he?'

'His name is Trilochan Das. His hut was burned down by the zamindar's men many years ago. He hadn't paid his taxes—'

'Who is the zamindar of these parts?'

'These villages fall within your estate, Chhoto Babu,' Bhujanga explained. 'But the incident occurred before my time—nearly thirty years ago. Udhavnarayan was nayeb then. His favourite sport was setting the ryots' houses on fire.'

'But even you have done nothing to better his lot.'

'He doesn't let anyone go near him.'

The villagers now told Nabin the whole story. Following the burning down of his hut, Trilochan had left the village with his wife and children. Many years later, he had returned, alone, and in a state of complete insanity. He had known no one and spoken to no one. The only thing he had recognized was his hut and the little patch of land on which it stood—land that had belonged to his forefathers. He had lived in it ever since, guarding it fiercely. And, strangest of all, he kept himself alive by eating the earth of his own land. He ate nothing else. People threw him food from time to time but he left it untouched.

Now, Trilochan spoke for the first time. 'Babu,' he said very gently. 'Can you give me some water to soak my *chiré*?'

'He's asking for water!' Nabin exclaimed 'And *chiré*!'

'That is something he repeats over and over again. It means nothing. He's a dangerous lunatic. Don't go any nearer.'

Ignoring the cries of the villagers, Nabin strode up to the man and said, 'Yes. I'll give you water and *chiré*. And anything else you want. Will you come with me?' Even as he said these words, the man gave a wild cry and leaped on Nabin Kumar, felling him to the ground. And, in a flash, before anyone knew what was happening, he had bitten a hunk of flesh from his zamindar's breast. The flesh, dripping blood, was still in his mouth when Dulal fell on him. Pulling him up by his long, grey hair, Dulal cuffed and kicked him with demoniac frenzy. In a few minutes the man was dead. Bhujanga lifted the unconscious Nabin from the ground and cradled him in his arms. The blood, spurting in jets from the wound, drenched his shirt and uduni.

# Chapter XXXIX

The vast crowd of spectators that had gathered at Princep's Ghat that morning was being kept in order by white cavalrymen of the armed guards. The sun blazed down on new uniforms and polished medals as, sitting on their sleek, well groomed horses, they rode this way and that, controlling the mass of people that pushed and jostled to catch a glimpse of the huge battleship that had just cast anchor. The new viceroy of the realm would emerge from it any moment now and set foot on Indian soil.

Rows of officials stood waiting on the bank, ready to greet him who had been dignified with the highest position in the land. But their eyes were mildly curious. The new viceroy was an Irishman and no one had ever heard of him. Lord Nashe, sixth Earl of Mayo, had been selected for the viceregalship by Disraeli against strong opposition both within and outside his own party. But Disraeli had stood firm and Mayo had set sail for India. Then, in mid-ocean, news had arrived that Disraeli was dead and that his arch enemy, Gladstone, was the new prime minister. A dismayed Mayo prepared himself for recall—it was but natural that Gladstone would choose his own viceroy for the dominions—but the order never came. Queen Victoria, as he heard later, had expressed her disapproval. It was not meet, she had said, that a chosen representative of Her Majesty should be treated in so cavalier a fashion. It would tarnish the image of the British Empire. Gladstone had seen the force of her reasoning and desisted.

Murmurs of admiration rose from the crowd of natives as the new viceroy stepped on the deck to the boom of cannon. Tall, broad-chested, with massive shoulders, he looked like a god from one of their own myths. And with that splendid physique went a face that combined virility with gentleness; strength with sensitivity. The Indian masses had seen many Englishmen but not one as impressive.

The viceregal lodge lay only a stone's throw away from the

bank and the new viceroy was to walk the short distance. He went slowly, nodding encouragement to the bands of soldiers on either side, dressed in plaid kilts and playing Scottish melodies on bagpipes. Arriving at his destination he walked up the steps to where Sir John Lawrence awaited him in full regalia, his chest ablaze with medals. But his face looked worn and his manner was weary. The truth was that John Lawrence was a soldier and the mantle of viceregalship sat heavily on him. Bureaucratic red tape tried his patience and he often found it difficult to keep up with diplomatic etiquette. He dressed informally and tended to lapse into the vernacular when conversing with natives. These were grievous defects in one who represented Her Majesty's government in India and held the highest position in the land. This morning he waited in a fever of impatience. He was wearing the viceregal robes for the last time. His successor had arrived to assume charge.

The arrival of the new viceroy affected others of the city not so favourably. All other movement at the ghat had been suspended, and the river was dotted with vessels as far as the eye could see. The bajra containing Nabin Kumar's party was anchored midstream, there being no possibility of landing for several hours. Nabin lay on his bed, eyes closed in deep sleep. A huge bandage covered his chest. Bhujanga hadn't taken any chances. He had had a kaviraj brought in from Dhankuri, who had cleaned and bound the wound with medicinal herbs. He had then boarded the bajra and set off with his patient for Calcutta. Now he sat at the side of the bed, his eyes fixed on his master's face. From time to time he held a mirror to the latter's nose and sighed with relief to see it clouded over.

It was late afternoon when the palki carrying Nabin reached the lion gates of the Singha mansion. Bhujanga had ordered the bearers to go very slowly and take care to step in unison. It was imperative that the palki did not swing for with every movement the blood spurted out, drenching the bandage. The moment the palki touched the ground, Dulal ran like one possessed to the house of Surya Kumar Goodeve Chakravarti. The latter had just sat down to a meal but Dulal's tears and impassioned pleas to come without losing a moment made him abandon it and rush to the house of the Singhas. Ganganarayan was away from home and a servant was dispatched to fetch him from wherever he was.

Goodeve Chakravarti loosened the bandage and inspected the wound. 'My God!' he exclaimed. 'Was he attacked by a cannibal? No ordinary man can bite off such a large chunk of flesh.' Then, losing his temper, he shouted, 'The wound is coated with dirt. Are you all numskulls? Didn't it enter your head to clean the wound with warm water and cotton?' Bhujanga assured him that the wound had been cleaned and that what he thought was dirt was actually kaviraji medicine. 'Rubbish,' Goodeve Chakravarti snarled at the hapless Bhujanga. 'To allow those quacks to mess around with the wound is adding insult to injury. Who knows what complications have set in?' And he proceeded to clean the wound with deft hands.

Kusum and Sarojini waited in the next room—Sarojini weeping bitterly and Kusum consoling her. Now Kusum came forward and spoke, using Dulal as her medium. Sarojini observed strict purdah from men but Kusum didn't. 'Dulal,' she called in her soft, clear voice, 'Ask Doctor Babu if the injury is a serious one. Will it be necessary to call in an English doctor?'

'The injury is external,' the doctor answered. 'It will heal in a few days. You may send for European doctors if you like but I see no need for it.'

'Dulal! Have you told Doctor Babu that the man who bit Chhoto Babu was a lunatic?'

'Who other than a lunatic would do such a thing?' The doctor replied. 'No sane person would bite another. *O he*'! You may tell your Ginni Ma that there is no cause for worry.'

Goodeve Chakravarti finished dressing the wound and rose to leave. 'If there is fresh bleeding,' he said, 'call me there and then. If not, I'll come tomorrow morning to check on him. Another thing. There are too many people in the room and the patient is likely to get disturbed. I would like the room cleared. Only one or two of you may remain. Make sure he doesn't move too much or try to sit up. The wound will bleed afresh if he does.' All the men now departed and Sarojini and Kusum were left alone with the patient. 'O Didi!' Saroj raised a tear-streaked face. 'A human bite is very dangerous. There's poison in the teeth.'

'Who told you that?'

'I know. There was a madman in our ancestral village. He bit another man and he went mad too.'

Kusum's hand went up to her shoulder in an involuntary movement. Saroj was wrong. She knew it from her own experience. Only, she didn't want to talk or even think about it. 'That's nonsense,' she consoled her sister-in-law. 'You heard the doctor say there was no cause for worry.'

'I don't believe him.' Sarojini shook her head from side to side. 'I'm so frightened. Will Bhasur Thakur[17] never come? My heart is thumping so hard I can hardly support myself.'

It took some time for the servant to find Ganga. He had left for Spencer's Hotel, following an urgent summons from Gourdas Basak. Madhusudan had returned to Calcutta and had been residing in Spencer's Hotel for the last two years. He had left his family in Europe, where the children were receiving an education. Madhusudan's friends and well-wishers had urged him often to leave the staggeringly expensive hotel and find himself a house in some respectable locality. But Madhu had turned a deaf ear to their advice. He had to live like an Englishman, he argued, if he was to compete with them. But, as a matter of fact, he was not competing very well. His speech had thickened with years of hard drinking and couldn't be comprehended easily. Besides, he was extremely irregular in attending court, preferring the company of friends and sycophants to that of his clients. He never charged the former if he took up their cases. If anyone insisted on paying he would declare in his expansive way, 'You may send me a bottle of burgundy, half a dozen of beer and a hundred langdas from the mango orchards of Malda.' In the circumstances, it was hardly surprising that within six months of his return, Madhu started having difficulties in meeting his expenses, both at home and abroad. The inevitable followed. He applied to Vidyasagar for a loan. But Vidyasagar was in a bad way himself. He had borrowed heavily to help Madhusudan out during his stay in Europe and now his creditors were threatening to sue him. Besides, he disapproved heartily of Madhusudan's lifestyle and

17 Husband's elder brother.

saw no reason why he should contribute to it. He hardened himself and refused.

Madhu's condition worsened every day and the more hard-pressed he was, the more he drank. His friends were alarmed at his rapid decline and tried to check it as best as they could. Gour's work took him to the mofussils from time to time and whenever that happened he left Madhu in Ganga's care. That is how Ganga was sitting at Spencer's Hotel the day Nabin came home.

On entering, Ganga found the room reeking of tobacco smoke (Madhu had started smoking an *albola* along with his favourite cigars) and Madhu lolling on the sofa in a dressing gown. He held two green chillies, their tips bitten off, in his hand and was rubbing them on his tongue with a distasteful expression. 'Ah Ganga! My dear boy,' he called out in welcome. 'See if these chillies have any bite in them. I feel nothing on my tongue. It is as dead as a doornail.'

'Green chillies! Oh, my God!' Ganga exclaimed in horror. 'What are you up to, Madhu? Do you want to kill yourself?'

'Don't sermonize, my dear . . . Let's celebrate your coming. Boy! Peg *lao*!'

'No, no, Madhu. Don't start all that. It's the middle of the day!'

'Ah! You're a vegetarian. I'd forgotten that. But don't ask me to follow in your footsteps. I'll drink whenever I please.'

'I'm not sermonizing, Madhu,' Ganga said, gravely. 'But I'll certainly say this. You've spent so much time and money becoming a barrister. You should settle down now, work hard and make money. Not live in this hotel like a waif and . . .'

'I'll never settle down in my life,' Madhu replied. Pausing a little, he continued in a saddened voice, 'Everyone advises me to make money. No one asks me why I don't write poetry any more.'

'I do. Why don't you write another great epic like *Meghnad Badh*? Your countrymen expect so much of you.'

'I am finished, Ganga. The Muse has left me. I've lost my gift. Living and dying are one and the same to me now. I'm afraid of taking poison. So I drink this instead.'

Madhu poured peg after peg down his throat, uttering the shattering cry, 'The Muse has left me,' at intervals. Ganga tried to remonstrate with him but Madhu brushed him aside. At last, not knowing what else to do, Ganga rose to take his leave. Walking out of the hotel he found his carriage waiting for him and heard the devastating news.

Once home, he questioned Dulal and Bhujangadhar in great detail about the nature of the accident and then rushed out again. He was back within the hour—an allopath, a homoeopath and a kaviraj with him. All three inspected the wound. The first two declared the injury to be superficial but the kaviraj shook his head doubtfully. Next, Ganganarayan went to Dr Goodeve Chakravarti. The latter told him plainly that he could collect as many doctors as he liked. But he would do it on his own responsibility. Surya Kumar would wash his hands off the patient. Ganga was in a quandary and decided to wait one more day.

Next day, Nabin was much better. He opened his eyes, jewel bright eyes in a worn, pale face, and smiled. 'How am I, Doctor?' he asked Surya Kumar. 'Will I live?'

'You'll have to work hard to die, young man,' the doctor smiled back. 'And wait a long while. Not less than fifty years.'

'Has he bitten off a great deal?'

'Very little,' Surya Kumar crooked his thumb and index finger till they met. 'Only this much. Nothing to worry about.'

'Can I see it?' Nabin tried to sit up but the doctor caught him with an exclamation. '*Arré! Arré*! What are you doing?'

'Take off the bandages. I want to see the wound with my own eyes.'

Ganganarayan and Surya Kumar hastened to dissuade him but Nabin brushed their protests aside. He would not rest without seeing the wound, he declared, and knowing how obstinate he could get, Surya Kumar had to loosen the bandage. There was a gaping hole, the size of a man's fist—raw and red with freshly oozing blood.

'It is just above the heart,' Nabin said, squinting down at it. 'My heart won't spring out of the hole, will it?'

'What sort of question is that?' Surya Kumar scolded. 'The injury is superficial and will heal in a few days. There's nothing to worry about.'

Lying back on the bed, Nabin shut his eyes and murmured, 'Make me well, Doctor. Make me well as soon as you can. I can't afford to waste my time lying in bed. There's such a lot of work waiting to be done. Will I be given the time?'

# Chapter XXXX

Dr Surya Kumar Goodeve Chakravarti was amazed at the change in Nabin. Nabin was the most cooperative of patients this time—a veritable doctor's delight. He submitted to the pain of dressing the wound without flinching and obeyed the doctor's orders with regard to food, medicine and rest to the letter. He never complained. Knowing the pain to be excruciating at times, Surya Kumar advised him to have a little brandy. Alcohol eased the pain and rendered it bearable. But Nabin refused outright. 'Don't ask me to touch that stuff again, Doctor,' he said. 'I've left all that behind me now.' But Nabin made one appeal, feverishly, over and over again. 'Get me back on my feet, Doctor. I have such a lot to do. My brain is teeming with ideas. I'm afraid, terribly afraid, that I shan't be given the time to carry them out.'

A week went by. Nabin gained steadily in health and strength. He felt well enough to sit up for several hours at a stretch and his appetite had returned. But the wound was not healing as well as it should have. There was no outward sign of sepsis or gangrene. But the hole gaped as large as ever and bled afresh with the slightest movement. Dr Chakravarti tried every kind of medicine but he couldn't stop the bleeding. He now decided to experiment a little. First, he sent for the two most illustrious homoeopaths of the city—Mahendralal Sarkar and Rajadhiraj Datta. The former had been an allopath of outstanding merit, being the second doctor in India to receive an M. D. degree. But he had switched over to Heinnemann's theories in his latter years. Rajadhiraj Datta was equally well known and had a roaring practice. They both gave it as their considered opinion that there was no gangrene. The wound would heal with the present treatment, they felt, and saw no reason for interfering with it. Mahendralal Sarkar suggested discreet doses of kaviraji herbs to augment Surya Kumar's foreign medicines. The two systems did not clash. Rather, one helped the other. Surya Kumar agreed and so did Nabin and Ganga. The decision seemed sensible to all three.

That morning, as Nabin reclined in bed, supported by pillows, a lively conversation ensued between the doctors surrounding him. 'O Kaviraj Moshai!' Rajadhiraj called out to Bhrigu Kumar Sen with a sneer in his voice. 'Do you know what happened at your Hari Sabha the other day?' Bhrigu Kumar Sen, who was a practising Vaishnav, prayed for his patients while dosing them with kaviraji herbs. He went on with his *jap* without deigning to make an answer.

'What happened?' Vishnucharan asked curiously.

'The strangest thing! It was in Kali Datta's house in Kolutola. You've heard of Kali Datta? So many people attend his Hari Sabhas that traffic gets disrupted in the street on which he lives. Kali Datta always leaves a vacant seat in the middle of the throng. He and his compatriots believe that Sri Chaitanya Dev comes in person to occupy it.'

'But what was the strange thing that happened?'

'I'm coming to it. A Kali *sadhak* called Ram Krishna walked up to the vacant seat and, before anyone could stop him, he stood on it and went off into a trance. The Vaishnavs were absolutely scandalized.'

'Who is this Ram Krishna?'

'He's the *pujari* of Rani Rasmoni's temple in Dakshineswar. You remember Ram Kumar Chattopadhyaya—the priest who performed the inaugural puja? Ram Krishna is his brother.'

'But Ram Kumar's brother's name is Gadadhar.'

'Yes. Gadadhar Thakur and Ram Krishna are one and the same. He got himself initiated at the hands of a Naga sanyasi who turned him into an *avadhut*. People say that his brains have got addled ever since. Now he goes off into a trance every other hour. One hand goes up into the air and the fingers get twirled as if in dance.'

'I've heard a lot about him,' Vishnucharan said. 'The renowned Ganga Prasad Sen, a veritable Dhanwantari, was called to Dakshineswar by Mathur Babu to treat him. But Sen Moshai wasn't able to do much. The man is a lunatic. He snatches food from the mouths of dogs; doesn't sleep a wink; and worships himself, instead of the Goddess, with flowers and bel leaves. And, strangest of all, I've heard people say that his back and chest are a glowing red colour. Most unnatural! Ganga Prasad Sen told me that his medicines had no effect at all.'

'Be that as it may,' Rajadhiraj said with a touch of impatience, 'what right had he to place his feet on an asan reserved for the Mahaprabhu? Being a Shakta, he had no business to walk into a Vaishnav's *akhara* in the first place and—'

Bhrigu Kumar Sen now released Nabin's wrist with a sigh and murmured, 'I was present on the occasion you mention. He's no ordinary man. His face glows with an inner light.'

'But to go off into a trance in the standing position!' Nabin exclaimed wonderingly. 'Is it possible?'

'It is not possible for you and me. But Ram Krishna is not an ordinary man. He's a saint. Mark my words. The day is not far off when he'll have a following larger than anyone has ever dreamed of.'

'I should like to have a look at him.'

'Get well quickly, Chhotku.' Ganga said. 'Then we'll go to Dakshineswar together.'

Nabin's brain teemed with ideas even as he lay in bed, and being impatient and impulsive by nature, he couldn't wait to implement them. The nayebs of all the other estates were sent for and the declaration of Ibrahimpur made known to them. A vast forest tract of Orissa and two low-lying fens in the Sunderbans were sold to enable him to buy a large piece of land in a suburb of the city. Here, Nabin had plans to set up a college of agriculture. Ganganarayan was shocked at this latest whim and tried to dissuade him. 'Our business is going through a bad patch, Chhotku,' he said. 'We've lost a lot of stock and we're having difficulty paying our creditors. Is this the time to throw our assets away with both hands?' But Nabin brushed his worries aside. 'Just think, Dadamoni!' he exclaimed excitedly. 'What a wonderful thing it will be! We should have had one in the country long ago. It will do more good, in my opinion, than Hindu College. Agriculture is the backbone of our economy and we have neglected it shamefully. All we've done is produce clerks to run the British government. I have plans to set up an agricultural college in every village of Bengal. We'll get farmers from Ireland to train the peasants. The Irish have highly sophisticated techniques of irrigation.'

It was late afternoon and the room was empty. Only Dulal lay sleeping on his mat on the floor. Nabin sat up slowly. A curious sensation overwhelmed him. He felt time to be running out; running out fast. He couldn't afford to lie in bed any longer. There was so much to do and so little time . . .

A strange restlessness seized him. He loosened the bandage on his chest, biting his lips to stop himself from crying out with pain. A deep sigh escaped him as the wound was revealed. It was as large and gaping as ever. Would it never heal? And again, that curious thought came into his head: 'What if my heart leaps out of the hole?' Ignoring the trickles of blood that had started flowing out of it, he put out a foot and stepped gingerly on to the floor. As he did so, he saw someone's reflection in the mirror opposite. It was there one moment and gone the next. He looked behind him. A stretch of innocent white wall met his eyes. There was no one there. Wrapping the layers of gauze anyhow around his chest he went to the door. The corridor was empty.

'What is it, Chhoto Babu?' Dulal sat up, startled. He had heard a sound and was shocked to see his master at the door.

'Nothing. I wanted to see if I could walk about a little. I found I could do it quite easily.'

'You shouldn't have left your bed. The doctors have forbidden it.'

Nabin lay down and pulled a sheet up to his chin. 'Dulal!' he called.

'Yes, Chhoto Babu.'

'You killed him, didn't you? I mean the man who bit me. Why did you do such a thing?'

'My blood was boiling in anger. I could have torn him to bits.'

'Do you believe in destiny, Dulal?'

'Of course, I do. We are all puppets in her hands.'

'You're right. Something, I don't know what, dragged me to the man. Why did I go so near? And why did he choose to attack me out of all the others? Destiny must have willed it. Otherwise—'

'Don't think about it, Chhoto Babu. You'll get well soon. All the doctors say so.'

'I'll get well, of course,' Nabin sighed and murmured. 'But

it's getting late. Very late!' The next moment he gave a startled cry. 'Who? Who's there?'

'Where, Chhoto Babu?'

'I thought I saw a shadow at the door. It slipped away—'

Dulal ran out of the room and down the corridor. But there was no sign of anyone. 'No, Chhoto Babu,' he said. 'There's no one outside.'

Nabin's brows came together in deep thought.

Next day, around the same time, Nabin stepped out of bed once again. Wrapping a shawl around himself, he walked softly to the door and then out of it. His heart felt light and almost happy. Here he was, walking about without any difficulty. If he felt strong enough to move about the house, why shouldn't he? How much longer must he remain confined to bed like a prisoner?

But as he walked down the deserted verandah, he was assailed by the strangest feelings. He didn't know where he was or what he was doing there. He looked around wonderingly. Who built this mansion with its vast ceilings and carved pillars? Who lived in these empty, desolate rooms? Had he walked into someone else's house by mistake? Even as he stood thinking these thoughts, a strain of music came floating to his ears. It was a woman's voice, sweet and soft, and it lingered in the air like an essence. A quiver of ecstasy passed through Nabin's frame. He had to find her. He had to find the woman who dwelt in this enchanted palace and sang her low, throbbing melody as she wandered about its halls and galleries. Pressing one hand to his breast he walked on.

Coming to a closed door he stopped short. Why, this was his mother's room! It was his own house. But who could be singing here? His mother was dead these many months. Putting out a hand he pushed the door open and got a shock. There were two women inside—one, sitting on a marble stool, with her back to the door, clashed a pair of cymbals to the beat of the other's song. All Nabin could see of her was the sheet of dark hair that swung to the rhythm of her hands. The other was a maid and it was she who sang. The women started up on hearing the door open and the one playing the cymbals turned around. It was Kusum Kumari. Nabin stared at her. He knew, of course, that she and Ganganarayan had moved into Bimbabati's room, but at that moment, his mind went blank. He didn't know who she was or how she came to be there.

'Why, Thakurpo!' Kusum moved swiftly towards him. Nabin recognized her now. His eyes, glazed and unfocussed, resumed their normal expression. 'I'm sorry,' he mumbled. 'I came here by mistake.' He didn't stop to answer her anxious queries but walked slowly back towards his own room.

# Chapter XXXXI

Nabin stepped out of the carriage, ignoring Dulal's outstretched hand. He wore an elegantly pleated Shantipuri dhoti and silk banian and held his father's silver-encrusted cane in one hand. A cap of gold lace sat jauntily on the fine black down on his head. His face was thinner than before and its bright fairness was considerably dimmed. It bore an uncanny resemblance, these days, to that of the famous English poet, George Byron.

Accompanied by Dulal, Bhujanga and others Nabin walked towards what looked like a vast sheet of water, dotted with palms and mangroves. A small hut, tiled with potsherd, stood in one corner.

'You see that fan palm, Huzoor? That marks the other end.'

'How much land?'

'Forty-nine bighas.'

'What you show me is water. I'm not planning to start a fishery.'

'There's very little water, Huzoor. The soil is excellent. All it needs is a bit of draining.'

Nabin looked around with lacklustre eyes. The area was a marshy swamp named Bali Ganj, situated at a little distance from the village of Rasa Pagla. It was submerged in water for the most part—a few rice fields and banks of reeds breaking the monotony. Clouds of mosquitoes swirled above his head though the time was early afternoon.

'Is there a river or canal anywhere near?' Nabin queried. 'I have to have some flowing water.'

'The nearest river is the Adi Ganga. But that's some distance away.'

'Do you approve?' Nabin looked at Bhujangadhar. Bhujanga shook his head. 'I'm of the same mind,' Nabin said. 'The river is too far off and the soil too wet. It will take ages to drain. We'll need to build quickly—quarters for a hundred peasants, bungalows for the teachers, storerooms and—'

'The land is going for a song, Huzoor,' the agent pleaded.

'Even if you invest in a few feet of earth you'll still save a lot of money.' But Nabin's mind was made up and he turned to leave. 'Let's look elsewhere,' he said to Bhujanga.

'Why don't you start a college in Nadiya, Chhoto Babu?'

'I will, very soon. I'll build one in every district of Bengal. But my first must be in the city. The Calcutta College of Agriculture will be larger and more prestigious than Presidency College. The latter is churning out half-educated clerks. I'll produce educated peasants. They'll learn farming techniques along with reading and writing and simple arithmetic.'

Sitting in the carriage, Nabin's hand stole up to his breast. The gauze felt cool and slightly damp. But examining his hand he gave a sigh of relief. There was no blood on it—not even the slightest smear. The doctors had managed to seal the wound after months of medication but the area hadn't healed properly. A mound of hard, red flesh had grown over it, out of which drops of blood oozed out, time and again, standing on its surface like drops of sweat. Nabin had to keep it bandaged all the time. Looking at him no one would dream that a bandage, often suffused with blood, lay just below his banian of rich China silk. The doctors had given him permission to move about; how much longer could a man like him be kept confined to bed?

Meanwhile, Calcutta was agog with rumour and speculation. Word had spread through the length and breadth of the city that Nabin Kumar Singha, son of that potentate among zamindars, Ramkamal Singha, was in dire straits. He, whose wealth had seemed inexhaustible, was now heavily in debt. He had lost his estates. The great houses of Calcutta were sold. Even the one that housed the Bengal Club was gone. Was it possible to squander away so much money in so little time? Would the mansion at Jorasanko be the next to go?

At first Ganganarayan had tried to stop Nabin from pursuing his foolhardy course. But seeing that his brother turned a deaf ear to his pleas, he gave up the attempt. The money was Nabin's—not his. Who was he to interfere? Kusum Kumari was of the same opinion. But other relations and friends were loud in their condemnation. Had Nabin gone mad? Did he really think peasants would abandon their fields and enrol in colleges? The idea was absurd.

But Nabin went on with his plans, ignoring the gossip and speculation that hummed around him. He was working like a maniac. Flouting the doctors' instructions, he rushed around inspecting land, talking to dealers and supervising construction. Bhujanga had gone back to Nadiya and opened a school for farmers. And Nabin had found the land of his choice for the Calcutta College of Agriculture—fifty-two acres of prime land near Tiljala, with a kuthi on it and a canal flowing through it. He had purchased it for the enormous sum of one lakh seventy-five thousand rupees and had already started construction. Letters had been dispatched to Ireland and some experienced farmers had confirmed their willingness to take up appointments. But through it all, every now and then, the old feeling haunted him. Time was running out. Swiftly—too swiftly. Whenever he felt like that, he raised a hand and pressed it to his heart. And more often than not, the hand came up wet and sticky with blood.

One day, as Nabin sat in his carriage on his way to the site, the last vestige of strength deserted him. He collapsed in Dulal's arms. The blood, spurting from his breast, drenched the bandage through and appeared on his banian. Dulal looked on in dismay as the stain spread and spread and spread . . .

Nabin was in a deep coma when Vidyasagar came to see him. He had been lying thus for the past three days, with rare intervals of consciousness. The wound on his chest had burst open, revealing a cavity larger and deeper than ever. Now it really seemed possible for the heart to leap out and fall, pulsing and pounding on the sheets.

Vidyasagar was far from well himself. His back ached constantly from the injury to his spine. But he had come rushing over the minute he heard that Nabin Kumar was critically ill. Though Nabin's behaviour had annoyed him from time to time, there was a fund of true love and affection for the boy in his heart. There was something so bright and beautiful about Nabin; so bold and divergent—Vidyasagar had seen no one like him. Looking down on the inert figure on the bed, he sighed deeply. Then, placing a hand on the boy's forehead and noting that there was no fever, he turned to the doctor and asked eagerly, 'He'll get well, will he not?'

'We hope so,' Surya Kumar answered.

'This young man never takes up a project without seeing it to the finish. He will complete the work he has undertaken even as he completed the Mahabharat.' With these words, Vidyasagar turned to leave the room. Ganganarayan stood at the door. Stooping low he touched the old man's feet and said, 'My wife wishes to offer you her *pronam*. Will you come into the inner quarters?'

'Why not?' Vidyasagar allowed Ganga to lead him to a room where Kusum Kumari was waiting. Kusum rose at his entrance and kneeling on the floor touched her forehead to his feet. Vidyasagar raised a hand in blessing and murmured a few words. As he did so, his eyes fell on the upturned face and something stirred within him—a memory. She had been a widow and it was Nabin Kumar who had stood principal sponsor at her marriage to Ganganarayan. Of all the widow remarriages Vidyasagar had organized this one had been the most successful. 'The country has great hopes of you,' Vidyasagar said, addressing Ganganarayan. 'She expects a great deal more from your brother and yourself.'

Sitting in the palki on his way home, he wiped his cheeks with his uduni. He hated tears but they came to his eyes unbidden every now and then. It was getting to be a nuisance.

Meanwhile, the city grapevine was busy spreading its tendrils. Some said Nabin Kumar Singha was dying of a diseased liver. What else could be expected of one who drank as much as he did? Others knew for a certainty that he had been stabbed in the abdomen in a whorehouse brawl. Still others had heard that a madman had bitten his heart out and chewed it on the spot. And there was a sizeable group which believed that he had poisoned himself—the ignominy and humiliation of his present existence being too grievous to be borne.

On the fourth day, Nabin passed into a high delirium. 'My mother,' he murmured, tossing his head restlessly on the pillow. 'I could smell the warm sweetness of her. I was sitting by the river, performing the last rites . . . There was a fire and I could smell her. She smelled the same as when I used to cuddle into her breast as a baby . . . My cat! . . . Krishna Kamal, where does all this money come from? . . . I ran off to the round pool to catch grasshoppers. It was afternoon . . . I hate arithmetic. The figures crawl towards me like big, black ants . . . English! Yes, I've learned English. It's the language of the rulers, after all! But there are countries without rulers. The common men rule. Yes, there are such countries. I swear there are . . . . *Sadhabar Ekadasi*! So much like my *Naksha*. The postmaster writes well. *Neel Darpan*—so powerful and fiery! And this—all jokes and fun! . . . He turned his face away on seeing me. I wonder why? There is so much work . . . I must live another thirty years—till the new century comes. Till the cannon from the fort booms a hundred times. Sahebs will speak fluent Bengali by then. See if they don't . . .

'Why don't roses bloom by themselves? The ashwatha springs from every cleft in the masonry. It is very bad of the rose . . . . Yes, I made a mistake. A terrible mistake. That's why my chest aches so. I thought he was a sadhu. Maybe that's why he bit me. Why did you bite me? I'm not a zamindar. I am neither a father nor a zamindar. You shouldn't have killed him, Dulal. Even if he bit me . . . I'm going. Others will come in my place . . . The world will grow beautiful . . . Who weeps? Who weeps all night in the streets? Is it the wind? Can the wind wail in a human voice? . . . I couldn't give you a child, Saroj. But it's all for the best. A man like me should not leave an heir. Vidyasagar will get you remarried after I'm gone. Then you'll be happy . . . ' At these words, Sarojini sobbed loudly and ran out of the room but Nabin went on and on.

It was late afternoon. The sun was sinking in the west and the sky was a play of light and shadow. All the doors and windows had been opened to let in the sweet, cool air of evening. Leaning over him, Kusum Kumari looked into Nabin's open eyes and asked tenderly, 'May I give you some medicine, Thakurpo?' Nabin stared at the face above his—a face like a camellia at dawn . . . swimming blue eyes like pools of deep water, beneath a brow as wide and smooth as the bank of a river . . . masses of rich, black hair, hanging in clusters and curling over the fair temples. Her eyes held his—radiant and luminous—and a light passed from them, entering his very soul.

Nabin turned his face away and sighed. Then softly, haltingly, he breathed a name, 'Va-na-jyot-sna,' even as his head sank lifeless on the pillow.

# *Chapter XXXXII*

It was a curious light—whether of dawn or dusk, one could not tell. Shadowy, chilly, with the sense of faint uneasiness that accompanies a change of props in a play. Like the awakening after a long, deep sleep, when everything is strange and unfamiliar and one seems to be floating in the infinite universe, groping for one's own little nest in vain. The fear, the desolation, the cold sinking of the heart as one hears the voices of loved ones calling from afar. 'Come . . . Come.' The knowledge that a long journey lies ahead and that time is running out . . .

Such a light suffused the city that day!

Nature has her own laws and so does life. The light of day succeeds the dark of night—invariably, unfailingly. Storm clouds at noon might darken the sky and a flood of moonbeams irradiate the night—but only temporarily. The cycle remains unchanged. If night descends on the earth—dawn is sure to follow.

It is a city of sound and movement; a city of light. Torches begin flaring in the streets with the first stealthy creepings of dusk, flashing from buggies, broughams and phaetons as rich babus wend their way to their evening entertainments. Lamps blaze in the windows of the wealthy. Light from crystal chandeliers form patterns of bright gold in the shadows of dark alleys. The streets throng with people. Middle class babus, making their way home at the end of a day's work, step across puddles and edge away from drains, the pleats of their dhotis held fastidiously in their hands. The jasmine-seller arranges his wares for the night in a deep barrel and the daily-wagers line up outside grocers' shops. Strains of kirtan, interspersed with the blowing of conches and clashing of cymbals, come floating out of temples and shrines, mingling with the monotonous murmur of religious discourse from the Brahmo Sabha and the sweet, solemn notes from church choirs. Muslims huddle together outside mosques after the evening namaz, their brows furrowed in thought, their breasts heaving with indignation.

They had mocked and reviled the Hindus all these years for their readiness in embracing the alien culture. They had kept themselves aloof and lived on their memories, seeing visions and dreaming dreams. But their dreams had shattered. Now, some among them had drifted away with the tide; others sat on the bank, waiting for the waters to engulf them.

Orderlies were busy arranging glasses and decanters of champagne, sherry and brandy on round tables in the balconies of houses in Sahebpara. Their masters would return any moment from their evening rides in the maidan and demand their chhota pegs. The memsahibs were dressing for dinner. Before donning their gowns, they stood naked before their Belgian mirrors and scratched viciously at the rashes on their breasts and thighs. White women were susceptible to prickly heat in the excessive heat and humidity of Bengal.

While the aristocrats of Simulia, Hatkhola, Ahiritola and Bagbazar were resting after their afternoon siestas, the members of the avant-garde were engaged in intellectual discussions. One such intellectual discussion went this way.

Looking out of his window, a young babu was charmed by the reflection of trees in the still waters of a pool. The blue-green of water and foliage had caught the last rays of the setting sun and turned to russet and gold. 'What beautiful scenery!' he exclaimed. 'Just like a water colour by Constable.'

'*O hé*!' A friend of his protested violently. 'You musn't use that word. It's obscene.'

'What word?'

'The first syllable of the painter's name.'

'O ho! ho! You mean I should say Thingstable instead! You're a veritable Mrs Grundy. But even the great poet, Shakespeare, used that word. In *Twelfth Night*. Don't you remember? Of course, he camouflaged it cleverly. "By my life, this is my lady's hand; These be her very C's"—capital C, you understand; "her U's", capital again; "and her T's" capital T and there's an n in and . . . Now, what do you make of that?'

'*Arré Chhi! Chhi! Chhi*! Is that all you remember of Shakespeare? Didn't Shakespeare use "dearest bodily part" and "peculiar river" for that word?'

'Ha! Ha! Ha! Dearest bodily part! Peculiar river! What wonderful, lively description! As good as a picture!'

This intellectual discussion became more and more elevated as the babus vied with each other to parade their learning, reaching dizzy heights with the opening of brandy bottles.

The city spilled over into the suburbs—virgin forest, once, dotted with the pleasure gardens of the wealthy industrialist-turned-zamindar. Houses, big, small and medium had mushroomed everywhere to accommodate the new generation of working babus, freshly migrated from villages. Weavers, barbers,washermen and oil crushers followed in their wake to minister to their needs. The Permanent Settlement had robbed many poor peasants of their land, not only in Bengal but in Orissa, Bihar and even distant Uttar Pradesh. These landless labourers flocked to the city's environs in thousands, ready to pick up any kind of menial work. Beyond the suburbs lay the villages, dull and somnolent with the fading out of daylight; little islands, linking hundreds and thousands of miles of dim silence . . .

Cities and townships; suburbs and villages; but no country! The land—from Kabul to Kanyakumari; from Dwarka to Burma—was governed by the British. But whose land was it? To whom did it belong? The people were such a medley of races and cultures. If the difference between a fiery Sicilian and a suave, sophisticated Parisian was great, how much greater was the difference between a wild Afridi Pathan from Baluchistan and a mild, devout Vaishnav from Assam! Though Indians all, they had nothing in common and hardly knew each other. There was no concept of country except in maps drawn up by the Survey office. Some sought it in the pages of the Mahabharat—others in the annals of Mughal history. For some, of course, it lay in the imagination.

And these were the islands in this vast ocean of darkness. These were the little pools of light. There were men who sat up nights, working by lamplight—each with a mission of his own. Some dreamed of a religion cleansed of all its impurities. Others of eradicating poverty and misery from the land. Yet others were striving for the spread of education and women's uplift. Some even saw visions of freedom; of being citizens of an independent India. Their eyes flashed with hope and anticipation. But these pools of light were few and far between, confined to the spaces of the mind for the most part and rarely, very rarely, spreading beyond the domestic hearth.

We are told that Queen Elizabeth of England bestowed knighthoods on those pirates who filled her coffers with Spanish gold. Queen Victoria went a step further than her illustrious predecessor. She dispensed titles in anticipation, dignifying those she sent out to India even before they reached her shores. For their task was harder. In them was vested the stupendous responsibility of draining the wealth of the land under cover of a benign and just administration. If one could see Lord Mayo now—handsome, cultured, the perfect English nobleman, sipping his brandy in the elegant drawing room of his palatial mansion in Barrackpore, one wouldn't dream that underneath he was really the leader of a band of marauders, out to despoil and plunder the country that he was pretending to govern. In this he was no different from Nadir Shah and Timurlane though, if the truth were to be told, the latter were as children in comparison to the Queen's viceroys in India.

Of course, nothing could be achieved without the help of some natives of the soil. These latter felt not a twinge of conscience when bartering their motherland for the crumbs that fell from their masters' tables. These traitorous thieves were trying to outdo each other even now—displaying their ill-gotten wealth in orgies of drunken merriment. But deep down they felt poor and deprived. Try as they would, they could never compete with their white-skinned compatriots. They felt like rats and weevils in comparision. And to shut out that terrible truth, they sank deeper and deeper in the pleasures of the flesh . . .

After the night comes the dawn, bringing fresh hope into the hearts of men. But Nabin did not live to see the light of that dawn. His last word uttered, he sank into a deep coma from which death claimed him.

It was ten o' clock in the morning and the light poured in from the open doors and windows. The sounds of weeping had subsided and a deep silence pervaded the mansion of the Singhas of Jorasanko. The lion gates had been opened wide, as befitted a house of death, and groups of servants stood huddled here and there, their faces blank and bewildered. Sarojini lay in a dead faint, her head on Kusum Kumari's lap. Kusum herself sat like an image of stone, her limbs motionless, her eyes stark and dry. Women tiptoed in and out and spoke in hushed voices but she heard nothing; felt nothing. A name kept pounding in her ears and in her heart, over and over again, to the beat of a thousand drums. It was her own name—yet, was it? No one had ever called her by that name except the boy who had once been her playmate and later, her brother-in-law. Why had he murmured that name even as he lay dying? What memory was he trying to awaken? Did the name have any significance? Did her life have any significance? Any value? She had been obsessed by that thought lately. Why did she go on living? In what hope? She would have gladly given up her life in exchange for that of Nabin's if that were possible. He had so much to give the world! She had nothing. She had wept and pleaded with God to spare him and take her instead. But God hadn't heeded her tears. She was only a woman, after all!

A slight commotion outside the house, accompanied by a patter of footsteps, came to her ears but Kusum did not move . . .

Bidhusekhar stepped out of the palki as it came to a halt at the gates of Singha mansion. His back bent forward a little but he drew himself to his former erect posture with his usual force of will. One hand resting heavily on his grandson, Pran Gopal's shoulder, he raised his eyes to the magnificent facade before him. This house—so dear to him that he had always felt it to be his own! It could have been his own, he thought wryly. He had held that power. But he had saved it for Chhotku and Bimbabati. Bimbabati had gone away these many years and taken his life force with her. He had aged quickly. Far too quickly. How old was he? He had been born in the first year of the century and it had thirty years more to go. Would he live to see it turning? He might if God willed it. Only, he would grow older and more feeble with each passing year. He sighed and turned to Pran Gopal. 'Come,' he said.

Going up the stairs was an agonizing exercise. He climbed a few steps, bearing the pain in his joints with a stoically impassive face, then stopped, panting with the effort. Ganganarayan came running down to take the other arm but

Bidhusekhar waved him away. 'I don't need help,' he said curtly, 'I can manage by myself,' and climbed another step. But seeing that Pran Gopal, though a sturdy youth, was finding it difficult to support his grandfather's weight, Ganga said, 'I'll get a chair, Jetha Moshai, and the servants will carry you upstairs.' Bidhusekhar's lungs were fit to burst by now and he had to agree. Ganga ran upstairs and brought his father's velvet cushioned mahogany chair and Bidhusekhar was carried to Nabin Kumar's room.

Nabin lay under a dazzling white sheet, his hands folded over his breast. His eyes were shut, as if in a deep, restful sleep. Bidhusekhar walked towards the bed, his hand still resting on Pran Gopal's shoulder. He opened his mouth as if to say something but no words came. The aged lips continued to tremble with unspoken words. Then, raising his head, he looked at the other people in the room, scanning their faces as if he sought someone. There was not a trace of grief or sorrow in his manner. 'Who is this?' he spoke at last. 'Is this really our Chhotku?' A loud sob from the back of the room was all the answer he got. 'Chhotku was so ill!' he continued in a voice of amazement. 'Why was I not informed?' Still no one answered. No one had the courage to tell him that being bedridden himself, he could do nothing for Nabin beyond distressing himself. Turning to his grandson, Bidhusekhar said, 'Gopal! I remember Chhotku at your age! He was very high-spirited; very wilful. But what intelligence! What memory! I don't seem to remember seeing him after that age. My mind is blanking out. The years between seem to have vanished. Chhotku's gone—you say. But how could he go without taking my leave?'

'Come to the other room, Dadu.[18]' Pran Gopal put his arm around the old man's shoulder.

'Yes. Let's go,' Bidhusekhar said tonelessly. 'There's nothing for me to do here.'

'Bara Babu!' Old Dibakar came forward. 'I was just saying—' Dibakar knew that with Bidhusekhar's arrival in the house, his permission had to be sought for whatever was to be done. He would take offence otherwise. 'I was just saying,' he continued,

18 Grandfather.

'that we had better take Chhoto Babu downstairs. Several gentlemen have come to pay their respects. Many more will come.'

'That's true,' Bidhusekhar replied. 'People will come in hundreds and thousands. We'll have the whole city at the gates. Chhotku has done so much good to so many. He distributed the Mahabharat free—'

'Come to the other room, Dadu,' Pran Gopal urged once again. 'You've been standing for a long time.'

Bidhusekhar turned his face and looked at Nabin Kumar once again. Then, wrenching his arm away from Pran Gopal's grasp, he rushed forward and threw himself on the corpse in a flood of grief as tumultuous and overpowering as a stream bursting its dam. 'Chhotku! Chhotku!' he wailed like a broken-hearted child. 'Why did you go away from me? *O ré* who will perform my funeral rites? Who do I have of my own but you? You're everything to me! Everything! *O ré* Chhotku! What great good fortune was ours the day you were born to our house! You're going to your mother, my darling boy! But why do you leave me behind?'

Bidhusekhar had seen so many deaths in his seventy years that people said his heart had turned to stone. His wife, several daughters and sons-in-law had left him one by one. His dearest friend, Ramkamal, had died in his arms. He had borne it all with stoic calm. No one had ever seen him break down like this. The news spread like lightning through the house and its inmates came crowding to the door to witness the astonishing spectacle.

Bidhusekhar held Nabin's face in his hands and repeated the same words over and over again, as he sobbed. Pran Gopal and Ganga tried to pull him away but he clung to the body more closely than ever. Others came to their help and the old man was hauled to his feet and led away. This had to be done for a number of distinguished visitors waited downstairs to pay their homage. Among them were the brother of the Raja of Posta and Rani Rasmoni's son-in-law, Mathur Mohan Biswas.

Bidhusekhar refused to go home. 'No, no,' he cried, jerking his head like a spoiled child. 'I won't go home. I must stay here—'

The body was to be taken to the burning ghat in the afternoon in accordance with the decree of the pandits. On hearing this Bidhusekhar rose from the bed on which he was lying and wiping the tears from his cheeks with the back of his hand, said quietly, 'I must go to Chhotku. I want to see him.' A change came over his personality as he uttered these words. His sagging face tightened with a return of the old indomitable spirit and his one eye flashed with authority. 'Not only that,' he continued, 'I'll take him to the *samshan* myself and perform the last rites. He died childless. Gopal, go tell Ganga.'

Overwhelmed with the responsibility of making all the arrangements, Ganga had no time to mourn his brother. He was rushing around like one possessed but his face was blank and his eyes dazed. His friends, Gourdas, Beni and Rajnarayan were downstairs and it was to them that he turned for support . . .

A new bedstead had been bought for the last journey. Covered with new linen and bedecked with garlands, it stood alongside the old, on which Nabin lay dressed like a bridegroom. Pran Gopal stood by the side of the bed, his eyes fixed on Nabin's face, which even now looked as fresh as a flower. Pran Gopal was a student of Presidency College. He was a brilliant scholar and had, even at this early age, read the complete works of Voltaire and Rousseau. His preference in political ideology veered towards the socialist doctrines of the Russians as opposed to the positivism of Kant. He had also read Nabin's translation of the Mahabharat, and though he had lost his boyhood closeness to his Chhoto Mama,[19] as he called Nabin, he had developed a strong love and respect for him and regarded him with awe.

With the lifting of the body, a piece of paper fluttered down to the floor. It was spattered with flecks of blood and had something written on it. Pran Gopal stooped and picked it up. But before he could read it a strange thing happened. A man came bursting into the room, his arms raised above his head, his feet stamping the floor in a joyful dance. '*O hé*, Nabin,' he cried excitedly. 'We were all wrong. You were wrong, too. And so were Debendra Babu and Keshab Babu. There's no God. Did

---

19 Younger Uncle.

you know that? No God at all. The old bastard, hunger, is the only god in the world. There's no one bigger than Him!' The man, though so wild and unkempt-looking that he was hardly recognizable, was Jadupati Ganguly. His family had fallen on bad times. Stalked by poverty and humiliation, a nephew of his had committed suicide a few months ago. Ever since that time, Jadupati's brain had shown signs of derangement. As the servants pushed him out of the door, one of the men in the room remarked, 'When a great man dies some people go mad. I've seen a number of cases like this.'

After the funeral party had left, Pran Gopal wandered from room to room of the near-empty house, feasting his eyes on its beauties. He had come to this house only once or twice before and felt overwhelmed by its size and splendour. Passing a doorway his eyes fell on Kusum Kumari. She sat cross-legged on an asan, her back straight, her eyes wide and staring. A little knot of women stood around her, trying to persuade her to rise. But she seemed to hear nothing; see nothing. She hadn't even noticed that Sarojini had been taken away. Looking at that pale, set face, Pran Gopal thought, 'Is this the new widow?'

The night was far advanced by the time everything was done and the men returned from the burning ghat. Pran Gopal came into his bedroom and prepared to go to sleep. As he bent forward to blow out the lamp, he remembered the piece of paper. It was still in the pocket of his kameez, where he had thrust it. He drew it out and held it to the light.

He recognized Nabin's writing though the lines were blurred and shaky, as if the hand that held the pen had trembled with weakness. When had he written all this? Late in the night, perhaps, when the household was asleep. He had risen from bed and taken up his pen for only thus could he assuage the burning in his breast.

'I never could sink completely in the pleasures of the flesh. Something, someone seemed to be pulling me back. Yet, I couldn't rise above them either. Desire beckoned to me constantly and I felt pushed towards it by an unseen hand . . .

'I was born to a race of hapless men and women, crushed even now, under the heel of a foreign power . . . I pronounce judgement on myself as I do on others. Progress and retrogression. The lines between them were blurred and I often mistook one for the other. Ah! Will this dark age never be spent? Will my countrymen never see the light? . . .

'Why am I paying for the sins of my fathers? . . .

'What we need is an amalgam. Of races, religions, knowledge and cultures. If they stand apart from one another they will avail us nothing . . .

'This pain in my breast. Is it God's punishment for my many mistakes? I've made mistakes—I don't deny them. But I've learned from my mistakes . . .

'I had hoped to see the new century. It isn't that far off. I had dreamed of hearing the cannon at midnight, booming a hundred times, ringing out the old and ushering in the new—the twentieth century! I can see it in my mind's eye. So bright; so joyous and beautiful! Oh Time that is yet unborn! I salute you! . . .

'I don't want to die. No matter what people say—I don't want to die. Save me! Grant me a little more of life. I yearn and yearn . . .'

Pran Gopal read the lines, over and over again. All the thoughts that had haunted Nabin Kumar as he lay on his sickbed; all that he had left unspoken in his delirium were here—in scattered phrases and fragments.

Youth is self-centred—devoid of sympathy. Obsessed with self, it isn't sensitized to the sorrows of others. Youth has too much fire and so its tears are few. Pran Gopal hadn't wept all day and he didn't weep now. He stood by the window, the scrap of paper in his hand. Of all the rambling sentiments penned by the dead man, only one took hold of his imagination. That of the cannon booming a hundred times—ushering in the twentieth century! Looking out into the night, he heard its footsteps in the distance. And his eyes glowed with the light of another, a more glorious world.

# READ MORE IN PENGUIN

# READ MORE IN PENGUIN